A PERFECTLY PARANORMAL CHRISTMAS

A PERFECTLY PARANORMAL ANTHOLOGY
BOOK FOUR

SAMANTHA MARSHALL   HELLUCY HOWE

LEISL LEIGHTON   MARNIE ST CLAIR

Published by A Perfectly Paranormal Anthology. For more information, email: leisl@leislleighton.com

Cover design – Samantha Marshall

Editors – Marnie St Clair & Leisl Leighton

Formatting - Leisl Leighton

ISBN: ebook: 978-1-922836-12-0; Print: 978-1-922836-13-7

❋ Created with Vellum

LOVE PNR? JOIN OUR PERFECTLY PARANORMAL PARAMOURS FACEBOOK GROUP

If you want to get to know the Perfectly Paranormal Anthology authors a bit more, get sneak peeks of what's coming up as well as giveaways, special offers and just some PNR fun, then join our Perfectly Paranormal Paramours Facebook Group.

Find us here:
https://www.facebook.com/groups/251663560162131

CONTENTS

BLITZEN

SAMANTHA MARSHALL

BLITZEN

A Merged Worlds
Novella

Samantha Marshall

Editing and formatting - Leisl Leighton Author Services

Cover - Samantha Marshall

All relevant correspondence may be directed through:

www.sliceofsammy.com

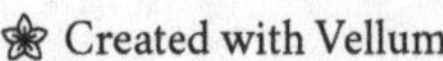
Created with Vellum

ABOUT BLITZEN

Nothing says relaxation like a post-Christmas cruise through the Bahamas – until Sin's ship breaks down in the middle of the Caribbean ocean, and relaxation becomes the last thing on her mind.

Despatched to a nearby island until the ship can be repaired, Sin's determined to salvage what remains of her holiday cheer. As a widowed mother to children long grown, she's used to amusing herself … but her solitude is swiftly hijacked by a blisteringly handsome man who goes by the name of Blitzen and may or may not be one of Santa's *actual* reindeer.

Despite making her no-dating rule more than clear, Blitzen wastes no time waging war on the walls around Sin's heart. Wherever she looks, he's there - rescuing her from over-zealous vampires, embroiling them in a piracy plot and walking around shirtless as though his chest and abdomen weren't weapons all of their own.

All Sin wants is to get home to her family … but to do that, she'll have to put her faith not in the miracle of Christmas, but something far, far worse: true love.

To love lost.
To second chances.
To magic.
To those who have the courage to believe.

1

WHATEVER FLOATS YOUR BOAT

"Hi, yes, I have a reservation?"

The maître d' perused the guest list down the length of his hooked nose, lips pressed into a prim line. "Under what name?"

"Um." Sin scuffed a canvas shoe against the polished floorboards. "Lucinda Watkins?"

The lone digit which had been trailing the length of the guest list halted. "Is that a question or a statement, madam?"

"Uh. A … statement?"

"I see." After a cutting look at her acid washed t-shirt and mint shorts, the maître d' returned to his examination of the guest list. "Ah, yes. One of the cruise ship refugees."

Sin shifted her canvas tote to her opposite shoulder and tried not to look like a cruise ship refugee. "Shining Star Cruises said—"

"No explanations are necessary, madam." He straightened his formal waistcoat with a crisp snapping motion. "I personally oversaw the negotiations with Shining Star Cruises, and am only too aware of the current … situation." The maître d's face creased in distaste as he motioned Sin further into the restaurant. "Since you do, indeed, have a reservation, it is my duty to welcome you to the Hibiscus Lounge. Follow me, if you please."

Sin's host turned with militant precision and strode away, leaving her little choice but to scurry along behind with her tote bag clutched to her chest.

The restaurant's layout had likely been fashionably minimalistic not so long ago, but with the *Shimmering Wave* emptying a goodly portion of its passengers onto the resort's shores, extra tables had been crammed into every available space. The maître d' navigated the maze of furniture and patrons with ease, patent leather shoes clicking together as he stopped beside a small, two-person table in the furthest corner of the restaurant. Sin fancied it'd been intended as an insult – but since the location put her right next to one of the open windows overlooking the beach, she was more than happy to drop her tote and flop into the elegant wooden dining chair.

"Your menu, madam, and some water."

Sin managed a nod of thanks, snatching up the iced water and draining the lot in several large, inelegant swallows. Her host made a choked noise as he retreated, but she was well past the point where the opinions of others mattered – after the last few days, a cool drink, a comfortable chair and the reassurance of dry land underfoot were the epitome of decadence.

Why had she let her children talk her into this again?

Sin set the glass back on the table and let out a weary sigh. Being surprised with a ticket for a tropical cruise on Christmas morning had been as exhilarating as it was terrifying – a fact her children well knew, just as they'd known that giving her the gift in front of her grandchildren would protect them from both her wrath and any attempts to give the ticket back.

Now, some two weeks or so later, the cruise she'd always dreamt of but never imagined actually taking had turned out to be a nightmare plagued by engine troubles, leaving several thousand passengers stranded in the middle of the Caribbean Sea on a cruise liner with no power.

The next time someone suggested Sin could use a break, she'd tell them exactly where they could shove their holiday and book a massage instead.

"There's nothing *wrong* with my life," she muttered, glaring at the foiled lettering on her menu. "I'm happy just the way I am."

"Excuse me."

Sin blinked and looked up. A man stood beside the table, dressed in bright pink board shorts with black tropical flowers and a loose black tank whose armholes were so large, several acres of tanned muscle were on display. Sin caught a glimpse of a tattoo before she forced her gaze up to his face, which boasted a square jaw dusted lightly with salt and pepper scruff, a tumble of black hair streaked white at the temples and impossibly dark brown eyes with thick, long lashes. Oblivious to her struggle to breathe in close proximity to so much excruciatingly attractive masculinity, he smiled, creasing his face with lines that said he smiled genuinely and often, and putting Sin in serious danger of passing out.

"Is this seat taken?" The stranger gestured to the chair opposite. "I forgot to make a reservation and with the cruise ship unexpectedly emptying passengers, the maître d' said this was the only unoccupied chair. I know it's rather forward, but would you mind if we ate together?"

"Uh …" Hoping the natural heat of the tropical evening hid her shock and simultaneously cursing her sweaty, grimy face, Sin shook her head. "No?"

"No, you don't mind, or no, you're waiting for someone?"

"I don't mind," she managed, tangling her fingers so tightly in the pristine white table cloth it was a wonder they didn't snap. "Please, sit. I'm here by myself."

Now, why had she said that? What if he was some kind of axe murderer and a fifty-something Australian woman stranded on a tropical island in the Bahamas was exactly his flavour? With over 700 islands in the area, the vast majority of them uninhabited, it'd be the perfect environment for a smiling assassin to snatch her away, never to be seen again.

"My children know I'm here," Sin blurted, pushing as far back in her chair as she could manage. The table seemed to shrink as he sat down, and though there had to be a veritable rainbow of scents wafting in through the open windows, she swore he smelled of nutmeg and pine. "They're not here themselves, but they know where I am."

The stranger smiled again, broad and easy and oh dear heavens, she was either blushing or having a hot flush, neither of which were going to improve the current state of her complexion.

"It's wonderful to have a close family," he said, voice as smooth and warm as her favourite blanket. "Is your husband resting in your villa?"

"Ah. Oh. No? Well. I mean … he's dead." Sin stared at the fine woodgrain of the table, trying to stop the words from tumbling out of her mouth – but they were determined, and she was tired, and so she added, "Not recently. Fifteen years ago, actually."

There was a protracted silence, and she dared glance from beneath her lashes to see him eyeing the two wedding rings she wore on a chain around her neck. Releasing her death grip on the table cloth, Sin snatched them up and stuffed them inside her t-shirt.

"I'm sorry to hear that," the stranger said at last. His smile was softer as he offered a hand. "I'm also embarrassed to realise that my manners have lapsed terribly – my name is Blitzen."

"Uh …" Sin stared at the extended hand as though it might bite. "That's … a very unusual name."

His smile didn't waver, his broad, strong fingers remaining firmly on her side of the table. "So I'm told."

"I guess I'm Sin." With no other recourse that wouldn't cause offence, she slid her hand into his. It was dry and warm, the skin calloused just enough to send pleasant shivers up her arm. What must he think of her clammy grip? Retrieving her hand as quickly as she could, she wiped it on the leg of her shorts. "It's short for Lucinda. My husband used to call me Cinders, but when he died I didn't want to use that any more. I also didn't want to go back to Lucinda because it felt so staid and my daughter, who was twelve at the time, suggested Sin because it 'sounded edgy' and even though I thought it was ridiculous it stuck and oh my stars why am I still talking?"

Blitzen's grin had only widened as she rambled, and Sin dropped her face into her hands to avoid the potent virility exuded by the simple curve of his lips. She was fifty-six, for goodness' sake, and she'd never had the inclination to even *look* at another man since Hugh died. Why was she now noticing the virility of a strange man's lips? How in the world were lips even virile, anyway? They were *lips.* All they did was frame a person's mouth, which in turn was nothing more than a hole in which to insert food in order to prevent starvation. Nothing special, and certainly nothing alluring about them.

At all.

Ever.

She was saved by the return of the maître d', his down-the-nose sneer replaced by one of quiet reverence as he bowed – actually bowed – to Blitzen.

"Sir." He produced a notepad with a flourish, materialising a pen from somewhere in the vicinity of his left ear. "My apologies again for the seating arrangements."

"It's not a problem, Devon. I should have thought to book ahead."

"The fault is not yours, sir. The sudden residence of a malfunctioning cruise ship in our waters is hardly something one could plan for." Devon twisted his mouth into what might have been a smile in some cultures, but seemed to Sin to be more like a grimace of pain. "Are we ready to order?"

"Sure. I'll have the usual, thanks." Blitzen pushed his unopened menu aside and favoured Sin with yet another mind-melting smile. "And you?"

"I … will … uh." Sin flipped open her menu and pointed to a random spot on the page. "This?"

One of Devon's immaculate eyebrows peaked. "The children's nuggets and chips? I'm afraid those are only for patrons under twelve."

"Oh. Um … well." Sin coughed politely, her face growing warmer by the second.

"Can I suggest the Caesar Salad?" Blitzen reached over the table to tap the menu with a calloused finger. "It's best with bacon."

"I love Caesar," Sin blurted, nodding. "And the whole Roman Empire. Oh my gods I'm still doing it."

Blitzen flicked an amused glance up at the scandalised maître d. "One Roman Salad for the lady, if you please."

"Indeed." Devon pocketed his notepad without bothering to write a single word, retreating with a disapproving sniff.

Sin snatched up the cloth napkin from the table, her heart going so fast she wondered if it was possible to have a heart attack from simple proximity to an incredibly attractive man. Oh yes, doctor, she'd say. I have my checkups regularly, but he had these *forearms,* and they were so brown and *muscular,* and oh dear gods save me but he's leaning them on the *table* and I can't help but stare …

"Is that a bird?" Blitzen's aforementioned forearms flexed as he stretched towards Sin, trying to see her hands where they fussed with the napkin.

She looked down and cleared her throat. "Oh. Um. Yes. A crane, to be exact."

Feeling even more self conscious than before, Sin placed the intricately folded fabric napkin on the table where he could see it. The bird's long neck was pointed upwards as though about to take flight, wings spread wide in glorious display.

"Amazing." He brushed a finger down the crane's back. "How did you do that so fast, and in such detail?"

"Well." Sin inspected her fingers, which were even now tingling with the aftermath of her ability. "Magic."

"Your magic manifests as origami?" Blitzen pushed back his chair to crouch beside the table, inspecting her panicked creation from a different angle.

"I … no?" She resisted the urge to rub at the single, thin blue line on her forearm that marked her small, very particular magical talent. "My magic gives me the ability to reproduce something I've seen as art out of whatever materials I have on hand."

Blitzen shook his head, awe etched into his unfairly attractive features. "Your fingers moved so fast they were a blur."

"Yes. Well. That's part of it – the speed, I mean." Sin cleared her throat again, wishing she could sink through the chair and into the floor. "I run a small business selling my creations."

"A woman of not just talent, but intellect, then." Resuming his chair, Blitzen reached for the crane and then stopped with his hands poised in mid-air. "May I?"

"Oh! Uh, sure. Go ahead." She bit her lip as he scooped the crane up in surprisingly careful fingers, twisting it this way and that before positioning it on the table beside him. "You … uh … don't have a mage mark?"

"Hmm?" He glanced up, those deep brown eyes so large and dark they stole her breath. "No, I'm not a mage."

Sin shifted in her chair. How rude would it be to ask him exactly what he was, then, if not a mage? Would it tarnish the perfection of his raw, earthy energy if he turned out to be something unpalatable? Did it make her prejudiced to even think that, let alone voice it? And what business was it of hers, anyway? Just because those perfect forearms didn't bear the obvious mark of magic, it didn't give her the right to pry into his private affairs just to salve her own curiosity, or—

"I don't mean to sound bold, since we're practically strangers, but …" Blitzen straightened from his examination of the crane to offer his own napkin, expression so boyishly hopeful that Sin accepted it before she'd had the chance to think. "Do you take requests?"

"Um …" She flipped the napkin back and forth in trembling fingers. "That depends. What would you like?"

He tipped his head to the side. "How about a reindeer?"

"A reindeer." Sin let out a sigh of relief. "Sure. I've done a lot of reindeer in the last few weeks; they're very popular in the lead-up to Christmas."

"Excellent." Blitzen watched avidly as she began to fold the napkin. "So, since we have nothing better to do while we wait for our food, why don't you tell me a bit about yourself, and how you came to be here?"

No. What a perfectly terrible idea. Sin began to shake her head, lining up a very polite excuse involving broken cruise ships and fatigue, but then she glanced into those decadent brown eyes and her thoughts took flight like a puff of startled butterflies. Drowning in the overwhelming intensity of the man opposite, Sin's fingers picked up speed, her mouth opened and she began to speak.

2

BAD MANNERS

It had been a long time – a long, long, *long* time – since Blitzen could recall enjoying himself so thoroughly. Food had arrived at some point, and though his empty plate insisted he'd made the required fork-to-mouth motions to eat it, he couldn't recall a single bite.

He didn't care.

The woman across from him, her face flushed and her dark brown hair a mess of humidity-induced waves, commanded his attention the same way a strike of lightning owned the midnight sky. In the last hour Blitzen had memorised the creases framing her grey-blue eyes, the swooping curve of her lips, the way she crinkled her nose when she concentrated, and the speed at which her nimble fingers flipped, folded, poked and prodded at every fabric napkin he slid her way. So far he had a crane, two reindeer, a sea turtle and a unicorn in his origami collection, each intricate piece lined up at the edge of his place-setting as though guarding his meal was their life's calling.

Sin, a far more apt name for the sensations she invoked in him than Lucinda would ever be, spilled words with a speed and generosity nothing short of incredible. She didn't seem to realise Blitzen had long exhausted his meagre reserves of charm and social grace, or that he'd been gently massaging the conversation in the direction he wanted it to go. His initial aim of gathering information remained – and he *had* gathered information, his lunch companion a veritable font of anecdotes about the days she'd spent stuck at sea on the powerless cruise ship, along with her immense relief when the local islands had banded together to offer temporary accommodation to the passengers when it became obvious the luxury liner required far more complicated repairs than initially hoped. His original plan had been to move about the restaurant and subtly question a variety of people, but the soft tingle of Sin's magic tickled the edges of Blitzen's senses in such a way that he couldn't bring himself to leave. Every word she spoke enchanted him, every blush and flighty gesture increasing the unaccountable urge to follow her wherever she went.

A fuss from the front of the restaurant dragged Blitzen from his thoughts. The wait staff parted to reveal a tall man in a bespoke suit, the chill of his aura a perfect match for his pale skin and the long, white hair that hung perfectly straight to the centre of his back. Ebony pupils punctured eyes of darkest navy that swept the crowded tables until they locked onto Blitzen, the only sign of recognition a subtle dip of his chin.

Blitzen set his cutlery down on his empty plate as the man approached their table, the clean lines of his suit emphasising the muscles from which his broad frame had been hewn. Sin's gushing litany faded as the newcomer drew up alongside them, setting an envelope by Blitzen's left hand. "We have to go."

"Always in such a rush." Blitzen waved a hand across the table and adopted what he hoped was a lazy smile. "Sin, this is my longtime friend and colleague Elias. Eli, this is the lovely Sin, who was gracious enough to share her table this afternoon."

Elias inspected Sin much the way one might inspect a bug about to stepped upon. Tension crept into his frame in increments, though his posture didn't change and his face remained impassive. "A pleasure."

"Hi," Sin whispered.

The single, trembling word roared through Blitzen with the force of a flood; before he knew quite what he was doing, he was out of his chair, pushing onto his toes to bump chests with the much taller man who'd arrived so abruptly. "You're scaring her. Back off."

Elias blinked, once, sole indicator of his shock. He held Blitzen's gaze for a fraction of a second before stepping smoothly to one side, sweeping long hair behind subtly pointed ears in order to execute a flourishing bow. "My sincerest apologies, my lady."

If Blitzen could have rolled his eyes, tossed Elias out the window and rewound time to prevent the last five minutes ever happening, he would have. Instead, he snatched up the envelope Elias had given him, flipped it open and tugged out the short note tucked inside.

Lights are on but nobody's home.

Damn. A malfunctioning cruise ship was difficult enough, with or without Nyk's cargo on board – but if the captain wasn't answering Elias' hails, they had a bigger problem than he'd feared.

"I pray you can forgive my lapse in manners," Elias continued. "I was so focused on my duties that I didn't pause to think. It was not my intention to make you uncomfortable."

Sin pursed her lips. "Doing your duty is admirable, but it's no excuse for bad manners. If I caught either of my children behaving the way you just did, I'd have something to say about it – and they're adults, just like you're supposed to be."

Elias' jaw dropped. Blitzen's laughter exploded free, obliterating his concern over broken ships and silent captains with such force that he dropped back into his chair, crumpling the ominous note in his fist.

"Sir." Devon arrived at the table with a polite cough, and since Blitzen's shoulders were still shaking from the force of his mirth, all he could do was wave a hand in invitation to speak. "I must protest. Your companion's display is ruining the ambience."

Elias snapped upright with such speed that Blitzen laughed even harder, wiping tears from his eyes with the back of one hand. Devon's lips pinched in disapproval as a giggle came from Sin's direction, the sound as pure and melodious as any musical instrument Blitzen had ever heard.

Still. The maître d had a point; they were drawing attention he'd been hoping to avoid. With a deep, shuddering breath, Blitzen let his laughter die. "Sorry, Devon. It wasn't intentional, I assure you."

"It never is, Sir."

"Eli, do me a solid and head home; I'll join you as soon as I'm done here."

Elias' jaw snapped shut with a click. "If you insist. Good day, my lady."

"And to you, Elias." Sin's words tumbled over one another like a river over rapids, but her tone was firm. "If we meet again, I hope you'll remember what you learnt today."

"I shall keep that in mind." Elias gave Blitzen a sharp look, then stalked back out the way he'd come.

"It's unlike your companion to interrupt so forcefully, Sir." Devon made a show of tidying and stacking the empty plates, but the lilt of question was heavy in his words.

"Elias gets carried away sometimes." Blitzen conjured a broad smile for the delightful woman opposite him. "Sorry about the interruption. Can I buy you dessert to make up for it?"

"Oh." Blue-grey eyes flicked towards the window, Sin's bottom lip rolling inward until it hid behind her teeth. "No, thank you. I'm quite full of Caesar's salad – I mean, Caesar salad – and even though it's barely one o'clock, I've had a really long few days. I'd prefer to go to my room and rest."

Disappointment surged. "I understand. Are you here long?"

"Oh … Uh." She chewed her lip harder, and Blitzen shoved his hands under his knees lest he reach out and tease it free with his thumb. "I don't know. The cruise ship …"

"Broke down. I heard."

Devon, standing by the table with the dirty dishes stacked precariously on one hand, sniffed. "The understatement of a lifetime, Sir."

"Yes." Sin dropped her gaze, colour spreading across her cheeks. "I'm sorry to be such a bother."

While Devon choked on platitudes, Blitzen watched the blush creep underneath the collar of Sin's t-shirt, where a lump disguised the wedding rings she wore. He should be concentrating on the mystery of the cruise ship and what it meant for Nykolaas' shipment, but instead he burned to ask how much of Sin's heart still belonged to the husband she'd lost. One thing was for sure; no matter what else was going on in his life, he wasn't letting her walk away without a fight.

Blitzen braced both forearms on the table and adopted what he hoped was a charming expression. "If you're not leaving the island any day soon, can I buy you dessert another time? Tomorrow, perhaps?"

Sin's face turned slack. "What?"

"Sir." Devon coughed again, the sound losing its customary polite echo.

"Hmm?"

"There's the matter of the bill. Shall I—"

"Add it to my account." He waved a hand as Sin began to protest. "No, no. Consider it penance for Elias' intrusion."

She dipped her head. "All right. Thank you."

Devon coughed again. "And the napkins, Sir?"

"Napkins?" Blitzen's eyes fell on the collection of origami Sin had created for him. Something dark and possessive swept over him, and his skin itched in preparation for a shift. "They're mine."

"Ah. Of course, Sir." Devon took a measured step away from the table. "I shall add them to your account alongside the meal."

Blitzen watched the maître d walk away, aware his nostrils were dilating as though he'd run the length of the island and back again but entirely unable to do anything about it.

"Are you all right?" Sin asked quietly.

He startled, the urge to shift dissolving as quickly as it had appeared. "Fine. I think I must be tired, too."

She stared at him, brows lightly furrowed and gaze only partially focused, as though she could somehow look beyond the surface to the alternate shape beneath.

"Say yes." The words were out of Blitzen's mouth before he could stop them. "To dessert. Tomorrow."

Sin's gaze lowered to the table, where her fingers fiddled restlessly with the edge of the cloth. "I don't date."

"Gelati." He was begging now, and gods, he didn't care. "I'm not asking for anything more than the chance to buy you two scoops of whatever flavour you like. Please."

"I …" Sin dragged her canvas tote into her lap, then sighed. "I'll be out on the beach in the morning; if you happen to wander by, then I'll let you join me for gelati." Her eyes narrowed. "Only for gelati."

Blitzen couldn't help it, he grinned like she'd just handed him the world on a platter. "I'll be there."

3

WHERE THE SUN DOESN'T SHINE

He wasn't coming.

Sin released the watch charm that dangled from her bracelet and stared out over the brilliant cerulean ocean. Why she'd expected Blitzen to show, she wasn't sure. After all, she'd made it clear to both him – and herself – she wasn't interested in a date. She didn't date strangers with dazzling smiles and excellent forearms. She didn't even date people she knew, whose smiles were mediocre and forearms average.

She didn't date at all.

Ever.

Sin reached up to grip the pair of wedding rings on the chain around her neck – hers, and Hugh's, together forever. The pain of his loss was a familiar ache, not faded so much as well-worn, a scar she cherished with a smile as soft as it was sad. She'd done her best to raise Charlotte and Faulkner in a way Hugh would've been proud of – and since they both sported smiles in the face of life's daily hardships, Sin figured she'd done well enough. Putting food on the table and keeping a roof overhead meant there'd been no time for a relationship, even if she'd wanted one.

None of those truths explained why she'd pulled on her most flattering bathing suit, though. Or why she'd knotted a soft sarong around her waist and tugged her hair into an artful clump at the base of one ear that was contrived to look as casual as it was pretty.

Who was she trying to impress, anyway? Blitzen's smile could melt an opponent at twenty paces and his muscles no doubt had their own fan club. He wasn't the sort of man to look twice at a fifty-something mother of two turned entrepreneur; particularly not one with a runaway tongue and fingers that needed to be constantly in motion – gods, had she really given him origami made from napkins? What was *wrong* with her?

Sin huffed a laugh, turning her gaze from the ocean to the small array of artistic creations in the sand by her lounger. Unsettlingly handsome men aside, she'd intended to sit on the beach and craft a little – so the hours spent in the shade of a palm, cool drink in hand and the idyllic Caribbean scenery stretched out in front of her? No loss. The shade was moving now, however, and Sin had no desire to go several rounds with the tropical sun, most particularly since she spent the majority of her normal daily life indoors. With a final glance up and down the empty beach, she tugged her tablet from her tote and opened the camera. After snapping a few shots of her latest creations, she sent them to Charlotte with the caption 'holiday whimsy, or worth selling?'

Her heart pecked out of time as she pictured her daughter's smiling face. Charlie had given up her full-time position in marketing to have children, and while they napped and grew and laughed and played, she worked part-time for Sin's art business. Even with two little ones underfoot and a third on the way, Charlie's marketing genius was beyond reproach – no matter how many people cooed over Sin's art, she was pragmatic enough to understand she'd never have been as successful as she was without her daughter's sharp brain on her side. Working closely together meant they spoke at least once a day, yet Sin hadn't been able to get hold of Charlie since arriving at the island.

"They're fine," Sin muttered, returning her tablet to her tote and carefully packing her artwork alongside. "The time difference is huge. Stop looking for a reason to panic."

With her bag a comforting weight on one shoulder, Sin wandered along the beach. The sand tickled between her bare toes, alternately hot and then cool as she passed from sunlight to shade and back again. The ocean was a gorgeous shade of aqua, the waves a soft, foamy wash. The whole scene was lovely, down to the last, sparkling grain of silica, until Sin fancied she was walking through a postcard.

Perfect.

Lonely.

"Excuse me."

Sin jumped, catching at her sunglasses lest they slide right off her face. She'd walked all the way back to the resort, so lost in her reverie she'd failed to notice deck chairs draped with guests and smiling waiters serving cocktails and snacks. Less than a handspan to her left reclined an elderly woman in an enormous sun hat, a crochet blanket draped over bony knees. Sitting on the edge of the chair beside her was a much younger man wearing nothing more than a microscopic pair of shorts, his skin a smooth, burnished gold and auburn hair slicked back from his forehead in a gravity-defying wave.

"I'm sorry." Sin took a step backward, offering an apologetic smile. "I didn't see you there."

The younger man closed the book he was holding with a sharp snap. "You almost trod on my grandmother."

"Again, I am so sorry. I was lost in my own thoughts and I—"

"You're off the cruise ship," interrupted the elderly woman. "Like us."

"Oh, uh … yes." Sin cleared her throat and tried another smile. "I'm afraid I don't recall meeting you before today."

The woman sniffed. "Rude. Nathaniel, introduce me."

"My grandmother is, in fact, none other than the great Dame Garadova. I'm her aide and protege, Nathaniel Garadova the Third."

"Oh. Right." Sin took another step back. "Lovely to meet you."

Nathaniel Garadova the Third put his book on the deck chair behind him and pushed to his feet, closing the distance between himself and Sin in one long, lean stride. Standing so close that Sin's nose clogged with the scent of fake tan and expensive cologne, he nudged his sunglasses down his nose to reveal a pair of eyes the colour of old blood. "You don't have a clue who we are, do you?"

"Vampires." Sin tried to swallow her sudden spurt of nerves without drawing attention to her throat in the process. She still didn't recognise the name – though, apparently, she should – but irises that specific shade? Definitely a vampire thing. And if they were out in the sun … "Daywalker nobility?"

"Royalty." Nathaniel drew out the word so that it was a purr. A bony knuckle nestled beneath Sin's chin, forcing her head up. "Day-walker royalty."

Sin pulled away from the unwelcome touch. "I don't know much about vampire culture, but issuing veiled threats in return for a sincere apology is rude wherever you are."

Dame Garadova let out a sharp laugh.

"So, you have teeth after all." Nathaniel smiled, a slippery thing that displayed his fangs without conveying a jot of positive energy. "What were you doing with the jägare yesterday?"

"I don't know what you're talking about." Sin turned to leave but the vampire moved to block her path.

"I can smell your blood, you know," he murmured, mirroring every step she took. It was like a dance, mesmerising and terrifying all at once – and though Nathaniel was the one doing the following, Sin was struck by the understanding that she wasn't doing the leading. "Perhaps that should be the price for your insult; a sip or three, from a vein of my grandmother's choice."

"Enough!"

Nathaniel's eyes widened a fraction of a second before he disappeared, leaving Sin teetering breathlessly on the balls of her feet in the loose sand. Warm, strong hands gripped her elbows and it took a long moment to realise the face bent over hers was one she knew.

"Blitzen," she managed.

Black hair tumbled haphazardly over his forehead, the white streaks at his temples all the more obvious in such a state of disarray.

Sweat beaded a bare chest dusted with black and white hair, his complete lack of shirt giving Sin an excellent view of more muscles than she knew the names of, along with the stylised reindeer tattooed on the left-hand side of his ribcage. Caught in some sort of proximity-induced trance, Sin's eyes dropped lower, where bright blue board shorts hung dangerously low on sculpted hips. She had the sudden urge to catch the undone laces between her fingers, and though she wanted to believe she'd tie them, there was a naughty voice inside her mind that whispered if she gave the slightest tug, she'd get to see … well.

Everything.

"Are you all right?"

The words came through a haze, and Sin wondered idly if she was going to faint. His voice was hard liquor and hot nights, warming her insides in a way no man's words had ever done before. She shook her head, forcing her eyes up to his. "Why are your shorts undone?"

"Huh?" Blitzen blinked, the muscles in his face flickering as they tried to decide which emotion was the most important to display. Sin watched the bunch and flex of his tanned skin, the nutmeg and pine scent of him chasing out the last vestige of Nathaniel's menace and restoring clarity with the speed of a slap.

"Oh, gods," she said, twisting her head back and forth. "There was—"

"It's taken care of," Blitzen assured her, the corners of his eyes crinkling as she tried to pantomime words with her hands. His grip gentle, he angled them so she could better see the beach.

Nathaniel lay flat on his stomach at the water's edge, soft waves licking at his face and completely ruining the artifice of his hair. One arm was trapped beneath him and the other twisted behind his back, the wrist held almost casually in the grip of Elias, who sat cross-legged on the vampire's spine in his bespoke suit as though it were the most natural thing in the world.

"That's my grandson your bodyguard is manhandling, jägare."

Blitzen's lips firmed, but he didn't remove his attention from Sin's face. "Eli's only demonstrating the same courtesy your grandson bestowed on the lady."

"How fortunate that you swept in to save her, like the true hero you are." Dame Garadova unfolded her frail body, the limbs exposed by her one-piece swimsuit just short of skeletal. "Do you feel grateful for your rescue, Mrs. Watkins? You certainly seemed enamoured of your new benefactor at lunch yesterday."

"What?" Sin pivoted on her heel to glare at the vampire hobbling slowly but surely towards her. "How do you know my name?"

"I know a great many things." Dame Garadova wobbled precariously in the sand, and to Sin's astonishment, Blitzen held out an arm. "Thank you, jägare."

Sin blinked at the unfamiliar syllables, each one of which rolled off the vampire's tongue as though she were born to utter them. The cadence of the word held import, the kind of weight which wanted to make her retreat despite having no idea what it meant.

"I gave that title up long ago." Blitzen's face remained open and his smile easy, but there was a warning in the timbre of his voice that made Sin's skin pucker. "For someone so well informed, I'd expect you to know better than to use it."

Dame Garadova, however, simply laughed and patted the arm upon which she now rested. "I am ... how shall we say? Old fashioned. Nathaniel! Stop embarrassing yourself and apologise to that elf. It's time for my afternoon massage."

Elf?

Sin eyed Elias as his head tipped to the side, ostensibly to catch whatever apology Nathaniel mumbled around a mouth full of sand and seawater. It was impossible to see at this distance but she remembered Elias' pointed ears from the day before – not a sweeping, accentuated point as most fae sported, but a far more subtle, not-quite-human point.

"I didn't know there were such a thing as elves," her mouth said. Her cheeks coloured at the involuntary faux pas but Blitzen merely chuckled.

"They prefer to keep a low profile." He fell silent as Elias flowed to his feet, breezing past Sin with the barest jerk of his chin.

The elf propped himself against a wooden pillar and watched as Nathaniel scuttled up the beach to his grandmother. Dame Garadova's lip curled at the sandy arm she was offered, but when Blitzen cleared his throat, she transferred her weight to Nathaniel and allowed him to escort her back into the resort.

It was only once the elegant glass door swished shut behind the pair that Sin realised two things. One: the loungers which had been crammed with people were now empty to the last, both staff and guests fleeing the confrontation with such haste that the idyllic scene was marred by crumpled towels, spilled drinks and discarded paper umbrellas.

Two: the man who'd stood her up so very casually that morning – not that it was a date – was currently right beside her, wearing a pair of unfastened board shorts a deep breath short of scandalous, and a grin so steamy that Sin hoped fervently her bathing suit wasn't flammable.

"You look beautiful," he said, glorious brown eyes skimming her body before returning to her face. "I hope they didn't scare you too much. Vampires are an unusual lot."

Sin pressed her lips together as words fought their way up and down her throat, pitching battles at the back of her tongue and swinging wildly to and fro in the cathedral of her mind – but though each and every one of them would be satisfying, not a single one was worth wasting the breath it would hitch a ride on.

So she drew herself up, tugging the knot on her sarong to ensure it was tight, and levelled Blitzen with the coolly professional expression she reserved for particularly difficult clients. "Thanks for your help, but if it's all the same, I'll be on my way now."

Blitzen's chiselled jaw dropped, but she refused to be distracted by the intriguing scruff of his stubble or the rough magic of his cheek-bones. Instead, Sin stepped around his poster-perfect astonishment and onto the resort's outer decking, heading for the safety of her villa.

"Sin." The deck creaked as Blitzen chased after her, inserting that gods-blessed body between herself and the resort proper. "Wait, please. I know I'm a little late, but I can explain."

"You call this a *little* late?" She cocked a brow ... and then the rest of her head for good measure, a move that never failed to induce the proper level of grovelling in her children.

Colour crept across Blitzen's toy-boy tanned cheeks, his expression twisting into one of rueful embarrassment. "Okay, I deserve that. I had something come up for work, and I lost track of time. I'm sorry."

Sin waited, and when he didn't add anything more, let out a shaky laugh. "That's your explanation?"

"Yes?"

"You seriously expect me to believe that you had something come up for ..." Sin raked her eyes down his almost-naked body and back up again, hoping the slap of colour blooming on her face would be mistaken for temper. "... Work?"

"Yes." Blitzen shifted from foot to foot. "I'm hoping you'll give me a second chance. Maybe this afternoon?"

"Not on your life." Sin shook her head. "You took advantage of my good nature yesterday, when you interrupted my lunch, and then again when you coaxed my agreement to meet this morning. Not only did you deign not to show up as promised, but after bodily removing a testosterone-driven menace from my personal space, you somehow think you have the right to stand exactly where he did. I'm no sheep to be herded home by the big, bad wolf. Just because I don't date, doesn't mean I'm an idiot. I know red flags when I see them and you, buster, have an entire collection."

Blitzen's eyes were saucer-wide by the end of her speech, both hands raised as though to ward off a blow. "I wanted – I had to – it's not—"

"Forget it." Sin snorted and stepped to the side, brushing up against one of the resort's outdoor tables as she squeezed past his bulky frame. The patrons had left in such a rush that their food was untouched, cupcakes sweating beside a bowl of jewel-bright gelati slowly surrendering to the kiss of the tropical sun. "This whole thing has been a waste of time."

"Sin, please." Blitzen's hand caught her arm, spinning her to face the man who was either admirably determined or insufferably dense. "I'm not asking much. Just another chance at sharing the dessert I promised."

Sin groped behind her, fingers closing around the rim of the bowl. In a motion that was likely nowhere near as smooth and badass as it felt, she shoved the half-melted mess straight into Blitzen's face, deriving an unholy amount of satisfaction from the way the pink and orange confection stuck to his skin while the bowl dropped to shatter between his bare feet.

"Thanks for the gelati, Blitzen. It was great."

4

ALL IT TAKES IS A MOMENT

litzen braced both forearms against the tiled wall of the shower and let his head hang, minutes sluicing by while Sin's damning words reverberated inside the cavern of his mind.

"I know red flags when I see them and you, buster, have an entire collection."

Gods damn him there and back again, he was *such* an asshole.

A loud, officious knock intruded on his perfectly maudlin brooding session, drawing Blitzen's brows into a waterlogged frown. "Go away, Eli."

"No." The bathroom door swung open, swiftly followed by the door to the shower. Elias leaned into the spray, paying homage to the near-scalding temperature with the barest flicker of a grimace, and flicked the tap off. "Trying to block me out with heat is a low blow, even for you."

Blitzen didn't bother moving from his position against the wall. "What do you want?"

"World peace, a rare steak and free haemorrhoid cream for pregnant women everywhere."

Laughter rumbled deep in Blitzen's chest and he lifted his head at last, expelling water from his hair with a quick, hard shake.

"You fucking heathen!" Soft, fluffy darkness cloaked Blitzen's head and shoulders. "Try this: it's a modern invention called a towel. The ladies love them."

Blitzen grunted and scrubbed at his hair for all of five seconds before he tugged the towel free and gave it a considering once-over.

"No. Fuck," Elias threw his hands in the air, his innate elegance transforming the otherwise simple gesture into poetry in motion. "You cannot send the pretty human a stack of towels by way of apology. Gods, Nyk, why did I have to be paired with the stupidest reindeer?"

"You chose the stupidest reindeer, that's why," called a voice from outside the room.

Blitzen froze. Elias grinned like the true asshat he was. "Oh, yeah. Nyk's on screen."

"I hate you." Blitzen wrapped the towel hastily around his hips. "Truly, passionately, and completely."

Elias looked, if anything, more cheerful. "You say the nicest things when you're sulking."

"I'm not sulking!" Blitzen stormed into the common room, the familiar hardwood floors flexing beneath every heavy step. He pulled up in front of the enormous screen hanging on the back wall and glared at the man dominating the middle of it. "I was *thinking*. In a non-sulky way."

"I'm afraid I agree with Elias on this one, B." The newcomer coughed politely. "In all my long years, I've never met anyone who champions sulking like you do."

"Fuck you, Nykolaas Klausse, and whatever fucking reindeer you rode in on."

Nyk's bright blue eyes twinkled in his handsome face. "Vix! B says I have to fuck you."

"Oh, shit." Blitzen's eyes went wide. "You did not."

From offscreen, a female voice screeched, "You tell that good-for-nothing, flea-infested excuse for a camel's *scrotum* that when I get my hands around his neck I'm gonna squeeze until his antlers fly off like fucking *rockets*!"

Nyk laughed, the gleeful sound packed with mischief and enough cheek-dimple action to last a lifetime.

"Great," Blitzen muttered. "Thanks."

"Most welcome – but I didn't call to watch you squirm." Nyk lifted a hand glittering with gold rings, raking long fingers through hair whiter than snow and styled sharper than any catwalk model's. His face, however, lacked the mirth which had wreathed it moments earlier. "We've got problems."

"Yeah, I know." Blitzen blew out a long breath, propping both hands on his hips. "I'm assuming Eli told you he couldn't raise the captain of the *Shimmering Wave*?"

"He did, but that's not what I was referring to." The father of Christmas crossed both arms, his brilliant green shirt whispering against the black and burgundy plaid waistcoat that hugged tight to his lithe frame. "As of a few hours ago, a massive area surrounding the stranded cruise liner's gone dark. Nobody can see or speak to anyone inside the zone, and nobody can reach out."

"Damn." Blitzen eyed his oldest friend, noting the sharp hollows in his cheeks. "How much power are you burning so we can have this conversation?"

"Too much," Nyk admitted. "We need to keep this succinct – Eli's message last night noted the captain of the *Wave* wasn't answering hails. Have you been in contact with him since?"

"Sort of." Blitzen grimaced. "Eli and I paid the *Shimmering Wave* a visit last night – but the captain won't be saying anything to anyone ever again."

Nyk blinked. "Dead?"

"Messily dead. The skeleton crew, too." Blitzen scrubbed a hand over his face. "The security system's hard drive is missing, the ship's logs have been cleared, and … your shipment's gone."

"Fuck." Nyk tipped his head back to stare at the ceiling, giving Blitzen clear view of the thin scars marking his throat. "Fuck a fucking fuck-duck."

"Pretty much." Blitzen sighed. "Eli and I didn't announce our intention to drop by, but we weren't too worried about being seen, either – I'm willing to bet whoever murdered the captain initiated the communications blackout to prevent us from raising the alarm."

Nykolaas pinched the bridge of his nose. "Gods damn it."

"There's more."

"Of course there's more," Nyk muttered. "The sabotage of a cruise ship, the murder of her crew and the theft of an entire load of charity-funded Christmas gifts isn't anywhere near enough bad news for one day. What else? What the actual fuck else, B?"

"Vampires."

Nyk snorted, continuing to inspect the roof for a long, drawn-out moment before he sighed and walked out of frame. Blitzen waited while glass clinked in the background, followed by the trickle of liquid and the unmistakable rattle of ice. When Nykolaas strode back into view, he had a tumbler of liquor in one hand, the other thrust almost casually into the pocket of his blood-orange slacks. The combination of colours he'd thrown on should have clashed but somehow he made it work, owning both the chic cut of his tailored wardrobe and the veritable rainbow it came in with the same aplomb he handled a team of rowdy reindeer shifters, a kingdom of snippy elves and, last but not least, the entire glittering empire that was Christmas.

"Right." Nyk tossed back the contents of his tumbler in one determined swallow. "Anyone we know?"

Blitzen ran a hand through his damp hair and shook off the excess moisture. "Dame Garadova and her grandson, Nathaniel."

"Daywalkers." Nyk crinkled his nose. "I don't know much about Nathaniel, but Dame Garadova has been a thorn in the crown's side since the day she was born. Just enough royal blood for a title, not enough to ever rule, and a chip on her shoulder because of it." He puffed air into his cheeks, held, then expelled it in a rush. "I suppose it's too much to hope they've got nothing to do with this?"

"Hard to say." Blitzen lifted one shoulder. "The run-in we had wasn't related to the cruise liner ... but Dame Garadova has a reputation for the shadier side of life. I'd wager everything I have that she's involved."

Nyk flicked a look from beneath his snowy brows. "You own an ancient patchwork quilt, a tarnished silver spoon and two rusty horseshoes."

Elias snorted. Blitzen flipped him off.

"Lack of materialism aside, I agree." Nyk set his glass aside and straightened his waistcoat. "All right; I'll get in touch with Lilith and see what I can learn about our Daywalker friends. I might also see if Dash can drum up duplicates of the *Wave's* passenger manifest, too." He glanced back at the screen. "Do you two need backup? Vix and I could be there in—"

"No." Blitzen slashed a hand through the air in emphasis. "You're exhausted. There's a reason we all scatter post-Christmas, and unless you're going to mend the rift you've been ignoring a good three centuries, it's going to stay that way. Eli and I can handle this."

Nykolaas growled in the back of his throat. "I thought we agreed not to bring that up."

"Actually, you *decided* that we shouldn't bring it up, and I chose to ignore your decision," Blitzen snapped. "Don't fight me on this, Nyk. Battling Sin was bad enough – I haven't got the energy to deal with you, too."

"Sin?" Nyk's ire disappeared in an instant. "Who's Sin?"

Blitzen's brows slammed together. "Just a passenger from the cruise ship."

"Who you know by their first name?"

"Yes."

"And who's mad at you."

"Yes."

"Because?"

"None of your damned business."

"Oh, no, you don't." Nyk's cheeks dimpled. "Eli?"

The traitorous elf by Blitzen's side snapped to attention. "A human woman, sire. A mage, single band, non-combative magical denomination. She captured Blitzen's attention during lunch yesterday."

"Really." The corners of Nyk's eyes crinkled in delight. "How much of his attention?"

"Shut up, Eli," Blitzen hissed.

"All of it, sire." Elias stepped and twisted, deflecting Blitzen's left hook without batting a single one of his perfect, snowy eyelashes. "He was in the process of charming her when I arrived at the restaurant, and despite the gravity of our situation, found time to ask her on a date this morning."

Nyk crowed a triumphant laugh, yanking his hand from his pocket in order to slap a raised knee. "A date! How did it go?"

"Ah." Elias coughed delicately. "He stood her up, sire."

"I did not!" Blitzen crossed both arms over his chest and tried not to pout. "Investigating the cruise ship took longer than we'd hoped, and I didn't make it back in time. She wasn't impressed."

"Hmm." Nyk propped one hand on his hip. "Non-combat magic, you said?"

"Yeah." Elias bent to scoop one of the origami reindeer from the coffee table, holding it up for Nyk's inspection. "She makes art."

Blitzen's chest grew tight. "Give that back."

The elf returned it at once, while Nyk's expression sharpened by several degrees. Blitzen dismissed them both in favour of checking the reindeer over, ensuring Eli hadn't caused any damage with his carelessness.

"B." Nyk's voice was gentler than Blitzen had ever heard it. "You need to fix this."

"I'm working on it. I'll keep an eye on the vampires while Eli visits the nearby islands—"

"Not the ship." Nyk waited until Blitzen met his gaze. "I meant the situation with Sin."

Confusion washed through Blitzen, followed swiftly and surely by the ignition of his temper. "If you think I'm going to use her to make this job easier, you can forget it."

"I'm not suggesting that. I'm talking about the fact that you like her." Nyk lifted his chin, daring Blitzen to disagree. When he didn't, the father of Christmas grinned like a kid on the proverbial morning. "I've never seen anyone get territorial over a folded dinner napkin before."

Blitzen sighed. "After what happened earlier, I'll be lucky if she stops to wipe her shoes on my corpse."

"Apologise properly, then." Nyk's gaze flickered, ghosts shifting in his expression. "Make it count, and maybe you'll get another chance."

Blitzen ran a finger down the origami reindeer's spine, the weave of the fabric catching on his callouses. "It's going to be very difficult to keep our secrets, solve murders, track down pirates and watch vampires while attempting to get back into Sin's good graces. She's too smart not to notice."

"So tell her everything."

"*What?*" Blitzen's jaw dropped. "Have you lost your mind?"

"No. If she's the right one – and only you can answer that question, B – then you'll have to tell her at some point anyway." Nyk shrugged, as though they were discussing the latest range of doll shoes rather than revealing the truth of not only his own identity but the entirety of the North Pole. "If it turns out she's not the right one, then we wipe her memory. No harm, no foul."

Something dark and ancient stirred in Blitzen's gut. "Touch her and I'll tear out your throat."

Elias gasped, but Nykolaas only grinned. "You already know."

"Don't be dumb. I've spent the sum total of little more than an hour with her."

"Sometimes," Nyk murmured, his expression soft and sad and unbearably ancient, "all it takes is a moment."

5

APOLOGIES ARE LIKE ASSHOLES

Sin stood on the deck of her holiday villa, fingers curled over the wooden railing as she watched the setting sun paint the sky in shades of tangerine and watermelon. A platter of tropical fruit sat untouched on the table by her hip, alongside a meticulously layered cocktail whose bell-shaped glass wore a paper umbrella and a sliced strawberry with all the flair of a burlesque dancer on opening night.

Life could be worse. She could still be trapped aboard the cruise ship in her suffocatingly small cabin, or threading between passengers attempting to drown their nerves at one of the ship's many bars. Instead, she was staying free of charge at an island resort so exclusive it wasn't advertised on any tourism brochure, eager staff only a click of the intercom away.

Sin turned her back to the sunset, inspecting the darkened outline of the villa's sharply angled roof. It was an elegant, two-story affair coiffed in rich amber wood and bright white paint, both chic and inviting at the same time. Carefully placed plant life added pops of colour both inside and out, and the veritable horde of windows ensured the villa was flooded with sunlight no matter where the sun sat in the sky. Sin had awoken that morning feeling like a princess in a fairytale.

She'd trade it all in a heartbeat for a single minute of time with her children.

Three days had passed since she'd first set foot on the island's pristine shore, during which time not a single device in the resort was able to reach the outside world – and nobody seemed to know why, or how to fix it. Sin clenched her fist around the rings at her throat, taking comfort in the cool cut of the metal against her skin. The emails she'd sent to Charlie on her first morning languished in her outbox, still marked with connection errors no matter how many times she tried to resend them.

Her head swam and the villa blurred, emotion knotting her lungs until breathing became impossible and all she could hear was the off-kilter thump of her heart as it slammed against the inside of her chest. When warm arms swept her close, Sin didn't bother to protest. She turned her face into soft cotton and set about soaking it with her tears, losing herself in the strength of her saviour. It was only when her sobs faded and she drew a shuddering breath full of nutmeg and pine that her brain thought it pertinent to point out she was supposed to be alone.

She shoved backwards with a gasp but Blitzen's tree trunk arms held her firmly in place. Somehow, they were curled together on the white wicker daybed, plump pillows propping Blitzen at an angle that was not quite sitting and not quite lying down. The smooth fabric of his board shorts were all that stood between the hot, hard muscle of his thighs and the back of Sin's legs, the gauzy beach cover-up she'd thrown on over her bathing suit having somehow rucked up around her hips.

"Easy," Blitzen murmured when she shoved at him again, panic lending her a strength that had absolutely no effect whatsoever on the man who'd appeared from thin air to hold her while she cried.

"What are you doing here?" Gods. Was that her voice, all cracked and hoarse?

Blitzen smoothed a hand over her hair, pushing back tear-damp strands and providing comfort in a single, fluid motion. "I was passing by and noticed you were upset."

"You were passing by?"

"Yes."

"Passing by a *second story balcony?*"

Laughter rumbled in his chest, banked thunder that vibrated through Sin's frame everywhere they touched. "Yes."

"And you noticed I was upset."

"Yes."

"So you ...?"

"Asked if you were all right." Again, that hand in her hair, infinitely gentle. "You didn't answer, and when I touched your shoulder, you collapsed."

"Into your arms."

"Not quite – you might have bruised knees tomorrow, but I did manage to catch you before you hit your head."

Sin pressed her lips together as a suspiciously hysterical giggle made a bid for freedom. Her mind was a whirl of spent panic and lost tears, the face-sized wet patch on Blitzen's grey tank testament to their final resting place. The soft light of a nearby lamp caught the white hair at his temples until it blazed with a life of its own, casting the rest of his face in shadows. When, exactly, had it gone from sunset to night-time? Sin had no idea, but it seemed the least impossible thing in the long list of impossible things her brain was conveniently composing on her behalf.

"I locked the doors," she said at last.

The corners of Blitzen's eyes crinkled. "I didn't come through a door."

"I squashed a bowl of gelati into your face."

"I appreciated the poetic irony."

Sin gathered herself as best she could, puffing up her chest and rapping the back of her knuckles against his dampened breastbone. "I'm angry with you!"

"I've been trying to apologise for the last two days." He cocked a brow. "I sent flowers."

"I made them into a crown and gave it to a teenage girl watching her younger brother swim in the pool."

"I sent muffins—"

"The young couple in the next villa over were very grateful."

"… and then bath oil—"

"Letitia, the cleaning lady, said baths were her favourite thing."

"… before I realised you weren't particularly interested in tokens of my regret." He had the gall to bop her on the nose. "So I decided to apologise in person."

Sin's words all tried to get out of her mouth at the same time, resulting in a strangled sort of sound that was part growl, part gurgle. She was alternately flattered and irritated, which on top of her recent distress felt like far too many intense emotions to experience at any one given time – but if she thought about *not* experiencing them, she was back to noticing how broad Blitzen's hands were as they spread down her spine, or the uncomfortable heat that prickled low in her belly every time he smiled.

"Apologies are like assholes," she snapped. "People like to dress them up in pretty packaging but at the end of the day, they're little more than an avenue for the delivery of a hot, steamy, meaningless pile of shit."

Blitzen coughed out a laugh that very quickly became a wheeze as Sin poked him firmly in the centre of his washboard abs. This time, when she shoved at his chest, his arms loosened enough for her to scramble to her feet, tugging industriously at her cover-up until it did what it was supposed to and covered her up. That done, she stuck her nose in the air and stomped on shaking legs back to the balcony rail, snatched her cocktail from the table and took a long sip.

It was only as the deliciously tart mixture of liquor and fruit juice slid down her throat that yet another thought flickered to life, and Sin swung back to accuse her uninvited guest of an entirely new crime. "Did you arrange this drink and fruit platter?"

Blitzen looked up at the starry sky, his guilty expression all the answer Sin needed. She loosed a frustrated growl but the cocktail was really rather good, so instead of tipping it over the balcony, she took another sip … then gathered a handful of tropical fruit and threw it at his stupid, handsome face.

"Sin." Her name came out a purring rumble, the effect unfairly potent given Blitzen was wiping cantaloupe out of one eye. "I know you're mad about the date, but I can explain."

"You said that last time – and it wasn't a date." Sin prodded at the umbrella in her cocktail. "You broke a promise, and where I come from, that's a serious offence. There's not a single thing you can do – or say – that would convince me to listen to whatever cock-eyed explanation you've come up with this time."

"No?"

"No."

"Not a single thing."

"Not. A. Single. Thing." She jabbed her finger at him with every word, poking holes in the spell he'd tried to weave with his unsolicited comfort and unfairly broad shoulders.

Blitzen picked a perfect sphere of watermelon out of his lap and slid it into his mouth with a thoughtful expression. The lamplight caressed his throat as he chewed, muscles flexing with a drawn-out swallow that had Sin hiding behind her cocktail glass.

Gods, how was someone so infuriating so damned attractive?

"Why were you crying?"

"Huh?" She glanced up in surprise, then back down at her drink before he managed to make eye contact.

"Why were you crying, Sin?" Blitzen's voice was gentle, a temptation against which she had no defences.

She sighed. "I miss my children."

"Your children?"

"I've been trying to get in contact with them since I arrived, but there's not a single device on this island capable of connecting with either Earth or Mu." Sin swallowed another mouthful of her cocktail in the hopes it would wash away the tremor in her voice. "I need to let them know I'm okay, and make sure everything's right at home."

Blitzen swung his legs off the daybed, pushing upright in a symphony of movement that the lamp wasted no time highlighting to best possible effect. Heedless of the fruit that dropped from his clothing and slithered from his skin to glop pathetically on the deck, he padded towards her on bare feet. Drawing up at a respectful distance that felt simultaneously too close and too far away, he ducked his head until they were at a level, the deep pools of his eyes reflecting the stars twinkling overhead.

"If I can get you in touch with your children," he said quietly, "will you give me a second chance to explain what happened the other day?"

Sin gaped. "What?"

"You don't have to forgive me – all I'm asking is for a chance to speak. Once I'm done, if you really never want to see me again, then you won't."

"You … can connect me with my children?"

He nodded once, sure and steady as the rising moon.

"I … I …"

"You can talk to them first, so you know I'm genuine." Blitzen cocked his head, no laughter in the lines and angles of his face, only a curious intensity that was far more alluring – and dangerous – than the charming version of him had been. "All you have to do is promise to listen."

The aching twist in Sin's heart demanded she accept at once, her hands already moving to set the cocktail glass back on the table. She arrested the motion midway, forcing her fingers to remain still and her pulse to steady.

"Do we have to go somewhere?"

"My house."

"Alone?"

"Elias can be there, if you wish."

Sin screwed up her face, caught between the sensible course of having another person on hand, and that person being Elias, who'd unsettled her on both occasions they'd crossed paths so far. "And if I don't wish?"

"He's got plenty he can do," Blitzen answered, raising his voice ever so slightly, "until I tell him it's all right to return."

There was a muffled curse from somewhere below and to the right, where a thick copse of vegetation cloaked a pretty little water feature in the villa's back garden.

"So I'm alone with you, in your house, which is …?"

The corners of Blitzen's eyes creased again. "On another island."

"Gods," Sin muttered, passing a hand over her face. "You really are an axe murderer with a taste for middle aged Australian women, aren't you?"

The vegetation by the water feature sniggered.

"Fuck off, Elias," Blitzen said mildly. His warm fingers nudged Sin's arm away from her face. "I'm not an axe murderer, I promise. I prefer a seax."

The way he said the word was so scandalous that Sin couldn't help the way her breath hitched. "A *what?*"

"It's a kind of short sword, or long knife. Gives a much more personal touch to my murdering sprees, and is useful in the kitchen to boot."

She bit her lip. "You're teasing me."

"A little." Blitzen turned his hand palm up, fingers splayed in invitation. "Well, my lady? Do we have a deal?"

This time, she did set the glass on the table. "I get to talk to my children."

"For as long as you like – and as I said, I'm not asking for forgiveness; only a chance to explain." His lips twitched. "I'd add 'and apologise', but I wouldn't want you to think I was trying to show off my asshole."

Sin's blush crept up her cheeks and down her throat – but for her children, she'd face the most fearsome of demons. Or, in this case, the most fearsomely handsome man she'd ever come across.

She set her hand in his, shivering at the contact. "Deal."

6

THE MAKINGS OF A BELIEVER

*B*litzen's throat dried as his fingers curled around Sin's. Lamplight washed over skin still kissed with a blush and glinted in eyes the grey-blue of a stormy sky, picking out each individual lash and setting the almost sheer fabric of her cover-up aglow. She'd fitted on his lap like the missing piece to a puzzle he had no recollection of starting, surrendering her fear and grief to the solace of his arms and the warmth of his heart.

Nyk had been right.

All it took was a moment.

"I'm a shifter," he murmured, tongue clumsy and words thick. "Don't be afraid."

Changing shape was such a natural thing that he never really stopped to think about it. Now, for the first time in his inordinately long life, Blitzen was acutely aware of the sweeping itch of fur erupting across his skin. The grinding of his bones beat a staccato rhythm for the dance of muscle and tendon, magic easing the transition between forms so that instead of untold agony, he felt only a tingling rush.

"Gods above us." Sin's whisper was filled with awe. "You're a … you're a reindeer."

Blitzen shook himself from nose to tail, settling his fur. When Sin didn't bolt, he twisted his head towards her, pausing with his nose just out of reach. She continued to stare, taking in the long lines of his legs and the sweeping planes of his back and shoulders, the pulse at her throat thumping double time.

"Blitzen," she began, then stopped, a furrow appearing between her brows. "Wait a minute. Blitzen the reindeer?"

"Yes," he replied, snorting a laugh when she jumped. "Blitzen the reindeer."

Sin pressed back into the railing. "You can talk."

"So you've heard."

"No, no, no." She shook her head, lips creasing in spite of the way her breath came a little too quickly. "I've met a bunch of shifters over the years, and not a one of them could talk in their animal form."

"I'm not *just* a shifter. I'm a magical shifter."

One of her hands crept upward until Sin regarded him from between the spread of her fingers. "Blitzen, the magical shifting reindeer."

"That's right."

"I'm dreaming." A tiny giggle preceded a quick shake of her head. "I have to be."

"Do you often dream of me?" Blitzen asked, daring to nudge at the back of her hand with his nose.

"What? No!" Sin swatted his snout and then gasped, fingers returning to stroke a wondrous path through the fur at his jaw. "You're so soft."

Her caress stirred his blood, drawing a rumbling sound from deep in Blitzen's chest. His lashes fluttered, attempting to close so that he could focus entirely on the sensations Sin was creating – but he'd made a promise. Keeping his movements slow, Blitzen folded his legs beneath him. "Get on."

Sin froze. "You did *not* just say that."

"Why?"

"I can't … I can't *ride* you!"

"You can ride me any time you like." The fervent response was out before he had time to think about it, and gods damn him if it didn't sound more like a prayer than a casual quip. Blitzen cleared his throat and angled his head, his antlers casting long, jagged shadows over Sin's torso. "It's perfectly safe."

Sin paced back and forth in front of him. "I can't just … I'm wearing my bathing suit, for the gods' sakes. What if I get cold? And I need … I need … some things. I can't just mount a magical reindeer shifter and ride off into the night! There are … responsibilities. And … and … notifications to make. What if the cleaning lady turns up, and I've mysteriously disappeared—"

"Sin." Blitzen waited until she turned to look at him, hoping his battle against laughter wasn't as obvious on his reindeer face as it would be on his human one. "I promise I won't let anything happen to you, and Elias will ensure your absence is anything but suspicious. I know you're nervous, but if you want to talk to your children, you need to climb on my back."

She blew out a long, trembling breath. "Low blow, playing the children card like that."

"Did it work?"

"Maybe." Her eyes narrowed. "Look, I'm really not sure—"

"Let me show you." He flexed his shoulder muscles, causing fur to ripple down the length of his spine. "Trust me, Sin. Please."

The moment hung suspended between them, a sparkling instant on a gossamer thread. Blitzen's chest ached as though he'd run for days without stopping, every fibre of his being straining for her answer. Sin's lips thinned into a narrow line as she approached, curling her fingers into the thick fur at the base of his neck. Muttering under her breath, she nonetheless swung a leg over his shoulders, sliding into position on Blitzen's back as though she'd been born to ride.

He was up in an instant, moving before Sin had a chance to change her mind. "Hold on tight."

"What are you – that's the edge! Blitzen, that's the *edge of th—shiiiiiit!*"

His forelegs cleared the balcony rail, hindquarters launching them into the air with a single, gargantuan push. Magic tingled in his veins, a gift so rare that only nine reindeer shifters in all the Merged Worlds claimed it as their own. It had set him apart from his kin, so many years ago, turning a soulful young man into an angry outcast – and then it had bound him to a new family, a purpose beyond anything he could ever have imagined. A life he'd thought complete, until a chance meeting at a table for two had introduced him to a woman unlike any other.

"Blitzen!" Sin screamed, the wind scattering her words into the night. "We're flying!"

"Do you like it?"

"Do I like it? Do I *like it*? You turn into a magical flying reindeer and leap off a two-story building and you have the nerve to ask me *if I like it?!*"

She wasn't truly scared. In this form, with his sense of smell so much richer, he could tell. True terror had a specific stink, the kind that coated the back of the throat and lodged in the nostrils for weeks, no matter how many times one washed or gargled or spat or cleansed. Sin's scent was citrus and roses, as complex as the woman to which it belonged, and edged with the same heady excitement Blitzen experienced every time he took to the air.

The island stretched out below them, large enough to support an exclusive luxury resort with all the trimmings, yet small enough to fly over in a matter of minutes. Tiki torches flickered around the resort's main building, solar lamps marking the paths between villas. Guests strolled beneath snoozing palms, ate on the restaurant's outer decking and danced at the outdoor bar, lost in the joy of the live band and the liquor sloshing in their glasses – and not a single one of them thought to look at the sky, where the silhouette of a woman on a reindeer passed by.

Except, of course, for the lone figure framed in the window of her villa, stooped spine draped in a loose-woven shawl and skin so paper-thin that the lights in the room behind her picked out the bones underneath. Dame Garadova lifted a gnarled hand as they shot overhead and though Blitzen couldn't see her face, he rather fancied she was smiling. Not necessarily the nice kind of smile, either.

"Was that …?"

"Saw her, did you?" Blitzen resisted the urge to turn his head, focusing instead on the soft puff of Sin's breath on his cheek. "Yes. I'd hate to sound like I'm ordering you around, but Dame Garadova's not the nice kind of vampire. If I were you, I'd keep my distance."

The island gave way to the sea, gentle waves tipped in white and stars twinkling at their own reflections. Sin's body relaxed as they flew, and Blitzen was struck by the instinctive way she moved – as though they were one being split into two parts, rather than two entirely separate entities.

"Dame Garadova called you a strange name at the beach the other day," she said eventually. "Juh … Jug …"

"Jägare."

"Yes. What does it mean?"

Blitzen crinkled his nose. "Hunter."

"Is that your surname?"

"No." He chuffed a laugh, felt the tightening of her fingers in response. "Jägare is a title, of sorts. It's no longer accurate but vampires have a flair for the dramatic, particularly if they think it'll gain them an advantage." He hesitated, torn between pushing too hard too soon and needing the truth. "What did she ask you?"

Sin's body shifted in a shrug. "She wanted to know why I had lunch with you. Old ladies are nosy creatures no matter their species, apparently. Why? Do you know her?"

"Only by reputation. But there is … more going on than there seems, and I'm almost certain the Garadovas have something to do with it."

"I thought we were done with giving me the run-around."

"We are." Blitzen inspected the horizon where the blurred shadows of other islands slumbered beneath their inky blankets, secrets tucked safe to their chests. "Talk to your children first, Sin. Then I'll tell you everything I know."

She was smart; he'd seen it in her eyes, heard it in her voice, had proof of it in the success of her business. With the right inferences, Sin would start to put the pieces together – and judging by the sudden weight of her silence, there was an excellent chance she was already replaying the events of the last few days in her mind, searching for the clues her fellow passengers chose to overlook.

The familiar shore of Nyk's Carribean island slipped out of the darkness, waves lipping gently at the glittering beach. Blitzen followed the sharp rise of the land until he spied a large house built into the side of the tree-studded bluff overlooking the open ocean. It was a perfectly balanced mixture of carved stone and polished glass, modern convenience intertwined with exquisite elven craftsmanship – a unique combination found only in places where Nykolaas Klausse might wish to rest his godly head.

Any other night, Blitzen would sweep down to the balcony outside his room, shifting on the fly. Given his passenger was nowhere near as athletic as Elias and therefore likely to protest the sudden disappearance of her mount, he circled around to the square patio that opened off the main part of the building, alighting on the slate pavers with the barest click of hooves.

Sin slithered off his back with a grunt, both hands going to her knees. "I'm not built for flying."

"You're built just fine." Courtesy of the sensor light which had blinked on behind her, Blitzen could see every svelte curve her cover-up attempted to disguise. In an effort to sound a little less like a pervert, he added, "It does take some getting used to, though. Or so I'm told."

She muttered something under her breath, straightening to take a better look at the house. Blitzen tried to picture it through fresh eyes, the smooth stone walls etched with characters from a language so rare as to be almost extinct, accompanied by lovingly sculpted accents and thick panes of handmade glass with curlicued leaves and vines frosted around their outermost edges.

"It's lovely." Sin moved to the patio door as though in a trance, fingers feathering over the carved handle. "Such craftsmanship."

Calling the shift from deep within, Blitzen returned to the body possessing opposable thumbs and moved to stand at her side. "The elves take pride in their work."

"The elves." She drew her lower lip between her teeth. "There you go again, making me think impossible things."

Unable to help himself, he bent so that his next words ghosted across the shell of her ear. "Nothing is impossible, Sin."

She jumped, then slapped both hands over her eyes. "Oh, gods, are you naked?!"

"What?" Blitzen glanced down the length of his body. "No?"

"But you just turned into a reindeer!"

"Actually, I'm fairly sure I just turned into a man."

"How can you possibly still have clothes on?" Her fingers twitched, as though she fought the temptation to peek. "Where do they go?"

"The answer to both of those questions is 'magic'." Blitzen curled a lock of silver-streaked brown hair around one finger and tugged softly. "I'm dressed. Promise."

He unabashedly took advantage of both her shielded eyes, and the angle of his body, to admire the soft flesh peeping out from her décolletage until Sin swallowed heavily and lowered her hands. Blitzen stepped around her, opening the door with a flourish.

"The house is old, but solid," he said, flipping on lights as he made his way through the large living area. Comfortable furniture blended lounge and dining, with several rustic stools pushed beneath the lip of an enormous island bench. The kitchen stretched down the western wall, modern appliances tucked between elegant cupboards and sturdy shelves. "Can I get you anything?"

"No, thank you." Sin trailed in his wake, eyes wide and voice breathless. "How many people live here?"

"Depends; Elias and I come here every year, right after Christmas. The others to and fro as duty allows but in most cases, we're on our own."

"You and Elias." Colour crept into Sin's cheeks. "Are you ... uh ... it's none of my business, but ..."

"Would I have asked you on a date if we were?"

She coughed, turning to inspect the small wooden carving of a pine tree which sat on a sideboard. "I don't know. Would you?"

Blitzen bristled, eyes narrowing to slits. He deserved the remark, in a way; he'd proven faithless by not showing up on the beach when promised, and it was obvious she'd taken his state of undress as something more nefarious than merely a shifter in a rush … but instinct insisted there was more to Sin's attitude than a dented ego. He wanted to demand answers but they were already on shaky ground – if not for his ability to contact her children, Blitzen had no doubt Sin would have refused to come here at all.

"The answer to both of those questions is no." He managed to keep the frown from his face, but the way she flinched let him know it was more than evident in his voice. "Elias and I are friends and work partners, nothing more – and I don't break my word without good reason."

Without waiting for an answer, Blitzen strode to the spiral staircase in the back corner of the room and began to descend. The lower floor contained a second living area with several long couches, shelves packed with books, a thick rug and the screen he used to speak with Nyk suspended above an old-fashioned fireplace. Though Blitzen could count on one hand the amount of times this particular hearth had ever been put to use, it was nonetheless laid with logs and kindling, ready to be lit at a moment's notice.

He'd flicked the screen on by the time Sin arrived, her footsteps hesitant on the stairs. Keeping his focus on the electronic device in front of him, Blitzen tapped his way through several prompts to the video connection lobby. "Call code?"

"Oh! It's really working?"

"Of course." He glanced over one shoulder. "I promised, didn't I?"

The corners of her mouth tightened, and Blitzen sensed he wasn't the only one fighting to hold onto their temper. For some reason, the notion caused him to smile, chasing his irritation away as though it had never been.

"The resort couldn't get a connection of any kind." Sin edged closer, eyes glued to the screen. "So it's not that I didn't believe you. More that I didn't want to get my hopes up."

"You don't believe in optimism?"

A soft laugh slipped from her and, when she looked at him at last, her eyes glittered with amusement and an old, old pain. "My husband died when my children were very young, leaving me to raise them on my own. I learnt very quickly that optimism is nowhere near as useful as pragmatism."

"You had no-one to help you?" The question was out before Blitzen could stop it, and the dimming of her eyes had him cursing his impulsivity. "I'm sorry. That's none of my business. If you won't believe in optimism, or in me, then how about I tell you this house has magical conduits which are usually dormant but, given the recent communications issue, have been charged so that we might access the outside world?" He waved a hand at the screen. "The conduits won't hold charge for long, but it'll be long enough for our purposes."

"All right." Sin lifted her chin, but her voice held the hint of a wobble that hadn't been there before. "Call code is AFM-354-982-Z."

Blitzen tapped the code in, ushering Sin forward as a box popped up demanding authorisation. "All yours. Feel free to make yourself at home, and talk as long as you like. I'll be upstairs making some supper."

"Supper?" She paused with her finger mere moments from the screen.

"Since you promised to hear me out after speaking with your family, we might be here a while." Blitzen raised a brow. "I might not be human, but I still need to eat. And I figured you might get hungry, too."

Sin's eyes traced the length of his torso before flicking guiltily back to his face. "Right. Uh, supper would be great."

"It's a date, then." Blitzen winked, then retreated up the stairs. He was almost at the top when Sin's indignant shout floated up after him, stretching his smile so wide it was a wonder his face didn't crack.

"I don't date!"

PIN DICK

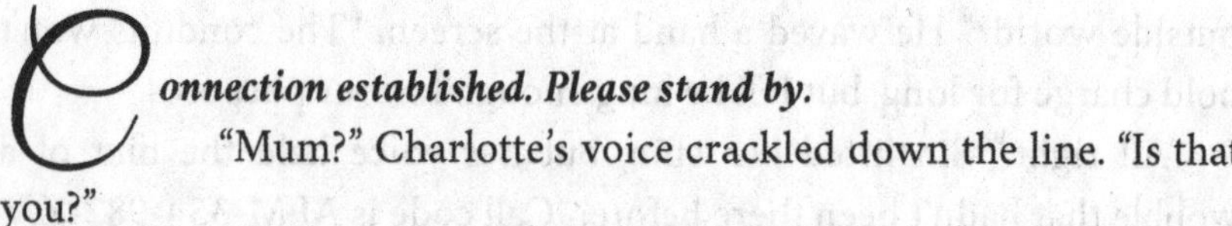

Connection established. Please stand by.

"Mum?" Charlotte's voice crackled down the line. "Is that you?"

"Charlie." Sin's heart expanded as the on-screen static cleared, revealing the achingly familiar setting of her daughter's lounge room. Afternoon sunlight picked out the auburn highlights in Charlotte's hair, pulled into a messy knot on the top of her head. Green eyes peered out of a face dusted with Hugh's freckles, a genetic marker he'd once laughed was the only evidence that Charlie was his own. "Are you all right? The kids? Garrett? Faulkner and Pierre?"

"Mum. Oh, gods, it really is you." Tears shimmered in Charlie's eyes. "Fork! *Fork!*"

"What is it?" Faulkner's smooth baritone preceded him into the frame, a lean slip of a man with ash-blonde hair, deep blue eyes and a voice so pure he'd been dubbed the 'king of modern opera'. "Mum? You're all right!"

"Forget me, are *you* all right? Is everyone—"

"Whoa up a minute." A tall, broad-shouldered angel stepped into the frame, his wings a mottling of grey feathers and his hair so dark as to be almost black. He curled an arm around Charlie's shoulders and squeezed her close. "Sin, it's a relief to see you well."

"Hi, Garrett." Sin offered her son-in-law a shaky smile. "Thank you, but I'm fine."

"Fine? *Fine?*" Charlie's voice rose to fever pitch. "Your cruise ship was sabotaged and people have been murdered and kidnapped!"

Sin blinked. "What?"

"It's all over the news," Faulkner confirmed, slipping his hands into the pockets of his slacks. "The ransom demands are astronomical."

"Ransom ..." Sin shook her head. "There must be some kind of mistake. The ship malfunctioned, and Shining Star Cruises sent the passengers to nearby islands until they could arrange to get us back home. I'm being very well looked after at a luxury resort, except that I couldn't get in contact with you because the network was down ..." She paused. "Did you say *murder?*"

"And kidnapping," Charlie cried, throwing her arms up in the air. "Pirates broke into the cruise ship while it was dead in the water, murdering the captain and some of the crew. Apparently the *Shimmering Wave* was carrying a load of charity-funded Christmas gifts for the local islands, which have now been taken ... along with some of the passengers and crew. They've cut off all contact to your section of the Bahamas, and have been broadcasting messages across every network they can access threatening to harm people unless their demands are met." Her daughter drew a shuddery breath, eyes wide and wet. "We had no idea where you were. If you were even alive!"

"Hey." Garrett curved a wing around Charlotte in addition to his arm, pressing a soft kiss to her hair. "She's okay, Charlie. She's okay."

"I know, but ... gods."

"I don't understand." Sin shook her head, the thoughts she'd so neatly lined up scattering like leaves in the wind. "There's been no mention of sabotage or murder here, nobody who's behaved in a way ..."

"So, you have teeth after all." Nathaniel smiled, a slippery thing that *displayed his fangs without conveying a jot of positive energy. "What were you doing with the jägare yesterday?"*

"Mum? You've gone pale." Faulkner stepped closer to the screen, one hand extended as though he'd catch hold of her arm. "Maybe you should sit down."

Sin stumbled backwards until her calves met one of the many couches in the room, whereupon she collapsed across the cushions in a daze. "When did the messages air?"

Garrett clicked his tongue against the roof of his mouth. "A couple of hours ago. Until then, we simply assumed the cruise ship was passing through a black spot."

"Okay," Sin murmured, her mind spinning. She felt as though she were trying to read a book with half the pages missing, something she detested even under the best of circumstances. In this case, however, she was willing to bet a certain magical flying reindeer had a large portion of those missing pages in his possession. "Okay. I just ... okay."

"*Are* you okay, Mum?" Charlie gripped Garrett's arm until her knuckles turned white. "Really?"

"I'm fine, I promise. Just shocked." Sin scrubbed a hand over her face. "How are the children? And the baby?"

"Fine. Pierre's with them now." Faulkner smiled at mention of his lover, a fellow opera singer and one of the most genuine men Sin had ever met. "We were baking cookies while Charlie caught a nap."

"The baby's fine," Charlie added, brushing one hand over the swell of her belly. "Growth is normal ... due date is still up in the air, though the doctors predict we're about half way through. So, June, maybe?"

Sin breathed out a sigh of relief. While cross-species breeding was nothing unusual, each of Charlie's pregnancies had presented a unique set of circumstances that kept even the most skilled doctors guessing. The first had gone the full forty weeks of a normal human gestation and all had assumed little Genevieve had inherited her mother's human genetics – until, shortly after her first birthday, she began to grow a pair of angel wings. By contrast her younger brother, Saul, had stayed in his mother's belly almost a month longer than was normal for a human baby, bringing him far closer to an angel's gestation period. At almost three years old, however, he had his father's eyes and hair but hadn't grown the wings to match.

Hearing the third baby was healthy was exactly the blessing Sin needed. "I'm so glad," she said, her throat thick. "I'm so glad you're all okay."

"Oh, Mum." Charlie leaned into her husband. Faulkner's face grew, if possible, more serious than usual. "We're so sorry we sent you on this cruise. We only wanted—"

"No! Don't you dare apologise, Charlotte Annabelle Watkins-Dovecote." Sin closed her eyes and drew a long, steadying breath. "Would you like to hear about my adventures the last few days?"

It was a cheap distraction, and they all knew it – but every single one, including the ever-calm and grounded Garrett, arranged themselves on the lounge room couch. Sin spent a moment rearranging her own pillows and as she did, she spotted a basket of brightly coloured wool and a crochet hook stashed beneath the coffee table. Guilt filtered through her as she gathered both basket and hook, but she'd feel inordinately better with something to occupy her hands – and if Blitzen truly took exception to her using whoever's supplies these were, she'd replace them the moment she was back home.

"All right." Selecting a ball of yarn in a deep raspberry pink, Sin tied a slip knot in the end and began to crochet. "So, it goes a little something like this."

Her family listened in rapt astonishment as she related all that had happened since she'd stepped off the cruise ship. Sin spared no detail, drawing comfort from the squeals and gasps punctuating her tale, imprinting their faces on her heart while she spoke. When it was done, her family sat in contemplative silence – until Charlie got a particular twinkle in her eye.

"Blitzen, huh? Is he who I think he is?" Her daughter leaned as far forward as her pregnant belly allowed and lowered her voice to a stage whisper. "More importantly, is he hot?"

Sin coughed, poring her energy into crocheting in the hopes it would hold off her blush. "I don't know."

"You don't know?" Faulkner tipped his head to one side. "Ma, it's pretty easy. Is the guy a hunky hunk of man cake that lights your fire?"

"Faulkner!" Sin's fingers picked up speed, magic tingling up her arms. "You know I don't date."

"You should." He crossed both arms over his chest, a sure sign her son was digging in both heels. "It's been how long since Dad died? Fifteen years? Don't tell me you're still holding a torch after all this time."

"Fork," Charlie murmured. "Don't be unfair. She's been looking after us."

"We're adults now," Faulkner pointed out. Then his face softened, and he relaxed enough to brace both forearms on his knees. "I worry about you, Mum. I want you to be happy – we all want you to be happy."

"I don't need a man to be happy, no matter how pretty he is," Sin huffed.

"Ohhhhh!" Charlie squealed. "You said he's pretty!"

"What? No, I just—"

"She likes him," Faulkner agreed, grinning. "Mum and Blitzen, sitting in a tree, K-I-S-S—"

"*Faulkner*." Sin's cheeks were on fire, and she could only imagine what colour they'd turned. "Stop it. He's upstairs, for the gods' sakes!"

"We know. You told us, remember?" Charlie's brows waggled. "You're having a midnight meet-up once this conversation is done."

Sin made a strangled noise in the back of her throat. "Stop that. He's cooking supper, but it's not a date."

"It could be," Faulkner offered. "He sounds like he's interested."

"He stood me up!"

"Forgiveable, if the reason is good enough," Garrett put in. "And he must be interested considering the trouble he's gone to, just to get you to hear that reason."

"Not you, too," Sin groaned. "You're the sensible one."

The angel cocked a brow. "I am?"

"Yes!"

"I'll ask a sensible question, then."

"Good."

Garrett cleared his throat. "If you're not attracted to this Blitzen person—"

"Of course not!"

"… then what's that in your hand?"

Sin blinked, then looked down at her crochet. Thanks to the whisper of magic that ran through her veins, she'd just tied off on the finished item – an impressively large, incredibly pink penis, complete with two neat, round testicles at the base.

"Sin? Are you all right?" Blitzen appeared at the bottom of the stairs, a quizzical frown marking his forehead. "There's a lot of shouting going on down here."

With a scream, Sin threw the crocheted penis into the air. It cut a gently scything arc across the room, only to bounce off Blitzen's face and drop into his outstretched hands. He stared down at it in astonishment while half a world away, Sin's family howled with laughter.

Gods. Could she crawl underneath the couch and just never come out? That was an option, surely. Or, even better, she could take up the remaining yarn and quickly crochet a rug beneath which she could live out the rest of her hideously embarrassed days in well-deserved solitude.

"Uh …" Blitzen held the penis up between thumb and forefinger. "What's this?"

"Dick," Faulkner wheezed, tears streaming down his cheeks.

Blitzen glanced between the penis and the screen, and back again. "You must be the children."

"This is Fork, and this is Charlie," Garrett's words came out choked. "They're the children. I'm the extra."

"As am I." Pierre wandered into view, as slight as Faulkner though marginally taller. His irreverently styled hair was currently dyed a bright shade of green, the perfect foil for charcoal eyes and the striking tattoos covering both arms and one side of his neck. He looked at the screen and took a half step back. "*Sacre bleu*, why is there a giant pink dick in the hands of that incredibly attractive man?"

"Mum made it," Charlie announced, and all three of the traitors dissolved into uproarious laughter.

Sin's entire body flamed with the heat of her embarrassment, her mind reaching for anything that might help scrape together what remained of her dignity. "It's … for pins."

Charlie and Fork collapsed against each other, laughing so hard Sin feared they might pass out. Garrett's face was blotchy from the effort of trying to keep his amusement contained, while Pierre only looked more confused.

"A …" He cleared his throat. "*Mon dieu.* A pin dick?"

"Pin dick," Charlie wheezed. "Pin dick!"

"I suppose that would work." Blitzen lifted the penis to eye height. "The shaft is more than firm enough."

Sin couldn't take a moment more. She launched herself across the room, grabbing at the yarn abomination. Blitzen lifted it out of reach, looping an arm around her waist when she crashed unceremoniously into his chest.

"Give me that," she hissed, clenching both fists in his tank and giving a solid tug.

"Oh, no." Blitzen's eyes danced, humour creasing the corners. When Sin pushed onto her toes, fingers stretching, the band of his arm slid to her lower back – and all at once, just like that, the world stood still.

Their two bodies fit seamlessly against one another, a perfect echo of plane and curve culminating in the astonishingly small space between their faces.

Sin found herself trembling, breasts pressed shamelessly against the pectorals of her much stronger, unfairly masculine opponent like some ditzy heroine in a cheesy story. She swallowed.

Blitzen's chocolate gaze dropped to her mouth.

She sucked in a breath. Her lungs filled with the scent of nutmeg and pine, the heat of his skin warming places that had no business being warm. Her knees wobbled, leaving her at the mercy of this man and his muscles, each and every one of them more perfectly sculpted than the last. His forehead bumped against hers, soft puffs of breath ghosting across her lips as he said, "I think I'll keep it."

Keep it?

Keep what?

Clarity rushed back, and Sin shoved away from Blitzen as though he'd just threatened to tip a bucket of iced water over her head. Which would have been a mercy, really, because she was unfathomably hot all over, her breath coming in the kind of gasps she usually only attained after running far too long on the treadmill.

"You." She jabbed a shaky finger in Blitzen's direction. "Don't do that."

Lazy, wicked heat suffused his expression. "Don't do what?"

"Don't—" Smell so good. Look so perfect. Tempt so badly. Sin shook her head. "Just … don't."

When she swung back to the screen, it was to find her family no longer laughing. Instead, Charlie had a hand pressed to her mouth, eyes brimming with moisture. Garrett had both arms wrapped around her, chin resting on top of her head and a decidedly smug smile on his face. Pierre had drawn up hard against the back of the couch, gripping Faulkner's shoulder while her son in turn clutched at his wrist, the two of them wearing shellshocked expressions.

Sin drew herself up and played the only card she could think of. "Who's looking after my grandchildren?"

"*Merde!*" Pierre yanked Faulkner off the couch, and the two sprinted from the room. "Ginny! Saul! Uncle Pierre said only one cookie, remember?"

The shrieking laughter of two small children echoed down the connection.

"Ginny," Faulkner shouted. "It's rude to fly inside the house. Get down here this minute."

Garrett carefully shifted his wife to one side, pressing a kiss to her temple. "I believe that's my cue."

In less than a second only Charlie remained, green eyes narrowed. "Very clever, mother dear."

"I don't know what you're talking about," Sin said loftily.

"Of course not." Charlotte's eyes slid to where Blitzen stood with the pin dick – *crochet penis* – in hand. "Are the news reports true?"

"I've only just seen them myself," he admitted. "But from what I know, yes."

Charlotte inched forward until her face took up the entire screen, her voice low and hard. "That there is my mother. She's the most precious woman in all the world, and I'm trusting you to keep her safe. Got it?"

"Charlie," Sin murmured, but in the fashion of children everywhere, even supposedly adult children who were mothers themselves and should, therefore, know better, her daughter acted like she hadn't heard a word.

"I understand." Blitzen inclined his head as though to a queen. "I'll protect her with my life."

"I expect nothing less." Charlie pursed her lips. "We're not finished talking, you and I."

Another slow nod. "Once this is over?"

"Once this is over."

"Charlie!" Sin propped both fists on her hips. "That's enough."

Charlotte leaned back with a smile. "For now. I love you, Mum. Stay safe."

"I love you too," Sin answered, blowing a kiss at the screen. "Take care of each other."

"We will." Charlie glanced in the direction of the kitchen. "I think they're going to need my help."

"My love to the kids," Sin whispered.

"Of course! Next call, I'll get them to say hi." Charlie reached for the screen, then paused to offer a cheeky wink. "Remember: if you can't be good, be good at it."

The connection cut out, leaving Sin alone in the room with Blitzen and his recently acquired yarn phallus – which, for some reason, he'd decided to tuck into the side pocket of his board shorts, the mushroom head peeping out the top as though afraid of missing the show.

Blitzen caught the direction of her gaze and grinned. "Supper?"

"Ugh." Sin closed her eyes. "I'm not sure about supper, but I could really use a drink right about now."

"Cocktail?"

She cracked an eyelid. "Not. Funny."

"You'd prefer something harder, then?"

"Blitzen!"

He burst out laughing, and Sin couldn't help the twist in her lower belly, nor the way her breath caught at the sound. This man … oh, he was trouble.

"I'm sorry – I couldn't help it. Jokes aside, we have plenty of rum." Blitzen gestured up the stairs, twisting so that the thing she absolutely wished she had never crocheted remained firmly out of reach. "It's the official drink of the Caribbean, after all."

"Rum sounds perfect." Sin levelled him with a glare from several steps higher up. "Then it's your turn to talk."

"In that case, I better make it a double."

8

THE TRUTH ABOUT SANTA

After the amount of energy he'd expended to get Sin exactly where she was – sitting across from him at the kitchen bench with an expectant look on her face – Blitzen hadn't anticipated the catastrophic case of tongue-tie that had crept up on him somewhere between pulling hash browns out of the oven and adding marshmallows to matching mugs of cocoa.

He pushed one of the mugs across the polished marble bench top, fiddled with the arrangement of cookies he'd baked, stacked the hash browns into a perfectly aligned tower … and sighed. "I don't know where to begin."

"Hmm." Sin stared at the offerings in front of her, plucking a cookie from the top of the pile. "How about the beginning?"

"If only it was that simple." Blitzen braced both hands on the bench and let his head hang. "I'm sorry I stood you up the other morning."

"So you've said." Sin lowered her cookie, fiddling with the outer edge until crumbs coated the white marble beneath. "After what I just heard about the *Shimmering Wave* being sabotaged and people having been murdered, I'm wondering if it really matters any more."

"Oh, it matters." He huffed a humourless laugh. "I was late to meet you because Elias and I flew out to the *Shimmering Wave* when the captain didn't answer our hails. We discovered the charity gifts had been stolen, and then stumbled over the murdered captain and crew."

Sin opened her mouth, closed it, opened it again, closed it again. Her fingers twitched. The crumbs she'd scattered over the bench formed into the tiny, intricate shape of a star.

"Well." She shook her head, snapped the cookie in half and took a bite. "That's not only horrifying, but a fairly valid reason for skipping our not-date."

"I didn't …"

"Kill them?"

"Gods, Sin, of course I didn't kill them," Blitzen spluttered, taking a half step back. "What the hell do you think I am?"

She shrugged the kind of shrug a person utilises when they've ridden the rollercoaster of emotions far too often in a short space of time. "Well, at first I thought you were an unfairly attractive man. Then I thought you were an asshole. After that, I discovered you were a magical flying reindeer who hangs out with an honest-to-gods elf. Then Dame Garadova addressed you as 'hunter', and you weren't the least surprised or upset about the whole sabotage-theft-murder scenario. So … really, given what I think has been proved bizarrely incorrect so many times, can you blame me for asking?"

"No." Blitzen examined the worn floorboards between his feet. "I *could* have killed them, but I swear I didn't."

Sin barked a laugh rough with cookie. "Santa's reindeer kill people?"

There. She'd said it. An odd mixture of triumph, relief, fear and sadness knotted tight in Blitzen's gut, and he found he couldn't lift his head to meet her eyes.

"Sometimes." He screwed up his face. "Nykolaas is … an anomaly. One of three Primal Gods in all existence – beings conceived by the raw, unbridled energy that manifested when Mu and Earth first began to merge. He's half of a pair; light to dark, snow to sunshine, however you want to put it. He and his counterpart manifested in the territory of Odin, the Allfather, King of the Norse gods. Odin gave—"

"Odin?" Sin's voice carried her astonishment. "Santa was raised by *Odin*?"

"Nykolaas," Blitzen corrected gently. "And no. Odin gave the babes to his most trusted warriors – a group called the Wild Hunt."

Cookie crumbs peppered the bench, and then the floor, as Sin coughed and choked.

Blitzen nudged her cocoa closer until she scooped it up and drank. "As the children grew, they demonstrated a unique ability: they could sense another's soul, and thereby ascertain who was …"

"Nice," Sin whispered. "Or naughty."

"That's the sanitised version, yes. They became the pride of the Hunt, deciding who was to be rewarded and who required punishing." Blitzen offered a rueful smile. "Every now and then, though, they disagreed. I was one such case."

"You? But Dame Garadova called you—"

"Hunter, yes." Blitzen returned to his former spot at the bench and snatched up a hash brown. "I was born to a remote clan of reindeer shifters in the frozen reaches of Mu. When they discovered my ability to fly, it was believed to be a curse. I was barely a teen when they tied me to the trunk of the clan's most sacred tree and walked away forever."

"Blitzen …"

"I survived by abandoning my honour in favour of theft and violence." Blitzen's smile was sharp, the memory sharper. "When the Wild Hunt caught me, Nyk and Inkhe fought over whether I should be punished, or granted mercy. In the end, Odin offered a deal; swear to follow Nyk for the rest of my days, or surrender to Inkhe and be … cleansed."

Sin nibbled the last of her cookie, though judging by the saucer-wide set of her eyes, she didn't taste a lick of it. "You chose Nyk."

"I chose life," Blitzen clarified, determined she understand the truth of it – of him – before they took further steps in their very private dance. "I bought myself time to look for an opportune moment in which to slip away. But Nyk … he has a way about him. By the time my opportunity arrived, I adored him so much that I didn't take it."

"Oh." Sin's face softened. "So you were ..."

"The first reindeer? Yes. Over time, we collected the other eight." Blitzen rubbed a palm over his chest, unable to put into words the strength of his feelings for his chosen family. "Eventually we came across a kingdom of elves who'd lost their light, and left the Hunt to help them. Together, we laid the foundations of what would become Christmas."

"All right." Sin picked up a new cookie and bit into it with grim determination. "What do you and Nykolaas have to do with the Caribbean, a broken cruise ship, and the murdered crew?"

"At first, I wasn't sure, either – but Eli and I have been doing a bit of poking around the last few days, and we've pieced together a theory." Blitzen finished the last of his hash brown and chased it down with a hefty swig of cocoa. "First and most importantly, Dame Garadova claims royal Daywalker heritage. It's a tenuous enough link that she'll never see an actual throne, but it's there nonetheless."

Sin screwed up her face. "So she went to great pains to point out when we met."

"Right." Blitzen squashed the instincts which demanded he seek swift and bloody retribution from the vampires who'd treated Sin so callously, and crossed his arms. "The problem is, Dame Garadova has a predilection for engaging in disreputable activities and then demanding her royal relatives bail her out when things go sour. About six months ago, said relatives got tired of the endless cycle – so when the lovely Dame and her grandson Nathaniel were caught smuggling, they were handed over to Lilith."

"Lilith." Sin shivered. "I've never met her, but as far as both goddesses and queens go, she sounds terrifying."

"I've met her, and can confirm she's equally as terrifying as you'd think – but she keeps her people in check, and she takes the reputation of the vampire community very seriously. Lilith excommunicated both Dame Garadova and Nathaniel, cutting them off from family and fortune, and tossed them out on the street." Blitzen lifted one shoulder in a shrug. "Elias tracked down a private bank account in Nathaniel's name containing enough money to sustain them temporarily – with the latest transaction being two tickets for a Caribbean cruise."

"Wait." Sin blinked. "They were thrown out of their homes … so they decided to take a holiday?"

"Yes and no," Blitzen chuckled. "Every year, Nykolaas anonymously oversees several Christmas charity drives, the proceeds of which are sent all over the world. If you total up the net worth of the goods for the Caribbean alone, it's well into the millions." He raked a hand through his hair. "Nyk can't be everywhere at once, so Eli and I come here every January to ensure the gifts are handed out to children who need them – while the other reindeer split up to watch over different charities in other parts of the world."

"Question." Sin held up a chocolate smeared finger. "Why does Santa Claus organise charity drives when he gives gifts out for free?"

"Balance." Blitzen grinned at the confused look on her face. "Christmas is about the spirit of giving, right? Nyk gives to everyone on what you'd call the nice list – no, that hasn't changed over the years – but he also wants to offer people in the grey area a chance at atonement."

"And if you donate anonymously to a charity, you're acting in the spirit of Christmas rather than for your own gain." Sin huffed out a surprised laugh. "Clever."

"We like to think so."

Sin finished her cookies in silence, including the tiny star shape she'd constructed from crumbs, then took several long sips of cocoa. "So … let me get this straight. Your theory is that after being cut off from vampire society due to a life of nefarious misdeeds, Dame Garadova and Nathaniel realise they'll eventually run out of money. Rather than atone for their sins or get an honest job, they decide to book a ticket on a tropical cruise that just so happens to be carrying a shipment of charity gifts worth a small fortune. After boarding, they somehow manage to sabotage the ship, steal the gifts, murder the captain and some of the crew, kidnap a group of people for ransom purposes … and then what? Stash the loot and lounge on the beach until they get paid?"

Blitzen winced. "I know it sounds a little far fetched—"

"You *think?*"

"… but it makes a certain sense."

"About as much sense as me sitting down to supper with one of Santa's magical flying reindeer." Sin leaned back on her stool, looking as skeptical as Blitzen had feared she might. "Do you have any proof?"

"Suspicious transactions from Nathaniel's account which could account for down-payments on a band of mercenaries – but without us catching the vampires doing something dangerous or recovering the stolen shipment, none of it will stick."

"Of course not," Sin muttered, wrapping her fingers around her mug. "That would be far too easy, wouldn't it?"

Blitzen busied himself with the dishes, giving her as much space to think as he could manage. He knew exactly how outrageous his theory was – he and Eli had scoffed at it themselves, and they were the ones who'd composed it. Still, for the time being, it was enough to make Nykolaas suspicious. And *that* was enough to warrant Blitzen and Eli being given strict instructions to monitor the vampires as closely as possible.

"Let's say I buy your idea," Sin said finally. "There's still one thing I can't work out."

Blitzen set the final baking tray in the drainer and turned around. "What?"

"Where do I fit in?" She flattened a hand on her chest. "I'm nobody special, yet I'm sitting in Santa's kitchen while the first and, presumably, most senior of his magical flying reindeer hands out sensitive information like candy canes on Christmas Eve. Why?"

"Those are two different questions." Blitzen tugged a tea towel from the oven's handrail and began to wipe out a mixing bowl, keeping his voice even and his movements smooth and steady. "The truth is that the day we met, I was looking for information. I didn't know the captain and crew were dead or the charity gifts gone, but a broken-down cruise ship is unusual enough to warrant investigation.

Since the restaurant was the first place weary cruise liner passengers were being directed, it was my first stop, too."

"So, you chose the lone, vulnerable middle-aged woman to work your charms on?"

"Not exactly." Blitzen tossed the towel in the sink and rounded the bench, propping his backside on the stool beside hers. "I asked Devon who I might best prod for information, and he waved me in your direction."

"*Devon?* Snooty, sniffing, judgemental maître d, Devon?" To Blitzen's surprise, instead of getting angry, Sin's expression softened. "I guess he chose well – when I'm nervous, my mouth runs non-stop."

"One of my favourite things about you," Blitzen murmured, daring to brush an errant lock of hair away from her face. "I might have sat down to play you, but by the time Elias showed up … it was real. You shine, Sin, with a light unlike anything I've ever seen. I couldn't walk away from it then, and I can't now."

She ducked her head. "I don't date."

"Why not?" Blitzen nudged the pair of wedding rings dangling from her throat. "Are you still in love with him?"

Sin reached to curl her fingers around the jewellery, hand brushing Blitzen's and sending a frisson of awareness up his arm. "That's a very difficult question to answer."

"Try. Please."

She blew out a long breath. "I would never have married Hugh if I didn't love him, nor agreed to bring children into the world. But … he's been dead fifteen years, eight months, two weeks and three days now, and the Cinders he loved died with him." Sin tugged on the rings, causing the thick chain to dig into her skin. "I keep these as a reminder of the promises I made; to love our children, to look after them above all else – but I moved them to a chain around my neck because it hurt to look at my finger and be constantly reminded of all I'd lost. I'll always love Hugh … but it's the kind of love you feel when you look at an old photograph. Faded and old, not because I don't care, but because I had to close that door and move on, or I'd have drowned."

"I understand." Blitzen's hand shook as he closed it over hers, brushing a thumb along the ridge of her knuckles. "That new woman. Does she have room for someone else?"

"I don't date." It came out like a whip, eyes squeezing even more tightly closed. "And I don't see what that has to do with my question."

"It has *everything* to do with your question." Blitzen hooked a foot around the stool, giving Sin plenty of time to escape as he dragged it around to face him. When she didn't, her body caged between his spread knees and her hand trembling inside his own, he leaned forward until they shared breath. "Nykolaas gave me permission to bring you here because he knows that I don't date, either. I play for keeps."

Sin's lashes shot up, framing grey-blue eyes wide enough to drown in. Her lips parted ever so slightly, her breath speeding up. Her breastbone bumped the back of Blitzen's fingers, still twined around her own. When her free hand slid across his knee to brace against his thigh, he thought he might go mad.

"Blitzen," Sin whispered – and oh, there it was, the breathless hitch to her words. "I don't … I don't know how to …"

He kissed her.

With his lips, with his heart, with every shining filament of his soul.

Sin surrendered instantly, gasping into his mouth when he buried a hand in her hair. She tasted of chocolate and cookies, of lust and magic, of broken promises and second chances.

Blitzen had meant to go slow but he couldn't stop, releasing Sin's hand to sweep her onto his lap. Her knees slid around his hips, breasts moulded to his chest, and when she wrapped her arms around his neck, the needy sound he made wasn't remotely human. Sin's curves were satin and sunshine beneath his hand, her mouth eager as she shifted restlessly.

"I'm going to lose it in my shorts like a teenager if you're not careful." Blitzen panted the words against her lips, a choppy sentence broken by kisses and the insistent roll of Sin's body against his own.

"Oh, gods," her voice wobbled, thick with an emotion that shattered the swell of Blitzen's need. "I don't ... I can't ... I haven't—"

"It's okay." He gentled the fire of his kiss, smoothing a hand down her spine to flatten it over her lower back. "It's okay, Sin."

She shook above him, a war taking place behind the stormy portal of her eyes. There was passion in this woman, so much passion, so carefully and thoroughly locked away. Letting it out all at once would be glorious – but it'd hurt her, too, and that was something Blitzen couldn't countenance. So he gentled her with lips and hands, guiding her away from the precipice until Sin choked out a sob and buried her face in the curve of his neck.

"I don't know if I should be grateful or embarrassed," she said at last. The movement of her lips against his skin went straight to the near-painful throb of his erection, causing it to flex against the confines of his shorts and drawing a half groan from his lips. For some reason, the sound made Sin giggle, and she lifted her head to glance at him through tear-laden lashes. "Sorry."

"Don't apologise." Blitzen's voice was gritty and rough, as though he'd tried to swallow a handful of gravel. "I pushed you, and that was unfair."

Sin's lashes fluttered, then she lifted her chin. "It takes two, as I recall ... And I wasn't exactly protesting."

"Do you think you should be?"

She tapped the tip of his nose with one finger. "Not for the reasons you're assuming."

"Oh?" Understanding hit with the speed of a falling star, dousing the last of his arousal. "He left you."

"Broken and alone," she confirmed, a soft, worn kind of sadness wreathing her face. "It wasn't Hugh's fault. Logically, I know that. But ... fear isn't logical."

"I'm not going to die," Blitzen said firmly. "I am, in fact, very difficult to kill."

"Good to know." Sin's lips curved, but that sadness, it was still there. "This island, though ... it's a stolen moment in time, a break from our normal lives. You don't truly belong here, and neither do I."

I belong wherever you are. The words hovered on the top of his tongue, but Blitzen swallowed them down and rolled his eyes. "That's the worst breakup line I've ever heard, and we're not even dating."

She blinked. "I'm not breaking up with you."

"So we're still together?"

"We … You … Oh!" Sin's brow furrowed, that awful sadness dissipating as she smacked a hand against his chest. "You're infuriating."

"One of my many talents." Blitzen nipped at her nose, earning a rusty laugh in response. "At the risk of sounding glib, how about this: I like you. I think, if I'm reading the signals right, that you like me. Since neither of us date, why don't we agree to not-date for the foreseeable, if uncertain, future, and simply … see what happens?"

A glimmer of light twinkled in Sin's eyes. "Just like that?"

"Just like that." He cocked his head, wondering if she could hear the rustling of feathers as his heart spread its wings. "Two people, not-dating, hunting for stolen Christmas presents, watching potentially murderous vampires, eating cookies and crocheting phalluses during family video calls. What do you think?"

This time, her laugh wasn't the least bit rusty. "I think I've either lost my mind, or you're more charming than you realise."

"Maybe both, because if you think I'm charming, then you have to be a little bit crazy." Blitzen grinned, then gestured at the clock. "It's late. There are a tonne of guest rooms here. Would you like to borrow one for the night? I'll send word for Eli to watch your villa, and we can head back in the morning. No pressure, just an option."

"I *am* tired …" Sin chewed on her lip. "And I suppose it'll give Elias a chance to poke around a bit without looking suspicious."

"So that's a yes?" Blitzen swallowed around the lump in his throat, breathing in the unspoken words that hung in the air between them. "You'll stay?"

Colour dusted Sin's cheeks, but she nodded. "I'll stay. But that doesn't mean we're dating!"

Blitzen's lips curved into a wicked smile. "Of course not."

9

NOT AS EXPECTED

After spending several weeks in a bed other than her own, Sin had expected the disorientation of waking in unfamiliar surroundings to have faded. It lingered, however, chasing her out of bed and into a scalding shower filled with all manner of toiletries which, while lovely, only served to remind her how far she was from her own home.

Decidedly male voices filtered through the bedroom door, causing Sin to clutch reflexively at her towel. She recognised Blitzen's rumbling baritone. Memories of the kiss they'd shared woke parts of her body that had, until the night before, been happily dormant. After debating whether to climb out the window – and then swiftly recalling the house was built into the side of a cliff – Sin tossed the towel aside and wriggled back into her tankini and matching cover-up. The gauzy fabric provided little in the way of actual armour, but was still infinitely better than being practically naked with temptation incarnate in the next room.

Once she was dressed, Sin padded to the door, took a deep breath and pulled it open. There'd been enough supplies in the bathroom that she'd been able to brush her teeth and her hair, meaning she was as put-together as one could be when one had agreed to an impromptu sleep-over without so much as a pair of shoes or lip balm.

"There you are." Blitzen's face creased in a smile which threatened to make Sin's knees wobble. "I hope we didn't wake you."

"No, I was up." She edged further into the room. "Is someone else here? I thought I heard—"

"I'm afraid that would be me. Good morning, my dear."

Sin froze, jaw dropping, as Blitzen stepped aside to reveal the large screen dominating the far wall. The man within was nothing short of breathtaking, wearing tailored slacks the colour of red wine, a paler red shirt with the sleeves rolled back and a plaid emerald waistcoat that hugged his lean torso like a lover. His snowy white hair was styled in a modern sweep that sat as neatly as his closely trimmed white beard. His skin was a strokable gold, the perfect foil for sleek white brows and curling white lashes, from between which twinkled a pair of periwinkle eyes. Though he looked to be in his mid-thirties, age fairly leaked through the screen, tempered by a welcoming smile and deep creases at the corners of his eyes that said he laughed well and often.

"Sin?" Blitzen gestured to the screen. "This is my friend, Nykolaas Klausse."

"So formal, B." That perfect face pulled into a grimace. "Please, call me Nyk."

Sin swallowed. Tried to speak. Coughed. Wondered if she should just go back to her room and sleep until this incredible, impossible being went away. As usual, her mouth had other ideas, and it chose that exact moment to shout, "You're supposed to be fat!"

The being who'd insisted she call him Nyk tipped back his head and laughed. It was a full laugh, rich and rolling, the kind of laugh that wrapped a person in unconditional affection … and it didn't sound a whit like 'ho, ho, ho'.

"I'm so sorry," Sin gushed. "It's just that the illustrations and stories featuring you are so incredibly, horrifically wrong, it's a wonder they've been allowed to stay in circulation. It's not every day I meet a real-life god, or, you know, talk to one on the screen, and despite

Blitzen telling me all about you it's really rather intimidating and oh my gods I'm still talking."

She slapped both hands over her mouth, digging the tips of her fingers into her cheeks for good measure. Blitzen was grinning from ear to ear, face alight with the same kind of laughter that still exploded from Nykolaas. Sin closed her eyes, pleading with her legs to take her back to the bedroom – but they wouldn't move, her toes digging so hard into the plush carpet that a sharp inhale might cause them to snap off.

"Sin." Blitzen's voice, rougher and deeper than Nyk's, the tone intimate in a way that should have frightened her more than it did. The same calloused hands that had caresssed her into a frenzy of need the night before coasted lightly up the outside of her arms. "I'm sorry if we surprised you, but I need to talk to Nyk about the ship situation and this is the only screen in the house."

The ship. How could she have forgotten? Sin's eyes snapped open, breath catching as she discovered Blitzen's face so close to her own that he might as well be licking the back of her knuckles. The thought brought a fresh wave of heat to her cheeks, as well as a coiling ache deep inside that she smothered with ruthless speed. She took a slow, deliberate step back, equally relieved and disappointed when he didn't try and follow. A kiss was one thing, and though she'd decided not to regret it, that didn't mean she was about to allow it to happen again. At least not until she'd had a moment to regain her equilibrium.

"Have there been more developments overnight?" Sin asked, lowering her hands just enough that words wouldn't come out muffled.

Blitzen grimaced and behind him, Nyk did the same. It was impossible not to compare the two, each attractive in their own way – but while Sin appreciated Nykolaas the way one might appreciate an incomparably beautiful work of art, it was Blitzen, with his silver-streaked temples and rough-edged charm, who put her in danger of spontaneous combustion.

"Not really," Nykolaas answered. "I was just letting Blitzen know that Shining Star Cruises have agreed to provide a copy of both the crew and passenger manifests, since the *Shimmering Wave* lost all its data. As soon as I have it, I'll forward it through."

"What about Dame Garadova and her grandson?" Sin shuddered at the recollection of Nathaniel's gleaming fangs. "Judging by what Blitzen said last night, they're dangerous whether involved in this situation or not."

"I agree," Nyk said, his smile beatific. "That's why I've asked Blitzen to enlist your help in bringing this matter to a close."

"*My* help?" Sin pressed a hand to her breastbone. "What in the world could I possibly do?"

"Nyk ever so kindly pointed out that the Garadovas have already taken an interest in you, and might do so again." Blitzen glowered at the screen. "If we were to spend more time together, I'd have a legitimate excuse to both keep you safe, and poke around the resort without it seeming suspicious."

"That makes sense, and isn't too different from what we discussed last night." Sin tipped her head to one side. "So why the frown?"

"Because now I feel like we're using you as bait, and I'm not comfortable with that idea." He slashed a hand through the air. "I promised your family I'd keep you safe. I plan to keep my word."

Sin raised a brow, temper sparking. "Don't I get a say in this, since it's me we're discussing? Or does the fact that I allowed you to kiss me naturally translate to ownership of my life and my choices?"

"What?" Blitzen blinked rapidly. "Of course not."

"Are you sure? Because it sounds to me like—"

"Wait a minute." Nykolaas leaned forward, grinning like a cat who'd got the cream. "You guys kissed?"

"None of your business," Sin snapped, daring to wave a reproachful finger at the god on the screen. "How would Mrs Claus – Klausse – feel if you talked about your bedroom activities like a child with a bag of lollies?"

"My apologies." Nyk's smile dissolved, shadows darkening his periwinkle eyes until they were almost unrecognisable. "And, for the record, there is no Mrs Klausse."

There is no Mrs Klausse.

A simple enough sentence, but weighted down by so many layers that Sin felt their impact as physical blows. She knew the look Nyk wore; she'd seen it on her own face in the early years following Hugh's death. Lifting a hand to the wedding rings at her throat, she gentled her tone. "I'm sorry for your loss."

"Thank you." He jerked his chin in a stiff nod. "I know this situation is stressful and dangerous, and I have no wish to intentionally endanger you, but there's more at stake here than the simple loss of some Christmas gifts. The longer things draw on—"

"You don't need to convince me." Sin smiled to take the sting from her interruption. "People have died, and if there's something I can do to bring them justice, however small, I will."

Nykolaas pressed his lips together, then nodded again. "Thank you."

"You're welcome."

"Stay vigilant, both of you." Nyk's gaze drifted to the left, where Blitzen practically thrummed with tension. "And take care of each other."

The screen went dark.

"Sin?" Blitzen cleared his throat. "Listen, I …"

"Don't." She held up a hand and counted silently to three, snuffing out the fuse his comments had lit and filling her voice with the resulting frost. "Impeccable forearms, hot lips and a verbal non-dating agreement don't give you the right to start throwing your weight around as though you own me. If the next words out of your mouth aren't 'I'm sorry', then I won't be held responsible for my actions."

Blitzen scuffed a bare foot against the floor. "I'm sorry."

"Good." Sin lifted her chin. "Now, if it's all the same to you, I'd like to return to my villa."

1 0

TAINTED WATER

Shorts with pockets were better for sulking.

Not that he *was* sulking, of course, but if sulking had to be done, it was better when there were pockets.

Blitzen sighed, kicking a stone off the path in front of him. Elias had been notably absent when he and Sin returned to the villa – though the remains of a meal, a rumpled guest bed and a pair of lacy women's underpants caught in the light fixture attested to the elf's presence at some point or another. The evidence of Elias' insouciant house-sitting style had pushed Sin's mood from irritable to downright furious, and somewhere between climbing onto a chair to retrieve the scarlet g-string, and shoving said g-string into Blitzen's pocket, she'd chased him outside, declaring the need for an hour or so to herself. And when he'd opened his mouth to protest, she'd locked the door in his face.

Rather than loiter on the back deck like a lost puppy, Blitzen had elected to spend his newly acquired free time locating Elias for an update on the vampires – preferably over a plate of the resort's tropically themed nachos and an ice-cold beer. With the thought of refreshments urging him forward, Blitzen stepped into the air-conditioned interior of the resort's main building.

Several staff members waved and wished him a good morning but he kept his pace brisk as he passed them by, excusing himself while he dodged sleepy adults and laughing children in brightly coloured outfits.

"Sir." Never one to be put off by a purposeful stride, Devon appeared beside Blitzen as though summoned from thin air. "If I may have a word?"

"That depends," Blitzen replied, slipping behind the resort's enormous reception desk. "I'm looking for Elias. Have you seen him?"

Devon pursed his thin lips. "Not since late yesterday evening. I believe he was engaged in a drinking competition with a group of youths willing to wager good money on their egos."

"And since?"

"I'm afraid I had a personal matter to attend to this morning, sir, and have only just arrived." The well-worn lines between Devon's brows deepened. "It's the very reason I'd like a few moments of your time."

"Is everything all right? Your daughter?"

"Coral is well, thank you. The chair you delivered last Christmas has enabled her to move about the island as well as any of us." The barest hint of a smile flirted with Devon's lips, fading as quickly as it had appeared. "It was my father who summoned me, and his message I'm tasked with delivering."

Though Garvon owned several local islands and the resorts built upon them, he rarely left his home. Instead, he'd installed his many children as managers of the family interests. Devon and his siblings served not only as very capable businesspeople, but also as liaisons between their father and the outside world. Though Garvon himself was no stranger to Blitzen, the delivery of a message was unusual enough that all thoughts of finding Elias scattered.

"In here." Blitzen ushered Devon into the small but well-appointed office behind the reception area, closing the frosted glass door behind him. He ignored the comfortable chairs and elegant desk in favour of the coffee machine in the corner kitchenette, brewing himself something dark, strong and exotic before he turned to face his host once more. "Okay, go."

Devon made a small moue of distaste. "At least some milk, or sugar?"

"Nope. Blacker than my soul, or not at all." Blitzen sipped for effect, savouring the boutique coffee; yet another arm of Garvon's sprawling empire. "There's nothing quite like this anywhere else in the world."

"Because that specific flavour combination is exclusive to this resort," Devon replied, his nose lifting the slightest amount – only to drop again, an uncharacteristically resigned sigh escaping him. "My father is, as are we all, adversely affected by the communications blackout blanketing the area. These waters are our home, and these pirates have invaded it, threatening not only our guests, but our people. While the insult was aimed at you and your Nykolaas, the danger is very much here, and my father believes the best way to solve both problems is to work together."

"Hmm." Blitzen sipped again. "If he's expecting me to snap to attention, he should know better."

"Oh, no, sir." Devon shook his head. "Rather, he'd like to put you in charge of the entire situation. Whatever you require of us, you have only to ask and I will see it arranged."

"Oh, good. More pressure," Blitzen muttered. "First Nyk, then Sin's family, now your father—"

"Who, sir?"

"Sin." When his companion continued to look confused, Blitzen rolled his eyes. "The woman whose lunch I interrupted the other day."

"Ah. The one who defaced my napkins." Devon nodded. "Thankfully for my napery, she's not been back to the restaurant since."

"That's because she was with me." Blitzen drained the last of his delicious coffee and set the cup in sink. "She's my ... mine."

"Good gracious, are you sure?"

"Weren't you sure when you met Flick?"

"Of course, but I ... But we ... Oh dear." Devon screwed up his face. "My condolences, sir."

Blitzen snorted a laugh. "Be nice."

"I'm afraid I'm rather at the end of my tether at the moment. There's much to catch up on, and no spare time to catch up on it." Devon unbuttoned his shirtsleeves and set about rolling them up, the closest Blitzen ever saw him come to acknowledging the island's tropical climate. "I'm certain Sin is endearing once one gets to know her, and I wish you both every happiness."

"You looked like you were trying to pass a melon when you said that."

Devon sniffed. "It was about as painful, sir, but one must make sacrifices in the line of duty from time to time."

If Blitzen didn't know Devon as well as he did, he might have been offended; instead, he slung an arm around the other male's shoulders and steered him towards the coffee machine. "You sound like you need one of these more than I did, and that's saying something."

"Perhaps." Devon retrieved a clean cup from the stack atop the machine, tapping his fingers against the porcelain. "Shall I instruct my father's men to continue searching the oceans for some sign of the pirates?"

"Yeah." Blitzen clicked his tongue against his teeth. "Is there a way to keep watch over the other islands affected by the blackout, too?"

Devon rolled his lips inward, setting the cup just so beneath the coffee machine's spigot and pressing several buttons in a complicated pattern. "I can send a message with the regular ocean patrols. It will take time to get word to us if there is something worth noting, however."

"It'll still be easier than trying to overfly each island myself."

"Good point, sir." Devon pressed the final button and the machine roared to life, the smell of grinding coffee beans filling the air. "I shall be sure to keep you updated."

"Thanks." Blitzen tugged open the door and stepped into the foyer. "Now all I need to do is find Elias, and we can get this show on the road."

ON ICE

Though the villa was in no way as welcoming as her own home, Sin was nevertheless relieved to be back. A change of clothes, a tall glass of iced tea and the miniature raspberry cheesecake she'd ordered the day before – but never had the chance to eat, thanks to the sudden appearance of a certain magical flying reindeer – went a long way to restoring her equilibrium.

Thinking of Blitzen tugged Sin's brow into a frown, and she set her cake fork on the granite countertop to rub at her temples. Tossing him clean out of the house felt a little dramatic in retrospect, particularly when he'd done nothing other than prioritise her safety. It was just … well. This whole thing that wasn't a thing, yet was *most definitely a thing,* had her on the back foot. The more time she spent with Blitzen, the more she liked him, and the more she liked him, the more uncertain she felt about the way forward. An hour or so to reset, perhaps indulge in some art and crafts, was just the thing she needed.

Toasting thin air, Sin drained the last of her iced tea and set the glass down on the bench. As she did, her eye caught on the canvas tote she took almost everywhere. The corner of her tablet peeped out of it. Odd; she could've sworn her tablet had been on the dining room table yesterday, along with her business journal and several of her latest creations.

Sin crossed the lounge to her tote and peered inside. The tablet and her business journal lay within, alongside a small painting she'd done while still aboard the cruise ship. Her mobile phone was there, too, rather than on the dressing table beside her bed, along with the travel wallet containing her passport and other paperwork, which had been carefully stored at the bottom of her suitcase, underneath all her clothing. The sundries she normally kept in the tote – lip balm, sunglasses, tissues – were gone. A cursory inspection of the area revealed them underneath the coffee table, as though someone had upended the tote in a hurry so they could stuff the other items inside instead.

A shiver trickled down Sin's spine. She didn't really know Elias – assuming he wouldn't steal from her simply because he worked for Santa Claus was so far beyond naive it bordered on insanity. In fact, it made a certain kind of sense; Blitzen had sent word they'd be staying the night rather than returning to the villa, giving Elias ample time to uncover all Sin's valuable information, drop it in the most convenient bag at hand, then plant the g-string as a distraction so she wouldn't immediately notice the tote was missing.

What he thought to gain from having access to all her paperwork, she didn't know, but when Blitzen returned to the villa, Sin was going to demand they find out. Only … what if Elias returned first? Sin was just a human, her magic's sole use the creation of art – crocheted phalluses notwithstanding. Elias, meanwhile, was a strong, muscular elf who'd already demonstrated not only excellent combative skills, but a sour demeanour to boot. What chance did she have, really, if she confronted him alone and he turned on her?

None.

Nada.

Zip.

Zero.

Gods, she was so stupid. She shouldn't be waiting for Blitzen like some mythical damsel in distress; she should be getting the hell out of dodge while she still had the chance.

With trembling hands, Sin shoved all her precious items back into the tote and raced into her bedroom. Dropping the bag on the bed, she flipped open her suitcase and tried not to think about Elias handling her underwear while she extracted several clean pairs and thrust them into the tote. A spare bra followed, along with a clean t-shirt and shorts; enough to get her through a couple of days if things really did go south. After a quick detour to the bathroom, she added her hairbrush, toothbrush and toothpaste to the stash, along with a spare lip balm and the chargers for her devices.

"Coat." She whirled towards the wardrobe. "Or some kind of wrap in case it gets cold—"

"Hello, Lucinda."

Sin leapt back with a gasp. A man stood inside the wardrobe; tall, broad, somehow familiar – though it was hard to put a name to a face partially hidden by her dressing gown. For a long moment all she could do was stare, but when the man's lips pulled wide into a vicious grin, revealing a pair of wickedly curved fangs, reality rushed back in and Sin did the only thing a self-respecting, fifty-six-year old woman would.

She screamed.

Loudly.

"Shhhhhh." A broad hand covered her mouth as the vampire stepped out of the wardrobe, revealing a perfect slick of auburn hair, artificially tanned skin and eyes the colour of old blood.

Nathaniel Garadova.

"Ah, yes," he said, backing Sin up until her legs hit the bed. "You recognise me now. I see it in your eyes – such an intriguing shade of grey, with the barest hint of blue. I thought so the day we first met, you know, but now that I'm seeing them dilated with terror? Oh, yes. Very pretty, indeed."

His body bumped against hers, forcing Sin back onto the bed. Her tote bag dug uncomfortably into her back, a pale contrast to the cool vampire pressed against her front, sticky blood coating his arms and hands. The metallic scent gripped Sin's lungs and she retched, her stomach turning a swift somersault. Nathaniel swore, yanking her head towards the side of the bed so she could deposit her iced tea and cheesecake all over the bedroom carpet.

"It was you," she managed at last. "Elias wasn't trying to steal my things. You were."

"You thought the *elf* was trying to rob you?" Nathaniel laughed, high pitched and grating. "He was so drunk he could barely finish the job he'd started with the cute little housekeeper. Ending his life was one of the easiest things I've ever done."

Sin froze. "You … killed him?"

"What else was I supposed to do?" Nathaniel made a tsking noise in the back of his throat. "He was in my way, after all. It was a shame I had to make it quick, but the female? Oh, she made the loveliest dinner."

Sin's nausea returned with a vengeance, but this time, so did her temper. The entire time she'd been doubting Elias, this asshole had been hiding in her wardrobe – and now, thanks to her own foolish actions, she was going to become just another statistic on the news: 'middle aged mother of two, murdered in paradise'.

No more art.

No more snuggles with her grand-babies.

No more opportunities to fight with Blitzen, or, worse, to see where the attraction between them might lead.

Nothing but darkness and wasted opportunities.

Fire burned at the back of Sin's throat, her eyes blurring with tears. "No."

"What was that?" Nathaniel's weight shifted as he leaned closer.

"I said, *no*."

Sin swiped a hand through her own vomit and rolled, flinging the sloppy mess into Nathaniel's face. The vampire howled, stumbling away from the bed to scrub at his eyes and mouth. Sin pushed to her feet and ran, slamming the bedroom door behind her in the vain hope it would buy a few extra seconds. She took the stairs two at a time in her haste to descend to the front door, clutching at the metal knob as she fumbled with the lock. The mechanism had just begun to turn when an arm banded around her waist, snatching away her chance at freedom.

"Bitch," Nathaniel hissed. Sin kicked at the vampire's legs but he ignored the blows, dragging her back to the stairs – only instead of going up he went down, where the villa's small basement housed the laundry facilities, a glass-fronted wine fridge and an enormous chest freezer which was currently open, a wide smear of blood trailing down one side and across the floor.

She screamed again, something her body seemed determined to do without her conscious volition. When Nathaniel shut her up by shoving a wadded-up rag in her mouth, Sin was irrationally grateful; she'd never been a victim and starting now seemed rather pathetic, if she stopped to think about it. Although, really, how *could* one stop to think about something like that when there was blood all over the floor, as though a body had been dragged—

Sin blinked.

The drag marks didn't go towards the freezer at all. They went away from it, as though whatever had been put in there had, against all odds, opened the lid and crawled out.

At the exact same moment she understood what she was seeing, Nathaniel said, "Where the fuck is the elf?"

Laughter echoed off the walls of the basement, a feat Sin would have predicted impossible if she wasn't hearing it for herself. Elias limped out of the shadows, his skin so pale that the tips of his fingers and toes were blue. Dried blood painted a macabre pattern down his torso and matted the long, white hair which was nowhere near long enough to disguise the fact that Elias was as naked as the day he'd been born.

"Pro tip, asshole." Elias' hand flashed, air whistled and Nathaniel let out an ear-splitting shriek as a kitchen knife buried itself in his thigh. "If you want to kill a frost elf, don't toss him in the freezer."

"You stupid little weasel," Nathaniel wheezed, pulling Sin directly in front of him. "You just gave up your only weapon."

"I've got plenty of weapons." Elias held out a hand, ice crystals forming on his palm. Slowly but steadily they grew, merging together to form the most beautiful, delicate dagger Sin had ever seen. "That knife was a gift."

"A gift?" Nathaniel pressed his cheek against Sin's, the sticky blood on his face sliding across her skin. "The only gift I need from you is your death."

"The present wasn't for you, dipshit." Navy eyes caught Sin's and while her heart rabbited in her chest, Elias winked. "I prefer to impress the ladies."

Nathaniel froze, no doubt realising the same thing Sin had – the knife buried in the vampire's thigh was bare millimetres from her dangling hand. No amount of supernatural speed was enough to stop her fingers from closing around the handle and pulling the blade free, twisting in her captor's grip with a strength born of terror and the desperate desire to *live*.

With a furious scream muffled by the rag in her mouth, Sin drove the blade straight into Nathaniel Garadova's smarmy face.

1 2

THE LAMB HAS TEETH

*B*litzen had just unlatched the villa's front gate when a mind-melting scream erupted from inside the building. He was running before it cut out, colliding with the front door hard enough to see stars as he staggered sideways into the garden. Though the scream had been terrifying in and of itself, the lack of it was far worse; he'd been around long enough to know the difference between someone choosing to stop making a sound, and being *forced* to stop making it.

Shaking out his sore shoulder, Blitzen gave up on the front door and vaulted the side fence. Though the villa had been designed to lure guests to the second story balcony and the attendant view, there was a tiny courtyard on the ground floor complete with hanging plants, wrought iron furniture and, most importantly, a set of folding French doors that were far flimsier than their front-of-house counterpart. Blitzen didn't bother stopping to check if said doors were locked; he caught up one of the heavy iron chairs and tossed it into the delicate assembly of wood and glass.

He was through the resulting hole before the wreckage had even hit the floor, hurdling furniture as he raced towards the stairs.

89

The metallic tang of blood assaulted his nostrils, urging him into the basement as fast as his legs would go. Two men struggled in the centre of the room, blood slicking their bodies, the floor, the walls. Blitzen recognised Elias at once, his body like quicksilver in spite of the injuries pockmarking his torso. A conjured ice-knife flashed in his hand as he defended Sin, who'd managed to press herself into a corner of the room so she could pull a piece of wadded up fabric from her mouth.

Rather than trying to arrest his momentum, Blitzen embraced it, bellowing in rage as he shifted from man to reindeer. Elias, who'd spent enough centuries by Blitzen's side to understand a warning when he heard it, abandoned all sense of decorum and leapt in the opposite direction, leaving his opponent stranded in the middle of the room.

Blitzen lowered his head, ramming the asshole with every ounce of strength he possessed. The pointed tips of his antlers sank deep, eliciting a high-pitched scream that cut off as Blitzen scooped his enemy into the cradle of his antlers, wrenching his head up and back to fling the body over his shoulder.

"About time," Elias gasped, limping backwards until he was squarely in front of Sin. "I hate vampires."

"Vampires?" Blitzen's hooves scrabbled on the slick concrete as he spun around, taking a second look at the creature picking itself up off the floor. "Nathaniel."

With his clean-cut, beach boy persona stripped away and what appeared to be a kitchen knife embedded in the side of his face, Nathaniel Garadova the Third was barely recognisable as he hissed and spat at Blitzen – only to turn tail and run, disappearing up the stairs at superhuman speed. Blitzen launched forward with a roar, shifting back to a man just in time to sprint into the stairwell. He took the stairs two at a time, but when he reached the top, the villa's front door lay splintered on the lawn, sunlight bathing the foyer's tiles in golden light.

Of Nathaniel, there was no sign.

Blitzen's heart thundered in his chest, demanding the battle which had been stolen from him – but over the top of that rose an image of Sin, covered in blood as she cowered in the corner. Since the likelihood of Nathaniel returning to the villa when so badly outnumbered was infinitesimally small, Blitzen decided to ignore the missing door and jogged back down the narrow steps to the bloodied basement.

"Blitzen, is that you?" Sin's voice was muffled, and it took several moments and a lot of rapid blinking to register that she was bent over the large freezer against the western wall, the top half of her body swallowed by the cavernous interior.

"It's him." Elias slumped against her legs, the conjured ice-knife pressed against his ribs. "You can tell by the crashing."

"Bull in a china shop," Sin agreed. Her head popped up, and she pushed sticky hair out of her face with a bloodied hand. "Help me, will you? She's too heavy."

"She?" When Sin continued to look at him expectantly, Blitzen crossed to her side and peered into the open chest freezer. "Fuck!"

"Don't get queasy on me now, mister I-just-stabbed-a-vampire-with-my-antlers." Sin pointed at the freezer. "Elias said he needs the cold to heal, and the less things are in here, the faster it will work."

"That's right." Blitzen braced his hips against the battered but somehow still functioning freezer and leaned inside. A woman's body awaited; short, curvy, dark hair, eyes wide and face frozen in a rictus of terror. Someone had very messily torn out her throat, and the arteries in both wrists and elbows had also been savaged. The way she'd been stuffed into the freezer made it impossible for Blitzen to see her other major pulse points, but given the feral glint in Nathaniel's eye and the evidence he *could* see, there was little doubt in Blitzen's mind that those other pulse points would be equally messy. As he scooped the poor, deceased creature into his arms, Blitzen caught a hint of scent beneath the blood and death; his heart twisted. "This is Letitia."

"I know." Elias lurched unsteadily to his feet, expression hollow. "She didn't deserve to die that way."

"Nobody deserves to die that way." Sin brushed her fingers over the dead woman's cheek. "I only knew her as the housekeeper, but the way you said her name … did you two know her?"

"Yeah," Elias grunted, toppling himself into the depths of the freezer. "I liked her."

For anyone else, it was a cold epitaph; for Elias, it was akin to declaring his undying love. Blitzen glanced down at the woman's face, then back at the elf who'd been his friend for more centuries than he'd bothered to count. "You okay?"

"I will be." Elias lifted his hand to reveal the stab wound in his ribs. "Missed my heart, but only just."

"That's not what I meant."

Navy eyes locked on Blitzen's face, barely visible pupils turning to vertical slits. "It's what you're getting."

"All right, boys, that's enough." Seemingly unperturbed by the inhuman ocular display – and the corpse – Sin inserted a hand between Blitzen and Elias as though refereeing a soccer match. "Elias needs to rest." She gave Blitzen such a pointed look that he stepped back, then turned to smile at the elf in the freezer. "Thanks for your help back there."

"Any time." Elias coughed, then spat out a mouthful of blood. "Shut the lid, would you?"

"Of course." Sin reached to do just that, then paused. "I'll make sure she's taken care of."

The briefest flicker of grief twisted Elias' features. "Thanks. I appreciate that."

Sin shut the freezer, which managed to seal in spite of the large dent in the side, and then propped both her elbows on top. "Are you injured, too?"

"No," Blitzen murmured, awed by the incredible fortitude of the woman in front of him. "You?"

She sighed. "Bumps and bruises, nothing more. If not for Elias, I'd have been in that freezer right alongside Letitia."

Blitzen's arms ached with the need to wrap her tight, to feel her body against his – but since he was holding the aforementioned Letitia, and dropping her was a mite too disrespectful for his tastes, he settled instead for saying, "I guess I owe him one for saving you."

Muffled laughter echoed from inside the freezer, and to Blitzen's astonishment, when Sin lifted her head she, too, was grinning.

"Elias didn't save me, silly," she chided. "He gave me the knife so that I could save myself."

13

LIONESS

While Elias did whatever it was injured frost elves did when shut in a freezer, Sin ensured Letitia's body was ensconced in the second guest room. After quietly retrieving the poor woman's g-string from the pocket of Blitzen's board shorts, she shooed him out with instructions to call whoever it was that needed to be called when murderous vampires lost their minds. To his credit, despite the million and one questions stamped all over his gorgeous face, he went, closing the door quietly behind him.

Alone at last, Sin turned to examine her deceased companion. Compartmentalisation was a skill she'd perfected when her husband died – her children had needed their mother, after all – and she employed it with ruthless precision as she manipulated Letitia's limp limbs back into the underwear she'd lost, then into one of the complimentary bath robes that hung in the wardrobe. Despite choosing a room that didn't have evidence of Nathaniel Garadova's presence stamped all over it, no amount of tugging at the hems of the fluffy robe could hide the damage done to Letitia's throat – so Sin took a towel from the attached ensuite, dragged a chair to the head of the bed, and let her magic go to work.

Her fingers shifted into hyper speed as they tore and tucked and folded and wove, producing a passable scarf in a matter of minutes. Sin carefully wound the scarf around Letitia's neck, twisting the loose ends into a decorative knot Charlie had once shown her.

"I'm so sorry," Sin whispered as she sat back. "This is the best I can do."

Memories stirred; Nathaniel's body pressing hers into the mattress, cruel fingers twisting into her hair as he yanked her down to the basement, the horrific crunch as she rammed the kitchen knife into his face. Sin blinked the images away, focusing instead on folding Letitia's hands over her stomach and pulling the blanket up to her shoulders. Then, as she'd once tucked her children into bed when they were young, she perched on the edge of the mattress and finger-combed the tangles from Letitia's hair, humming a soft lullaby.

Tears wet her cheeks and her breathing grew choppy, but she didn't stop – not even when the bedroom door opened and a group of people filed quietly into the room. It was only when a pair of warm hands clasped her shoulders that Sin fell quiet, wondering if the shadows in Blitzen's eyes were mirrored in her own.

When he nudged her away she relented, following him out to the villa's balcony, where the tropical sunshine and brilliant jewel tones of the beach seemed offensively bright. Blitzen pushed something into her hands, but as Sin blinked blearily, she registered not the glass of liquor he offered, but the strands of black hair twisted around her fingers.

"Letitia was always so cheerful when she came to clean the villa," Sin said, meticulously gathering the loose hairs and poking them into the pocket of her bloody jeans. "The day I gave her the bath oil you sent, she thought it was the most wicked joke."

"She had a very naughty sense of humour," Blitzen rumbled, his deep voice cut with gravel. "Even as a child, she laughed at the most inappropriate things."

"You've known her that long?"

"Elias and I have been coming here for years." Blitzen blew out a long breath, his gaze turning misty. "I taught Letitia how to play poker as a child … and then, when she complained she couldn't beat the adults, I taught her how to cheat."

"Oh, gods." Sin swallowed. "So she and Elias …"

"Not a once-off," he confirmed, staring out over the ocean. "Letitia adored him as a little girl, crushed on him as a teen and pursued him relentlessly once she hit adulthood. He held her at arm's length for a few years, but finally melted about a decade ago. They were both adamant it was nothing serious, but he never saw anyone else in the months between visits and I'm certain she didn't, either."

Sin opened her mouth to say 'I'm sorry,' but instead, what came out was, "I'm going to pull Nathaniel Garadova's teeth out one by one, and then I'm going to make them into a set of matching jewellery for Letitia's family."

Blitzen blinked … and then he laughed, a rusty, broken sound wet with tears. When he lifted his arm, Sin didn't think; she pressed herself to his side and buried her face against his chest. The scent of nutmeg and pine eased into her lungs, loosening something inside her that had been wound far too tight. Her next inhale felt like the first breath she'd taken in weeks, and when she raised her hands to sip the liquor Blitzen had given her, the tremor that had wracked her bones disappeared.

She savoured the rich, full flavour of the liquor as it coated her throat before saying, "You came for me."

Blitzen rumbled, his arm tightening around her ribs. "I'll always come for you."

Two hours ago, the level of intensity in that solemn promise would have terrified her. Now, all Sin felt was gratitude and warmth – a blossoming giddiness in the centre of her chest that grew and grew and grew. While it would've been easy to blame the sensation on adrenaline, Sin was past lying to herself. The feelings were her own, her heart cracking free of the chrysalis in which she'd encased it for so long …

And it wanted Blitzen.

This man, who'd frightened and angered and charmed her, who'd smiled and frowned and argued. The magical flying reindeer who worked for the real, honest to goodness Santa, who'd apologised badly and then properly, who'd kissed her with a fire unlike anything she'd ever felt before, and now offered comfort without coddling.

Sin blinked through a fresh wave of tears, holding her world-bending epiphany as close as she'd once held her babies. The longing to share her feelings with Blitzen created a sudden ache at the back of her throat – but doing so with Letitia's lifeless body so close seemed disrespectful, so she breathed her way through the sensations and then lifted her glass until the sunlight turned the dark amber liquid the colour of molten bronze. "This really is delicious."

"Caribbean spiced rum," Blitzen answered, flicking the side of her tumbler. "Brewed on a nearby island by one of Devon's many siblings."

"Huh." She took another sip of her drink, just in case her mouth decided to misbehave, and swallowed heavily. "What now?"

He didn't even pretend to misunderstand. "Elias will be a while, and Devon's people are going to be preoccupied with ensuring Letitia's properly cared for."

"As they should."

"Agreed … but that means the only people available to chase her killer are you and me."

You and me. A fierce smile dawned on Sin's face, the whirlwind in her heart gathering momentum. "I like the sound of that."

"I thought you might." He huffed a laugh, then sobered just as fast. "Do you have any idea why Nathaniel was at the villa in the first place?"

Sin divulged her discovery of the things Nathaniel had tried to steal and the terror-laden events that had followed. Blitzen listened in silence, his hold on her never wavering, and when she finished, he twisted so that he could look her in the eye.

"I'm sorry you doubted Eli. No," he held up a hand when she opened her mouth, the corner of his curving ever so slightly. "Don't apologise. I can see why you thought what you did, and I don't blame you. But I swear, Sin, neither Elias nor I would ever lift a finger to hurt you."

"I know."

Relief flooded Blitzen's expression at the simple certainty of her statement. "Good. Now, the trick is to work out where Nathaniel is, so we can bring him to justice."

"I'll bet anything you care to name that Dame Garadova will know." Sin's eyes narrowed. "Nathaniel is her grandson and protégé, after all."

Blitzen's shoulders dropped, and Sin had never seen anyone look so world-worn as he did in that moment. "I already asked resort security to swing by her villa to detain her. Unfortunately the place was empty when they arrived, with nothing so much as a speck of dust to show either Dame Garadova or Nathaniel had ever stayed there."

"Gods." Emotion crawled up Sin's throat. She closed her eyes to breathe through it. "Now what?"

"We need to rest, and clean up, and think. And …" Blitzen paused, and the atmosphere took on a tension that had Sin's eyes popping open. "Your villa's a mess. The resort is offering to make alternate arrangements, but in my opinion, it's not safe for you to stay on the island while Nathaniel's at large. If you're amenable, I thought we could grab your stuff and head back to my place?"

Blitzen, who'd flown as part of the wild hunt and served as a reindeer under Santa Claus for more centuries than she dared to count, was fidgeting like a teenage boy because he was worried about her answer. In spite of the horror of the day, that simple piece of knowledge had bubbles popping in her blood, and Sin couldn't help but smile up at him. "Are you inviting me to move into your house?"

"I …" Beneath the smattering of blood and grime, his cheeks darkened. "Well, I just thought …"

"Hey." Sin flattened a hand on his chest, savouring the glorious cut of his pectorals beneath her fingertips. "I'm more than happy to stay at your place; I'll feel safer there than anywhere else, and it'll be easier to figure this whole thing out if we're under the same roof."

He blinked. "Really?"

"Yes. Really." Sin stared into those deep brown eyes, words tripping unbidden over her tongue to sparkle in the space between them. "Take me home, Blitzen."

14

MELTED CHEESE

*B*litzen cut the video connection and tossed his phone on the bedside table. It seemed more than a paltry six hours since he'd last spoken to Nykolaas, but the clock didn't lie – in a meagre quarter of a day, Nathaniel had turned Blitzen's involvement in the case of the missing Christmas gifts from professional to personal, reminded him his knees weren't what they used to be, and claimed ownership of several of the white hairs that graced his temples by threatening both Elias and Sin's lives.

Gods, Sin. Turning away from the memory of his own panic, Blitzen shucked his towel and located a fresh pair of board shorts. An exceptional scrubbing and three rounds of shampoo had succeeded in getting him clean, but there was an itch to his bones that wouldn't settle, not even after he'd called Nykolaas to deliver as full a report as he was able. Even though Sin was safe in her guest room, every second Blitzen was away from her made him edgier, until he'd been anticipating the call's end with a breathless impatience that bordered on rude.

"Get it together," he muttered, running a hand through his still-damp hair and then flicking the water off his fingers with a grimace. "She's fine. She's here. Relax already."

When he entered the common room Sin's door was firmly closed, so Blitzen padded upstairs to the kitchen. He wasn't much in the mood to cook but in the time it took for the coffee machine to warm up, he threw together a respectable collection of open-faced sandwiches and slid them under the griller. Since he wasn't sure if Sin preferred tea or coffee, he stuck to hot chocolate for both of them, arranging the mugs and the sandwiches on a tray for the journey back downstairs. Her door was ajar when Blitzen approached, but he nevertheless balanced the tray on one arm in order to knock as politely as possible.

"Come in."

Blitzen shouldered his way inside to find Sin lying on her stomach on the bed, her chin propped on one pillow and her phone propped on the other. Though the screen was small and at a slight angle, he could see her daughter, Charlie, along with two small children who went abruptly silent as Blitzen approached.

"Sorry to interrupt." He set the tray on the end of the bed and gestured at the spread of food. "I thought you might like something to eat."

"Thank you." Sin's smile was somewhat strained, but she'd lost the haunted expression that had dominated her features immediately following Nathaniel's attack. She'd showered, too, and wore a fresh pair of denim shorts beneath a simple lavender t-shirt that was just fitted enough to hint at the curves underneath. Blitzen's mouth went dry as he remembered exactly how those curves felt underneath his hands – and quite suddenly he wasn't hungry for food, but something far sweeter. Oblivious to the sharp turn of his thoughts, Sin gestured at the little screen in front of her. "Meet my grandchildren, Genevieve and Saul."

"Ginny!" The sweet-faced little girl with steely blue eyes, soft auburn curls and wings of palest grey thumped herself in the chest. "I'm Ginny!"

"Nice to meet you, Ginny. I'm Blitzen." Breathing through the thunder in his blood, Blitzen braced both hands on his knees so that he was at a better height with the phone. "And you must be Saul."

Wearing a sombre expression more suited to an adult than a toddler, his hair a tangled mess in the same shade of iron grey as his father's and a half-eaten stick of carrot clutched in one hand, Saul gave a slow nod. "Bizzen?"

"Yeah, that's right," Blitzen grinned. "What have you got there?"

"Cart." Saul held the carrot a little higher, then bit it as though to illustrate a point. A thoughtful look pinched his mouth as he chewed, and after a moment, he held the carrot towards the camera. "Some?"

"Ohhhhh yessssss," Ginny clapped her hands in delight. "Bitzen needs lots of carrots, because he's one of Santa's rain-deer!"

Charlie made a choking noise and Sin winced, pink creeping over her cheeks. "Uh, I may or may not have outed you."

"Is that so?" Blitzen let the amusement bubbling in his gut warm his voice, straightening enough to pat his bare stomach. "I do need a lot of carrots, Ginny, you're right – but Saul's growing too, so I think it would be better if he ate his, and I ate mine."

Another very serious nod from Saul, followed by Ginny crossing both arms over her chest. "You don't have carrots on your plate. I can see it from here. You've got *cheese*."

"That's because reindeer eat more than just carrots," Blitzen said, tapping the side of the tray. "I need lots of different vitamins to keep my muscles strong. How else would I help to pull Santa's sleigh?"

"Satta," Saul whispered, dark eyes shining. "Butta dino ferme!"

"He brought a dinosaur for Saul at Christmas," Ginny translated, her tiny wings flaring in excitement. "And I got a dolly! She's so pretty. Did you pick it for me, Bitzen?"

"Uh..."

"There's lots of presents to be organised for lots of different children," Charlie cut in, nudging Ginny's wing away from her chin. "It would be very difficult for Blitzen to remember exactly which ones he chose – and by the time he did, his lunch would be cold."

Ginny pouted. "I suppose. He's got a lot of lunch."

"This isn't all for me," Blitzen told her, lowering his voice to a stage whisper. "I made extra so that I could share it with your – uh – Nana?"

"Gramma!" Ginny cried, cheeks creasing with laughter. "Her name is Gramma, silly!"

"Of course it is." Blitzen gave both children a gentle smile. "Gramma's had a tricky morning, so I thought she could use something to eat and drink."

"Yes!" Ginny clapped her hands again. "Then you can kiss her!"

Charlie's jaw dropped. "Ginny!"

"What?" Ginny looked up at her mother in surprise. "You said Gramma should kiss him some more. I heard you."

There was a muffled groan from Blitzen's left, and he glanced to the side just in time to witness Sin pulling her pillow over her head. "Is that so?"

"Yeah," Ginny answered, her tone rising with indignation. "Mama said you are nice and a total hottie, and that if Gramma doesn't kiss you more then she has lost her marbles." The little girl's brow creased in consternation. "Which is silly, because I've never seen Gramma with any marbles."

"Okay, Ginny, we really have to let Gramma and Blitzen go now," Charlie said, her cheeks slapped with colour. "They have things to do."

"Fine." Ginny heaved an enormous sigh. "But I really wanted to know about the kissing—"

Charlie put a hand over her daughter's mouth. "Bye, Mum! Talk to you later!"

Sin made a muffled noise from beneath her pillow that might have been an answer, but may also have been a scream.

Blitzen cleared his throat. "Nice talking to you again, Charlie. Pass on my regards to the others, would you?"

"Sure," Charlie answered, looking like a rabbit caught in a hunter's trap. "Uh. Have a good lunch."

"Oh," Blitzen answered, his voice deep and rough even to his own ears. "We will."

Charlie squeaked, snatching at the tablet. Less than a second later, the screen went black.

Blitzen grinned. "Total hottie, huh?"

15

STRUCK BY LIGHTNING

The warm darkness created by her pillow was so comforting that Sin pondered the practicalities of staying there forever. Sure, it'd make showering, eating and toileting a little difficult – but if it meant never having to acknowledge what Ginny had said in her childhood innocence, it might be a worthwhile trade-off.

"Ginny looks just like you." The bed dipped as Blitzen settled beside her, the clank of crockery hinting that he'd either dragged the tray of food closer, or set it on his lap. "Well, really, I suppose she looks like Charlie – but Charlie looks just like you, so the comment stands. And Saul is the spitting image of his father. Is Garrett as serious as his son?"

"Yes," said Sin's mouth. She frowned, then yanked the pillow off her head and heaved it at Blitzen. The cotton-covered projectile hit him square in the chest and bounced off, disappearing down the side of the bed to leave him blinking those unfairly decadent brown eyes at her in surprise. Unwilling to be swayed by the acres of smooth, tanned skin and lovingly sculpted muscle on display, nor the intricate curlicues of his stylised reindeer tattoo, she shoved a shaking finger in his face. "And yes, you are a total hottie, and no, I'm not sorry!"

"Fair enough," he replied, lifting something off the tray. "Sandwich?"

Sin's jaw dropped as she stared at the slice of bread in his hand, a thick layer of melted cheese over something she might have been able to identify if she wasn't distracted by the way Blitzen's forearm flexed as he leaned closer ... and stuck the corner of the aforementioned sandwich into her open mouth.

"Mmf!" Instinct had her biting down, melted cheese and perfectly crisp bread giving way to warm ham and creamy avocado. Sin let out an entirely inappropriate sound of appreciation that, if she were so inclined, might be labelled a moan – but she wasn't that way inclined, so it was definitely not a moan.

At all.

Nope.

"Good?" Blitzen bit down on the opposite corner of the same sandwich, lashes fluttering as he chewed and swallowed. "Oh, yeah. So good."

When he offered another bite, Sin leaned in, the magic of his presence as potent as the moment they'd met. It was only when her hand braced on the heated steel of his thigh that her breath caught, the sensory shock causing her to jerk back. "I can't."

"Why not?" A crease formed between his brows. "Food allergy?"

"What? No," Sin ducked her head, hair sweeping forward to create a curtain between them. The morsel of sandwich she'd swallowed sat like lead in her gut, and she pressed a fisted hand against it. "Dammit, Blitzen, someone *died.* How can I sit here and flirt with you over a late lunch when Letitia's never going home? How is it fair that my heart pounds out of time when I look at you, when hers will never beat again? I know what it's like to be left behind, how your entire world falls apart. How can I possibly—"

"Sin."

The single word, his voice so soft, hit harder than a shout. Wrapping both arms around herself, Sin stared resolutely at her knees. "I stabbed someone. I took up a knife and I stabbed someone in the face, and I don't even feel bad about it. What does that make me?"

"Alive, for a start." Crockery shifted as he set the tray aside, and a moment later warm fingers brushed her shoulder. "When I was on my way back to the villa and I heard you scream ... gods. There was nothing I wouldn't have done in that moment to get to you. *Nothing.* Do you understand?"

"No."

"Liar." His fingers drifted upwards, gently tucking her hair behind one ear. "Defending yourself doesn't make you a bad person. In fact, feeling twisted up inside proves your moral compass is well and truly pointing north. Being sad over the loss of a life is natural ... but what we have here, now, between us? That's not wrong, either. We're not disrespecting anyone, we're taking comfort in each other. Giving support and strength in a time of need."

Sin rolled her lips inward and pressed them together as hard as she could.

Blitzen sighed. "I'm glad you stabbed Nathaniel. Doing so not only saved your life, but probably Elias' as well. Does that make me an asshole?"

"Of course not!"

"Then why is it different when applied to yourself?" The rough warmth of a knuckle nudged at her chin, and against her better judgement, Sin lifted her head. "You went through something traumatic, and when I think about how close I came to losing you ... gods."

Her throat threatened to close, but her mouth, oh, it was determined. "It's okay."

"No, it isn't." Blitzen shook his head in emphasis. "I've been trying to go slow, to keep things light until you're ready – but after this morning's attack, I can't hide it any more. You've got my heart in your hands; right where it belongs."

Sin touched his jaw, the salt and pepper scruff teasing the skin of her palm. There was no subtlety in this man, no games; nothing but a raw, brutal honesty that cut her to the core even as it wrapped her in a thick, protective shield.

"I'm scared," she managed, and yeah, those were tears spilling down her cheeks. "I've lost once before, and the thought that it might happen again ..."

"I know." His deep brown eyes burned, thumbs gently wiping the moisture from her face. "But I'll never leave you, Sin. *Never.*"

Sin opened her mouth to say he couldn't promise such a thing – Hugh had said the same thing – but instead, she said, "I think I'm in love with you."

The smile that bloomed on Blitzen's face was worth every moment of heartache and uncertainty that had led to this point. It creased his cheeks, lit his eyes, made his skin glow with an infectious kind of joy that caused Sin to splutter a wet, embarrassed laugh as he tumbled her onto the mattress.

"See, that's where we differ, because I *know* I'm in love with you." He nipped her nose, the ridges of her cheeks, paused with his lips so close that Sin's tingled. "Tell me no, and I'll stop."

Panic clutched at Sin's throat, threatening to close it over. If she let go, truly let go, there'd be no going back – and to love and lose a second time? She couldn't. *Wouldn't.*

Except, whispered a little voice in the back of her brain, it's already too late.

The warmth which had blossomed in her chest on the villa balcony returned with a vengeance, smoothing the sharp edges of Sin's panic. The fear and trauma she'd carried so long trembled, struck by the reality of that single, sparkling thought.

Blitzen was under her skin, swimming in her blood, his name etched on her bones. It didn't matter if she walked away in the next minute, or stayed for as long as they both had – they belonged to each other.

It was already too late... which meant Sin had only one answer.

"Yes," she breathed, and sealed her mouth to his.

Blitzen rumbled deep in his chest, lowering his weight so that every impossibly perfect inch of him pressed against her. Though she'd started the kiss, Sin happily surrendered when he buried a hand in her hair, parted her lips with his own, and set about branding his name on her soul from the inside out.

Her hands trembled as she stroked them down his bare back, tentatively at first, then with growing confidence as he hummed and arched beneath her touch. Blitzen's body was a wonderland of silk over steel, the landscape of his musculature marked by scars and blemishes that spoke of a life lived to the fullest. When his hand slipped beneath her t-shirt, the pads of his fingers were just the right blend of hot and rough.

"Blitzen," she managed, the syllables barely intelligible between kisses.

"I know." Though his erection lay hard and thick against her thigh, he made no attempt to rush, sliding his hand up her ribs until the tip of his thumb traced the bottom edge of her bra in perfect rhythm with the movements of his tongue. "Gods, Sin."

Her gasp was throaty. "I …"

Sin felt the bunch of his muscles and then Blitzen was gone, kneeling beside her on the mattress. His black hair was tumbled, tanned skin flushed with desire, and gods, she wanted to lick every inch of his chest, wanted to trace the lines of his abdomen with her tongue, to explore what lay beneath the straining fabric of his shorts.

Only … he wasn't moving. Uncertainty whispered through her veins, drawing Sin's brows together until she recalled the last time they'd kissed. She hadn't known how to deal with the sudden avalanche of sensations and feelings that had threatened to sweep her under and it had only been Blitzen, with his enormous heart, who'd soothed her down from a precipice she hadn't been ready to leap off of.

The knowledge that he was doing it again coated Sin's bones like honey, rich and sweet, giving her the courage to sit up, gather the hem of her t-shirt and pull it off over her head. She didn't know how to be sexy, so she simply dropped the garment on the floor and then looked back at Blitzen. His jaw had gone slack, body vibrating as his eyes traced a slow path down her throat, drinking his fill of the black and violet bra that cupped her breasts before dropping to her abdomen, where the faintest spiderweb of stretch marks over softened skin marked her as a mother. "Sin …"

"It's okay." Heart in her throat, Sin hooked both thumbs in the waistband of her shorts. "Yes?"

"Fuck." He shook his head, eyes glued to her hands. "Yes."

Sin unfastened her shorts and slid them off, kicking the bundle of denim onto the floor with her t-shirt. Her panties were plain black, chosen for comfort rather than appeal, but the look on Blitzen's face made her feel as though she wore designer lingerie. With a dry throat, she twisted her arms up behind her back, curling her fingers around the clasp of her bra. "Yes?"

"Yes," he wheezed, and that bulge in his shorts, it jerked. "May I?"

Sin opened her arms in invitation and Blitzen pounced, lips catching hers as he undid her bra in one smooth, easy movement.

"Here." Wondering who this strange, wanton woman was, Sin guided his hands to her bare breasts. "Oh, gods."

"No gods," Blitzen breathed, brushing both thumbs over her nipples and sending bolts of lightning straight to her core. "Just us."

"Just us." She arched into his touch, but it still wasn't enough. "You're wearing too many clothes."

"If you think I'm letting these go, you can think again." Blitzen bent his head, shifting one hand so that he could draw her nipple into his mouth and suck. Sin gasped as pleasure short-circuited her senses. Her thighs clenched together. She was suddenly, achingly aware of how empty she was, her body insisting that no matter how good she felt right now, Blitzen knew how to make her feel even better.

"I need you," she said, pulling at the waist of her panties. "Right now."

Blitzen mumbled something nonsensical against her breast, nudging her onto her back. Sin went gladly, wriggling out of her underwear while he shifted his mouth to her other breast. Letting out a sound somewhere between a moan and a scream, Sin writhed in his arms, trying without success to reach the fastening of his shorts.

Her body was on fire, Blitzen's every caress a lightning strike to her senses. When he showed no sign of stopping his dedicated appreciation of her breasts, Sin did the only thing she could think of – she smacked him in the side of the head with her panties.

He laughed against her skin, angling his head so her nipple slipped from his lips at just the right angle to have Sin's hips bucking. "Yes?"

The word was wicked and rough, the teasing grin almost more than she could take. It'd been decades since she was naked in front of someone other than her children, but rather than feel vulnerable, all Sin could think about was how *not* naked her companion was.

"Shorts," she demanded, pointedly tossing her panties across the room. "Off."

Grin widening, Blitzen rolled off the bed. Despite having ordered him to go, Sin opened her mouth to protest his absence – but as he tugged his shorts down over his hips, all she managed was, "Oh."

Blitzen with clothes on was hot. Blitzen half dressed, hotter. Blitzen naked, mussed, and aroused? H-O-T-T-E-S-T.

He wore his nudity with ease, the soft brown of his skin suggesting the sun had kissed him as a baby, and he'd managed to keep some of the warmth for himself. Powerful thighs flowed into a backside Sin wanted to bite, but it was the erection jutting out in front that took her immediate attention.

"I'm clean," he said, voice tender in spite of the fact she could see his pulse jumping. "And I take a contraceptive draught the elf doctors make, but if you want me to—"

"No." Sin shifted her gaze to his face with effort. "I trust you." Colour threatened to bloom on her cheeks as she added, "I'm clean too."

Blitzen crawled slowly back onto the bed, his body fluid and graceful as a cat. When he drew level with Sin's feet, he paused to kiss one ankle bone and then the other, the gesture both warming her heart and firing a fresh wave of lighting into her blood. He nipped at her shin, and in reply, she slid her legs wide enough for him to shift between them. Rather than pounce, Blitzen began the slow, exquisite process of kissing his way up the inside of one leg. By the time he reached the top of her thigh, Sin was gasping and squirming, and when his tongue flicked out to caress the bundle of nerves at her apex, she cried out.

"I want to taste you," he growled, caging her hips in his hands. "I want to put my mouth on you until you scream."

He licked her again, holding her down when she would have bucked right out of his grip. Sin wheezed his name, somehow managing to catch hold of his hair and tug.

"Hmm?" Blitzen's expression was lazy and wicked as he glanced upward.

It was the most erotic thing Sin had ever seen, leaving her struggling to find her tongue. When she did, her words were little more than breathless pants, strung together in the vaguest approximation of sound. "It's been a long time."

"I know."

The depth of care in his voice, oh, it threatened to undo her. Swallowing the sudden lump in her throat, Sin said, "I don't want to go over alone."

"Then we go together."

Tears blurred her vision as his next kiss landed in the crease of her thigh. Sin sifted her hands through his hair as Blitzen continued his slow, torturous journey up her ribs, pausing to scrape his teeth over the side of her breast before nipping his way along her collarbone and up the side of her throat. His body settled in the cradle of her thighs as he claimed her mouth for a kiss, his tongue sweeping against hers while the blunt head of his erection nudged at her entrance.

Sin wriggled her hips in a desperate attempt to get that hot, hard length where she wanted it, the friction of her movements drawing gasps from them both. Bracing himself on the mattress, Blitzen broke the kiss and leaned back far enough that he could meet her eyes – and then he slid into her, a maddeningly slow invasion that was the most incredible torture Sin had ever endured.

She clutched at his shoulders as her body stretched and clamped in turn, the simple, steady thrust igniting her blood until she was little more than a creature of sensation.

"Blitzen," she panted, her hips hitching of their own accord.

His lashes fluttered, a low groan catching in the back of his throat. "Okay?"

"Good," Sin managed. Her hands slid down his back to his butt, fingertips digging in as she tugged. "You can – ohhhhhhhhhh."

Her voice trailed off as he slowly withdrew, then slid right back in all over again, only to repeat the process. Each time Blitzen thrust, he gained a little more speed, applied a little more pressure, learning her body as she learned his. Sin urged him on with breathless gibberish, rolling her hips in time to Blitzen's, their dance as ancient and natural as the Earth itself. He kissed her hard and deep, mimicking the rhythm of his hips with his mouth and tongue, stoking the fire until Sin wasn't sure where she left off and he began.

"Sin, oh fuck, Sin, I—" Blitzen's hand clamped over her hip, urging her legs around his waist. When she complied, he shifted his grip, changing the angle of her pelvis and increasing the intensity of every thrust. "Hold on."

There was little else Sin could do, because his lovemaking turned from calculated to frenzied and gods, it felt so good that the roof could have caved in and she wouldn't have cared. Blitzen thickened inside her and they cried out in unison as she shattered around him, the clamping of her internal muscles dragging him over the edge exactly as he'd promised. They rocked together through the waves of ecstasy, limbs tangled and lips locked, and it was so damned perfect Sin knew that whatever happened in her life from this moment forward, she'd never, ever be the same.

16

THE TRUTH ABOUT LAUNDRY

As it turned out, the sandwiches Sin laughingly called toasties were just as good cold as they had been warm. It may have had something to do with the way Blitzen reclined against the head of the bed with Sin curled into his chest while they ate – and the shenanigans that followed after she started licking crumbs off his pectorals – but either way, he'd never eschew a cooled toastie ever again.

Reality, however, could only be kept at bay for so long. By mid-afternoon, Blitzen found himself showered, dressed, and perched on the couch beside Sin, a cup of iced coffee in hand as he watched her examine the items Nathaniel had tried to steal.

"Tablet, phone, business journal, travel papers, passport ... and this painting." Sin's brows knit. "As far as I can see, nothing's been tampered with."

"What about the painting?" Blitzen cocked his head to one side as he eyed the image. "Is that the island where the resort is based?"

"Yeah. It was such a lovely scene, lush and tropical, framed by the sea ..." She shrugged. "Maybe Nathaniel just wanted a souvenir?"

"And maybe I'm the tooth fairy," Blitzen muttered. "There are a

113

literal boatload of passengers staying at the resort right now; why would Nathaniel specifically come after you?"

"I don't know. I'd never met him before that moment on the beach, and even that was by chance."

"Was it?" Blitzen sipped his iced coffee, eyes narrowed in thought. "The wounds Letitia suffered at his hands are almost identical to those inflicted upon the *Shimmering Wave's* crew." He hesitated, but when Sin didn't balk, added, "It's not unheard of for vampires to tear out a throat in order to hide the puncture marks left by their fangs."

"You think Nathaniel killed the crew?" Sin shivered. "I suppose that would incriminate him in the sabotage and theft of the gifts, too. Were the crew members drained of blood like Letitia was?"

"No – but not even the most gluttonous vamp would have been able to drain them all. A few mouthfuls from each would have been enough to fill him without raising the alarm." Blitzen took another sip of his drink, then set it on the table to run both hands through his hair. "That still doesn't answer the most important question: why you? Did you know any of the ship's crew?"

"Not really." Colour crept into Sin's cheeks. "I don't sleep well away from home, so I decided to use my night-time hours creatively. I got this idea to make a travel journal-come scrapbook to give the grandchildren, and I thought it would be fun to make the book from the cruise-branded notepad in my room."

Blitzen's jaw dropped. "You can do that?"

"Of course." Sin shrugged. "Anyway, I thought the pages would be more interesting if I tea-dyed them before I bound them, so I used the tiny kettle and tea bags in my room to get it done." She shot him a shy smile. "Wet paper crinkles as it dries, though, which isn't great for book pages. At home, I just iron it, but there's nothing like that in the ship's cabins – so early one morning I took a stack down to the laundry and convinced the woman there to let me use one of the ironing stations."

"And she *let* you?"

Sin nodded. "Beatrice liked the company and we're similar enough in age that conversation was no problem. In fact, we got along well enough that I went to the laundry more mornings than not, and when Beatrice left the ship, she gave me her employee code so I could keep ironing paper while I waited my turn to disembark."

Blitzen blinked. "Surely that violates the terms of her employment."

"I said as much, but she just laughed and said, 'If they can find someone else willing to wash dirty underwear at all hours, they're welcome to do so.'" Sin's brows drew together. "The night before I left the ship, I went down to the laundry and there was a woman inside, wearing crew uniform pants and a tank. She'd upended a basket of clean laundry on the floor and was hunting through it. When I explained I was a friend of Beatrice's and only needed to use the iron, she said she'd run out of clean uniforms, and was trying to find a shirt before she was late for her shift."

Icy fingers trailed down Blitzen's spine. "What did you do?"

"I helped her, of course." Sin tapped a finger against her chin. "It took some doing, but we finally found a uniform shirt that fitted. She was so grateful for my help, she promised not to tell the Captain that Beatrice had shared her employee code with me."

"Gods." Blitzen swallowed. "Did you tell her your name?"

"Of course. Hers was Drew." Sin looked at the ceiling for a long moment. "Her name tag said McIntyre, I think."

"Drew McIntyre." Blitzen dug his phone out of his pocket and pulled up the cruise ship's crew manifest. "Martin, Maverick, McDonald … McIntyre."

Sin leaned against his shoulder so that she could see the screen, where the face of Drew McIntyre smiled back at them. "That's a man!"

"Looks like it. Here; scroll through the rest of the crew photos, see if any of them match the woman you met." Blitzen handed over his phone and even though his gut knew the answer, he sat silent while Sin checked the entire manifest.

"She's not here," she whispered, hands trembling. "Which means …"

"Whoever was wearing Drew McIntyre's uniform was an imposter," Blitzen agreed. "And you might be the only person left alive who saw her face."

17

ART VERSUS LIFE

$\mathscr{A}$s the sun sank towards the horizon, shading the sky in vibrant pinks and oranges, Sin leaned back to massage her blurring eyes. It had taken several hours, but she'd sifted through the enormous list of passengers who'd been aboard the cruise ship with her, mapping out where each person had been sent once the ship was evacuated and examining each passport photo in the hopes that one of the faces matched her recollection of the woman in the laundry room.

Whilst Blitzen had helped as best he could, it quickly became apparent that sitting still for long periods of time was not his strong suit. After he'd knocked over two cups of iced coffee, made Sin more chocolate milkshakes than she could consume in a week and rearranged the things she'd carefully laid out on the house's large dining table not twice but three times, Sin had suggested in her politest voice that his skills might be better suited to something else.

Anything else.

His sheepish apology had been followed by a scorching kiss – and then Blitzen whipped out his phone, strode to the balcony and spent the next few hours talking animatedly to one contact or another while she worked in blissful silence.

"Is it safe to come inside?"

Sin peeked between her fingers to see Blitzen framed by the tropical sunset, hair adorably mussed and roguish smile dialled up to full wattage. Dressed in only a pair of low-slung board shorts, fingers curled into the architrave overhead, every single one of his glorious muscles was on shameless display.

"You make it sound like I'm dangerous." Sin tried to sound annoyed, but her voice came out soft and thick. "I'm an artist, not a warrior."

He tipped his head to one side, expression hidden by the shadows slowly lengthening across the room. The moment crystallised in Sin's mind, capturing an image her fingers itched to paint – if she didn't melt from the sheer potency of the man first.

"An artist who raised two young children on her own, built a business empire, and isn't afraid to take even the most intimidating beings to task." The light gilding his cheeks shifted, and though Sin couldn't see the smile, the warmth of it reached her from across the room. "You're no retiring wallflower, Lucinda Anne Watkins."

The way Blitzen said her name, as though his tongue were a flame looking to set each syllable alight, made Sin shiver. She fluttered her lashes coquettishly, but couldn't get the image of the woman she was now dead certain had to be one of Nathaniel's mercenary accomplices out of her mind.

As though he shared the same thought, Blitzen's wicked smile faded and he jerked his chin at the table. "Anything?"

"Nothing. Whoever the woman pretending to be Drew McIntyre was, she's not here." Sin sighed, moving her fingers to her temples. "I have, however, formulated a long list of questions."

"Such as?"

"One: Why would Dame Garadova and Nathaniel go to the trouble of hatching what appears to be an incredibly complex scheme involving sabotage and murder in order to get the Christmas gifts *and* the ransom for them, only to risk it all on a home invasion?" Sin drummed her fingers on the tabletop. "It doesn't make sense – and leads me to question two. If the Garadovas didn't have any money, how did they hire mercenaries in the first place? Closely followed by number three: if the vampires intend to share whatever money's accrued from this entire ridiculous debacle, how are they planning to have enough left over to live off themselves? I know you said the gifts alone are worth a small fortune, but surely they'd need a sizeable band of piratically inclined people to enact the kind of operation we're talking about."

"Four," Blitzen added, moving to lean against the table beside her. "Why did Nathaniel murder Letitia the same way he murdered the captain and skeleton crew, but only stab Elias in the heart with a kitchen knife and hope for the best?"

"Five: if Nathaniel went to the villa purely to kill me so that he could tie up a loose end, why attack Elias and Letitia in the first place?" Sin threw her arms into the air. "Not to mention trying to steal my stuff?"

"All good questions." Blitzen slid his phone onto the table. "I sent the picture of fake Drew to Dash, and he did a bit of computer genius-ing. He said—"

"Wait, wait, wait. Dash as in Dasher?"

"Uh … yes?"

Sin massaged her temples a little more firmly. "One of Santa's reindeer is a *computer genius?*"

"Yeah." Blitzen's eye crinkled in the corners. "We don't spend the three hundred and sixty four non-Christmas days of the year twid-dling our thumbs and munching hay, you know."

"I …" Sin's cheeks warmed, and she cleared her throat. "Of course not. Carry on."

"The long and the short of it is that Dash compared the image of fake Drew to everything he had on hand and he thinks – emphasis on the thinks – that he can see her in the footage of the hostages." Blitzen tapped the picture on the table. "Which means, if he's correct, there's a good chance the hostage situation is fake."

"How confident is he?"

"Confident enough to tell me, but not confident enough to poten-tially risk the lives of eight people when the deadline for the ransom hits in two days' time."

"Two days?" Sin repeated, aghast. "Please tell me there was something in those videos that points towards a specific location."

Blitzen shook his head. "Nothing. That was the initial reason Dash analysed the footage – the fake Drew spotting was just a bonus."

"Hmm." Sin slid her hands from her temples to the base of her jaw. "Okay, let's focus on what we *do* know. One, the way Nathaniel killed Letitia pretty much proves that he, and by extension, his grandmother, are involved in what happened to the *Shimmering Wave*, and the theft of the charity gifts."

"Correct."

"And since they've conveniently left town, so to speak, the only foreseeable way to catch them is to draw them out." She lowered her hands to the table and straightened her spine. "If they're hunting for me, I could use myself as bait to—"

"No." Blitzen's strong hand gripped her jaw, his face filling her field of vision. "No, Sin. I won't put you in danger like that."

"I'm already in danger," she mumbled, the positioning of his fingers garbling the words. "Letitia died because Nathaniel was after me."

"*No.*"

Sin wrenched her face out of his grip, shoving out of her chair for good measure. "Damnit, Blitzen, what else is there? All we have are loose ends, and nothing to tie them together. Without some kind of clue …"

Huh.

She picked up the painting Nathaniel had tried to steal, a tiny, rushed watercolour that had been little more than a practice piece as she reclined on one of the cruise ship's many sunbaking decks.

"What?" Blitzen stomped around the table until he was in front of her again. "What is it?"

"The ship," Sin murmured, tapping at the painting's rippled surface. "I painted this while I was on board the ship."

Blitzen glanced at the picture. "So?"

"If there's anywhere in the world that might contain a clue to the Garadovas' location – or the stolen gifts – it's going to be on the ship, right? Fake Drew may not have left a trail, but one of the other mercenaries might have."

Blitzen blinked slowly, and she could almost see the cogs turning in the depths of his chocolate eyes. "It's a long shot, but it's possible … and visiting a dead ship is worlds better than offering you up as a sacrifice."

"I said bait, but whatever." Sin waved the incipient argument away. "Can you fly us out to the *Shimmering Wave* without being seen?"

"Provided we go at night, sure." A wicked smile spread across his face. "Unlike Rudolph, I don't glow in the dark."

"Perfect." Sin turned to regard the sun, now almost completely hidden behind the horizon. "I'll get my shoes and – wait."

"Hmm?"

"Does Rudolph's nose really glow red?"

Blitzen winked. "Once this is over, you can ask him yourself."

FLOAT LIKE A REINDEER

With the stars to guide him, Blitzen cleft the air on soundless hooves, Sin clinging tightly to his back. The ocean stretched out below, her inky surface broken here and there by the faintest brush of moonlight on a cresting swell. Since the cruise ship was completely without power, it was all-but invisible against the black-on-black horizon – so much so that as Blitzen circled in to land, Sin's fingers clenched convulsively in the thick fur around his neck and didn't relax until his hooves clattered on the wooden decking.

He expected her to dismount immediately so he could return to human form but she stayed in place and whispered, "Do you see that?"

"See what?" It was dark, and the shadows upon shadows cast by the cruise ship's bulk made it difficult even for Blitzen's night vision to pick out details.

Making a frustrated sound in the back of her throat, Sin grabbed one of Blitzen's antlers and dragged his head around until it was almost backwards on his neck. "That."

Far across the water, so tiny that they appeared as fireflies, bobbed a string of flickering lights. Progression was slow, but they were definitely moving – and then, one by one, they went out.

Blitzen blew out a long, slow breath through his nostrils.

"I thought so, too," Sin murmured, letting go of his antler. "Unless I've lost my mind, none of the islands in that direction are inhabited."

"No. They're not." Blitzen shifted from hoof to hoof, glancing at the shadowy cruise ship and then back in the direction the lights had come from.

As though reading his thoughts, Sin said, "The cruise ship isn't going anywhere – but whoever had those lights certainly are."

"Hold on." Swivelling on his haunches, Blitzen raced for the edge of the ship. Sin plastered herself against his neck as he reached the railing and leaped, magic and muscle taking them back into the air.

Rather than waste energy on climbing, Blitzen stayed close to the ocean's surface and poured all his effort into crossing the Caribbean as fast as reindeerishly possible. After a while, the blurred outline of something moved beneath the water – then it became two, then three, then five. Dipping lower, Blitzen allowed his hooves to drum the crest of a swell and was rewarded with a shimmer of grey and a splash in return.

"Oh," Sin breathed, holding so tight to his fur that Blitzen knew he'd have bruises later. "What are they?"

"King Garvon's people."

"*King?*"

"King of the Caribbean," Blitzen confirmed. "The waters here are full of merpeople, and Garvon rules them with a fist both fair and firm." He paused a beat. "He's Devon's father."

"He's *what?*" Sin spluttered. "Devon's a prince?"

Blitzen snorted a laugh. "I suppose so, although he's never used a title. Even Garvon only pulls his out on formal occasions."

"How considerate of him."

Her dry tone made him laugh again, but since no amount of levity changed the fact that there was a lot of ocean to cover, Blitzen returned his concentration to the horizon. The stars continued to keep him on course, and Garvon's people came and went in the water below, silent reassurance that they weren't alone – but it was at least half an hour before he glimpsed the shadowy outline of cliffs up ahead.

The island which grew from the gloom was so small it could barely claim the title. Dropping as close to the surface of the water as he could without actually swimming, he circumnavigated the entire thing in less than five minutes before ending up back where he started, brows creased and ears flat to his skull.

"I didn't see anything, did you?" Sin's whisper was so soft that if she hadn't spoken directly into his ear, Blitzen would have missed the words over the sound of the waves.

"No." He hesitated. "I might need to go higher, but we risk being seen."

Sin smoothed one hand down the side of his neck. "I think it's worth the risk."

"All right." Blitzen inched upwards, keeping a close eye on the surrounding area for anything untoward. When he was level with the top of the cliffs, he began a second slow circle … and had barely moved when Sin gasped and smacked him in the chin.

"Look!"

This time, he could see where she pointed; a narrow fold in the rocks they'd missed from the waterline. Blitzen followed the cleft carefully as it zigged and zagged before emptying into a snug little cove just big enough for a compact boat. The beach itself was empty, but the sand above the waterline held the unmistakable furrow of a hull – and halfway up the cliff, almost invisible thanks to the way the rocks jutted all over the place, was the pitch-black mouth of a cave.

Rather than try to climb an unfamiliar cliff in the dark, Blitzen tucked his legs up and his head down and managed an awkward landing in the mouth of the cave. Sin clung to him for a good minute, the sound of their collective breathing overly loud in the still night – but when nobody jumped out to attack, she let out a soft groan and slid to the ground.

The space was tight for both a woman and a reindeer, so Blitzen returned to human form. The air was cool on his sweaty skin, his lone pair of board shorts doing absolutely nothing to shield him from the draft coming up the tunnel. Swallowing his shiver, Blitzen crawled to Sin's side and helped her to her feet. "Are you all right?"

"A little stiff, but otherwise fine. What about you?"

"Same." He tugged her against his chest, something deep inside settling when Sin's arms curled around his waist. "I'm going to wager there's nobody here, but I've been wrong before. If you want to wait—"

"No." She poked him in the ribs. "I don't want to wait here in supposed safety while you creep off alone into the tunnel of doom, so don't waste your breath asking."

"I just—"

"*Blitzen.*"

He sighed. "All right."

"Good." Sin drew back to cup his jaw, and Blitzen couldn't help but turn into the caress so that he could kiss her fingers. He couldn't see her face properly, but he felt her body soften and his blood surged enthusiastically southwards. The resulting twitch had Sin gasping out a laugh. "Really?"

"Oh yes," he breathed, tugging her closer.

"We might be in mortal danger!"

"I like mortal danger." He nipped at her nose, her lips, then forced himself to step back. "That said, I'm not an idiot. If there's something here to find, we'd best find it before whoever owns those lights decides to come back."

"Agreed." Sin peered back at the cave's entrance. "What about your friends from before? Will they help us?"

"If we need it – but for now, the less people sneaking about in here, the better." Blitzen turned away from the glittering stars and tucked Sin's fingers into the waistband of his shorts. "No lights until we're sure we're alone, okay?"

"Got it." Sin shifted a little closer and though her fingers trembled, her voice was steady. "Let's go."

19

PASSWORD

Sin had never been afraid of the dark. Even as a child, she'd found the night sky beautiful, and never balked at having the lights off to go to bed. There was something decidedly different, however, about the kind of darkness in the tunnel – a pitch so intense it crawled across her skin leaving goosebumps in its wake. If not for her anchor in the back of Blitzen's shorts and the image of Letitia's mutilated body burned into the back of her brain, Sin would have turned back the moment she lost sight of the cave's entrance.

Though it seemed like an age, it was likely no more than a few minutes before Blitzen stopped walking. Sin's fingers skimmed the waistband of his shorts as he turned to face her, warm lips brushing her forehead.

"Light," he whispered. True to the warning, a soft click preceded a flood of light in the tunnel. Instinct ushered Sin forward, where the curved planes of Blitzen's bared chest provided enough shelter for her eyes to adjust. His hand sifted through her hair, voice rueful as he murmured, "Sorry."

"At this point, a bright light is the least of my worries." Sin frowned against his chest. "Although … where did you have that stashed?"

He chuckled softly. "These shorts do have pockets, you know."

Sin humphed against his sternum, earning a second gravelly chuckle. When Blitzen's hand shifted from her hair to her chin, she chanced the glare and lifted her head. The light which had seemed so brilliant only moments ago was little more than the dull beam of a tiny flashlight, Blitzen's face a landscape of shadows.

"I'm sorry you got dragged into this shit show," he murmured, feathering a thumb along her jaw. "But I'm not sorry it gave us an opportunity to meet. When this is over, I'm going to take you on that not-a-date I promised back in the restaurant – and then I'm going to take you home and make love to you until we both pass out from exhaustion." He leaned in close, warm breath ghosting over her face. "Fair warning: I have a lot of stamina."

Despite the fact that she'd already been on the receiving end of said stamina and was more than happy to repeat the encounter, Sin raised an eyebrow. "Awfully confident for someone who stood me up the last time, don't you think?"

Blitzen growled and lowered his head, lips teasing Sin's until she was pressing into his warmth, his strength, breathless from both the tingling contact and the lack of anything further. The kiss was a promise without words, whispering to the heart of her that he would never let her down again.

Sin believed him.

"All right," she breathed against his lips. "When this is over ... yes."

"On that note." Blitzen's hand slid down to her waist as he twisted to shine the torch further into the tunnel. Several paces ahead, the walls dissolved into yawning darkness – and the path dropped clean away to infinity.

"Oh my gods." Sin took an involuntary step back, heart lurching into her throat. "Oh my *gods.*"

"It's one way to put off uninvited guests, isn't it?" Blitzen's arm tightened in reassurance. "I don't have the sharpest nose in the shed, but there's no new scents here. Nothing to hear, either, so I'm fairly confident we're alone." He glanced back the way they'd come. "For now."

Sin swallowed as she stared at the void ahead, every single one of her brain cells supplying increasingly vivid thoughts on how many bones they would have broken if Blitzen hadn't stopped when he did. "How did you know it was there?"

"The air pressure changed." He pressed the flashlight into her hands. "I need you to wait here for a minute, while I check things out."

Though she liked the idea of being left alone in the tunnel about as much as hot chilli sauce, Sin firmed her grip on the flashlight and nodded. Blitzen pressed another kiss to her forehead and backed away, tossing her a broad wink before he stepped off the ledge and dropped from sight.

Adrenaline drove Sin's feet to the lip of the precipice, where she held her breath, waiting for the familiar fear to rise. He'd left her alone, after all – but her heart only snorted and kept right on beating. Blitzen wasn't Hugh, and though it wasn't fair to compare the two, there was a humming in the depths of her soul which promised he wouldn't leave her. When the now-familiar form of a large reindeer floated into view, Sin smiled. "Well?"

"Funnily enough, it's hard to make much out in the dark, save that I was right – there's nobody here."

"I take it that means we're going down for a better look?"

Blitzen pressed himself up against the side of the ledge. "Correct."

Tucking the flashlight into the waistband of her shorts, Sin slid onto his back and held tight. There was an eerie, hollow quality to the air that made the hair stand up on Sin's arms, her instincts insisting that somewhere out there, something big lurked, ready to eat her at a moment's notice. Gritting her teeth against the sensation, she swung to the ground as soon as they landed and brandished the tiny flashlight, but it wasn't powerful enough to do more than illuminate a tiny circle of loosely sanded floor.

"I know where the lights are," Blitzen said. His body shimmered and warped and quite suddenly he was a man again, pointing off into the distance. "If we're lucky, they might even turn on."

"Oh, goody," Sin muttered, eyes firmly on his sculpted back muscles as she followed him across the cavern. "Just what I always wanted; some maybe-lights."

Blitzen tossed a grin over his shoulder. "I live to provide."

Sin grunted, far too occupied by keeping her flashlight trained on the sandy floor to respond. Thirty paces later Blitzen stopped, and she lifted the meagre beam of light to illuminate a compact generator hunched against the back wall of the cavern.

"Will it have power?" Sin squinted, but couldn't see anything in the way of power cords or even a can of fuel conveniently left around for them to find.

"I'm hoping so." Blitzen paced from one side of the generator to the other, bending to examine a small array of buttons set into the front. "There's a certain brand of generator that runs on Lemurian crystals. Expensive, but if Dame Garadova's got a hand in this, she probably stole it anyway."

Sin blinked. Lemurian crystals grew in Mu, thanks to a complicated process shrouded in mystery. They worked like solar panels, absorbing and storing sunlight which, with the correct know-how, could then be used as a source of power. A piece as small as Sin's thumbnail could run an entire house – and was worth about as much. Something big enough to run a generator ... yikes.

Blitzen, seemingly unconcerned by the potential fortune inside the generator's metal shell, shrugged and pressed one of the buttons. The machine coughed to life, filling the cavern with a pleasant hum. One by one, heavy duty lanterns blinked on around the space, illuminating the underground grotto as brightly as if it were midday.

Unlike the hewn walls of the tunnel, the underground chamber looked natural. Tiny specks of what might have been salt, silicate, or even quartz glittered in the lantern light, and the roof stretched high enough overhead it was little more than a hint of stone among the shadows. The layer of sand on the floor was scuffed with footprints, drag marks and oddly shaped hollows – but it was the neat stack of wooden crates to Sin's left that captured her attention.

"The stolen Christmas gifts," she whispered, drifting closer. Shining Star Cruise's logo was stamped onto the outside of the crates, alongside the logo of the charity who'd organised the donation. "I didn't realise there were so many."

"It's a well-known charity drive," Blitzen answered, tugging his phone out of his pocket. He tapped the screen and then set it to his ear. "Nyk? We've found the shipment."

Tinny expletives filled the air, and Blitzen grinned. Sin shook her head, leaving him to converse with Hot Santa as she explored the rest of the cave. Now that the lights were on, it wasn't nearly so threatening – and by some stroke of luck, the enormous lanterns also pumped out heat, the feeling akin to actual sunlight licking over her skin.

A small fold-out table sat at the base of one of the lanterns, and Sin's heart kicked as she recognised a laptop on the surface. Wiping her palms on her thighs, she opened the lid and jabbed the power button. The device didn't take long to boot, flicking through several loading screens before displaying a soothing desktop background and a password box. After a cursory rummage through the nearby case didn't produce anything with a password conveniently written on it, Sin crossed her arms and stared at the screen. If there was to be any information about the Garadova's plans, surely it would be on the laptop? Otherwise, why else would it be here? She was in no way a computer guru, however, and didn't need to ask Blitzen to know he wasn't, either. Maybe he could call Dash—

Sin paused.

Bent at the waist until she was eye-level with the screen.

"What have you got?" Blitzen appeared at her side, sliding his phone into the pocket of his shorts. When she didn't immediately answer, he crouched to get a better view of the computer. "Sin?"

"I found this in a bag on the table. Figured it might have some information we could use." With shaking hands, Sin typed a single word into the password box. The computer chimed acceptance, the login screen dissolving in favour of a dreadfully familiar workspace.

Blitzen glanced between her and the screen and back again. "How did you guess the password?"

"I didn't." Sin swallowed heavily. "I used my own password – because this is an exact replica of my home computer."

20

AN EYE FOR AN EYE

"I didn't ..." Sin waved a hand at the computer. "I don't understand. I don't have anything to do with this, I swear!"

"It's all right." Despite the roaring in his head, Blitzen gathered her into his arms and sat them both down on the sandy floor of the cavern. "Everything makes sense now."

Sin let out a hollow laugh. "There's a replica of my computer in a *pirate's den*. How can that possibly make sense?"

"They're trying to set you up," Blitzen said, gentling his voice as much as he could. "Think about it – there's already footage of you in the cruise ship's laundry with one of the thieves. It wouldn't take much for a hacker to find out what kind of computer you have at home and replicate it. Alongside your personal information, they can manufacture evidence to frame you as the mastermind of this entire operation."

Sin's jaw dropped. "But ... I don't keep any personal information on my home computer; all my important data is on either my tablet or my phone."

"Which Nathaniel Garadova tried to steal." Blitzen rubbed a cheek across the top of her head. "Now that I think about it, this laptop answers a lot of the questions we were asking earlier. If the Garadovas have a fall person, they can not only shift the blame from themselves, they can also get rid of the mercenaries too – allowing the vampires to keep not only the ransom, should it be paid, but the entire stash of gifts as well."

"But … but … what about the ambush at the villa?"

"I'd wager Nathaniel was trying to make it look like *you* killed Letitia. Maybe even turn me against you by involving Elias." Blitzen's stomach knotted. "It would certainly explain the difference in Letitia's messy death, and the awkward stabbing Elias received; Nathaniel was setting things up to look as though Elias interrupted you mutilating the body, you struggled, managed to stab him with the knife and pushed them both into the freezer in order to escape."

Sin's throat bobbed. "I'd never do something like that."

"It doesn't matter – if Nathaniel had succeeded in killing you, there'd be no way for you to argue your innocence. He was probably intending to dump your body somewhere along with the items he'd stolen and this replica laptop, probably with the kind of injuries that made it look like you bled out after the fight with Elias." He clicked his tongue against the roof of his mouth. "You'd be convicted post mortem, the pirates would be rounded up … while the Garadovas walk away."

"Why me? What would I possibly – wait." Her face went even whiter than before. "They picked me because I happened to walk into the laundry at the same time as Fake Drew, didn't they?"

"Yes. In that respect, you made their job easy." Blitzen sighed and wrapped her tighter in his arms. "At least now that we've found the stolen goods, we can stop this getting any messier."

Sin rested her head against his chest, lashes damp against his bare skin. "You say that. You're not the one almost framed as a criminal mastermind."

"I guess not." Blitzen frowned around the cavern. The scuffed sand testified that there'd been a far more complex setup here not so long ago – likely removed as the deadline for the ransom drew closer. "There has to be another cave."

"Huh?" Sin lifted her head, blinking blearily up at him.

"There has to be another cave," Blitzen repeated, more certain with every word. "Even if you discount the impracticality of getting the charity crates up to the tunnel we entered through, I've never met a vampire without at least one backup plan in place."

"You're right, but …" She scrubbed her face, cleared her throat, and took a deep breath. "What about the hostages?"

Blitzen stretched out an arm and hooked the laptop off the table. It didn't take long to get into the system's files, revealing several well-laid out documents listing each of the hired pirates, and the entire plot Sin was supposed to have concocted – along with a hostage hoax to garner more money than the Christmas gifts were worth on their own.

"Those *assholes*." Sin scrambled upright on wobbly legs. "Forget being upset – now I'm just angry. There has to be a way to bring the Garadovas to justice."

"There will be; starting with the discovery of their actual entry and exit." Blitzen squinted at the shadowy walls of the cavern before pointing off to the left, where drag marks in the sand led towards a thick pool of shadows. "That way. Come on."

Situated almost directly below the tunnel they'd come in through was a waist-high recess that appeared to have been used as a storage space. From the outside it looked like a dead-end, but when Blitzen stuck his head and shoulders inside, there was a crawlspace hidden behind a fold in the rock.

Sin eyed it doubtfully. "Will you fit?"

"I think so." Blitzen tugged the tiny flashlight from her pocket and shone it into the hole. "It curves out of sight, but I can smell the sea."

"All right." Sin drew a deep breath and nodded. "I'm right behind you."

Blitzen bent to steal a kiss, then stuck the flashlight between his teeth and dropped to his hands and knees. After a bit of shoulder wriggling, he was through the opening and into a tunnel wide enough to crawl along without bumping the walls or roof. Sin followed close behind, the only sound they made that of their own breathing and the soft shush of sand against skin.

Despite the fact he could move with ease, it was a relief when the tunnel ended, spilling them into a low-roofed cave dripping with stalagmites. The sand stretched out for almost ten metres before it began to drop away, eroded by the softly lapping seawater seeping in through the cave's narrow mouth. Framed by the starry night sky beyond was a small but sturdy rowboat, pulled far enough up the beach that high tide would be unlikely to wash it away.

"See? Backup plan," Blitzen murmured, ducking between stalagmites as he made his way down to the boat. It was in good condition, held in place by several lengths of marine-quality rope and a metal loop that had been hammered into the cave wall. "Good."

Sin curled her fingers over the boat's timber rim. "How is this good, exactly?"

"Right now, the Garadovas are in hiding. The only way to dispense justice is to draw them out."

"Okay." Sin nodded, then wrinkled her nose. "I'm still not following."

Blitzen pursed his lips. "This all hinges on the gifts, right? Without those, there's no money. If we steal the gifts back, then the Garadovas will have no choice but to come to us."

"*Steal* the *gifts?*" Sin paced the length of the cave and back again, her slighter height having no issue with the stalagmites dangling from the roof. "Assuming I agree to this crazy idea – which, for the record, *is* crazy – there's only two of us, a literal ship-load of wooden crates, and this tiny rowboat. It doesn't add up."

"That's because you're not one of Santa's reindeer." Blitzen tapped the side of his nose and winked. "I have just the right combination of magic and balls to make this work."

"Balls," Sin repeated, her voice flat. "You're asking me to believe magic and *balls* are going to solve this."

"I'm asking you to trust me." Blitzen tugged her stiff body into his embrace and kissed her, coaxing with hands and tongue until Sin sighed and melted. "And my balls."

"Oh, for—" She wrenched back, but a laugh snuck out before she could smother it. "You're saying that on purpose."

"Let me prove it." Blitzen led her back to the tunnel, crawling through with renewed determination. Once they were in the main cavern, he stuck a hand deep into the pocket of his shorts. "Every reindeer who oversees a post-Christmas assignment keeps a basic emergency kit at their place of residence. I don't bother with it, for the most part, but I have gotten into the habit of carrying around … this."

Sin eyed the tiny square of hessian he produced with a skeptical expression. "A rustic handkerchief?"

"Not quite." Blitzen turned the little square inside out, the magic woven into the fabric producing a hessian sack large enough for both Blitzen and Sin to climb inside. "Ready for a spot of theft?"

"With a reusable shopping bag?"

"Of the Santa Claus variety."

Sin blinked at the sack, then over at the neatly stacked wooden crates. "You're not serious."

"Oh, but I am. Watch." Blitzen moved to the nearest crate and laid one hand against it. The sack in his other hand rustled, magic crawling up his arm, across his chest and down the other side. The crate beneath his palm began to shrink.

And shrink.

And *shrink.*

When it was about the size of a shoebox, Blitzen dropped the crate into the open sack and moved to the next, grinning at an astonished Sin. "Well? Are you a believer now?"

She nodded, eyes round and jaw slack as he continued to shrink the crates and add them to the sack. When Blitzen was about half way through, Sin gave herself a shake and ran to the table, where she rummaged through the laptop bag until she discovered a notepad and pen. By the time she returned to Blitzen with the laptop itself under one arm, she sported a smile that was positively feral.

"Balls, you said, right?" Sin held out the laptop and he obligingly took it in hand, waiting until the sack's magic shrank it to the size of a matchbox before adding it to the stash. "I figure someone's coming back here soon enough – so I left a message."

"Dare I ask?"

Sin took hold of the open lip of the sack, jolting as its magic flowed into her body, then set her free hand against one of the remaining crates and watched it shrink. When the crate was cradled in the palm of her hand, she flicked a look at Blitzen from beneath her lashes. "I wrote 'naughty children don't get presents' and signed it 'jägare, xoxo.'"

Blitzen laughed and scooped another crate into the sack. "Perfect."

BEFORE THE DAWN

At no point in her life had Sin ever imagined finessing a magical sack full of twice-stolen Christmas gifts down a narrow tunnel deep in the belly of a nameless Caribbean island. Nor watching one of Santa's reindeer deposit said sack into a pirate's secret rowboat, only to ask her to hitch him to the front of it ... like a sleigh.

"You've got to be kidding," Sin muttered, even as she assessed the thick length of mariner's rope that secured the boat to the wall.

Blitzen didn't bother dignifying her comment with a response as he freed the rope and handed it to her.

Magic tingled in her fingers, her wrists, her elbows – and then Sin took the inordinately heavy rope in her hands and set to work. It was a small talent, really, to see a thing in her mind and just *know* how to craft it, nowhere near as impressive as the mages who made portal stones or powerful medicines ... but when she showed the finished harness to Blitzen ten minutes later, he looked at her as though she'd performed a miracle.

"It's going to be a sketchy take-off," he warned, ensuring the gifts were properly secured. "There's only one of me, and I'm already tired. Make sure you're hanging on tight."

Sin watched the play of muscles in his forearms, a million protests forming and dying on her tongue. "Okay."

Blitzen transformed without further comment, moving into position at the front of the boat. Sin slid the rope harness into position and twisted it together, securing the free ends to the forward oar rings on the rowboat. The anchor points were wrong; there was no rational, logical, or scientific theory in which the boat would even get airborne. The combined weight of Sin, the boat and the sack of gifts seemed ridiculous when compared to Blitzen, no matter how large and muscular he was in his reindeer form … yet here she was, climbing onto Blitzen's back with little more than hope and magic to guide her forward.

Energy crackled over Blitzen's fur, tiny sparks of power that left afterimages on the back of her retinas. He pranced in place, testing the harness, and Sin was forced to lay flat against his neck or risk falling off. No sooner was she settled than Blitzen sprang into the shallows, the boat bumping unsteadily along behind. Sparkling droplets filled the air and Sin braced herself for the bite of the ocean – and then they were out in the open, stars twinkling above and cliffs rising all around. The narrow passage twisted and turned, jagged pieces of rock jutting from the sides of the cliff, each one sharp and solid enough to wreck a poorly navigated craft – or to gut a reindeer, should he make even the slightest mistake.

Blitzen rumbled deep in his chest, picking up speed. Sin fought the urge to close her eyes as the cliff drew closer, closer … until, with a tremendous heave, Blitzen shot straight upwards. Against all odds, the rowboat sailed along behind, the speed of their flight causing the gathered top of the sack to ripple in the wind. Something that might have been a scream, or might have been a laugh, erupted from Sin's chest as they burst into open air, the ocean a rippling wave of midnight silk below.

"All right," she whispered, stretching so her words dropped directly into Blitzen's ear. "You win. I believe."

He chuffed a laugh, the sound warming Sin to the very core of her soul.

When the now-familiar island containing the tropical resort came into view, the sky had begun to lighten in preparation for dawn. Lights were on in the main building and a few of the villas; tiki torches burned around the vacant expanse of the resort's dance floor and bar. Blitzen angled towards the shore, and Sin tightened her grip as she realised he was aiming for the long, elegantly manicured pathway that led from the island's single pier to the resort's grand front entrance.

The ground rushed up at neck-breaking speed, coating Sin's throat with the acrid taste of bile. Blitzen, however, barely stumbled as he touched down, powerful legs harmonising with the land in the space between one hastily swallowed scream and the next. The rowboat came in behind them, hitting the beach with an echoing crack before sloughing through the sand and clumping up onto the pathway as though it had been made for just such a purpose.

In spite of the early hour, a small group of people had gathered outside the resort by the time Blitzen drew to a halt near the door. Devon stood at the front, impeccably dressed in a white shirt beneath a black waistcoat and slacks, his hair as immaculate as his disapproving expression. His staff scattered on command, one disappearing back into the resort proper while the rest came racing down the steps towards Blitzen, leaving Devon alone except for—

"Elias!" Sin cried. The frost elf wore a loose t-shirt and a pair of faded denim shorts, his long hair gathered into a braid and pale skin peppered with bruises. He let out a grunt of surprise as Sin cannoned into him, squeezing as tightly as she dared. "You're out of the freezer!"

"Of course you're a hugger," he muttered, body stiff and unforgiving. "Why wouldn't you be?"

"You almost died," Sin snapped, burying her face in his t-shirt. "And you did it saving my life. Hug me back, or I'm never letting go."

The elf clicked his tongue against his teeth, but his arms crept around Sin and he patted awkwardly at her back.

She lifted her head, seeking those dark, dark eyes. "I'm sorry about Letitia."

"So am I." For a moment, she worried he'd let go – until Elias let out another, far more shuddery sigh and dropped a surprisingly tender kiss to the top of Sin's head. "Thank you."

Someone cleared their throat, and Sin glanced over her shoulder to see Blitzen standing on the top step. He was once again in human form, sweat slicking his skin and hair a tumbled mess. He gave Elias a grave nod. "You good?"

"I'll do," the elf replied.

"Good." Blitzen waved a hand over his shoulder, where the resort staff were tugging the sack of gifts out of the boat. "Devon's going to secure the load and put out a call to King Garvon. We'll have reinforcements by dawn."

Dawn. There was weight to the word, the kind of weight that sent a shiver down Sin's spine. She stepped back from Elias, rubbing at her arms. "Do you really think the Garadovas will attack so quickly?"

"Oh, yes. Dame Garadova's smart enough to know that the longer they wait, the longer we have to recover our energy and gather reinforcements." Blitzen ran a hand over his face, and Sin's stomach twisted as she noted the way his muscles trembled with fatigue. "The only respite we have is that they're Daywalkers – they'll attack when they can use the sunlight to their advantage."

"Pre-dawn's already lightening the sky! That's not a respite, it's a coffee break."

"Indeed; and yet it will have to do. The only comfort I can offer is that we have most excellent coffee." Devon came gliding up the steps, mouth set in a prim line. "That, and my father's warriors are en route. They'll be here before true dawn breaks."

"Thank you." Blitzen offered a hand and Devon, after grimacing at the sweaty, grimy skin, shook it. "I appreciate it, and I know Nykolaas will, too."

"It is for all of our benefits, but your gratitude will be noted." Devon tugged a handkerchief from his pocket and wiped his hands. "Since time is of the essence, I came here to suggest that perhaps, while the coffee brews, you both might like a shower? If I send word to the kitchen, we might even be able to arrange for a meal."

"A shower and a meal sound great." Blitzen slid his arm around Sin's shoulders, angling her towards the resort's perfectly polished front door. "Keep the preparations moving – we'll be back before you know it."

SHARK INFESTED WATERS

shower and a meal did wonders, but Blitzen would have given a great deal of his earthly possessions for a nap. Despite three double shot espressos, his eyelids drooped the moment he leaned against the reception desk, where Elias was sifting through the contents of the laptop he and Sin had liberated from the pirate's grotto.

"Anything?" Sin's voice was subdued as she joined them, but still sudden enough an interruption that Blitzen jumped. Her brown hair was damp from the shower, her clothes baggy enough he assumed they were borrowed. As Blitzen blinked blearily, she frowned and pressed a fourth mug of steaming coffee into his hands. "You should lie down."

"So should you."

Her eyes narrowed, but Elias came to the rescue by tapping the laptop's screen with a long finger, diverting Sin's attention. "Whoever set up these fake documents did a good job. We're lucky you recovered this before anything went live."

"While I was still alive, you mean," Sin grumbled.

Elias cracked a sharp grin, but any reply he might've made was drowned out by a loud, whooping alarm. Blitzen cursed, tossed the scalding coffee down his throat in one go, then coughed and cursed again. By the time he'd caught his breath, the reception area was full of running people, some with determined expressions and others with tight, frightened faces.

"Tsunami warning," Blitzen shouted as Sin looked at him in question. When she blinked, pointing at the calm, entirely unthreatening ocean clearly visible through the floor to ceiling windows, he added, "It's the most severe alarm Devon has. Emergency procedure dictates all guests retreat to the main building where they can be safely locked in an underground bunker."

"Underground? For a *tsunami?*"

Elias slammed the lid of the laptop closed. "King Garvon and his subjects – Devon, most of the staff here – are merpeople. There's underwater access to the bunker, and plenty of supplies to keep the guests inside safe until the danger subsides and a rescue can be mounted."

Sin's mouth opened and Blitzen knew she was longing to ask more, but he shook his head. There was only one reason Devon would have sounded that particular alarm – and he saw it confirmed in the man's face as he strode purposefully up to the desk.

"Sentries have sighted several watercraft approaching the shore." Devon's voice somehow carried through the blaring siren, each clipped syllable as clear as the last. "Both the craft and the visible occupants are armed."

"Can we do anything before they land?"

Devon's lips thinned. "The main craft are surrounded by a troupe of jet-skis trailing electrified netting. We can't get close."

"Long range?"

"Already attempted. Our uninvited guests have shielded hulls and personal armour. I could request heavier artillery, but it'd never reach us in time."

Blitzen nodded, unsurprised, and turned to the map of the resort on the back wall. "Station teams in these locations, and tell them to wait for my command. I'm trusting the two of you to get everyone else into the bunker, and make sure they stay there."

Elias face darkened. "The fuck I'm going to—"

"You're barely out of the freezer," Blitzen snapped, jabbing his friend in the sternum. "You might be mobile, but don't try and convince me you're combat ready."

"We need everyone we can get," Elias argued, stepping in until their chests bumped. "If things go sou— *fuckingfrostbittenshitonastick!*"

Blitzen watched as his friend doubled over, clutching his ribs. "You were saying?"

"You're an asshole," Elias hissed, glaring from beneath lowered brows. "Did you have to punch me in the *stab wound?*"

"If it gets the point across."

"Come closer, and I'll get the point acr—"

"Enough." Sin stepped between them, hands raised. "If Nathaniel's on one of those boats, he'll be looking to finish what he started, and I'm no warrior. Elias, I know this is hard, but I don't trust anyone other than Blitzen to keep me safe. Please, will you stay with me?"

As far as ruses went, it was one of the most obvious Blitzen had ever seen – but Elias grunted and let out a stiff nod. "Fine."

"Thank you." Sin patted the frost elf on the shoulder, then brushed her lips over Blitzen's cheek. "Be careful out there."

He caught her chin, swooping in for a kiss so searing they were both panting when he broke away. "I'll be back soon."

Ignoring Elias' hissed promises of retribution, Blitzen jogged out the front door, heading straight for the beach. The alarm still wailed. The insistent sound throbbed in his ears and made his brain ache – or maybe that was the caffeine from the inhuman amount of coffee he'd chugged in the last half hour.

Either way, he couldn't help but grimace as he approached the lone figure standing beneath a beach umbrella, one hand shading her brow as she looked out over the water. Clad entirely in the deep blues and greens that made up the uniform of King Garvon's ocean people, and with a short blade sheathed on one hip, she cut an impressive shape against the steadily rising sun.

"I didn't think they'd let you lead this one, Daph."

The head of King Garvon's mer-knights cut him a sharp glance, the smooth skin of her cheeks shimmering silver-gray for a fraction of a moment. "Letitia was my cousin."

"My point exactly."

"Consider it extra motivation to get the job done right," Daphne answered. "Or should I be saying it was a good excuse to work alongside you again?"

Blitzen snorted, letting his gaze wander over the watercraft rapidly approaching the shore. "I'm taken now. You missed your chance."

"Lucky I bat for the other team, then, or I might just have to cry myself to sleep tonight." She winked, then followed his gaze out to sea. "My knights are ready. Are you?"

"Always."

"Excellent." Daphne smiled, revealing wide, triangular teeth that were in no way human. "Come then, brother of Christmas. Let us show these vampires what happens to fools who swim with sharks."

23

LEVERAGE

"**C**oming?"

Sin tore her gaze from the blurry silhouette of Blitzen and his companion to find Elias watching her expectantly. "Huh?"

"I said, are you coming?" The frost elf had one hand splayed over his ribs, face tight with discomfort. "To the bunker."

"I …" Sin glanced back at the beach and her heart stuttered.

A small fleet of sleek black watercraft pulled into the shallows, figures in black combat gear, bristling with all manner of weaponry, making a mockery of the idyllic sand and cerulean seas.

Blitzen sprinted to the waterline, morphing from man to reindeer in a shower of salty spray. The impressive spread of his antlers seemed somehow smaller when facing so much aggression, even though Sin had seen him use them to devastating effect.

Fingers banded her wrist. "He'll be okay."

"They've got guns! And is that … Elias, that's a plasma cannon!"

Elias let out a frustrated sound in the back of his throat. "Watch."

As the enemy turned towards Blitzen, raising weapons he had no hope of avoiding, Sin opened her mouth to scream – and the water erupted, warriors in deepest green and blue seeming to materialise from nowhere. Fins flashed where legs should have been, and Sin found herself jerking backwards as blood sprayed into the air. "What was that?"

"My father's knights." Devon let out a low, rasping laugh that made the hair on Sin's arms stand on end. "The people of the deep are far more varied and dangerous than the pretty stories of popular culture describe."

"Oh." She swallowed. "I guess that makes sense."

Elias gave her wrist a gentle tug. "Come on. Bunker."

Sin wanted nothing less than to walk away. Blitzen was out there, fighting for the island, for Nykolaas … for her. She looked up at Elias, whose navy gaze was soft with understanding. The elf *was* a warrior, and he'd been sidelined; if he had enough faith in Blitzen to enter the bunker without complaint, then she could do no less.

"Bunker," she agreed quietly.

"Okay." Elias glanced at Devon. "Lead on."

"Of course. This way, please." Devon ushered them through the sunny foyer and into the same restaurant where Sin and Blitzen had first met. The sounds of fighting faded as they entered the attached kitchen, industrial appliances gleaming and partially chopped ingredients abandoned on the stone bench tops. Towards the back of the kitchen were two doors; Devon pushed through the first and held it, an expectant look on his face.

Sin nodded her thanks and stepped through, pausing as she found herself behind the tropically-themed bar. Stools had been placed upside down along the length of the bar itself, and beyond, the dance floor was empty, the tiki torches ringing the border extinguished. A palm-frond roof cast the area in dappled light and shade, creating an intimate mood even during the day.

"Not far now," Devon promised, leading the way across the polished dance floor. "The entrance is just around the corner, between—"

A figure stepped from the shadows of a nearby booth, blocking the way. He wore pale grey dress shorts and a mint polo, auburn hair combed and set with meticulous care. In any other setting, his golden skin, lithe muscles and designer loafers would have completed the preppy look – but the illusion was ruined by sharp eyes the colour of old blood and a smile marked by fangs.

"That's far enough," Nathaniel purred.

"Fuck." Elias shoved Sin behind him and she went without protest, clinging to the back of his denim shorts. "Of course you're too much of a coward to be down on the beach."

"Those pawns are doing exactly what they're meant to. I, on the other hand, have something far more important to resolve." The vampire reached into the booth and dragged out a child, lifting her into the air by the back of a pretty floral sundress. The little girl looked about six, with sleek black hair in a messy braid, pale skin and delicate features. Wadded up fabric blocked her mouth, eyes the colour of the ocean shallows wet with tears. Her wrists had been bound and her legs—

Sin gasped.

Instead of legs, a grey and black tail ending in angular fins hung from the bottom of the child's dress.

Devon drew a sharp breath. "Coral?"

"Double fuck," Elias muttered. The fight went out of him, and when Devon made to rush forward, he grabbed the other man's shoulder. "Don't be dumb."

"That's my daughter!" Devon cried.

Sin's blood turned cold as she looked the child over a second time, noting the similarity in features between the two. "Eli—"

"I know who she is," Elias growled low in his throat. "Look again."

"Yes," Nathaniel invited, angling his body so they could see into the booth. "Look again."

Partially hidden by the vampire's bulk were a pair of feet in strappy sandals. Sin squinted, following those legs up over white capris and a dusky pink blouse to the too-pale face of a woman whose cheeks blossomed with bruises, her dark hair a messy tangle and her throat stained with blood.

"Flick," Devon croaked. "Oh, gods, *Flick*."

"Your wife is delicious." Nathaniel licked his lips, cleaning a drop of blood from the corner of his mouth with an appreciative hum. "Seafood has always been a favourite of mine."

"Is she alive?" Sin couldn't stop the wobble in her voice, nor the way her nails dug into Elias' skin.

"For now." Nathaniel smiled, cold and cruel. "How long she stays that way depends entirely on you."

"Me?"

"Correct." The smile twisted into a supercilious sneer. "My grandmother and I spent months planning the sabotage of that ship. *Months.* Our only variable was the exit strategy – until you wandered into the ship's laundry, providing the perfect scapegoat. But you couldn't just lay down and die, could you? Oh no. You had to fall in with that stupid reindeer and start poking your nose where it didn't belong."

"Sorry to disappoint." Sin choked a wet laugh. "So now what? Surely you don't think you can still salvage this."

"Why not?" Nathaniel tipped his head to the side, the movement sharp and not entirely natural. "The communications blackout holds. Nobody knows the truth except the three of you, and that blasted reindeer. All I need to get our plan back on track is a little leverage. The deal is simple – surrender yourself to me, and the kid and her mother go free."

Sin glanced at the unconscious woman in the booth, then at the mer-child dangling from Nathaniel's fist. "All right."

"No!" Elias whirled, eyes wide. "No, Sin."

Her knees trembled, but Sin lifted her chin. "I won't stand by and let Coral be hurt. I can't."

"Gods, don't you see that's the whole point?" Elias shook his head. "Blitzen will do *anything* to keep you safe, Sin – even let these assholes escape. The minute Nathaniel has his hands on you, it's over."

"She's a child, Elias." Sin blinked away the tears blurring her vision. "I won't leave her in the hands of a monster. Blitzen will understand."

The furious agony on Elias' face said he knew she was right. Swearing under his breath, the frost elf stepped aside, giving Sin a clear path to the vampire across the dance floor.

"Slowly," Nathaniel warned, holding Coral against his chest like a shield. "Try anything funny and the kid dies."

Sin complied, taking steady, purposeful steps until she could lift one hand and stroke Coral's cheek. "It's going to be all right, sweetheart."

"For the girl, at least." Nathaniel's chuckle was cold. "Not so much for you."

"Yeah." Swallowing around the lump in her throat, Sin glanced over her shoulder at Elias. "Thank you. Again."

"For what?"

She smiled. "The knife."

Elias blinked.

Sin turned back to Nathaniel, gathering what little magic she had. The design in her mind was simple. Useless, really; a half-formed notion of doll's clothes made from repurposed children's clothes. It was enough, though, to make her fingers tingle, to allow her hands to move faster than a human should have been able to move.

Faster, even, than a vampire.

The hand that had been stroking Coral's cheek shifted, yanking the wadded fabric from her mouth and throwing it into Nathaniel's face. The little girl didn't hesitate, latching an open mouth full of teeth – shark's teeth – onto her captor's forearm and biting down until he gave a startled shout and dropped her into Sin's waiting embrace.

"Dead!" Nathaniel screamed, clawing at the fabric covering his face. "You are *dead!*"

As Coral's bound arms looped around Sin's neck, she used the last of her magically-induced speed to flick open the pocket knife she'd swiped from Elias' shorts, grunting as she drove the blade hilt deep into Nathaniel's ribs. "Fuck you, asshole."

24

OH GRANDMA, WHAT SHARP
TEETH YOU HAVE

It took Blitzen less than a minute to realise that the full-frontal attack on the beach was a distraction. While there were a few strategically placed warriors of skill, most of the enemy fought so terribly Blitzen almost felt bad as King Garvon's mer-knights stabbed, slashed and disabled whoever was closest at hand – until he remembered what these pirates had conspired to steal, and the innocent people who'd been murdered so they could steal it. After that, he didn't feel a whit of regret as he scooped the assholes into the cradle of his antlers and tossed them deeper into the sea.

When he at last reached the shore, Blitzen shook the water from his fur and made his way cautiously up the beach. The resort's elegant outdoor areas were deserted, hats and towels lying alongside half-emptied glasses and the occasional paperback novel, abandoned by panicked guests the moment the tsunami siren began to wail. The fact it was *still* wailing, signalling that not all the island's residents were present and accounted for, had Blitzen straining his senses as he approached the building proper.

The entrance to the secure bunker was situated beside the kitchen garden, in a secluded courtyard that was central to the resort without being overtly obvious. Two mer-knights stood by the open doors, one with a clipboard in hand and the other clutching an energy rifle. They nodded to Blitzen as he approached, melting from reindeer to human mid-stride. "Who's missing?"

"Uh." The male with the clipboard cleared his throat. "Sir Devon, his mate Flick and their daughter Coral, Elias Frostwhisper and Lucinda Watkins."

Blitzen cursed. "Where were they last seen?"

"I don't know, sir."

"What do you mean, you *don't know*? I left them by the reception desk less than twenty minutes ago!"

"Don't tell me you're surprised, jägare." Dame Garadova dropped down from the roof, diaphanous peach kaftan billowing as she landed with a predator's grace. "Or did you really expect I'd be unprepared for eventualities just like this one?"

Blitzen held up a hand when the pair of mer-knights made to step to his side. "Get inside the bunker and seal the door."

"Sir—"

"It wasn't a suggestion," Blitzen growled. "Keep the guests safe, and leave the rest to me."

One of the knights made a choking sound of protest, but they backed slowly away. A few moments later the doors to the bunker slammed shut, locks thudding into place.

Dame Garadova raised a thin brow. "You realise I cannot let them live, now that they've seen me here."

"You think you can best me *and* these doors?" Blitzen snorted. "Good luck."

"I won't need it." Her lip curled just enough to show the tip of a fang. "Not only are you going to surrender, you'll open those doors for me voluntarily."

Blitzen barked a laugh. "No way, in this world or the next, would I stoop to helping you."

"Not even if your mate was in danger?"

The air in Blitzen's lungs turned sharp. He opened his mouth to demand answers when the tsunami alarm cut off, the sudden silence as deafening as the constant noise had been. And into that silence ... someone screamed.

"Oh, my." Dame Garadova tilted her head, eyes crinkling with mirth. "I wonder who that could be?"

Then she was gone, moving so inhumanly fast Blitzen had no hope of tracking the direction. He took off towards the screaming instead, bulldozing several neatly potted plants and a row of unlit tiki torches as he transformed into a reindeer mid-stride. His hooves skidded on the pavement, legs straining for speed as they propelled him around the edge of the building and into the resort's outdoor bar and dance area.

Elias and Nathaniel rolled across the ground, the vampire screaming incoherently as he struck out with increasingly frenzied blows. Uninjured, Elias would have been more than a match for his opponent, but his barely sealed wounds made every movement sluggish, his face taut and pale as he worked to avoid wildly flailing fists and fangs. Beyond the pair stood Sin, a child cradled against her chest and blood spattering her clothes. She was edging towards a shaded booth on the far side of the dance floor – where Devon crouched over the limp body of his mate, Flick, frantically patting at her cheeks.

Blitzen allowed himself a sparkling instant of relief that the unearthly sound came from his enemy rather than his love, and then succumbed to the roaring storm of rage that thundered in his blood. Lowering his head, he charged straight at the pair on the ground. Elias threw himself sideways at the last possible moment and Blitzen's antlers hit Nathaniel hard, piercing flesh to grind against bone in a well-practised movement that used both strength and momentum to maximum advantage.

The vampire's screams changed cadence as Blitzen lifted his head and flicked – but instead of flying free, Nathaniel ignored the various places he'd been impaled and clung tight. Pain erupted in Blitzen's jaw as the vampire kicked him square in the face with both feet, shattering bone with his supernatural strength. Before Nathaniel could repeat the strike, Blitzen reared up on his hind legs and shifted forms, sending his foe crashing to the ground when the antlers he'd been clinging to dissolved.

"Blitzen!"

Dizzy from the pain in his jaw, Blitzen nonetheless forced his body to turn, snatching whatever Elias had thrown out of the air on pure instinct. When he opened his hand he found a pocket knife, the blade already out and stained with blood. Curling his fingers around the handle, Blitzen whirled back to find Nathaniel crouching on the dance floor – in full sunlight. The vampire squealed and spat as his wounds healed in a matter of seconds, leaving only torn fabric and bloody smears as proof of Blitzen's efforts.

"Fucking Daywalkers," Elias muttered, body trembling as he staggered upright. "Fucking sunlight." He bared his teeth at Nathaniel. "Fuck you, you gods-damned son of a frostbitten ice troll."

Nathaniel screwed up his face and let out an ear-piercing scream that twisted Blitzen's insides into a horrific knot.

"*Enough*." Dame Garadova appeared before her grandson, her voice a whip of command that stunned Nathaniel into silence. "You should be peeling the female's skin from her bones, not losing your grip on reality."

Fury and nausea warred in Blitzen's gut. Raising his free hand to his face, he cupped his broken jaw and said through gritted teeth, "Berserker."

"Very good, jägare. Perhaps you're smarter than you look, after all." Dame Garadova inclined her head. "My grandson does have a habit of losing himself when things get a little … how do you say? Overstimulating." She snapped her fingers and Nathaniel's glassy eyes locked onto his grandmother. "Fortunately for me, I've worked with him since he was a babe – my sweet darling responds to every command I utter, no matter what state he's in."

"Fucking precious." Elias spat on the ground. "What a bond you have, Grandma Psychopath and Little Berserker. No wonder Lilith banished you."

"It's no fault of mine Lilith has softened over the centuries. Still, we digress." Dame Garadova straightened her spine, every inch the noblewoman. "You, jägare, are going to return those gifts to me, and then my grandson and I are going to walk out of here unchallenged."

"No." Blitzen flipped the knife into a defensive position. "Never."

She tsked, sliding both hands into the pockets of her trousers. "I was expecting that answer, and yet, I'll admit I'm still disappointed. Nathaniel?" The sharp cadence of her voice drew an answering hiss from the creature crouched behind her. Dame Garadova smiled. "Kill the reindeer's mate."

25

REST IN PIECES

In movies, when the heroine froze to the spot, Sin was the first one to shout at the screen for her to move. Yet as Nathaniel Garadova barrelled towards her with madness in his eyes, all she could do was stare.

"Sin!" Someone yanked on her clothes, dragging her aside just in time for Nathaniel to breeze past. Devon stepped into view, almost nose to nose as he pulled her t-shirt a second time. *"Sin!"*

"What?"

"Take Coral and—" Fabric tore and then Devon disappeared. Sin's jaw dropped as he sailed through the air, clearing the entire dance floor before crashing into the outer wall of the resort and dropping out of sight behind the bar.

The shocking violence woke her like a slap. Clutching Coral close, Sin threw herself on top of Flick just as Nathaniel's clawed hands swiped through the place she'd been standing.

"Coral," she managed, her voice hoarse. "Can you shift back to your legs for me, sweetheart?"

The little mershark shook her head. "I can't shift. When I'm on land, I need my wheelchair – but *he* threw it away."

Gods.

"Okay. Just … whatever happens, don't let go of me, all right?"

"I can't. My wrists are tied."

"Right. Good point." Sin struggled into a sitting position, looking around for Nathaniel.

The vampire didn't hurry; he stalked them like an animal closing in for the kill. There was no way Sin could fight him and win – but with Devon gone and both Blitzen and Elias fighting an impossibly agile Dame Garadova, there was nobody else to save them.

"I won't let him hurt you," Sin whispered, pressing her lips to Coral's hair to hide the way they trembled. "Don't be afraid."

"I'm not." Coral glanced up, face serious but, somehow, calm. "Are you ready?"

Sin opened her mouth to ask what she should be ready for when the child twisted towards Nathaniel and flung an open pepper shaker into his face. The vampire squealed as the fine granules hit his eyes, and Sin didn't stop to think – she shoved to her feet and ran.

There was nothing subtle about her attempt to flee, particularly with Nathaniel spitting and howling. The noise caught Dame Garadova's attention and she shoved Elias aside, moving to intercept Sin instead. For a single, ridiculous moment Sin wondered if she could possibly hip and shoulder the elderly vampire out of the way – but then Blitzen was there, no longer a man but a reindeer bellowing in rage. His full-body charge knocked Dame Garadova to the ground, hooves cutting deep into her skeletal body.

"Grandmother!" Nathaniel's voice cracked. "No!"

Sin didn't dare look; she just kept running. They were almost clear when Coral made a breathy noise of warning and something caught Sin's ankle, sending her sprawling. She skidded across the floor to collide heavily with the front of the bar, body curled protectively around the mer-child in her arms.

"Grandmother," Nathaniel repeated, his voice sounding more normal by the moment. "Are you all right?"

"Am I all right?" Dame Garadova wheezed. "Your grandmother just got run over by a reindeer, and you're asking if I'm *all right?* If I hadn't snatched up the knife that fool dropped, he'd have smashed my skull!"

Sin propped herself against the reassuring solidity of the bar, groaning as several parts of her body protested vehemently. Coral clung to her with a vice grip, but apart from some surface scrapes, seemed miraculously uninjured. Good sense dictated she move, but she could only watch as Dame Garadova struggled upright, Elias' pocket knife gripped in one hand. Blitzen lay at her feet, blood streaming from a gash in one of his hind legs. Despite the agony he must be suffering, his head was up, body positioned between the vampires and Elias.

Nathaniel hesitated, drifting towards his grandmother. "Let me—"

"No, you idiot." Dame Garadova pointed the knife in Sin's direction. "Do what you should have done days ago, and *kill the woman!*"

Sin cast around for something to use as a weapon as Nathaniel turned her way, but the dance floor was inconveniently spotless.

"Don't worry," Coral whispered, "If he gets too close, I'll bite him again."

"Good idea." Sin pressed another kiss to Coral's dark hair, praying her fear didn't show on her face. "You're very brave, sweetheart."

The little girl flashed a brief, humourless smile, and then they both looked up as Nathaniel's shadow blotted out the sun. He tore off his ruined polo, revealing a chest smeared with blood but otherwise completely unmarked – healed by the sun thanks to his Daywalker heritage.

"I'm going to tear this into strips," the vampire growled, bunching the shirt in his fists. "Then I'm going to tie you up and make you watch while I bleed the mer-child dry. After that, the two of us will share some long overdue alone time." Nathaniel spread both arms and grinned. "Ready to play?"

A loud boom echoed, and Sin screamed as the wood at her back shuddered. A ghastly hole appeared in the middle of Nathaniel's chest, through which she could clearly see the rest of the dance floor. Silence cloaked the area – until the boom echoed again and Nathaniel dropped to his knees, the hole in his torso doubled in size.

Devon stepped out from behind the bar, a plasma shotgun gripped in white-knuckled fingers. His hair was dishevelled, skin dirty and scratched, and he limped as he approached Nathaniel … but he didn't hesitate as he shoved the muzzle of the rifle against the vampire's forehead and pulled the trigger a third time.

"No," Dame Garadova cried, watching her grandson's headless body collapse. *"No!"*

"For Letitia." Elias' voice was thready, arms wobbling as he pushed to his knees.

Devon poked Nathaniel's remains with the toe of a patent leather shoe, then nodded in satisfaction. "For Letitia."

"Mongrels," Dame Garadova hissed. "My grandson was—"

Blitzen flowed up off the ground, caught hold of the wrist that held the pocket knife and twisted with such force, bones snapped. Dame Garadova's face went white, the knife falling from nerveless fingers to land in Elias' outstretched hand. The frost elf drove the knife into the vampire's chest, her scream cut short as Blitzen wrapped both hands around her head and gave a violent wrench.

"An asshole," Blitzen said as Dame Garadova slumped to the ground. "Your grandson was an asshole. Just like you."

YOU'LL DO

The cleanup went faster than Blitzen expected.

Or … perhaps it was as tedious as the cleanup of any other messy situation, and he just didn't notice because his only priority was Sin.

When the resort's medical team arrived, Blitzen insisted they check Sin first. After rallying enough to give him the kind of glare that could make a male's pride and joy wither on the spot, she directed the healers to Coral instead.

Once Blitzen was reassured neither had suffered more than a few bruises and scrapes, he allowed the healers to transfer him to the resort's infirmary alongside Elias. Under normal circumstances they'd have had a room each, but there were enough wounded mer-knights that sharing quickly became a necessity. The healers insisted on an intensive round of hands-on magical treatment, which Blitzen endured while watching Sin demand to stay in the room with him, then demand Elias join them once he was stabilised, then proceed to fuss over how the room should be rearranged to accommodate everyone concerned.

"Your friend took quite a beating," the senior healer reported, elderly face weathered and green eyes bright. "And on top of the previous assault, too. He needs time, and ice, but he'll heal. That, I can promise." He patted Blitzen's knee. "You had a narrow escape of your own – a hair further and that knife would have sliced the tendons in your ankle clean through."

Blitzen wrinkled his nose. While his ankle had been painful, it was the jaw that hurt the most; so much so that even after the bones had been mended, his entire face continued to ache.

Sin chose that moment to perch on the edge of the bed. "I'll make sure he rests."

"I have no doubt." The healer chuckled, then glanced up as Elias was wheeled in. The frost elf rested in a special bed whose mattress and sides were lined with sheets of ice, each one bespelled to meet his specific needs. He lay so still and pale beneath the single cotton cover that if Blitzen hadn't seen a restorative sleep before, he'd have feared the worst. As it was, he had to bite his tongue to stop from urging the healer to his feet faster, or to demand a translation for the way he hummed and tutted over the chart attached to Elias' bed.

"Hey." Sin poked him in the arm. "He's going to be fine."

"I know." Blitzen turned to Sin, her face etched with lines of fatigue no amount of showers or hot meals could cure. "Nyk said the same thing."

Sin's eyes narrowed. "I still can't believe you called him while the healers were trying to knit your broken bones. It could have waited, surely."

Blitzen was saved from answering by the arrival of Devon, who strode into the room with his favourite clipboard in hand. Like the rest of them, his face bore minor scrapes and bruises, fatigue creating shadows in the hollows of his eyes. He'd eschewed rest in favour of a quick wash and a fresh set of clothes, and had been overseeing the cleanup effort as though he hadn't blown the head of a vampire off with a shotgun mere hours earlier. "A word, sir, if I may?"

Blitzen lifted a brow.

"One of the surviving mercenaries has revealed the location of the device blocking incoming and outgoing communications. I've despatched a team of knights to take care of it." Devon tapped his pen against the edge of the clipboard. "I've also spoken with the Daywalker Consulate, who report that as per the rules of exile, the remains of both Esmeralda Garadova and her grandson, Nathaniel, will not be claimed for traditional burial." A flash of inhumanly sharp teeth. "If the North Pole has no objections, it's been suggested they be fed to the sharks."

Sin gasped, but Blitzen only grinned. "The North Pole has no objections. Frenzy away."

"Excellent." Devon made a swift mark on his paperwork. "I've also prepared a report on the situation for Nykolaas Klausse, on behalf of the resort and the mer-kingdom as a whole. Shall I forward it to your device?"

"Ugh." Blitzen screwed up his face. "If you have to."

"Wait." Sin held up a hand, her face pale. "That's … that's it? We're feeding the vampires to the sharks? Just like that?"

Devon regarded her down the length of his nose. "Are you saying they deserve better?"

"No, I just …" She swallowed audibly. "Real sharks, or mer-sharks?"

"I'm not at liberty to say." Devon's teeth flashed again. "Coral, however, is looking forward to her dinner tonight."

Blitzen watched the conflicting emotions play out on Sin's face before she said with quiet ferocity, "I hope it's the best meal she's ever eaten."

It was only the subtle flutter of Devon's lashes that suggested he was surprised by the response. He inclined his head. "I'll convey your sentiments when I see her next." An officious click of the tongue. "Whilst I'm here, Mrs. Watkins, I should like to add that once the communicatations blockade is lifted, we'll be contacting Shining Star Cruises to arrange the departure of all stranded passengers – meaning that if you so wish, I can have you home to your family by tomorrow morning."

Blitzen's lungs seized. He'd known this moment would come, but he wasn't ready to let Sin go; not even for the few weeks it would take to heal and handle the North Pole side of things in order to chase after her. Part of him had hoped for another night at least, a few stolen hours in which to promise the future she deserved; only now, thanks to Devon's efficiency, he wasn't going to get the chance. He knew her well enough to recognise the yearning in her expression, the catch in her voice as she opened her mouth and said, "Will there be a memorial service for Letitia?"

Blitzen blinked. "Huh?"

Devon looked equally as mystified. "I beg your pardon?"

"Letitia," Sin repeated firmly. "Will there be a funeral? A memorial? I'm not sure of mer customs."

"There will be a funerary rite in a few days," Devon allowed. "Once we've ensured our guests, both living and deceased, are returned safely to their homes."

Sin nodded. "Then I'll stay."

"*What?*" Blitzen and Devon shouted in perfect unison, then cringed as the healers across the room shushed them.

Sin looked back and forth between them, a smile flirting with her lips. "Well, for a start, I won't leave while Blitzen and Elias are injured – but I'm certainly not going anywhere until I've attended Letitia's funeral." She paused. "If that's allowed, of course."

"Er ..." Devon looked as thunderstruck as Blitzen felt.

"But ... your family," he managed.

"Oh, I want to see them, and I know they want to see me, but this is more important." Sin began rummaging in the pockets of her borrowed hoodie, which was large enough to fit Blitzen – and a necessity given the air conditioning in the room was set cool enough for Elias' comfort rather than their own. She made a noise of satisfaction and withdrew her hand to reveal an elegant, tear-drop shaped pendant suspended on a copper chain. The pendant itself was clear, and when Blitzen leaned forward, he noted a single black hair twisted into an intricate design within. Sin cleared her throat. "When I was sitting vigil with Letitia, some of her hair caught on my fingers. I put it in my pocket, and completely forgot it was there until I was getting changed earlier. I enclosed the hair in a pair of necklaces, and I ... I hope you don't mind, Devon, but I wondered if you'd give one to Letitia's family."

Devon went very, very still. "And the other?"

"It's for Elias." Sin lifted her chin. "When he wakes."

Blitzen's head spun. "When did you make them?"

"While you were with the healers." A self-conscious look from beneath her lashes. "I needed something to do besides worry."

"Let me get this straight," Devon said, his voice flat. "Though you could fly home to the children for whom you've pined since your arrival, you wish to stay here with the lover you've only known for a few days and attend the funeral of a woman you barely knew? A woman in whose memory you crafted not one but two delicate necklaces of undeniable skill, which would no doubt fetch a high price if put up for sale?"

"Yes," Sin said.

Devon's eyes locked onto her face, a predator's regard. "How much of my napery was harmed in the creation of these masterful works of art, Mrs. Watkins?"

"None," she replied, then winced. "Although … you'll find the waiting area outside the healing grotto is missing a lamp. Sorry about that."

Blitzen looked at the pendant anew, noting the clear glass in which the hair was ensconced, the delicate wire wrapping, the copper chain. "That used to be a *lamp?*"

"Um …" Colour crept into Sin's cheeks, but she didn't retract her hand. "I'm afraid so."

With gentle fingers, Devon plucked the pendant from her palm. With his other hand, he drew his phone from his pocket, thumbed the screen and held the device to his ear. "Flick? Yes, love, it's me. Can you do me a favour – on Mrs. Watkins' guest information, who's listed as her next of kin? A daughter? Yes, that will do. Would you call her as soon as the blockade is lifted, please, and arrange an all expenses paid trip for Mrs. Watkins' entire family to be here in time for Letitia's memorial? No, there will be no end date. They may stay as long as Mrs. Watkins wishes to stay. Thank you, love. Yes, I'll be there soon." Devon hung up and glanced back at Sin. "A lamp, you say."

Sin, face slack, simply nodded.

Devon tsked, then leant in and pressed a soft kiss to her cheek. "You'll do, Mrs. Watkins. You'll do."

"Thank you," Sin managed.

"Thanks are unnecessary, when you have given us such a gift. Blitzen is a very lucky man, to have someone with a heart as large as yours." Devon clicked his heels together. "Now, I'm afraid I must go. The evening meal will arrive soon, courtesy of our incredibly grateful chef. Enjoy."

"Thanks." Blitzen watched Devon walk out, then turned to Sin. "A *lamp*."

"Why does everyone keep saying that?" She laughed, tears glimmering in the corners of her eyes. "Yes, Blitzen. A lamp."

"How did you melt the glass? Shape it into a pendant? Extract the wire from the innards? Make the chain!?"

Sin bit her lip. "Magic."

"And …" his heart tripped. "The decision to stay?"

She reached to cup the side of his face. "Love, Blitzen. I love my children, but I also love you – and I'm not letting you out of my sight ever again."

"Thank the gods for that." Something restless inside him settled. "I feel the same."

"Love, or the need to keep me close?"

"Both." Blitzen threaded his fingers through Sin's hair and drew her in for a kiss. "You're mine, Lucinda Anne Watkins, and I am never, ever letting you go."

"Good."

~ The End ~

♥

Thanks so much for reading!

I HOPE you enjoyed Sin and Blitzen's story, and that it puts you in the mood for some post-Christmas celebrations!

So ... do I write other stuff? You bet I do! Keep up to date with all the latest shenanigans at:

www.sliceofsammy.com

IF YOU ENJOYED this latest peek into the magical Merged Worlds, then I'd love it if you would leave a review – not only does it help an author out, it lets me know that I've hit the mark and put a smile on your wonderful face. So, please and thank you in advance!

♥

LOVE A FREE BOOK?

Learn to let go... or burn.

Dating Noah Acheson has always been gentle, predictable and above all, safe – but when the softly spoken foxkin breaks the rules of their carefully crafted relationship, Deanna cuts him off, retreating to her private sanctuary deep in the Australian bush.

Stinging from Deanna's rejection, Noah returns from a brief stint fighting fires in New South Wales to face an infinitely more vicious fire front in Victoria. Though his broken heart still very much belongs to Deanna Schellponte, he's determined not to chase her – until the wind changes, turning the fires towards pack land, and Deanna is reported missing.

With fire raging all around, Noah races into the bush to find the wolfkin he loves. To survive, Deanna and Noah must confront not only the fury of Mother Nature... but the ghost whose memory tore them apart.

ALSO BY SAMANTHA MARSHALL

(Featuring Headless)

A Perfectly Paranormal Easter

(Featuring Foiled)

A Perfectly Paranormal Christmas

(Featuring Blitzen)

COMING SOON

Sorcery and Sacrilege

(Book four in the Weaver's War series)

To find out more about these awesome tales, check out my website:

www.sliceofsammy.com

ABOUT SAMANTHA

Hi, I'm Sam!

I've been writing my whole life, scribbling stories on anything close to hand – from the shopping list to napkins to post-it notes (don't mention post-its to hubby haha).

I grew up reading fantasy of the likes of Anne McCaffrey, Terry Pratchett, and their peers. I'm also a lifelong vampire fan, along with all things spooky. In my late teens I was introduced to paranormal romance and discovered a whole new layer of storytelling with a bit of a spicy edge! Taking what I learnt from all of the above, I devoted myself to creating full-bodied characters, meaty plots, epic adventure, and a little bit of naughty sauce on the side.

I completed a Diploma of Professional Writing and Editing after high school and spent the next several years in my writing cave, working on a novel that is now in a drawer somewhere, followed by a couple of others who shared the same fate. (What can I say? I'm a recovering perfectionist.)

I came close to debuting my novel career in 2009, then ended up pregnant and took some time off to have kids. I debuted for real in 2019 with *Sorcery and Stardust* and won ARRA's Favourite Debut Romance Author for 2019, which was extremely cool!

I write speculative fiction that is a fusion of multiple sub-genres and therefore doesn't fit particularly well into any of them, but after many years and a lot of angst, I'm okay with that. I love all my characters and their stories for different reasons, but have a soft spot for an excellent villain and a tortured protagonist.

I currently live in southeast Melbourne, Victoria, with my hubby, two kids, a Golden Retriever, and a turtle. I volunteer with the Romance Writers of Australia, and I'm passionate about great writing, interesting characters, chai tea and happily ever afters.

And if you want to get to know the Perfectly Paranormal Anthology authors a bit more, get sneak peeks of what's coming up for the APP Anthologies, as well as giveaways, special offers and just some PNR fun, then join our Perfectly Paranormal Paramours Facebook Group.

Find us here:
https://www.facebook.com/groups/251663560162131

ACKNOWLEDGEMENTS

I have to admit; I've had the beginnings of this novella planned for well over two years now. From the moment we all sat down as an anthology group and picked out the holidays to explore during season one, I've been waiting for Christmas to roll around so I could get inside Blitzen's head and craft him a deserving partner. In spite of this enthusiasm, the writing of this novella was drawn out by personal and real-life challenges, and there was a point I feared it might never get finished.

And yet.

Here we are.

I'm incredibly proud of the resulting story, and I'm ever so grateful to my fellow APPA authors – Leisl, Marnie, Helen – for encouraging me to keep going even when our deadline sailed merrily on by with a cheerful wave. Without their endless support, I can say with confidence you would not be reading this right now.

To you, dear reader, thank you for coming along on yet another sparkly adventure. If you're new, I hope you loved your first foray into the depths of my imagination; if you're a repeat offender, then welcome back. Here's your wine and cheese – kick off your shoes and relax.

There is, to my great joy, so much more to come.

♥

MISTLETOE AND MEDDLING

HELLUCY HOWE

MISTLETOE AND MEDDLING

Tales from the Fae Court
Book Four

~

Hellucy Howe

ABOUT MISTLETOE AND MEDDLING

Can new love eclipse old fears?

When Lord Treymeron Aphiski arrives at the Palace of Elrodel for his Tri-moon apprenticeship, he's hoping for a fresh start - but never in his wildest dreams did he imagine he'd be made assistant to Queen Dianathke's chief advisor.

Lord Athys Castniidae, Earl of Rengarth is not only capable, kind and generous, he's also incredibly handsome and has a lovely sister to boot. Inca is every bit as witty and intelligent as her brother, and together they mentor Trey in his first assignment; planning the palace's Yule solstice celebrations.

The festivities are threatened when an unknown creature attacks the palace, forcing Trey, Athys and Inca to sideline their preparations to investigate the mystery. But Trey's confusing attraction to both Athys and Inca continues to grow until the truth is revealed, forcing them to either make a stand or lose everything they've struggled to achieve.

Too bad Trey's spent his entire life hiding from the spotlight, Athys is keeping secrets and Inca … well. Be careful what you wish for this Yule, because you just might get it.

I dedicate this story to those of us who fight a daily battle of limiting beliefs, societal expectations and personal issues. We don't have to prove ourselves to anyone because we're perfect as we are.

AUTHOR'S NOTE

Aside from the adventure, this is a love story. I believe in love and I write speculative fiction, so my characters and worlds are not those people may expect. If you are offended by love in all its forms, then this book may not be for you.

Within these pages, I have stepped outside the standard boundaries of male/female – one of my main characters is two natured and could even be classified as alien, despite the 'human' form. I hope you can keep an open mind and see that love is love, no matter what form it takes.

TREYMERON

*T*hrap, thrap, thrap.

Treymeron Aphiski glared at the door, offended by the interruption to his quiet time. Of all the skills he possessed, why couldn't seeing through an opaque piece of wood be one of them? He still wasn't certain agreeing to participate in the Tri-moon training program at the Palace of Elrodel had been the best idea, but it was too late to back out now. Plus, his goal of finding a life and a career somewhere other than home at the Papillion duchy could only happen if he left that home. But the palace was huge, bigger than his expectations and it made him uneasy.

Frowning, he scanned his messy room, then shrugged and grabbed the jerkin he'd tossed over a chair. Dodging haphazardly placed furniture and open boxes, he struggled into his tunic as he crossed the room. He eased the door open a handspan and peered out. The opposite grey stone wall of the hallway was all he could see through the narrow opening, then a movement down low caught his eye.

Marda, the house brownie, touched her forelock. "Sorry to bother you, Lord Treymeron, but this here is Athys Castniidae, Earl of Rengarth. He said you'd be expecting him." She gestured at someone he couldn't see, then a tall, smiling Fae-male stepped around Marda, peering back at Trey through the narrow gap.

Wow.

His tongue clove to the roof of his mouth as he clutched the edges of the door in frozen befuddlement and stared at this very tall friend of his brother-in-law Dario.

Whose smile was the stuff of dreams.

And aimed at him.

Open-mouthed, unable to look away, Trey simply blinked while the brownie's words of introduction seeped into his skull, then drifted away like thistledown. His Adam's apple bobbed on a hard swallow. He realised, for the first time ever, he was suffering no discomfort in holding the gaze of someone who wasn't a parent or a sibling. This was a stranger. One whose gaze skewered him, yet offered warm recognition as well.

He should look away, because staring like this was surely rude, but he couldn't. Why couldn't he sever the connection? But, how could he – anyone – look away from this astonishing vision of masculine magnificence?

Accented by a single beaded braid caressing the right side of his face, glittering blonde hair swept across Athys' aristocratic forehead and haloed his head, neck and shoulders in lustrous splendour. Teal eyes glowed with a gilded radiance belied by the faintly knit brows in his long, narrow, creamy-gold face. Add in a blade of a nose, high cheekbones, well-shaped lips above a smooth, firm chin, and Trey stood shivering. He clamped the door between desperate fingers; Athys was an entrancing Golden God and he wanted to lick the handsome warrior anywhere he could.

That was when Trey's mouth ran away with him. "You're Athys? Are you sure? Because I was told Athys was away until tomorrow and it's not tomorrow yet."

The corners of Athys' beautiful lips ticked up in a smile, while Trey continued to gawp like a landed fish, mentally kicking himself for the foolishness of his words. When would he learn to put his brain in gear before he opened his mouth?

The Golden God's voice was as deep and sinfully delicious as the rest of him. "I'm definitely Athys and I'm back a day early." The deep timbre invaded the narrow gap between them like Trey's favourite sweet and creamy cheese-filled pastry, wrapping him in scrumptious yumminess. "I thought we could chat and get acquainted before the official Tri-moon program gets underway in the morning. Does that work for you, Treymeron?"

Eyes drifting shut, Trey basked in warm sensations, as they seeped through the pores of his skin; deeper and deeper, until the beautiful tendrils wrapped and stroked his parched soul. It was blissful. He wanted more. In fact, his inclinations were pushing him to climb Athys as if he were a tree, then cling tight and, and …

And that was no sane way to think about the Fae-male with whom Dario had arranged Trey's Tri-moon stay. He swept his tongue across his lips; was there a drugging scent in the air here? Some sort of craziness induced by pollen?

"Treymeron? Hello? May I come in and speak with you?"

The warm honeyed strands were still cuddling him, but oh! Words, issuing from the Golden God's attractive mouth, suddenly registered in his loopy mind; his eyes shot open on a gasp. "Holy snapping swamp turtles! So sorry, your lordship. I don't know what came over me. Of course you may, but how is it that you're here? I mean, it's not that you aren't wanted; you're more than welcome." He jerked the door wide, a flush scalding his face. Heaving in a breath, he fought for serenity and control. Athys was high in the Queens' regard. Wouldn't it be wonderful to be in such a valued position? To know where you fit in the world?

Athys smiled. "Thank you, Treymeron."

As he moved aside, the suite's disorganised chaos was revealed and Marda's hands flew to her cheeks. "My Lord Treymeron! What have you done to your room? It was so neat, so well-prepared, and now look!"

Peering around, Trey swallowed. "I'm sorry but I wasn't comfortable." He threw her a challenging stare. "You said I could make myself at home."

The brownie threw her hands in the air. "But there's furniture and cushions everywhere!"

Athys glanced into the room; there was no doubt he was taking note of the mess.

Trey bit his lip. "I haven't finished." He smoothed a hand down his rumpled jerkin. "If you'd returned tomorrow, like you said, this would've been neat and tidy once more."

Now Marda's hands were clasped at her bosom. "But you're changing everything!"

He winced. "I know, but if this is my room and I'm to live here for the next few months, I need to have things organised in a way that doesn't make my neck crawl."

Athys bit his lower lip, but nodded gravely. "Understandable. That sensation is never a welcome one."

The little brownie was peering around. "Where are the flowers I specially picked?"

Trey flushed. "I know you went to a lot of trouble and I really appreciate it, but …" He bit his lip. "I'm sorry, they stunk the room up, so I threw them out the window."

Her face screwed up. "The brithaglio lace doilies?"

He tilted his head, pointed to one side of the room. "Stuffed in a closet."

"And the antique bronze figurine crafted by the famous Farrugio?"

His hands went to his hips. "That disgusting satyr leering over the terrified nymph? So hideously unpleasant! I can't get over how ugly it is! I had to embalm it in those lace thingies before I shoved it in the back of the closet and covered it with other stuff. It gives me the heebie jeebies! That Furruglio guy must have been some kind of pervert!" He trailed off at the expression of horror on the brownie's face and clapped a hand over his mouth as he took a step back.

A snort came from Athys but Marda let out such an outraged howl, it caused a painful ringing in Trey's ears. Shaking his head, he retreated further, only stopping when something hard clipped the back of his calves and threw him off balance.

"Oh shite!" Arms windmilling, he toppled, rear end forcefully meeting the sharp edge of the box he'd backed into, before he bounced sideways and down, to where the solid floor awaited. The momentum flattened his upper body, forcing his feet and legs high into the air. For a moment he feared a somersault was inevitable – but then he rocked forward and his feet slammed back to the floor. Pain filled him and he groaned. Miserably aware of the flush rising from his chest, flowing inexorably up his neck, spreading until it swamped his cheeks with glowing humiliation, he sagged. Was it possible the floor could crack open, let him fall through, then snap shut again?

A scream rent the air. Probably Marda. Through his agonised daze, he was vaguely aware of Athys shoving the door wide and striding in.

The beautiful Golden God dropped to his knees and leaned over Trey's supine body. "Treymeron! Look at me!"

Forcing his eyes to meet Athys' worried gaze, Trey was vaguely aware of Marda wailing about the disordered state of his rooms, but who could care about that with this adorable Fae-male looming over him? What was pain when beautiful hair fell forward to cocoon them in a shiny curtain? When those enticing lips shaped words …

Which dropped like stones. "Marda, please stop! They're only things. If you like them so much, put them in your own room."

The harsh order jolted Trey out of his haze. He focused on Athys' concerned face, now filling his field of vision.

"Shite, Treymeron! Are you hurt?" Large warm hands slid down his arms, ran over his body, his legs and back up his torso, finally cupping either side of his jaw. "Tell me where the pain is."

Trey grimaced weakly. "I was *trying* to make a good impression." He huffed a weak chuckle, his eyes falling away. "Waste of time. Oh well – I'll definitely have bruises, just as my pride does. But you know what they say: 'Pride goeth before a fall.' Or before a bumble foot, tangoing with randomly scattered boxes. Can you tango with boxes? Who would lead as you slide across the floor? The floor! Is it damaged? If it's scraped, I'm happy to work off any repairs. I'm—"

"Very talkative." The hands on his jaw gently raised his face until he again met the crystal blue eyes inspecting him with focused concern. "You didn't appear to hit your head, so you're not dazed. Which means …"

They were interrupted by a litany of 'squees', which accompanied the skittering gallop of little paws crossing the room.

Athys tensed, spinning to face the threat. His hand flew to a sheathed knife at one hip. His nearest leg maintained a kneeling position, but the other leg was suddenly drawn up beneath him, weight on the ball of the foot. "What's this?"

"Oh, that's my Pinkerpush." The tiny duskit raced to Treymeron, trembling as she scaled him to snuggle under his chin. He cooed, raising his arms to cradle her and smoothed his jaw over the softness of her downy head.

Reaching out slowly Athys stroked Pinkerpush's ear. "A duskit. I'm impressed." His fingers dropped so Pinkerpush could sniff them. Trey watched as Pinkie stared up at Athys; her deep blue eyes blinking from a face covered in bright purple fur, before her soft wet nose snuffled his fingers - folk were always fascinated by Pinkerpush. Athys was approved with the swipe of a tiny tongue. Shifting his finger to caress the satiny cheek, he grinned as he refocused on Treymeron. "I see Pinkerpush is quite young; how long have you had her?"

A wobbly smile bloomed. "Pinkerpush was orphaned last winter in a Vulpiawolf attack. I was caring for her and then she wouldn't leave."

"She must feel safe with you."

Trey nodded. "I hope so. I've grown to love her and I'd be lost if she left now."

Athys nodded. "That's understandable." He studied Trey's face intently. "Now, where do you hurt? Any areas of sharp pain?"

Trey's hands fluttered weakly. "No, I'm okay. Oh, wait, my bum aches."

"Hmm. Well you did hit the floor with a wallop, so that wouldn't surprise me." Athys continued to scan him. "Fortunately, I didn't feel any obvious broken limbs or sprains, and nothing looks odd. Are you okay to get up, Treymeron? Here, let me help you."

Trey's eyes drifted shut. "I'm alright and just call me Trey. I'll get up momentarily. Ohh!" A shoulder under his armpit hoisted him like a baby. "How'd you do that? You're a big guy, but I'm no weanling."

Athys chuckled as he gently lowered Treymeron to sit on one of the rearranged dining chairs. "One of my many talents."

Marda appeared next to them, wringing her tiny hands. "Do my lords need assistance? A healer perhaps?"

Trey shook his head. "No, no. Thanks anyway, Marda. Really, it was just a trifling thing. Nothing exciting, or serious like an earthquake—"

A dull roar vibrated the entire building, sending objects rattling and floors, doors and walls moving in a series of waves. The magical colour plumsplat radiated through the ether in frantically shooting sparks.

The chair tipped enough to send Trey sliding into Athys, while Pinkerpush went flying. They crashed to the floor in a twisted heap. Trey found himself lying half on, half off of a very broad chest, legs intertwined, and his face buried in the side of a warm neck. Both of Athys' arms banded tightly around a shaking Trey, then Pinkerpush tried to burrow between them, chittering furiously.

"What in thunder just happened?" Trey could only mumble as he forced himself to breathe, in and out, in and out ... The scent of Athys filled his nostrils, a delightful aroma of cinnamon and rosemusk. The movement of his mouth as he spoke pressed his lips into Athys' skin. "Ooh, sorry! I'm not kissing you, although it probably seems like it. But a kiss would be more forceful, done with intent and ... Icklegolia! Me and my silly mouth!" Beneath him, Athys started to shake and his mirth burst from him in a loud chuckle. Trey pulled slowly away, forced his aching body into a sitting position, his skin burning as a blush crept up his features. Squeeing again, Pinkerpush crawled into his lap.

Marda was staring at him with fearful awe. "I d-don't care about the room changes, Lord Treymeron, I really don't! You-you caused an earthquake. That's powerful magic. Please say you weren't angry with anything I said or did!"

"No! No! That wasn't me!" Panic welling, Trey flapped his hands wildly and Pinkerpush's claws gripped his jerkin as he let her go. "I can't … I didn't … I wouldn't …" His voice grew louder with every word.

Large hands clasped his. "Ssh, I've got you." Athys pulled him closer. "Marda, that wasn't Trey."

Marda didn't look convinced. "But he said … he said the word, then it happened." She pointed at Pinkerpush. "And he's got a familiar."

Trey gasped. "A familiar? Pinkie? No!" He bit his lip. "No, she's my fosterling and my friend, but not my familiar."

"Although, I can see why you might think so, Marda." Athys nodded, one arm cupping Trey's trembling shoulders. "But that was no earthquake. If you look around, you'll see there's no real damage other than a few small things falling over."

Marda frowned. "But there was noise and shaking and magic – I saw plumsplat sparking."

"You're right about that, Marda. It was magic." Athys rubbed Trey's upper back. "But it was portal magic. Very badly constructed portal magic, too, which is why it resembled an earthquake."

"It felt wrong." Trey wearily scrubbed one cheek. "The magic was off."

Athys' mouth thinned. "The magic was 'off', as you put it, because whoever tried to cast the spell didn't know what they were doing."

Trey's brows furrowed. "How do you know that?"

Athys' lips twisted. "Because I've been present when Queen Dianathke does portal magic and it's nothing like that."

2

ATHYS

Studying his new charge, Athys drew in a slow breath. Suddenly, the Tri-moon program was wonderfully more inviting and a lot less annoying than he'd believed it was going to be. Lord Treymeron Aphiski, the 'favour' he'd agreed to accommodate for his battle-brother Dario, had turned out to be the cutest Fae-male he'd ever had the pleasure of meeting. Look at all that shining, wavy dark hair simply begging to have its softness tested. He'd already found Trey's slim, bronze-skinned face to be soft but firm under his finger-tips, and those eyes … The delectable violet hue, more brilliant than any spark-amethyst Athys had ever seen, impaled him.

Swallowing, he forced his vision lower, along the straight-ish nose – what was a tiny bump, or two? – to the generous mouth and cleft chin. His tongue itched to trace that very same pathway, and the faint burn of annoyance that had been roiling in his gut since Queen Dianathke had agreed to Trey's presence unravelled and dissipated like a hot wind over the Vansitarkan Badlands.

"Are you sure you're okay, Trey?" Athys pulled his legs in and rose to a crouch. "Because I need to check in with the Queen after that mucked up portal magic; see what went wrong and why. As her closest adviser, she'll be expecting me. How about you come along? If you're feeling up to it, I can introduce you."

Trey gawked. "Introduce me? To the Queen?" His hands fisted, then re-opened. "She's probably very busy."

Athys held back his grin. "Likely she is, but not too busy to greet the son of an old friend." Plus, if he considered the condition she'd imposed on him for agreeing to host Trey, there was no way he could arrive in her presence without the company of this gorgeous nobleman.

Violet eyes shining, Trey swallowed; his lips curled into a fleeting smile. "Alright, if it isn't too much trouble." His eyes immediately dropped, his nose burying itself in Pinkerpush's fur, nuzzling briefly before he tucked the kit into the neck of his jerkin.

Ah, he was shy; Athys mentally shrugged. If Trey was the reserved type, he'd be more likely to stick like quicksand to the only person he knew, something that could only make Athys' job easier.

Scooting to his feet, Athys held out his hands. "Here, let me help you up."

Hesitantly, Trey accepted his grip. "Let's hope we can stay upright this time."

Athys tilted his head. "Well, nobody was expecting an earthquake." He retained his grasp on Trey's hands, until he was sure his protege was steady enough to stand on his own.

Trey frowned. "But you said it was badly done portal magic."

"And so it was. Because it caused a disruption."

"A disruption?" Marda's voice was slightly muffled. "Hah! That there was an earthquake, your earlship."

Athys sighed. "Very well, Marda, just for you we'll call it an earthquake – of sorts." He focused on Trey. "You okay?"

Trey flushed as he glanced up, nodded, then pulled his hands free.

Athys turned and headed towards the entry. "Good. Let's go then. I'll help you finish your room later." He held the door open, waiting for Trey to step through. "Got your key? You'll need to lock up."

Trey glanced towards the closet. "I can't lock Marda in." Sure enough, when Athys looked that way, he could see Marda ferreting around in the wall cabinet.

"Marda? What *are* you doing?"

The brownie reappeared, hair ruffled, expression defiant as she clutched a large lace wrapped object. "The Farrugio statue. You said as I could put it in my room. If Lord Treymeron doesn't want it, I reckon I'll have it." Her glance shot from Athys to Trey. "If that's really okay?"

Nodding vigorously, Trey clapped his hands together. "Marda, I'm totally fine with the idea. It's brilliant. You're welcome to take it and, since you like it so much, I'm happy for you to keep it as long as you want."

Marda's expression held trepidation. "Are you certain sure, Lord Treymeron?"

He grinned. "Absolutely, Marda! I know you'll take excellent care of it and there couldn't be anyone better to do so." He gestured towards the open door. "Better take it to your room before you get called to further duties. Athys and I have to go somewhere anyway."

"Oh, yes, you're right." Gifting him with a beatific smile, Marda hurried away down the corridor holding her precious cargo.

Meeting Athys' gaze, Trey dusted his palms across each other. "Ready when you are."

With a chuckle, Athys clapped him gently on the back of the shoulder. "Not sure whether to call that move cunning or manipulative, but you'll be back in Marda's good books anyway." He shook his head, still chuckling. "Come on."

Locking his door, Trey followed. He lost count of the number of hallways, rooms and stairs they traversed, but his sense of location enabled him to remember the way they'd come. "I hadn't expected Elrodel to be such a big place."

Athys paused in front of a wooden door heavily carved with vines. "With so many folk living here?"

Trey gulped. "Mmm. It's daunting."

Athys grinned sympathetically. "You'll become used to it sooner than you think." He opened a door, revealing a room lined with chairs except for the double doors in the end wall. In front of those stood a pair of guards, who nodded when Athys came into view. One reached to open a door, but the other stayed his arm, his expression challenging.

"Lord Athys, we know the Queen is expecting you – but she said nothing about you having a companion. Who's this?"

"Ah, she must've forgotten." Athys gestured. "This is my new aide, a gift from her majesty. Lord Treymeron Aphiski, youngest son of the Duke of Papillion, meet Sir Nasper Immaday and Sir Frith Limacodi."

Stepping forward, Trey grinned as he offered his arm in polite greeting. "Hi. I only arrived here this morning, so good on you, noticing I'm a stranger, Sir Nasper. Although, now you know who I am, I'm not one any longer. A stranger, I mean. Right?" He tilted his head. "I bet you've got to be really on the alert in your position. Can't be certain who might turn up, so that makes your job super important." He nodded. "Such a pleasure to meet you and I'll be sure to let the Queen know how diligent you are."

"Er, right." Sir Nasper cocked an eyebrow at Athys as he slowly extended his arm to link briefly with Trey's. "Welcome, your lordship. The Duke of Papillion? Good bloodlines there. Yessiree."

As Trey stepped past Sir Nasper to greet Sir Frith, Athys' attention was caught by Sir Nasper elevating and lowering his eyebrows several times. He glanced quickly to see Trey well-occupied some distance away talking with Sir Frith, then turned back. "Something wrong, Sir Nasper?"

The guard leaned closer, his voice lowering to a whisper. "Erm, your, ah, aide, you said? He seems a little unusual – nothing wrong with him, is there?"

Annoyance welled, but Athys concealed it. "Wrong in what way?"

"You know." Sir Nasper tapped the side of his head a few times.

"No." Athys' annoyance flared into anger. "I don't know." He cocked his head, smiled in bland invitation. "Why don't you tell me."

Sir Nasper grimaced. "The way he spoke. Who the hell speaks like that? Compliments someone on their alertness and diligence?"

Athys couldn't keep the curtness from his voice. "Someone with manners." Passing Sir Nasper, he rejoined Trey and smiled at the second guard, now holding the door open. "Morning, Sir Frith."

"Morning, Lord Athys." He waved them through, closing the door behind them.

They were in a smaller antechamber, also containing chairs along the walls, but no occupants other than the two of them. Athys kept going until he reached the door on the opposite wall. He made for the latch, but Trey stretched out a hand.

Athys met his worried gaze. Was it too much to hope Nasper's action had gone unnoticed? "Yes, Trey?"

Trey tugged at the hem of his jerkin, patted the tiny bulge that was Pinkerpush. "I did something wrong back there, didn't I?"

"No." Athys' voice was firm. "You were all that's pleasant and polite. Some folk simply don't recognise those things."

Trey's gaze shifted. "Yeah, nothing new, really."

"Don't worry about it." Athys patted Trey's hand. "His problem; not yours." Now was not the time to take this further, despite his seething displeasure, so he opened the door. "In you go, our Queen is waiting." With a resigned shrug, Trey walked through the opening; Athys followed quickly.

"Athys!" Queen Dianathke's voice snapped sharply. "What took you so long? Do you have any idea who attempted that atrocious portal magic? The whole palace shook! Portal magic in the wrong hands is capable of destruction on a major scale - we can't have unknown threats running around loose."

"Indeed we can't, and my apologies for my tardiness, Your Majesty." Athys bowed. "I came as quickly as I could. I know the portal wasn't cast by yourself, but I'm not aware of anyone else at Elrodel who can do such magic."

The Queen tapped her lower lip. "Hmm, now you say so, neither am I; that's very strange." Her rich brown hair rippled as she paced to and fro across the carpet of her personal receiving room. "We need to locate the culprit forthwith and find out what the goddess they think they're doing." She turned again and her soot-ringed, blue eyes landed on Trey. "Ah, Treymeron Aphiski, I presume? Welcome. You've a bit more of the Neptulidae line in you than most of your siblings."

Trey's eyes were wide. "Oh. Um, greetings, Your Majesty. Yes, I'm Trey." He bowed. "It's been said I take after my mother; thank you for the compliment." As he straightened, a furry little head popped out from under his hair and squeaked at him.

Queen Dianathke's gaze sharpened. "Who's that?"

"Oh, this is Pinkerpush, your Majesty." Trey ran his fingers up and down the little creature's back as she snuggled into his neck. "An orphaned duskit I've fostered."

The Queen nodded. "Last winter was very nasty." She pursed her lips. "This year I've decided our Yule shall be extra special to compensate. As Athys' personal aide, you'll be involved with arranging that – after you apprehend the fool who's mucking around with magic they've no idea how to control.

You hear that, Athys?"

He looked up from the pile of paperwork he'd been shuffling through, and bowed again. "Absolutely, Your Majesty."

"Good." Queen Dianathke waved a hand. "Ah, excellent. You're emptying your workbox - having me instal a paperwork box for you was a brilliant idea but, for now, just stash those papers in your office. Apart from Yule preparations, finding the failed portal caster is your top priority." She smacked a fist into the palm of her other hand. "Bring that idiot to me as quickly as you can."

"Very well." Athys folded the papers and tucked them inside his own jerkin. "I have a question about portal magic which may assist us in finding the culprit. If I may, Your Majesty?"

She inclined her head. "Proceed."

"Since it is Your Majesty's specialty, would you know whether the palace experiencing a physical disturbance means it was the actual site of the intended portal?"

The Queen snapped her fingers. "Ah! Very good question, Athys, and straight to the point. The answer is no. The palace experienced the ripple effect from the portal's collapse. The epicentre isn't far away, judging by the force of the shaking. You'll recognise the site by the burnt and flattened state of its surroundings."

"Perfect!" Athys bowed again. "By your leave, Your Majesty?"

She waved her hands to shoo them away. "Of course! Go. Haven't I already said so?"

Athys grinned. "Okay, Trey, let's be off. We've work to do."

The Queen's laugh tinkled. "Indeed, we both do." Her attention shifted to Trey again. "Thank you for coming to stay, Trey. I believe you might turn out to be just what Athys requires. Good day." She turned away as Trey executed a quick bow and hurried after Athys, already striding for the door.

Back in the anteroom, nervous words tumbled and rushed out of Trey's mouth like a stream over rocks. "Your aide, Athys? That seems a bit of an elevated position for a Tri-moon apprentice, but Her Majesty and Sir Nasper both called me that – would you mind explaining, please?"

Athys cleared his throat. Having learnt things about Trey from Dario, he'd been dreading this moment. "Ah yes. Well, it's like this. When Dario contacted me to ask for a Tri-moon position for you here, he also told me you were looking for somewhere away from home." He rubbed his forehead. "I mean, a new home, even a career, and he said you might need guidance because you'd never lived anywhere but Papillion with your family and their support."

Trey's mouth straightened and he looked away. "I can't really argue with any of that, but it doesn't explain the position as your aide."

Athys drew a breath. "Dario asked me to help and guide you – something I'm both pleased and happy to do – however, I couldn't do it if you were simply a Tri-moon apprentice. Not only am I very busy, but the Queen's assistant would *not* be paired with a Tri-moon apprentice."

Trey frowned. "No?"

Athys shook his head. "Lower palace functionaries will be handling the few we have."

Hands fiddling with his jerkin, Trey stared. "So, I'm *not* a Tri-moon apprentice?"

Again Athys shook his head. "I discussed things with Queen Dianathke and, at her suggestion, you've been apprenticed to me with the official position of aide."

After eyeing him for a moment, Trey nodded. "I guess that makes sense." He inclined his head. "You can only be the guide Dario asked you to be by having me in the position of your aide for the length of the Tri-moon apprenticeship. Have I got that right?"

Athys grimaced, then sighed. "Almost. But it's not just for the length of the Tri-moon program, Trey. It's permanent if you'd like it to be."

3

TREYMERON

"*P*ermanent?" Trey's eyes widened. "Did you say ... You mean ... Did nobody think ... I'm not going home?"

Turning, Athys grabbed Trey's wildly flapping hands. "Ssh, Trey, it's okay. I wanted to sit down with you and have a sensible existential discussion about what you wanted out of your life and lead up to the announcement gently, not spring it on you. Unfortunately your question caught me on the hop."

Wits skittering as if he was caught in an ocean's tide pull, Trey was vaguely aware of being guided to the seats against the wall. Something was crushing his chest, making every breath a struggle, and he could hear his heart pounding in his ears. His vision tunnelled and twisted until he was faced by a weirdly unfocused version of Athys, whose mouth opened and closed almost noiselessly.

"Trey!" His name came to him faintly and he became aware of Athys chafing one of his hands, leaning so close his knees were spread to bracket Trey's legs. The intense concern in Athys' expression helped anchor Trey – somebody in this strange place cared about him. For the moment, it was enough.

When Trey's ears popped, it was like a key being turned in a lock.

Blessed air flowed into his starved lungs, then his sight straightened and hearing rushed back in a crashing wave of surf.

At first, he could only tremble and shake his head, but Athys kept an anxious watch and continued patting his hand until he was much calmer.

Athys dropped his head to peer between the fall of Trey's hair. "Come on, please talk to me. I'm sorry I sprang that on you; I was warned you don't do well with surprises, but I didn't expect the severity of your response. I won't make that mistake again. Are you okay?"

Between uneven pants, Trey managed a feeble chuckle. "I'd like to defend myself; that was a huge surprise." He shook his head. "Wow, Dario must have told you lots about me."

Athys returned a nod. "Very perceptive, our Dario." He smiled. "I believe he has a soft spot for you; he was quite explicit in describing your character, your skills and what you'd need. That was what made me realise the Tri-moon program isn't right for you and why I took it to the Queen. She was the one to create the position you've been assigned, even if I did make the suggestion. It's not just a fluffy title, Trey, it's a real job and you'll work hard."

Taking a deep breath, Trey swallowed, then swallowed again. "It's not just because you know Dario, then?"

Massaging one temple, Athys looked away for a moment. His lips firmed as he met Trey's eyes again. "Okay, Trey. I'm going to be frank. Dario and I are old friends, battle-brothers in fact; he knows I have personal experience being someone who doesn't fit the generally expected world shape. According to what he said, you also struggle with that. It's another reason why he asked for my assistance to help you, but this isn't just a favour. I do need an assistant and when he described your abilities … Well, I just felt you and the position would be a perfect fit."

An expression of wonder filled Trey's face. "You really believe that."

Athys nodded vigorously. "Absolutely I do. Plus, I want you to know I'm really pleased to find myself with a capable aide at my side."

"Capable?" Trey pulled a face. "I put my foot in things all the time. Look at how I offended Marda by rearranging my room and shoving things in cupboards."

"And look at how you finessed your way back into her good books."

"Oh." Trey rubbed the back of his neck. "The ugly statue. I told her she could take it because it gave me what I wanted."

"While also giving Marda something she obviously desired." Athys smiled. "That's a skill."

Trey snorted. "Could've been a fluke."

Athys grinned. "Maybe. There's plenty of time to find out."

"But what if it doesn't work? We might rub each other up the wrong way, long term, or I might offend someone important, or ..." Trey swallowed as Athys pointed a finger at him.

"No, Trey. I'm sure you can invent any number of 'why the position won't work for you' excuses, but that's not what's important. If the arrangement doesn't work, for whatever reason, it won't be the end of the world – you can simply choose to return to Papillion and resume your life there."

"I can?"

Athys snorted. "Of course you can. You're not a prisoner here."

Trey blushed. "Oh, no, I didn't think I was. I mean ..." He waved his hands and sighed. "I suppose we take it one day at a time then."

"My thoughts exactly." Athys studied him. "Colour's coming back into your face. Good. Are you feeling well enough to go back to your rooms and sling furniture?"

"I'm feeling better." Trey frowned. "But aren't we meant to go looking for the portal maker?"

Athys nodded. "We are and we will, but it's late in the afternoon. I'll send out messages to a few people I know, get them searching for clues and we'll collate the information tomorrow. We can use what's left of today getting you settled in. Okay?"

Relief swamped Trey. There'd been so much that was strange about the day; he needed to get some familiar things out of his baggage and spread around his rooms to make them more like home and he wouldn't be happy until he had. "Okay."

~

Straightening the small framed artwork, depicting Papillion Estate's Old Lady Willow, Trey stepped back, rubbing his chin. It was one of his favourite paintings by his sister Zhulija. He stared at it, memories cascading; a knock at the door jerked him from his revery. Nobody was outside, but a covered tray sat on a small semi-circular table next to the door, and from the scents wafting his way, he guessed it to be dinner. He carried the tray inside and popped it on the sideboard, noticing that it contained enough dishes for two. Either he was thought to have a large appetite, or somehow, someone knew Athys was with him.

"How about this, Trey?" Athys' voice carried across the room. "Would you like these cushions here?"

He twisted to look and Athys stepped back, gesturing to his handiwork. "I've kind of nested them and I think the rich colours go well together – almost invites you in to sprawl and be comfortable. What do you think?"

Trey nodded. "Yeah, I like it, but it's time to stop – dinner's just arrived."

Athys approached and reached for the tray. "Great, I'm hungry. Let's take this food to the table and admire your garden view while we eat."

The tray held several covered dishes, clean plates and cutlery, which Athys transferred to the table before sliding the empty tray to one side. Trey joined him in removing the covers to reveal the prepared food, a bit nervous about what would be underneath. Back home at Papillion, his likes and dislikes were known and he was used to the types of dishes served. Food here was unlikely to be totally to his liking, but he had no wish to go hungry or appear fussy, so he was relieved to see that at least one of the bowls contained salad with vegetables he both recognised and liked.

"Oh, yum." Athys grinned. "There's a layered vegetable pie and it's still warm." He cut a slice and lifted it on to his plate. "You want some, Trey?"

Mouth twisting, Trey eyed the pie. "I've never had that before. I'm not sure …"

"Okay." Athys nodded. "What if I just provide you a mouthful to taste?" He indicated Trey's plate. "I can see you like salad – are the other foods unfamiliar to you?"

"Mostly." A flush crept up Trey's neck and into his cheeks. "I recognise the sweet yam wedges, but do you know what they're sprinkled with?"

Forking one up, Athys took a bite, chewed and swallowed. "Mmm. Salt and herbs. Quite delicious. Would you like a bite?" He offered the fork to Trey.

Hesitantly, Trey leaned forward and nibbled a piece off, consciously avoiding where Athys had taken his bite.

But Athys shook his head. "You call that a bite, Trey? That tiddly bit isn't enough."

Trey grimaced. "I'm sorry, but for me it's not just about taste. Sometimes I can't handle the texture or how things are put together."

"How about you take a tiny bit from each dish, then? You'll be able to try whatever you like and make a judgement one way or the other."

An expression of relief crossed Trey's face. "Your suggestion is a good one. Thank you."

Swallowing the rest of his mouthful of herbed yam wedge, Athys waved a hand. "No apologies, Trey. We're all different and we've all got preferences. It doesn't offend or upset me that you need to work yours out; you *are* in a new environment after all. It'll take you a while to get used to palace food offerings and you can bet the last acorn from the oak tree, you're not the only one in the palace with food issues."

The rest of the meal went smoothly. Trey took little samples from most of the dishes, but there was one that he couldn't bring himself to touch. It was mud coloured with dark brown lumps in an oily liquid in which bubbles rose and popped constantly. He noticed Athys didn't have any either. He pointed to it. "What's that?"

Athys wrinkled his nose. "Fermented black mollusc beans. Some folk say it's an acquired taste. Not for me, though."

Trey felt his stomach turn over. "Nor me." He placed some food he thought Pinkerpush would eat on another plate and put it on the floor.

"Pinkerpush, here's your dinner." Pinkerpush's purple furry head poked up from amongst the cushions Athys had stacked earlier; she slid off the sofa and came to investigate. Trey was pleased when she ate most of the food he'd selected. He found and filled a bowl with water, then showed her where she could find it. She mewed, rubbing against his legs.

When they'd had enough, Athys repacked the tray. "I'll place it out on the table in the corridor. For future reference, if you're not planning to eat in the dining hall, just tell one of the house brownies whereabouts in the palace you'll be for the next meal and a tray will be delivered. It's standard procedure here and all you need do to ensure you're fed on a regular basis."

"That's simple enough." Trey rubbed his chin. "What about snacks? Is fruit available?"

Athys nodded. "There's a fruit and nibbles table in the dining hall for those who get peckish between meals."

Trey rubbed his hands together. "That's good to know; I love fruit."

"You're not alone." After casting a glance through the window, Athys reached for the tray. "Not long before it'll be dark; time for me to go."

"Oh, but it's still early."

Athys shrugged. "Yeah, sorry, Trey, but I've some other things to take care of, so I'll see you in the morning. Meet me in my office at nine bells and we'll get started on finding the portal culprit. Okay? Can you remember where my office is?"

Rising to his feet, Trey smiled; his memory never let him down. "Sure. I'll be there. Ah, do you think it would be okay if I go to the library tonight?" On the way back to his rooms earlier, Athys had pointed out a few places that Trey would need or find useful; his office for one, but also the dining hall, the adjacent kitchens and the passage leading to the library.

Athys was heading for the door at a fast pace, so Trey had to rush to reach it first, then hold it open, since Athys' hands were filled with the tray. His mentor nodded. "Of course you can visit the library. It's a great idea. Sorry I need to rush off, but I've just realised how late it is. Good night, Trey." He paused briefly to leave the tray on the little table, then he was off down the hall, steps brisk.

Trey scratched his head, watching until a bend in the corridor concealed Athys from view. It wasn't very late … but Athys appeared to be a rather busy male. Maybe he was going to attempt some of that paperwork the Queen had given him? Oh well, Trey was happy to have the time to go off to explore the library.

Pausing only to grab his room keys and Pinkerpush, he left his suite and headed down the corridor. When he reached the passage, he discovered that it was L-shaped, and the library itself was doorless. The hallway simply widened, opening onto a semi-circular stone plat-form from which three curved steps led down into the foyer of a large main chamber.

Standing just inside the entry, Trey smiled as he scanned the room; it had a number of tall, free-standing bookcases filled with books and scrolls, in addition to shelves on the walls, which were also were over-flowing with tomes. There looked to be rooms off the main chamber and the area beyond the foyer contained a few seating areas and even some desks, all arrayed over a rectangular burnt-orange carpet, which had a leaf pattern in various greens. With a sigh of pleasure, he descended the steps and went to explore. He'd never be lost for some-thing to do with a library of this calibre available to him. Some things never changed – the wonderful homey scent of books was one of them.

He selected a couple of volumes to study and took them to a desk. One contained maps, the other was titled 'Diary of Spell Magics', and a quick flick had shown it to be handwritten. He opened that one first and discovered it contained some great spell ideas, drawings of herbs, plus recipes for crafting soaps, rituals and candles. Running a finger beneath a line of writing he found particularly interesting, Trey shaped the words in his mind, thinking about the ramifications of such a spell. This one contained a lot of words, but his studies had revealed that magic was more about intent – something often obscured by verbosity in his opinion. He'd been working for some years now, reducing spells to their base form. Analysing the purpose, the restrictions and why each one was set up in the form of its presentation. He settled to work through the book.

Sometime later, the scuff of a footstep, a scrape of tanned bark leather on aged stone, was just loud enough to invade his concentration. He stilled, then tipped his head to one side, peering through a few stray strands of hair to the library's small raised foyer.

A Fae-female moved into view and smiled at him. Startled by her height, Trey swept his hair aside for a clearer look. He judged her to be as tall as Athys – something unusual for a Fae-female, as was the solid muscle she was packing. Silvery blonde hair fell loosely to just past her shoulders and her lips were rosy as she smiled.

"Hello." She descended the steps to the library floor. "I hope you don't mind me invading your quiet time."

Trey smiled back. "Oh, no, it's fine. Plenty of room. I'm Treymeron Aphiski – just call me Trey."

She nodded. "Welcome to the Palace of Elrodel, Trey. I'm Inca and I'm closely connected to Athys."

4

INCA

Inca took her time crossing the carpet, studying Trey as she moved closer. Moonlight shafts illuminating a window caressed the wavy inkiness of his hair, lit the black and violet beauty of his eyes and wreathed him in a faint silvery sheen. She shook her head. The moon and the darkness were hers, yet they embraced him like a long-lost lover. Noting his gaze, she smiled faintly, having already heard Marda talk about the intensity of his focus.

"Thanks for the welcome." He tilted his head. "Something funny?"

She shrugged. "Not really. It's just that hardly anybody ever comes to the library, yet you've found it on your very first day."

He raised an eyebrow, then spread his hands, palm upwards. "Athys showed me and frankly, I like books."

"A bookworm, are you?"

He chuckled. "More like a book dragon."

She frowned. "You hoard books?"

Trey sighed. "No. Sorry, just a family joke. Although I do have a few books of my own at home."

Nodding, Inca took a seat, leaving a couple of chairs between them. "Papillion Duchy, right?"

Those spark-amethyst eyes connected with hers again. "You've heard that too? Word gets around quickly here."

She grinned her agreement; communing with Athys was more than helpful. "Lots of folk enjoy tall tales and gossip. Plus, you're new so you'll be a fourteen-day wonder."

He grimaced. "So long." Pursing his lips, he leaned back in his seat. "I thought there were some Tri-moon apprentices? Surely they'd be good gossip fodder?"

"Absolutely." She relaxed into her own chair, unable to cease admiring his dark good looks. "But they're only of five-day mild interest."

This time both brows rose. "Why am I a 'fourteen-day wonder' while they're only a 'five-day mild interest'?"

Her grin surfaced again. "Because you're permanent and they're not."

His mouth twisted. "Permanent." He looked away.

She cocked her head. "You don't like the idea?"

Shrugging, he flicked another glance at her. "Day one. Too soon to decide. Strange really. It's what I'd convinced myself I wanted, but now it's been tossed in my lap, I'm second guessing."

She nodded. "That old adage of being careful what you wish for."

"As you say." He drummed his fingers lightly on the desk, cast her an assessing glance. "Mind if I ask where you fit in around here?"

It was her turn to shrug. "You could say I'm on the night crew."

"What do you do on the night crew?"

A wry smile. "Run it, mostly."

His eyes widened. "Impressive. You're the night version of Athys in terms of position, then?"

"Among other things." She laughed heartily. "Very perceptive. As I said before, Athys and I have a very close relationship."

Stiffening suddenly, he glared at her. "So you and Athys are partners? In a romantic sense?"

Inca's mouth fell open. She snapped it shut. "By the twin-horned goddess, no! Our connection is as brother and sister. Romantic? Ew." She shuddered. "What a thought."

Releasing a huge breath, he propped his chin on his fisted hand. "Sorry. It seemed the most obvious link considering he's male and you're female."

Her lips twisted and she wagged a finger. "We're Fae. We come in all types, shapes and sizes, as do our romantic relationships. You're extremely intelligent, you should already know that."

He twined his fingers together, turning them over and over. "You're right. I … Yeah, at a grass-roots level, I do have that knowledge." He continued to twist his fingers, shot her another sideways glance. "You called me intelligent. We've just met, how can you make that judgement so quickly?"

"It's a talent of mine." Her smile was knowing. "Plus, I told you folk are already talking."

"What?" Puzzlement filled his voice. "Why?"

She raised a hand and started ticking fingers. "You arrived today and you've met the Queen, you're Athys' new aide, you're very particular about having your things a certain way, you're a witch with a familiar, you caused an earthquake, you like to wave your hands around but you're polite and well mannered." She paused, grinning as he gaped at her. "Very impressive, wouldn't you say?"

Recovering, he snorted. "Perhaps if it was true."

"It's all false then?"

He waved a hand, noticed the other was rising and hissed, then flattened both hands to the desk. "Some of it's true; the rest is twisted or a half-truth. I thought I was coming here as a Tri-moon apprentice and only found out differently this afternoon. I'm not a witch and my so-called familiar is an orphaned duskit who thinks I'm her mother or something. I had nothing to do with the failed portal magic that most folk thought was an earthquake. I do wave my hands around, but it's my natural inclination and everybody has those. My parents instilled manners into me, so my politeness stems from me having learned those manners, and yes, I like to arrange my things to suit me, but who doesn't?"

She was grinning again. "All very innocuous when stated like that, but you'll have a hard time changing minds – especially the house brownies, they're a superstitious lot."

He dropped his head into his hands. "No wonder you wanted to meet the 'fourteen-day wonder'. I'm probably being labelled a weirdo or an oddity."

Her face hardened. "Didn't we just cover this in the relationship area? Let me be clearer. Neither Queen Dianathke, Athys, nor myself allow disrespect or name calling and come down very hard if it appears. The Fae are an extremely diverse race with multiples of sub-species, all with their own idiosyncrasies, beliefs, proclivities, likes and dislikes; very few folk are alike. If we get right down to it, everyone of us is an oddity or a weirdo in some form or another."

Trey's hands flew up in front of his chest, both palms facing her as he lurched into speech. "Icklegolia! I'm sorry if I hit a nerve but I've too often come up against that kind of prejudice in the past." He shook his head. "Your attitude, this stance, makes me feel loads better."

"Good to know." She stared at him; should she even be here? She rarely wanted to take time off her duties to interact with someone - yet, this time she'd found she couldn't stay away. Trey was as gorgeous in the radiance of a moonlit night as he'd been in the ambiance of a sunny afternoon; the change of time and conditions had certainly not negated the draw she felt. The question was: why was she so instantly fixated on this unknown newcomer? What was it about Lord Treymeron Aphiski that … A very small, super cute, violet and navy furred animal chose that moment to crawl out from around his neck, drop to the desk top and blink sleepily at Inca.

"Oh, look at you!" Having a chance to see the duskit babe so close was fascinating. Lifting from her chair, she moved forward, but the action startled the little duskit into skittering across the desk and diving over the edge into Trey's lap. Her actions shoved his books askew and one toppled to the floor.

Inca clicked her tongue. "Sorry, Trey, didn't mean to scare your little one; Pinkerpush, I believe her name is?" She craned her neck in an attempt to see over the desk, then shrugged. "She'll come around later I hope, but since I'm up, I'll get your book." Which she did, but as she straightened, the book's title caught her attention and she stilled, before placing it carefully back on the desk. Her brows rose. "'Diary of Spell Magics'. Interesting choice of subject matter for someone who denies being a witch."

A sheepish expression crossed Trey's face as he tapped a finger on the diary. "I suppose it is, but not everyone who can do magic, or shows interest in the study of it, is necessarily a witch."

"I'll give you that. Where do you fit?" She continued to watch him, switching on her deep stare and simply waiting. Most folk eventually caved under so much pinpoint intensity and hurried to fill the uneasy silence; babbled answers, told her what she wanted to know. That was the nature of interrogation and due to her skill, she was an old hand at it.

But neither her hunter's focus, nor the quiet, bothered Treymeron Aphiski at all. He stroked his little duskit with one hand and gazed contemplatively down at the book while tracing the letters on its front cover with the other. After a while, he flipped the volume open, turned a few pages and began to read.

That was when Inca understood his interest in the book had swamped his recollection of the surrounds and he'd forgotten she was even there. Despite her stunned disbelief that he'd been able to resist her compelling glare, she was both annoyed and reluctantly amused. Deliberately, she stepped forward and placed her palm directly over the pages.

His head shot up, gorgeous lips mutinous. "Hey!"

She quirked an eyebrow. "So are you able to do spells, or are you just studying them?"

He stilled. "Oh, I thought we'd finished that conversation. Give me a moment." Frowning, he fingered the edge of a page, his head tilted as he thought. A gasp finally escaped his mouth. "No, no, we hadn't. Icklegolia! I'm sorry for my rudeness. I let my interests carry me away, as usual. Maman has lectured me about it so often, you'd think I'd remember by now."

It was Inca's turn to frown. "Wait. Did you just replay our conversation in your mind?"

He nodded cheerfully. "Everyone in the family says my memory is too good by half and they can never get away with anything."

"Really?" Inca crossed her arms, her interest heightened. "What sort of things do you prefer to remember?"

Trey's smile faded. "I'm not sure I understand. It's not a preference, it just is – I remember stuff."

Her eyes narrowed. "What stuff?"

He swallowed. "Well, pretty much everything. Is – is that a problem?"

By the goddess, it sounded like he had an eidetic memory. What a bonus. As the discovery sank in, Inca smiled. "Not in the least. It'll be extremely useful in your position."

"Whew." He relaxed in his seat. "I was getting worried for a minute, thought I'd done something wrong."

Inca laughed. "No. Now, about the spell book – what's your interest in it?"

He shrugged. "There's all kinds of magic and I study it a lot. At first, it was by chance that I came across spell-craft information in our library back home, but I found it intriguing to compare to, so I looked for more. It seemed that the more notes and books I unearthed, the more fascinating it became."

"In what way?"

He indicated the book in front of him. "The words. So many words in these incantations, all directed at a single goal and I began to ask myself this: if the objective is so focused, why not a single word or short phrase?"

Inca stared at Trey in confusion. "But words are the nature of a spell, aren't they?"

He shrugged, his eyes a dark sparkle. "Are they?"

She nodded. "That's what I've been told. The descriptive nature of the incantation gives detail and provides parameters."

Hands rose and gestured briefly, before he noticed, then his lips tightened and he clenched his fists. "Many of them babble on in rhyme for a few lines and end with 'so shall it be' or something simi-lar, said three times. I'm still deciding whether three times is for emphasis or because the number three is believed to be a magical seal. If I ever meet a witch, I'll ask them to clarify. Anyway, I've been studying spell books where I can find them and stripping the convoluted rhymes back to the barebones of their goal."

She rubbed her chin, trying not to sound too incredulous. "A single word or phrase."

"Yes." His enthusiasm lit up his features. "I search for the focal point of the spell. If the intent is strong enough, why couldn't the spell be comprised of one or two words? Surely there's lots of achievable magic without the confusing incantations."

Brows knit, she shook her head. "I don't know. I – I believe spells and incantations all require some level of rhyme and chanting. I don't have any real knowledge, but from my understanding, that's the way of it for witches."

He scrabbled around in the shelf under the desk until he found a writing stick and paper. Mewing indignantly at being jostled, Pinkerpush clambered back onto the desk and crouched near Trey's hand. Turning the book sideways so that Inca could also see, he pointed at a page. "This spell runs on for several lines, but all that 'into the air we rise and hover' stuff can be pruned back to the actual goal of levitation." He wrote the word 'levitate' on his paper. "Do you see what I'm getting at?"

She stared, almost shivering as the full force of his lambent violet eyes skewered her. "Maybe, but what's the point?"

Crumpling the paper into a loose ball, Trey tossed it from hand to hand. "I suppose you could say studying types of magic and dissecting them into their combination of working elements has invoked my professional interest."

"Why?" Inca rolled her lips in and out as she watched his lush mouth. "It's not as if spells can work without all their parts interacting, is it?"

"They can't?" Trey chuckled, then focused on Pinkerpush. She'd hunkered down to watch the ball of paper arch backward and forward between Trey's hands. Her ears were curved at attention and her head was twisting from side to side as she followed its trajectory. As Trey lobbed it yet again, one paw shot out to bat the paper out of the air. She pounced on it, drawing a laugh out of Inca.

Reaching close, Trey prodded the duskit gently. "Hey, Little Miss Cheeky, how about we play your favourite game?" She chittered at him, paws clutching the balled paper. When he circled a finger around, before raising it higher in the air, her chittering developed an excited edge. "You want to fly, Pinkie?" Moving his finger closer to her prize, Trey hooked the paper free and cupped it in his palms. Pinkerpush stood up and faced him in an expectant manner. She mewed and tapped a paw on the desk.

Inca folded her arms. Was Pinkerpush impatient or was she giving a signal?

Laughing, Trey raised his cupped palms to a prayer-like position and blew into them, then he ejected the paper ball in a flicking motion through the back of his clasped hands. The rounded sphere struck Pinkerpush in the chest and exploded in a tiny, but intense, puff of purple flame. It flared briefly, then vanished. All that remained was a fine mist of lilac ash, which drifted over Pinkerpush. As the ash sank into her fur, she rose slowly from the desk until she was hovering in the air an arm's length above it, legs outspread as she voiced a barrage of excited squee-ing sounds.

Inca gaped. "What in all the demon hells?" From the corner of her eyes, she saw Treymeron grinning at her. "How did you …" Her voice died away as she watched Pinkerpush make swimming motions with her front paws and wiggle her tail until she turned a somersault, all the while mewing quietly as if talking to herself.

"That's right, Pinkie, now it's time to float on your back, remember?" Trey made a horizontal swirling motion and, with another mew, the duskit promptly rolled to present her belly to the roof. "Oh, good girl." They watched her for a few minutes as she continued to move her paws like a swimmer in water. "Okay, it's time to come down now." Reaching up, Trey closed his hands around Pinkerpush's torso and she relaxed into his grasp. He pulled her close, patting her back. "That was fun, hmm?" When she chittered softly, sagging in his grip, Trey smiled and tucked her under his chin, where she snuggled in and sighed. Then he looked at Inca and raised one eyebrow, his expression smug.

She took several deep breaths and rubbed the back of her neck as she tried to make sense of what she'd just seen. "I've lost the plot. You said you couldn't do magic, but you just performed some." She fixed him with a gimlet-eyed glare. "If that doesn't make you a witch, what *does* it make you, Treymeron Aphiski?"

He shrugged, grinning. "I said I'm not a witch and it's true; I can't do their spells. But I also commented about the existence of other forms of magic – and that's where I fit."

Inca's hands went to her hips. Cunning as well as gorgeous. "What? You deliberately misled me?"

He shook his head. "No. You asked about the spell book and that's all we talked about. My magic is neither related to, nor founded on, witchcraft or rhyming spells."

She tapped a foot. "Okay, I'll bite. What kind of magic do you perform?"

He grinned again; this time the action revealed suddenly sharp fangs. "Oh, *I'm* the one who bites, Inca – my magic is draconic."

For a moment, she just stared, then she slapped one hand to her forehead. "Dammit! You even gave me a clue when you joked about being a book dragon." She rolled her eyes. "And how could I have forgotten your brother Mak, not to mention your multiple-great-grandpa Old Venny? Gah!"

He simply laughed.

5

TREYMERON

On his way to the dining hall the next morning, Trey replayed his evening with Inca. He'd enjoyed it; she'd been great to talk to and he couldn't get over how attractive she was. Since her announcement of the fact, it was obvious to Trey that Inca and Athys were sister and brother; they had a similar build. Athys had deliciously firm pectorals slimming down to his waist and hips, while Inca had beautifully firm … pointedly shaped … um … and a waist which flared into hips and … He threw his hands in the air. "Icklegolia! Embarrassed by my own thoughts. Pathetic."

But, when he recalled her large frame and solid muscles, it dawned on him that she fit his ideal as much as Athys did. Her breasts weren't large, probably because she was super fit. Naturally, he was as prone to boob admiration as any other Fae-male but, for some reason he'd never been able to pinpoint, being able to snuggle up to a sweaty, lickable, hard-muscled chest did it for him. Turned him on. Made his cock perk up and really take notice. Helped him get his rocks off in spectacular fashion.

Large-breasted females just didn't have the same impact. But Inca, with her smaller, firm breasts and her warrior's physique, was well, very inviting to someone who was a lover of both males and females. In his puberty, he'd been sexually active with both genders because he couldn't choose between them. He had a strong liking for anyone with a tall, sturdy frame, and preferred his females to be more than delicate sylphs – after all, you needed something of substance to fill your hands with. His footsteps faltered.

Holy snapping swamp turtles. He was attracted to *both* Athys and Inca – although, if he could choose, it would be Athys. Hands down. Also, he'd always been monogamous in a relationship and had no plans to change *that*. Not to mention, he was assuming a reciprocal interest that was more than likely non-existent. "Great going, Trey." He'd been here twenty-four hours and was getting way ahead of himself. The only concrete thing, apart from his intense admiration of two different folk, was his new job - which he needed to prioritise if he wanted to keep it.

Becoming aware he was standing in the passageway next to the dining hall's entrance, Trey shifted his weight from one foot to the other and ran a hand through his hair. The conversational mayhem rolling out into the corridor put paid to his private thoughts. He rubbed one ear fretfully; why hadn't he organised a breakfast tray to be delivered to his room? Could he do that for every meal? He considered the idea, then grimaced. Probably not. Oh, it was possible, but it would only create extra work for the house brownies and – he pulled another face – he really did need to meet other folk who lived in the castle, make an attempt to get to know them, instead of succumbing to his naturally introverted nature. Especially if this venture worked and he ended up building a new life here.

From her shoulder perch, Pinkerpush patted his cheek, chittering what sounding suspiciously like encouragement. "Yeah, Pinkie, I know. I can't hide forever and we're both hungry." Clenching his fists, Trey forced himself through the doorway, then paused to take stock. The large room contained various sized tables and accompanying chairs, set up in random clusters. Many of the places were filled and he winced again as the noise of multiple conversations assailed him.

As Athys had described, the half window between the dining hall and the kitchen was set in a side wall. Sweat beading on his brow, Trey threaded between tables, nodding and smiling vaguely as he passed other Fae-folk. Swiping hair from his damp forehead, he peered through the waist-high aperture. House brownies moved quickly in every direction, from ovens to counters, from pantries to work stations, while others carried platters of food through a connecting door to the dining hall. The trays were placed on a long bench arranged against the wall between where he stood and the connecting door. There'd been a table further along adorned with used dishes and utensils.

Rolling his lips in and out, Trey rapped his knuckles on the wooden sill. "Excuse me, could I get some assistance, please?" At the sound of his voice, two male brownies at a nearby work station looked his way, glanced at each other, then approached slowly.

Staring up at him, one brownie swallowed, twisting his fingers together. "Yessir? Something wrong, sir?" The other one hung back, eyes huge.

Trey's eyebrows slid up. "Wrong? Oh, no, nothing's wrong. It's just that I've got Pinkerpush here." Sliding the duskit from his shoulder, Trey held the little creature where she was easily seen. "She eats fruit, nuts and vegetables, which I see there's plenty of, but I want to put some things in a bowl for her and I wondered whether you have one I can use. Something we can designate specifically for her use."

A smile dawned on the brownie's face. "Certainly, sir, that's very thoughtful of you. We can write her name on it. And a water bowl, wouldn't you think, sir?"

Relaxing, Trey smiled and nodded. "Yes, that's brilliant. May I ask your name? I'm Treymeron or Trey if you prefer."

The second brownie gasped, hands flying to his cheeks, while the one talking to Trey gulped and a flicker of trepidation crossed his face before he spoke again. "If it pleases you, Lord Treymeron, sir, this one is called Nutley. Marda has shared knowledge of your powerfulness with all of us, Lord sir, and this one hopes his forwardness has not caused any offence."

Silently cursing Marda, Trey fought the urge to pat the little brownie – he'd probably be more frightened than reassured. "Thank you, Nutley." He kept his tone gentle. "You have been wonderfully helpful and I would be pleased if I can speak to you if ever I need further assistance for Pinkerpush or myself."

A hesitant smile formed and the brownie looked at Pinkerpush, now perched on the counter sill. "This one is at your service. Would it be okay, Lord Treymeron, sir, for this one to stroke little Lady Pinkerpush?"

Trey nodded. "Of course, Nutley. Just hold your fingers out in front of her nose so she can take your scent first. She startles easily." Nutley followed the instructions, smile broadening as the duskit sniffed his fingers, then stretched her neck until her head rested on his palm. He looked a bit unsure, but Trey encouraged him. "Just tickle her under the chin, Nutley, she loves that."

The look of wonder on Nutley's face when he stroked a diffident finger along Pinkerpush's jaw and she mewed, closed her eyes and snuggled in, warmed Trey's heart. The second brownie eased closer, gaze flicking between Trey, Nutley and Pinkerpush.

"If it pleases you, Lord Treymeron, sir, this one is Kester. Would it be alright for this one to pat the Lady Pinkerpush also?"

Trey smiled warmly. "Of course, Kester. Like I explained to Nutley, if you just take it slow, so Pinkie doesn't become startled, you're more than welcome." Now certain Marda had warned her fellow brownies to beware of him as some kind of witch, he was pleased the adorability of Pinkerpush disarmed their fear, giving him a chance to prove he was not a danger. Trey would take any advantage if it helped him in his quest to make a place for himself. They didn't know him of course, and …

Understanding was a blinding flash of light; if he knew nobody here, then he was an unknown to them also. No older siblings had discussed him in advance, nor was there was any hearsay, and both those things meant he had no prior reputation. He was a stranger in every way. Ergo, he could start as he meant to continue, be himself, own who he was. Recalling Inca's steely admonition from the night before, he simply had to look around the room to confirm how right she was concerning the variations in the castle's Fae-folk. Different was the norm here, so *he* would *not* stand out. Closing his eyes as the knowledge sank in, Trey couldn't help grinning. This might just be one of the most wonderful discoveries of his life; all he had to do was seize the chance and take advantage of it. He hoped it proved easier than it sounded.

~

HE ARRIVED AT ATHYS' office door five minutes before nine bells. At first, he wondered whether he should knock and wait, but if this was his place of work, knocking seemed ridiculous. *Begin as I mean to go on.* Trey turned the handle, pushed the door open and went in.

Then swallowed hard. Athys was as beautiful to Trey this morning as his memories of the previous afternoon had painted him. During the night, Trey had begun to doubt his reactions, question the intensity of the other Fae-male's appeal to him, but the allure was still there and he could only stand and stare, wondering if someone like Athys could ever be drawn to one such as him. He sighed. With his luck, this male of his choice was probably sexually straighter than a bee's line to nectar.

At his entry, the Golden God stopped shuffling papers from one side of his desk to the other and smiled. "Ah, Trey. There you are – right on time, too. Excellent." He tapped a finger on a few papers centred on his desktop. "Just as I'd planned, we have some reports to follow up. According to what I've read so far, the shaking was felt a fair distance away – even down and across the river at Castle Synternesse. Sounds like it was milder over there, though, which means *we* were closer to the actual site of the attempted portal."

Focusing on his mentor's words, Trey nodded thoughtfully. "That narrows down things somewhat. What else do we have?"

Indicating the papers he'd separated from the pile, Athys grinned. "These three reports talk about lights and sightings. Here, take a look." Trey accepted the papers being held out and studied the top one, then flipped to the next and the next. "All in Elrodel village – I'm guessing that's not far from here?"

Athys nodded. "Several leagues to the west; you wouldn't have seen it on your way here, since Papillion Estate is to the east."

"We need to talk to these folk face to face." Trey handed the papers back.

Athys raised his eyebrows. "We do, but don't you need more time to read the information? There's quite a bit of detail to take in."

Trey shook his head. "I'm good. I've got everything. In addition to the noise and the shaking, the baker saw intense flashes of light further to the west, the herbalist was harvesting plants along the river bank and heard voices yelling in a language he didn't recognise, and the blacksmith said the sky split open, spat a whole lot of lightning, then slammed shut."

"Oh that's right; you possess an eidetic memory." He rubbed his hands together. "That will be so-o helpful. Probably for both of us." He chuckled. "Not to mention your dracon magic; you really put one over on Inca with your levitation display. The pair of you really hit it off, eh?"

A blush rocketed up Trey's neck and spread to his cheeks. He fidgeted uneasily, his earlier thoughts flooding back. "Er, yes, we did and I think she really liked Pinkerpush too. She was super easy to talk to and a lovely person. Considering we only met last night and all that. Once she pointed out that she's your sister, I wondered how I'd missed it. Quite beautiful really. I mean you both are. I mean being such pretty blondes, but Inca's more silvery and you're so golden and – by the goddess, I do ramble on! Did I mention how much she likes Pinkerpush?" His face now burned like a forest fire.

Those gorgeous teal eyes were sparkling, but to Trey's relief, Athys didn't follow up any of his more embarrassing conversational gaffes. "Yes, we definitely have a family connection. How is Pinkerpush this morning?"

At mention of her name, Pinkerpush poked her head out from the neck of Trey's tabard and chittered sleepily at Athys. He chuckled again. "Looks like she found a comfortable spot to nap."

Tray stroked her head, feeling more comfortable as they focused on Pinkerpush. "She's pleasantly full. Nutley and Kester fell over themselves to find the choicest tidbits for her breakfast bowl."

"Nutley and Kester?"

Trey waved a hand as Pinkerpush subsided into a sprawl inside his jerkin – he'd started wearing the garments longer and with a tie belt so she didn't slip out the bottom edge while sleeping. He'd have to think about a lap bag or something when she got a bit bigger – not that she'd ever be large, since duskits were naturally small. Probably for the best with the brilliance of their sparkly violet and navy fur coats; hard to stay hidden from predators if you were a beacon of brilliance. "Oh, they're a couple of the kitchen brownies who helped me; they were thrilled to meet Pinkerpush and couldn't have been more helpful."

Athys laughed. "Marda's been talking, I gather."

Rolling his eyes, Trey smiled ruefully. "Yeah. They said Marda had spoken about my 'powerfulness'." He shook his head. "Which had them terrified at first. Pinkie helped me dispel their fears. They were much happier when we left."

Still grinning, Athys came around his desk and stopped in front of Trey. "Of course they were; they'd made friends with the witch and his familiar. They felt safe and important."

Trey stiffened. "What? Why?"

It was Athys' turn to gesture. "Because they ended up with first-hand information to share – details about the new witch and his cute familiar. The brownie network will be humming."

Scowling, Trey crossed his arms. "That's ridiculous. I'm no witch; therefore it's ridiculous to call Pinkerpush a familiar."

Athys chuckled. "So we swap the title of witch for draconic mage. But I hate to break it to you, Trey, having a small off-sider who happily involves herself in your magic means Pinkerpush will only ever be seen as your familiar."

Rubbing his forehead, Trey frowned. "Happily involves herself in … oh! The levitation. Yeah, she loves that." His lips twisted. "You must have gotten up really early to get all the details from Inca."

Athys scratched his neck as he looked away briefly. "Yes indeed. Inca and I swap information every day at sundown and sunrise. We never miss our appointment."

Trey smiled. "That's why you had to rush off yesterday evening. Of course." He nodded wisely. "Very important for the day chief and the night chief to fully brief each other. I totally understand."

Smiling crookedly, Athys strode for the door. "Come on Trey. The sooner we get to Elrodel village to interview our three best leads, the sooner we can locate the portal perpetrator." As he passed Trey, their arms brushed and the brief contact sizzled wonderfully – a heated delight Trey savoured with closed eyes.

Until Athys' words broke through his meditation. "Oh! Yes, of course." Trey stepped forward with alacrity, wondering how a Fae-male he'd only met yesterday could have gotten so deeply into his system. Because he knew, without any shadow of doubt, he would follow his Golden God to the ends of the Fae-demesnes and beyond, if it was asked of him.

Maybe even if it wasn't. He shook his head. What did that make him? Desperate, that's what. He was nothing special; the only thing he had going for him was being born into a respected, rich family with a noble lineage. Someone as wonderful as Athys would want a partner who could meet him on equal footing, rather than the third child of a duke whose only recommendation was a colour coded journal of hand-crafted, one word spells.

6

ATHYS

s they took off from the flight arena in the palace courtyard, Athys circled while waiting for Trey and their two Fae-guards. Rising to join him, Trey grinned, before glancing around, interest clear on his face. Athys tried to see their surrounds as if it were all new to him.

Around the castle a forest towered, with a well-beaten wagon track the only break - had the trees always been such a variety of greens? The red earth of the wagon path stood out against it, as did the varicoloured blue stone of the multi towered and many floored castle. Was it always so pretty? Probably, he'd just been too busy to notice.

Shaking his head, Athys glanced around, found his group all hovering near, and, for Trey's benefit, pointed. "We'll follow the track. It's easier than flying to get above the trees." There were nods all around and they were off.

The village was set in a natural clearing where the tall forest monarchs gave way to smaller trees and bushes, until finally the greenery thinned to bushes and wildflower clumps at the edge of the open space. The small hamlet filled much of the available space with buildings of all shapes, sizes and materials. Some were of wood, some of mud bricks and others of thick-woven withies daubed with mud to seal out the elements. The common element in all the buildings was a thatched roof.

Athys aimed for the two venerable oaks that had failed to get the message they were in a clearing. From well-anchored roots, their massive trunks grew proudly skywards and the main street curved either side. The pair of trees, with their huge canopies, created an island of greenery in the centre of the village, one that was frequently used as a gathering place by the villagers. He pointed them out to Trey. "Land near the oaks."

Trey fluttered straight down, but Athys descended with more care, scanning for anything of danger or interest. He was peripherally aware of the two guards, Sir Frith Limacodi and Sir Cadbury Janusidae, flanking him. Sir Cadbury had flown slightly lower and touched down first, then Athys, with Sir Frith hard on his heels.

Looking around for Trey, Athys finally located his assistant reverently stroking the bark of one of the oak trees. Unexpected relief welling, Athys moved to join him. "Thought you'd gotten lost for a moment."

Trey's eyes were shut, his features relaxed. "This ancient called to me."

Smiling, Athys laid a hand on the bark. "These two oaks are amazing examples of their kind." To his utter shock, the trunk above his and Trey's palms rippled and moved until a face formed. Eyelids opened slowly and a pair of deep brown orbs, swirling with the still silence of trees and the wisdom of ages, regarded them.

"Thank you, Twahirren." The voice rumbled sonorously, yet the rustle of leaves twined through it. "Most kind of you to say so."

Athys froze, completely unable to form thoughts or words as the eyes, fathomless but gentle, watched him solemnly. His heart thudded, heavy and deliberate, as he gaped; not only had a tree come alive, it had seen to his core and recognised his nature. Had Trey picked up on it? The guards? What was he going to do? To say?

The choice became irrelevant as Trey's jubilant voice redirected the weighty silence. "Yesss! I didn't imagine it. Greetings, Ancient One."

The deep-set eyes blinked, then focused on him. "Ah, I thought I sensed the blood of another ancient and there you are. Greetings, Sapling of a Venerated Bloodline."

Athys' attention sharpened. What was this?

Beside him, Trey cocked his head. "Another ancient? Are you referring to Old Venny?"

Oak leaves rustled above them. "Indeed, the Ven-drake *is* the one to whom I refer. Is he well?"

Relaxing slightly, Athys pursed his lips as his memories of helping Queen Maerovana put down the rebellion of the previous River King flooded his mind; a time when he and many others had discovered that Old Venny the tinker-trader was actually an ancient dracon connected to the Aphiski family.

Trey was nodding. "Last I heard the Ven-drake was very well, Ancient One. It's so wonderful to meet you. I'm Trey."

Branches creaked. "Hmm. So quick to trust me with your name, Sapling Offspring of the Ven-drake."

Reaching forward, Trey patted the trunk. "Only part of it, Ancient One, and it's not my deep-name."

Athys frowned. Deep-name? He mentally filed the words to ask Trey about later.

Above them, leaves rustled again. "Good to know you understand the importance of that, Sapling Trey." The old oak's voice was filled with approval. "You've been well taught."

Athys saw the back of Trey's head as his assistant bowed briefly. His dark hair was dappled blue-black in the intermittent sun rays able to squeeze between the oak leaf canopy. It was pretty and Athys had to link his hands together to restrain the urge to stroke the gleaming strands.

Trey was grinning. "My thanks. As for Grandpa Venny, I haven't seen him for a while."

A dry chuckle shivered the tree. "The Ven-drake comes and goes as he pleases, but he will come to check on his sapling at some point, especially after the recent disturbance. Maintaining vigilance over their young is natural for fleshly creatures."

Trey cocked his head. "Not just natural for 'fleshly creatures', as you call us. You can't tell me you don't check on your own saplings, from time to time, Ancient One – I wouldn't believe you."

Another chuckle shivered through the oak. "You are smart, Sapling Trey. The Ven-drake must be pleased. Are there more of you?"

"Yeah." Trey rolled his eyes. "I've a brother and five sisters. Two of the girls are younger than me, the rest older. Oh, wait! Maman has not long since birthed a new baby - Eskander Keyvan - so I've two brothers now. I believe Grandpa Venny has met them all briefly, and he spent quite a bit of time with my older brother not that long ago." He glanced at Athys. "You were there too, I believe, Athys?"

Athys nodded, grimacing. "Correct and what a mess that was."

"Ahh." The old oak's mouth ticked down at one corner. "That would be when the former River King of the Mirkdowd was excised from his crown. Rotten to the core that one. Diseased heartwood. Spreading his blight to his subjects." The tree shivered. "Not good when a charmed entity loses their way."

Cocking his head, Athys raised an eyebrow. "Charmed entity? Is that some level of ancient? I didn't think Eskavon was one."

The old oak snorted. "Not an ancient, but a chosen one of bestowed power, trusted by a mature magical entity. Unwisely as it turned out."

It was Trey's turn to snort. "Doubt anyone who was involved in that fiasco would disagree."

"Hmm, hmm," the old oak pondered. "So the male half of the new Mirkdowd ruling couple is your brother and you're here with the assistant of one of the current Fae rulers – it appears the Ven-drake's blood breeds strong and true."

Trey shrugged and grinned. "Yeah, my siblings and I are getting around a bit. Tindresse, one of the twins, is over the river at Castle Synternesse as we speak." He glanced at Athys. "Which reminds me, I need to ask how to send a message to her; she'll be annoyed if I beat her to it."

Athys frowned. "Annoyed to hear from you?"

Trey grinned. "Yeah; sibling rivalry, plus she'll think it won't occur to me because I'm a male. And if I get in before she does, well it'll be on … fun with Tin and Trey."

Blinking in confusion, Athys turned Trey's words into a question. "Fun with Tin and Trey? What is that?"

"Don't you and Inca engage in sister/brother one-upmanship?"

Staring, Athys rubbed his jaw, uncertain how to answer. "Er." He pursed his lips. "Not sure that we do."

"Really?" Trey spread his hands. "It'd be so easy. You're both here, one of you works day and the other night."

"That's true."

Trey tilted his head. "Well, for example, Inca could say 'I circumnavigated the palace in five minutes' and then you could go out and do it in four minutes. Next time you see her, you'd rib her about being the better sibling. So naturally, she would go out and try to break your record and so on."

Athys blinked some more. "Why would Inca or I wish to rush around the outside of the palace each day and night? It seems pointless and tiring."

Trey shook his head, dark locks flying. "It's not the action that counts, it's the competition between you. Being able to say you're faster, or better, or something."

Stroking the smooth skin of his chin, Athys considered. "Inca and I are very busy; what would this gain us?"

Trey threw his hands into the air. "It's a game! It's about having fun with your siblings. Surely you and Inca have fun together?"

Athys swallowed. Why did his mouth feel so dry? In the background, the old oak's bark lips had turned up and his leaves rustled. Was the tree laughing at his discomfort? He ignored it, as Trey stared, waiting for an answer he wasn't certain he could give. He wet his lips and stumbled into speech. "Er, yes, we try, um, sometimes, but …" Feeling a little desperate, he glanced at the accompanying guards. Would he be able to use them to deflect Trey from pursuing this topic? Unfortunately for him, they were doing their job, studying the area, so he returned his attention to Trey – at least he could admire the view of this gorgeous yet puzzling male. Not knowing how to answer, he clutched at duty. "Ah, is this really relevant right now? With what we're here to do?"

Biting his bottom lip, Trey looked away. "No, probably not; I've gotten a bit distracted." His eyelids flickered. "Sorry. I do that a lot – you'll very likely find it annoying." A quick glance. "My father does."

Eyes widening, Athys shook his head. "Trey, I'm *not* your father and I've no wish to be." Be seen as a father to the focus of his interest? *By* that interest? Bile surged, forcing him to swallow several times.

Sir Frith chuckled. "Both of you're a bit too close in age for that, anyway."

Athys' voice held an edge of vehemence. "Agreed." Relief welling, he pointed at Trey. "Plus, there's no need to apologise for being you; Inca and I have both talked about—"

Trey was nodding. "How different all Fae-folk really are. Yeah, okay. Point taken. Own myself. Duh. I even had that talk with myself this morning."

Sir Cadbury cast him a sideways look. "You talk with yourself?"

Frowning, Trey met his gaze. "Of course. Usually when there's no one else to talk to. At least you get the answer you're looking for."

His hair swung, as he tilted his head thoughtfully and Athys' fascination grew - was it as soft as it looked?

Trey spread his hands. "Most of the time you get the right answer, anyway. Don't you talk to yourself? Doesn't everyone?"

Sir Cadbury's face registered astonishment. "No, I don't. I can't speak for others though. You're a very intriguing individual, especially with that duskit." He nodded to where Pinkerpush had nosed free of Trey's jerkin and was blinking blearily around, and snorted. "Don't worry about not fitting in, the palace is a hodgepodge of the interesting."

Athys clenched his fists. Sir Cadbury found Trey intriguing? The strangest feeling roared to life inside him – he felt protective of Trey, that was natural. What wasn't normal was his desire to push between the two of them and fend Sir Cadbury away. His jaw bunched as he fought against saying the words: *I saw him first!* What was wrong with him? For sure, Trey was his assistant, and yes, he'd agreed to mentor him, but … he closed his eyes. *I need to face it. He's gorgeous and … I'm jealous. The fit of my pants when I think about him, scent him, is a dead giveaway. I'm in lust.*

Swallowing, he opened his eyes and deliberately stared at Trey, who was now petting Pinkerpush. Attraction surged. Yep, definitely lusting. He tamped the feeling down and cleared his throat. "You're not in the least annoying, Trey, and the palace is definitely a hodge-podge of the interesting. A great way to describe it. Now let's get on with the interviews we came here to do. Good day to you Oak Lord." He bowed to the tree and turned towards the bakery. Behind him Trey's voice sounded.

"Until later, Ancient One." His footsteps rustled through the carpet of oak leaves behind Athys. He drew alongside, Pinkerpush peeking out from his collar and flashed a grin. "Who are we interviewing first?"

~

KAZEMBARD, the dwarf baker, combed fingers through his short beard. "Ah was standing outside my back door, breathing in some cool air." He tapped his chin. "Ah'd just taken some dwarf bread from the ovens and the kitchen was hot, ya know?"

Athys nodded. "You saw something? Heard something?"

One hand turned palm upwards. "There came the shaking and the roaring noise; so violent ah had to hang on to the door post while it all went on and on. In truth, ah reckoned the door post was going to give way, maybe even the whole building was about to collapse. Ah was wondering if one of the ancient dragons was a-roaring about and such, so ah stared up at the sky and just prayed. That's when ah saw the flashes of light towards the west. It was still day, ya know? But them flashes of light were brilliant, eye blinding almost. In the old days, ah would've been clutching my beard in both fists, but ah'm a baker now – had to trim most of it off so it wouldn't contaminate the products."

"I see." Fighting a grin, Athys glanced at Trey. "Anything you can think to ask Kazembard?"

Withdrawing his gaze from the western sky, Trey cleared his throat. "Just one thing, if you don't mind, Kazembard?"

The dwarf offered a bow. "Ah am pleased to be of service, young lord."

Trey returned the courtesy. "Thank you. You said: 'flashes of light', so I'm assuming more than one or two." Trey tilted his head. "Did you have a chance to count how many flashes there actually were?"

Kazembard grinned. "Eh, a very good question, young lord. There were quite a number, ya know? Ah can't be perfectly certain, but ah think it was either nine or ten."

Massaging his chin, Athys considered. "Nine or ten? Good to know. Alongside the shaking and roaring? Did it all stop at the same moment?"

Kazembard squinted as he thought. "Eh, ah believe they did. Not instant silence, ya know? Just kind of died away after the last flash of light." He spread his hands. "That's all ah've got. Now, how about some dwarf bread to take on home?"

Athys and the guards politely refused Kazembard's offer, but when the dwarf looked hopefully at Trey, it was plain he didn't have the heart to issue a rebuff. Athys raised a hand to cover his smirk as Trey smiled weakly.

"Why thank you. I'm sure it'll be very tasty." Trey held the solid, paper wrapped bundle diffidently as they moved on, unable to ignore Sir Cadbury's mutters.

"That stuff'll break your teeth, Lord Trey, see if it don't." Pinker-push sniffed at the package, then subsided, but her mew didn't sound very enthusiastic.

~

THE HERBALIST'S shop was closed. A sign on the door said: Busy herb hunting. Back soon.

Athys sighed. "Damn, he's not here."

Tapping fingertips against his thigh, Trey was staring at the sign. He glanced at Athys and raised an eyebrow. "Not very helpful."

Shrugging, Athys met his gaze briefly before studying the sign again. "It tells us what we need to know: Myrtis isn't here. Let's try the blacksmith." Trey rolled his eyes but fell into step beside him as their group crossed the street and aimed for the westward-situated smithy.

As they approached, Athys was pleased to identify smoke rising from the chimney. The blacksmith's barn was a large, sprawling building, with some empty animal pens off to one side. Clanging noises began to impinge on their hearing, the noise just short of deafening as they turned in through the entrance. Fortunately, it died away almost immediately.

Athys took advantage of the silence to call out loudly. "Anthracite? Got a moment to talk?" After a couple of thumps and thuds, followed by hissing, a thick-set female troll emerged from the gloom at the back of the barn, wincing and flinging an arm over her eyes as she stepped into the light. Removing wads of cloth from her ears, she looked their group over.

"Athys Castniidae. Good to see you." Anthracite closed her eyes, rubbing the lids with long, thick fingers. "Bet you're here about the lightning I saw when the ground shook and thundered. You're always niggling about the details." She opened one eye; it landed on Trey. "Who's this then?"

Athys grinned. "Details are important." He gestured. "This is Lord Treymeron Aphiski, second son of the Duke of Papillion."

"Huh." Anthracite studied Trey, one eye still shut. "You're a pretty one. If you want to drop by and share some stew with me at some time, I'd be keen."

Trey's eyes rounded. "Erm, nice to meet you, Anthracite, and ah, thanks for the stew offer."

Athys fought back a growl, but there was still a gruff tone in his voice. "He's busy. Now, what can you tell us about this lightning you've reported?" The nerve of her, trying to move in on Trey – not on his watch.

Opening her second eye, Anthracite studied them a moment longer, then shrugged. "That's what happened. I was outside checking on my goats when everything went to hell. The sky split open, spat out multiple zigzags of lightning, then slammed shut – and this all while the world shook and screamed around me. The shaking knocked me flat and I was lying on my back in one of the pens." She wrinkled her top lip, revealing sharp teeth. "It was pretty intense."

Remembering what Trey had asked Kazembard, Athys pursed his lips. "Any chance you saw how many flashes of lightning occurred?"

Anthracite nodded grimly. "There were ten blindingly intense bolts. I slit my eyes for protection, but the flashes were so brilliant they couldn't be shut out; glowed through my eyelids. There were definitely ten."

Trey frowned. "Anything else you can recall?"

Switching her gaze to his, Anthracite's top lip wrinkled in a snarl; her fangs glistening. "Yeah. A fence broke, my goats ran off in terror and I haven't seen them since."

"Right then." Trey rubbed the bridge of his nose to hide his smile. "Thank you, Anthracite, you've been very helpful."

~

THE HERBALIST HAD STILL NOT RETURNED. STARING at the locked door, Trey sighed. "She could be gone all day if she's collecting herbs."

"She could be." Athys tapped his lower lip pensively. "In that case, we might as well go back to the palace and try again later."

"Okay." Turning back towards the oaks, Trey commenced walking.

Athys' eyebrows rose. "We can just lift off and fly from here, you know."

Trey waved a hand. "Yeah, but it just occurred to me we didn't ask the ancient oak about the event and nobody else would have."

Falling into step, the guards on their heels, Athys decided to humour Trey. "Because nobody else knew the tree was a sentient being."

Trey flicked a glance at him. "Except Great-Grandpa Venny."

Athys saw no point arguing. "Right."

They reached the oak island and Trey marched up to the old tree. "Excuse me, Ancient One?"

The tree opened its eyes. "Hmm, hmm. Greetings again, Sapling Trey – what can I do for you?"

Trey explained their mission while Athys waited and the guards watched. "We've been trying to collect as much information as we can about the event which happened yesterday. The ground shaking, the noise, the um, lightning flashes. Some folk thought it was an earthquake, but Athys and the Queen said it was portal magic cast wrongly. The baker and the blacksmith say there were also ten flashes of lightning and I – we – just wondered if there's anything you might have noticed or felt or sensed?"

The old oak's eyes flicked from one to the other of them before returning to Trey. Leaves rustled above them. "Hmm. Indeed it was portal magic, of a sort. You had that right, but cast wrongly? It wasn't, no, but it probably would seem so. Hmm, yes."

Trey pushed cautiously. "What do you mean it wasn't cast wrongly? Athys and Queen Dianathke both say it wasn't right."

A few leaves fell. "Hmm, hmm, wasn't right – that's also true. Hard to identify something not from this world, hmm yes."

Athys stiffened. "Other-world portal magic? That's why it grated on me?"

"Other worldly or other dimension, hmm, yes. It grated on me, too."

"Well now." Athys frowned. "Anthracite reported shaking and noise, watching the sky split open for ten lightning flashes, then slamming shut again."

"Hmm, indeed, yes a portal opened and yes, it closed again, mostly." The old oak's lips twisted. "Not lightning, hmm, no. Flashes of light, one for each of the ten beings falling through to our world before the portal collapsed in on itself to a tiny point. Hmm yes."

7

TREYMERON

"Ten otherworldly beings came through to our world?" Trey goggled at the Ancient Oak. "Holy snapping swamp turtles!" He shifted his gaze to Athys, who looked equally shell-shocked. "That might explain the herbalist reporting she heard voices yelling in a language she didn't recognise." Hearing his agitation, Pinkerpush chittered and brushed her head comfortingly against Trey's chin.

Sir Frith swung towards Athys, face frozen. "Otherworlders? What are we going to do, my lord? We've no idea what they are or what they're capable of – they could be monsters, they could cause terrible damage."

Trey was fascinated to see Sir Cadbury place a hand on his fellow guard's shoulder. "Easy there, Frith." Even his formality had vanished.

Athys narrowed his eyes. "I want this information kept quiet; we don't need mass panic as the locals invent weird bogies." His gaze swung to each of them. "I'll inform Queen Dianathke of course, but no one else, so if word gets out I'll know where the leak originated. Are we clear?" Both guards nodded.

Trey didn't know whether to be excited or terrified as he focused on Athys. "Will we be searching for these ten offworlders?"

After pursing his lips for several moments, Athys nodded. "Our original mission was to locate the perpetrator of the portal; the Queen will need to be updated, but I doubt our orders will change." He frowned thoughtfully. "Now that we know the truth, it's even more imperative to locate whatever they are – if they're not dangerous, they may be in need of assistance. Let's return to the palace and break for lunch. I'll see the Queen and we'll reconvene at the flight arena in the early afternoon."

Approaching the window between the kitchen and the dining room, Trey looked through to see if Nutley or Kester were available. They hurried over as soon as they saw him.

Kester clasped his hands together. "What can this one do for you, Lord Treymeron? Can this one provide food for the Lady Pinkerpush?"

Trey smiled. "Well, yes, if that's not too much trouble … but there's something else." The two brownies smiled and stared and waited, so Trey produced his wrapped package of dwarf bread. "I was down in the village and I was given this freshly baked loaf of dwarf bread. It's not really something I eat, but I wondered if there are any dwarves or other folk at the palace who might enjoy it? I'd rather not throw it out, especially as it was a gift."

Kester's eyes widened. "Ohhh, Lord Treymeron – that's a brilliant idea and so generous and thoughtful of you. In fact there is and they will be very grateful." He accepted the loaf and turned to hand it off to Nutley, who took it with much reverence.

Relieved to have the dwarf bread off his hands, Trey smiled again. "Okay. Ah, I'll just wait here for Pinkerpush's food, shall I?"

Kester shook his head. "No, no, Lord Treymeron. You take a seat and this one will bring you the Lady Pinkerpush's food straight away."

Choosing food for himself as quickly as he could, Trey took his plate to an empty table and sat. Seconds later, Kester and Nutley were beside him. One carried food and the other a water bowl, which they both placed reverently on the floor next to his chair.

Kester beamed. "Here we uns are with a feast for Lady Pinkerpush." Nutley nodded and smiled so much, Trey wondered if his head might fall off. Neither brownie showed signs of leaving so Trey took the hint.

Lifting Pinkerpush out of his jerkin, he set her on the floor, then smiled at the two kitchen brownies. "Pinkerpush and I thank you both very much." Seeming to understand, the duskit sat up, balancing on her back paws and chittered. Faces alight with joy, the two brownies bowed, then scampered away.

~

WHEN TREY RETURNED to the landing arena, Sir Frith and Sir Cadbury had already arrived. He joined them, faltering briefly when he saw they stood with Sir Nasper, who cocked his head and smirked on sighting him.

"Greetings, Lord Treymeron. How's your work going on day two of your stay? Are you as diligent as me?" Sir Nasper nudged Sir Frith. "I feel I can ask you these things now that we're no longer strangers – so to speak."

Sir Frith eased away, frowning at him. "Speaking so is unwise and unacceptable, Nasper."

Trey straightened. He hadn't needed the confirmation of Sir Frith's admonition to know Sir Nasper was mocking him. Meeting the male's eyes for the few seconds he could cope with, he nodded, then altered the direction of his gaze to the male's cheek, deciding to ignore the provocation. "Thank you for enquiring, Sir Nasper, I'm doing fine. Are you on your lunch break?"

Sir Nasper wrinkled his nose. "I was, but orders came for me to report here and wait for Lord Athys."

Trey nodded again. "Looks like we're working together, so you'll be able to take note of my diligence yourself."

At that moment, Athys arrived, with five extra guards. "Good, you're all here. After the information we discovered this morning, Queen Dianathke believes our mission requires a bigger contingent of folk. I'll fill you newcomers in on the details later, but know that, for now, it's classified information. Trey, you know Sir Nasper, of course and this is …" He gestured to each guard as he named them. "Sir Harlyn Chantuzidae, Sif Tanda Vendagyre, Sif Chetanzi Ambiiday, Sir Kitkun Oloden and Sif Meilani Tenekarx. Everyone, this is Lord Treymeron Aphiski, my aide." Murmurs of greeting filled the air. Trey smiled at the two male and three female additional guards, putting faces to the new names as he scanned their larger group – eight guards, himself and Athys. Was that because there were ten offworlders?

Athys gestured towards the landing arena. "We're flying back to the village to see whether the herbalist, Myrtis, has returned and then we'll be going hunting. Everyone clear?"

There was surprise on a few faces, but murmurs of acceptance until Sir Harlyn voiced his thoughts. "Hunting? For what?"

Athys' mouth stretched into a dry smile. "Yule supplies and unexpected gifts."

~

THE 'BUSY HERB HUNTING, BACK SOON' sign still graced the door of the herbalist's shop. At Athys' signal, the group gathered close and listened to his update on the portal investigation.

Sir Nasper frowned. "You're saying ten monsters from another world have invaded?"

Athys narrowed his eyes. "No, I said ten entities came through a portal originating on another world. We have no idea what they are, where they are, or why they came here, but until we do, we keep an open mind. Labelling them as 'monsters' is jumping to conclusions. Until they prove otherwise, unfamiliar things are not automatic enemies or bogeymen. I shouldn't need to say this, Gentlefolk, but whoever or whatever we might find, we treat with dignity and respect, unless our lives are in danger. Does everyone understand?" He scanned his squad one by one, waiting until each nodded.

Turning from his absent-minded study of the herbalist's window, Trey gestured towards the far end of town. "I think we should start by asking Anthracite which way her goats ran when they bolted."

A snort erupted from Sir Nasper, but Trey's confidence was bolstered by Athys' expression of intrigue. "That's interesting. Why?"

Suddenly Trey found himself the focus of everyone's attention and swallowed. Out of the corner of his eye, Trey saw Sir Cadbury elbow Sir Nasper with a hard jolt to the ribs. Looked like Sir Nasper was going to be an ongoing problem. He shrugged; been there, seen it all before and had the scars to prove he'd survived.

He kept his gaze firmly on his Golden God. "The goats were terrified and trying to escape whatever it was, so whichever way they ran, we probably would do well searching in the opposite direction."

A smile lit Athys' face. "Of course! Great deduction." Even most of the guards looked impressed. Except for Sir Nasper, whose expression was sullen. Athys faced towards the smithy. "Fall in, two by two and keep vigilant. Trey, you're with me."

As they made their way along the street, Trey smiled, politely greeting everyone they passed. Most answered or returned the smile – at the same time keeping a wary but interested eye on the squad of guards behind Athys and himself. Patrols were common, but usually in groups of two, three or four; ten was as good as shouting to all and sundry that something unusual was afoot.

Trey's watchful gaze landed on a dwarf and a dark elf chatting at a trestle table outside the inn. The dwarf lowered his ale tankard, his regard holding curiosity, but the dark elf's regard brimmed with suspicion. A large fox sat adjacent to the pair, ears pricking up as it eyed them. The dark elf eased a hand under the table, but the fox whined and laid a paw on his arm.

The dwarf cleared his throat as he rubbed the metal of his tankard. "Ya goin' lookin' for the source of the earthquake, Lord Castniidae?"

Athys paused, nodding. "Yes, you have any information that might assist us, Sir Dwarf?"

Twisting fingers into his beard, the dwarf shrugged. "Nah, I doubt it. I was north of the Rubiconia at the time; felt the shakin', heard the roaring noise and all – impossible not to – but that's all I've got."

"Thanks." Athys offered a casual salute. A smile briefly twisted the dwarf's lips, but the dark elf turned his head and spat, then propped his head on his palm and observed the squad with a flat expression and flinty eyes.

Trey couldn't help admiring the midnight blue hair arranged into four braids. One fine, beaded pair hung either side of his narrow face, while the other two, containing the remainder of his hair, descended over his ears and down his neck to his chest. The braids were banded with several colours of twine and the tie-offs included small feathers, in colours to match.

"Saw nought." The dark elf's voice was deep and surly, his stare hard. Trey's empathic senses identified scorn radiating from the dark elf.

Beside him, Athys tipped his head to one side. "I see from your colours that you're a member of the Third Scintilla, out of Delgado Medea. You've come a fair distance – is your Arikini still Novnea Tolderoth, and did he send you out?"

Trey's head whipped around to stare at Athys. What was this? A chair scraped, drawing his attention to the inn's annex again. Flanked by the fox, the dark elf had pushed to his feet, head tipped to one side as he scowled. "How do you know of that which you speak? You are not of our brethren."

Athys dipped his chin. "You're right, I'm not, but I've been to a lot of places in the Fae Demesnes."

The scowl deepened. "You imply you have been to Delgado Medea and that—"

"Do the last rays of the setting sun still illuminate the Cache of Laltahini before turning the Oxidean Lake golden?"

"Ai-ee!" The dark elf's voice was a stark whisper. "You *have* been there!"

The next words to drop from Athys' lips were guttural, harsh and completely unintelligible to Trey, but the dark elf stiffened, his eyes deep pools of shock. "You – you …" He swallowed, touched tightened fingertips to brow, throat and chest. "I am Byue Tanetzotl." Then he broke into a spate of words in the same raspy dialect Athys had used.

Mouth hanging open, Trey watched as Athys made a beak of his fingers and thumb to touch brow, throat and chest exactly as the dark elf had done. Then Athys inclined his head. "Thank you. Please ensure you convey my regards to Arikini Novnea."

The dark elf nodded. "That will I definitely do, but if you would permit, I would like to accompany your group, so that I might give a true report to my Arikini, regarding the incursion."

Athys nodded. "That is acceptable to me." Trey drew a deep breath, his senses zinging with excitement; this was his first day working with Athys and nobody could call it dull, least of all him. The dark elf, Byue, bowed to the dwarf, then turned and strode rapidly to join the squad from Elrodel. The fox accompanied him. Trey was surprised when both Byue and his fox focused their attention on him.

The dark elf bowed. "Byue Tanetzotl and this is my friend Volpiere."

"Welcome." Was that strangled voice his? Trey cleared his throat. "I'm Treymeron Aphiski." He felt a stirring at the opening of his tunic, saw Byue's eyes drop and Volpiere's ears prick, their gazes fixed on his chest. "A-and this is my companion, Pinkerpush."

Byue nodded. "An empathic pair such as Vol and myself. We sensed it. Please tell her it is an honour to meet her."

Trey frowned. "You can tell her that. You sort of just did."

Now Byue's brows were knit. "No." He waved a hand. "I only have telepathic connection with *my* linked partner, Vol. That's why I asked *you* to communicate my message to *your* linked partner."

Trey knew he was gaping. "A telepathic link? You have that?"

Byue stared back. "You haven't?"

8

INCA

$\mathcal{A}$ slight smile gracing her lips, Inca watched a hand-waving Trey pace back and forth across the library floor. He was adorable, but she wasn't about to reveal *that* little tidbit. Not yet anyway.

"And then he and Volpiere taught Pinkie and I some lessons to work on, to help us find our telepathic connection and, let me tell you, we've got lots to learn, but … it's amazing." He paused to throw his hands wide. "Ah-mazing."

Inca chuckled. "I bet." It didn't matter that she already knew all this, she couldn't look away to save herself. "So Byue and Volpiere accompanied you on the otherworlder hunt?"

Trey's hands flew up to clap together at the side of his chin, fingers pointing up towards his eyes, which shone as he nodded. "They did! Byue's great – he shared so many tips and hints. Plus, Volpiere allowed Pinkie to ride on his back for a while. She had a wonderful time, didn't you, Pinkie?" Thus addressed, the little duskit perched on the nearby desk, sat up on her hindquarters and mewed, her huge eyes glowing. Trey cupped the side of her head, his fingers flexing as he tickle-stroked. "Yeah, Pinkie, I know."

So. Much. Cuteness. Inca loved it. She rubbed her chin. Why was she so drawn to him? Wasn't there something in the old Twahirren tales about kindred spirits? Or perhaps it was another branch of the Fae? It would come to her eventually. Grinning, she prompted Trey again. "Did the hunt find anything? Were the goats as helpful as you believed they'd be?"

Continuing to pet Pinkerpush, Trey raised his head and grinned back at her. "They so were. Anthracite told us Munster, Mork and Menace fled to the south-east. In fact, she was just about to go looking for the three of them, but after finding out what we were doing, she asked to come along too. Athys and I thought it a good idea – extra brawn, you know? Especially with no idea what we might find."

Leaning back in her soft-chair, Inca nodded. "Go on." So what if she already knew the story? Trey was riveting and beautiful.

"Yeah, so based on where Munster, Mork and Menace hied off to, we went north-west until we reached the Rubiconia River and just on the bank there was this mess of mud and torn up ground and one lightning-struck tree, which was still smoking. At least, I thought it was hit by lightning, but there were other opinions – it'd certainly been blasted by something – Athys said the energy from an out-of-control portal might have done it, too." Trey pursed his lips. "I think I need to study portal magic." Then he shrugged. "Time for that. So, after inspecting the site carefully, it was agreed upon as the landing place for the otherworlders. Plus, the warriors, that's really everyone bar me, decided it was also a fight scene."

Inca played along. "What did they fight?"

"Each other." Trey's hands spread. "You probably know Sif Meilani and Byue are excellent trackers and they said a couple of the outworlders, maybe three, fought like crazy, then one fled west and after a time, the other nine followed, with one of them heavily supported by two others." Trey shook his head. "Amazing how they can tell that from torn-up ground and the weight of footprints, isn't it?"

It was Inca's turn to nod. "So they went west."

"Yeah, west. And that direction only leads to the Vansitarkan Badlands."

Inca shuddered as memories she'd rather not examine surfaced. "It does. An awful place of heat and cold, rocks and desert sands – all populated with unusual wildlife."

Trey's brows knitted. "So I've heard, but have you ever wondered how it can be both hot and cold?" He shook his head. "Unless the reference is to the temperature difference between night and day?"

Inca tipped a hand side to side. "Partly. For certain, it's cold at night, but there are areas where heat and cold seemingly exist side by side and without any sign of a barrier, you can step from one to the other. At night those cold areas are frozen."

Pursing his lips while he thought caused Inca to shift restlessly in her chair. That mouth; a lovely shape, very mobile and oh so tempting. She almost licked her own lips, but clamped them tight to prevent it. What would Trey do if she kissed him?

Oblivious to her dilemma, he subdued his waving hands and tapped his fingers together instead. "That would indicate the presence of water, don't you think?"

She swallowed against her desire for him, focused on what he'd said and shuddered. "As someone who's been out in the badlands, I had to wait to collect the icicles just before they were melted by the rising sun and when they thawed, I had water."

Trey frowned. "Yes, but has anybody dug down under the sand in the cold areas to see if water keeps the area frigid?"

"I didn't." Inca shrugged. "Nor have I heard of anyone who thought to do that. It would be time consuming and tiring; most folk, if they have to go in there, don't want to remain very long."

"Huh!" He tapped fingers together. "And yet, nine, no ten, outworlders went that way."

Inca chuckled softly. "Well, they wouldn't know what they were getting into now, would they?"

It was Trey's turn to shrug. "True. Anyway, Athys had us splitting into pairs to cast around; we covered a wide area, always keeping in sight of the next pairing, but not one of those offworlders turned back. We even went as far as being able to see where the badlands began and their trail kept going." He sighed. "That's when Athys made the judgement to stop, said we weren't equipped to venture in." Wrinkling his nose, he turned his head to peer out through the glass patio doors at the night-dark courtyard garden with its bench seats.

Inca watched him. "You don't think that was a good choice?"

Trey sighed. "Of course it was." He wrenched his fluttering hands down, staring at them in frustration. "It's just … Well, it was a bit anticlimactic if you understand what I'm saying. To go from that, to marking some damned fallen trees, as possible selections for the Yule log, was such a letdown."

"Can't disagree." She chuckled. "And you found the missing herbalist."

He tilted his head. "I guess Athys told you about Myrtis."

She smiled wryly. "You could say that."

"Yeah." He flung his hands in the air. "Another letdown. We passed him leading the goats back to the village. He was annoyed because they'd eaten herbs in some wild garden he'd been maintaining. Although I'm not certain how a garden can be called 'wild' if you're maintaining it. What do you—"

A dull boom reverberated through the room, quickly followed by another and another. Inca shot out of her chair, bounded up the library steps and out into the corridor. As she ran, she yelled over her shoulder. "Come on, Trey, and bring paper and a writing stick!"

The booms were still coming; a solid and relentless barrage. It sounded as if the palace was under attack. Inca paused as she reached the main passage and glanced over her shoulder to check for Trey. He'd just turned the bend out of the library hallway into the corridor and had Pinkerpush tucked under one arm as he ran. She wasted no more time and rushed towards the noise. A few seconds later, she rounded the corner into the palace foyer and ploughed into the back of a group of guards strapping on their leather armour and checking their swords.

She drew a deep breath and amplified her voice. "Report!" Faces turned in her direction and several guards spoke simultaneously, but she understood none of their garbling, and the repetitive booming only made it worse. She was gesturing fiercely, trying to cut the noise in a one-handed cancelling motion when a loud, shrill whistle rang out from just behind her. It pierced the hubbub and drew everyone's attention.

Trey's voice was calm. "Speak one at a time." Flicking him a grateful smile, Inca noticed his hands shaking as, without looking, he tucked Pinkerpush into his jerkin. The duskit made no objection and quickly disappeared from view.

Scowling, Inca pointed at Sif Tanda. "You. What do you know?"

With a deferential inclination of her head, the guard responded, speaking between the deafening, evenly spaced 'booms'. "There is a single unknown creature attacking the main gate, Lady Inca. It's very strong and hasn't responded to any spoken overtures in an intelligible manner. The gate guards are struggling to hold the gates closed."

Inca nodded sharply. "Right. Our attacker isn't a winged creature then. I'm assuming you lot were planning to get out there and help them brace the gates?" She raised her voice over the mumbles of agreement. "Keep with that plan, but Sif Tanda, Sir Cadbury and Sir Kitkun stand back a ways with weapons at the ready. Do what you must if the creature breaks through. I'm going up to the battlement above the gate. Trey, you're with me. The rest of you, go!"

Several fully armoured guards plunged out the door, but Inca was hard on their heels as she sprinted for the nearest stairway to the ramparts, her speed so great she let her wings take over and carry her up the stairwell. The slapping of feet from behind changed to the flutter of wings, letting her know Trey was following. Reaching the upper walkway, she turned left towards the gate, flitting along until she was directly above it. Below, she could hear the gates creaking with every booming thud, but they held. She smiled grimly, fully aware of the massive thickness of the oak planks and how well bolstered with spells they were. The attacker wasn't likely to throw them down, but it wouldn't do for her to be overconfident.

Gripping the inner edge of the parapet, she dropped to her feet, furled her wings and eased silently into the nearest gap. Balanced carefully, she leaned out just enough to see whatever was attacking. Copying her, Trey peeked out through the next crenel. Thus revealed to them, the creature was a tall, wingless, heavy-set biped with long hair and it was hurling itself at the gate with single-minded ferocity.

She made a trumpet of her hands and called down loudly.

"You there! Cease and desist!"

Hearing her, the creature looked up. Lips drawn into a snarl revealed pointy teeth below deep-set, dark eyes narrowed in a thunderous scowl. The intensity of rage beat at her empathic senses, so she drew on her moon-linked power and raised a personal shield as she continued her study. The bipedal form was Fae-shaped and troll-sized, but had a different appearance than any troll she'd ever seen. Its nose gave off the dull sheen of metal and one of a pair of arms extending from its sleeveless jerkin also appeared metallic, but ended in a rough break just above the wrist and was trailing ... were they strings? There were several hanging bits of thin stuff in different colours. Inca had never seen anything like it – this had to be one of the offworlders.

As they stared, it shook a fist at them and roared something lengthy that sounded like speech but made no sense in any language she knew. When she shook her head in frustration, it – no, *he* – snarled and rammed himself into the gate yet again.

Inca fisted her hands. "Stop that at once!" He looked up again, spat to one side, then balled his upper body for another attack. She backed out of the crenel-gap and quickly turned to Trey. "Can you strengthen the gates with a spell?"

Nodding as another booming noise reverberated around them, he jerked out his writing supplies and jotted a word on it before scrunching the paper in his fist, raising it to his mouth and breathing into his closed hand. When he flung the balled paper out and down, Inca saw the flare of his purple flame before the resulting lilac ash responded to another hiss of breath from Trey and fell to coat the top of the gates' timbers. For the barest second, the two gates glowed lilac before fading back to their natural colour.

The barest sound of footsteps on stone had Inca spinning to see who had joined them on the parapet. A dark elf nodded in greeting before taking his own look at the out-of-control creature beneath them.

"Ha!" Byue Tanzenotl drew back and fumbled in a pouch at his waist, before withdrawing a slingshot and some pebbles.

Inca's mouth fell open. Pebbles? A slingshot? What in the name of the goddess? Of what use were damned little pebbles going to be? Was the dark elf an idiot? Oblivious to her derision, Byue wasted no time leaning out through the gap and firing at their male attacker.

Trey's fist pumped, just as a howl of pain and outrage sounded. "You got him! Keep it up."

Inca grabbed Trey by the shoulder and pulled him around to face her. "We'll need more than that! A creature strong enough to continuously hit the gates like he's been doing is unlikely to be stopped by just a slingshot with a silly pebble. What other spell can you do?"

He shook his head. "Whatever Byue shot, it wasn't a pebble. It splattered, burning the creature somehow. There's something nasty in those pellets he's firing." He gulped suddenly. "Please don't say you want me to kill the creature. I'm not sure if I—"

Inca bared her teeth. "If necessary! He'll certainly be killed if he gets inside, and he may hurt or kill some of our folk. Better him than us – now think!"

Frowning, Trey hastily smoothed another piece of paper onto the wall of the parapet, flexed his writing stick and scribbled something. Dropping the marker, he balled the paper, breathed on it and leaned out to drop it down on the behemoth beneath. Bursting into purple flame, the paper sizzled briefly then turned into a shower of ash.

The light of the flame had their attacker staring up in puzzlement, then the ash rained down onto his upturned face and trickled into the neck of his garment. His eyes immediately widened as he brushed at the light coating of ash. For a moment, nothing appeared to happen. Inca stared, wondering what Trey had done – was it even useful? Then the creature flinched away from his own fingers, eying them blankly.

Trey spun to the dark elf. "Byue! Fling some more of whatever you're using. Quickly."

While the dark elf scrabbled another piece of ammunition into his slingshot, their attacker smashed himself into the gate again. He bounced off, staring at the gate in a combination of fury and pain-filled perplexity. Trey grinned his satisfaction as their attacker reacted to his first spell. He watched as the creature rubbed at his shoulder, then howled at his own touch and shook his hand violently. Yep, the second one was working too.

Byue launched another piece of exploding shot, then another and another. Each one found its target, hitting the large being in the shoulders and arms. Shrieking at every impact, he lifted his hands to rub the spots, but every touch made him scream more. He was staring at his fingers in bewildered fear when more of Byue's strange ammunition hit. Screeching, their attacker tried to dodge, but as Byue continued the barrage, the male began to back away from the gates. Finally, he turned and fled.

Inca breathed a sigh of satisfaction and took note of his direction. Tomorrow they would track the flesh-and-metal creature and see where he went. But for now … she turned to Byue. "What was your ammunition? I owe you an apology – I thought your weapon useless at first."

Byue smirked. "A pellet containing a burning mud. They burst on impact."

"Wow." Inca shook her head as she swivelled to Trey. "What was your second spell? It took a while to begin working."

Trey grinned. "Super sensitivity. Anything that contacted him caused severe pain, even his own touch."

She stared at him doubtfully. "Well, I could see that something did, but how did you make it more painful?"

His grin widened. "I wrote it to the power of 10, making it expand exponentially."

Inca's mouth fell open, then she winced. "In combination with Byue's burning mud? Ooh, that's nasty."

9

TREYMERON

"What's for breakfast this morning?"

Trey looked up from his plate as Mikasi Opostidae, apprentice gardener, pulled out the opposite chair and hung her pack over the ear-post. As a dryad who always carried a seed pod from her tree with her, the gardening position suited her down to the ground.

Almost snorting at his own pun – but that would mean explaining it – Trey swallowed the mouthful he'd been chewing and filled his fork again. "I've got pancakes and berries with syrup – that's today's special. I think there's nutcakes too, if they take your fancy."

"They certainly take mine." Kitkun Oloden – *Sir* Kitkun, actually – grinned at the both of them as he pulled out the chair catty corner from both Trey and Mikasi and plunked his plate and cup on the table. He was one of the guards who'd been on the offworlder search. As a junior guard still learning the ropes, he'd since confided to Trey how pleased he'd been to join the mission. "I asked for extra berries – I'd love to know what the cook does to them to make them so delicious."

"Me too." The third member of his new friend group, Quanah

Ethmidae, used his foot to drag out the remaining chair at the square table. "Hope I've got time for seconds."

Trey laughed. "You're a bottomless pit."

"I'll say." Mikasi jostled the newcomer with her elbow as she eased around him, heading for the buffet.

Twisting in an attempt to mitigate the jab, Quanah grinned and slid into his seat. "Gotta keep my strength up." He was a strapping young Fae-male apprenticed to Verdigron, the castle's weapon master, so that made sense – especially once he'd explained to Trey how a weapon master was a 'specialty blacksmith'. Back at Papillion, a smith was just that – someone who handled all the estate's forging needs, but now he was living in one of the two castles forming the core of the Fae Demesnes, the homes of the Queens. Both castles housed a large complement of guards, allowing him to understand the necessity for a master smithy specialising in weaponry.

Beside him, Pinkerpush lifted her head and squee'd a greeting to both the newcomers. She'd emptied her bowl and now licked a paw to smooth across her whiskers. Kitkun leaned down to stroke her sleek head. "Oh and a good morning to you too, Pinkie." She twisted her head to nuzzle his hand, then switched her gaze to Quanah. He stretched forward, cooing to Pinkie and she chittered a reply, watching him hopefully.

He glanced at Trey. "Okay if I give her a berry?"

Mouth full again, Trey nodded. His friends played by the rules, but not everyone did. At first, he'd been recognised only as Athys' new assistant. But as he became a more familiar, and accepted, figure in the castle's corridors and social rooms, other Fae had thawed towards him. He was a little suspicious of some of them at first – after all, he was in a position which held some power. But he'd learned subterfuge from the best. Those folk who thought they could circumvent protocols by going through him to get a fast track to Athys had quickly been set straight. He'd earned respect and made new friends – particularly the three now sharing his table.

Kitkun pushed his plate away and wrapped his hands around his hot tea. "Any further sign of Metal Creature?"

Trey shook his head. "No. He's clever. Injured and alone, yet we can't find him. And him going to ground somewhere in the Vansitarkan Badlands doesn't help." That was somewhere the Queen had not yet authorised them to go.

Quanah listened with interest. "Weren't there ten of them, or something?"

Trey shrugged. "The ancient oak said ten beings came through but none of the others have been seen anywhere."

Kitkun hummed. "Just that mud bath near the Rubiconia where they apparently brawled, before they all disappeared into the Badlands." He frowned. "Do you think it's possible that the one the other nine followed is the one who attacked the palace?"

Mind gearing up for the day ahead, Trey nodded at Kitkun. "You know, that's a really good assumption and something Athys and I have already discussed. Truth is, we don't know, although we've got lots of theories." He shrugged. "Anyway, I've got to get going." He stacked Pinkie's bowl with his own as he rose.

Quanah waved a hand. "Leave it. I'll take your dishes back when I get my seconds."

Scooping up Pinkie, Trey settled her in the new cross-shoulder bag he'd had made by one of the brownie leather workers. "Thanks, Quanah, I appreciate it. See you both later." He snatched up his beaker of tea, waved at a returning Mikasi and hastened from the dining hall.

Fast walking down the corridor to the office he shared with Athys, Trey shivered. It had snowed the previous night and was still snowing. From his windows, he watched the fat wet puffs of whiteness drifting down in a steady curtain, his thoughts so tied up in his family back at Papillion, he nearly made himself late for work. Even cupping his hands around a beaker of hot tea didn't fully warm him. "I think I need gloves, Pinkie. What do you think?" She chittered drowsily as he sipped his tea. "Hmm yes. This maple syrup adds just the right touch of smoky sweetness. I like it."

Taking another sip, he conjured up the day's 'to-do' list in his mind. He thrived on lists. Started new ones and worked through them every day. His list folder sat prominently on his desk and even Athys sometimes added things to it for Trey's consideration.

This morning, as Trey let himself into their office, Athys was munching on some grapes, plucking them from the stalk and tossing them into his mouth as he leaned against Trey's desk. "Ah, there you are." His eyes lit up. "Hot tea? Great!" He straightened, crossed the room to lift the insulated beaker from Trey's hands and took a sip.

Trey's mouth fell open as he watched Athys smack his lips together. "Mmm, maple syrup, yum." He gulped another mouthful, before handing the beaker back to Trey. "Here you go." Flooded with uncertainty, Trey hovered in the doorway. Was Athys eating the last of his breakfast or were those grapes out of Trey's secret food stash?

Downing another grape, Athys jabbed a thumb over his shoulder. "You need to stock up your secret snack drawer, there's not a lot left." Trey's heart lodged in his throat; Athys was an important person and important people could be officious. Was food in the office even allowed? Would he be sent back to Papillion in disgrace? He bit his lip. Surely not just because he'd organised a bit of a food stash; he got hungry a lot and with Pinkie still a baby, frequent snacks were necessary. Maybe he should have asked for permission first. He quelled his panic and slowly shut the door behind himself. "Oh, really?"

Athys nodded, crunching another grape. "Sorry, but after this, there's only a few toffees left."

Trey gaped. "Last time I checked, there were little cheese packets, crackers, a couple of pieces of fresh fruit, some dried fruit, some nuts and—"

Athys flexed his jaw. "They were rather delicious." He glanced sideways at Trey. "Some popped corn kernels would be a nice addition, don't you think?"

Swallowing hard, Trey nodded. "Uh, so this is okay then? Um, having food in my desk?"

Athys' eyebrows skyrocketed. "Of course. Why wouldn't it be? You eat, I eat, Pinkie has growing needs."

Trey's hands fluttered. "Oh! Well, um, yeah. Popped corn. You're right; that's a great idea. Don't know why I didn't think of it. I'll get some. Today. Okay?"

Athys tilted his head and narrowed his eyes as he considered Trey for a few moments. "You know, having an accessible food stash in our office is a fantastic idea – I don't know why I didn't think of it sooner. You do have some brilliant innovations." He winked and grinned. Trey sighed with relief and considered visiting the lavatory; the stress lump in his throat had passed on down through his stomach and was nestling in his intestines. Clutching his beaker, he swallowed as Athys returned to the desk and grabbed Trey's list folder.

Tapped the listed items, Athys rolled his lips in and out. "Okay, guards collected one of our pre-marked selections for the Yule log yesterday and will be out guarding the folk attending the Yule 'gathering party' planned for this morning. Assuming the snow stops – and I've been advised that it will." He glanced up at Trey. "I know you thought to go along, but the Queen wishes to speak with you and morning's her favourite time for business, so you'll be attending her instead."

Trey choked. "The Queen?"

Alerted by the wheezing gasp, Athys glanced up. "Yes, the Queen."

"Q-Queen Dianathke?"

Athys frowned. "She *is* the only Queen here, right now, so yes, Queen Dianathke." His frown deepened as he crossed the room to Trey. "You look like you're about to pass out – have a bit of our tea." He pushed the beaker to Trey's lips and hot liquid poured in, scalding his tongue. Trey spluttered, but at Athys' urging and, with a controlling grip on his mentor's arm, he took a more cautious sip. It was difficult to get a grip on his scattered wits with his gorgeous Golden God looming over him, easing closer and closer, teal eyes glowing like suns, well-shaped lips taut with concern – almost near enough to kiss …

Flushing, fighting his wayward desire, Trey pushed back when the beaker was thrust towards his mouth a third time. "That's enough! I'm okay!" He averted his eyes, breath sawing in and out and hands trembling, his feelings a jumble of attraction for Athys and panic at facing the Queen. His fear of the Queen triumphed.

How would he be able to talk to her? He was Treymeron Aphiski and she was one of the co-rulers of their realm; he was a younger son with no real prospects other than the chance she'd given him, here at the Palace of Elrodel. His entire body shook. His hands flailed and he was vaguely aware of tea slopping but he had no room left for concern about tea. His thoughts ricocheted every which way in his brain.

Perhaps he could hide? His eyes shot to the cupboard on one wall. Too small, but maybe he could try to bend and twist and … no. No, better if he pretended to be deaf, except he'd just been talking so that wouldn't work either. What if he were suddenly taken ill? Then—

Athys' large form suddenly blotted out his skewed, tunnel-vision view of the room; a firm hand relieved him of the beaker of tea, moving it … somewhere. The hand returned and fingers cupped his chin, tipping his face until he had no choice but to stare wildly into Athys' warm golden orbs. "I've got you, Trey. You're fine. There's nothing to fear. I've got you."

He struggled in Athys' grasp. "But the Queen a-and I'm getting it all wrong! I should have asked! I should have written everything on my list! I didn't … and you, Inca, the Queen—"

The strength of another arm sliding around his back beneath his half-mantled wings eased and reassured him. Athys' voice was firm. "I've got you, Trey." The teal in his eyes had been eclipsed by gold; they were full of reassurance but Trey could only maintain eye contact for a few seconds.

Dropping his face into Athys' shoulder, he shuddered and shook and gasped – breathed in the familiar scent of cinnamon and rose musk; unaware and uncaring that he'd turned his head until his nose and mouth were plastered to the skin of his mentor's neck. All the while, that reassuring hand rubbed his back, another cupping the rear of his skull, holding him while he struggled with his inner demons and self-perceived inabilities; while the build up of weeks of change hit him like an avalanche sweeping everything away – including the bedrock of his life as he'd always known it. There was nothing left but sparkly fog – he spiralled ...

Later, when he came to himself again, Athys was talking quietly in his ear, although it was a while before Trey could understand the words. Eventually, he recognised a story he'd heard lots of times growing up, one his mother used to tell and Old Venny, the tinker-trader. It was relaxing and familiar and helped to ground him. He raised his head slightly, but not so far that he cut himself off from that marvellously soothing, cinnamon and rose musk scent. "I-I'm okay."

Athys maintained his hold on Trey, continued the back rubbing. "You sure?"

Trey managed a weak nod. "I-I'm sorry. I- " He swallowed, throat dry. "I had a-a meltdown. On you. Dung beetles and s-swamp turtles! I'm so sorry."

The back rub never paused. "No need to apologise, Trey. I'm guessing you've had too much change, too quickly and haven't been able to adjust, am I right?"

Trey drooped, his head cushioned by that perfectly positioned shoulder. "Yeah. I'm trying hard, but I haven't quite g-gotten my routine worked out and there are times when I-I feel like a fish flopping on the river bank."

There was a slight pressure on the top of his head – had Athys just kissed his hair? No, surely not. But it came again, more firmly, and his breath hitched. "It's fine, Trey, and let me tell you, you're definitely *not* failing or doing anything wrong. You're so amazing you take my breath away."

Swallowing hard, Trey raised his head, managed to meet those beautiful eyes. "W-what?"

Athys' expression was gentle as he scanned Trey's face. "Goddess, Trey, your eyes. They're so dazzling I could drown in them, I'd like to kiss you, but I don't want you to think I'm taking advantage."

Trey's eyes widened. "You would? No! I mean yes! I mean, you're not advantaging me. I ..." Abandoning his words, Trey stretched up and jammed his mouth to that of Athys, who, having deciphered Trey's mixed-up pronouncement, met him halfway. Athys' lips were warm and soft, and that feeling of warmth bloomed slowly through his entire body. It lit dark places and pushed back the feelings of inadequacy Trey had been lost in.

Managing to free his arms, he wound them around Athys' neck and gripped strands of hair, tangling his fingers in the satiny length. When Athys' tongue licked at the seam of his lips, he parted them almost shyly, heart beat accelerating, although there was nothing of reluctance in the kittenish licks he returned and shared with his golden god. He felt his knees weaken and thrilled at the feeling of Athys' arms firming even more tightly around him.

When their lips parted, both of them panting lightly, their noses rubbing together, Trey swallowed. "Wow."

A smile tickled Athys' mouth. "Couldn't have said it better. I love the way you taste."

Heat flashed up Trey's neck and into his cheeks. "Oh. That's amazing. I mean, it's great because I'd be happy to do this some more. If you wanted to. I mean, I want to, but if you don't, I'd understand. Icklegolia, no! I wouldn't understand because you said I taste—"

When the firm delicious sweep of Athys' smiling mouth cut off the babbling inanities of his sparkling mind, he welcomed the new kiss eagerly.

10

ATHYS

*L*ifting his lips from the deliciousness of Trey's mouth, Athys surprised himself by admitting the truth. "I've wanted to kiss you since the minute I laid eyes on you."

Trey's eyes widened. "What? But I'm – I was a crazy, bumbling mess!"

Athys chuckled. "A gorgeous, crazy, bumbling mess. I didn't like you hurting yourself, even though I got to pick you up and cuddle you sooner than I'd dared to hope because of it."

Trey's voice emerged as a whisper. "It wasn't just me, then." Cheeks pinking, he raised his face to peep upwards.

A tide of heat spread through Athys and his elation revealed itself in the silly grin he could feel decorating his face, in the tightening of his arms around Trey. "It absolutely wasn't just you. I felt like I'd been struck in the head by a dwarf hammer – I couldn't take my eyes off you."

Trey's hand slid across Athys' chest to rest over his heart as he caught his bottom lip between his teeth. A shy smile bloomed, sweet as the first blush of sunrise. "I've been calling you a 'Golden God' since that time."

A shout of laughter burst from Athys. "I love it! Golden I definitely am, my skin colour anyway, but a god? That's definitely pushing it and I'm fairly sure you're the only one to think so." Tingles shot through him as Trey's lips moved against his neck; he could almost see the happiness radiating through Trey's skin.

Trey tipped his head back, his lashes lifting in another shy peep. "And I'm the only one who matters, so that clamshell is closed. You're *my* golden god."

Still chuckling, Athys gently rocked Trey from side to side, lowering his head to rub his chin against Trey's cheek. "You're adorable. How am I so lucky?" He thought his heart would beat right out of his chest and sprinkle them with happy glitter as his mind and soul recognised his mate. Tears sprang to his eyes. His mate. What a blessing he'd been given – but it wouldn't be an easy path. He'd have to reveal … no, not going there … not yet. He'd have to take it slow and easy, after all there was—

"Athys!" Trey reared back. "What about Inca? How will she feel about this?"

Rubbing a finger across the tip of his beloved's nose, Athys fought down a grin. "Oh, she's totally in favour of you and me. Don't worry."

That delicious mouth pursed. "I hope you're right; I don't want to get on Inca's wrong side – she's as ferocious as you are!"

Athys couldn't help laughing again. "Well, there's only one entity more ferocious in this palace and she's waiting on us."

Trey gulped, his Adam's apple visibly bobbing. "Queen Dianathke?" His eyes narrowed. "Us?"

Athys grinned. "Yes and yes." His mouth softened. "She definitely wants to talk with you, but I'll go in with you – provide some support so you can be Trey-monster instead of Trey-munchkin."

Trey's mouth fell open. "What in the name of smelly snapping swamp turtles did you just call me?"

Still grinning, Athys turned Trey towards the door. "Let's go; she's waiting. Put your Trey-monster suit on."

"Athys!"

BOOM!

The palace rocked. The guard contingent outside the Queen's receiving rooms were lost to view as Athys became airborne and his ability to see anything but a vague cartwheeling smear of stone, or to distinguish the difference between walls, ceiling and floor, vanished. He hit the floor with a bone-jarring thud and lay there, trying to regain his breath, his wits and his hearing.

Desperately hoped Trey was okay, Athys manoeuvred until he had his hands and knees beneath him, then raised his head and began to assess their situation. His first fear was eased when he saw Trey dragging himself to a sitting position, but all three of the Queen's day guards were still down – although, thankfully, moving. One had rolled to her side, another was raising a hand to his forehead and the third was just drawing her legs up.

Using the nearby wall as a crutch, Athys scrambled to his feet. At a glance, the walls of the corridor appeared undamaged, despite some settling dust.

BOOM!

Athys fell sideways against the wall, but managed to stay upright.

Trey's low-voiced gasp reached him. "Just like the other night! Metal Creature must be back."

Athys gritted his teeth. "You're right. We're close to the main gate; I'll go and see what I can do while you stay and help these guards." He spun and staggered back the way they'd come, staying close to the wall as a precaution.

BOOM!

The third blast made him glad he'd done so – his proximity to the wall was the only way he managed to stay on his feet.

Lurching around the corner into the foyer, he discovered several wounded guards, sitting with legs outstretched or laying haphazardly across the tiles. Healers and some of the least injured were starting to help their less-fortunate comrades. Slowing, Athys wove between them and hastened into the central courtyard, where the recently fallen snow had melted to muddy slush. Breath harsh, he strode for the main gates, which were both still intact, although part of the nearby wall had cracked. A squad of fully armed guards and another squad of stonemasons, all coated in mud, swarmed about the wall.

"Hold that stone!"

"Seal the gap!"

"We need more stone setter!"

BOOM!

They all went flying, their attempts to repair the damage thwarted with every explosion. Fewer folk rose to the breach after each blast. It had to cease. Gritting his teeth, Athys drew his fulgar blade and aimed for the gates.

A panting guard offered a ragged salute. "It's the metal-and-flesh creature, my lord. He's trying to batter the wall down this time. He's very powerful."

Athys nod was grim. "Thanks, Sir Ladvig. Open the postern gate – I'm going out." With a doubtful glance at him, the guard set to unfastening the magic-reinforced locks and bolts on the small gate built into one of the two larger gates. They continued to rock and shudder with every new barrage but Athys was certain the force of the current strikes wasn't as strong as earlier. Easing up to the open postern gate, plastering himself against it for support, he peered out towards the assault zone.

The creature had his only hand plus the side of his head pressed to the damaged wall and was scowling heavily. He appeared to be listening, but the sensation of rage emanating from him was as visible to Athys as the sun. The mix of flesh and metal parts was easier to see in the daylight – the nose, plus the arm broken off above the wrist with the lengths of trailing coloured strings. Although, those had now been wrapped around the forearm; Athys wondered if that was to keep them out of the way? It didn't matter. He could see the creature reaching into a weapon bag for something and that was more than enough for him. Glaring, he stepped out through the gate, fulgar blade at the ready.

As expected, his movement drew the creature's attention and it – he - straightened suddenly, mouth twisting into a pointy-fanged snarl. Athys gestured at the wall. "Stop your destruction."

The eyes of Metal Creature swept over him, then focused on the short length of his fulgar blade. He pointed at it and laughed, but Athys simply waited; he'd come across this reaction before. In truth, his Twahirren-made weapon was not well known; the very short blade was more like a long knife than a sword, however that was for a very good reason and his confidence in it was tried and true.

Metal Creature moistened his lips and jerked a thumb at the castle. "Da mihi portam potestatem!" His tone was demanding.

Athys frowned and shook his head. "No idea what you said, but based on your behaviour so far, my answer's not going to be pleasant."

The pointed fangs made a snarling reappearance. "Scis quis ego sum?"

Athys shrugged, his free hand turned palm upward before he turned it over and pointed into the forest. "You get one chance. Leave and never come back, or be captured and suffer the consequences." He brandished his blade. "Choose wisely."

Snarl deepening, Metal Creature charged. "Aarggha!" Both arms rose to point at Athys. One hand formed into a claw, but the other – did the creature think to bludgeon him with that broken metal arm?

Sending his solar power flashing into the fulgar blade, Athys aimed. Then watched closely as the sun bolt erupted from the weapon's tip and smashed into the remains of his opponent's metal gauntlet. A shower of sparks flew up, the broken strings caught on fire and the concussive blow halted Metal Creature in his tracks, sent him staggering.

A mirthless grin formed on Athys' mouth. "Not laughing now, are you?"

Metal Creature rocked and shook his arm violently, lips twisting in pain. His eyes flickered to the fulgar blade in puzzlement, then widened as Athys pushed more power into the weapon, the re-charge lighting it up like a brilliant shaft of sunlight. With a roar, Metal Creature turned and bolted for the trees. Perhaps he wasn't as stupid as some of his behaviour had indicated.

Furious, Athys aimed at the creature's arse and fired the bolt. A mingled shriek of pain and anger rewarded him as his bolt landed on target. The creature dropped and rolled, but was back on his feet in seconds. He kept going and quickly disappeared into the forest.

Glowering after the fleeing male, Athys was swamped with the churning need to chase, to hunt the thing down, but Queen Dianathke wanted to capture the beast, so he fought the urge. Her Majesty had handicapped them by refusing the request to seek and destroy – despite acknowledging the need for answers, there were times Athys regretted Queen Dia was nowhere near as bloodthirsty as her cousin, Queen Maerovana.

Capping his quivering anger, Athys extended all his Fae sensory abilities in the direction the male had fled; he needed to be certain it wasn't returning. At least the creature had gone in the totally opposite path to what had been planned for the Yule collecting party, which meant they were all safe. He was pleased about that, but the angry side of him wanted an excuse to follow ...

Stiff with reluctance, he turned back towards the postern gate, then his eyes fell on the cracked wall. How had Metal Creature done that? Because the stone was too hard to damage with his body, as he'd been attempting to do when ramming the gates during his night attack. Moving closer, Athys saw huge black smears across the damaged stonework and a few tiny globs of black stuff on the ground. He picked up one of the larger pieces, a pebble-sized chunk, turning it over in his hand – it smelled resinous. Some sort of pitch? But pitch was a syrupy gel, so something else must have been added to solidify it. As he fingered it, some sort of powder flaked away, but was that just to thicken the stuff or did it have some other, more sinister, purpose?

Frowning, he checked the ground again and spied some long sticks with blackened tips. He picked one up and sniffed it, recognising the scent of fire. Maybe this was how Metal Creature had caused the explosions; light the stick on fire and apply it to the black substance? Which meant the chunky stuff in his hand may explode if flame was applied.

Athys turned the pebble over, rubbing it firmly. He felt it warm in his fingertips – and stopped immediately. Friction was, more than likely, a very bad idea. He scanned the wall and the ground again, working things out. Metal Creature had put together some sort of explosive to take down the wall. So, why hadn't he used it on the gates? Turning, Athys studied both the gates and the wall – what was different about them? Then it hit him.

"Shite! He's worked out the gates are bespelled for strength and the walls rely on the solidity of the stonework." Coupling that information with the power of an explosive element? Athys grimaced as he studied the result. Well, the stonemasons could repair it and the mages would bolster it – but, after this, they'd be working spells of protection on all of the walls as well.

ARRIVING at the doors to the Queen's offices, Athys found Trey gone and new guards on duty; four instead of three. There were also some house brownies sweeping dust and cleaning blood stains off the floor. Sif Tanda Vendagyre, Sif Chetanzi Ambiiday and Sir Ackerly Cabbegoth were now backed up by Sir Frith Limacodi; all held weapons at the ready. Sif Tanda sported a small bandage on one cheek, Sir Ackerly had a black eye, and the other two sported some minor grazes and bruising, but they were all on full alert.

Athys' voice emerged sharply. "Everyone okay here?"

Sif Chetanzi nodded. The three bars on her tunic made her group senior. "The injured have been seen to."

Athys returned her nod. "Good." He glanced around in puzzlement. "Where is my assistant, Lord Treymeron?"

Sif Chetanzi indicated the door they were all guarding. "Varli, came out and invited him to go within for his meeting with Her Majesty."

He couldn't help raising his eyebrows. "Invited? Yeah, let's go with that. Okay, I'll join them." The guards all bowed as he passed. He kept his face impassive, but deep inside, he was desperately hoping Trey was okay.

As he stepped into the antechamber, a house brownie seated at a tall desk came to attention. She began to descend to floor level via the small curving stair attached to the side of the desk, but he waved her away. "Sit, Varli. It's just me. I can let myself in."

Her voice was an indignant squawk. "But, my Lord Athys! One doesn't just burst in on our Queen! This one must announce you, as is proper!"

He strode briskly across the room. "It's fine, Varli, thanks anyway." He clicked the latch and thrust the door open.

Varli howled and pointed. "Wait, my Lord!"

The sound of a frustrated sigh drifted out through the entry. "Such noise, Varli! Just let the Earl of Rengarth in. I keep telling you there's no need to announce me to my high-level court people."

Varli fisted her hands on her hips and shouted from her desk. "Your Majesty is a Queen and should not look upon herself with such disdain! The protocols must be observed and since Your Majesty appointed this one to the task, this one must see to it."

The Queen's frustration vanished in a laugh. "I chose well – you're as bristly as a hedgehog. It's okay, Varli, let Lord Athys come in; I was expecting him."

"As Your Majesty commands." Despite her words, Varli continued to glare at Athys as he headed inside the Queen's private receiving room. His lips were twitching, but he kept his face averted so she didn't notice.

Queen Dianathke rose from a seat in the window embrasure; the strands of her brown hair rippled like a living being, with even the colour sometimes shifting from deep umber to mahogany then chestnut and all the shades in between. She scanned him carefully. "Well, you look alright, Athys. I presume the attack is over, since you're here?"

He bowed. "Indeed it is, Your Majesty." His anxious glance flew to Trey, who'd risen from one of a pair of chairs facing the window seat.

Queen Dianathke gestured. "Be at ease, Athys. I haven't upset young Treymeron and he wasn't injured in the attack, merely shaken up, as was I. We've been having a lovely chat over a restorative beaker of flamuisge."

Athys met Trey's gaze and, apart from a pale complexion and the rubbing of fingers up and down his thighs, Trey did appear to be okay. He nodded at Athys, who sighed; tension he hadn't realised he'd been holding, flowed out like water. "Flamuisge sounds like a great idea, my Queen. Mind if I have some?"

She waved a graceful hand towards a side table. "Do help yourself and then I require your report, if you please." He did as he was bid, filling them in on what had transpired and the conclusions he'd reached between sips of flamuisge.

At the end, Queen Dianathke frowned. "I don't understand why the creature's so intent on getting in here. It's obvious from your story he doesn't understand elvish and that just makes things more difficult. If we could ask him what he wants …"

Athys swirled the liquid in his beaker. "Why the attacks at all? I mean, yeah, he wants something, but why couldn't he have just knocked on the door, so to speak? We're not monsters."

The Queen laughed.

He shot her a wry look. "Well, not all the time."

Trey swallowed. "Could he have had a bad experience?"

Athys snorted. "Other than dropping in on a strange world through a portal, then getting into a brawl with the entities who came through with him?"

Trey rolled his eyes. "Smart arse." The Queen snickered and he blushed. Athys wanted to kiss his sassy mouth but kept quiet as Trey continued. "Beg pardon, Your Majesty. I meant whether he might have had a run in with some folk from our world – maybe because of the language problem."

Rubbing the back of his neck, Athys chuckled. "Or his arrogance. *That* came through loud and clear despite the language barrier."

Fluttering his hands, Trey paced a few steps. "Okay, I'm clutching at straws here and I could be far off the mark, but …" He glanced between his companions. "He came through a portal. Now he's attempting to break into a place where someone else can do portal magic – could he be trying to find a way to go back where he came from?"

Athys rolled his shoulders, trying to ease the aches and kinks – walls and floors weren't soft landing places. "Possible, but how would he know to come here?"

Trey grimaced. "A creature of flesh, metal and wire? How do we know what skills he possesses?"

Queen Dianathke's lips kicked up. "You think he can sense my portal magic, Treymeron?"

He turned both hands palm upwards. "It was a thought, but the idea of him sensing Your Majesty as a power is probably too far fetched."

She pursed her mouth. "Except that I've been using a focus crystal to make portals recently. Could he be sensing that?"

Trey tilted his head. "The portal or the focus crystal?"

Queen Dianathke nodded. "It could be either, I suppose, but I activate the crystal with a drop of my blood, so I just wondered whether that's the draw."

Athys nodded as Trey croaked, "Blood magic? That's what you use?"

TREYMERON

"Why is it so cold?" Sir Kitkun Oloden huffed warm air into his cupped hands.

Trey shook his head, his smile revealing small, pearly eye fangs glistening in the late morning sunshine. "Poor you." Although not currently snowing, the stuff lay in drifts of sparkling white, and while Trey could simply turn up his inner draconic furnace in response to the outer temperature, not everyone was so lucky. Hats, cloaks, scarves and mittens were everywhere. And there was a lot of red, which only served to remind him of Queen Dianathke's reference to her use of blood magic. He shuddered - yes it strengthened your power, but it was too close to deeper world magic for him.

Kitkun's glare shifted between Trey and Quanah Ethmidae, both of whom showed no reaction to the cold. "The pair of you are dressed in finery, with not even a nod to the season." Some of the Fae folk milling about were also able to adjust core body heat by using their own magic, but Kitkun fell into the group of Fae who were forced to don hooded cloaks, or other warm clothing, to protect themselves from the elements.

Trey glanced down at his own maroon velvet cloak, cream shirt, navy tunic and hand-tooled, apple leather boots over dove grey trousers. "Apart from Pinky's new fancy carry bag, this gear was a parting gift from my parents when I left Papillion. Wearing it in today's Yule procession to the memorial of the most famous of the Fae-monarchs indicates I'm honouring my folks and my new baby brother as much as King Oberon and Queen Titania." He peeked under his cloak at Pinky, who was currently snoozing happily at his side in her plush bag.

"New baby brother?" Quanah's sideways look revealed the gleam of dark blue eyes beneath his sable lashes. "So now there's eight Aphiski offspring?"

Trey smiled. "Yep. We've welcomed Eskander Keyvan to the tribe. Two of my sisters have birthed Fae-lings also. One female and a set of twins, one female and one male."

Kitkun's brows rose. "Sounds like a story there."

"Wait!" Quanah tilted his head. "Isn't one of your sisters mated to Duke Dario Eribifax, the Unseelie Beast?"

Trey nodded cheerfully. "Absolutely. Zhu and Dario have a baby girl."

Kitkun goggled. "The Unseelie Beast with a daughter? Wow! I pity any of her future suitors; he'll be vicious!" They were all laughing when Mikasi Opostidae squeezed between the throngs of finely dressed Fae-folk to join them.

"Hey!" The grin stretching her lips was electrifying. "I'm so excited!" Her voice almost a squeal. "Today the traditional Fae-rade to the Shrine of King Oberon and Queen Titania and tomorrow the first day of the Yule celebration with the midnight feast! Have you seen the size of the Yule log? Or noticed how the palace is so-o delightfully scented with cinnamon and fir-trees?"

Sobering slightly, Trey grinned back at her. "Hard not to. The folk who collected all the greenery have outdone themselves. There's sprigs of mistletoe above all the doorways, with wreaths and swags of holly, fir and ivy everywhere."

The elbow in Trey's ribs had him twisting to glare at Kitkun. "Hey! What's that for?"

The junior knight winked. "All that mistletoe – you'll have to manoeuvre some cutie underneath it."

Immediate thoughts of Athys sprang to Trey's mind as he recalled the delicious kisses they'd already shared. The first one in their offices had been echoed many times now. He licked his lips. "Maybe I'm thinking of someone. How about you lot?" He'd be very happy to kiss Athys again and the desire had, so far, been mutual.

But was he reading too much into their kisses? He rubbed the back of his neck. What if Athys didn't want a full-fledged relationship and only wanted a fling? Would he, Trey, be out of a job if things between them didn't work out? Did Athys replace his assistants frequently?

Quanah chuckled, drawing Trey out of his spiralling dilemma. "I've definitely got my eyes on a sweetly curved elf and all of that mistletoe."

Before anyone could comment, Queen Dianathke drew the full attention of the gathering as she flitted to a landing on the flight plat-form. She spread her beautiful aqua and black wings out, fluttering them occasionally as she smiled at the gathering of Fae-folk; all eager to participate in the annual Yule Fae-rade in honour of their original rulers and the grandparents of both current Queens. The watching crowd quietened.

Crisp in the expectant silence, Junamia, the Queen's herald, sounded her forest-horn from the bottom stair of the dais. "All hail Queen Dianathke, joint ruler of the Fae Demesnes." The crowd roared.

When the cheers faded, the Queen spoke. "Thank you all for attending the annual rade to the shrine of my grandparents, the beloved and mighty Queen Titania and King Oberon." Another round of excited cheers filled the courtyard. "Many other Fae-folk will join us on the way and we'll be met at the memorial by Queen Maerovana and her court, who are walking from Castle Synternesse. It's a long rade so I hope you've all wearing your most comfortable footwear. Let's begin."

Trey watched two guards help the Queen descend the stairs from the dais – no more flying. It was a surprise to no one when Athys appeared beside her. The Queen had no consort, so as her most senior courtier, Athys' place was beside her at the head of the procession. Behind them, the lines would wind back in order of rank and seniority, except for Trey, who was staying with his group of friends, amongst the other apprentices and juniors.

Mikasi clasped her hands under her chin as she watched the procession forming. "This is so exciting! My first Fae-rade ever! Look at everyone wearing their most sumptuous clothes. It's such a feast for the eyes."

Quanah's mouth twisted. "I'd rather a feast for my stomach, despite this being an unmissable event."

Kitkun laughed. "You'll just have to wait for tonight's banquet."

Winking, Quanah produced an apple from his pocket. "I'm prepared." Even as he joined in the ensuing laughter, Trey continued monitoring the procession. Junamia was calling names from a long list, and finally, their names rang out.

"That's us!" Mikasi jumped up and down, face aglow, ringlets bouncing.

Kitkun chuckled. "Well, stop bobbing around and let's go." The four of them took their places, adjusting their speed to avoid treading on heels.

Quanah peered down the hill at the extensive crowd drifting along in the wake of Queen Dianathke and Athys. "We're a long way from the front. I'd have thought you'd be right up there, Trey, what with your job and all. Not to mention you're the Duke of Papillion's son." He regarded Trey, his voice a puzzled rumble.

Trey shrugged. "We're juniors." He also had his orders. With Metal Creature still on the loose, Athys had spread his protective assets out along the length of the rade. From his central placing, Trey could fly in either direction and throw out some magical protective spells. He had several pre-written spell papers in his scrip, but he wasn't about to divulge work secrets without the authority to do so, despite Quanah being his friend.

A frown drew Quanah's brows down. "But Kitkun's a guard; shouldn't he be in his squad?"

Kitkun waved a hand. "If you look around, you'll see lots of junior guards nearby."

Had Kitkun worked out why the younger guard contingent were all around them? Trey flicked Kitkun a sideways glance, lifting his empathic shields slightly – could he pick out Kitkun's emotions from the crowd and get a sense of his thoughts? He sent out an energy feeler and immediately regretted it. A myriad of emotions from surrounding Fae-folk slammed into him; a pain-filled blast of mixed excitement, anticipation, pleasure, amusement, curiosity, eagerness, pride, love and satisfaction – plus so much more he didn't want to identify. He struggled to close his shields. Clutching his head in both hands, clenching fistfuls of hair, he couldn't stop the groan spilling from his lips as he staggered to a stop. "Icklegolia."

Pinkerpush stirred from her carry bag beneath his cloak with a mew of concern. His trembling fingers found her soft warmth, burrowing into the satiny folds of furred skin at the side of her neck.

At the same time, Mikasi tipped her head to peer into his face. "Trey! What's wrong? You've gone white as the snow."

At war with his shakiness, Trey forced himself to straighten, then had to swallow a wave of nausea. He cast her a tight-mouthed parody of a smile. "Empathic shield slip. Not concentrating fully." Let her think so, anyway.

Her eyes widened, features sharp with concern. "Do you need—"

He held up the hand not clutching Pinky. "I'm okay." Her brows rose as she glanced doubtfully from his still-twitching fingers back to his face. "Really, I am." Finally, she nodded, but when he resumed walking, she stayed close, her shoulder bumping his arm occasionally. He leaned into her, pushed back lightly. "Thanks."

As his senses calmed, he found he could focus them outward once more.

And discovered Kitkun was still lecturing Quanah. "As Trey said, we're juniors and this is where we were told to congregate. We all received orders – surely you did too?"

Pulling a face, Quanah glanced around. "Truth? I didn't really look at the instructions I was sent. I simply figured I'd hang out with you lot."

A chuckle burst from Mikasi. "And you got it right without even knowing." Quanah stared at her in puzzlement and she giggled again. "The herald called your name along with ours – so you followed instructions without even knowing you had."

They all laughed and continued bantering while they strolled along. Trey found himself glad to be in sunlight, even if it was only shedding light rather than warmth. It'd been a couple of weeks since the second attack from Metal Creature, and it had mostly snowed. They still had no knowledge of his whereabouts and without proper shelter, it was possible he'd perished. But, why had he attacked them in the first place? And what of his other nine companions – where had they gone?

The lack of further attacks was a good thing, but Trey's curiosity about Metal Creature had led him to look for information in the library every evening. With Athys always away on top secret night missions, they couldn't spend any time together, so Trey returned to his other love – knowledge. Books, scrolls and tomes called to him; plus, Inca always came in on her break. She'd bring beakers of tea for them both, and often a muffin, cake or cookies. He found talking to her as easy as talking to Athys and, despite their physical differences, it was easy to see the pair were related. He glanced around, wondering where she was positioned in the rade ...

Thinking back, he realised he hadn't heard the herald call her name. He pursed his lips. Had he been so caught up in conversation that he'd missed it?

"I haven't seen Inca around. Did anyone hear her name announced?" All three of his friends peered at him as if he'd taken leave of his senses.

Quanah's hands turned palm upward. "You *never* see Inca during the day."

Trey stared. "What?"

Mikasi's brows rose. "Trey, she's a nocturnal Fae. Didn't you know that?"

He blinked a few times. "No, but nocturnal … That's why I've only seen her at night then. I mean, she is the night commander and all. How silly of me." His hands fisted. "I was just … oh never mind."

Clapping him on the shoulder, Kitkun smiled. "Don't worry, Trey. She'll be asleep in her quarters."

Trey let the subject slide, but he continued thinking about both Athys and Inca and how much he really liked both of them. He was almost certain he was in love with Athys, but an image of Inca, the plush pinkness of her mouth and the deliciousness of her female form floated into his mind. Only to be superseded by mouth-watering thoughts of Athys' firm, biteable muscles and how tempting his bewitching lips were … Trey clenched his fists. He *wanted* to be with Athys, so why couldn't he banish thoughts of Inca? How could he be attracted to both of them at once? Was it because of Inca's strong family resemblance to his Golden God?

He let out a huge breath – that had to be it. So, as his relationship with Athys developed further, the attraction to Inca would surely settle. He smiled, feeling infinitely better.

By mid afternoon, their rade had reached the outskirts of Elrodel village, with the shrine not far beyond that. The rade filled out further as folk from the village eased in to join them, spilling from buildings with joyous laughter. Greetings were exchanged between friends, family and loved ones, and a groan came from Mikasi as the process slowed them even more. "My legs! They'll never be the same."

Trey cupped a spell paper for stamina between his palms, fired it up and wafted the resulting magical ash over himself and his friends. He stepped close to many of the nearby young guards, and repeated the process with more of his stock. None of them were accustomed to walking and the guards would be useless if they were needed and had walked themselves into exhaustion. Athys had assured him the Queen had agreed to use her powers to keep her guard contingents imbued with strength as well. Of course, that had made him curious about the kind of powers she possessed; perhaps she'd be willing to discuss it? Then he swallowed: he must be mad, to think of voluntarily chatting to Queen Dianathke as if she were one of his siblings. She and her cousin weren't simply ruling because of their royal bloodlines – they were also powerful and capricious.

From below, a shout echoed, then a scream. Stiffening, Trey craned his head, but could see nothing. He bit his bottom lip. Should he—

A wild roar rang out, followed by more screaming and a hiss left his lips. Flipping his cloak to the centre of his back, he spread his wings and rose a short distance into the air. The area near the front of the rade was a sea of milling bodies, but many Fae were backing off from what appeared to be a violent melee.

He grabbed the small reed tube he'd been provided with, thrust it between his lips and blew the short, long, short succession Athys had taught him. Shouts, gasps and curses erupted around him as the junior guard squads below responded to his call to arms. Good, he'd done it correctly and—

Agony twisted through him. He gasped and crumpled, curving over the sudden pain arcing beneath his ribs. What was this? He clutched at his midriff, expecting blood from whatever had been fired at him – but there was nothing. No damage. Just the pain, which was fading even as he focused. Seconds later, it was completely gone. He peered down at himself in perplexity. What had caused it? Maybe he needed to see a healer? But …

Oh! Horror surfaced as the truth dawned; because the pain – it hadn't been his. What he'd experienced was reflected, empathic, the pain of another … His blood turned to ice.

Athys!

Goddess, no!

Terror flooded Trey and his instincts took over. Without waiting for the guards as he was meant to, he flashed down the hill over the heads of the confused crowd, wings beating fast and furious and every beat of his heart sounding his beloved's name.

Speeding closer to the turmoil, he identified many of the guards he knew, barricading Queen Dianathke's flanks and rear, even as she shouted and gestured, magic flying in sparks and bolts from the glimmering red jewel cupped in her palms. The red lightning she wielded splashed out over the heads of several guards who'd crouched before her so she could work while they fired their bolt thrusters. Metal Creature, still standing despite all the firepower released by the guards, roared unintelligible words and continued forging his way forward, one small step at a time. How?

As Trey stared uncomprehendingly, one of the Queen's bolts hit Metal Creature's shoulder, but the lightning only sizzled across the strange covering he wore, in little balls of weird fizzing light, then sheeted to the ground, the power slowing him but not doing any real harm. He continued his snail shuffle towards the Queen, his face split by a mad grin of triumph.

Looking the group over from above, Trey couldn't see Athys in the guards surrounding the Queen and he swallowed heavily. No, him being the type who'd take the fight straight to Metal Creature, rather than simply stand back and defend, told him Athys wouldn't be with the guards. Which meant …

Hovering out of the line of attack, he forced himself to scan the dips and hollows of the ground around Metal Creature. Yes, there! Athys, his Athys, his own Golden God, lay in a sprawled unmoving heap, between the Queen's group and their enemy. Oh, by the goddess, please let his Golden God be alive. He had to get to Athys, but there was still the enemy to deal with.

The enemy, who, even as he slowly closed the gap to the Queen, was brandishing a metallic blue-black gauntlet, where days ago he'd had nothing but a ragged stump with coloured trails of strings. And even as Trey stared, aghast with terror, Metal Creature's new gauntlet began to glow. He was aiming the forefinger straight at Athys, who lay limp and defenceless in his path …

"NO-O-O-O!" Acting instinctively, clarity of thought wispy as sea mist, Trey sucked on all his powers, grasped at his volatile emotions, drew on the very core of his being, flattening any barriers he came across, until he coalesced every infinitesimal particle he could gather into one massive roiling uncontainable storm, then …

Red and gold fire flashed from him in a tsunami of boiling fear and rage and love. It passed above the motionless form of Athys and hit

Metal Creature square in the chest, detonating with a deafening boom. The crazed behemoth froze, all forward movement truncated as the tornado of furious power erupting from Trey, wrapped him up and flung him backwards. He hit the ground in a shower of sparks and rolled several times to lie face down in the village street.

Staring uncomprehendingly, Trey gasped and wheezed, shivered and shook, his entire body a searing maelstrom of surging energy. What the hell had he just done? He glanced around and found everyone had stilled to stare at him, eyes rounded, mouths gaping as the shock held them motionless. All except Queen Dianathke, who wore a little smile as her fingers continued to grip and stroke her glowing red jewel as if it were a beloved pet.

What did he care about what they thought? He turned his back on them to seek Athys, flexed shaky wings and dropped into an unsteady glide before he wobbled to a landing right where he wanted to be. Beside his Golden God. Trey trembled as he laid his ear against Athys' chest. For a moment, he could hear nothing but his own sawing breaths, then he was rewarded with the steady flutter of a heart beat and relief rolled over him like the tide. He closed his eyes, tears leaking from the corners to soak into the material of Athys' tunic.

But when the silence was broken by the sound of heavy footsteps echoing on the cobbled street, he lifted his head. A figure appeared from behind the Ancient Oak, a male who slowly approached Metal Creature, then dropped to a crouch by his side, turning him over to scan his features with a look of desperation and despair. He shook his head, his voice a deep rumble.

"Kellay, *quare non audies nos?*"

Metal Creature's eyes opened. "*Quia ego non amo te verbum!*"

Trey could only wonder what the words meant. He stayed still, ready to throw his body across Athys' if necessary, but wanting to see how this played out. If the newcomer could get Metal Creature under control, that would be a favourable outcome ... but then his eyes widened.

Having slowly and shakily raised his gauntlet, Metal Creature pointed it at his companion and let loose a pulse of brilliance. His companion had time to drop to the ground, and the energy pulse hissed as it arced over his prone body into the snow, where it fizzled and went out.

Anger flashed across the newcomer's face as he raised himself to a crouch and looked up. "Kellay!" He shot to his feet, a snarl stretching his lips as he aimed a blast of his own at Metal Creature. It was a weaker pulse, from some sort of hand-held device, but it hit the gauntlet, which lit up like an exploding star.

Kellay Metal Creature screamed and pointed the gauntlet, now pulsing brilliantly with the invasive power, back towards his companion – who attempted to roll away. The gauntlet followed, a vicious grin spreading across Kellay's face as he tracked his compatriot. Intense light flared, crashing around the gauntlet, over, under, through and finally, out through all of the fingers. This time, Kellay's blast sizzled straight into the other male entity, who was desperately scrabbling across the snow in an attempt to avoid being shot, but the pulse splashed into him anyway and catapulted him backwards in a surge of energy. When he hit the ground, he lay limp and unmoving.

The gauntlet, having ejected the unwanted energy pulse, sizzled violently, then burst into flame and Kellay spat out something unintelligible as he dragged the gauntlet through a mound of snow.

Once the flames had died down, Kellay Metal Creature struggled to his feet and turned to the hushed and watching Fae. He brandished the gauntlet, but it was now completely black and lifeless. He glanced to his prone companion, a feral snarl twisting his mouth, and took a step towards him.

"Now's our chance!" It was Sir Cadbury's voice. Trey threw himself over Athys, as the guards thundered past. From his sprawled position, Trey watched as Kellay Metal Creature fled from the charging guards into the gloom of the forest and was quickly lost to view.

12

INCA

ursting into the library, Inca continued down the steps at a limping run. "Here you are! I should have guessed."

Still shaken by the day's events, Trey scowled. "Okay, so I'm predictable. What of it? You're later than usual tonight – and you're limping. What happened?"

Her eyes narrowed. "You sound out of sorts, Trey. And to answer your last question, I hurt myself."

He continued to scowl. "You've been sleeping all day – what'd you do, fall out of bed?"

This time her eyes went wide. "Wow. You *are* in a mood."

Grimacing, Trey swept a hand through his hair. "Sorry. That was extremely rude of me. It's just that Athys was badly injured and I'm a bit upset by the day's events."

Pleasure was a warm glow inside her; he was worried. She spread her hands wide, then winced and rubbed at her sore midriff. Maybe she shouldn't have relied on just internal healing powers; the palace healer would've helped with the more severe damage. Maybe later, although one more changeover would probably complete the healing. She shrugged. "I'm not to blame for that. Besides, you staged a rescue and saved, ah, a member of my family – something for which we're absolutely grateful and you should be proud of."

Trey tensed. "You've seen him?" His lips twisted. "I suppose you *are* his sister, but the healers took him away and I wasn't allowed to go with them. It's been killing me."

She exhaled roughly, then grimaced at the resulting pain through her side. "He's definitely as alive as I am, but some injuries take more time to heal than others. He'll be fine tomorrow; being Twahirren, we heal quickly."

He sagged in his seat; oh, he *definitely* cared that Athys was okay. She took note of his heavy swallow. "Thank the goddess. But that blasted Metal Creature got away." He scowled. "I'd like to teach the pond-scum a lesson."

A chuckle escaped her, followed by another explosive breath as the pain lanced through her ribcage. She raised a hand to cup the area, massaged gently. "From all accounts, you blew Metal Creature Kellay through the ether like a wood chip, just as he did to Athys. That's not enough for you?"

He narrowed his eyes on the motion of her hand across her ribs. "No. He got up and ran; Athys is still suffering." He dragged a hand through his hair again. "Holy snapping swamp turtles! Why wasn't I strong enough to take him down permanently?"

She stilled her self massage. "Wow, so fierce." She tilted her head. "And we both know you could've burned him to a crisp with that dracon flame you have, so don't try to tell me you weren't physically or magically strong enough."

His head dropped. "I couldn't do it. What sort of warrior balks in a crisis?"

A sigh whispered from her; he was so adorable. "The smart sort. Killing is a last resort." She eased her hand across her ribs. "Athys was brought down by an explosive substance. The same stuff Kellay used to attack the palace and breach the wall. He was hiding in the forest and Athys was taken off guard. Yes, Kellay escaped, but you know the guards captured his companion?"

He looked up, a smile lurking at the corners of his mouth. "Yeah, I saw that."

She grinned. "That's actually why I was looking for you. We have him locked up and nobody's been able to work out what he's saying."

Trey's stare was sceptical. "You think I can? I'm not a linguist; that's my sister, Tindresse."

It was her turn to nod. "So I understand, but I'd still like you to come and see him. Is that okay? Will you come?"

Trey closed the book he'd been studying. "Since you ask so nicely." He slid from his seat, then lifted a sleeping Pinkerpush and transferred her into her snuggle bag. "I'm ready."

THE CAPTIVE WAS in a barred cell, wrapped in a blanket and seated with his back to a wall, legs stretched out in front of him. He looked up as Inca and Trey appeared, his gaze flickering from one to the other of them, but he didn't move from his position.

Glancing at Inca, Trey raised his eyebrows. "What do you want me to do?"

She waved a hand. "Use your magic, get him talking in a language we can understand so we can work out what his friend Kellay is trying to do."

Trey rubbed his chin. "I don't think that gives enough for my magic to work on – it's too abstract an idea without knowing what his language actually is."

"Kellay?" The male had drawn his legs in and was in the process of rising to his feet. "*Quid accidit ut* Kellay?" He pushed a swathe of black hair back from his face and glared at them. "*Si tu nocere ei ...*" The words sounded threatening.

Trey spread his hands, palm up and out at shoulder height, and added a shrug. "I'm sorry. I don't know what you're saying."

The dark-haired male narrowed his eyes and pursed his lips. Then he cocked his head. "Kellay?"

Inca already knew words didn't work; she waited to see what Trey would come up with. He'd proved himself very resourceful and he was a gift they were definitely keeping, for more than one reason. She caught her lower lip between her teeth – would he be resourceful in bed too?

Trey grimaced, shrugging again. "Kellay." He jerked a thumb away from himself and acted out running – although he did it on the spot, pumping his arms and looking over his shoulder as well. Inca fought to hold her chuckle in and failed. Luckily, the harsh laughter of the male in the cell covered her mirth.

He clenched his fists. "*Et cucurrit tunc.*" His lip curled. "*Porcos.*"

"Huh." Trey rubbed his chin again. "I think he understood my play acting."

"He did." Inca nudged him. "That's more than anyone else has thought to do. Keep going. You're clever."

Pushing a lock of hair out of his face, Trey turned back to the captive. Once again, he jerked a thumb away from himself. "Kellay." Then he prodded his chest. "Treymeron." Lastly he pointed at the male and spread his hands as if asking a question.

The tall, heavy-set male squinted at him briefly, then looked away. A moment later, he met Trey's gaze and pointed at him. "Trey-mer-on?" He enunciated it slowly.

Trey grinned. "That's right, I'm Treymeron." He thumbed himself in the chest. "Treymeron."

The male nodded, then he pointed to Inca. "*Eius?*" His tone was questioning.

She answered for herself. "Inca."

He studied them for a moment, eyes narrowed, then he pointed to each of them. "Treymeron. Inca." His lips twisted as he gestured to himself. "Zett. Zett *ex* Berengaria."

Satisfaction welled in Inca, then Trey pointed to himself again. "Trey." He pointed to the other male. "Zett?"

Zett frowned. "Trey? Treymeron?" He arched his eyebrows.

Trey nodded and spread his hands wide. "Treymeron." Then he mimed bringing his hands closer together. "Trey."

Nodding, Zett repeated his motions. "Zett *ex* Berengaria." He narrowed the distance. "Zett."

Inca clasped Trey's arm. "Oh great job, Trey! I'll be able to pass on your discovery that sign language works. It's slow, but it's something. Still, I think I'll advise we get Tindresse involved, as you suggested." She pursed her lips thoughtfully. "We might have to send someone to Papillion for her."

Trey chuckled. "Oh, she's closer than that. Tin is tri-mooning at Castle Synternesse, so it'd be easy to send Zett over there or have her come here."

Beaming, Inca rubbed her hands together. "Better and better." She eyed him. "Let's call it quits for now – we've had a long, trying and painful day." She coughed. "Or rather, you have." She threw him a brief, speculative glance; had he picked up on her tiny faux pas?

Trey massaged the back of his neck. "You were right the first time – we all have."

Apparently he hadn't noticed; her stomach churned with disquiet. The secret inside her chafed more every day with the growth of her love for Trey. She and Athys – Athys and she … Swallowing, she summoned a smile. "As you say. We'll go then." Turning to Zett and careful of her ribs, Inca bowed, then waved. By her side, Trey followed her lead. To her pleasure, Zett bowed and waved in return, before resuming his seat and rewrapping himself in the blanket he'd been provided with.

She wanted to weep, she wanted to fist pump. Thanks to Trey, they'd made progress – with Zett anyway.

IT WAS close to the end of her shift when Inca returned to the library. Trey would have taken himself off to bed hours ago, but his wonderfully addictive scent was all over the place here and she couldn't stay away. Inca rotated her shoulders, feet shuffling as she slowly descended the steps. Sighing gustily, she twisted her neck from side to side. It had been a close call and she was aching and sore after the terrible day. She knew she wasn't thinking clearly; that what she really needed was rest and to hand the reins back to Athys, but it wasn't quite time. Eyes closed, she stopped at the base of the steps and breathed in deeply; Trey's strong scent was already providing solace.

The sound of a chair scraping on the floor brought her head up, her eyes flying open.

Trey stood at his usual table, gorgeous lips pursed. "You're tired."

She swallowed the rush of excitement, tilted her head. "I am." Her eyebrows rose. "It's only an hour or so until dawn; I didn't expect to find you still here."

He shrugged. "I've been busy." Frowning at her, he stepped around the table. "You should sit. Come on, let's get you into a comfortable chair."

When he cupped her arm in guidance, she resisted, stared searchingly into the delicious depths of his violet gaze. "Wait." Her hand came up, fingers nestling against his chest."I'm thrilled you're still here and I'm tired enough to be reckless."

He continued to frown at her. "What?"

She was sick of all the subterfuge. She moved her palm, stroked a small circle on his chest. "I'm in love with you, Treymeron Aphiski."

His mouth fell open as he backed up. "*What?*"

Inca went with him, step for step, just as if they were dancing. Her palm smoothed out towards his shoulder, then back again. "I'm going to kiss you."

Trey swallowed as she leaned closer. Looking torn, he held up a hand, stopping her from making the connection. "I'm sorry, Inca, but no."

Head tilting, she bit her lip. He was rejecting her then. Pain fought with elation. "No?"

Reaching down, Trey grasped her hand and removed it from his chest, clasping it within both of his. Rolling his lips in and out, he pinned her with his bewitching eyes. "You're beautiful, Inca, and even though I think I do love you, I truly love another and he – I-I saw him first. I've chosen him, because we've already formed a connection. But you know, if you'd been first, then maybe I'd be having this conversation with him."

The ache in her heart eased and a smile teased her lips. "So you're rejecting me because I came in second." She slanted her head. "I can't tempt you to change your mind?"

His throat moved convulsively. "No. Even though being in love with both of you has confused me, I've made my decision and I'm not fickle. I'm also monogamous in a relationship, so please, don't go there either."

Her mouth fell open, eyes rounding. "No! That's not what – I wouldn't." She swallowed. "I, too, am monogamous." She sighed; she was, but this was going to be difficult to deal with.

His voice trembled. "In truth, any partner of yours would be blessed; you're lovely inside and out. It's just that …"

She nodded. "You're taken. I get it. Athys is a very lucky male."

His smile was shy. "To have me? Thanks for the compliment." His brow furrowed. "Wait, how do you know Athys is my love?"

She snorted. "After you made such a glorious spectacle of yourself saving him? Who wouldn't know?"

He didn't deny it. "B-but you weren't even there!"

Satisfaction welled inside her that he'd noticed she wasn't at the rade. "The Queen told me, so did a lot of other folk who witnessed the event."

"Oh."

She continued to gaze at him, saw perspiration break through the skin at his temples and watched a blush steal up his cheeks. When he tried to draw his hands away, Inca's grip tightened. She leaned forward until they were almost nose to nose. "You shouldn't need me to tell you what a blazingly wonderful Fae-male you are. You've a lovely, caring soul. A willingness to help others and a generous heart." Her eyes caressed him. "So easy to fall in love with – you're also gorgeous to look at, you possess amazing magical skills, analytical thinking and perfect memory. If that's not enough, you're able to do things with flame because of the draconic bloodlines you possess. It's been delightful watching you stretch and grow into your own strengths and abilities." Her silver hair sparkled in the lamplight as she shook her head. "You're one in a million; what chance did I have to resist?"

Trey was gaping. Inca released his hands, tucked fingers under his chin and pushed up until his lips closed. All he did was blink and breathe and stare at her. A smile formed as she regarded him. "Guess what, Trey?"

"Ungh?" His eyes widened even further as Inca leaned in.

She smirked. "I'm going to kiss you anyway." He tensed, but she only brushed his warm, soft cheek with her lips before she drew away.

Tears sparkled in his eyes. "Inca." He swallowed.

She leaned forward once more, repeating the caress of her mouth on his cheek, before offering her own trembling smile. "Thanks, Sweet Pea. Now, remember what I just said." Still grasping a hand, she tugged at him gently. "Because there's something you need to see. Would you trust me enough to come along and let me show you?"

He eyed her, nibbling at his bottom lip. "Okay. Just let me grab Pinky." She waited while he tucked the sleeping duskit into her nest and slipped the bag over his shoulder. Then she led him out of the library. They met no one as they traversed several corridors to a corner stairwell, which they climbed to the next level.

Inca guided him left. "This way."

Slowing, Trey cast her a troubled glance. "I've been told this floor has suites for senior officials."

She glanced at him. "You're right, but it's okay. You're welcome up here." She touched his arm. "Come on."

Instead, he stopped dead, slapping both palms to his hips. "Why? What's going on, Inca? We're going to your rooms? I've already explained—"

She held up a finger, shaking her head. "This is not about me attempting to change your mind, Trey. Please trust me."

He blew out a heavy breath. "Fine." He gestured between them. "This is me, trusting you. Lead on." Every door they passed was labeled with the names of the occupants; two corridor twists later, Inca stopped outside a door showing the name Castniidae.

She held her hand up, palm facing him. "As most palace folk

understand it, Athys and I share this suite as brother and sister. I'm now going to repay *your* trust in me, by entrusting *you* with some information that is very private and personal. Something only a few folk know the truth of."

Trey was frowning, hands now clutching the fabric of his trouser legs. "You don't have to do that, Inca. I'm happy to go on as we've been doing. I—"

"That's the thing, Trey," she interrupted him, smile wistful. "With your closeness to Athys, to me, you have to know."

He swallowed again. "I understand, I guess – but why can't you or Athys simply tell me what it is?"

She shrugged. "We could, but it's better this way." She fiddled with the lock and opened the door. "After you."

He hesitated, then met her gaze again as the door swung back at her push. "Okay, this is me, still doing the trusting thing."

Her heart bled for him as he walked into the room.

13

TREYMERON

Stomach roiling, Trey stopped in the centre of a living room filled with things he was too worked up to pay attention to. Hearing the door shut and the lock click, he spun to face Inca, not expecting the haunting sadness that had overtaken her face as she crossed the room. Stopping with her hand on the latch of the inner door, she cast Trey a tense look.

"Yes, I've locked us in and I'm sorry if that intensifies any suspicions you're harbouring, especially after my confession of loving you. I'm thrilled that you love Athys, which probably seems strange, but you'll understand – after."

Trey's gaze flickered to the door she stood in front of. "He's in there?" Then, he shook his head. "No, forget that. I know it's a foolish question – he must still be recovering after today."

Inca's mouth twisted. "Well, technically, yesterday now. Night's all but gone."

His eyebrows shot up. "Icklegolia! I've been up all night?" He scrubbed the nape of his neck as she nodded. "Used to do that at home when I got engrossed in my studies."

She smiled. "Back at Papillion, you mean?"

He spread his hands. "Yeah." Sighing, he faced the bedroom door.

"Okay, show me how badly he's wounded, since I've worked out that's what all of this has been leading up to." He gulped. "Athys isn't going to die, is he?"

Shock spread over her face. "No! No, Trey, that's not what's going on. I apologise for giving you the wrong idea." She glanced out of the window. "We're out of time. Over the next little while, as night becomes day ..." She sighed. "Just please wait and talk with Athys, okay?"

What the hell was happening? Trey frowned. "I don't understand. Athys is in here, isn't he?"

She returned his scowl. "Promise me you will wait to speak with Athys. He'll be out of it for a while. Please, promise. This is important."

He threw his hands up. "Fine, I promise."

"Thank you."

She opened the door and entered the bedroom. Trey followed uncertainly.

He didn't expect the huge, empty bed. Where was Athys? "Inca? I thought you said Athys was in here! You've misled me! What's going on?"

She didn't look his way. "You'll see." She sat on the side of the mattress, removed her boots and swung her legs up.

"Inca!" His hands fisted as he forced her name out between clenched teeth.

She shook her head. "Wait."

Frustrated, he watched her wriggling until she lay flat and still, closing her eyes on a sigh. He stared uncomprehendingly. Was she asleep? Unconscious? Should he call a healer? How long was he supposed to stand here? She'd made him promise to stay, to talk to Athys, but—

Limned by dawn's early light, her motionless figure blurred. He squinted and made out her steady, even breathing. Sleeping then. He scanned her milky pale skin and silver blonde hair, unable to deny that she was beautiful. His heart ached. But, he loved Athys and he'd denied her because she *wasn't* his Golden God.

Trey's breath stalled in his lungs as her body was suddenly bathed in a broad shaft of sunlight. The strengthening sunrise eclipsed the dawn, chasing away the last vestiges of the night. As the light played over her, Inca's milky skin deepened to a creamy hue, her silvery, moon-blonde hair intensified to match the golden sunbeam and the shapely muscularity of her body, so similar to Athys'…

Open-mouthed, eyes starting from his head, Trey staggered backward until he hit the wall. As the sun continued to brighten, he was riveted by the altering shapes of hands and limbs; frozen to the spot as all the traces of femininity in Inca's body hardened. Even the face was changing. The jaw was more square, the lips firmer, the nose had become bolder and—

Surely this was impossible? He'd never heard of such magic; he'd come to this room with Inca, but now?

Now, the figure on the bed was his own Golden God.

VISION BLURRING AGAIN, legs like jelly, Trey sank, his back sliding down the wall until his bottom was on the floor. Unable to come up with any thoughts that made sense, he dropped his head into the crease of his raised knees, wrapped his arms around his legs and let his overwhelmed mind shoot rainbow sparkles in random patterns. He was barely aware of Pinkerpush nosing her way under one arm and into his lap; of her paws reaching up to pat his cheeks and chin; of her soft mews of concern comforting him as he trembled and rocked, unable to fully comprehend what he'd seen.

He was finally drawn from his personal form of catatonia by Athys' warm, deep voice. "Trey." A hand closed around each arm, forcibly drawing them away from his legs. He cried out as light flooded the little cocoon of darkness he'd made and he slowly tipped his head to squint upwards. Athys was crouched in front of him, radiating concern from every line and angle of his body.

He sighed. "Dammit. I never intended to terrify you, Trey."

A tidal wave of fierce anger roared through Trey. "Yeah? Well, what the hell did you think was going to happen? I'm with Inca and she's babbling on and on without making any sense and suddenly she dies or something and fades away and then you're there and – and what the hell is this? Where's Inca? My friends said she's nocturnal, so is she in hibernation now? Did she somehow sink through the bed to be preserved in some secret compartment underneath until nightfall? And what about you? You said you had night missions, or did I fail to understand what you actually meant?"

Athys held up his hands. "Ssh."

But Trey couldn't stop. "I won't shush! I need to know why you hide during the night and Inca hides during the day. What are you – two people in one body? How could that happen? Were you meant to be twins and lost a body? What—"

One of Athys' hands covered Trey's mouth firmly, pushing his head back until it rested against the wall. Trey turned his head, squirming to get free, then punched and kicked out with his arms and legs; within seconds, he and Athys were in a full-on wrestling match. Pinkerpush shot away and leaped onto the bed as the two of them rolled across the floor; Trey screaming and flailing and Athys grimly silent as he fielded every one of Trey's blows without returning any.

Their brawl ended with Trey spreadeagled on the floor, wrists gripped by Athys, his feet and legs anchored to the floor as his warrior-trained mentor sprawled atop him. Gasping, Trey stared upwards, opened his mouth to shout or scream, but Athys forestalled him by sealing their lips together. Trey kept his mouth in a hard line, but the brush of familiar warm lips across his, the taste of cinnamon and rose musk he'd grown to adore, the little sipping kisses at the corners of his lips and across them, the gentle sucking of his bottom lip between Athys' teeth, combined to derail him. Until he responded, no longer able to hold out against a recognised pleasure, which, once he relaxed into it, quietened and soothed his abused and ragged senses.

Finally, Athys lifted his head, eyeing Trey with deep concern. Trey simply stared back; still confused and hurt, but his brain had kick-started again.

Athys moistened his lips. "I'm sorry about this, Trey. Will you please let me explain? I wasn't trying to hurt you."

Trey swallowed, his voice emerging as a whisper. "Good to know that much, but can you say the same for Inca? I did reject her, after all."

Sighing, Athys pulled a face. "Actually, I can say the same for her. I was actually trying to protect me, her, us." His sigh was frustrated. "The truth is, I'm Twahirren-fae. Ever heard of them?"

"The two-natured Fae-folk? Yeah, but they're rather secretive from what I've been told."

Athys nodded. "We often suppress who we are, for reasons I'll explain in a moment." He took a breath. "Inca and I are one person, but not, as you said earlier, two people in one body. I'm Inca and she's me."

"But … you …" Trey blinked as he tried to process. "I'm sorry, that doesn't make sense."

Athys drew a breath. "Okay, well, we're two aspects of a single person – that's the nature of a Twahirren. Each aspect controls the body for half of a planet rotation, so one aspect is always day and the other is always night. It isn't a choice we make, it's a genetic thing, like eye colour. Generally, the two aspects of a Twahirren are the same sex, but in some rare cases, like my own, the two aspects are of different sexes. It's a difficult thing for folk to accept, even in a world where species variety is considered standard."

"That's why you and Inca are always on about accepting folk at face value."

A wry smile crossed Athys' face as he inclined his head. "Indeed."

Trey frowned. "But what about sleep? If you're up all day and Inca you is up all night, when do you get any sleep?"

Releasing Trey's wrists, Athys rolled to one side, propping his head in the palm of his hand. "This is where I confide my vulnerabilities. You must decide if you want to hear them and, if you do, agree never to divulge them without my permission, even if you end up hating my guts for all this subterfuge."

Not having even the slightest qualm, Trey nodded. "I wish to hear and I'll keep your secrets. I swear on the honour of my draconian bloodline."

Athys nodded. "Thank you. In truth, Twahirren-fae sleep during the changeovers between their two aspects. The length of time is no longer than one hour, but during that hour we cannot be roused and are completely vulnerable."

Trey gaped. "So two hours a day, maximum? How is that enough time for any folk to rest and recuperate? And yet, you clearly do." His hands flew to his cheeks. "I've just realised you're over the really bad injuries you received during the rade – how is that possible? You were unconscious and seemed near death – I was so afraid for you, but the Queen said … she knows, doesn't she?"

Athys inclined his head. "She does and those questions bring me to the next secret. We have accelerated healing abilities. Despite that, I was too severely wounded for my abilities to completely heal in one changeover."

"That's why you, um, why Inca was limping and in pain overnight."

"Yes." Athys shrugged. "As I said earlier, I'm Inca and Inca is me. There's just one of me, but I split my two given names so that everyone would think I was two people. If you and I are to succeed in a relationship long term, you need to know everything I just revealed. And," he swallowed, his heart in his eyes. "I want long term with you."

"Do you now?" Anger gathered as Trey thought of all the things he'd confessed to Inca, thoughts he'd trusted her with, stuff that he hadn't been ready to share with Athys – only it had been Athys all along. "Just as well I refused to allow the Inca-you to kiss me then, wasn't it? Were you testing my fidelity, or my honour? Did you get a good laugh out of it?"

A horrified look crossed Athys' features. "Laugh at you? No! Goddess no. I was testing how much you trust me."

Pushing himself to his feet, Trey could only stare incredulously. "That makes no sense! How does me refusing the advances of someone I didn't know was *you* give any indication of how much *I* trust *you*?"

Grimacing, Athys rose to his knees. "I was afraid. I've always been afraid. Being me - Athys Inca Castniidae - saw me rejected and spurned by my parents, excommunicated from my clan and turned out into the world alone while I was still a child."

Trey blinked away tears. "By the goddess - that's horrible! How did you manage?"

"It wasn't easy." Eyes pleading, Athys extended a hand, palm up, towards Trey. "But, all of that can wait for another time. Here and now - I love you and I want a future with you. Can you forgive me?"

"I don't know. There's no denying I love you, and have from the very beginning." Trey glanced at Athys' hand and huffed a bitter laugh. "Strangely enough, I even love Inca and it's been driving me nuts trying to work out why I'm in love with two different folk - except now I've discovered that I've really only fallen for one entity, and I'm not sure where that leaves us. From the very beginning, I shared all of who I am, while you merely played a part. *You* might think you've been hiding, but it feels like deception to me."

Athys slumped. "There was no intention to deceive, only to protect myself. I've really stuffed this up."

"I'd say so. Now I need some time to think." Trey paused. "Do I still have a job?"

Head jerking up, Athys glared. "Of course you damn well do! I may be an idiot, but I'm not a lowlife."

Gathering a snoozing Pinkerpush from the bed, Trey nodded. He swallowed around the huge lump in his throat, ignored the slow trickle of tears from the corners of his eyes. "Thanks." He shut the doors quietly as he left.

14

ATHYS

Queen Dianathke rustled her papyrus. "You've not been very helpful today, Lord Rengarth. You know I wanted your input on these last minute Yule plans."

Head in hands as he hunched in a nearby chair, Athys vaguely registered the use of his true family name, but his mind was filled with thoughts of Trey. Why had he made his announcement without ensuring Trey was properly informed about Twahirren? Why had he sprung the change on Trey in such a shocking way? No wonder he'd fled.

He scrubbed his scalp. "I should've been named Idiot-Misery."

Queen Dia's voice was dry. "Fortunately, your parents were more intelligent than that."

He shook his head. "I've managed to alienate my mate! When I was young, before I'd reached the age to reveal my second form, my parents both warned me of the difficulties I'd face; I should've listened harder."

Her pen scratched as she worked. "I can imagine it isn't easy for any of the two-natured, but even more difficult for you, with the appearance you present to the world as both female and male. Also, being ostracised by your family as a pre-pubescent child has left a deep scar. You operate in constant fear of it happening again."

He grunted. That was an understatement.

The scratching ceased and she tsked, pinning him with a look. "Really, Athys! Grunting is not an acceptable form of communication here. Where are your manners? At least both of your aspects are two-legged folk. Think of your fellow Twahirren who share with wolves, bears or others; their lot wouldn't be easy when it comes to mating either. Now, don't assault me with silly noises again."

Sighing, he raised his head. "Apologies for my lack of manners, Your Majesty. As for my fellow Twahirren, right now, I couldn't give a fat flying squirrel about them."

The Queen chortled. "That's what I've always liked about you Athys – you're straightforward and you don't pull any punches. Too bad you didn't do that with Trey."

He huffed. "But I gave him lots of time to get to know Inca and I – he even admitted he loves both of my aspects."

"Well, most of my subjects here at Elrodel worked out how much he loves you, with that brilliant demonstration he gave. The way he blasted that Metal Creature was lovely." She tapped her pen on the desk. "Too bad you were unconscious at the time."

He groaned, dropping his head again. "Thanks for reminding me how easily I was taken out." The Queen's chair scraped. The sharp blow to his forehead was unexpected and painful. "Ow!" He stared at her indignantly as she reseated herself.

"You've never been a fool, Athys. Stop acting like one. You were ambushed because you'd bested the Metal Creature face to face and he feared you."

His jaw clenched. "I should have seen an ambush coming. It's humiliating that I didn't. An ambush isn't a fair fight."

She shot him a pointed look. "And yet you did the same thing to your mate."

His breath hissed between his teeth. "Hell."

She smirked. "There's a lovely mark on your forehead. Maybe I should've tried knocking sense into you sooner."

Glaring, Athys rubbed at the sore spot. "The mate of a Twahirren-fae has to be able to accept their two-sided nature before any mating can happen. I admit I made a mess of the revelation, but it's too late to change that."

Queen Dianathke pointed her pen at him. "Finally, light dawns in that witless mind of yours."

His glare intensified. "Hey!"

Her teeth gleamed as laughter lit her features. "So you mucked it up. Fine." She shrugged. "Accept it and move on, but Trey didn't reject you outright, so there's something to work with. Make a plan and fix it. Your brilliant and delightful mate is the perfect addition to my coterie of useful Fae-courtiers." She pointed her pen a second time, jabbing the air with every word she spoke. "Don't. Let. Him. Get. Away." She watched him. "Are we clear? And before you ask, yes, that *is* the royal 'we'."

He threw his hands up. "I don't want Trey to 'get away', as you put it, but I can't simply tell him he's my mate. You know I can't – that law is in place to protect folk from being pressured or tricked."

She rolled her eyes. "Yes, I do know – since I'm currently one of the law makers and I get to review all the laws with Maerovana annually." She pursed her lips. "Try your hand at courting Trey."

He goggled. "Courting? But he already loves me! He said so."

She scrunched her eyes shut. "Goddess save me from arrogant males!" Her eyes reopened and drilled him like a goblin's blow-dart. "The problem, as I understand it, is that Trey is currently uncertain of *you*. So court him, romance him, *convince him* you're a worthy mate; show him he comes first in your thoughts and isn't simply being taken for granted." A sarcastic moue of her lips. "How I'll be able to bear the demotion I don't know."

His mouth fell open. "A joke?"

Her hand slashed the air between them. "Never mind that. Focus. This is probably the most important plan of your life. The happiness of both of you rests solely on what you do now and, if luck is with you, somehow he'll work out that you're his mate and he's yours." She eyed him narrowly. "Do you understand, Athys?"

He gulped and nodded at the same time, his voice emerging as a husky whisper. "Yes. Yes, I've got it. Thank you, Your Majesty."

She waved him away. "Just take your mopey face out of my sight and get on with it."

Hastily, he bowed and departed her royal presence.

RETREATING TO HIS OFFICE, Athys snatched up a pen and grabbed a sheet of papyrus. Rubbing his forehead again, he reviewed the Queen's stinging verbal attack and grimaced. She was right. He'd been nothing but an arrogant insensitive dolt, getting to know Trey thoroughly – he'd even had a dossier and inside information from his long-time friend, Dario. And what had Trey been given? Nothing. He'd had an unfair advantage over his mate from the start. The thing was, he hadn't known Trey *was* his mate. At first. He scrubbed his hair, fingers snagging in one of his coming of age braids. Irritably he jerked free and started writing.

Some time later, he glanced over his list and bit his lip. Treats, gifts, poetry. It didn't look like much, but there were a huge variety of options to fit those broad parameters. All kinds of foods, cute items, different poems, even a range of poets he could employ. He'd need a sub-heading for each. He bent his head and applied pen to papyrus again.

First ...

PEEPING around the corner of the dining hall two hours later, Athys watched as Trey frowned at his plate. He'd enlisted Nutley's help and, in addition to the traditional elements of the first Yule meal comprising nut bread, dried fruits and cheeses, Trey's platter held a red rose with a scroll wrapped around the stem. The twine bow had been horrible to tie and looked a bit wonky but he'd done it, and writing Trey's name on the outside of the scroll had buoyed his spirits.

He flexed his fingers, crossed them and held his breath as he recalled the line of poetry he'd written. *'I'm stunned by the violets growing in your eyes.'* He'd almost changed 'growing' to 'glowing' and was now wishing he had.

His heart lodged in his throat as Trey raised the rose to his nostrils before unrolling the scroll. Athys pulled back when Trey, face giving nothing away, glanced searchingly around the room. He fisted his hands. Maybe Trey didn't like the compliment he'd agonised over. Had he been an idiot to attempt something so far out of his comfort zone?

He risked another look, only to see Mikasi attempting to take the scroll. Trey snatched it out of her reach, re-rolled it and tucked it into the inner pocket of his jerkin.

Sagging against the corridor wall, Athys' breath was uneven. Trey hadn't been overwhelmingly enthusiastic, but he'd kept the scroll from his friend and pocketed it, so maybe there was hope. He bit his lip as he considered what his next offering should be.

~

FROM A SIDE CORRIDOR, Athys held his breath as his love walked past on the way to his rooms. Would Trey stop at his hall table? After waiting a few moments, he peered down the corridor and tensed. Trey had lifted the domed lid covering the plate and he was staring at the little round cake, iced with tiny violets and his name.

Athys thanked the goddess because Kester had agreed to spare one of the cakes baked for the Yule party that afternoon and personalise the icing. Trey slowly replaced the dome and Athys drew back. Did Trey like it? Did he think it looked mouth watering? After a few moments, the sound of a closing door reached his ears. He eased forward and was overjoyed to see the empty food table.

Trey had taken the cake into his room.

TWO HOURS LATER, Athys strode down a hall on his way to the ballroom for the Yule party. He'd missed the start, but he'd been labouring over a poem for Trey and for that very reason, he was certain the Queen would forgive his tardiness. Taking a reassuring breath, he fought his nervousness by stopping at a side lounge and checking over his outfit in the available looking glass.

He'd dressed as the Forest Lord and his outfit was in soft browns and leafy greens. On his head was a fitted headpiece made of small branches, a slightly tattered relic of a previous year, but still good enough to use. He adjusted the cuffs of his fine silk shirt, smoothed imaginary wrinkles from his heavily embroidered velvet tunic and reached lower to adjust the hang of his raw silk trousers. Finally he scanned his apple leather boots, ensuring they were still as spotless as when he'd put them on – just a few minutes previously. By the goddess, he was a mass of nerves.

Sighing, he turned and went on through the palace until he reached the ballroom and the queue of folk waiting for the herald to announce their names. He'd love to ease in quietly, but he was certain Queen Dianathke wouldn't like that; she loved the fussy pomposity of her parties and balls.

Finally he reached the head of the line. Junamia's clear voice proclaimed him loudly. "Athys Castniidae, Earl of Rengarth." She waved him through.

Standing to one side of the doorway, he scanned the massive room; the beauty of the decorations took his breath away. The Yule Organisational Committee organised by Trey had done a marvellous job. The walls were adorned with masses of greenery and offset with flowers, berries and ribbons. There were bunches of mistletoe positioned above every doorway and in all the corners. Swathes of net draperies were interspersed with beribboned pine swags, wreaths of grape vine, bowls of poinsettia and pots of huge cream roses twisted with trumpet lilies. The gardeners were a credit to themselves; he'd suggest Queen Dianathke thank them personally if she hadn't already done so.

He looked for Trey, finally locating him laughing and chatting with his friends Mikasi, Quanah and the young knight, Sir Kitkun. Once more checking his pocket for the newest gift, he turned their way and started to weave a path through the throng of partying Faefolk. To his annoyance, a giggling group of dryads gathered between him and Trey, bouncing and gyrating to the music being played.

"Hey Lord Athys, dance with us?" The dryads' many twiggy fingers clutched his arms, refusing to let go until he let himself be drawn into their dance. When he eventually managed to slip free of them, Trey and his group had gone.

Walking and searching, Athys slipped through the crowd until he found them in a corner. They were pointing at the mistletoe and making kissy faces at each other. Quanah bent in an attempt to kiss Mikasi properly, but she simply grinned as she spun out of reach. Then Quanah turned towards Sir Kitkun and held out his arms, but Kitkun shook his head. Athys glared. Quanah had better not think of kissing Trey. He strode forward.

"Hey, Lord Athys, could you further explain the lunging techniques we were working on the other day? Bonzo here says it works better if your feet angle like this." He demonstrated and Athys was suddenly caught up in the technicalities of training routines, exasperation at the three young knights for thwarting him eclipsed by his professionalism and genuine desire to help. When he was able to take his leave and move on towards Trey, it was to find he and his group had disappeared again.

He sighed, frowning as he looked around. A hand at his elbow startled him; Sir Cadbury, another of his oldest friends, smiled and held out a beaker of something. "Flamuisge to celebrate your recovery, Athys. Brilliant to see you healthy again, so quickly. I know you or Inca possess healing powers of some sort, but I'll let you keep your secrets." He winked. "Metal Creature almost did you in. If it wasn't for the bold actions of young Lord Treymeron ..." Sir Cadbury shook his head. "He's got a bad case of hero worship – very awkward for you, I'm sure."

Fists clenched, Athys didn't bother to restrain his sharp words. "You're wrong and I request that you *not* speak about Trey that way because, no, I don't find his feelings awkward." He glanced around, ensuring their privacy, and lowered his voice. "He's my mate, Cad, but he hasn't figured it out yet."

Sir Cadbury's eyes rounded. "Oh! My apologies. I meant no disrespect, Athys." He grinned. "That's marvellous. He's an amazing Faemale – a few unusual habits, but hey, who hasn't got some? I'm fully on board with accepting differences and idiosyncrasies after all of the years you've been preaching at us. Outward appearances can conceal a lot of valuable skills, even a wonderful personality, so ..."

Athys froze. How could he have been so stupid? Idiosyncrasies, differences and outward appearances?

Suddenly he knew what he had to do.

15

TREYMERON

Standing with his friends near the buffet tables, Trey didn't know whether to laugh or cry. "Can you see where he is?" Responding to his distress, Pinky nudged her head up under his hand clutching the edge of her satchel. His fingers slipped through her silky fur, her tiny mew grounding him for a few moments.

Then Kitkun nudged him, grinning. "Lord Athys has just gotten away from the three members of my training squad, but now Sir Cadbury has stopped him to share a drink and a chat."

Frowning, Trey glanced sideways. "Sir Cadbury? I wasn't aware he was part of our avoidance plan."

Swallowing a bite of fruit tart, Quanah laughed. "He wasn't, but it plays right into our scheme, so we'll take it."

Chest heavy and eyes burning, Trey stared at a platter of cakes, biting his lip as he thought of the single cake delivered to his room. These little cakes were iced and dotted with coloured sugar crystals, but they were nowhere near as pretty as the one Athys-Inca had left for him. The candied violets next to his name, swirled across the pale pink icing in loops of dewberry butter cream, had hit him where it hurt. He sighed. What was Athys-Inca trying to achieve with his – her – *their* gifts? Displeasure hissed bitterly from between his lips. He didn't even know the true name of the one he'd fallen in love with. And these gifts? Were they love, persuasion or pressure? He closed his tired eyes. "I don't know what the point of the gifts are."

One hand rising to rub his chest, Trey acknowledged he was heart-sick, mind-sick, brainsick – hell, just broken – without Athys-Inca or Inca-Athys. He'd deliberately stayed away from the library at night, only slipping in once, late in the afternoon, to follow up on a new idea. Standing in the foyer, he'd thrown out a quick 'metal' seeking spell – and been pleased to get a response. A single small scroll in language he couldn't understand. He patted the pocket in Pinky's carry bag, relieved to find the strangely notated paper still there. He must show it to Athys and— He sagged. "Blast it."

Kitkun's voice sounded near his ear. "I reckon they're apology gifts."

From his other side came the soft leafy rustle of Mikasi. "They could be, or what about love gifts?"

Reaching across in front of Trey, Quanah picked up some cheesy herb bread and shrugged. "They could be an apology, maybe he's courting you – the reason doesn't really matter. You told him you had to think about things and by giving you constant gifts he's ensuring you do. Look at you, Trey. You're miserable without him. Work out what you want before the pain you're broadcasting kills all of us."

Mikasi snorted. "Twiggy dry rot! Quanah, you heathen, we're not gonna die of lovesickness." She shoved his arm. "Because of course they're in love, but you think Lord Athys is courting? I didn't think of that. What about Lady Inca – she must be helping her brother. I'll bet she's the one giving him ideas. It's getting near evening so she'll be here soon. Are you going to talk to her, Trey? Maybe she can give you some helpful inside information about Lord Athys."

A fresh wave of unhappiness crashed over Trey, blurring his vision until he could no longer see the cakes. If they only knew the truth, but he refused to break a confidence, had only told his friends that he and Athys-Inca had quarrelled and he was taking a break to think about the reasons behind their argument. But what if—

A hand gripped his shoulder. "He's moving!" Kitkun's voice was a low hiss. "Looks like he's in a hurry, too."

"I told you." Mikasi spoke with a note of exasperation. "It's almost evening; he's probably going to meet Lady Inca."

Trey clenched his fists but held his tongue; he was safe from Athys-Inca but soon he'd be seeing Inca-Athys. He groaned – they were the same entity, so what the hell was he talking about? Ickle-bloody-golia, how did this two-natured thing work? He didn't really want to avoid them at all; he wanted to run straight into their arms and speak of love, hear of love, talk about forever. Instead they were doing this crazy dodge and chase because – because ... He swallowed. Because he'd seen something he hadn't expected and hadn't known how to handle, so he'd fled.

He swallowed again, throat tight. All along Athys-Inca had preached acceptance of differences because they were different too. Even more, they'd revealed their nature to very, very few – and why was that? The truth smote Trey like a thunderbolt. They were afraid of not being accepted, just as he had been, and when they'd told him, what had he done? Run like a frightened rabbit.

Trey scrubbed at his eyes, feeling sick. Sure he'd a right to his feelings, but when had he considered theirs? Because, in telling him, they'd stripped themselves bare, offered their secret on a platter ... another truth forced a gasp from his trembling lips. Wow, they really did love him and they'd showed that love further with the little gifts – Trey would treasure that amateur line of poetry forever. A tiny smile crossed his lips. It was time to stop running, time to face up to his love and sort things out. He fisted his hands and turned.

Quanah was craning his neck to see over the crowd. "No, Mikasi, he's not leaving the room; he's going the other way. Look at him churning through the gathering! A male on a mission, that one. Now, he's reached the dais and gotten Queen Dianathke's attention."

Kitkun tipped his head to one side. "Wow. Look at the expression on the Queen's face."

A low whistle came from Quanah. "She looks stunned. Wait, she's smiling and patting his arm. She's signalled her herald."

A knowing descended on Trey like crystals of snow, shivering him all the way down to his toes. "No, wait! We've got to talk." He whipped Pinky's bag off over his head and handed it to Mikasi. "Here, hold Pinky for me!"

With urgency filling him, he pushed into the crowd, twisting, dodging, slipping sideways past groups of Fae-folk, mumbling apologies to those he collided with, but all the while making a beeline for the dais. He kept going when the notes of Junamia's horn wound through the room and she made her announcement.

"All embrace silence for the words of Queen Dianathke." The room of Fae-folk quieted and the Queen's tinkle of laughter embraced the lull sweetly.

Forced to halt, Trey was yet close enough to have a clear view of the dais. Their Queen stood near the edge of it and aimed a brilliant smile into the throng. "I'm pleased to see everyone enjoying themselves. Lord Athys and his assistant Lord Treymeron have worked hard to organise this event and many of you helped them bring their plans to reality. I thank everyone for that help, but now, Lord Athys wishes to speak. He is well known to all of you and a friend to many, so I hope you will all listen, as this subject is close to his heart."

Pale but looking determined, Athys-Inca stepped up to flank the Queen. "Your Majesty is most kind." He shook his hands out and cleared his throat, then offered a thin smile. "You may have already guessed the topic I wish to speak of: acceptance of our differences. No matter who or what we are, we all deserve to be accepted at face value and not judged. We are Fae and the name covers a very broad spectrum of folk."

Peering closely, Trey noticed the drops of perspiration appearing at Athys-Inca's temples. Holding his breath, he eased forward another pace as his love continued.

"I have preached this for years—" There were a few groans and mumbles from the crowd, but Athys-Inca held up their hands to quell the noise. "I know, I know – you're tired of hearing me say it. Fair enough, but tonight I am going to reveal why this subject is much closer to home, for me, than any of you had any idea of." He moistened his lips. "I'll try to be as brief as possible. When I first left my homeland, it was because I'd been found too different for even my unusual people and pushed out of society. Arriving here after many adventures, I found a place, and other Fae-folk, with whom I enjoyed being. I was welcomed, invited to stay, and worked my way through various occupations until reaching my current position." He swallowed. "But I did that without revealing my true nature – the reason I was rejected by my own folk – to anyone but our two Queens and the one or two very close friends I made."

Murmurs of interest and speculation filtered through the room. Trey, his belief of what was happening confirmed, eased forward another step. Throat dry, he twisted his fingers together. A gesture reflected in the movement of Athys-Inca's hands.

"In truth, I was afraid of rejection; it's a foul thing to push folk away based on looks, mannerisms or even behaviours resulting from physicalities they were born with. Thus did I begin to champion anyone who needed it, and to advise any folk perpetrating such rejection that their behaviour was neither welcome nor acceptable. I have become known for my stand, and I always planned to reveal my true nature, but the time never seemed appropriate and, as the seasons passed, it became easier to leave things as they lay." His mouth twisted. "Fear is powerful, and given even more power when you don't face it head on, don't release the poison it engenders. So this was the position I placed myself in and how long it would have continued, I don't know … But recently, something changed for me."

He rubbed his chest, something Trey totally identified with – his own was tingling like crazy. There were a few gasps, but otherwise the room was silent, all eyes trained on Athys-Inca.

He smiled. "I fell in love. So deeply in love that my life has been turned upside down and inside out. Unfortunately, I botched up the revelation of my nature and left my love feeling shocked, terrified and betrayed. I didn't blame him when he told me he needed time to think about things. When I thought about how I'd carried out my plan, I believe I too would have reacted as he did but, because he distanced himself from me, I was wretched. Even Her Majesty took me to task and told me to fix it."

Queen Dianathke wrinkled her nose. "Don't even try telling me you didn't deserve that little punch I gave you."

Rubbing his forehead, Athys-Inca grinned. "I won't." He turned back to the rapt and silent crowd. "I made a plan to woo my beloved and arranged a series of little gifts for him. It was encouraging when he didn't refuse them, but the situation remained unaltered."

Eyes wide, Trey's hands flew up to hide his trembling lips. Athys-Inca *had* been courting him!

"It was only this evening I realised that I couldn't reconcile with my love and expect him to live the lie my life has become, that I understood I have to back up my beliefs and my teachings by sharing my true nature with everyone." He paused and drew a very deep breath. "So. This is it." He scrubbed a hand through his hair, glanced at the nearest window and grimaced. "The shadows lengthen; I must hurry. I am of the Twahirren-fae. For those who don't know, all Twahirren have one body but that body has two faces. I am no exception to that rule, but what got me thrown out is that, where the dual nature of other Twahirren is same sex – that is, two male entities in one form – I am two different genders." He stared at the watching Fae-folk expectantly; they stared back, making no sound.

He gestured at himself. "Here you see me: Athys Castniidae, Earl of Rengarth, but even my name isn't quite correct." He drew himself up proudly. "I was born, and named, Athys Inca Rengarth. My second physical form is female, but she is still me, only you have all known her as my sister, Inca. I have no sister and she has no brother – we are one entity, one form with two different faces. I have the face and form of a male in daylight, but at night, I change shape and become my female form, whom you all know as Lady Inca. At dawn and dusk, I change to and fro between my dual faces; in the one shape I am fully male and in the other I am fully female, but it is still me, Athys Inca Rengarth. There is actually no 'Inca' – all I did was use my second given name to hide my secret and I took the name Castniidae to fit in with other Lepidopter-fae."

Many Fae-folk were now gaping, exclaiming, calling out questions, but they quietened when Athys held his hands up. "I can only apologise for my actions. I meant no ill; I was simply afraid. As it is now almost time for my change and I am no longer intending to hide who, or what, I truly am, I'm just going to lie down here on the dais, let my change happen and the action will, hopefully, answer all your questions."

A sob shook Trey – Athys had already answered all of his questions, all bar one. Another sob escaped him, carrying the word with it. "Why? Why do this?"

A tall, stately Fae-female next to him smiled sympathetically. "Many Fae-folk get a little crazy when this happens to them."

Trey dashed his tears away. "C-crazy? What do you mean? When what happens to them?"

Her smile broadened. "Why, when Fae-folk find their mates, of course."

The universe collapsed on to Trey, planets and stars a dizzying whirl across his mind. "Mate?" He swayed, the stars aligned and suddenly the accuracy of her words smacked him right between the eyes. "Oh my goddess, we're mates!"

16

ATHYS

rey's words rang clearly through the hushed chamber and Athys homed in on his voice, spinning to seek him out. Both hands across his mouth, Trey stood to Athys' right in the third row back from the dais. Athys knelt down and extended a hand towards him. "Yes, my beloved Trey, we are indeed mates."

The crowd parted, creating an open avenue between Athys and Trey. Weak smile dawning, Trey moved hesitantly forward and accepted the proffered hand. He gulped a couple of times before he found his voice. "You've already worked it out – thank the goddess. I was so stunned the words just burst from my unruly mouth. I was terrified I'd broken the law."

Hands trembling, Athys drew Trey up on to the dais before him. "No laws broken, my adorable mate. Not one." Holding Trey's hand firmly in his, he smoothed his other palm up Trey's arm to his shoulder and across his back, drawing Trey into his arms. To Athys' delight, Trey responded by pressing himself close and sealing their lips together.

The kiss was as warm and wonderful as Athys remembered. Eyes closed, noses rubbing as they tilted their heads, he enjoyed the added deliciousness of Trey's sandalwood, sage and lime scent wreathing up

312

around him. His heart thudded wildly as he took his time sampling the smooth firmness of lips eagerly moving against his own. Then Trey nipped at his lower lip and Athys readily opened his mouth for the teasing thrust of Trey's tongue, meeting it with the warmth of his own.

The sudden tingling in his feet told Athys the sun was about to set. He drew his tongue from Trey's willing and addictive mouth, dropped a kiss on the tip of his nose and rested his forehead against Treys. "Sorry, sweetheart, but my change is starting."

Trey's eyes opened wide. "Icklegolia! We need to get you lying down then. Come on, I'll help." He looked around, then tugged on Athys' arm. "Holy snapping swamp turtles! We're the centre of attention!"

That was when spontaneous cheering, applause and hearty shouts of congratulations broke out. Athys couldn't help himself; he laughed.

Queen Dianathke prodded his shoulder. "Excellent work! You've provided a wonderful highlight to our Yule celebration – it'll definitely eclipse tomorrow's mummery." She smiled widely at a suddenly uncomfortable Trey. "A true mating is always inspirational. Now, I'm sure you'll want to keep Athys company during this. Yes?"

The tingles were spreading upwards. Athys swayed. "I need to lie down."

The Queen pointed. "I've arranged for a daybed to be positioned just there." It was arranged near the edge of the dais further to the right and near the wall where the dais ended. "I had it placed to your specifications; it's where anyone may come to view the proceedings if they so wish, but not stuck out in the open as to be fallen over by revellers. And, it's wide enough for Trey to sit or lie with you as he desires. So come along and let's get you settled."

Nodding in relief, Athys allowed Trey to support him. He was surprised when another large form flanked him, tucking a shoulder under his, on his other side. Fighting to hold off the change until he'd lain down, he glanced sideways.

Sir Cadbury glared at him. "What a gobsmacking fool you are! Fancy thinking any of us would be unable to accept you and your twin nature when most of us would die for you. Just as we know you would for us."

From Athys' opposite side, Trey pointed. "No talk of death, Sir Cadbury – though I take your meaning. But nobody's dying today, or anytime soon. Athys and I have just found one another; we've yet to complete our mating ..." He trailed off, a blush crawling up his neck and into his cheeks.

Athys managed a soft laugh as he dropped on to the daybed. It was covered with a plush, navy and maroon velvet quilt, which felt heavenly to his weary body. Ignoring the gathering onlookers, he stopped the fight to hold back his shape-shift and let his consciousness fade ...

WHEN HE CAME TO, only six Fae-folk were gathered around him. Well, five really, because Trey was sitting cross-legged on the bed, holding his, no, *her* hand, with Pinky on his lap. Athys allowed her gaze to drift over Trey's friends: Mikasi, wearing Pinky's carry-bag, was in between Quanah and Sir Kitkun; next was Sir Cadbury and finally Queen Dianathke.

The Queen nodded firmly. "There you are, Athys. You're well?"

Her croaky reply emerged in a soft voice. "Yes, thank you, Your Majesty."

She stooped and patted Athys' cheek. "Good. Now you can relax, because while your change was certainly show stopping, nobody ran screaming in disgust or terror. Indeed, the prevalent consensus of opinion was about how stupid and ridiculous your Twahirren-Fae tribe were, to expel you from their midst. A judgement I heartily agree with, but that narrow-minded belief resulted in an action for which I will be forever thankful, because you came here, where you, and what you do, are priceless." She patted his face again. "Have a little something to drink, perhaps a bite or two of food." She winked, her glance moving between both Athys and Trey. "Because as soon as you're feeling up to it, I'll get the musicians to play the Rhynfallia mating dance for you to partner each other in." Turning, she walked back towards her throne, her hand raised to signal a page to attend her.

Sir Cadbury drifted closer. "Well, as usual, Her Majesty is a force of nature, but she was correct. From what I could see, not a soul had anything bad to say about who and what you are."

Athys blinked. "Are you certain?"

Sir Cadbury nodded. "Absolutely."

She dragged herself to a sitting position, anxiously assisted by both Trey and Sir Cadbury. She grinned. "Relax, you two – I've done this zillions of times."

Raising an eyebrow, Sir Cadbury smirked. "Zillions?"

Athys tuned a hand palm upward. "Well, twice a day for my entire life – surely that counts as zillions?"

Bending forward, Trey dropped a light kiss on her mouth. "That depends on how old you are, my love. However, he's right, Athys. Lots of other guards have reported in, offering to help guard you, and they all said that same thing. Folk are annoyed about how you were treated and, apart from being fascinated, couldn't give two owl hoots about your dual nature."

Nearby, Sir Kitkun hovered with a tray containing food and drink; Quanah had a second tray while Mikasi stood between them, arms folded. She was nodding. "The only annoyed people were us, on Trey's behalf. He told us you'd had a disagreement, but he wouldn't tell us what it was about, so your shape-shifting nature was a huge surprise." She glanced at Trey. "I just don't understand why it upset you to the level it did, Trey."

He grimaced and parted his lips, but Athys spoke first. "Because I took him to my rooms to watch the change without telling him what would happen. He had no idea – then I shifted in front of him and he discovered two folk were actually only one."

Quanah swallowed, hard. "Good heavens! That was harsh."

Looking to Trey, Athys met his love's forgiving amethyst gaze. "You're correct. I was an idiot. After he got over the shock, he told me how disappointed he was in me, said he had to think and left me wallowing in my stupidity. I deserved it, but I was miserable and hopeless until Queen Dia bopped me with her fist and told me to get my act together. That's when I began planning my gifts." She shot Trey a wink. "Sorry for my rotten poetry."

Staring down his nose, face pink, Trey shook his head. "It's not rotten, I treasure every word of it. Now get some of this food and drink into you – we have a dance to perform."

Chuckling, Athys checked out the two trays, then her eyebrows shot up. "I can't possibly eat all that food!"

Mikasi laughed. "It's not all for you – we thought to share your little supper, and Quanah is a bottomless pit."

Quanah frowned protestingly. "Hey!"

SO THEY DANCED, performing the pair-bonding dance in front of the entire attending court; twisting, turning and whirling in the elegant Rhynfallia all Fae-folk learned – some as children, some as adults. It was played at every ball or revelry, sometimes for fun and practice and sometimes for a mating. Athys and Trey only broke eye contact when one or other of them followed the pattern of the dance into a spin and thus it went on, until the music swelled towards the final stages of their mating dance.

Riveted by Trey's graceful swirls, the lithe fluidity of his supple body and her own utter joy as her mate swayed back into her arms, Athys couldn't hold her words in. "You're adorable, Trey, and I'm so in love with you."

Her love's steps never faltered, but the blown kiss, the blushing, shy smile blooming on Trey's delicious mouth, was equally as joyous. "My Athys. You're every dream I never thought to have fulfilled."

Lost in each other, they leaned into the final glide, their wings mantling as the pattern of the dance required. Trey's were the sooty charcoal, splotched with violet, cobalt, green and cream, of his Lepidopter swallowtail heritage, while Athys flashed out her Twahirrenstyle wings of sunlit gold mixed with splashes of lunar silver. Blue eyes aglow, she smiled, her outward breath a gust of happiness. "How did I get so lucky?"

An enormous smile wreathed Trey's features. "I'm the lucky one." He leaned forward, pulled the neck of Athys' jerkin and shirt aside and blew a small stream of purple flame across, what felt to Athys like her collarbone, as he created his mating mark. Athys stood very still, pleasantly surprised to discover the flaming wasn't the least bit painful. It even tickled.

When Trey eased back, Athys grinned. "What did you mark me with, my love?"

Trey's answering smile was gleeful. "The outline of four winged hearts, purple like my magic. Each one carries at its centre one letter of my name."

Athys cupped the back of Trey's head and placed her other palm at Trey's left temple. "I love it." She drew on her power, her thoughts full of her sun and moon/gold and silver duality and the perfect image sprang to her mind. When she removed her palm, a yin-yang-style golden sun and silvery moon graced Trey's temple. Leaning forward, she kissed the mark. "Now you wear my sun and moon for all to see."

Smile wobbly, Trey bit his lip. "I couldn't think of anything more you."

A hand clasped Trey's right shoulder and Athys' left one. The Queen's smile was as radiant as theirs. "I am pleased to see this day for one of my oldest favourite courtiers and one of my newest. You, Trey, are so right for Athys and now, I believe there's only one thing left to do – you've claimed each other in front of witnesses, danced the Rhynfallia and shared mating marks – that leaves the blood exchange."

Facing a smiling Trey, Athys closed the small gap between them to lightly kiss, then nibble and nip at his lips, one of her fangs nicking the fleshy fullness; she eagerly licked up the slight well of blood. Seconds later, she thrilled at the tiny sting from one of Trey's fangs piercing her lower lip. When Trey sucked it into his mouth, his tongue laving up the answering bloody trickle, Athys closed her eyes, savouring the resulting heady zing of their blood tie taking effect.

Queen Dianathke's voice rang out, amplified by her magic to reach all corners of the massive chamber. "Having fulfilled the requirements of our bonding rituals, in front of us all, on this wonderful Yule eve, I declare and recognise the true mating of Athys Inca Castniidae, Earl of Rengarth and Lord Treymeron Cosmo Aphiski, henceforth to be known as Earl Consort of Rengarth. I am certain that all here join me in wishing them a long and happy life together."

And everyone did. The cheering, shouting and applause was deafening. Athys was glad of Trey's support as the acceptance of herself, of Trey and of all she'd championed flowed over her in such overwhelming waves, her knees wobbled. She found her equally shaky voice. "This is amazing."

Trey leaned in and kissed her lips. "No, it's you who is amazing, my Athys. Just you."

THEY EXITED the ballroom in the early hours of the following morning. Midnight had brought the traditional Yule celebrations to their Goddess, Aine-Holly, and her consort Cernunnos, The Green Man, at the Winter Solstice with darkness at its peak. From this night forward, the days would once again grow longer and the night hours reduce.

Athys gripped Trey's hand. "I've never had so much mistletoe held over my head in my entire life as this one night."

Trey laughed softly. "The kisses were more than worth it. I think …" He fished in Pinky's satchel, careful not to disturb her slumber. "Yes, a piece of mistletoe has been stuffed in here as well." Athys snorted. Trey nudged her. "Don't pretend you're not happy; I can feel the truth through our mate-link."

She grinned at Trey. "Our mate-link – such a beautiful combination of words." Her grin faded. "Something I'd begun to despair of achieving, thanks to my idiocy."

Trey held up a finger and wagged it. "Ah, ah, ah. We've sorted all of that out. Let it go and take me to your rooms so we can banish the bad memory with good ones."

Athys increased her pace. "You have such brilliant ideas and – they're *our* rooms now. We can move your things afterward."

Trey's eyebrows waggled. "Afterward?"

Athys chuckled. "Well, after you and I've recovered from boning each other so much we can't walk."

Trey increased his speed, tugging Athys along with him. "Now that is a most excellent idea, my love. Walk faster."

By the time they reached their quarters, they were almost running and they'd laughed so much, Trey's breath was coming in gasps. Athys unlocked the door, dragged Trey inside, then lifted Pinky's bag over Trey's head and tucked the little duskit carefully amongst the sofa cushions.

Trey checked to ensure she could comfortably breathe, stroked her sleeping head lightly, then turned to stalk Athys, pushing her against the bedroom door to indulge in another kiss. Leaning back, his hands smoothed over Athys' midriff and continued upwards. "I love how firm and muscled you are even as a Fae-female."

Athys grinned. "Just as well you do because if you wanted voluptuous curves …" She shrugged. "I don't have them."

Tugging at her clothes, Trey shook his head. "Don't care. I fell in love with your Fae-male form first, then, when I thought you were your own sister, I fought against my attraction to two different folk, but couldn't help admiring how alike you are in build."

A look of wonder filled her face. "Most males don't have a taste for solid, small-breasted females."

It was Trey's turn to grin. "Such a female is perfect for someone who enjoys both sexes but has a leaning towards males. I think you're hot in both your forms." He flicked the latch on the door and walked Athys backwards to the bed. "Time to get naked."

Athys' under-lash glance was sultry with promise as she removed her clothes, never taking her eyes off Trey as he dispensed with his. When she held her hand out to him, Trey grabbed it eagerly and moved with her to fall onto the bed. He twisted beside her, but she rolled on top of him, her lips snaring his in a fiery kiss.

Full of love and desperate with desire, Athys wound fingers into Trey's dark locks and tangled their tongues together. Trey's palms caressed her skin, his fingers shaping muscles, cupping her bottom and stroking up her back. His touch made her feel good, better than good; it had her thrilling to the understanding that she was wanted for herself. She was finally able to accept she'd found the place and person to whom she belonged and it was time to show him that he was perfect for her too.

Kissing and licking her way from his mouth to his neck, then lower to his chest, their lovemaking developed into a loving tussle as his lips and tongue adored her skin in turn. They rolled to and fro, each of them seeking to explore their mate. Every lick, every kiss, every nibble, every caress of fingers and hands on nipples, drove their desires higher. Then Athys wrapped her hands around Trey's cock, chuckling as his eyes rolled back in his head and he let out a gasping groan. Her hands slipped up and down, using his leaking pre-cum to ease the glide of her palms. "I think I win this round."

Trey's eyes snapped back open. "Shut up and ride me, mate – we're not in a competition." Even as he spoke, his fingers slid between them, into the wetness between her thighs, to find and finger the stiff nubbin of her clit until she began frantically lifting herself so he could stuff his cock where they both wanted it. While he pushed up, she shoved down, both of them crying out their pleasure as his cock hilted itself, snug and deep, inside her. Then they were lost in a storm of thrusting and writhing, their bodies sliding up and down, in and out as their mutual enjoyment built, second by second.

Brilliant blue eyes meshed with violet as their loving lifted them to the heights of rapture, gripped them with paralysing force and flung them into a maelstrom of delight. Waves of spasming bliss overcame Athys, and she felt her violently aroused sex grasping and releasing Trey's deliciously plunging cock in joyous frenzy, until he gasped beneath her, clutched her hips firmly, pressed his head back into the pillow and came, splashing his seed deep inside her. When their tornado of passion gradually subsided into a state of blissful contentment, Athys collapsed over Trey and they hugged bonelessly while lovely aftershocks continued to shudder through both of them.

Finally lifting her head, Athys smiled into Trey's glowing eyes, ran a finger across his adorable mouth and sighed. "I've been carrying a hard-on for weeks, from the moment our eyes met and you toppled over backward, giving me a marvellous excuse to get my arms around you."

A sappy grin widened Trey's lips. "You too? Wow. The moment our gazes met I thought I'd been struck with an axe handle; your brilliant golden male beauty stunned me. Then I met you as you are now and your glowing silver radiance simply took my breath away."

She grinned back. "I couldn't stay away from the library at night, knowing you were there. It's been so difficult not sharing my dual nature with you – I wanted to confess from the start, but I couldn't understand why, until us being mates dawned on me."

Trey shook his head, the pillow rustling beneath him. "I was so pulled to you, so in love with you, but I didn't work it out until that Fae-lady I was standing near said that new mates often acted a little crazy – and that axe handle walloped me again." He chuckled. "I loved those nights we shared in the library." He glanced up under his lashes. "Actually, I love the library – Oh! Athys!" A babble of words spilled from him. "During our, um, separation, I went to the library and cast a metal-seeking spell. A single scroll was revealed. It was tied with the Sand Seers red ribbon, denoting a prophecy, but it was in a language I couldn't read. I gave it to the Queen while your shift was taking place. She said she was sending our otherworld guest across to Castle Synternesse and she'd send the scroll as well – the paper will likely be given to Tindresse to unravel."

Satisfaction filling her, Athys nodded. "That's good news. Now we just have to keep watch for Kellay Metal Creature – it's strange he hasn't attacked since the night of the Fae-rade."

Trey yawned and his eyes were heavy. "Yeah, he's licking his wounds, I reckon."

Athys rolled to one side, enfolding Trey into her arms. "You're probably correct." She kissed Trey's mouth, then the tip of his nose. "You're tired, beloved. Just relax and sleep; I've got you."

Eyes closing, Trey's voice was a soft whisper. "I thought we could share more loving …" His words faded and his breathing deepened.

Resting her forehead against Trey's, Athys smiled. "We will, my love, we most definitely will." Outside the window, a bird sang to welcome the dawn and Athys recognised the familiar tingle starting at the soles of her feet. She smiled and relaxed into her change.

They'd face the new day and a whole new life, together, as mates did.

GLOSSARY

Note: This series is speculative and based in Faery – a land I call the Fae Demesnes. The family around whom the stories are based are Lepidopter-Fae: that is, Fae-folk with butterfly/moth wings. Other Fae races also exist.

Main characters in this story:

- Lord Treymeron Cosmo Aphiski – Fae-lord from the Papillion family of the Lepidopter-Fae.
- Earl Athys Inca Castniidae – Fae-lord, formal title Earl of Rengarth, claims to be from the Castniidae family of the Lepidopter-Fae, but actually from a rare race of the Fae called Twahirren; first appeared as one of Queen Maerovana's guards in Book 2 *Ancestors and Expectations*.

Treymeron's Parents:

- Duke Papillion – Yanvian Cosmo Aphiski
- Duchesse Papillion – Azura Gracilla Neptulide Aphiski

His siblings in birth order: (for more information, see Main World Glossary)

- DeMaksim Yanvian Aphiski – Main character of Book 2: *Ancestors and Expectations*)

- Lyssica Fern Aphiski – Main character of Book 3: *Blizzards and Beginnings*
- Janeska Lyria Aphiski – twin to Tindresse
- Tindresse Azura Aphiski – twin to Janeska
- Treymeron Cosmo Aphiski
- Armelle Gracilla Aphiski
- Zhulija Juniper Aphiski – Main character of Book 1: *Filigree and Fate*
- Eskander Keyvan Aphiski

Mates and consorts of Aphiski siblings so far:

- Cherith Vanitheriel Beriaden – Main character of Book 2: *Ancestors and Expectations*; DeMaksim's mate/consort
- Dario Calaspon Eribifax a.k.a. The Unseelie Beast; Main character of Book 1: *Filigree and Fate*; Zhulija's mate/consort
- Kynthlord Emryn Arion Phengaris / Kynthcat – Main characters of Book 3 *Blizzards and Beginnings*; Lyssica's mate/consort

The Fae Queens, cousins who decided to unite the Queendom and rule jointly:

- Seelie Queen Dianathke Morgana (Palace of Elrodel)
- Unseelie Queen Maerovana Titania (Castle Synternesse)

Other characters:

- Ackerly Cabbegoth (Sir) – male knight/guard at the Palace of Elrodel
- Anthracite – female troll blacksmith in Elrodel Village
- Byue Tanetzotl – male dark elf
- Cadbury Janusidae (Sir) – male knight/guard at the Palace of Elrodel

- Chetanzi Ambiiday (Sif) – female knight guard at the Palace of Elrodel
- Frith Limacodi (Sir) – male knight/guard at the Palace of Elrodel
- Harlyn Chantuzidae (Sir) – male knight/guard at the Palace of Elrodel
- Junamia – Queen Dianathke's herald at the Palace of Elrodel
- Kazembard – male dwarf baker in Elrodel Village
- Kellay – Metal Creature
- Kester – male kitchen brownie at the Palace of Elrodel
- Kitkun Oloden (Sir) – junior male knight/guard at the Palace of Elrodel
- Lanvig Cecidos (Sir) – male knight/guard at the Palace of Elrodel
- Marda – female house brownie at the Palace of Elrodel
- Meilani Tenekarx (Sif) – female knight/guard at the Palace of Elrodel
- Mikasi Opostidae – female dryad who always carries a seed pod from her tree with her; apprentice gardener at the Palace of Elrodel.
- Myrtis – male herbalist in Elrodel Village
- Nasper Immaday (Sir) – male knight/guard at the Palace of Elrodel
- Novnea Tolderoth – Arikini of the dark elves of the mountain fortress of Delgado Medea; male
- Nutley – male kitchen brownie at the Palace of Elrodel
- Pinkerpush – female duskit; Trey's companion
- Quanah Ethmidae – strapping young Fae-male apprenticed to
- Verdigron, the castle's weapon master (a higher-rank blacksmith)
- Tanda Vendagyre (Sif) – female knight/guard at the Palace of Elrodel
- Metal Creature – alien attacker; Kellay

- Varli – female house brownie at the Palace of Elrodel
- Verdigron Ypsoliday – male blacksmith specialising in weapon mastery
- Vinny – stable youth at Papillion
- Volpiere – male fox
- Zett of Berengaria – captured offworlder

Terms:

- Arikini – dark elf chieftain, can be male or female
- Scintilla – a dark elf military grouping
- Sir and Sif – male and female titles for knights/guards
- Fulgar blade – lightning blade

Foreign language phrases and meanings:

- *Da mihi portam potestatem* – Latin for: "give me the gate power"
- *Scis quis ego sum?* – Latin for: "do you know who I am?"
- Kellay, *quare non audies nos?"* – Latin for: "Kellay, why won't you listen to us?"
- *Quia ego non amo te verbum!"* – Latin for: "Because I don't like your words."
- *Quid accidit ut* Kellay?" - Latin for: "What happened to Kellay?"
- "*Si tu nocere ei...*" – Latin for: "If you've hurt him ..."
- "*Et cucurrit tunc. Porcos.*" – Latin for: "He ran then. Swine."
- "*Eius*" – Latin for 'her'

Places:

- Cache of Laltahini – tomb of an ancient and famous, dark elf wise woman
- Castle Synternesse
- Delgado Medea – fortress city of a race of dark elves

- Elrodel Village
- Oxidean Lake – lake adjacent to Delgado Medea
- Palace of Elrodel
- Papillion Duchy
- Vansitarkan Badlands

Other races:

- Dark Elves – skin grey-blue, hair deep blue
- Dracons
- Eldwytch mages
- Goats – Munster, Mork and Menace belong to Anthracite, the troll blacksmith in Elrodel
- Redcap goblins
- Trolls of various types,
- Shapeshifters of various types
- Shapeshifter Sand Seers – folk of the Changeling clans who practice
- divination
- Undines, type of water-Fae
- Vart-demons – type of demon
- Water-Fae of various types

Various animals, including some I have invented for my own purposes:

- Blush-cheeked chirpers – little birds
- Devil-rabbit – an evil rabbit, minion of The Bodach
- Duskit – a purple blue multi-coloured little creature. Cross between a kitten, a squirrel and a possum: Treymeron fosters Pinkerpush; Yanvian fosters Dash, Splash and Crash
- Fox – one named Volpiere is partnered with the dark elf, Byue Tanetzotl

- Kynthcat – lion-like cat with a mocha coat, chocolate mane, pale glowing eyes, gnarled, curving horns and a whip-like tail with a fluffy tip
- Vulpiawolf – a type of wolf with a spiky rough body pelt, legs without fur and a spiked tail tip. They're greenish grey in colour and smell like wet fur.
- Wood bunnies – as opposed to just bunnies or rabbits.

There are also appearances by Goddesses, Gods and their consorts in some of the stories, although none in this story. See main world glossary for more information.

ALSO BY HELLUCY HOWE

FILIGREE AND FATE

Dario and Zhulija's story in:

A Perfectly Paranormal Valentine

ANCESTORS AND EXPECTATIONS

Cherith and DeMaksim's story in:

A Perfectly Paranormal Halloween

BLIZZARDS AND BEGINNINGS

Lyssica and Emryn's story in:

A Perfectly Paranormal Easter

MISTLETOE AND MEDDLING

Treymeron and Athys' story in:

A Perfectly Paranormal Christmas

ABOUT HELLUCY

Meet Hellucy Howe, a Book Dragon who teethed on romantic fairy tales and went on to voraciously devour anything paranormal. Writing was also second nature but became something to do in secret when the stories of her young child mind were ridiculed. Homes were populated with books and hidden caches of story notebooks inspired by a fertile brain and a massive creative streak.

She became a Professional Reader and a Closet Scribbler, convinced no one would want to look at the mad ramblings of someone who hates getting dirt under her fingernails and knows ironing was invented as a torture method.

Nowadays, Helen loves inventing paranormal and fantasy romance from the comfort of her cosy study with a hot cup of tea beside her laptop and her little spaniel, Lexie, snoring at her feet. With her anthology contribution of 'Filigree and Fate', Helen was dragged kicking and screaming from her closet, into the deer-in-headlights world of being a Real Author.

And if you want to get to know the Perfectly Paranormal Anthology authors a bit more, get sneak peeks of what's coming up for the APP Anthologies, as well as giveaways, special offers and just some PNR fun, then join our Perfectly Paranormal Paramours Facebook Group.

Find us here:
https://www.facebook.com/groups/251663560162131

ACKNOWLEDGMENTS

My heartfelt thanks go to the other authors in the APP anthologies - Samantha, Marnie and Leisl - for your continuous encouragement, professional advice and wonderful friendship.

With the help of all of you, a goal I'd never thought to achieve, and had actually struck off of my goals list, has come to pass. I'm eternally grateful for your persistence, ladies, and drinks are on me. ;-}

HEARTS CURSED

LEISL LEIGHTON

HEARTS CURSED

A Gods Cursed Novella
Book 4

Leisl Leighton

Published by Leisl Leighton as Permien Press. For more information, email: leisl@leislleighton.com

First published 2022 in the A Perfectly Paranormal Christmas Anthology.

Cover design – Samantha Marshall

Editor – Marnie St Clair

Formatting - Leisl Leighton

❀ Created with Vellum

ABOUT HEARTS CURSED

Cursed to live alone, fated to be blood-bound ...

After being trapped in the HeartsBlood Gem for almost 3000 years, Ilia Silvia is pissed. She'll never be so needy or naive to trust any of the Gods again. Not only that, once she's finished helping Korinna and Tamuel, the witch and the cupid who freed her, she plans on finding a way to take her revenge on those who betrayed, trapped and used her.

But first, she must separate her life-force from Dawn, the baby who made her corporeal with her powers, and help find Korinna's long-lost father Triptolemus – oh, and avoid all the Christmas cheer that sets her teeth on edge. Three seemingly impossible tasks. Until she realises the man she's been having sexy dreams about just might be the answer, even if he is wearing a Santa suit.

Trip O'Dem has lived without a memory for over 2000 years. All he knows about himself is that he enjoys farming, is immortal, and can grow things with his blood. It's been a lonely existence, except for Christmas time, when he truly comes alive. Then he sees a 'Christmas angel' in his field and starts having non-stop sexy dreams. Dreams that also indicate *she* is the answer to the mystery of who he is. Problem? She seems to hate Christmas, and there is a fury inside her so great it threatens to swallow them all whole.

Surely it's nothing that a bit of Christmas spirit won't be able to handle? But there is more at play than he knows. Will their cursed hearts betray them, or will a Christmas miracle save them all?

DEMETER'S SACRIFICE

"*I* do not wish to do this, my beloved boy."

Triptolemus' eyes met Demeter's, steady and sure as ever. "You must, D. You know it is the only way."

"But I do not wish to lose you," she said, hating the quaver in her voice. If it was anyone but he, she would smite them for witnessing her weakness.

"I will still be here."

"But you will not be you. And you will not know me. You will know nothing."

"I will know this." He gestured to the snow-laden pine forest around them, his expression peaceful.

To her, in this moment, the prettiness of the green frosted branches of the conical-shaped trees wasn't peaceful at all. It was a slap in the face given the ugliness of what she must do with the spell they'd crafted.

He sighed, turned back to her and said, "My need to do my work will remain. It will be enough."

"Will it?"

"It must be." He swallowed hard, stood tall, chin raised, vibrant green eyes full of all the love and life and giving that was so much a part of him. A part of him she was about to steal away. "Do you think I wish to leave my beloved when I know my disappearance will hurt her beyond endurance? To leave before my daughter is born, to never know her, not even at such a time she is strong enough to utilise her powers and endure the burden of foreseeing in a way even Cassandra could not?"

He took a deep breath, but not soon enough to cover the throb of grief in his voice; a throb she wished she could take away but couldn't. Not for him; not for her; not for any of them. Because he was right.

They had to do this.

He continued calmly when most would fall prey to their emotions – including her. "I wish I could stay. I wish this burden was not ours. But you cannot unsee what you saw. And I cannot allow myself to be used by one of the Old Gods for such ill purposes." He took a shuddering breath, shoulders straightening further so he looked like one of Ares' soldiers. "Promise me you will make sure my beloved does not suffer."

"I promise."

"And promise me you will look after Korinna like she is yours."

"Persephone will take her as one of her Soteira. She will want for nothing. And we will ensure she is hidden for as long as we can."

He nodded, then looked away over the snow-tipped pine trees surrounding them, before, fists clenched at his side, he said, "Do it now, before I change my mind."

She lifted her hand to start the spell, but hesitated. Instead of touching the edges of her magic, she reached out to touch his handsome face, to glory in the spring green of his eyes – a green that represented his ties to her and Persephone and Gaia, and marked him for this fate.

They'd tried everything to change the path of destiny that led to the future she'd seen – but the power fed into him, that caused his birth, had been warped by Perses' ancient curse, and nothing could undo what had been done except for this. "I vow, with all the love for you I have in my heart, that I will find some way of bringing you back to us."

His eyes widened. "No! I do not ask that of—"

But the Eternal Well had already heard her vow, the rolling knocks in the distance cutting off his protest.

Tears filled his eyes. "What have you done?"

"What must be done to ensure a happy ending." The rolling knocks were a sign that the Eternal Well had accepted her vow, had written it into the Halls of Power and tied her existence to its fulfillment.

"But there is no happy ending if you die."

She smiled softly as she cupped his face one more time. "My dearest boy, the son of my heart if not my body, have some faith in me."

Then, because she could stand the torture of this goodbye no longer, she cast the spell they'd created, taking everything from him that made him who he was except the power in his veins and the immortality that would forever mark him as different from all humans on this Earth he so loved.

A difference that would see him wander, a lost soul, never able to settle in one place for long, never to belong, eternally hearts cursed and lonely because of a cursed prophecy.

It was the only thing that would keep him safe. The only thing that would keep his daughter safe until she was ready.

The spell made him jerk and clench his teeth, frothing at the mouth for interminable minutes until, finally – thankfully – he passed out.

She caught him, cushioning his fall, laying him in the cold snow under a large pine tree next to the bags of coin that would help him in his new life. After making certain he was safe under the shielding branches and wouldn't be covered in the snow now falling from the sky, she turned and opened a portal to her home.

She stepped through and immediately knelt down beside the pond of foreseeing she'd had Cassandra make for her before the other woman's constant foreseeing had driven her insane. Until Korinna was born and grew old enough to handle the power of foresight that would be hers, someone among the pantheons must still be able to see and understand and try to stop the danger that was coming for them.

Not that anyone but she, Persephone and Triptolemus believed in what she'd seen.

Her brothers and sisters and all their children were nothing if not consistent in their belief that they were untouchable. As far as Zeus and Hades and the others were concerned, they had defeated the Old Gods once, and were certain they could do it again even if one of them did make it past the Void. The Gods and Goddesses of other pantheons were no better in their egotism.

They relied too heavily on Cassandra and the Fates.

Idiots, all of them!

They went on and on about the hubris of humanity, but honestly, hubris, thy name be … insert any name of any God or Goddess that ever was or ever would be!

They were concerned only with their power and how to hold on to it.

So, short-sighted. But she wasn't. She had seen the future and couldn't deny it.

She waved her hand over the waters of the pond, looking, searching to see if her actions today had created the change they desired.

The dark future was still there, but it was fogged, parts of it flickering and changing over and over as the echoes of her actions affected the ripples of time. And there was a coming birth, not long after Triptolemus' baby girl was to be born, whose life seemed twined with hers. She would need to dabble in that boy-child's life and the life of his parents to ensure a favourable outcome. She sighed. So much to do.

She hoped it wouldn't be too little too late. She wished she could talk to her Triptolemus. He always made her feel better. Her chin wobbled. "Please, Eternal Well, don't let the sacrifice my beloved boy made today be in vain."

There was no sign her plea had been heard, but then, that wasn't really the way the Eternal Well worked. Still, she wouldn't stop praying to it. Even a Goddess as powerful as she was needed to pray to something.

Roping her thoughts back in, she stared at the ripples before her.

There was a face in the water now. A woman's face. The image glowed strangely – first blood-red, like the gem she'd wrested from Tiberinus a century ago, then changing to the colours of dawn. Could this be the soul trapped in the HeartsBlood Gem? Is that why she'd been so determined to take it? She'd never quite known what to do with it, having no interest in the prophecy that tied the soul inside the gem to God Killer powers. She'd put it with the rest of her collection of powerful gems and trinkets. Perhaps she needed to look at it again.

As she watched, the ripples from that image bled out and linked with the ones of Triptolemus' fate.

The soul in the gem and her precious Triptolemus were linked in some way.

How, she didn't yet know, but it was something when she'd had nothing before. Something that might help her fulfill her vow despite the unfortunate prophecy. Now, she just had to figure out how she could use it to her advantage while bypassing that particular prophecy.

She had no plans to die now or in the future.

She had to see this war with the oncoming darkness that was Perses through to its conclusion. A conclusion she would force to go her way, even if she had to sacrifice her heart.

1

Ilia sat bolt upright, hands clutching at her chest. Her heart thundered under her ribs – so hard, so fast, it felt like it might tear itself in two. "Fuck-fuck," she gasped, blinking sweat from her eyes – or was it tears?

Both. "Fuck."

Her chest was hot. She looked down to see glowing pinkish-gold light. It had to be Clodia, the evil ancient witch now trapped in the HeartsBlood Gem she'd melded into her chest months ago.

But how could the bitch-witch be doing this? It had taken Ilia centuries of being trapped inside the gem to figure out how it worked, and centuries more to be able to affect the person wearing it. There was no way the evil old witch could have discovered those secrets so quickly and used them against her.

So what the fuck was this?

"Wait a minute." The gem usually glowed red, not pinkish-gold. Maybe this wasn't Clodia. Maybe this had something to do with her newly acquired powers.

She still knew so little about them. Her own powers – part of the reason she'd been blood-cursed into the gem in the first place – had been burned out after fighting Clodia in the Void. These ones had

349

been gifted to her when Tamuel's use of an ancient spell from the Eleusinian Mysteries Grimoire and Dawn's burgeoning powers, so incredibly strong even though she'd just been born, had given Ilia a corporeal form.

It still made her shudder that part of that spell had used blood magic. All those times Tam had used the sigil spell, she'd never realised it used blood magic, even though the sigil had to be carved into the skin. There were many spells that only worked if made a part of the worker in some way. The blood was just a by-product of the carving – or so she'd thought. But when he'd used it on her – as it had always been meant to be used, to make a worthy spirit corporeal – she'd realised just how important the blood was in the working of the spell. She'd been so shocked – and it had happened so quickly – she'd not been able to stop him. Then after, she'd been so overwhelmed by the new life she'd been given, everything she'd lost a fresh wound in her heart, she'd barely been able to say anything.

Then, after they'd got home and she'd come to terms with what had happened, it had seemed churlish to make a fuss when Tamuel's intent had only been good. As had Korinna's use of blood magic with the Eleusinian Mysteries Grimoire and the ring she'd got from her long-lost father. Although, from what they'd been learning, that had more to do with the qualities of their blood being magical. So it wasn't really blood magic in the way she knew – and hated – it. It was something else entirely.

But blood magic – it wasn't good. Look what it had done in this instance – tied her to the baby whose magic had been instrumental in letting her live again and in getting them out of the Void.

Thinking of it made the power in her chest flare brighter.

Fuck. She put her hand to it, feeling its warmth, its urgency. She couldn't go out there like this. The others would worry – and they already worried enough.

She had to think of something else.

The dream. Yes. Her dream. She needed to try to remember it. It had felt important.

She closed her eyes, breathing slowly, bringing the feeling she'd woken with back to the fore.

Fragments of her dream fluttered to life, but stayed foggy and elusive. All she could grasp was that it had been a thing of import – a great hope and a terrible loss.

She gasped, eyes snapping open. The dream must have been about her sons.

But why could she not remember?

She hissed a sound of frustration. She wanted to remember. Her memories of her sons, in the brief moment she had with them before they were torn from her because of some stupid prophecy, were all she had of them.

That and the fact she had failed them by trusting in the wrong God.

After both Mars and her uncle's betrayals, she had stupidly trusted Tiberinus when he said he could help her find her sons. Desperation, innocence and gullibility had worked together to make her agree to give her blood to the River God. He said he would use it to help track down the She-Wolf who had taken her sons after her uncle had ordered them – and her – killed because some idiot had intoned a prophecy about them that made them a threat to his rule. Instead, Tiberinus had drunk of her freely given blood to sever her soul from her body and tied it to the powerful gem he was desperate to use, but couldn't without a living soul inside it – a soul that must be hers, he'd told her, because of the incredible untapped power she held inside and the prophecy.

At the time, she'd assumed he meant the one about her sons, but she'd later come to realise it was another one about someone known as the God Killer. Somehow she was tied into that prophecy, although she still had no idea why. Even with the strength of her powers, she couldn't kill a God – much to her disappointment. It would make revenge so much easier if she could.

Of course, the fact she was nowhere near powerful enough to kill a God hadn't mattered to the Fates or Tiberinus, and she'd been trapped inside the HeartsBlood Gem for thousands of years. Her one hope had been that, one day, she'd come into the possession of Tamuel and Korinna, the two lovers who were the key to her freedom.

She snorted. Some freedom. It, like everything else in her life, had come with a catch. In this case, a baby-sized one and the tether that tied them together.

It could be worse. She could be tied to some arsehole God. At least this way, she was tied to gorgeous little baby Dawn, who she'd come to love. Even though every moment spent with her was like a stab in the heart because it reminded her of how little time she'd spent with her boys.

Remembering them was a joy, but also a terrible, unbearable pain. Pain she clung to with everything in her despite the fact that her failure to find them and stop their bleak future from playing out, one killing the other in the name of power, plagued her sleep.

She lifted a shaking hand and roughly swiped at the sweat on her brows, the tears that wet her cheeks and dribbled off her chin. "Enough sitting here thinking about a past that cannot be changed," she said into the silence of her room. "I've got work to do and a future to plan for."

An image of a man – the man she kept dreaming about – swept across her mind. Her heart throbbed with a knowing: somehow he could heal her of her pain.

She blinked, forcing the image away, lip curling at the stupidity of such a romantic thought. The only person who could heal her pain was herself. And she didn't want to. Because if she did, she might lose the very thing that kept her going day after day – her need to find those responsible for all that had happened to her and make them pay.

It had been so satisfying taking down Clodia and trapping her in this gem. She wanted to experience that feeling again.

The thought made her heart thunder; the glow in her chest brightened.

Damn it!

Taking herself in hand, she breathed deeply, slowly until finally – finally – her heart stopped thundering and the glow in her chest faded.

Now the only glow was the one that the sunrise – shining its rays through her bedroom window – gave to her skin. Thankfully, the dawn light that had glowed from within her after her 'birth' had ceased doing so months ago. It had been awkward leaving Stevens' House radiating like a sunrise. But then, that was the price you paid when an ex-Cupid and a powerful newborn baby witch used an ancient forbidden spell and their magic to shove the power of Ostara, Goddess of Dawn (among other things), into you to turn you from a spirit into a living, breathing being with a power she couldn't quite yet control.

But she was learning. Speaking of which, she better get on with her day, because Korinna and Tamuel would need more leads to follow to try to find Triptolemus. Despite what she'd been able to share what she'd overheard when in Demeter's possession about the reason Triptolemus had been stripped of his memories and hidden, they still knew so little. Every lead she found had turned up nothing more than a confusion of myths and legends that didn't lead to where he was now or how they might get his memory back.

Korinna was handling it well, but Ilia knew the other witch was upset over their lack of progress. Not to mention, the thing that had escaped from the Void at Easter was still out there and, while they guessed it had something to do with the danger they faced, they knew precious little else. It hadn't made itself known to them yet – but it would, and when it did, they needed to be ready.

The only way they could be was if they found Triptolemus and helped him gain his memories back. What she'd overheard Demeter say had been clear on that at least.

Typical, the Goddess hadn't said anything more helpful they could really use to track him down. But then, when was the last time a God or Goddess had ever been helpful?

She sighed.

So, a lot to get on with today. Not to mention, she still hadn't found anything useful about how to break her connection with Dawn. Except of course, the entry in the grimoire she'd read months ago that suggested blood magic would do it – that it would create a bond that would snap and supplement the life-force bond she shared with Dawn under certain circumstances. What circumstances, it didn't say. Not that she would ever consider using it. Who knew what more it might do to that precious little baby? Blood magic always asked for a price.

She shook her head to dispel the unpleasantness and threw the covers back. She needed a hot shower and a nice hot shot of espresso and then she could get on with her day.

Twenty minutes later, after the shower had beat the trembling from her muscles and the cold from her bones, she dried and dressed herself. There wasn't much she could do with her waist-length dawn-gold hair, darkened into an almost normal light brown by the water. It would spring into a riot of unruly curls the minute it started to dry, so she tied it into a messy knot and headed downstairs.

Her pink bunny slippers slapped quietly on the carpet runner of the stairs. It always made her smile when she shoved her feet into them. She wondered if Tamuel had known it would when he gave them to her not long after they returned from Roma at Easter. Violetta had been appalled by the gift, telling him it was inappropriate given how and when Ilia had been brought back to life, but Ilia didn't think so. She was with Tamuel. It was kind of funny how grotesquely cute they were – virulently pink with ears so floppy they flipped around wildly when she walked.

She bent, giving the ears a little pat as she made it to the bottom of the stairs, then straightened and stopped dead.

"What the Hells!"

It looked like the house had vomited up Christmas decorations. There was a massive pine tree opposite the front door, its limbs reaching up to the vaulted ceiling and decorated with bows and baubles and lights. If this wasn't enough to scream 'Christmas is coming!', wreaths had been hung and wound around every available surface, lights twinkling in their faux-pine depths. It was then she noticed a wreath with colourful baubles, bows and lights had been wound around the staircase banister. She'd been so busy staring at the bobbing bunny ears on her slippers that she somehow hadn't noticed.

"Hells."

Tamuel had said Jules was mad about Christmas, but she hadn't thought it would be like this. Jules had been too ill and tired with morning sickness last year to do more than slap up a few decorations and a small Christmas tree. Although, she had forced Bas, Tamuel and Korinna to watch multitudes of candy-cane sweet Christmas movies with her. Given Ilia had been trapped in the gem, which at the time had been fixed inside Tamuel's chest like it was in hers currently, she'd been privy to everything he saw. Unless she purposefully tuned out, she'd had no choice but to watch. Tam had said she should tune out if she didn't like it, but given she only had the energy to do that for short periods of time, periods she kept for when Tam and Korinna had sexy times together – which was a lot! – she hadn't had the energy to withdraw for so-sickly-it-made-her-want-to-vomit movies.

The only one she could stand had been Scrooged – that Bill Murray was kind of cute in a scruffy way and it was pretty funny when he was being slapped around by the tiny and violent Ghost of Christmas Present.

Not to mention, she could kind of see his point of view. Of course, that was before he'd turned into a sap at the end of the movie, got his second-chance love and learned his lesson, which he then proceeded to share via a lecture to the viewer, as if they hadn't been able to figure the moral out themselves.

Socrates had a bloody lot to answer for when he introduced moralistic thought to the world.

"Bah humbug!" she muttered to the cheerily blinking lights surrounding her before stomping down the hallway.

It too had Christmas cheer in abundance, as did every room she passed. Was there no place she could escape to except for her bedroom to get away from all this? Maybe the kitchen—

"Hells," she muttered again as she stopped in the kitchen doorway.

It hadn't been spared from the Christmas 'cheer' as she'd hoped. All around her, wreaths and twinkling lights hung and there was a veritable elves-reindeer-Santa palooza on the dresser *and* the window-sills by the breakfast nook. "And I'm expected to eat in here?" she muttered.

"Good morning. Say morning to Aunty Ilia, Dawn."

She whipped around. Jules stood at the kitchen sink, baby Dawn in her arms, waving at her. Well, not so much of a baby anymore – she was almost eight months old.

Trying not to wince at the Christmas apron Jules wore, which bore a winking cartoon Rudolf with the words 'Naughty *and* Nice' under him, Ilia forced herself to enter.

"You're up early."

"Not really." She always woke at sunrise, even now the days were getting longer and daylight came earlier and earlier.

"You're the first to see all the Christmas decorations," she said proudly. "What do you think?"

"Umm … None of this was here last night before I went to bed."

"I know. I wanted it to be a surprise for everyone," Jules said, satisfaction filling her voice. "I got up during the night and used my magic."

Ilia gasped. "You didn't just … poof this into existence, did you?" Because if she had, that meant Jules had more than Goddess-given powers. It meant she had the power to create worlds. And destroy them.

Jules chuckled. "My bank account wishes I could! No – I bought it all. Haven't you noticed all the packages arriving over the last few months?"

"Nope." She'd been too busy trying to find a way to separate herself from Dawn and to help Korinna and the others find Triptolemus. "I've spent most days down in the library."

Jules threw up her hands. "You see! This is exactly why I wanted to do this. We've all been so busy concentrating on finding the elusive Triptolemus, we've forgotten all about why we're doing it in the first place."

"I thought it was so he could tell us what big bad is coming for us and how to stop it. And to help undo the blood-curse on his and Korinna's magic."

"Well, that of course. But isn't it also to preserve this?" She waved her hand around.

"What? A home?"

"No … well yes. And all it encompasses – family, friendship and love."

Which is exactly why she hated it – it reminded her of everything she'd lost and was never to have.

Jules didn't notice her bleak expression though, her attention on Dawn as she jiggled her up and down, making the baby giggle. "But I meant we also need to preserve fun. We need to celebrate the joyous things, otherwise, what's the point of living?"

Ilia really didn't have an answer to that – living for her had just been existing for so long, and still kind of felt like that, despite the new life she'd been given.

Jules tipped her head and shook it sadly. "You see! You need to be reminded about fun."

Ilia glanced around her. *This* was fun?

Jules waved her hand expansively. "Et voila! Great start, isn't it?"

Start? This was just a start?

"I have so many fun activities planned leading up to Christmas." Activities? She hid her shudder as Jules spun around and said, "What do you think?"

"It's …" She swallowed hard. "Very bright. Cheery."

"Oh, I'm glad you think so. I wasn't certain the tree in the foyer was big enough or that I'd hung enough lights."

"No, there's enough. Of everything."

Jules beamed at her. "I love Christmas so much."

"Really?" she drawled. "You wouldn't be able to tell from this."

Jules laughed and said, "I know it's a lot … but go big or go home, right?"

"Umm … right. But … I thought witches were supposed to celebrate Yule."

Jules made a pffing noise. "Given I didn't have any power for most of my life, I missed out on all the things the rest of the Coven enjoyed this time of the year – especially heading OS to where it's cold and snowing so they could properly do all the rites and rituals. So I took Christmas as my own." She reached for a bowl as Dawn jigged in her arms, the baby almost knocking the rice cereal onto the floor.

Ilia rushed forward and grabbed it before it landed. "I bet your Coven wasn't happy about that."

Jules took the cereal from her then pulled a face. "Thanks – and no, they weren't. They gave Violetta a really hard time for letting me get so invested in it, but she never let that stop me. She wanted me to have something that was mine, so she did all she could to celebrate with me."

"That was nice of her."

Jules nodded. "More than nice. It showed me how much she loved me, which was the best present I could have every year. And now I have my magic, I can go to town like I've always wanted. I can't wait for Dawn to see the choo-choo in the lounge room. And if you like the lights in here, wait until you see what I've done outside. I think it's pretty special."

"Must be," Ilia said, thinking she'd have to wear very dark sunglasses if she was to venture outside any time in the next month. "Umm, does the Christmas cheer extend all the way down to the library?" Hells, she hoped not.

"No." Jules grimaced. "I tried one year to put a Christmas tree down there but the ghosts kept stealing the decorations and hanging them off the chandeliers and turned the tree into Yule logs which they shoved into various corners, so I never tried again. Although, now I have my magic I might be able to set a spell that stops them. Do you think I should?"

"No!" Jules blinked at the almost-shouted word. Ilia smiled hastily, trying to cover. "I mean, you don't want to upset the ghosts or your Coven do you? The library is a witching space, so maybe it's best not to open that can of worms."

Jules sighed. "You're probably right." She glanced around and smiled. "Maybe I'll just put a few more decorations in here to brighten it up a little more."

A little more? If it got any brighter, she'd have to start wearing sunglasses in here too. But instead of showing her dismay, she turned to the coffee machine and said, "Now you have your powers, shouldn't you give this away and embrace Yule as the rest of your Coven do?" She glanced up to see Jules staring at her.

"Are you crazy? And miss all this?" She gestured at the house around her.

"Of course, what was I thinking?"

"How could I deprive Dawn? I want her to have the best of both worlds. Besides, it's just so joyful."

"Yes." The kind of joyful that shoved itself down your throat and choked you. But she couldn't say that to Jules or give away just how much she didn't like it – Jules had been so wonderful to her since Oestra, helping her in many ways to acclimatise to this new life and being so good about the fact Ilia was linked like she was to Dawn. She'd also been a great learning partner, given both of them now had magics they'd never had use of before.

All the Stevens had been amazing in fact. She'd sooner eat one of the Christmas wreaths than hurt any of them with how she truly felt about anything.

Just then Dawn leaned out of her mother's arms towards Ilia, making grabbing motions with her hands. Jules laughed. "Can you hold her while I finish getting her rice cereal mush ready? She's extra impatient for it this morning – mummy's breast milk just wouldn't do, would it, Sweetums?" she said to the baby, rubbing noses with her, making Dawn chuckle. Then the baby leaned away and put her hands out towards Ilia once more. Jules laughed. "So impatient."

"As Her Majesty dictates," Ilia said smiling. She took the baby, holding her close, breathing in the delicious scent of her – powder and breastmilk and something greener, fresher and incredibly warm; a smell that she could only describe as of the dawn. Which made sense given the Goddess' star she was born under and the reason for the name she'd been given.

"Why so hungry this morning?" she asked as she jiggled the baby.

Dawn lifted her chubby hands and cupped Ilia's face, looking up at her out of her big, indigo eyes with the gold of dawn's light flickering in their depths. Then she shook her head, expression serious in a way that only a baby with her magical heritage could.

"So this impatience isn't about hunger?"

She glanced at her mother – busily pouring boiled water into her dried cereal. She made a little sound of longing.

"So you are hungry?"

A nod. Then those remarkable eyes met hers again and she shook her head quickly.

"Ah, but it's not *all* about hunger?"

Dawn tipped her head, little mouth screwed sideways as if considering the question, then tapped her head.

"You had a dream?"

A shake. Then she touched Ilia's brow and cocked her head in question.

"My dream?" An enthusiastic nod. "You want to know about my dream? But I can't remember." Even as she said it, images flickered to life in her mind. Not of her sons as she'd thought the dream must be about, but the man who featured in her dreams more and more often.

In her mind she saw him now as clear as day, the man waking in a snow-frosted pine forest, confusion and pain on his handsome face; walking aimlessly, heavy bags slung over his shoulder as he tried to find shelter and answers; falling into a depression when no answers were forthcoming, his efforts to remember only bringing incredible pain that drove him to unconsciousness time and time again.

Time passed, dark and bleak, with him wandering, lost, alone, bereft – oh, how she knew those feelings! Time shifted again before the memory of them could grab too tight a hold, then the image stopped, to show him being given shelter by an impoverished farmer and his family; it showed the moment when he'd touched the few seeds the farmer had left to him, dried husks that would never have grown, but at his touch, sprang into seedlings and multiplied. And with their growth, a new passion inside him was born.

After helping the farmer and others sow the seedlings into one bumper crop after another, the man had to strike out on his own when the community realised he was not aging and that his talent with growing things had more to do with magic than a green thumb. Despite the help he'd given them, they'd come after him with pitchforks.

These scenes were repeated over and over in different places, a flickering cascade of images that made her slightly nauseated. Then it settled into an image of him wearing light khaki shorts, a dark blue t-shirt, feet encased in heavy work boots – modern clothing – as he worked under a hot sun, sweat glistening on his brow.

She swallowed hard. "Are you seeing this too?"

A firm nod.

She wanted to ask why the baby saw the man too when she never had before, but the questions that popped out were, "Who is he? And why do I keep seeing him?"

Dawn blinked at her, then flattened her hand against Ilia's brow.

The kitchen swirled around her, fading to nothing. She was flying high above the ground.

No, not flying. Falling.

The ground rushed up to meet her.

She screamed as she fell into the dream she'd woken from that morning.

rip looked up as a scream echoed across the hills. Birds, squawking and flapping, flew out of the nearby trees to circle above the field he worked. Something had disturbed them, but he couldn't see what. The scream could have been possums in heat – they did make a horrible sound. Although, they usually kept their activities to night.

The scream didn't repeat and the birds settled down into the trees on the other side of the field, so Trip shrugged then arched to stretch his back. Sweat stung his eyes – he wiped his arm across his forehead but the sweat was back a minute later.

He swiped at it again, then dug the fork into the soil. It slipped in his hands. He wiped them on his jeans, ignoring the slight sting. It didn't matter. Nothing mattered but getting this field finished.

More sweat stung his eyes. This time, he lifted his shirt and rubbed it over his face. As he lowered the shirt, his gaze caught on his watch.

Shit! It was well after lunch. Daphne should be back by now with the emptied trailer so they could do another load before she left to pick up her youngest son. Where was she? He had more than a full load for her. Not that it was enough. The flooding river had dumped so much rubbish into the field.

Why the fuck had the flooding rains come now? And right after the hail that had ruined his orchard, stripping it of fruit and leaves. It was perfectly biblical. What was next? A plague of locusts?

No. He wouldn't let any of this ruin his appreciation of the season.

Christmas.

Just the thought of the coming season made him smile.

He loved Christmas. Learning about Christmas and helping to spread the joy was the second bright light he'd had after waking to this memory-less existence, with only the bags of gold left beside him and the clothes he wore as clues to who he might have been. He'd long ago stopped trying to push past the pain that came every time he endeavoured to remember – a pain so terrible, he'd inevitably pass out. Trying to remember only led to frustration and depression. He'd almost given up on everything at one time, but thankfully he'd stumbled on the fact he could make things grow and help people with that talent. He always had to move on before those he lived near realised he wasn't aging and that his talent was fuelled by magic. But it made life bearable.

It was lonely though. He could never get close to anyone. It hurt too much when he moved on. But then he'd discovered Christmas, and it was something that helped him get through the rest of his year. The thought that, for this short period, he could be with people and share in the fun and the joy ... it was magical.

It's why he'd started up his Christmas tree farms all those centuries ago. It meant he could keep that feeling with him all year. Even in this country where the seasons were all turned around and it was summer when it should be winter.

It was beautiful though – although not right now, after the mess Mother Nature had dropped on him a few days ago.

He glared at the ruined field. Then up at the sky.

It was crystal blue, not a whisper of the storm that had caused the disaster in this newly sown field. Just the sun, beating down on him mercilessly as he worked.

But that was the weather here all over – unpredictable. Even after ten years of living on this farm in the Central Highlands of Tasmania, he hadn't got used to it.

He still wasn't sure why he'd come to a place where it rarely snowed and was hot at Christmas, but he had. The feeling inside him, the one that always told him it was time to move, made it impossible to go anywhere else. So he'd journeyed here and bought a derelict property and turned it into a successful Christmas tree farm; one of only three in Tassie.

He also grew other seasonal produce and had a good fruit orchard too.

Or *had* had a good fruit orchard. Many of those trees had been stripped of leaves, fruit and buds by the storm. It would take months to repair the damage. He'd planned to get started right after he fixed this field and planted the pine tree seedlings that were slated to be his crop of Christmas trees in four to five years.

Which was why he had to get this done soon. He didn't want to miss the summer growing season. If he did, he'd have nothing but four footers to sell in four years' time.

Which wasn't at all acceptable!

He was known for his six to eight footers. He couldn't give his customers less.

He ignored his stinging hands and the ache in his shoulders from hours of digging and carrying and dumping the stones and rocks and other debris scattered across his field and returned to work.

Not long after, a rumbling jangling sounded behind him and he turned to see Daphne driving up in his ute with the now empty trailer.

She waved at him and smiled. And even though he was hot and sweaty and not a little annoyed at having to be out here doing this when he should be tending to the trees they were going to sell this year, he smiled and waved back.

Daphne didn't deserve his grumpiness. She'd lived a hard life and he was happy to do anything he could to make it a little easier. After her shit of a husband had just up and left, taking their life savings with him, leaving her with two young boys and another on the way, she deserved every good thing he could do for her.

Given his situation, he knew he shouldn't have let any of them get so close to him, but after coming across her labouring so bravely alone in the old stockman's cottage with no power or hot water, her boys crying because they didn't know what to do, he had to help. Then it had just seemed natural to renovate the stockman's cottage to make it a lovely place for her and the boys, and to offer them jobs because they needed them. The closeness thing had just kind of happened without him realising.

Now he had Daphne and her boys in his life, he couldn't imagine having to do without them. Although, sometime in the next five to ten years, when they noticed he wasn't aging, he would have to tear himself away from this little accidental family.

It would tear a hole in his lonely heart.

He would grieve their loss, but he would move on. He just had to hope he had as long as possible with them and didn't give himself away before then.

Thankfully, the magic that lived deep inside him and seeped out into the growing things around him, helping them to thrive, did so in a non-flamboyant way. A way that in this modern world where people didn't believe in magic anymore, he could pass off as a very green thumb. People didn't blink over the furfie he told over a secret fertiliser mix that helped his Christmas trees and other produce grow so quickly. They just kept trying to get him to sell his secret formula, and took any advice he gave when he refused to sell it to them.

The ute pulled up beside him and Daphne hopped out, her brown bob glinting in the sunlight. Instantly her hands went to her hips and she scowled at him. "Trip O'Dem! Did I not tell you stop and drink a bottle of water before I left with that last load? Just look at the state of you."

Oh crap. He'd forgotten about the water the moment she'd driven away. He'd just wanted to get back to fixing his field. He had to start the planting. Had to. He was running out of time.

"Did you even drink any of the water in that bottle I gave you?"

He grimaced a smile at her. "Umm, maybe." He'd meant to take a mouthful, but given how dry his mouth was, not to mention a little lightheaded, maybe he hadn't. When the need to work came on him, it kind of took over. It was difficult to explain that to other people, especially Daphne, who seemed to like to mother him as much as she mothered her boys.

She reminded him a little of someone, but he couldn't think who. Maybe his own mother.

He winced as pain spiked through his head at the thought of a woman he couldn't remember. Thankfully Daphne didn't see it – she had bent to swipe something off the ground.

She straightened, and, with thunder in her eyes, shoved it in front of his face. "No, you didn't. It's full. See! You just dropped it on the ground the moment I left, didn't you? Without even opening the cap!" She shoved the bottle into his chest and let go – he had to drop the fork to grab it. "Well, why are you staring at me like that? Drink up. The whole thing. And I expect you didn't stop to eat the sandwiches I packed for you either?"

He looked sheepishly at her as he unscrewed the cap on the bottle.

She sighed loudly then poked a finger at him. "How you managed to survive before I came into your life, I have no idea."

"Neither do I."

His words seemed to placate her, because her mouth twitched as if she was fighting not to smile. Hands back on her hips, she said, "Well. You need to eat. Now."

"I'd just like to finish—"

"I'm not going to let you load up the trailer until you do." She shook her head at him.

"You don't need to baby me," he said, then took a swig of the water. Gods, the cool wetness felt so good sliding down his throat. He swallowed convulsively.

"If you don't want to be treated like a baby, then perhaps you should act your age."

Easier said than done, given he'd never met anyone else who was well over a couple of thousand years old – at least, he guessed he was

– and so had no benchmark to judge how someone his age was supposed to act. So he mostly just tried to act like a thirty-something human man, which was the age he resembled.

He finished drinking the water, wiped his hand across his mouth and held out the empty bottle. "Happy?"

She rolled her eyes and pointed at the Esky she'd placed by the fence that morning. "Sandwiches."

Knowing it was pointless to argue, he went to the Esky, pulled out the Tupperware container – it contained two big sandwiches filled with ham, cheese and salad, just the way he liked it – put the lid back on the Esky and then used the sturdy container as a seat.

He bit into the sandwich and couldn't help the groan of pleasure that rumbled in his throat.

She threw him an 'I told you so' smile along with an eyebrow twitch that said, 'but what did I expect, you male-idiot', and then went to work, picking up the smaller branches and rocks and putting them in the trailer.

By the time he'd finished the two sandwiches, she'd cleared half of what he'd freed from the mud and was trying to drag one of the bigger branches over to the trailer.

"Here, let me get that." He reached for the branch.

She dropped it. "Oh, Trip. Your hands!"

He looked down. They were red-raw and blistered. No wonder they stung. But he'd been so focused on work, he hadn't even taken the time to look at them. "They're fine," he said. And they would be. He healed quickly. But that wasn't really the problem right now. He couldn't let the blisters pop or his skin crack and bleed. It would be disastrous if it did.

He'd been careless. Stupid.

He stomped over to the ute and pulled his thick work gloves out of the glove box. He should have put them on this morning, but he'd been too focused on getting started and hadn't thought beyond that. Thank the Gods Daphne had noticed now. He hated to think of what might have happened if she hadn't.

His blood should never come into contact with soil. It was another thing he didn't know the why of, just the certainty of the unfortunate consequences that would follow if it did.

It was the reason he never forgot his gloves. Even his preoccupation with getting to work shouldn't have made him forget. It was too important. So why had he?

He didn't know.

He really wasn't himself today.

"Trip, what are you doing?" Daphne grabbed his arm as he pulled on the second glove. "You can't be thinking to do more work!"

3

$\mathcal{T}$rip stared at her as if she was the one being unreasonable. "Of course I am. This field needs to be cleared and then ploughed and the soil prepared so I can plant the seedlings by the end of the week."

"You can't do all that in a few days! Especially with those hands. You need to come back and let me clean and put some salve on them. Then rest for a day or two. When Charlie gets back from Launceston with the replacement fake-snow making machine, he can take care of this."

"No. I need to do this now." He yanked his arm from her tenacious grip, ignoring the look of worried confusion on her face. "Just let me work." He stomped to where he'd dropped the fork.

"But … what's the hurry? If you don't get it done until next week or the week after, it will still be fine. We'll still have trees in four to five years, especially given how good you are at growing them."

"No, it has to be done now." He grabbed the fork and shoved it under a rock, groaning at the effort to lever the bloody thing out of the sucking mud.

"Trip! Stop."

"I can't."

"Why?"

"You don't understand."

"No, I don't. Why don't you tell me?"

He opened his mouth to explain, but all he could do was make a croaking sound. Because he couldn't explain. He just knew it had to get done. He was running out of time. "I just … I just need to get back to work."

"Trip!"

"Isn't it time to go pick up Gideon? Don't you need to take him to basketball practice?"

She glared at him. He glared at her.

Finally, she threw her hands up in the air. "I give up. Fine. Let those blisters pop. Get sepsis. See if I care." She stomped off across the field towards the far gate – it was the closest one to the stockman's cottage, which was nestled in the hill just beyond the neighbouring field of Christmas trees. As she got to the gate, she turned and shouted, "Just don't come running to me when you wake in the night with a fever and need help."

"I won't," he shouted back, knowing that, of course, in the event of that unlikely scenario, she would come running faster than a speeding bullet. Superman had nothing on her when it came to helping others.

The woman truly was a gem.

She opened the gate, then slammed it behind her, the clanging sound of metal against metal making birds fly up out of the nearby gumtrees in a flurry of squawking and flapping wings.

Daphne didn't even look up at them as she disappeared amongst the Christmas pines that were for next year's buyers.

Trip grimaced. Crap. He'd really upset her. He'd have to do something nice later. He'd think over what while he worked.

Shoving his hands more firmly into the protective barrier of the gloves, he got back to it.

He filled the trailer, made a run to the empty field behind his house where they'd dumped the rest of the stuff – he'd keep the wood for a bonfire for winter and maybe build a fence from the rocks? – then returned with the empty trailer and kept going.

The sun seemed to get even hotter as he made two more runs with a full trailer before returning to finish the last of the clean-up. His shirt was wet with sweat, his hands were stinging inside the gloves and his socks were so wet he was certain his feet were turning into prunes inside his boots. At some stage though, he thankfully stopped sweating. Although, his mouth was incredibly dry. He should stop and have one of the bottles of water Daphne had left. He'd grab one after he cleared this section.

He dug the spade into the soil, but almost fell as the world swayed before him, the horizon shimmering in a way it shouldn't at this hour of the day. Shadows had grown long across the paddock and the heat of the sun had faded. He stood there, clinging to the spade, suddenly burning hot and yet shivering at the same time. And his tongue felt large and sticky, almost like it didn't belong in his mouth.

Crap! His thoughts were sluggish, but not so much that he didn't realise what he'd done to himself. He was seriously dehydrated. He needed water. There were more bottles in the Esky. Which he'd put in the ute after he'd eaten. He just had to make it there.

He made it a couple of steps, using the pitchfork to steady himself as the world wheeled around him. Almost there. Just had to round the trailer and get to the door.

He stumbled on the overturned earth he'd worked earlier, arms pinwheeling as he tried to re-balance himself. But he bounced into the wheelbarrow he'd left leaning against the edge of the trailer, tripped over his own feet and smacked his head.

The loud dull clang of head hitting the side of the ute rang through the twilight around him as he stumbled. No, no, he couldn't let the blood-soaked kerchief hit the soil.

Somehow, he managed to catch himself on the trailer before he fell to the ground.

He stood there, shaking, taking in deep, unsteady breaths. Head spinning from the knock, he steadied himself and stared at the horizon to try to settle his vision. He couldn't pass out here – there was no phone reception and Daphne wouldn't be back for hours to check on him.

He tried moving, but his head rang and something wet dripped across his eye and onto his cheek.

Shit, no!

He grabbed his kerchief from his pocket and pushed it against his forehead, willing the bleeding to stop.

But it didn't and the kerchief was soon soaked through. He shoved it in his pocket and hauled his t-shirt off – a more than exhausting exercise, indicating just how badly dehydrated he'd let himself become – and pushed it against his head. It wasn't good enough. Blood dripped onto his chest.

Hells. He couldn't let it touch the ground.

He had to move. Had to get in his ute.

Using the trailer as a guide, he edged his way forward slowly. The world flipped sideways. The pressure in his head increased. He kept going.

A breeze had blown up as twilight settled around him, cooling his heated, dry skin.

Almost there. Almost there. The door to the ute stood open just a metre ahead. He could get there. He could. He just had to let go of the trailer and take two steps.

He let go, lifted his leg and …

The ground rose up to greet him. His gloved hands splayed out before him, hitting the dirt first. Then his arms gave way and he landed face first in the dirt.

There was a hiss as his blood hit the soil and sank in.

Before he could push himself up, greenery sprung up all around him, racing across the field until it was full of swaying fruit trees, South Esk Pines and an abundance of all the plants he'd ever grown in his life – a veritable garden of Eden.

No-no-no-no-no! How was he going to explain this?

He began to push upright. Then froze.

A woman, in a flowing gown the colour of night just before dawn, walked towards him through the greenery. She was short and curvy, with curling long blonde hair that somehow held dawn in its depth. She stared around her, her plump mouth puckered in a little 'oh' of surprise as if she'd never seen anything like this before – in truth, she probably hadn't.

She drew near to him and he sucked in a breath – in eyes that were the darkest purple lit by sunlight, he could see pain like a never-ending scream.

How could she have endured so much pain?

A voice he knew from his dreams whispered, *"Drink. You must drink of her blood. For she is made of dawn's light and the rejuvenating qualities of birth and rebirth. She is of the eternal stuff of life now, like the Old Gods; like you were. Her blood holds magic and knowledge of ancient things within. Drink of her and you will be returned."*

What the fuck?

"Drink. Drink her now. She has come to you. She is the one we've waited for."

"No!" He would never do such a thing.

"No?" the woman questioned as she stopped next to an apple tree that held a single apple. Her gaze raked over his form. "You can see me?"

He nodded.

"Holy crap!"

"Holy crap indeed." He couldn't keep talking to her from this position flat on his stomach in the dirt. Sucking in a breath, he pushed to his knees slowly. The world moved again but somehow she remained steady. Solid. He concentrated on her and managed to sit back on his haunches without falling over. "Who are you?"

She just stared at him then plucked the apple from the tree and took a bite, brows rising a little as she chewed. He watched her, mouth dry, as she continued to eat the fruit that had been born from his blood and whatever magic happened when it touched barren soil. The action was mesmerising, stoppering all thought until there was nothing but a core left.

"Who are you?" he asked again.

She dropped the core on the ground beside her and said, "The question is, who are you? And how did you do this?" Her gaze left him to take in the still-growing trees and plants around them.

"I didn't ..."

Her gaze collided with his once more.

The breath left his lungs at the impact. Her eyes, they were extraordinary. He'd not seen eyes like that since—

He clutched his head as pain spiked through him.

"Are you okay?"

"I'm ... fine," he managed after sucking in a shaky breath. He waved at his head. "Just hit my head, that's all."

Her gaze went to the cut on his brow. "Here, let me take care of that." She waved her hand. There was a small breeze of air around his brow and then the pain of the cut was gone.

"Thank you. Although I wished you were here earlier to stop this from happening," he said, giving up all pretence that he had nothing to do with the magical growth. She would notice pretty quickly that as the blood stopped flowing, so the greenery stopped growing.

Her eyes widened as they flickered between him and the greenery. "Your blood. It did this." It wasn't a question; rather, it was said on a breath of horror. "Blood magic. You did this with blood magic." She took a step back, as if suddenly afraid of him. "I can't be here. I can't be a part of this." She turned.

He held up his hand. "No. Stop. Don't go!"

But it was too late. She'd already disappeared.

"What the fuck?" The words exploded out of him as he scrambled to his feet, suddenly not the least bit dizzy. "Where did you go? Who are you? And why should I drink your blood?"

He cried the words into the darkening sky, but there was no answer.

He stood there, the new greenery the only movement as it rustled in the breeze that had sprung up.

He must have imagined her. Yes, she was a result of a knock on the head and the worry about how he would explain to his neighbours, to Daphne and her boys, about his suddenly lush and fertile paddock.

Even so, he couldn't stop himself from going to where she'd stood, to find the imprint of high heels in the grass and the apple core where she'd dropped it.

She *had* been real.

But what in all the Hells did it mean? And what was he supposed to do now?

Even more importantly – how was he supposed to explain this field to Daphne and the boys? Because he sure as shit knew there was no way of keeping it from them.

Perhaps they would believe in Christmas miracles?

4

Ilia reeled as the sensation of falling suddenly stopped. She couldn't believe she'd screamed like that. But it had been terrifying, so … kind of justified. Her heart still pounded in her chest though, her breath sawing through her lips.

"Get your shit together, girl," she panted.

She breathed slow and deep until things started to settle around and inside her. As it did, she gathered her spiralling thoughts: whatever this was, it wasn't a dream.

There was no fogging around the edges, no flipping from one place to another, no sense of timelessness. Plus, the falling had felt real.

In fact, all of it was too real, too vivid. And as she breathed in deeply, she realised it wasn't only sound and image she was getting, but also scents.

A vision? Was this a vision?

Yet it didn't quite feel like that either.

Then what was it?

Did it matter?

No. She had to stop wasting brain energy on questions she

couldn't answer and concentrate on what she'd been brought here to witness.

The man from her dreams was in front of her, digging up a muddy field, his entire attention on what he was doing.

It was strange to see him in this way. So tired and frustrated and … driven. He was usually pretty jovial in the dreams she remembered, despite the loneliness that always seemed a part of him.

She hovered over the scene for a time, watching him work. A ute drove up. A woman with bobbed brown hair, sporting similar work attire, hopped out and began to berate him into eating and drinking.

Ilia smiled. She liked the woman.

Then he said something to piss the woman off – typical male – and she left. The man returned to his work. He worked long and hard, never stopping even though he was sweating up a storm and must feel the effects of the hot day.

She dropped closer when he tripped, hitting his head on the ute.

He tried to get in but didn't make it. Ilia wished she could help him as he fell to the ground, the cut on his brow bleeding profusely.

Then suddenly, green things began to spring out of the ground – trees and bushes and flowers of all types, shapes and sizes – and within minutes, the muddy, ruined paddock had turned into a strange garden; a mix of orchard, vegetable garden and pine forest.

It was so lush and inviting, she wanted to go down and explore it; find out how it had suddenly come to be. The male seemed to be the source – but how?

Suddenly, she stood on the field, the springiness of lush grass under her feet, the scent of wildflowers and summer fruits hanging heavy in the air around her.

What the fuck?

Despite her confusion, she couldn't help walking closer to the man. He was looking wildly around, then he sucked in a breath.

"No!" He shouted, seeming to stare right at her.

"No?" She stopped next to an apple tree that a single apple had grown on, gaze raking over him as his raked over her. "You can see me?"

He nodded.

"Holy crap!"

"Holy crap indeed." His voice, deep with a slight huskiness, wove around her, reminding her of the warmth of a fire in the hearth and the enticing scent of cinnamon and honey. *Home. He is home,* her mind whispered. The whisper stole all other thought.

He didn't seem to be struck so dumb though. He pushed to his knees slowly, swayed a little, his remarkable eyes fogging before refocusing on her with a kind of desperate need that made her shiver. "Who are you?"

She didn't respond, didn't quite know how to. She looked down, noticed she had plucked the lone apple from the tree, and without thinking, took a bite. Oh by all that was holy! She'd never tasted anything so delicious. Sweet and tart and crunchy and juicy. It was perfect – and exactly what she needed. She ate greedily until there was nothing left but the core. Nothing had ever satisfied her quite so much as that apple.

And all the time she was hyper aware of him watching her with something in his eyes that made her heart expand in her chest with a deep warmth she'd never felt before.

"Who are you?" he asked again.

"He's not ready for you to tell him yet," the voice in her mind – a voice she'd heard in her dreams – said. It was right. *She* was barely ready for this – whatever it was. And yet she wanted to know him.

She dropped the core on the ground beside her. "The question is, who are you? And how did you do this?" Her gaze left him to take in the still-growing trees and plants around them.

"I didn't ..."

Her gaze returned to him, and she noted that he was still bleeding, his face pale, eyes fogged with pain and exhaustion. Blood dripped from his chin, onto the ground.

Around her the trees and plants kept growing, but slower than before.

He clutched at his head as if in severe pain.

"Are you okay?"

"I'm ... fine," he said on a shaky breath, obviously anything but fine. He waved at his head. "Just hit my head, that's all."

Her gaze went to the cut on his brow. "Here, let me take care of that." She waved her hand, using a spell she'd learned from Bas. A small breeze blew up around them, weaving around his head as magic sparked over his cut. As it went to work, she couldn't help but truly look at him – for he was so much more real now than he'd ever been in any of her dreams.

He was a big man, even kneeling in the dirt. Her mouth dried as she took in the breadth of his shoulders, the bulge of his pecs and biceps under his t-shirt, the way his sweat-damp hair clung to his forehead and how his excessively long dark lashes framed his leaf-green eyes. Most males, Gods and human alike, could suck it as far as she was concerned – except for Tamuel and Bastien of course – but there was something about this man. And it wasn't simply that he was glorious. There was something else. Something that called to a place inside of her she'd thought long dead, and made it surge to the fore.

She longed to go to him, touch him, enfold herself in his arms and never let go. It was a wild thought, one she'd never had in her long life, not even when she'd thought herself in love with Mars. This was deeper and fuller and wider. It was like ... oh! She sucked in a breath. It was a bit like the feelings she'd had for that brief moment of joy after giving birth, when she'd held her boys and knew she'd never love anything like she loved them.

What the ever-loving fuck?!

Something changed in his eyes and he straightened as the pain left him, her magic having done its work.

"Thank you." His lips tilted a little as he gestured at the new growth around them. "Although I wished you were here earlier to stop this from happening."

She gasped. Did he just infer what she thought he had? Her gaze flickered between him and the greenery. "Your blood. It did this. Blood magic. You did this with blood magic." All her warm, fuzzy feelings fled before panic. She took a step back, trembling. "I can't be here. I can't be a part of this." She swung around, wondering how the Hells she could get out of this vision-thing she was in.

At the thought, the lush field and the handsome man wavered and disappeared and she was back in the kitchen, little Dawn in her arms, the fresh taste of apple lingering on her lips.

What the Hells! Why had she seen that? Why had she been there to witness the use of blood magic?

He hadn't seemed evil. But if he used blood magic, he was.

And if that was true, why had Dawn shown him to her? Breathing hard as if she'd been running, she stared at Dawn. The baby didn't seem disturbed at all. "Did you see that?"

Dawn shook her head and tapped Ilia on the brow once more.

"Just me?"

Dawn nodded.

Well, that was a relief. "Why did you show that to me?"

Dawn covered her eyes and then uncovered them. "I needed to see it?" Dawn nodded. "But why did it seem so real?" The tartness of the apple was still so clear on her lips.

Dawn flattened her palm on Ilia's chest, then drew it away, fluttering her hands to indicate flying. "I astral travelled?" Well that made a bit more sense for why it had seemed so real. She'd actually been there.

Dawn made a cooing sound that caught Ilia's attention again.

Ilia leaned in and whispered, "I wish you could speak so you could tell me why I needed to see him like that. Why is he so significant?" Was he part of the big evil they were supposed to fight? It made sense given he'd used blood magic. She shuddered again.

Dawn's little forehead puckered and she stroked Ilia's cheek as if to soothe her.

Hells. She was pathetic. Shoving her fear aside, she kissed Dawn's downy head and said, "It's not your job to soothe me, little one. I should be soothing you."

Dawn shook her head and patted Ilia's cheek.

The stubborn gesture made Ilia chuckle.

"It's remarkable how you communicate so well with her," Jules said, joining them with the bowl of cereal in her hands. "I wish I could understand her half as well as you do."

"It's the link," Ilia said, gesturing to the now-invisible magic thread that tied their life-forces together. It was part of the magic that had given her life, and had tied them together in the most inexplicable way ever since.

As well as sharing certain thoughts and emotions, she could understand the baby, and the baby could understand her, in a way that should be impossible. That was the up side. The down side was that the thread meant she could never go too far from where Dawn was. They'd found out the hard way how dangerous it was if one of them got too far from the other a month after Dawn's birth and Ilia's rebirth.

She rubbed her chest in memory of the sensation of her heart slowing and almost stopping the day Jules had taken Dawn to the Coven's paediatrician for a check-up.

Dawn's heart had almost stopped too before Tamuel and Korinna's quick thinking had saved the day.

Since then, they'd barely been more than the distance between the top floor of Stevens' House and the area where the Coven library lay underneath it.

Dawn reached for her cereal, almost knocking it from her mother's hand.

"So impatient," Ilia chided. She set the baby down in her highchair then returned to the coffee machine to continue making her espresso, leaving Jules to feed Dawn – an exhausting process of avoiding grabby hands, singing 'here comes the choo-choo' and cleaning up the half of it that always seemed to dribble down the baby's chin. Despite how advanced she was in other areas, Dawn certainly hadn't mastered eating.

But Jules handled it the way she handled everything else – without fuss or nonsense and as if she'd been doing it all her life.

It was hard to watch, reminding Ilia she'd never got to do any of that with her sons.

She clenched the edge of the kitchen bench and tried to ignore the feeding behind her, fixing her attention on the coffee machine.

Come on, come on.

It seemed to be slower than usual. She just wanted her espresso – a truly magical invention the humans had created that was better than the nectar of the Gods – and then she could escape and think more clearly over what had just happened.

Something that was difficult to do in a room overstuffed with an excess of tinsel and glitter and winking lights that were starting to make her head pound.

Finally her espresso was done. She picked it up and breathed in the nutty-bitter aroma – glorious. The scent lit up her nerve-ends and chased away the last prickling cold that witnessing the use of blood magic had left behind. She sipped cautiously – even better than it smelled. This Columbian roast was better than the Costa Rican one Bas had sourced a few weeks ago.

Even so, the taste of apple lingered.

Hells. She'd eaten an apple made of blood magic! What might that have done to her? She closed her eyes and checked her magic and the flow of her aura, but didn't notice any changes. The only lingering effect was that she could still taste the apple clearly. She breathed out a long sigh.

"You okay?"

"Uh-huh," she said and bolted down the rest of her coffee, needing it to scald the taste of that delicious apple from her traitorous tongue. It didn't quite work, so she set up another cup. Hopefully two would do it. As it poured, she turned back to Jules and said, "I think I might go down to the library."

"This early? Is that wise? Especially alone. You know what happened last time."

As if she'd forget. The family ghosts, the ones that lived in the Melbourne Coven Library, which lay below Stevens' House, had been attracted to her right from the moment she'd ventured into the cavernous space a month after they'd returned from Roma. Thankfully she'd been with Tamuel and Korinna and they'd managed to chase the ghosts away before they did more than rush around her too fast. They'd thought it was just curiosity at first, but it became obvious pretty quickly it was something more than that, given they had to chase the ghosts away every time she entered the library.

Then she'd made the mistake of going down there by herself. She'd actually thought Bas was down there – but he'd slipped out via portal when Jules had sent him a text asking him to get more nappies, and so the place had been empty.

Except for her and the ghosts.

They'd rushed her as soon as she'd stepped off the bottom stair, taking her by surprise. One got through before she managed to throw up a shield, taking over her body. It had left her weakened for days after she'd eventually pushed it out – unfortunately not before it had made her eat and drink way too much. She didn't think she'd be able to look at chocolate or Fanta ever again.

She hid her shudder at the memory and said, "I'll be fine. You don't have to worry about me. I'm a big girl. Besides, I've been working on my shields since then with Bas and Tam. They're pretty strong now."

"Are you sure? I can come down now. Dawn is finished her breakfast – and I wanted to do some research on Earth magics. I thought maybe if we could pinpoint the type of magic Triptolemus used, it might help us track him down. From what you overheard Demeter say, he was left with some of his magic."

"That's a good idea."

Jules beamed. "I thought so. It will be good to get a start on it before anyone else comes down to work."

"You want to bring Dawn down to the library?"

The few times the baby had been down there, she'd screamed loud enough to make the chandeliers shake.

"Umm, I could go wake Bas."

"Don't be silly. I know he, Tamuel and Korinna didn't get back until the middle of the night." They'd been tracking down leads on Korinna's father. All they had to go by was a muddle of contradictory mythology and history about Triptolemus that now made them uncertain if he was a God, a demi-God or something else entirely when they'd always thought he was a minor God in service to Demeter. They also had the Eleusinian Mysteries Grimoire, which he'd apparently written. Despite that fact making his standing in the pantheons even more unclear, it had at least opened up a treasure trove of spells and diary-like entries thanks to Korinna's magically cursed blood. What it couldn't tell them was where he was now.

She wished she could be more help in tracking Triptolemus down, but apart from what she'd overheard Demeter and Persephone say on the matter, she'd been pretty much useless in the hunt for the ancient God/demi-God or whatever he was.

All she could do was keep going through the ancient texts they had in the library and see if there was something there they'd not found before. An almost-hopeless task given she had no true idea what the Hells it was she was looking for, either about Triptolemus and his whereabouts or what the big bad was that had forced Demeter to take all his memories and send him out into the world without ...

"Holy crap!" She slapped herself in the head. The man in her vision-dreams! He'd grown things with his blood. It was like what Korinna had done with the ring and her blood earlier this year. Maybe he hadn't used blood magic at all, like with Korinna, because he was the same as her. Which meant ... "That's what you were trying to show me!" she said to Dawn. "I was just too stupid to see it!" And so full of fear she'd stupidly thought a man with such gentleness in his eyes could be part of the evil they were meant to battle.

Jules stared at her. "Too stupid to see what?"

She shook her head. "I don't want to say anything in case I'm wrong. But I really do need to go down to the library. Now."

"But the ghosts—"

"Don't worry." She raised her shield with a wave of one hand. "See. I'm already protected." She didn't wait for Jules to respond, just chugged down her second espresso – even though she was now less worried about the taste of apple in her mouth – then ran for the stairs to the library.

If she was right, this would change everything. For Korinna. For her family. Even, maybe for her.

Because, if she was right and the dream-vision male was Triptolemus, then their search was over and they would soon have all the answers they'd been looking for.

And maybe then, she could fully concentrate on how to cut the life-force bond with Dawn and free them both.

5.

Ilia raced down the stone stairway, the slap of her bunny slippers echoing loudly through the stairwell.

Lights flickered on in the library as she entered, as they'd been spelled to do, so that by the time she took the last, cautious step into the space, it was fully lit by the bone chandeliers that hung from the arched stone and wood ceiling.

The ghosts rushed her as she came to a halt, their hands outstretched, pale eyes gleaming brightly in even paler faces.

She flinched as they bounced off the shield, their impact like something poking at her mind – not bad, but not exactly pleasant. They quickly regrouped and rushed her again. She put her hand out even though the shield would keep them at bay.

They bounced off it again. It didn't hurt, but it also didn't tickle – a little worse than the first time.

Obviously it affected her more than it affected them – they rallied and came at her again.

The shield held, but this time the impact was more than a poke at her mind; it was a slap. She stumbled back a step, shocked at how much it hurt. She hadn't read anything about it hurting when things impacted a shield like that. Did that mean the shield wasn't working properly? Hells, could they get through? She was so stupid to have tested it with nobody around. Should have waited for Jules. Even if she had to put up with the Christmas cheer that had been vomited all over the house.

One of the ghosts picked itself up from where it had been thrown faster than the others and came at her again. Hells. What was that spell Korinna had used to chase them away?

She couldn't remember, so giving in to impulse, she raised her hands and called on the power she was still only learning to use; power that still didn't feel like it belonged to her.

Pink and golden light sparked on the tips of her fingers, then flared brightly. And as it did, the glow in her chest started up again too. Bugger. But she didn't have time to worry about it now. She waved her hands, the power sparking again. "Come closer and you'll get a taste of this. And I promise, you won't like it." She was guessing of course. She had no idea if the light and power of the dawn would bother them at all, but given they lived mostly in the shadows, it was her best bet.

All of them stopped except the one that had come at her first. She willed the power to spark out towards it, and as it flew across the space between her and the ghost, an arc of power from her chest flew along with it. The moment it touched the spirit, it began to writhe, its mouth open, screaming. Then it began to flicker, like bad reception on a TV. The other ghosts shrieked in terror and ran away, followed quickly by the one she'd hit, his form still flickering.

"Good. Run! There's more where that came from."

Actually, she wasn't sure there was. The magic – both in her fingers and chest – had disappeared as fast as it had come and left her trembling.

Hells. She wasn't used to using magic like this despite the training she'd been undertaking with Jules. And whatever the glow was that emanated from her chest, it packed a powerful punch. Aside from her trembling limbs, she also felt weak and dizzy.

It must have something to do with the way she got her power.

Maybe the baby was giving more than one aspect of her power. But, was she sharing it willingly or was Ilia stealing it without knowing?

Hells!

She really needed another thing to worry about and try to figure out like she needed a chastity belt!

The bloody Gods were sadists, fucking with her once again. They asked for and took too much over and over and over in their need to play their stupid games and screw with those they thought 'lower beings'.

Someone needed to make them pay – she only hoped one day that that someone would be her. Or, if not her, that she would be there to see it when they got what they deserved.

Her anger was a warmth growing in her chest. A warmth that heated to a blaze, brightening the space around her as it snapped and crackled, pushing to get out. "Crap. Not again. What the Hells is going on?"

Calming herself with breathing exercises had worked this morning, so she endeavoured to do that again, closing her eyes, breathing deeply and thinking calming thoughts.

An image of the man from her dreams, the one she thought might be Triptolemus, sprang into her mind, and as it did, the angry heat in her chest changed, its blazing edges softening to a welcoming warmth that filled her with calm and clarity.

And longing.

The sensation was so strong, air punched out of her and her eyes snapped open.

Just then, something began to rustle and whisper from the depths of the library. Something else made a horrible moaning sound, coming from the direction of the Black Magic and Dangerous Books section. Then a voice whispered from somewhere close by, *"Blood. Your blood. He drinks your blood."*

Hairs lifted on her arms and the back of her neck. "What?" She spun around, looking along the closest stack as far as she could. "Who said that?"

There was no answer. She must have imagined it.

Shaking off the jitters, she started towards the area where the computers and reference shelves were.

"Blood. More blood. Blood for the drinking. Blood for the thinking. Blood that is life. Blood that is strife. Blood that is giving. Blood that is taking. Blood that is destiny always in the making."

She stopped, fear whispering across her skin, drying her mouth. She wanted to run. But she couldn't. Wouldn't. She was sick of other beings playing with her for their own sick reasons. She had no idea how or why it was in some God's interest to torment her with her fear of blood magic, but she wasn't going to play their games. Squaring her shoulders she shouted, "Shut up! Just shut the Hells up. I don't want to hear anything more about blood or what it can do. If you don't have something to tell me that will help me find Triptolemus or free myself from Dawn, then just fuck right off and leave me alone!"

"Blood is your destiny." It was little more than an echo in the distance.

"No. It bloody well is not!" No pun intended of course. She snorted and then yelled, "Screw you!" The words rang around her, echoing through the library.

All other sound ceased. Even the moaning from the Black Magic and Dangerous Books section. Surprised that whatever it was had actually listened to her, she slowly turned and continued over to the reference shelves, centring her mind back on the job ahead.

All she had to do was find the right way to work the magical reference book Jules had been building ever since getting her powers back. If she could do that, and if the realisation she'd had upstairs was right, she'd have good news for Korinna and everyone by the end of the day.

She was glad to see that Jules had left the catalogue reference book on the desk in front of the shelves – she'd obviously added more to it yesterday; it seemed even thicker than before. She still had a lot of work to do to include links and references to every book, grimoire and magical object in the library, but she was well on her way. And it was easier to use than the online system, or poring through drawers and drawers of card catalogues.

But it could still be a bit tricky, because if she didn't pose her question right, or think about the right thing, then it could send her to grimoires and journals that had proved completely unhelpful.

The difference today was that she had what she thought was a current image of Triptolemus in her head. All she had to do was open the book, place her hands on the pages, and bring that image to mind with the right question that would lead her to him.

It shouldn't be difficult to think about him. She seemed to think of him more and more these last few weeks and now it took nothing at all to picture his handsome face. Or hear the sound of his voice. Or see the leaf-green of his long-lashed eyes.

Whoa, was it getting hot in here?

She wiped her hand across her brow and then reached for the reference book. Her hand trembled, fumbling on the latch.

She shifted her shoulders, trying to rid herself of the itch that chased between her shoulder blades and ran down her back, prickling and tightening between her legs. She squeezed her legs together and clenched her fingers hard against her palms until the biting sting of her fingernails digging into flesh helped to push away the unwanted sensations sliding through her.

Ridiculous to have that reaction for a man she'd never even met in the flesh. She'd long ago vowed never to give into that kind of need again; the consequences of the one and only time she had were just too high.

Never again.

So, stop being stupid and just open the damned book.

The sting of where her fingernails had bitten into her palm helped to keep the frisson of want at bay as she flipped open the reference book and put her hands on the pages. She filled her mind with his image – the one she'd seen only a short time ago – and posed a question as she had every day since coming here. Although, rather than the question being, "Where is Triptolemus?", this time it was, "The man in my vision, is it Triptolemus?"

The page under her hands warmed.

It had never done that before.

She snatched her hand back as a crawling sensation brushed across her palm and fingers.

Oh! The page was filling with writing – the names of treatises and pieces of information and the grimoire or book she'd find them in.

And every single one of them held the same name within the descriptive line:

Triptolemus.

Then her eyes caught on a particular section she'd never seen before.

Triptolemus: Golden God of the Harvest. He who made the Garden Gems from his tears mixed with a piece of Demeter's heart. Servant and partner of Demeter and Persephone here on Earth. Instigator of the Eleusinian Mysteries. Holder of the sacred blood.

The sacred blood? So she'd been right. It had been a property of the blood that enabled him to grow things, not blood magic.

Her knees dipped as relief rushed through her.

She forced herself to read on but then stopped as her gaze hit the words a few lines down:

Triptolemus – he and his line forever destined to be God Killers.

What? There was a prophecy about them being God Killers? But hadn't Tiberinus said there was a prophecy about her and her sons being God Killers, which was part of the reason he'd chosen her, rather than any other powerful witch, to power the HBG?

There couldn't be two prophecies about God Killers, could there? Or was it the same prophecy?

How entwined were they? She thought she was involved in this because Korinna and Tamuel were the only ones who could have freed her from the gem. But what if it was so much more than that? What if ...

Her mouth dried.

No. Those feelings for him she'd been drowning in, the reason she kept dreaming about him – it was nothing but lust and the need to find him. Nothing more. Nothing deeper. Because she couldn't do deeper. Not now. Not ever.

How could she ever be a part of this amazing group of people and their close-knit family? No matter how much she might long for it, she couldn't have it. She was too broken. Too unworthy. The need for revenge that drove her too much a part of her. She didn't want to let it go; not for them, not for anything. It gave her purpose. But she wasn't so gone not to understand that if she stayed with them, that darkness inside her would mar their love, their friendship, their family. She couldn't do that to them. She couldn't destroy something so good.

Which was why she had to separate herself from Dawn. Why she had to leave them, no matter what they said.

But if they found out about this connection, they'd be unlikely ever to let her go. They'd keep trying to bring her back to them because that's who they were. So she couldn't show this to them. She didn't want them to start to believe things that just couldn't be. It was already going to be difficult enough to leave given they already treated her like family. It would be so much worse if they thought her connected to them, to Triptolemus, in some deeper way.

But how could she hide this?

She slammed the book shut, losing the page with the words that caused the hairs on her nape and arms to stand up.

Closing her eyes, she intoned a spell:

"Hide this entry where no one can see.

Hide it away, show no one but me.

Three time three times three times three,

By the power of dawn light, so mote it be."

The power spiralled up, ruffling her hair, then fell to wind around the book. Something tightened, there was a pop and the spell fizzed away.

It was done.

She blew out a slow breath. She wished she could empty the knowledge from her own brain. But she couldn't. Damn the Gods and Goddesses and their machinations, tying her into them once again.

Eyes prickling with tears that had more to do with anger than anything else, she took in a shuddering breath, looked up at the ceiling and shouted, "Fuck you, whoever is responsible for messing with me like this. Fuck you and all your children. I don't know how, but somehow I will make you regret using me like this. I swear it."

Three rolling knocks sounded in the distance.

She stilled.

Shit.

Fuck.

But she hadn't used the word 'vow'. So why had the Eternal Well treated her rash statement like a sacred vow?

Bloody fucking Hells. Why did the universe seem to have it in for her?

Hot tears poured down her face, heated rage bubbled in her chest, the glow of her power shining through her skin once more. She wished she could just let it go, let it lash at those who'd caused this pain, but she didn't know exactly who was involved beside Tiberinus – and she knew there were others involved. So no taking her revenge yet.

Besides, she had things to do first.

It took her longer this time to push the power back, to stop the glow in her chest, but once done, she whispered harshly, "Fine. I said I'd find him and I will. But then I'm done." She opened the book again and put her hands on it, filling her mind's-eye with Triptolemus' image once more. "Just show me where he is."

6

The woman smiled at Trip, her eyes, like the darkest purple-blue of the night sky, glinted at him with something secret and knowing. Her smile widened as she opened her mouth and licked the apple juice from her lips – the action gripping him in the groin and tightening his balls. He groaned at the memory, hand tightening around his erect cock – a cock that seemed to spend more of its time erect than not, ever since he'd seen the woman in his field a few days ago.

Day or night, she was there, with him, the long gown that looked like something from Roman times draped over her, hugging in all the right places and showing off the shadow between her pert breasts.

In these daydreams – the ones that kept coming to him whether he wanted them or not – this was the moment she dropped the apple core to the ground and reached for the clips on her shoulders holding her gown together.

She didn't disappoint now.

With that knowing look, she slowly – so slowly and sensually it stole his breath – undid those butterfly-like clips and let the gown fall, showing off skin the colour of rich cream and nipples swollen and softly pink.

Still smiling, she reached out her hand and said, "Triptolemus. I am here for you. Come. Drink of me and all will be well."

Even the pained dissonance that strange name – so like his, but not – caused every time she said it did nothing to rid him of the desire that heated his blood and made him want to touch, to take. And to want things he'd always stopped himself from wanting.

Connection. Belonging. Love.

Impossible things, but within these dreams, the impossible seemed to be within his grasp.

He rose to his feet, reaching for her and—

There was a loud bang and then a voice said excitedly, "Oh my God. Trip! Have you seen the field? Oh, God ... My eyes! My eyes!"

Trip snapped out of his daydream with a horrible jolt to see Daphne standing before him. She'd turned around and had her hands clasped to her head. There was a sound coming from her that sounded suspiciously like smothered laughter.

He quickly tried to tuck himself back into his pants – a difficult task given how swollen his cock was. Although, with her sudden entry – not to mention the laughter – it was quickly deflating. "Umm, well, it wasn't ... I mean ... I wasn't ..." His eyes lit on the box with the inflatable Santa and his reindeers that he was supposed to be working on for the Winter Wonderland in time for their first customers this weekend. He had been reading the instructions when the daydream had taken over and ... He coughed. "I was about to erect the inflatable."

"I think you were doing a good job of it too," she said on a definite snort. "Is your inflatable tucked away yet? It's rather awkward to talk to you like this." She turned before he could answer, her eyes alight with laughter.

"I didn't mean for you to see—"

"Well, obviously you didn't. Nothing to be embarrassed about though, as I tell the boys. Masturbation is a healthy part of life. I'm kind of glad to see you do it too."

"What? Really?" He blinked completely taken aback before his mind zeroed in on the last part of her statement. "What do you mean 'do it too'?"

She snort laughed. "Well, I think that would be obvious."

Oh, Gods! He didn't want to hear that. Daphne was like a sister. The last thing he wanted to think about was her doing *that*! Face as red as his Santa suit, he stammered, "I ... Umm ... Wh-what did you come racing in here for? Is something wrong?"

Her eyes lit up with excitement. "Oh. Yes. That's why I barged in rather than knocking." She began to pace, excitement in every step. He'd never seen her this way before. "It's just so wonderful. I can't believe it really, even though I saw it with my own eyes."

She looked at him expectantly. A sinking feeling gripped his stomach and tightened his chest. Oh no! Even so, he couldn't help but ask, "Saw what?"

"The boys saw it this morning and came to get me. It's a ... It's a ..."

"Christmas miracle?" Trip groaned inside as the words fell from his lips. They sounded lamer than he'd imagined. There was no way she would believe—

"Yes! It's a Christmas miracle. A true Christmas miracle!"

"Really?" he asked before he could stop himself.

"Well, you've obviously seen it if you're calling it that – and don't think that we won't have a conversation later about why you didn't tell us when you first saw it. But for now, I'm too excited to be mad at you. All that growth in that destroyed field. Trees and plants I've never seen before. And endangered South Esk Pines too! Plus there's fruit trees and other produce springing up everywhere. All grown in only a few days. It's our own Christmas miracle! Who would have imagined?"

"Umm ..."

"Isn't it exciting?" she asked, hands on hips, hair uncharacteristically dishevelled, brown eyes glowing with excitement and ... jubilation?

Exciting wasn't the word he had in mind. Terrifying was more to the point. "I just ... didn't think you believed in such things."

"As miracles?" Her eyes widened in surprise. "Of course I do. I know you, after all."

Shivers prickled down his spin and he stilled, his breath once again caught in his chest. Oh Hells. What did she know? "I ... Wh-what do you mean by that?"

She walked over to him and cupped his cheeks – her hands warm against the sudden chill in his skin. "You came into our lives like a miracle. Everything was lost and I didn't know how I was going to keep feeding the boys, let alone clothe them and get them to school. There wasn't enough work around here and I had no money to pick up and move elsewhere. I'd been sitting there crying after the boys were asleep, when my contractions started and I had no idea what to do or where to go and then ... you appeared. I was so afraid you were going to kick me and the boys out regardless of the fact I was about to drop a baby, but you didn't. You took control and got me to the hospital and looked after the boys and then, the biggest miracle, you offered us all jobs and a place to stay, then took us in while you fixed the stockman's cottage up so it was not only liveable but lovely. What do you call that if not a miracle?"

"Umm, being neighbourly?"

She choked on a laugh as she blinked tears from her eyes. "I had neighbours, and not one of them did anything for us when we were tossed out after my husband left and took all our money. You were the only one who helped, and you did so without even knowing us at all." Her hand dropped to his chest as she smiled up at him and said softly, "You made me believe in miracles that day and every day since."

"Well ..." What did a person say to that? He took her hand and held it in his. "You were a miracle for me too. I never knew how badly I needed a frie— an assistant like you. You take care of all the things I didn't like doing – housework, bookkeeping, managing the shop and helping with the cooking and baking of the goods we sell. And Charlie, well, he's taken to farming like one born to it. And without Harry and how savvy he is with computers and social media and the like, the business would not be what it is today. And Gideon, well ... I never knew how much joy a baby would bring."

Daphne chuckled. "Don't let him catch you calling him a baby. He's a big ten-year-old now."

"He sure is. And a born salesman to boot. I think we sold more in the shop last Christmas than we've ever sold before, and that's mainly up to him working there alongside you for the first time."

She smiled, wide and proud. "It was pretty special. But it would never have happened if you hadn't taken us in and treated us like family." She touched his cheek. "And we are, family."

He swallowed hard. "Yes." They were. And he couldn't ask for a better one. Even though in a few years, he'd have to say goodbye to them forever. But he didn't want to think about that now.

She cleared her throat and patted his hand. "Now, what are we going to do about this Christmas miracle?"

Hells. He'd hoped she'd got so side-tracked by their trip along memory lane that she'd forgotten. No such luck. "Umm ... What is there to do about it?"

She gestured expansively. "Get the word out, that's what! We can't keep this miracle to ourselves."

"Can't we?"

She gave him that look that made him feel like he was living on an entirely different planet to her. Although, maybe he had been – it would explain a lot.

"Of course not! Miracles like this need to be shared with the world."

"But do they?"

More of that look. "Are you serious?"

Like a cyclone bearing down on land was serious. He nodded slowly. "I just ... don't see how it will be of benefit to us."

"Of benefit to us?"

"Yes," he said slowly, landing on the 's' with an uptick that turned it into a question. "I mean, if we let people know, won't it bring reporters and tourists and ... attention." Attention he'd spent his life running away from.

"Well, that's the point."

"It is?"

"Yes. To spread the goodness of the miracle." She nudged his arm. "You of all people should understand. You're Mr Christmas."

"I am?"

"Yes. You love spreading the Christmas cheer and good will. I mean, look what you do for our ticket holders every year when they come to cut their trees. They get an experience here that they don't get at other farms, with the tractor ride and costumes and the food and drinks you serve and the goodies we sell, not to mention the Christmas Wonderland decorations you set up from the carpark to the shop and inside the shop and the fake snow you spray around. It's a proper outing and puts people in the true spirit of Christmas."

"Yes, well, I like doing that."

"And letting people know about this Christmas miracle is just an extension of what you already do."

Except, it had giant, sticky strings attached. Namely, all the questions about how it happened and the scientists and government folk who would come down with legal documents and insist on doing tests. He just knew they would somehow end up tying it to him, and that would lead to him being carted away by army people or the Men in Black and locked away in a dark room to be experimented on.

Okay, maybe he'd watched too many sci-fi shows with Charlie, Harry and Gideon, but there *would* be consequences. Not little consequences but CONSEQUENCES. Not least of which would be he'd lose this little idyll and the family that was his even faster than he planned.

Daphne was looking at him, excited expectancy written large on her face.

"Is it really? I mean, there'll be reporters and people traipsing everywhere."

She waved that issue away. "The reporters will come, take their footage, ask some questions and then go. We can deal with them."

"Can we?"

"Of course. And of course, they'll get the word out." Her eyes glowed as she began to pace in front of him again. "Just imagine. People will come flocking to see, to share in the miracle. They'll buy everything we have and we'll be booked out for the next ten years or more! Not to mention the tourists it will bring to the rest of the county." She spun to face him. "There's absolutely no bad."

Oh, there was bad. Lots of bad. Bad with a capital B. A. D. – as in Bloody Awful Disaster. He just couldn't explain it to her. The fact she believed it was a Christmas miracle was a miracle in and of itself, so he couldn't really expect another one to occur. Pity, because he hated to let her down but … "It's just … I like things how they are."

Her brow creased as confusion filled her eyes. "But Trip, don't you see, this could be the start of something big."

Oh, he saw. He saw more than she could ever know. He'd lived through people finding out a little too much about how the last 'miracle' he was responsible for had happened. There'd been excitement to begin with. And then there'd been pitchforks and torches and guns and the air filled with angry, frightened shouting and the acrid smell of thick smoke rising from his house, his pine trees and crops and orchards as they burned along with the field where it had happened.

While it was a few centuries on from that time, people hadn't changed that much. His Men in Black worries wouldn't be far from the truth and he would be subject to all sorts of horrible, invasive tests before he could say, "It's the magic of Christmas, not me!"

He took her hands in his. He had to stop her. "Please, Daphne. I came here to live a quiet life. What you describe … it makes me too uncomfortable. I don't want it."

"You don't want to bring joy to untold masses?"

He smiled crookedly at her. "Does it sound selfish to say no? No, I don't."

Her frown deepened. "You know, you don't have to hide yourself away like this. You have us now to protect you. And I know you love people – I see it every year at Christmas. Whatever happened in your past to make you live like a hermit for the rest of the year … it doesn't need to touch you anymore."

He let go of her hands, stepped back. "I just … I don't want it, okay?" She blinked, obviously startled by his stiff, firm tone. He didn't blame her – he never sounded so formal. But he couldn't help it right now. "Please, let's keep the miracle our secret."

She narrowed her eyes at him. "And how do you imagine we do that?"

"We don't tell anyone."

She sighed heavily. "You know the boys and I won't say a word if you don't want us to, but what about their friends? What about our neighbours? They're going to eventually see it. Not to mention we have the first of our Christmas tree bookings arriving this Saturday. You know a lot of them wander despite us telling them not to."

He chewed on his lip for a moment. "Well, given the people who've booked won't know that field was washed away a week ago, even if they happen upon it, they won't think there's anything miraculous about it." If they didn't look too closely and note all the plants that couldn't possibly have grown there.

She nodded reluctantly. "Okay, well, that might work for them, but what about our neighbours and the boys' friends? Cutter Thompson can see that field from his back paddock. And you know Gideon's friends often ride along the lane that runs beside that field when they're coming over to our place."

"We'll lock the gate to the lane, and your boys can tell their friends that I found toxic soil when I was clearing out the field and not to come down there. And in regard to Cutter … I guess we'll just have to hope he doesn't decide to suddenly put his cows in the back paddock. In the meantime, I'll get out there and trim it to try to make it look more normal." Although he'd have his work cut out for him. From experience, the things grown from his blood were pretty hardy. Even when he'd torn things out in the past, they grew back overnight. But he'd try.

She shook her head. "I don't understand why you're so against sharing something as wonderful as this. Particularly at this time of the year."

"I'm not asking you to understand. I'm just asking you to respect my wishes. Okay?"

Her mouth twitched from one side to the other, and for a moment he thought she was going to argue with him some more, but then she nodded. "Okay." She waved abruptly at the box that held the inflatable. "You better get on with erecting that, otherwise the Winter Wonderland won't be finished by Saturday."

He blushed at the overt reminder of what he'd actually been erecting when she'd burst in. "I will. Thank you."

She shrugged. "Don't thank me. I've not given up yet."

He chuckled. "I didn't expect you would. But I'm not going to change my mind."

"We'll see." She gave him a salute – their little joke because she'd always called him the captain of this mad little ship they called Snowy Hills Christmas Tree Farm.

He did fully intend on inflating the Santa and his reindeers, but as he went to pull it out of its box, the whispers of the daydream came back to him, enticing him like a siren song.

He shook himself, shoving the images away. He had work to do. He couldn't keep giving into the pull of the daydream and the need that tightened his balls every time he even thought about the woman and the way she'd looked at him. It was ridiculous really, the randy-teenager-esque bent of his thoughts. In reality, it hadn't happened like that. He'd been in pain and shocked then worried. And so confused. Not really sexy at all.

Yet, his mind kept pushing him to go there with the memory of that moment.

He tried to ignore it, but it kept calling to him. Calling to him, and without realising, he was falling … falling …

7

The last week had been filled with nothing but frustration and false leads. The reference book had sent Ilia and the others to books that referred to events that were similar to what she'd seen Triptolemus do with his blood in that field. It was comforting to know she didn't have to worry about the evils of blood magic, but so frustrating to not find anything else. There seemed to be nothing about what had happened after Demeter had removed his memory and taken much of his magic. Demeter's spell was effective in hiding him from everyone – including his own daughter. But they had to follow the leads even if they were centuries old, because they had nothing else.

Tamuel and Korinna went rushing off to check out the leads. They visited old churches, libraries and places of power across Europe and North and South America in search of more information. But they discovered no clues as to where Triptolemus might be now.

The desperation and hopelessness in Korinna's eyes every time they came back with nothing made something inside Ilia ache. She found herself rubbing her hand over where the HBG was embedded in her chest, blaming the ache on Clodia shifting and pounding at her prison in the gem even though she knew that wasn't it. This was about the glow that kept appearing, the sensation like a small burn, growing larger and hotter with every false lead, every distraught expression Korinna tried to hide. It was made even worse by the fact she was hiding knowledge of that entry about Triptolemus and his line being God Killers and how that possibly tied her to them. She wished she could tell them because, while it might not help find him, it would give Korinna some clarity about why this had happened.

But she couldn't. The consequences would make things so much more complicated and difficult for her with what she must do in the future. And ultimately, it would hurt them all more than her hiding it from them. What they didn't know couldn't hurt them, right?

The only thing she could do was to go back into the dream-vision over and over, trying to see something that might give her a clue as to where Triptolemus was. But she found no new information. The only thing it did was to fill her with an itchy longing every time she laid eyes on him as he knelt on the ground staring at her with those gorgeous eyes that made the cold she'd built up around her heart melt.

If that wasn't bad enough, she itched to touch his face, to brush over the bristles of his beard – hardly more than a few-days' worth of growth. She longed to brush her thumb over his plump lower lip, then follow with her lips. At least, that's what she'd done in her dreams every night since, and multiple times when in moments of despair she allowed herself to sink into daydreams that echoed the vision, but were hotter. Sexier.

Far sexier.

It actually infuriated her, the fact she kept losing herself to those stupid, hot daydreams. She wasn't some randy teenager. She was thousands of years old. At least, her spirit was. This body was only eight months old in a corporeal sense. But that was neither here nor there. She had learned long ago how disastrous giving in to hormonal lust was. Everything that had gone wrong in her life could be blamed on the fact she'd fallen head-over-heels in lust – she'd stupidly thought it love – with Mars and in doing so, exposed just how powerful she was, making her father take her boys from her and casting her, and them, away because of his fear, and bringing her to the attention of Tiberinus.

So, these useless, stupid, tempting feelings she was experiencing weren't going to go anywhere or help with anything. She had to ignore them.

But, by the damned Gods, it was getting harder and harder as each day passed, and she didn't know why.

The only good thing about spending so much time in the library was that she didn't have to participate in any of Jules' Christmas plans – cookie and cake baking, painting new Christmas baubles for the various trees around the house, an endless viewing of every Christmas movie on all of the streaming services, and the constant singing of carols that were played non-stop during the day, piped through speakers that seemed to have appeared in all main rooms of the house.

Every morning, Ilia turned on stealth mode, getting up super early to race from her room to the kitchen and then down into the library as quickly as she could before Jules or anyone else made it downstairs. And when they came down to the library, any time Jules or any of the others started to mention Christmas and family and tradition, she mysteriously had something to look up in the stacks and rushed off.

But waking morning after morning frustrated from sexilicious dreams, which really didn't help with quality sleep, was exerting a toll, and a week to the day after she'd had the vision of Triptolemus using his blood to grow things, she struggled to pull her mind out of the sensual fog the too-hot dream created. She spent longer in the shower than she meant to, trying to wake herself up – and trying to get rid of some of the sexual frustration with a bit of self-help – and so when she made it downstairs to the kitchen, Jules was already there with Dawn, getting breakfast. Bas was there too, helping. Both looked up as she entered, smiling.

"Good morning," Jules sing-songed.

"Is it?"

Dawn, who was in her father's arms, cooed and did her grippy hand-wave thing, her smile bright as her dad placed her in her high-chair. "Someone is a bit slug-a-bed this morning," Bas said, his voice low and rumbly.

She waved at Dawn, somehow managing a smile for the baby before turning to the coffee machine. "Just need coffee," she mumbled, trying to ignore the chirpy Christmas carols ringing through the kitchen from the speaker that unfortunately sat over her favourite kitchen appliance.

"I made cinnamon scrolls," Jules said, pointing at the table. "Help yourself. That is, of course, if those two have left any."

It was then she noticed Tamuel and Korinna sitting in the break-fast nook, sharing a kiss, a plate full of cinnamon scrolls before them.

"Looks like they haven't got to them yet," she said, turning away from the sight. Just in time to see Bas lean in to give Jules a kiss, his hands cupping her face in a way that spoke of love and adoration.

Hells.

She was in couples purgatory. Their loved-up antics were another reason she really didn't want to participate in all the Christmas goings on. Or keep hanging around like some sad third wheel after she'd separated herself from Dawn.

Seeing them and their happiness made her feel like shit. Not because she begrudged them that, but because of the jealousy that speared through her every time she saw couples being all coupley.

That was when she noticed the coffee machine hadn't been turned on. Crap. It would take at least fifteen minutes to warm up to a point where she could make a decent coffee. She flicked the button on, dithering. She really didn't want to stay in the kitchen with the loved-up couples and happy family going on all around her while Christmas assaulted her every which way she looked, but she needed her coffee.

Shit. She couldn't even go to the cafe a few blocks away to get one because it was too far from Dawn. Maybe she could take Dawn for a walk?

She glanced back, trying to avoid seeing Jules and Bas, who were still kissing. By the looks of things, Dawn hadn't had her breakfast, which meant there was no chance she could take her for a walk.

Shit-crappity-fuck! She turned back to the coffee machine, staring at it, wishing it would hurry up. She snorted, knowing it was a ridiculous thing to do. Wishing for things had never got her anywhere.

She almost felt like crying. She just wanted her Gods-damned coffee and to disappear down into the library.

Rage began to simmer in her chest, the glow starting to shine.

Fuck!

She snapped her arms around herself to try and hide it. She couldn't let the others see – they'd ask questions and get worried and would want to help and they already had too much going on to waste time on some stupid glowy power that kept emanating from her chest when she couldn't control her emotions.

She had to get out of here. She turned to leave, and almost bumped into Jules. She hadn't even noticed the other witch coming up behind her.

"Ouch!" Jules said, shaking her hand. Then eyes widening, she said, "Ilia. Your chest!"

Crap! The rage was swept away in a rush of panic. The glow went along with it.

"Are you okay?"

"I … I'm fine." She looked past Jules, thankful everyone else was too busy to notice what was happening.

"Is that the HBG doing that?"

Hells. She wished it was. It would be simpler to admit to that than the truth. She couldn't outright lie to Jules though – she was already lying every time she reported she'd found nothing new about Triptolemus – so she hedged by saying, "No. It just sometimes happens. Something to do with my body still trying to get used to Dawn's powers."

"Oh. But … it doesn't hurt?"

"No. As I said, I'm fine." She turned to leave.

"Ilia. Don't rush off, please. You've been working too hard – all of us have. So Bas and I have decreed this is a morning off for all of us.

We're going to bake Christmas cookies for the neighbourhood party this weekend."

"We?"

Jules gestured behind her at the others in the kitchen. Tamuel and Korinna were still kissing. "Even grandmama is helping. When she gets back from the meeting with the Coven representatives overseeing the Yule celebrations."

A prickle started behind her eyes at the generosity of spirit that made Jules always want to include her. But … "I don't want to intrude on a family thing."

"Intrude? Why would you be intruding?"

Ilia waved at them all, her gesture taking in the kissing couple and Bas, who was now feeding Dawn her cereal. "You're all family and … I'm not. It doesn't feel right."

"But you are family. Of course you are."

She edged away a little, not liking the bright look in Jules' eyes. "No, I'm not. I'm just the unfortunate hanger-on you're stuck with for now because I'm magically attached to your daughter."

Jules sucked in a breath, her hand going out towards Ilia. Ilia stepped out of reach so the other witch's hand just hovered between them. "None of us think of you like that."

"I do." She looked away, unable to meet Jules' eyes, to see the slight trembling of her mouth. "You've all been so kind, but … I'm not your family. And you're not mine. My family died long ago. It's foolish to try to pretend otherwise."

"Do you truly feel like that?"

"I do." Without another word – and without her coffee – she turned and ran out of the kitchen. She'd not wanted to hurt the other witch, but she was horribly afraid she had. However, it was too late to take back what she'd said. Even if she apologised, it wouldn't undo the truth in her words.

She couldn't take that back, no matter how she tried.

More out of habit than anything else, she headed to the library, almost tripping down the stairs. It wasn't until she got to the bottom that she realised she'd been so upset, she hadn't raised her shields. She tried to do so now, but was too upset and the glow started up in her chest.

Shit. Shit.

She didn't know if the glow was the reason, but, despite the temptation of her without a shield, the library ghosts stayed away, as they'd been doing ever since she'd used her magic on them.

But what the Hells was she supposed to do about this glow? She couldn't work like this!

She stood there, sucking in deep breaths, trying to calm herself, to push the glow back inside. It took longer than it ever had before, but finally, it faded and disappeared.

She blew out a breath. Hells, she needed a coffee now more than ever.

Trembling, she headed to the library's kitchenette and flipped the kettle on. There was no lovely coffee machine down here, but they did have instant coffee, which was nowhere as good but would do in a pinch if it was strong and sweet enough.

Then she'd turn her attention to trying to find where in the Hells Korinna's long-lost father was. Not only did she want to help Korinna, finding him was the only way she was going to be able to move on. And she seriously needed to do that – sooner rather than later.

She flicked the kettle on, got out a mug and added four heaped teaspoons of instant. And even though she would never usually sully a good coffee with sugar, she put in an equal number of teaspoons of sugar to balance out the bitterness.

As she put the sugar back on the shelf, there was a thump from the stacks just behind her.

She spun around, hands out, magic sparking on her fingertips, ready to fight off the ghosts. "Stupid, Ilia. You need to get your shields up."

But no ghosts appeared and the only sound she heard was a rustling coming from the Black Magic and Dangerous Books section.

She let out a trembling breath and lowered her hands. As she did, she noticed a book lying on the ground in front of the nearest stacks.

"Well, hello. You weren't there before."

She walked closer. There wasn't a gap in the shelves where it might have fallen from. So where had it come from? Had one of the ghosts dropped it there as an apology? But then, why not stick around so she knew?

Slowly, carefully, she picked it up and turned it over.

The cover was dark green, the lettering on the front so faded she couldn't make it out. Magic buzzed in her fingertips; more magic than she'd previously felt in any of the books here, except for ones that were locked up.

"Shit." It was obviously from the Black Magic and Dangerous Books section. But how had it got out and landed here? Biting her lip, she wondered what she should do. Something was urging her to open it up, but that was a stupid thing to do without anyone else here to help if something went wrong. The last time a book had opened of its own accord from the lock up, it had taken both Korinna and Tamuel to capture the entity inside it and push it back in the book and lock it away. With her magic still being so unfamiliar, she was no match for whatever lay inside.

Gingerly, she placed it on the table. She had to go back upstairs and get Korinna and Tamuel at least. Hopefully she wouldn't walk in on more lovey-doviness, although there was nothing she could do to avoid the Christmas joy.

She rolled her eyes. She really wasn't in the mood, but did she have a choice?

She'd taken two steps when a wind whipped around her, pushing her back towards the table. She stumbled, turning to catch herself on the table's edge before she fell. "What the Hells?"

She tried to push upright but the wind didn't let up, curving around her like arms to keep her there no matter how much she struggled against it.

Before her, the cover of the book flipped open, the pages fluttering up and over. Then just as suddenly as it came, the wind was gone and the book stilled.

On the open page was a picture.

Of a face she recognised.

Underneath, the confirmation she needed. A name. Triptolemus.

Without meaning to, she reached out to touch the edge of his strong chin.

And fell into a vision.

8

The world swung around her as she fell. Bile rose in her throat. Her heart beat fast and hard in her chest; her breath was a tight pain that couldn't seem to get out, not even in a scream.

She closed her eyes. Then, as quickly as it had started, the falling, spinning stopped.

There was no jolt as she steadied, although she appeared to be standing upright. On a firm surface.

She opened her eyes.

And there he was – Triptolemus.

He stood before her, much as he'd been when she'd first seen him in the vision.

Except this time, he wasn't injured and he was standing.

To full attention.

In every sense of the word.

A fact she immediately noticed because he was stark naked. Every single inch of his tanned and muscled body on full and delicious display.

If that wasn't hot enough, he smiled, a sexy smile that touched her in all the right places. A smile that was more wicked and enticing than anything she'd ever seen.

In fact, she felt that smile in every nerve and sinew in a way she'd never experienced before, even with Mars. And it was overwhelming.

Heat flared over her, through her and there was a sudden flood of wetness right in that most sex-starved part of her.

Gods, he was sex on a stick. Just plain lickable.

She wanted to fan herself but didn't seem to have control over her limbs. In fact, all she seemed capable of right now was to stare at him and feel unbearably itchy and hot and needy.

So needy.

His smile widened as his gaze roved over her, hunger flaring in his eyes. And amusement. "You're dressed differently this time."

"This time?"

He gestured at her, his cock flexing. "No Roman gown with clips." He touched his shoulder and suddenly all she wanted to do was run her hand over that firm breadth of skin and feel the warm silk of it, the strength of muscle beneath. And then lick it.

See. Definitely lickable. She roped her wandering thoughts back in, forcing herself to concentrate on this strange conversation, so unlike any she'd had in previous dreams. "I'm all out of Roman gowns with clips."

"Pity. I did like how they … draped."

Yea Gods! That pause. It did things to her insides that shouldn't be possible. But that pause brought to mind all the dreams she'd had lately of her undoing clips on a gown she barely took notice of as she reached for him, baring herself to him as he was bared to her now. "They did … drape nicely."

"Hmm. I think I almost prefer this though." His smile widened even further and he waggled his brows at her. "Do they flop when you walk?"

What? Then she noticed his gaze had dropped to her feet. Hers followed and she almost groaned.

Bunny slippers!

Why was she wearing bunny slippers in this vision? Sure, she had slipped them on this morning after tugging on her shorts and t-shirt before dragging herself downstairs and enduring that disastrous conversation in the kitchen. But never before had she worn her actual clothes in a vision. She'd always been draped in something distinctly closer to what she'd worn when she'd been alive the first time.

But this time, it was green shorts, a bright pink t-shirt and her purple bunny slippers.

Sexy … not!

She shifted. The ears flopped around.

Triptolemus chuckled.

Her knees wobbled at the husky wisp of sound. It wrapped around her, vibrated through her, caressed every erogenous zone on the way, leaving her tingling and even more needy.

"I never knew how sexy bunnies could be," Triptolemus said, voice still a low, aching rasp that made her nerves tremble and her nipples peak so hard she was certain they were very visible now through bra and t-shirt.

"Sexy?"

"Oh Gods yes. And who knew I was a leg man?"

She stared down – thank everything holy she'd shaved her legs that morning in the shower. "You are?" This was the strangest vision.

"Oh yes. Prior to this, I would have said I was all about your breasts, but looking at your legs in those short little shorts, capped off with those bunny slippers …" He licked his lips. "Oh Hells yes. I'm a leg man."

Her gaze went to his legs – thick, muscled thighs and defined calves dusted with dark hair over sun-kissed skin, narrow ankles, large shapely feet. "I find I'm rather partial to legs too." Her gaze roved back up, arrowing in on his thick erection. "I'm also rather partial to other things."

His erection flexed, brushing against the six-pack he sported. "All hail other things! I have to admit, this 'other thing' is rather partial to 'other things' as well."

Her gaze flew up to find his roving over her once again, finally coming to meet her eyes.

The impact stole her breath.

"You have the most extraordinary eyes. They're like the velvet dark of night kissed by the dawn."

Oh! What a thing to say. Her heart squeezed and warmed in a way that felt like she was melting. In a good way. In the best way.

"And your hair? It's been dawn-touched too. Like the rays of sun whispering over the hills, lighting the sky with gold and lilac and peach. And so silky-looking, I just want to wrap my hands in it and find out if it feels as soft as it looks. If it's cool or warm."

Her heart did that thing again, squeezing and warming in a way that would have worried her if not for the fact that other things were squeezing and warming. She never knew words could be so sexually powerful. She swallowed hard, touched her hair, fingers sliding through the lock falling over her shoulder. "I was going to cut it short."

"Oh no. Never do that. It's perfect the way it is. Glorious. In fact, it shines like a halo in the sun. You're like an angel. My Christmas angel."

"Pfft." She waved away the idea. "I'm simply a woman."

He let out an unsteady breath. "Nothing simple about you." He took in another breath, his muscled chest expanding, his tanned skin glowing in the strange light of this place. "Did you know you glow?"

Her lips twitched. "You're a poet and you don't know it?"

He laughed, the sound a brilliant burst around her, doing much the same as his chuckle had done earlier. She wanted to wrap herself in that laugh, in the warmth and joy of it.

In her long, long life, that kind of joy and warmth had been non-existent.

His laughter died when she didn't join him, didn't even smile. His gaze met hers again, the hunger intensifying in the depths of his brilliant, spring-green eyes. "I'm serious. You actually glow."

"It's the light of this place." She gestured around them at the garden they were in. The garden he'd created with his blood. "It's different here. You're glowing too."

He looked down at himself, raising his arms, turning them over. "No. My skin is simply reflecting the light. The glow in you comes from within. I noticed it the first time I saw you. And every time since."

Every time since?

Was he talking about the dreams? But that wasn't possible. They'd been her dreams. Not visions. Not astral travel or whatever this was. Just hot, wet, sexy dreams – more fantasy than dream – that she couldn't seem to shake no matter how much she tried.

So, how had he seen them too? She wanted to ask, but he got in first.

"So, my Christmas angel, do you have a name?"

"Ilia."

His brow quirked. "Ilia." He said her name like he was breathing it in, tasting it, and the sensation pleased him. "So, Ilia. How is it you glow if you're not an angel?"

"I was brought into this life with an ancient spell at dawn with magic that was Goddess-given by Ostara." She had no idea why she'd told him that, but the words just tumbled out.

He nodded. "Makes sense. The first time I saw you it was like I saw the sun's rays at dawn after being stuck in the dark all my life."

Again with the words. He was good with the words. Damn him. It was doing something to her that she didn't think she liked, but was powerless to stop. Especially given he wasn't using his looks and magnetism to pull her in like most males – God or man – would. Okay, he was standing there completely starkers, but he'd done nothing to take advantage of that fact. He'd just used humour and bantering and the loveliest compliments she'd ever been given.

And boy, it was working. Not that it needed to work. She'd been ready to jump his bones the moment she'd seen him; she didn't need anything else.

Yet … instead of moving towards him, she asked, "What's going on here?"

He glanced down at himself then looked up at her through his eyelashes. "A baring of souls?"

She snort-laughed, slapping her hand to her lips, mortified. She'd never made that sound in her long existence.

He laughed too, plush lips splitting wide, white teeth flashing, head tipping back, the laugh vibrating in his chest and throat. Such a laugh, it made her laugh with him. At him. At her. At this strange situation they were in.

Slowly, their laughter petered out. He took a slow step towards her, head tipped to the side. "What brought you here?"

"A book. There was an image of you. I touched it and then here I was. You?"

"I think maybe you brought me here."

"What do you mean?"

"I was about to get on with my day after …" He stopped, cheeks flushing and waved his hand. "Never mind. It's a long story. Needless to say, I was finally determined to stop getting sucked into the wet-daydreams when bam! I was sucked into this. I assume it was you who brought me here."

"I didn't mean to." She frowned. "Although, if it was me, why would I bring you here with no clothes on? I mean, I'm wearing the clothes I had on before coming here. Unless you weren't dressed when dragged here?"

"No, I was dressed." He raised a brow. "Maybe this is how you want to see me."

Heat rushed up her chest and into her face. He was right. She'd been imagining what he looked like after every non-fulfilling dream ended with her disrobing and him staying clothed, then disappearing before they'd even got to touch. She should lie about that, but … "Maybe. Or maybe it's about time that you're the one who's naked."

"All's fair," he said. "In love and war?"

Why did panic rise in her chest at that word? To cover, she snorted and said, "Love. That's hardly applicable to these dreams of ours. That's just lust."

"Is it? Is it only that? When you appear and look at me like that, it feels deeper than lust. It feels—"

"Whoa! Hold that thought right there, Mister. We don't know each other."

He looked down at himself then back at her. One brow cocked. "Really."

Heat rushed over her again. Almost against her will, she took a stumbling step towards him before managing to stop herself from rushing to him, giving more away than she was willing to. He had to meet her part way.

But he didn't move. Every part of him was tensed, as if waiting for something. She wasn't certain what, given the look in his eyes.

She licked her lips. He raised his brow, his erection twitching against his stomach.

"So?"

"So."

She might have wanted the words before, but now, she wanted more. Needed more. "Are you going to continue to talk, or are you going to come over here?" She had no idea where those words came from either – her one and only time spent with any male in this way had been nothing like this. She'd not been this bold, this forward. She'd completely followed Mars' lead. He'd taken. She'd given. And thought that was love.

So stupid.

But she wasn't stupid now. She knew this wasn't love, despite Triptolemus' inference that more was going on between them. For her, it was lust. Pure and simple. Not that lust was either pure or simple. But whatever.

Looking at him filled her with lust.

And by the evidence before her, looking at her filled him with the same. But still, he didn't move. "Please," she managed to say.

"Please what?" he asked, that smile widening a little more.

"Please. I need you. Now."

"Now?"

"Yes, now!"

"So demanding. Why are you always so demanding?"

"Because you like it that way."

"Do I?"

"Oh yes, you do."

She was shocked at herself but also delighted. It was freeing, this open, teasing talk. And so damned hot, especially with that look flaring in his eyes that mirrored the sensations firing through her.

And yet, he held back, sucking in an unsteady breath. "Oh, Ilia. I would like nothing more than to come over there and explore this. But given we seem more in control of things this time, shall we try to figure out why we keep being drawn back to each other? Or even why this is happening in the first place?"

Sexual heat fizzled inside her. She'd never been more disappointed in all her life, but Hells. He was right. Given this chance, she couldn't let the others down. "I know why. We've been looking for you."

"We?"

She nodded. "And then I found you in that vision. I think the quality in your blood that allowed you to grow those plants brought me to you, allowed us to talk briefly. But there wasn't enough information."

"Information? About me?"

"That. And where you are."

He glanced around him. "On my farm."

"Yes, but where?"

"Why do you need to find me?"

She paused. Was that really her news to tell? Not really. "Don't you want me to?"

His gaze heated once more as it raked over her from head to toe and back again. "Oh yes. I really want to. I want to see you in the flesh. I want to feel your skin under mine, not just reach for it and have you disappear. I want you here with me."

"I want that too."

"Good. Because I can't get you out of my thoughts. I don't think I even want to."

She couldn't get him out of her thoughts either. Although, she really wanted to. After this lust was slaked, she'd be able to. "Well?"

"Well what?"

"Where are you?"

"I'm—"

"Ilia? Ilia? Are you okay? Ilia?"

The words thundered around her, covering his answer, and before she could figure out what was happening, she was whisked away. "No!" she screamed.

She came back to herself with a thud and a horrible sense that she'd just wasted her one and only chance to get the information they needed. "No, no, no!" She slammed her hands back on the picture of Triptolemus, running her fingers over his face. "Take me back! Take me back! I'm not finished. I'm not finished!"

"Ilia!"

"She's hysterical."

"She's still lost in the vision."

Bas, Tamuel and Korinna stood around her. They must have pulled her out of the vision. But they didn't understand. She had to get back. To him. She had to find out where he was. Then she had to jump his bones. She hadn't got to jump his bones. Her skin felt like a live-wire was attached. Her nerves jumping. Heat flashed through her. Power sparked on her fingertips, in her chest. She began to fall again.

"Look at her chest! It's glowing."

"The gem. It must be Clodia doing this."

"No. Wrong colour. This is something else. We need to make her let go of that book."

Hands grabbed her arms, others wound around her waist. They pulled at her. Her grip on the book began to slip, fingers raking across the page, across that incredibly handsome face. She scrabbled to hold on, getting her clawed fingers around the edge of the book.

"Ilia, you've got to let go."

"No! No. Don't make me stop. I almost had it. Don't make me stop!"

"Ilia. It's taking your life's energy. It's affecting Dawn."

Those words. They got through.

Her grip slipped.

The arms around her, holding her shoulders, her waist, pulled and they lurched back.

And he was truly gone. "No, no, no! I didn't find him! I didn't find him!" Tears tumbled down her face.

"Find who?" Tamuel asked, his voice close to her ear – he was holding her up.

"By the Heavens. Look at that!" Korinna exclaimed.

"What?" Bas asked from Ilia's other side. He was holding her too?

"It's my father."

"Words are appearing."

They were?

She looked down and sure enough, words appeared across the bottom of the picture that had taken her into the vision with Triptolemus.

"Find me at Snowy Hills Christmas Tree Farm, Tasmania."

"Does that mean what I think it means?" Korinna asked, her voice wobbling.

"Ilia?"

She blinked, staring at the words. "Y-yes. I saw him. He was about to tell me where he was when you pulled me out. I don't know how, but he managed to tell me even though you ripped me away."

"We had to, Ilia. The book was killing you. And Dawn. It sucks on your soul's energy to power the visions it gifts. That's why it's locked away and has a warning attached for anyone who wants to use it."

Did it? She hadn't seen any warning.

"Why did you bring it out here and use it without one of us?" Tamuel asked.

"I didn't. It just appeared."

"It what?" Korinna looked at Tamuel and Bas, her eyes wide. "That's not possible."

Bas shook his head slowly. "No, it's not. The only way a book can get out is if someone takes it out."

"Or lets it out," Tamuel said ominously. "We never got to the bottom of who let the book out Korinna and I battled before Easter."

"We've been a bit busy," Korinna said. "Besides, its release helped us to find the solution to how we could blend our magic together and let Ilia out of the HBG, so it felt like the intent behind that was positive. And I have to say, this feels the same. If that book hadn't been let out for Ilia to use, we'd never have discovered where to find my father."

"You don't think it could be a trap?"

Korinna took Tamuel's hand. "This is the best lead we've had. We have to follow it."

"True," Bas said. "But you need to be careful. Whoever put this information before us like this is playing a dangerous game. Ilia and Dawn could have been seriously hurt." He turned to her. "Ilia, are you okay?" He grabbed her just in time – her legs suddenly gave out.

"I need to sit down."

"Here." He picked her up and walked to the couch where he lowered her gently so she was lying down.

It should have been a relief, but her head ached and her breathing was a little too slow and hard.

"Oh Gods. Ilia. What can we do?"

"Nothing. I'll take care of her," Bas said. "You and Korinna need to check out the address in the book, Tam."

"Are you sure?" Korinna asked, her voice wavering with worry and excitement. "Jules might need help with Dawn, and you with Ilia. Checking to see if my father's at that address can wait."

"No, it can't," Tamuel said grimly. "You're having more intense nightmares every night, Rinna. You know the darkness is drawing near. We need to find Triptolemus sooner rather than later.

"But … Ilia. Dawn. How can we go when they're like this?"

"Because Tam is right," Ilia managed to say. "I'll be fine."

Bas nodded. "We'll be able to handle this. They both should recover quickly now Ilia is no longer in contact with the book."

"Really?" Korinna's gaze bored into her with their hope and worry.

"Really. You need to go. Now." How could saying so few words sap her of all energy? But she held herself together because Korinna wouldn't go otherwise.

"See. They'll both be fine." Bas raised his brow at Ilia and he smiled grateful before his gaze went to Tam. "But just be careful, my son. Okay?"

"Of course. We don't know if that message is from Triptolemus or from something else entirely."

"We'll be careful," Korinna promised.

Portal magic prickled the air in front of the couch but Ilia didn't see them step through because blackness surrounded her and she passed out.

9

Trip slammed out of the vision as fast as he was sucked into it. He fell back on his couch with a thump. Breath exploded out of him.

"Shit!" He grasped at his chest, fingers clenching on his t-shirt as he struggled to breathe. His cock pressed hard against his shorts, still at attention despite his inability to catch his breath.

And in his mind, her face as clear as day.

Ilia.

He knew her name now!

Ilia.

It suited her, the name like sunlight shining from beyond a mountain, lighting the sky.

He smiled sappily, sinking softly into the couch, his hand going to his crotch and …

"Shit-crap-fuck!" He leaped to his feet, shoving his hands behind him. It had almost happened again. What in all the Hells was wrong with him? He'd never acted like this. Ever. And the fact Daphne had caught him masturbating last week and yet he was still at it like some horny teenager …

Something else was manipulating him. He was certain of it. But why?

He stared around his lounge room as if to find the answers there. When nothing came, he blew out a long breath, raking his hands through his hair.

Was this happening because they were meant to be together? That might explain the outrageous lust and also the deeper feeling that he knew her somehow. Was this the Fates' way of making up for the crappy hand he'd been dealt? Maybe. Although, she didn't seem too keen on that idea when he'd tried to bring it up. All she'd seemed to want was his body … and for some strange reason, his address.

We've been looking for you. Those were her words. Who was the mysterious 'we' and why did they want to find him? A crawling sensation prickled over his skin. Maybe he shouldn't have shouted his address out to her when she abruptly flew up and away from him.

Had she heard him?

Was she coming to find him? Would she just appear, like the best, most sexy Christmas gift he'd ever seen? Or would she be with the 'we'?

The front doorbell rang, making him jump.

He sucked in a breath. Could that be …?

He stumbled to the door as if in a dream. The doorbell peeled again just as he got there. He smiled. She was just as impatient to see him as he was to see her. He pulled the door open with such force it was a miracle it didn't tear off its hinges. "Thank the Gods you heard me. I—"

He stared at the handsome couple who stood on his front veranda. A man and a woman. He didn't really notice anything about the man because his attention was drawn to the woman. Not Ilia, but equally as mesmerising in a very different way. She stared at him with eyes that were the exact same colour as his. He'd never seen eyes that colour, other than when he looked in the mirror. "What …? Who are you?"

"Triptolemus?"

That name … Ilia had called him that. And like it had then, it made him feel a little sick as a bell clanged through his head over and over in time to the syllables. He winced and pressed his palm against his forehead where pain throbbed along with the clanging.

"Oh my Goddess, it's you! I can't believe we've finally found you!"

Found him? Were they Ilia's 'we'? And why wasn't she here with them? She was supposed to be here too. He felt it deep in his soul. "This ... isn't ... right," he managed to say around the pounding in his head.

"Triptolemus? Are you alright? Triptolemus?"

Hells. The pain in his head got worse every time the woman said his name. "I'm not Triptolem ... Triptol ... Tripto—" The pain threatened to fell him when he tried to say the name, so he stopped and said, "My name's Trip. Trip O'Dem." The name had been the only thing left to him when he'd woken all those years ago – that and the bags of gold – and as he said it, the pain slipped away.

"Trip." Her lips wobbled. "I like it."

He frowned. What did it matter if she liked his name? And yet, it did. And why was there something so familiar about her? The familiarity wasn't just in the fact they shared the same colour eyes. It was something else he couldn't put his finger on, yet he was certain he'd never seen her before in this life.

He cleared his throat. "Who are you?"

The woman's hand went to her throat. "Do you not recognise me? They say I look like my mother."

He stared at her, his chest tightening. Her mother? Had he known her mother? Maybe that's why she looked familiar. For a glimmering moment, a wisp of memory of a face very like hers shimmered in his mind's-eye before a stabbing pain sent it spiralling away.

Biting back another wince, he said, "I ... I've never seen you before. And I have no idea who your mother is."

"Oh, I ..." She swallowed hard, her upset obvious.

His chest ached. He wanted to touch her face, to tell her everything would be okay.

But she was a stranger. A stranger who might know Ilia.

For some reason though, he couldn't come out and just ask. Her name seemed locked in his throat. Instead, he asked, "Who are you?"

"I'm Korinna Soteira. This is my mat— My husband, Tamuel Stevens."

He shook his head. The names held an echo, like something long forgotten, but he was certain he'd never heard them before. "Doesn't ring a bell. Why do you think I'm supposed to know you?" The longer this conversation went on, the more he was coming to think they had nothing to do with Ilia. Because if they did, wouldn't they mention her?

"I ... I suppose it was foolish to hope you would." The woman blinked rapidly, her gaze flickering to the man she'd identified as Tamuel. He didn't say anything, just took her hand in his, holding it tight, and for a moment, Trip could have sworn that his dark eyes glowed violet as he met Korinna's gaze.

Power pulsed from both of them.

These people were not human. At least, not fully. He took a step back, panic a tight grip in his chest. Something inside him told him to run, that he could never let himself be caught by anyone else with magic.

Except, he hadn't felt that with Ilia. And she most definitely had magic.

This must be proof that these people had nothing to do with her.

He took a step back, reaching for the door. "I don't know what your business is here, but I want you to go."

The woman stepped forward, hands clasped together, eyes beseeching. "Please, don't. I've come a long way to meet you. There's things ... things I have to say. Things you need to know."

"I need to know nothing from you."

He went to close the door, but the man – Tamuel – waved his hand and the door sprang out of Trip's hand to slam back against the wall. "Please. Triptolemus. You need to listen."

Anger welled inside him, burning away the panic and fear that their presence brought, and the pain the sound of that name evinced. He gripped the door and yanked it from its position against the wall.

It wasn't easy to move, but he gritted his jaw and pulled until he slammed it in their faces.

The last thing he saw was the surprised expression on the man's face and tears in the woman's eyes.

Arms and legs trembling, he leaned back against the door.

"Well, that didn't go well," he heard the man say through the door.

"It's him. She found him. I can't believe it's really him."

"It is wonderful, my heart, but I don't think he was lying when he didn't seem to remember anything about you at all."

"I know. I have to admit that I thought if he just saw me it would break the spell."

"I hoped that too but … did you see the fear in his eyes? That doesn't bode well for making him listen to us."

"It must have something to do with the spell Demeter put on him to take his memories and keep him safe."

At the sound of that name – Demeter – Trip's legs gave way and he slid to the floor, the room swaying and swirling around him. Even so, the couple's conversation came through the door loud and clear, piercing the fog in his mind.

"But how am I to get through to him? I need him to listen. I need him to teach me about my birthright and to explain exactly why he did what he did."

"Maybe Ilia can help. She's the one who's been seeing him."

Ilia! They did know Ilia. They were her 'we'!

He tried to move, but his limbs were just too sluggish and his head too full of pain as their words swirled around him.

"Yes. But … if she comes, it means everyone has to come and they'll have to come by plane then drive because Dawn gets too sick going through the portal. And how can I ask Jules to leave right now with all her Christmas plans in place?"

"I don't think we have a choice. He obviously still has some of his power – did you see how he moved the door despite me holding it with my power? Not to mention what helped us to find him. Ilia's dreams then that vision and now the book!"

"And what about the thing Ilia says he did with his blood? Growing the plants in that field. Do you think his blood is what drew her in some way, because of what we did at Easter with my blood and yours, mixing them with the power of the ring and the power of Oestra?"

"I don't know. It's possible."

"But what does it mean?"

"I can't answer that. What I *am* concerned about is if the media gets wind of the miracle Garden of Eden growing in his paddock, they'll have a field day. It might even get so big an issue it could draw Zeus and the other Gods' attention – and we don't want any of them turning this way before we've discovered how to get his memories back."

"I'm sure there's things we can do to stop that from happening."

"True. You should try using your powers with your ring. If he grew all that from his blood, I'm sure yours mixed with the gem can help undo it all so it doesn't seem so … miraculous."

Trip held his breath as their words punched through his spinning thoughts. Could they take care of that problem for him? Perhaps he should go out, talk to them, ask for the help they seemed so ready to give. Especially given they did know Ilia. Were talking about bringing her down here.

Ilia.

Every time they said her name, it pushed aside the pain and confusion, the sound of it a burst of brightness in his mind like the most perfect of blooms, carrying her perfumed scent along with it, like night-blooming jasmine and roses as they were warmed by the sun's rays at dawn.

Ilia.

"She is the one. The one who will save you. You must get her here. You must drink of her blood."

The thought jagged in his mind, stopping him from spinning back into the wet-daydream again. He tried once more to get up, but his limbs were like jelly and he slid back to the floor.

The voices outside grasped his attention.

"… using your powers isn't what's worrying you, is it?" Tamuel was saying.

Korinna snorted. "Hardly. I'm feeling much more on top of them now. The Eleusinian Mysteries Grimoire has helped so much with that."

The what? Those words, they sounded like he should know them. No … like he *did* know them.

"I've still got so much to learn. There's so much I don't know. I mean, how did he do it? How did he grow things with just his blood? I didn't think we were supposed to be able to do any of that without the ring because of how our blood is cursed. I didn't see him wearing it on his hand."

The ring?

A vision of a ring, thick gold with a green gem set in it, appeared in his mind's eye. He'd had that ring on his finger when he'd woken, but he'd taken it off and hidden it before walking into the first village he'd come across. For some reason, he'd kept it hidden ever since.

So how did they know about the ring? He wanted to ask, but still couldn't seem to stand, or make a sound. All he could do was listen.

"… I don't know. Maybe Demeter took it before she wiped his mind."

He clutched his head as pain spiked through it again. That name. Pain came every time they said it.

"I can't believe she's disappeared. I thought now that I'd discovered all she'd hidden from me, she'd speak about it at last and tell me why."

"Does Persephone know where she's gone yet?"

Persephone. More pain in his head; but not as bad as the ache in his heart at the sound of that name.

"No. She has no clue. Seph is really worried. And she can't tell me anything either because she's bound by the vows she made to her mother. All we have is what Ilia heard Demeter say when she was in possession of the HBG."

"Well, we've got no choice. We have to ask everyone to come down here. Before he does something more to out himself than he's already done. Given Ilia is certain he's seen her in the dream-vision, he might listen to her."

Ilia? They would bring her here? He pushed past the pulsing pain and listened harder.

"First, we should go and deal with that field."

"Yes. Let's do that. Then we need to call Jules so she can organise flights to get them all down here."

"You don't want to go back and tell them?"

"No. I can't leave him. I want to stay close." Thick tears in the woman's voice. "I didn't think meeting my father would be like this."

Father? The word rang through his mind, stealing his breath, drowning out the sound of the male's reply.

She couldn't mean that word in relation to him. He was nobody's father. He hadn't made his vow to not get involved with a woman lightly. It was too dangerous, not only because he couldn't risk anyone finding out the truth about him, but because he couldn't risk passing on to a child his cursed blood, as she called it. And she was right. For surely it was a curse when he had to hide it from the world for fear of what would happen if the truth got out. Look what had happened with the small amount he'd spilled and the trouble that waited in the wings because of it.

These people obviously knew all about it. Perhaps they could get rid of the curse.

The thought brought energy to his limbs with a sudden rush, enabling him finally to push to his feet. He was still wobbly and it took a few moments of him leaning against the door to get his breath back.

There was a rush over his skin, akin to the lightning pricks of static electricity, and a gust of wind blew under the door.

What in the Hells? He managed to pull the door open.

They were gone, dirt and leaves whirling in a spiral a foot above the ground in the place they'd just stood.

10

"*D*amn!"

He swung around to make certain Daphne and her boys hadn't been around to see them disappear. Daphne wouldn't swallow a Christmas miracle again and neither would her boys.

But thankfully, there was no sign of them. They were either all working in the shop, getting it ready for Saturday, or preparing the tractors – Gideon had dressed them up like reindeers for last Saturday and there were some issues with antlers staying in place that the boys had been working on all week to delight their guests this weekend.

Would Korinna and Tamuel be back with Ilia and the other people they spoke of on Saturday? Could he wait until then? He supposed he had to. It wasn't like he knew where they were.

Although … he did. They said they were going to take care of the magically grown garden.

Limbs still a little wobbly, he raced as fast as he could to where he'd parked his ute. He barely had the door shut before he'd started it and was off down the lane that led to the field. He swore at every gate he had to stop at and open, not bothering to close them behind him as he'd told Daphne and the boys they must – he'd get them on the way back. He needed to speak to this Korinna and Tamuel. And he had no idea how long they would be at their task. They were dealing with magic after all. If his blood could grow a lush garden in a few seconds, then it shouldn't take them much longer to get rid of it – should it? He really didn't know how any of this worked. Something else he had to learn from them.

Hells. Why had he acted like such an idiot? They'd appeared just after he'd shouted his address in the dream to Ilia. Of course she'd sent them. He should have trusted them. He blamed years of living alone and barely trusting anyone. Well, he had to trust them now. They had answers.

And Ilia.

As he drove closer, a glowing green light rose above the hill between him and the field.

Korinna's magic. She was already at it. Hells.

He pushed down on the accelerator, the revving engine complaining loudly. He didn't care. He had to get there.

The light glowed and pulsed. In the morning sun, it wasn't too bright, but what if people on nearby properties saw that glow and wondered what was going on? Shit. He hadn't thought of that. His magic didn't have a colour. Things just grew. This was something different.

He crested the rise that led down into the valley where the field was. His foot hit the break and he jerked forward at the abrupt stop.

Green light flowed from Korinna's right hand, reaching out to twine around and cover the plants he'd grown with his blood. The man she'd called her husband – Tamuel – stood at her side, a blue and purple glow growing around him, feeding down his arm and into the hand clasped around hers.

Was he feeding his power into her in some way? What for? A dual power? Was that a thing? Once again, he had no idea.

But all those questions fled as the green glow fell on the garden he'd accidentally grown and started to press down. The plants began to disappear, turning into a fine green mist that settled on the ground.

As it did, hundreds of pine tree seedlings, like what had been there before the storm, appeared.

The green power fluttered then withdrew with a snap into Korinna's ring.

The young witch who claimed he was her father – he shook his head at the impossible to fathom thought – seemed to sag a little. Tamuel held her up, arm around her waist, his magic still feeding into her.

She straightened, smiled up at her powerful husband, then kissed him gently on the lips.

He returned her kiss before pulling away to wave his hand, his power changing as it flew from his outstretched fingertips. The air in front of them wobbled, then began to spin, sparking with blue and purple lights. The air split and a round … portal? He didn't know how he knew the word, but he was certain that was right … spun there.

They were leaving!

He hit the accelerator and began to honk his horn, shouting out the window, "Don't go. Don't go!"

They turned.

Fearful they'd leave despite the fact they'd stopped and were staring at him as he drove madly towards them, he didn't bother getting out to open the gate, just crashed through it.

To their credit, they didn't move.

He stopped the ute and jumped out. "The ring! You used the ring!" The words exploded out of his mouth on each pant of breath as he ran the last few metres to them.

She held out her hand, the ring and its green gem gleaming on the middle finger of her right hand. Exactly like his.

"You remember the ring?" she said as he came to a stop in front of her.

"I have one too."

She smiled slowly. "I know."

"I didn't know it could do that." He gestured at the field of Christmas tree seedlings.

"You weren't meant to know," Tamuel said.

"But you can tell me?" He couldn't look anywhere but at Korinna and the ring.

"We hoped you'd be able to tell us," Korinna said. "I'd hoped just seeing me would help you to remember."

He shook his head slowly, sadly. "I can't remember. I can't remember who I was before I woke up all those years ago. All I remember is this," he said, gesturing around him. "This life. And even that I struggle with. I have diaries, but there are so many by now, it's impossible to look over them, to keep up with it all."

"Well, we're hoping we'll be able to help you with that."

"They will. They can help. But only after Ilia is here. Only after you have drunk her blood."

The voice rang in his mind, louder than it had ever been in any of his wet-daydreams or even when he'd seen Ilia in this field.

"The blood," he said. "It's all in the blood."

Korinna looked down at the ring, and he noticed for the first time the blood on her skin, sizzling on the gem. "My blood? Your blood?"

He shook his head. "Her blood. The one you call Ilia. You have to get her here. Her blood is the key."

"What? Why? How do you know that?"

"A voice keeps telling me. I heard it first when she appeared in my field and then ..." he blushed a little, "... in dreams I've had ever since."

"Dreams? Tell me about the dreams."

His blush deepened. It was bad enough Daphne knew about his lascivious mind. If this woman was actually somehow his daughter, he most definitely didn't want her knowing how he lusted after her friend. But, if he was to get their help, he needed to tell them something more than he had to convince them. "She is standing there, like she was that day, but in the dreams she's wearing this Grecian-type gown with gold butterfly clips on the shoulders." Not in the most recent one, of course, but he most definitely wasn't sharing that with them. It was too intimate. Too ... everything. He cleared his throat and forced his mind back to the other dreams. "She reaches for me and tells me to drink of her blood, that it will make everything right. Except, come to think of it, it's not really her voice."

Korinna and Tamuel shared a look. "A Grecian gown? With butterfly clips?"

"That means something to you?"

"It's a message from Demeter. It has to be."

He winced at the name.

They looked at him. "Are you okay?" Korinna asked, reaching to touch his arm.

He let her, wondering at how good it felt, how right. He stared at her.

"Trip?"

He suddenly remembered her question. "Yes, it's just, some of the names you say, they give me pain."

She glanced at Tamuel. "Part of the spell?"

"Makes sense. From what Ilia told us, your mentor wouldn't want him looking into anything that might lead him to the truth until you were ready."

"So, it's true then. Ilia's blood is somehow the key."

Tamuel was grim as he turned his gaze back to Trip. "It makes sense. Her magic was always special and incredibly strong, which is why Tiberinus used her in the first place – only a special kind of witch could have survived being used like that in the HBG."

"She has rejuvenating powers!" Korinna blurted.

"Yes. And now she's linked to Dawn's magic, her blood must carry something even more special – an ability to conjure a kind of rebirth."

"Like she could reset Trip to what he was before!"

"Yes."

"Goddess. That's amazing. It's like what the old Gods used to do when they needed to share power or heal or just power-up. They'd even grow fangs to help facilitate it."

"Like Tiberinus did to Ilia," Tamuel said harshly.

Korinna's eyes flared wide. "Oh no."

"What?" Trip asked as Korinna began to wring her hands.

"If she knows this, she'll never come."

"What?" Trip's gaze zipped from one to the other. "Why?"

Tamuel grimaced. "It's the blood thing."

"The blood?"

Korinna grimaced. "Well, that's a rather long story about lies and betrayal, leading to her being held prisoner in a gem for thousands of years. Suffice it to say, she won't be on board with any kind of blood magic. Especially if you have to drink it."

He pointed at the ring and the blood that still stained its surface. "Do you hide your use of it from her?"

"No. It makes her uncomfortable, but she knows it's got more to do with the magical qualities in my blood tied to my birthright, and so isn't like the blood magic she fears. However, drinking blood to syphon power, even if it's to heal … I don't think we'll be able to talk her around to accepting that as anything but evil given her past."

No. This couldn't be true. "But she's been coming to me. She told me."

"It wasn't her."

"It was. She remembers the dreams. She's seen them too. I know she has, otherwise you wouldn't be here."

"That's true," Tamuel said. "But I know Ilia. I lived with her and the gem in my chest for months. She would never ask you to drink her blood. You said it didn't sound like her voice when she asked you to do that, right?" Trip nodded. "Something else is at play here, putting those words in her mouth."

"The same thing that brought her the book?"

"Perhaps," Tamuel said, expression becoming even more grim.

Damn all the devils in all the Hells! He was so close. For the first time in his very long existence, he knew he was close to remembering what he was supposed to be; who he was. But if Korinna and Tamuel were to be believed, being close wasn't going to get them anything. He would continue to live his life not knowing what all this was for. He would never know why this woman who stood in front of him was suddenly so terribly important to him. He would never know why his blood grew things and he never aged. He would always be alone.

Even though he'd always thought that was his future and was resolved to it, the possibility that had been waved in front of his face for a brief moment, of something more, of true, long-lasting connection, now made that future unbearable.

Despair took him in its maw.

Why was his life like this? Who had done this to him? There were no answers and there were never going to be any.

He turned to stare across his lands.

As he did, Ilia appeared on the other side of the field. She didn't look like she had previously – this time far more ghost-like. In fact, he could see the outline of the land and trees behind her. She smiled at him, blew him a kiss then turned and walked through the fence and up the hill, disappearing among next year's crop of pine trees.

"She's here."

"Who?"

"Ilia. There she is. Rising above the trees. Oh. She looks like a Christmas angel."

"I can't see her."

They couldn't see her? But suddenly it didn't matter as her voice, deep and huskier than he remembered, sounded in his ears.

"Look at these pine trees you grow. They could be nothing, withering and dying without the right care. But, you give them that so they can become healthy and green and stand as a sign of the promise of renewal. Hope is like that. Like these trees, you can make hope grow and flourish once more. You love this time of year for a reason – because it speaks to the need in your soul for family, love and forgiveness. Remember that now and go forth, in the spirit of Christmas, and find a way. Find a way to me. Find a way for me. I need you." She gestured behind him. *"Your daughter needs you. Find a way."*

"What?"

"You know."

"I do? How?"

"Who are you talking to, Trip?"

Before he could answer Korinna's confused question, Ilia disappeared in a flare of light as bright as the star of Bethlehem.

"What the fuck was that?" Tamuel said, shielding his eyes.

"Trip? Trip, are you okay?"

"Did you see her?" he asked, still unable to look away from where she'd hovered moments before.

"See who?"

"The morning star. The dawn's light. My Christmas angel. Ilia."

"What? No. She couldn't be here. She can't leave without Dawn."

"All I saw was a bright flare of light."

He shook his head. It didn't matter they hadn't seen her. "She was here and she gave me a message." One meant just for him because only he could figure it out. Only he could bring it to pass. Because only he had lived the life that he had leading up to this very moment in time.

The trees. His Christmas spirit. His love of what this time of year represented: light and laughter and sharing, the warmth of family and friends, the renewal brought around by kindness and forgiveness. They were true and everlasting, no matter if you believed in the old ways or the newer religions that had taken them as part of their celebrations.

The black of depression and despair faded. He spun to face Korinna and Tamuel. "I know what to do!"

Korinna blinked rapidly at his startling announcement. "Know what to do what?"

"To encourage her to agree. To see it's not evil. To make this work."

"You do?" Tamuel asked, putting his arm around Korinna. "How can we help?"

A smile curled his lips. "You can get her here, right? Ilia?"

They both nodded, Tamuel asking, "But what good will that do?"

"And you will stay?"

"Of course." Korinna said, taking his outstretched hands. He sighed happily at the feeling of oneness and homecoming that holding her hands brought to him. By the smile in her eyes, he guessed she felt the same way.

"Good. Then, invite Ilia and everyone who needs to come with her. We will share Christmas together and see if it won't shed a little of its Christmas magic and help us out in the way we need it to."

"You're hoping for a true Christmas miracle then," she said, not a little sarcasm in her tone.

He didn't care if she doubted. She would learn. "Not hoping. I am certain we can make one happen." He slung an arm around Korinna, the other around Tamuel and, guiding them towards his ute, said, "Now, tell me what you can."

"But what about the pain?"

"If I pass out from it, we'll know not to touch on that until I get my memories back." He squeezed Korinna's shoulder, grinning like a loon. "Now, we better get to it. There's a lot to do to get everything ready before they get here."

As they got into the ute and drove back to his house, he could barely contain his excitement.

Soon, very soon, he would remember everything – the good and the bad.

He couldn't wait!

She was coming. Today. In fact, she'd be here with Tamuel's family later this morning.

It was like a buzz under his skin, the knowledge, the certainty. He'd known it this morning before he'd even seen Korinna, who'd greeted him with the news.

She was so close now. And with her came the future. His future.

Or was it his past?

One was all tangled up in the other – for without a past, how could you have a true future?

For the first time in his life, he wished he didn't have hundreds of Christmas tree hunters coming. He wished he had the day free, set aside just for her. For her arrival. For the momentous *something* he knew she brought with her.

He glanced around. The car park was almost full. Daphne and Charlie were already in their Mrs Claus (the summer version) and elf costumes and were busy confirming the e-tickets for each booking. There was a queue lined up around the shop-shed, where Harry and Gideon were stationed along with Korinna, ready to greet hungry and thirsty travellers with a cold drink and whiskey cake before they headed off to hunt down and cut their trees. Tamuel was acting as traffic officer in the car park – also in an elf costume.

The nine o'clock session of Christmas tree hunters was about to begin. He couldn't ask them to go now and disappoint all these people. Part of his plan was about the Christmas spirit, about spreading and sharing the joy. Their being here was part of who he was and why he did what he did. He needed her to see that. To feel it. To understand what sharing herself in the way he needed her to would do for them; for the world. But not only that, deep in his bones, he knew that once he drank of her blood, things would be righted for them in a way they never had before.

He had to show her, to make her see. And this was the only way he knew how.

Daphne glanced his way, her brow rising in question. He waved and smiled in acknowledgement, then headed to get changed into his costume, nerves fluttering in his stomach.

She and the boys had been worried at first that Korinna and Tamuel were lying. That they were some kind of gold-digging couple come to benefit from his prosperity. But nobody who looked at him and Korinna could deny the familial connection.

Korinna had smoothed things over with the story that her mother, his high school sweetheart, had never told Trip she was pregnant because she didn't want to hold him back from his plans of travelling the world once they finished school – which cleverly explained how, at his age, he could have a daughter in her late twenties. Only after her mother's recent death had Korinna discovered his identity and tracked him down. Not to mention, both she and Tamuel were so kind and helpful – with wealth of their own given how they dressed and the helpful additions they'd made to the farm and its Christmas decorations – that both of them soon had Daphne and her boys onside. Daphne hadn't even baulked when she found out Trip had invited them and their family down for Christmas so they could all get to know each other at this most special time of year.

Daphne had immediately started planning menus for the next few weeks and things to do with their visitors once they got here. He was a little worried that he would have no time with Ilia as he tried to work some Christmas magic on her and get her to agree to the horrible reality that he must drink her blood, but both Korinna and Tamuel said they'd help with that.

There were so many unknowns though. Ultimately it came down to Ilia being willing to give while he only took, but there was nothing he could do about that other than focus on bringing the joy and family feeling that would convince her that drinking her blood was for good purposes, not evil.

He ducked around the back of the shed to his workshop. He grabbed his Santa suit off the hanger and headed into the change-room. He was actually glad he had something to do now to while away the time before her arrival.

Fifteen minutes later, dressed the part and having made certain the tractors and their trailers were all ready to go – and laughing at the amount of tinsel-covered gaffa tape Harry and Gideon had used to stick the antlers and red reindeer noses on the tractors – he hopped on to the one closest to the door, started the engine and with a rumble, drove out of the garage.

"Ho, ho, ho. Merry Christmas!" he called out as he drove around the corner and up to where people waited, eating whiskey cakes and drinking frosted cups of fruity tea that Korinna was passing around. "My trusty steed Rudolfer and I are ready to go Christmas tree hunting. Who's ready for a ride on my Aussie sleigh to come and hunt with me?"

Shrieks of 'me' lit the air as hands were thrust up, most of the kids grasping a candy cane that they'd already been given from the sack Gideon hauled around.

Trip laughed jovially and said, "Once you've finished your drinks and cake, those with a one on their tickets, hop on in. Those with a two, my helper-elf, Charlie, will be out with the other sleigh in a moment to take you to where the best tree hunting will be this year. Climb aboard and a-hunting we will go!"

Gideon and Harry helped everyone up as the sound of the second tractor chugging out of the garage lit the air. Cheers went up as Charlie drove it around the corner towards those waiting for him.

As soon as both groups were loaded up, he set off, winding up the hill towards this year's crop of trees.

The laughter and happy chatter carried to him over the rumble of the tractor engines and made him smile. This was what he loved.

~

ILIA HAD RECOVERED QUICKLY after the incident with the book draining her and Dawn's souls to power her vision, but the baby had not. It had been agonising, seeing her so listless as Bas and Violetta worked their magics and slowly brought her back to them. She'd tried syphoning some of her energies back through the link that tied them together and into the baby, but Bas and Jules had instantly noticed and demanded she stop.

"All you're doing is making yourself weaker, which isn't good for you or Dawn," Bas had said firmly. "Let Violetta and I take care of her."

"And for pity's sake," Violetta had said. "Don't touch any more books."

Not being able to do anything was frustrating, made worse by the fact Korinna and Tamuel were waiting on them all.

Their news had been the only light in a dark week. It was annoying that Trip couldn't come up to Melbourne, but given he ran a Christmas tree farm and this was December, she supposed it was difficult for him to leave. It wasn't like this was going to take a few minutes – there was much to discuss and the problem of returning his memory to overcome. So down to Tasmania she had to go. Which meant all of them had to go.

She'd been certain Jules and Bas would say no given Dawn's state and Jules' own plans for Christmas, but they'd readily agreed to the trip as soon as baby Dawn was recovered.

During the week while Dawn recovered, Triptolemus – or Trip, as Korinna had reported that he liked to be called – continued to feature in her dreams. Frustratingly, the dreams never went any further than they had. It was as if something was blocking them from taking that extra step and no matter how much she tried to push them to move forward, it never happened. She'd always woken in a sweat, panting and tingling all over with a need that just didn't want to be sated no matter how much she took things into her own hands.

It was a relief on the Saturday morning when they finally set off on their trip to Tasmania – a trip which soon became a horror from which there was no escape. Dawn had begun to cry and vomit the moment the plane took off and continued the spew-fest in the car they hired to drive to Trip's farm.

It seemed that travelling via portal wasn't the only kind of travel the baby didn't like – although this wasn't as bad as the portal travel had been. Still, she felt horrible for the poor little mite, but even worse was to discover that she was a sympathetic vomiter. Or a sympathetic dry-retcher. By some miracle she'd managed to keep her breakfast in her stomach where it belonged. She'd thank the Gods, but didn't want to give them credit for even that much.

And quite frankly, much more of dealing with the bile-laden scent of baby sick and her breakfast wouldn't remain where it was. If only she could crack open her window – but when she'd done that, Dawn had begun to scream, so she'd quickly closed it.

To have been locked in a gem for thousands of years then to be freed and made human once more only to deal with the ignominy of this! But really, who was she to complain? Poor little Dawn had suffered so much worse and none of it was her fault. She was as caught up in the machinations of the Gods as Ilia was. That fact made her so angry.

And with that anger came the glow.

Dawn began to scream and retch more.

Shit. Crap. Fuck.

Given the smell in the car, deep breathing exercises were out. So she had to find another way to calm the fire of fury inside her.

Her mind immediately threw up an image of Trip. And not just any image. The one of him smiling at her in that way he had just after he'd said all those lovely things about her.

The flare of rage inside her flickered and died, replaced by a curl of something heated, much lower, and curiously, a strange warmth around her heart.

Thinking about him like this calmed her in a way the sexy dreams didn't. Why? She didn't know. Just another mystery surrounding him. She wished she knew what tied them together in this way. She'd been looking for him, but something deep inside told her that wasn't why she'd begun, and continued to, have the dreams of him and had then been pulled into those astral visions.

The uncertainty of it troubled her. She didn't believe in coincidences. No, this felt much more like the Fates or some God or Goddess messing with her once again.

And she didn't like it one bit. Even though, she had to admit, she rather liked Trip. Not just because he was hot and she'd seen him naked and, oh boy, she definitely wanted to explore his glorious body. But because he was kind and gentle and loved growing things and helping people. Which made him unlike any other God or demi-God that she'd ever met – except for Bas and Tam of course.

She had felt excited to finally see him in the flesh, but with this realisation of more God-like meddling, and a deeper connection that whispered of something more than a good romp in bed with a sexy man, she now felt like she was heading towards her doom.

A shiver rippled over her skin and down her back.

She must have made a sound because Bas asked, "Are you okay?"

She forced a smile that didn't feel at all convincing, so she gave up on it and said, "Fine. I just want to get there."

"You and me both." His gaze flew to his daughter then back to the road.

Ilia rubbed the shiver out of her arms and turned to smile encouragingly at her tiny friend. Dawn's teary eyes met hers and somehow, despite how travel sick she was, the baby managed to smile.

Ilia returned the smile before whipping back to face the front. "How much further?" she asked Bas.

His gaze flicked to the sat-nav. "About twenty minutes."

"That long? Why does Trip have to live in the middle of nowhere, Tasmania?"

"Patience is its own reward," Violetta intoned from the back seat as Jules began to sing another lullaby to Dawn to try to get her to sleep.

"Patience kept me locked in a gem for almost 3000 years, so excuse me for not being a fan of its rewards."

"Patience got you out of that gem in the end."

She snorted. "Reward indeed."

"I know you don't mean that," Bas said, his deep voice a rumble beside her.

She swallowed hard and looked down at her hands. She'd picked the quick of her thumbnail raw. "No, I don't. I'll be forever grateful to all of you for what you did to free me."

"We know," Jules said in a breath between lullaby lyrics.

An annoying burn started at the back of her eyes. She sniffed and rubbed at them. "Bloody hay fever!" she said when she noticed Bas giving her the concerned side-eye.

He huffed a laugh and said, "Yeah, that kind of 'hay fever' has been bad for all of us this last year."

She glowered at him.

He masterfully ignored her as he took a rather sharp turn, then pointed to a hill rising before them. "Ah, we must be close. That hill is covered in Christmas trees. And look, there's the sign."

Sure enough, a large sign in green and red, all sparkly in the sun announced: Snowy Hills Christmas Tree Farm – Come for a tree, stay for the Christmaspalooza!

Hells-bells and all its demons.

Bas chuckled and she turned to see him glance at her quickly before returning his attention to the road. "Cheer up. A bit of Christmas won't kill you."

How had he figured out how she felt?

He chuckled again and said softly, "All the running away from Jules' Christmas madness has been a bit obvious."

"Bah humbug!" she grumbled.

That made him chuckle again. "I'm sure it won't be that bad."

"Little do you know." She stared blindly out the window, crossing her arms over herself to cover the shiver that wracked her again. Her suspicious and grumpy attitude had served her well over the span of her lifetime after being trapped in the HBG, and she wasn't about to change her stripes now.

Bah humbug indeed. She would give Scrooge a run for his money and no ghosts of Christmas Past, Present or Future would change her mind about one skerrick of it.

Hours passed happily and Trip was almost able to ignore the feeling of electricity building inside him. But when he pulled up in front of the shop with the last of the second group of the day, their Christmas trees in Charlie's trailer behind him, a prickling started over his back, making him sit bolt upright in his seat.

He swung around to search the car park.

There was nothing out of the ordinary – people were leaving with their trees netted up and strapped to the tops of their cars or poking out of SUV boots.

Except there – a car had just pulled in at a time when they were expecting nobody.

She was here.

A tall male with dark hair who bore a strong resemblance to Tamuel hopped out of the driver's seat. The front passenger door opened and sun glinted off hair filled with the colours of the dawn as *she* climbed out of the car.

His breath caught in his chest as she turned, her gaze finding him as quickly as his had found her.

She didn't move away from the car. In fact, she clung to the open door as if holding on for dear life. And the look on her face ... If the Hells had an expression, that would be it.

Even with that look of doom and horror on her face, her beauty and the immediacy of her presence hit him like a punch in the diaphragm.

He tried to breathe, but it was impossible.

The world swung in front of him, darkness encroaching on the edges of his vision, and then slowly and unceremoniously, he fell off the tractor in a dead faint.

12

"Did that Santa just faint? Bas, perhaps you should go and help him," Jules said as she pulled Dawn out of her car seat.

"He probably just tripped. Or it's a play they put on or something. Isn't there some movie where Santa falls off the roof?"

"And dies," Jules said as she moved to stand beside Ilia. "The father who finds him ends up having to take over the job of Santa."

"Well, bags that's not me."

"Bas!"

"It's him," Ilia said, still clinging to the door.

"That was Triptolemus? Bas, go help him!"

Bas muttered a curse under his breath before taking off towards the fallen Santa.

"Ilia? Are you okay?"

No. She wasn't. Far from it. How could just laying eyes on Triptolemus affect her like this? Longing and need filled her with warmth and a trembling that had nothing to do with lust. To cover her weakness and confusion, she snapped, "You know, I'm sure he'll be fine. Idiot shouldn't be wearing such a stifling suit in this weather."

"She's right," Jules said. "It's probably heat prostration."

"I'll go help Bas," Violetta said. "It's not like we can help him with magic. Not with all these people around."

Jules nodded towards the commotion where Korinna and Tamuel were pushing their way through the gathered crowd, Bas close behind them. "You better remind them. By the looks of things, Korinna might just forget."

"I don't know what you're worried about," Ilia said to Jules as Violetta hurried off. "Triptolemus is a God. He'll be fine!" She on the other hand felt like she was dying a little bit inside.

Overdramatic? Perhaps. But kind of true.

Everything was buzzing and fizzing and yet slowing down – fading, fogging.

"Ilia!"

Pain flared as she hit the dirt. Shouts sounded around her. Then arms went under her and she was lifted up, the movement making the world swirl around her.

Her eyes fluttered open to land on Tamuel, his elf hat and ears looking precariously tipsy on his head. "Nice costume," she muttered.

He glanced down. "Thank the Gods you're okay."

"Am I?" she asked before passing out.

Somewhere deep inside her mind, she was aware of being carried, worried whispers, the sound of a woman's voice she didn't recognise telling them to bring her and Trip inside and telling Charlie, Harry and Gideon to take care of things out there and reset for the afternoon. She had no idea why any of that was important.

But then the fuss faded and she lost all sense of herself as the world turned grey and stars swirled around her in a sickening way.

Oh Gods! It was just like when she'd been sucked into the Hearts-Blood Gem!

She couldn't remember a spell or blood magic being used but it was almost exactly like the experience of being ripped from her body as Tiberinus drank her blood, her soul sucked into the gem he pushed against her.

No-no-no-no-no-no! Not again! How could this happen to me again!

How? Why? What had she done to deserve this?

Nothing.

Not. One. Damned. Thing!

Rage filled her, huge and fiery, a tight ball in her chest that pulsed out and out and out as words formed in her mind to curse the being responsible for this. "I vow—"

"Whoa! Hold your roll, little missy!"

Hands grasped her shoulders abruptly, stopping her from spinning out of control in the grey and the sparks of light. She gasped at the suddenness, her rage still there, still a huge thing inside her, but kept at bay by the shock of being grabbed and spoken to like that. "Little missy! What are you? A cowboy?"

He laughed. "Some people think of me that way. I prefer to think of myself as a little bit of mischief."

A little bit of mischief? Who in the Hells was this? She tried to focus, but the light wasn't good. Everything was monochrome except for the pinky-orange glow coming from her chest. In that glow, all she could see was a male-shaped figure as he held her still while they floated in the greyness of this nothing place. "Who are you? What are you doing here?"

"I am here for you and Triptolemus."

"Okay." His voice was so familiar, but she couldn't place it. Even so, a little bit more of her anger drained away. "Is he okay?"

"He's just dandy."

She looked around her. "So where is he?" She really wanted to see him. Out of that stupid Santa suit.

"Waiting. We had to stop on our journey because you decided to go all nuclear on me."

"Wait, what?"

"You were powering up, your magics and were about to use them to explode the in-between. And I couldn't have that now, could I?"

"Couldn't you?"

"No. Also, you were about to make a rash vow – and the Lords of the Hells know, there's been far too many vows bandied about by you people over the years. I had a chance to stop one of you from making another stupid proclamation that would make my job so much more difficult, so I did."

"Okay, so all of that maybe explains the what-are-you-doing-here part of my question. But it doesn't answer the who-are-you part?"

"Ahh, well, I was hoping to keep that to a once-and-I'm-out kind of thing."

She shook her head, his round-about way of speaking giving her a sudden headache. Or maybe that was due to the fact she'd passed out and hit her head. "What are you talking about?"

"Let's go to Triptolemus and then I will tell you all." The shadow tipped his head. "Well, actually, that's a lie. I won't tell you all. Can't. But I will tell you what you need to know for now to get yourself out of this shit you're in. It would have been so much easier if you hadn't fought me like you have." He took her hand before she could respond to any of that and said, "Come."

Then they were flying again through the grey with its sparkling stars, but this time, there was no spinning, so she actually got to look around. Not that there was much to look at. Except, yes, there *was* something, in the distance. A pinprick at first, that looked like a strangely red star, but grew slowly until she realised it was some kind of portal.

She couldn't see through it – it was filled with a red-grey fog – but its edges spun and ruby and garnet sparks lit the space around them.

It was kind of beautiful.

But she didn't get long to appreciate it as they were suddenly flying through it.

To land in a field where a lone male stood.

He turned as they appeared through the portal, his eyes meeting hers.

Electricity. Fire. Sparks of all sorts. Plus that strange warm weakness she'd experienced when she'd seen him in that stupid Santa suit on that ridiculous tractor. They shot through her. Gods! She was more alive than she'd ever been in her life. She wanted nothing more than to reach for him, touch him, press up against him, the warmth of him against the warmth of her, and never let go.

It was insanity.

And yet, nothing had ever felt so true. So real. So complete.

And so fucking scary.

"What's going on?" she breathed.

Triptolemus shook his head. "I don't know. I saw you then everything went blank and then I was here." He pointed behind her. "He told me to stay and he'd be back soon."

She wanted to look at the male who'd brought her here, but couldn't take her eyes from Triptolemus. He was glorious. Still in that silly Santa suit, but without the hat and beard – he was holding those. But this Santa suit looked like no Santa suit she'd ever seen, the way he was wearing it now. The front was undone, showing not the pillowy cushioning that had broken his fall when he'd tumbled off the tractor, but the suntanned planes of his broad, muscled chest, his Santa pants hitched low on his hips, showing off that 'v' of muscle that led down to what she knew was his glorious manhood. They were like arrows pointing to a place of glory – one she wanted to see again. Maybe suck on like the most delicious lollypop before chucking off her clothes and shucking off any final inhibitions she might have to ride him like nobody had ever ridden a Santa before.

"Okay. Wow. You two really need to cool down or you're going to combust this place. And if you combust my little slice of the in-between, daddy's gonna be a little pissed."

The words broke through her sexual fantasy and she snapped back into her body with a little pop. By the look in Trip's eyes, he'd been having a similar fantasy. What the Hells? She couldn't seem to control herself whenever she saw him. It'd been getting worse since she'd first spoken to him in his field that day, taking over her life more and more. It was scary as fuck and yet, it felt so right. Like seeing him was coming home.

She shook her head, trying to sort herself out, but her thoughts were mostly a jumbled mess, tangled up in the ever-growing want and need for him. His gaze on hers. His hands reaching for her. That smile tilting his glorious lips. The warm pine and spring rain scent of him that twined around her. She longed for his touch, his heat, his hardness to surround her and fill her as those lips of his met hers and then took her on a journey around her naked body of glorious, building expectation as he joined with her and drove them both to their very own slice of heaven.

After which she wanted to hold and he held and never let go. Hells – the need for that was even greater than her need to ravage him and be ravaged by him.

"By the Gods! I didn't realise the Fates had bound your souls. If I had, I would never have bothered with the introductory dreams. But what's done is done and can't be undone."

Once again she was pulled from her fantasies by the male's annoyingly amused voice. But she still couldn't turn to face him, or seem to ask him what the fuck he was talking about and why he'd brought them here. All she could do was stare at Trip. At the breadth of skin exposed by his open Santa suit. Her fingers tingled, the need to touch, to spread her palm over his chest, all that muscle twitching as she stroked and stoked the fire that was ready to combust between them.

She sucked in a shuddering breath. Trip did the same. Her gaze flew to his.

In his eyes she saw the same bewilderment, the same questions, roiling around inside her. But she could also see that he too was slayed by this overwhelming *need*. Something in his eyes that filled up all the empty places and made her feel … whole.

She took a stumbling step towards him, hand outstretched.

He did the same.

The male stepped between them. "I can see now I might have made a slight error in calculations, although why you two couldn't have sated this need in the dreams, I don't know. but seriously, you have to pull yourselves together if we're going to get anywhere with this."

Taking in a shuddering breath, she finally managed to look at him. Her eyes popped wide as she took in the tall, thin, well-muscled, black-haired male with eyes that swirled with black and red and green, hinting at an old, old, power. And an old, old madness.

"You!" She'd seen him earlier that year when she'd lived in

Tamuel's chest. He'd helped them … kind of … because he was an old friend of Tam's.

"Moi?" the male said, hand to his chest, lips trembling with mirth. "Yes, I am me. Very clever of you."

"What? No, I mean, you're Loki!"

"Ah, ah, ah!" he said, wagging his finger side to side. "I am not Loki." Wind whipped up, his hair flying like wings away from his face as a red-gold glow surrounded him, his voice echoing and loud, like a voice-over from a movie trailer as he said, "I am the Ghost of Christmas Past."

"You are?" Trip asked as Ilia stood there, mouth open, eyes wide.

Loki sketched an absurdly elaborate bow, all hand flurries and bending down to almost touch his feet, before popping back up again. "At your service. As requested."

"What?" Ilia spat. "You requested this loon to pretend to be the Ghost of Christmas Past? Are you insane?"

Triptolemus frowned. "I don't think I did any such thing."

"Of course you did." Ghost of Christmas Past-slash-Loki grinned widely. "You asked the Gods for help with your little plan, did you not?"

"I …" he began, frowning deeply. "I had a plan, but I didn't ask for this." He looked around at the green field they stood in, surrounded by a forest of ancient pine trees that stretched up to the improbably blue-blue sky.

"Well, of course you didn't, because you weren't thinking big enough. But not to worry. I heard your plea and voila!" A hand flourish, another snap of wind, and a ruby red cape appeared around Loki's shoulders as his hair turned white and a beard grew to obscure the dimple in his chin. "Dressed for the part and all! How good am I?"

"Loki! Stop your nonsense and tell us why you brought us here!" Ilia snapped, wondering why she'd found him so amusing at Easter.

Loki pouted, swirling his cape around him like a chastened child. "But don't you like my cape? I went all out with it. See, it even has 'Ghost of Christmas Past' bedazzled on the back." He swung around, holding the cape wide to show them. "Just in case you confused me with the other two."

"What other two?"

"The Ghosts of Christmas Present and Future. I've got costumes ready to go for them too. Can't wait for you to see them. They're pretty spectacular if I do say so myself."

"What the Hells are you talking about?" Ilia shouted. "This is not a joke!"

Loki's eyes widened with offence. "A joke? Oh, no. This is not a joke. This is very, very serious. Especially if you two don't get your shit together and do what must be done."

Ilia opened her mouth to do some more shouting, but Triptolemus got in first.

"What must be done?" he asked quickly, a lot less shouty than she thought Loki deserved.

Loki turned to him, eyes flashing red and green like the lights on a Christmas tree. "We must go back to the past to save the future!"

13

Wind whipped up around them, the green place they'd been in turning into a tornado, like colour being swirled into paint.

The tornado cleared as quickly as it had started and Trip found himself standing in a snow-tipped pine forest, Ilia and Loki opposite him.

"Ta-da!" Loki said, swirling his cape as he spun around in a circle, snow flying up in little flurries around his leg.

Ilia wrapped her arms around herself, teeth chattering, breath a puff on the air as she glared at him. "What is so 'ta-da' about this, you insane little shit?"

Trip understood her annoyance but didn't think it was exactly wise to annoy or upset the God who had brought them here. He was about to say as much, but Loki just laughed, the sound ringing joyously around them.

"Ah, I love a bit of spunk in a woman. If you weren't tied down to this one," a nod at Trip, "I might just allow myself to fall in love." He fluttered his long eyelashes at her as, with another swirling gesture of his cape, clasped his hands to his chest. "You truly are magnificent, Ilia. I understand now why Tamuel was so keen on helping you last year. You're a lucky God, Trip," he said, waggling his eyebrows.

Trip didn't respond because his mind had got stuck on one word. "God?" he asked through a throat suddenly parched like he'd not drunk for a thousand years.

Loki's face went through a series of puzzled expressions, before landing on an 'ah'. "Oops. A bit too soon with the news, eh? Have to admit though, I thought Korinna or Tam would have clued you in."

"They've mentioned things, but never anything about being a God. I thought I was a witch or warlock or something, like my daughter."

"Oh, she's so much more than a witch – she has your blood, after all. You grew out of the power wielded by Demeter, Persephone and Gaia themselves." Trip winced at the names, but Loki went on. "The child of many and yet not truly of one. An immaculate conception. Or accidental conception is probably more apt. A bit too much of them trying things out, sprinkling their powers around at times that proved … birth-worthy. And suddenly there you were, grown out of Gaia's soil in amongst Dem's and Seph's favourite garden. A bit of a surprise. One they quickly got over when they realised what you represented for them, and what you could do."

"So he is a God?" Ilia asked. "There's a bit of confusion about that in the texts."

There were texts about him? This was crazy.

"Yes … and no. He's not quite like any other God, nor is he a demi-God. He is his own creation, so to speak. Which is why his power holds dangers that Demeter and Persephone and Gaia did their best to keep hidden."

"Is that why they took my memories?"

Loki waved his hands. "No. That happened centuries after. Not until you had the misfortune of falling in love and spawning a legacy of your own."

"Korinna?"

He nodded.

"Why was having her so dangerous?"

"You were already a danger to the pantheons and their reigns, like the Gods were to the Titans before them. But add children to that mix …" Loki sighed and shook his head sadly. "Not good. Especially given the prophecy."

"What prophecy?"

"Well, that's what we're here for. A little blast from the past." He waved his hand. A shimmering mirror appeared before them. In it, they saw two women sitting before a pool of water. One of them touched its surface, face bowed, a long tangle of white hair hanging around her face. The other woman waited at her side, hand on the white-haired woman's shoulder.

"Tell me what you see, Cassandra."

"The ancient one. A Titan of old. Perses the Unknown, father of Hecate. He did not get caught with the others and sent into Tartarus. He escaped into the Void, but was trapped in the Beyond. Now he is seeking a way out. And that way out comes closer with Triptolemus and his child."

Her voice changed, taking on an echoing, mystical strain as she said:

"Their blood is what can bind him; their blood is what can find him;

Their blood is what can free him; their blood is what imprisons him.

In all of the Realms from Heavens to Hells

Expanding out to control the Eternal Well

All will be lost to Perses' mad need, an endless maw devouring all power

If control of the blood magic isn't held by the One and his progeny in the final hour."

"Well, that's enough of that." Loki waved his hand and the vision shifted.

"Wait! Is there something about a prophecy to do with me?" Ilia asked.

"Probably was, but if you see everything, what's the fun in that?"

"Fun? This isn't fun. This is life and death!" Ilia looked very much like she was going to clock him. And a strange glow emanated from her chest.

"Ilia. He's here to help."

Her gaze snapped to Trip's, eyes ablaze. "Is he? Can we be so certain of that? He is the God of Mischief, after all. He can't help himself. I mean, why waste time bringing us together in dreams? Why not just tell us what we need to know if it's so important? He could have saved us months and months of searching and stress and despair. But no, because he's a God, he has to do things the difficult way. The way most likely to piss people off and obfuscate the truth."

"The truth! You can't handle the truth!" Loki said, doing an exact impersonation of Jack Nicholson in that army movie Charlie and Harry had made Trip watch half a dozen times over the years.

Obviously though his impersonation-joke was ill timed because Ilia's fury sparked in her eyes, the glow in her chest getting brighter.

She turned on Loki, demeanour menacing, flames burning in her eyes, heat coming off her in waves. "The truth! All I ever wanted was the truth. But all I've ever got from you bloody Gods and Goddesses is lies and betrayals and secrets. I don't think a single one of you is capable of being truthful."

Loki pouted. "That's not fair. I can be truthful. It's just often not fun."

"This. Isn't. Fun." She stepped towards him with every word.

"Maybe not for you."

Trip grabbed Ilia's hand before she could raise it to punch Loki a smacker right in his smiling mouth.

At his touch, the glow in her chest dimmed.

Loki laughed, clapping his hand. "Such drama. Such passion. It's no wonder I could never keep control of the dream-visions."

"What do you mean?" Trip asked. "If you weren't in control, who was?"

Eyes opening wide, he let his gaze run meaningfully from Trip to Ilia. "Us?"

Loki shrugged. "One of you? Perhaps both? But all that sexy stuff was definitely all you. Although, why you couldn't seal the deal, I have no idea."

Ilia looked away and Trip cleared his throat. "Umm, well, okay. But then what was your role?"

"All I did was put you together in the dreams because Demeter needed my help."

"But why would she ask *you* to help?" Ilia asked. "You're not even of her pantheon."

"Precisely the point. She could not show her hand, and she couldn't ask anyone she trusted in her pantheon to do so either, because same result – it would make her effort to hide you pointless. But who would look at little ol' me? I'm always doing something mischievous and silly. The Gods are so used to it now, they barely even glance at what I'm up to as long as it doesn't affect them."

"I still don't understand why she'd ask *you*. Why she'd trust *you*."

He touched a hand to his heart, flicking his hair back. "My innate charm and trustworthiness, obviously."

"Loki!" Trip snapped before Ilia could. "Be serious."

And suddenly, he was. The wind stopped blowing his hair back from his face, his eyes stopped spinning green and red, and the cloak ceased its heroesque billowing. "I've never been more serious than I am in my duty to Demeter. She helped me when no other God or Goddess would in a moment of darkest despair; an action I can never truly repay. But even if that wasn't the case, I would have given my help when she asked for it. I have felt Perses creeping back. The darker side of my magics quivers and wishes to prostrate itself to the power he could wield if he ever escaped. And I vowed long ago that I would never again prostrate myself at the foot of another God. So even if you do not believe that I would do everything I can to ensure Demeter's plans succeed, believe that I will put myself and my wellbeing front and centre. Perses *cannot* have me or my powers. And to ensure that never comes to pass, he cannot fully be allowed back into this world."

"Fully?" Ilia asked. "That thing that came out of the Void at Easter – was that him?"

Loki nodded. "A small part of him. Call it a scout."

"It's scouting us? Then why have we seen nothing of it?"

Loki pulled a face. "Why do you think I'd know what's in the mind of a mad Old One? I have no idea what that scout is scouting, or even how it might report back. All I know is it's here and that, sooner or later, it will make itself known. It won't be able to stop itself. And when it does, you all have to be ready."

Trip stared at the other God, noticing out of the corner of his eye that Ilia looked worried, the glow in her chest now completely gone. "Then why play with us like you have? Why not just come out and tell us what we need to know if things are so dire?"

"Because while I have more freedom to act than Demeter does, there are still eyes on the lookout all the time. Rules that are in place regarding how information about certain forbidden subjects can and cannot be shared without drawing the ire of the greater Gods. I may be mischievous, but I am not foolish." He crossed his arms, pouting a little. "Besides, I am not entirely to blame here. It's you two who couldn't seem to keep it in your pants. Every time I thought you were headed towards where you needed to go, you just kept dragging the visions right back to sexy-land. I should have realised then that you are soul-bound—"

"Soul-bound? What are you talking about?" Ilia said, jerking back a little. "We're not soul-bound."

"Of course you are. What do you think all of this …" he waved his hand between them, "is caused by? This isn't just simple lust. You are meant to be."

Ilia paled, as if she was scared. But why? The thought they were meant to be together thrilled through him, making him happier than he'd ever felt in his life.

But he didn't have a chance to question her, because Loki tipped his head to the side and said, "Huh, that's probably why your blood more than any other is the key."

"My blood?" Ilia asked, paling further, fear now definitely clouding her eyes.

Trip tensed. Hells. It wasn't time yet for that to be brought up. She wasn't ready to know.

Loki waved his hand again, blithely ignoring her. "Of course, I can't be held to blame for missing such a thing. I mean, it's not like it happens that often. And I was just a little too frustrated by the fact my little plan wasn't coming together quite how I wanted. I have to say, it's been quite tiring constantly pulling you back into the dream-vision so we could attempt to get to the good stuff. I swear, it wouldn't have even happened if I hadn't done a little spell on that book and made it cough up the address when Trip failed to tell you in time."

"That book? That was you? That almost killed Dawn and me!"

"Uh-uh-uh, no skipping to the Ghost of Christmas Present act. We're still in the past. Now, on with the play!"

He waved his hand and another mirror appeared before them, wavering like before but quickly resolving to show the same tall woman, her green eyes shining with tears, standing before a man dressed in a Grecian-style tunic, shaking her head as he pleaded with her.

"This is when you came up with the plan," he said to Trip. The scene sped forward to show them standing in this very forest, snow covering everything. "This is where the spell was placed and you sacrificed everything for the good of us all." He raised a brow at Trip. "So honourable. Ah, but wait, this is my favourite bit." Demeter waved her hands and the ancient Trip stiffened, his face a rictus of pain, before he fell, to be caught and lowered lovingly onto the snow. A handkerchief appeared suddenly in Loki's hand and he dabbed at his eye and said wetly, "So touching. Brings a tear to my eye every time."

"Oh for fuck's sake!" Ilia grumbled.

"Harsh!" Loki said. "But hush. This bit is what affects you."

They watched as Demeter made her vow, hearing her words clearly and the three rolling knocks that followed, signifying the vow was accepted by the Eternal Well – unbreakable, unshakable, causing death if not brought to fruition.

"Why would she do that?" Ilia asked. "It wasn't even specific. How did she know she could do it?"

"She didn't. She just knew it must be done so made a vow to ensure it, no matter the cost." He turned his gaze to her, something in his eyes that was pointed and knowing, but that she couldn't understand.

"But … I don't understand what this has to do with me? How am I a part of this?"

"Shortly after, she had a knowing about the gem and the spirit residing in it that she'd come into possession of. It was then she realised that you were the key to her completing the vow. It's funny how the Fates work, isn't it? Placing you in that gem so that you could then be of use when needed. An act of superior weaving, I have to say." He waved at the image again. "But look! This is where my Machiavellian mind truly came into its own for Demeter's plans."

They watched as the image played out, showing him bowed over the gem, Demeter behind him, a worried expression on her face. "You had already started to be able to make yourself known and she was worried you would use your persuasion on some poor bleeding heart to get you out."

"But nobody could get me out but Korinna and Tamuel. It was prophesied."

"I know. I was the one who came up with that prophecy," he said proudly, as if expecting congratulations. "Demeter was so grateful when I suggested it, because it was the only way to ensure you couldn't get free until in Korinna and Tamuel's hands. What she saw in her knowing was that you would only get to this point if they were the ones to free you."

Ilia stared at him, breath heaving. "You. Kept. Me. Enslaved. In. That. Gem. For. Two. Thousand. Years!"

"Uh-huh," Loki said, staring at the image of Demeter thanking him. "Pretty clever, huh?"

Ilia roared, lunging at him, the glow, like dawn's light, spreading in her chest once again, brighter this time.

Trip caught her as Loki went stumbling back, hands up. She

screamed and fought against the arms banding around her. "Let me go! I have to kill him!"

The power in her chest didn't lessen this time at his touch and was hot to the point of burning. But he held on. "No, Ilia. You can't. We need him."

"I don't need him. I don't need anyone."

"Ilia, please. Look at what's happening now."

Something in his voice made the fury hazing her sight and her mind fade just enough that she looked where he was pointing.

In the mirror a new image showed; one that was clearly of the present.

She and Trip lay on a bed, side by side, a glow surrounding them, their hands clasped.

Beyond them, Jules stood, sobbing, a limp Dawn in her arms. Bas, Korinna, Tamuel and Violetta gathered around her, hands raised above the baby, working their collective magics on her. But no matter what they did, she remained limp, face as pale as death, lips turning slowly blue.

"Dawn!" Ilia cried, the glow and her anger fading as quickly as they'd come.

"Ah, now we've got to the present," Loki said, spinning around. His hair changed back to his normal black as his cloak turned into a black-hooded one covered in black sequins, except for the green ones on the back that spelled out Ghost of Christmas Present.

14

*I*lia lunged towards the mirror. Trip let go of her just enough so she didn't face-plant into it. She would have thanked him except all her attention was on the precious baby in the image. "What's wrong with her?"

"She's dying."

"What? Why?"

"Because you're dying."

"What? No, I'm not." She pointed at her image. Both her and Trip's bodies looked relatively healthy given their unconscious state.

"Ah, but you are." Loki wagged his finger, swaying a little so that his cloak fluttered around him. "You have been since you were made corporeal by Tamuel and that rather powerful little baby. A single life-force, no matter that it's as strong as hers, isn't enough to keep the both of you going."

"But ... there was no sign of this before."

"Ah, well, yes ..." Loki shuffled away from her again. "I'm afraid I might have just precipitated that a little – only out of necessity, of course."

"You what?"

"The dark magic book that I put in your way to help facilitate an astral visit with Triptolemus here … It might have just sped things up a bit."

"How much is a bit?" Trip asked dangerously.

"Hard to know, really. You might have had a human lifespan to figure out how to separate yourself before. Now … given how quickly little Dawny is deteriorating …" Loki tipped his hand back and forth. "Probably Christmas day. Maybe a day less or a day more."

"What?" Ilia said, terror spiking through her. "This can't be. I can't let this happen. Tell me how to stop it from happening."

"Let Triptolemus drink your blood."

"What?" His words pulled her horrified gaze away from the baby she'd give her life for and she swung to face him.

Blood magic. He was suggesting blood magic! And not just any type of blood magic, but exactly what Tiberinus had used on her.

Fear, huge and clawing, scraped at her insides, making it difficult to think, to breathe. She shoved it down, shoved it back. "You can't be serious," she said, voice shaking.

"I am very serious. What do you think all of this is about?"

"Umm, getting Triptolemus' memory back?"

"Which this will do."

She shook her head, trying desperately to hold onto reason, to not let the fear take her over. "B-but h-how does that help Dawn? I-I can't even see how it will help Trip's memories come back."

"Well, I don't have time to get into the minutiae, but basically it comes down to the fact that the power you were born with, added to the power you got when you were reborn, not to mention the fact you are soul-bonded to him, makes your blood the ultimate cure-all for Trip here."

"But … I don't have my original power."

"Of course you do. What do you think that hot little glow is that keeps leaking out of your chest?"

She stared at him, shaking her head, unable and unwilling to accept what he was saying. "B-blood magic isn't the answer here."

"Of course it is. It is the only answer."

"It's never an answer!" Ilia snapped, fist pressed against her chest as she struggled to breathe. The glow in her chest pulsed in response. She thought it only activated with anger, but it seemed fear flipped the switch on it too. She tried to shove it all down as she whispered, "Blood magic only brings pain and betrayal and death."

"But if it will help the baby ..." Trip said.

"You only want this because it will help you!" she snarled, turning on him. She'd been right to hold herself back from him. He was just like any other God – always wanting something from her. Wanting to use her and betray her.

He took a step back from her anger, but to his credit, kept his calm. "I won't lie. Of course I want that. But if you hadn't agreed, I would never have pushed the matter. I would have spent my life by your side trying to find another way. But this ..." He gestured at the image hanging before them. "That poor little baby. We have to do everything in our power to save her. Surely you want that?"

"Of course I do." Just the thought of Dawn's life in danger ... Her anger fizzled once again.

Trip wasn't to blame for this. No. The brutality behind all this had a touch of the Fates about it. No wonder she'd found that entry in the grimoire that said blood magic, under the right conditions, would sever the link between her and Dawn and had found nothing else to help her.

Well, she hadn't trusted the answer then and she certainly didn't trust it now. Breath unsteady, she said, "But ... This can't be the only option. Blood magic is dark magic. It trapped me and used me and has been the cause of so much misery in my life and in others. I mean, look at what it's done to you, Trip."

He frowned. "What do you mean?"

She began to pace, the words tumbling out of her. "This is all happening because of the curse of blood magic. Perses means to use your special blood to break his way back into this reality, if what Loki has shown us is true. He means to use it for evil because that's what blood magic can only ever be used for."

"That's not true," Trip said. "Think what I can do with my blood. I grow things. I take something that is hardly living and make it flourish, turning it into something vibrant and new."

"That's not blood magic. That's just something special in your blood because of how you were created." Which was why she could feel the goodness in his soul, the kindness that made him want to give and share joy.

He was nothing like the Gods and Fates responsible for all this. She should have known that. After all, part of his legend was about him travelling the globe, sharing his skills and teaching humans how to provide for themselves. He stopped them from relying so heavily on the mercy of the Gods – which was always a good thing. Then he'd given up his beloved wife and unborn daughter to protect not only them, but everyone, from an evil none of them was strong enough to face at that point. And even after losing his memory, he had still travelled, sharing his skills and good fortune where he could, even spreading the joy of this ridiculous time of the year with his Christmas trees and food and drink and endless cheer.

But even with all his goodness, his kind intentions, he didn't understand the true evil of blood magic.

He came to stand in front of her, stopping her pacing, and took her hands. Looking deeply into her eyes, he said, "Blood magic isn't any more evil than what I do with my blood."

"But it is. It's very different. What you do brings life. Blood magic just brings misery and darkness."

He sighed. "Korinna told me you'd feel this way."

"She did?"

He nodded. "In the last week, she and Tamuel have filled me in on so much. Including what you've been through." He let go of one of her hands and touched her cheek. She couldn't help but lean into the gentle caress as she gazed into his beautiful eyes with their crystal green depths and long dark lashes. "I'm so sorry for all that was done to you. For all that you've lost. And I truly don't want to ever ask you to do something you're not comfortable with." He snorted a self-derisive laugh. "It seems stupid now that I thought I could somehow win you around to allowing me to drink of your blood by showing you some Christmas spirit. I thought the joy or family bonds or something might be enough to convince you. But I didn't know. I didn't understand, until what Loki said, how you were kept trapped and used. And I'm so sorry for it."

"You are?"

"Of course. That only happened to you because of me. Because you are the answer to my current problem. We might not be responsible for what Tiberinus did originally, but there is no denying that the Fates ensured you could be here, ready once again to be used. This time, by me." He let out a shuddery breath, the expression on his face filled with so much regret, shame and pain. "And I wish right now that I could just set you free of it all. I wish that I could say it's not necessary, that you don't have to do this. I want to be able to do that. You deserve to be free. But ..." His gaze returned to the image.

At his sucked-in breath, she turned to see that things had become worse with Dawn.

It was now dark, the glow surrounding the two bodies on the bed lighting the room, showing clearly the little body lying limply beside them, her parents kneeling beside the bed, hands grasping their daughter's, Korinna, Tamuel and Violetta standing behind them.

"How much time has passed?"

"A week since you fell unconscious," Loki said.

"A week! But you said she only has until Christmas."

"I did say that, didn't I. Which means, if we take much longer here, it could be too late. See, even as we stand here, time passes and things become more dire."

The image shifted to show all the adults in the room next to the bed, hands out, pumping power and their own life-forces into the baby, trying desperately to keep her alive. But they were weakening. Two demi-Gods, a demi-God-witch, a normal witch and a witch with Goddess-given powers did not have the life-force energy to keep them going indefinitely. Only a God or Goddess, with their full connection to the Eternal Well, the well-spring of all Godly powers and life-energy, could do that.

But they were trying. They wouldn't stop trying. They would all give their lives for Dawn.

As would she.

She glanced at Loki and Trip. Both looked so grim, so … griefstricken. They didn't want to bind her or use her for evil or their own selfish machinations, but still … How could she trust they all wouldn't end up paying some even worse price? Although, right now, she couldn't think of a worse price than losing Dawn.

As they watched, Violetta passed out, falling to the floor, having given too much of herself to keep going. Hells. Was she dead? Had she already made that sacrifice?

"Loki. Stop this!" she pleaded, gripping his shirt, shaking. "Please. Make it stop."

"There's only one way. You must allow Triptolemus to drink your blood. When he does, the link between you should prove stronger than the one between you and Dawn, severing the current one in favour of a new one, and the baby will be free."

"She will survive?" She yanked at his shirt.

He frowned down at the hands crumpling his costume. "And so will you. And Trip will have all his memories back."

"But she will be tied to me?" Trip asked.

"Of course. You will be sharing your life-force with her. You will be the one keeping her alive."

"So, you're asking me to leash her to me? How is that any different from what was done to her when she was used to power that gem?"

"Because you are soulmates," he said, as if that was obvious. "You are already tied together by the Fates and destiny and the Eternal Well in a way that cannot be undone by any other. But if it truly bothers you, I'm sure you can keep looking for a way to free her life-force from yours in the years ahead. That is, of course, if we manage to defeat Perses. Which, if you remember, is the point of all of this."

"That baby should never have been endangered to get us to here."

Loki winced. "I have to admit, that was never a part of my plan. But it's not easy to wrangle the threads of fate into submission. You try it sometime."

"Don't you even care she's dying?" Ilia asked.

"Of course I care. That's why I brought you here, to bring it to your attention and make you see what must be done. Because if I'm sure of anything, Trip's silly plan wouldn't have worked."

"What do you mean?"

"Let me show you some possible futures. Maybe then you'll decide."

15

oki waved his hand over the image. It changed to show what was obviously Christmas day, given the wrapping paper strewn around the base of the tree and the half-eaten meal on the table beside it. But nobody was at the table, they were all standing around it, an argument in full swing.

"Where are Daphne and the boys?" Trip asked.

"Who?" Loki asked.

"My friends. My employees."

"Oh." Loki shrugged. "Dunno. Tam probably spelled them to stay away from all the magic going on. Good thing too, given what's about to happen in this version of the future."

As they watched, the argument got more and more out of hand. Ilia couldn't believe the look on her face – betrayal mixed with an anger so deep it burned.

And the glow! It was coming out of her chest, expanding, growing brighter and brighter as Trip argued his case, and Korinna and Tamuel – the people she'd thought of as friends; the two people in all the world who'd always backed her up; who'd never let her down – took his side. The fury that lived inside her, fuelled by a total and utter need for retribution and revenge that had carried her through the ages, grew in the image. But now it was fuelled by the betrayal playing out in this version of the future.

It grew and grew and then exploded out of her, felling them all in one, horrifying burst.

Ilia stared, unable to blink or breathe, as her power, the power she'd thought lost, killed everyone in the room.

The Gods Killer. That was her.

"Oh Gods. Dawn," Trip whispered.

Ilia's gaze searched the image until she found what brought that broken sound to Trip's voice.

Attached as she was to Ilia, Dawn had been spared death. But death would have been better. The burst of power had pulled nearly everything the baby was from her, making her skin crack and bleed through terrible burns while she slowly withered as her life, her soul, was sucked from her.

But she was still alive, feeling all of it. Screaming. Such terror, such pain!

"No. No. Do something!" Ilia cried.

"There's nothing to be done," Loki said. "This would have been the future if I hadn't brought you here." He made a humphing sound, his expression flat as the scene played out before them. "If you think this is bad, wait until you see what happens next." He shuddered.

In the image, as the dust settled from her firestorm, the future-Ilia stared around her, tears flowing down her face to drop and sizzle on the still-burning embers of Trip's house. Slowly, so slowly, she moved towards the blackened, bleeding husk that was little Dawn.

She carefully knelt down beside the baby. Then holding out her hands, gripped a hold of the gossamer thread that was the link between them, and tried with everything in her to give back what she'd taken.

Some of the blackened skin around where the link joined them over Dawn's chest began to turn red, then pink. It was working! But not fast enough. The baby's breath was a slow shudder, her screams now mere whimpers as Death laid its foul hand on her.

She had to do more. But there wasn't much more inside her – so much had exploded out of her with the fury that had caused this. There was power all around her though – in the remnants of what was left of those who'd been her family – and yes, she knew now they were her family. She'd been so stupid to deny the truth of it before.

Despite the fact they were dead, their spirits had not yet departed and their power still buzzed in their flesh.

Heart breaking, she flung her hand out, creating links with all of them, and pulled from them. She took and took until first one, then another, then all of them was sucked dry and turned to dust, everything they were now inside her.

But it wasn't enough.

The baby was still dying.

So she flung out her hand again and created a link with the greatest power around her – Gaia. She was only able to do so because of the power she'd taken from Trip and Korinna. It allowed her to tap into something that was sacred, divine. And she took and took and took.

And as she did, everything died around her; the light was sucked from the world and into her to power her guilt-driven furious misery as she desperately tried to save Dawn.

The baby slowly turned from blackened char to healthy pink, but still, she didn't wake.

She had to wake. She had to. Ilia couldn't stand it if she lost another baby.

But as she held Dawn, the baby took her last breath and passed out of this world.

Ilia screamed to the Heavens, her fury so great now that time and space split open under its force. In that split was the pulsing grey of the Void, and the fullness of evil that waited there.

With a shriek of victory, something huge and black and terrifying spilled out, tendrils, like fingers, gripping the edges of the tear, pushing it wider, wider. Then as the sky rent in two, the evil oozed down to cover the land, sucking up all the souls she hadn't already managed to destroy.

Ilia screamed as the evil drank her soul.

And then she was standing once again in the place Loki had brought them to, watching the mirror-like surface fog once more, hiding the image she'd been sucked into.

Her cheeks were wet, her breath coming in great heaving gasps, Trip's arm around her shoulder, holding her up. She swiped at her eyes and managed to say, "That ... that can't be true! I wouldn't do that!"

"You would," Loki said sadly. He tapped her chest where the glow remained even now. "You almost let your fury get the better of you multiple times since I brought you on this journey. If Trip or I hadn't stopped you, it could have been disastrous."

"But ... I ... I don't have that kind of power. I can't take power from others."

"Of course you can. Why do you think the ghosts ran from you when you used your power to repel them? Why do you think they kept away?"

"Because my repelling spell worked?"

"No, because the magic you were created with, the birth magic for lack of a better word, is being twisted by your bitterness and fury. It can give and create, but it can also take and tear apart. You didn't just repel the ghosts, you started to undo them, taking the essence of them into yourself. They ran from you to save themselves."

"I didn't mean—"

"Of course you didn't." He waved his hand at the image. "Just like you won't mean to do this either. But the fact is, if you don't come to terms with allowing Trip to drink your blood, then this is the future we face."

"But ... if I know this is what lies ahead, I can avoid it. I can just say no."

"You can. But then this happens."

He waved his hand, showing another image. This time, rather than allow her fury to build, she simply refused them and walked out. Time sped forward to show her friends battling the evil that was Perses as he exploded from the Void and used Trip's and Korinna's blood to power himself, destroying all before him.

"I wouldn't leave them to fight alone. I'd be there to help."

"Yes. But without your blood giving him his memory, and you and Dawn being dead because you didn't find another way to separate from her, they fail. Even if you and Dawn are still alive, you are both too weak to be of true help." Another image showed her refusing, but staying to fight – and die – by their side as Perses once again drained Trip and Korinna of their blood and destroyed everything.

Before she could protest that possibility, another image followed, and another and another, a rolling horror of futures where she said 'no' and all of her friends died; and Hells on earth was born because of it.

"But … but … this can't be all on me. I'm nothing. I'm unimportant," Ilia said weakly as fresh tears streamed down her face. Her mind was in turmoil, a pain in her chest so bad it made it hard to breathe.

"We are all unimportant … until we aren't," Loki said.

"That isn't very helpful, Loki," Trip said, glaring at the other God.

"I'm sorry. I've used up my quota of helpfulness in getting you to here. The rest is up to you."

"But …" She cast around for some argument, some alternative. But the only question to ask was, "How do I know that the future will be any better if I allow Trip to drink my blood and tie my life-force to his?"

"Good question," Trip said. "Show her that future."

Loki raised his hands. "I can't. Because of the blood magic, that future is uncertain. The only certainty I can show you is this." He waved his hand.

Jules was placing Dawn on the bed beside where Ilia sat. She was sobbing and couldn't seem to let go of her daughter's hand, stop touching her head. Ilia leaned over and said something to her, then Bas added something else. A short conversation passed between Jules and Ilia, ending with Ilia smiling, tears in her eyes. Then Jules kissed Dawn on the forehead before rising to stand by her mate's side, supported by him, her family at her back.

The Ilia in the vision took a deep breath as she lay down, then turned to Trip, muttering something.

He nodded, cupped her face and whispered words that made her eyes widen, then before she could respond, he bit down on her neck and began to drink.

A desperate kind of hope filled all their faces alongside terrified grief as the link — suddenly visible — between Ilia and Dawn began to fade. The baby's lips became a little less blue, her skin a little less deathly pale.

Within a few minutes, the link was so thin and tight that when Dawn's eyes snapped open on a wail, her arms flailing, the movement was enough to snap the bond completely.

She was free.

Her mother and father grabbed her up, their cries of relief and joy obvious even though there was no sound.

Loki waved his hand again; the image disappeared.

"Wait! What happens next?"

"That I can't show you." Loki turned to face her, a look of triumph glowing in his eyes. "But as you can see, the only clear option to save Dawn is to allow the blood magic."

"But we don't even know if doing that will ultimately save everyone."

Loki frowned at her. "Never happy are you? What about the fact you just saw yourself saving Dawn? I thought that would be enough."

Ilia's lips trembled. He was right. It was wonderful. She didn't believe it before, but she couldn't argue with what she'd seen. She could free Dawn if she allowed Trip to drink her blood. Still, the very thought made her skin crawl and her mind scream — and caused the power to glow in her chest once more.

Lip trembling, she said, "I want to do this. I'm just ... I'm afraid the fear ..." She gripped at her chest, scrunching her t-shirt up in her hand, the glow getting brighter. "It burns inside me, wanting out. I'm afraid that I won't be able to stop it from doing just that the moment you begin to drink."

"It didn't, though," Trip said, gesturing to the now-blank mirror surface. "Loki showed you."

"He showed to a certain point. If only I could see more, it would help allay my fear that it might be worse."

"Worse than what I just showed you?"

She gestured futilely. "You don't understand. I need … something. Please, give me something."

Trip turned to face her, taking her hands in his, squeezing gently. "He can't. None of us can. We just need to trust. Trust in each other. Trust in ourselves. Trust that, whatever comes, we are family by choice if not all by blood, and we will stand together, facing whatever comes. And if your power starts to overwhelm you, then we will face that too. Together." He shot Loki a look. "That's what I wanted to show you in the weeks leading up to Christmas. The reason I love Christmas so much. The Christmas spirit. Not just kindness and generosity, but that love and friendship and family binds us together and makes us strong. That you are not alone in this. That this is something we all do, together. That it gives all of us something as we give something of ourselves."

He lifted his hands to cup her cheeks, thumbs brushing along her suddenly sensitised skin. "I might drink from you," he said softly, breath brushing over her face, "but I also will be giving you life-force energy. You might give of your blood, but you also get the freedom you want for little Dawn. And even though you will be tied to me, I will make certain it is not a bond you are restricted by." He dropped his hands to her shoulders. "We will go wherever and do whatever you want. This is my promise to you."

"After you've defeated Perses, you mean," Loki said dryly.

"Of course. But maybe before that too." He winked at Ilia and she couldn't help but offer him a small smile in return, glad, despite everything, that he was holding onto her. She needed his touch, to feel him there, with her. It made coming to this terrible decision not seem so … lonely.

"So," Loki said, waving his hand again to show the same image of the present they'd seen before. Dawn dying. Her family devastated and helpless. She and Trip lying unconscious on the bed, seemingly useless, but in truth, the only answer to stop Dawn from dying. "Have we resolved things? Has this little trip with the Ghosts of Christmas Past, Present and Future done the trick? Are you ready to address the problem at hand?" He turned to look at her, brows raised.

She chewed on her lip, hands worrying in front of her.

The problem at hand.

That's what she needed to concentrate on. Not some future she couldn't control.

This. This is what she could do. This is what her life had been leading to, whether she wanted it or not.

She'd been unable to save her sons, but this baby's life was in her hands and she could save her.

Surely she'd be able to rise above her fear and just let Trip do what he needed to do? He was right. She might be giving a lot but she was also getting what she wanted in return. Okay, it wasn't full freedom. But it was never really about *her* freedom. She'd only ever wanted freedom for Dawn. That little girl shouldn't have ever had to suffer being bound to Ilia.

Trip … well, he was an adult who could deal with the consequences of being bound to someone as bitter and broken as she was.

"Ilia." Trip ran his hands down her arms to take her hands in his once more, pulling them to hold against his chest, his skin so warm, his heartbeat a steady, sturdy drum-roll beneath her palms. "If you don't trust me, then trust yourself. Trust in the goodness I know you have inside."

"Goodness?"

He nodded. "Goodness. Look what you did, what you would sacrifice for love of that baby. You are filled with goodness, if you would only see it."

"I wish I could see me as you see me," she whispered.

A smile broke out on his face as he touched beside her mouth. "You will. You will come to see everything I see when you agree to this. You can't help but see it when your blood, powered by that goodness as it enters me, does everything we know it can, and more, as we fight for all that's good."

"How can you be certain?"

"That you are filled with goodness? You are standing before me, listening seriously to a proposition that terrifies you, all to save a baby and give my memories and my life back to me. What is goodness if not that?"

She huffed out a chuckle at his oversimplification and the fact he'd purposefully misread her question. "No. I mean, how can you be certain that it will all turn out right?"

He chewed on his lip for a moment. "I can't. But what's the alternative? A thousand futures filled with loss and destruction? Or a moment of faith that could lead to victory? Those are the choices before you. I hope you will choose faith. I hope you will choose to believe in me. But mostly, I hope you will choose to believe in yourself."

The warmth that radiated out from his touch was astonishing, making her catch her breath as it buzzed through her, filling her with something … something … wanted. Needed. And so big. But it was nothing as compared to his words. They filled her with something she hadn't felt in many thousands of years.

Filling her gaze with everything she felt inside, she said, "I believe."

His smile, it lit her up inside, as bright as the sun, calming the fury, dousing its flames. Then, still smiling at her, he said, "Right, Loki. How do we do this?"

"You wake up." Loki waved his hand and space wavered around them, swirling and dissolving; the only thing certain was Trip's grip on her hands, holding tight.

Then just before blackness took over and everything went away, she heard Loki say, "Damn it! I forgot to change cloaks. I'm still wearing the Ghost of Christmas Present. Odin be damned! What a waste of sequins!"

16

It was dark when Trip awoke in his bed. The room was quiet around him.

What time was it? For that matter, how did he get here? He couldn't remember coming to bed.

Hells. His head hurt.

He groaned.

Another groan sounded beside him. He flipped to his side to see Ilia.

She was awake and holding her head.

He didn't blame her. His felt rather like a sledgehammer had taken up residency and was busy marking every second with a thump against the inside of his skull.

But what was she doing there? How had she …

It all came rushing back and he slammed upright.

"Oh-oh-oh. Don't move the bed like that. I'm going to chuck." Then, so saying, Ilia rolled over and vomited all over the floor.

Sympathetic vomiter that he was, he rolled over to the other side just in time.

The door opened, letting in a shaft of light from the lounge room that slashed into his eyes. The thumping pain in his head blazed anew. "Yea Gods! Shut the door. Or turn the light off."

"They're awake," Tamuel shouted back into the lounge room.

There was a snort then a clatter as Korinna leaped up from the chair in the corner – she must have been sleeping – and rushed forward. Tamuel caught her before she could go more than a few steps. "Watch your step. They've both vomited."

"Let me take care of that," Violetta said, appearing behind them. She waved her hand and the smell of sick evaporated, replaced by a fresh citrus scent that helped clear the air but did nothing for Trip's nausea. He bent over and vomited some more. As did Ilia.

"Bas! We need you."

Tamuel's words echoed in Trip's head, adding to the pain of the sledgehammer. He held up his hand, managing to groan, "Please. Less noise. Less light."

Tamuel waved his hand and the light became a dull yellow glow.

Bas entered the room, his face shadowed with worry and fatigue. "Glad to see you're awake."

"Help her first," Trip said, pointing at Ilia as he pulled himself up gingerly to sit against the headboard.

Bas drew near the bed on Ilia's side, raising his hands, but Ilia grabbed his arm. "Where's Dawn?" she rasped.

His lips tightened, his breath hitching. "With Jules. Out there."

"She's sick?"

He nodded. "I can't seem to make her wake up. None of us can."

"Bring her in here."

"We just took her out there."

She shook her head slowly. "She needs to be here. It has to be exactly the same as what we saw or it might not work."

Bas' eyes widened. "You can help her?"

Ilia's face contorted before she pulled herself together, and nodded. "We can."

"But how? How do you know?"

"Loki showed us."

"Loki?" Tamuel asked as he came to stand at the foot of the bed with Korinna. "What has he got to do with any of this?"

"No time to explain," Trip said, worry for the baby making him able to shove the nausea away and ignore the pain. "Dawn will die if we don't do something soon."

"But how?" Violetta.

"Why?" Tam.

"Because," Ilia said, head dipping as she avoided all their eyes. "I'm sucking the life out of her."

"What?" Bas snapped, taking a step back. "Why would you do that?"

"She can't help it! It's that damned bond Dawn created when she helped Tam make Ilia corporeal. Dawn is feeding her life-force," Trip said.

"What?"

"How?"

"Why have we never seen this?"

The questions came from all quarters, pushing at him, at Ilia, making her wince and curl in on herself a little more. Not a physical thing – she showed her strength in that moment by pushing herself upright with trembling arms – but a soul-thing he felt deep inside.

He wished he could stand between Ilia and Bas as the ex-cupid glowered at his love.

Yes, his love. He loved her. It had always been there, he realised now, but he hadn't truly known it until the moment she had taken that step of faith – for him, for the baby, for all of them – despite what it was doing to her. He loved her as he'd never loved before. Not even Korinna's mother, who he was as yet to remember. But he knew without needing that memory.

Loki was right. She was his soulmate, and he would die to protect her. He would die to protect her right to choose. To be her own person.

Except, because of a twist of Fate, he couldn't do any of that.

All he could do was stand strong beside her as she saved them all.

Then he would spend his life paying her back for everything she'd lost because of this Gods-cursed destiny that seemed to be their lot.

He would vow it, but enough rash vows had been made that took no prisoners in their need to be brought to fruition. He wouldn't add to Ilia's burden; not for anything.

But he could make sure she knew he was here, with her. He captured her hand in his. She glanced over at him, squeezing back – so weak but still, the trust, it hit him square in the chest, making it difficult to breathe.

Strong. So strong. Even in the face of the fear that threatened to rip up out of her and tear them all apart. She was strong enough to push down the fear, to keep her power at bay, no matter what it cost her.

Had he thought it necessary to show her what the Christmas spirit was about? He'd been an unthinking idiot. She was the one who could teach all of them its true meaning.

He squeezed her hand harder.

It seemed to give her strength. She took in a steadier breath and said, "I don't know why I didn't realise I was using Dawn's life-force energy. It wasn't obvious before. Now it is. But Loki showed me what I need to do." She glanced at Trip, her eyes warming a little as she met his gaze.

"And what is that?" Bas asked breathlessly.

Her mouth trembled and he saw how hard it was for her to go on, and yet she did. "Trip must drink my blood. Doing so will create a link between Trip and me that is stronger than the one I share with Dawn. The creation of that link will break my link with her, and she will be free. Once free of me, she will recover quickly."

"And you're willing to do this?" Korinna asked quietly. "Even though it's blood magic?"

She nodded firmly. "It will save Dawn. That's all that matters." Her hand tightened on Trip's, squeezing so hard, if he wasn't a God, it might have broken his fingers. But he didn't protest, just let her hold on.

If it was giving her strength and comfort, she could break every bone in that hand and the other if she needed to.

"Gods, Ilia. I'm so sorry you have to do this," Korinna said, voice breaking. "I wish there was another way."

Ilia turned to meet her friend's gaze. "There isn't. Loki showed us. This is the only way."

"You trust what he showed you?"

She nodded, and so did he. "There are things we need to share with you, but not now. Now, you need to bring Dawn in here so we can save her."

"Why does she have to be in here with you?" Bas asked.

"The vision Loki showed us. She was lying here." She moved into the middle of the bed and patted the spot beside her. "And Trip and I were on this side. I think we need to do it exactly as we saw it to make sure it works."

"Okay," Bas said. He disappeared from the room. Everything fell silent.

"Is there anything I can do?" Violetta said, hovering near the end of the bed next to Tamuel and Korinna. "Anything to make you more comfortable?"

"Can I have some water?" Ilia asked.

"Me too," Trip said. His mouth had already been dry when he woke, now it was also burning, and tasted disgusting. "Maybe some mint to chew on as well."

"I'll be right back," Violetta said, disappearing out the door, leaving them there with his daughter and her mate.

"Where are Daphne and the boys?" Trip asked.

"In their cottage. I spelled them to stay there until we managed to wake you. It was harder than I thought it would be, especially with Daphne and Gideon. I had to keep sending them both back. They were determined to check on you – and Gideon kept mentioning Christmas."

"They always spend it here with me."

"Well, maybe they still can, given you've woken on Christmas Eve."

Ilia gasped. "Almost two weeks have passed?"

"Loki did intimate that time was passing much faster here than where he'd taken us to show us the past, present and future."

"But … he also said she had until Christmas. Why did he keep us there so long? We're lucky she's not already dead. We have to do this now."

Bas and Jules hurried into the room, Dawn's limp body cradled in her mother's arms.

"Jules," Ilia said, voice breaking. "I'm so sorry."

Jules shook her head, tears tumbling down her face. "Don't be sorry. Just make it better."

Ilia nodded sharply and patted the bed. "Lay her here, head next to my shoulder."

Jules lowered Dawn, then with a whimper, knelt beside the bed, one hand on her daughter's head, the other holding her little hand.

"You have to let go and stand back," Ilia said.

Jules' lip wobbled as the tears fell harder. "I'm not sure I can."

"You have to. We have to do this exactly as we saw it," Trip said, voice gruff with emotion.

"Come on, Jules." Bas took her hands in his, helping her up from beside the bed, holding her trembling form to his even as a world of grief and pain chased across his face. "We have to trust they know what they're doing."

"I do," Jules said. "I know Ilia will do everything she can to save my baby."

Ilia's face twisted again before she managed a watery smile. "You trust me with her life?"

"Of course. Always."

"Thank you."

Jules leaned down and kissed Dawn on the forehead, then Ilia. "Bring her back to us."

"I will." She took a deep breath then lay down, still holding Trip's hand. Then turning her head to meet his gaze, her astonishing eyes glowing in the dark, she said, "Do it now. Before I lose my grip on my fear."

He nodded, cupped her face and whispered, "I love you."

Then before he could even see how she might respond to that statement, he bent over her, his teeth elongating as Tamuel had said a God's teeth would for this very thing. Then, mouth suddenly watering, he bit into the sensitive, fragrant flesh of her neck.

17

*I*lia whimpered as Trip's new fangs sank into her neck – just like Tiberinus' had – slicing through her skin with hardly any resistance, piercing the artery that carried her life's blood through her body. But unlike with Tiberinus, she felt no fear, no revulsion.

Her entire world centred on those three little words he'd just uttered.

How could they carry such power?

But they did.

She felt them inside her, growing, feeding her soul as he fed from her life's blood.

He loved her.

It seemed improbable, and yet, she knew with a deep certainty, the like of which she'd never felt before, that he did.

He loved her.

And she loved him.

Maybe it was the soul-bond that Loki had talked about, forcing them to love each other. But she didn't think that was it. There was no feeling of being forced.

Only a huge sense of freedom. Like she was a bird who'd had her wings clipped but was suddenly able to fly.

That sense of freedom, it had started with lust, certainly, creating sensations in her body that made her feel more like herself than she ever had. That lust had been true. She had trusted it. And that trust had grown, fed by Trip's trust in her, his belief that she was good.

It was then solidified by the realisation that he wasn't the only one who felt that.

The people around her – her family, if not by blood, then by choice – all believed in her too. They believed in her goodness; had been trying to make her be true to that all these months as they'd shown their love and support and tried to enfold her into their family and make her feel like she belonged. They'd trusted her with the task of finding Trip. They'd trusted her enough to start to train her how to use and control her new magic. But the best thing of all – to use a metaphor suitable to this time of the year – the thing that had turned a lonely, damaged pine tree into a true representation of Christmas spirit was that they believed in her enough to save Dawn. To do exactly as she asked and stand back and let her do it.

That trust, added to Trip's – it was everything she'd never had and more. It filled her up inside and made her glow, not with fury and fear, but with love and happiness, and yes, Christmas spirit.

Joy. She felt joyous. She'd never in her life felt joyous before.

And it was the most marvellous sensation.

"Look, she's glowing all over," someone said reverently.

"The link. Between Dawn and Ilia. Can anyone else see it?"

"It's getting weaker."

"Where's the one between Trip and Ilia?" That was Korinna, her voice worried. "I thought they said that was supposed to appear to take its place."

"What happens if it doesn't?" Jules sounded worried.

"She'll die." Bas whispered. "She needs a life-force to help keep her alive."

He was right. She knew that now. Knew this was why Loki hadn't been able to show her any more of her future – she didn't have one. But that thought wasn't enough to mute her joy.

"What can we do?" Tamuel's pained question did, stabbing her in the heart.

"Nothing," she whispered to them. "You can do nothing. My life doesn't matter. Only Dawn's."

Trip lifted his head, his hand convulsing against her cheek, his tortured gaze meeting hers. "Your life does matter."

She touched his lip, his fang. "You must keep drinking."

"Not if it will take your life."

"You must. I give it willingly. For you. For Dawn. It's necessary. To save you all."

"No. I won't. It's not fair."

"A life for a life. It's the penalty we must pay. I've had more than my fair share, anyway. Drink. Before it's too late."

"Ilia," Jules said, bursting into tears.

She reached out her hand for Jules to take. "It's okay. These last months have been a gift I never thought to have. To be a part of your family." She turned back to face Trip. "To know love. True love. I leave you all far happier than I have ever been." She took Trip's head in her hands. He was still so weak from their trip to the in-between that it was easy to guide his head back to her neck. "Drink, my love. Let your touch be the last thing I feel."

"No," Trip moaned against her neck even as his fangs sank into her skin once more, as if the Fates and destiny were too strong for him to fight against. Another sign this was meant to be.

I don't want to lose you. I can't lose you, she heard in her head. Trip, somehow talking through the soul-bond as he drank. *Not now I've found you.*

"I will always be with you," she whispered.

Not how I want. Not how you deserve. The Gods ask too much of you. This was supposed to be a giving and a taking. A sharing. Now it's just all give from you and all take from me. As the words echoed in her head, he sucked harder, groaning against her skin as if the action pained him.

But she felt no pain. All she felt was rightness and a need. A need that was growing inside her. A need for the sharing he was talking about. A need for his life-force to be in her.

A need for … his blood.

As the thought hit her, fangs grew in her mouth, pricking her lower lip.

What? How? She wasn't a Goddess.

"Maybe not," a distinctly female voice whispered in her head. *"But you are Trip's soul-bound mate, equal to him in every way. Be equal now."*

Oh! Sharing. That's what this was truly meant to be. While he drank of her blood, she was supposed to complete the circuit by drinking of his.

But with him at her neck, how could she do it?

His fingers convulsed against her face, his wrist brushing up next to her mouth. Without thought, she turned and sank her new fangs into his skin.

The copper tang of blood rushed into her mouth followed by a rush of power and a scent that was like apples and summer fruit and the blooms that had grown in the garden he'd made with his blood. It filled her, making everything inside her grow and reform, settling into something new.

Something that was just her.

Something that was part of him too. But not in a cloying way. Not in a way that made her feel trapped. No. This was like when he'd told her he loved her, like when she realised she was part of a family, like when she realised she loved him, and felt freed by it.

And as that sense of freedom swept through her, there was a wrenching tear as the link binding her to Dawn snapped. But that tear didn't remain an open wound. It healed immediately, the frayed ends of the bond reaching, stretching, joining.

With him. With her love. With Trip.

He was hers and she was his and together they were flying to a freedom she never thought to have.

Somewhere in the distance, a baby wailed, accompanied by shouts of joy. Movement beside her as the slight weight of Dawn was lifted from the bed. She rolled over, closer into Trip, her arms tightening around him, her leg sliding over his as they twined together, both taking, both giving.

They were one.

And it was the most magnificent thing in the entire universe.

In her eyes, stars swirled faster and faster until they exploded, a magnificent firework, and she and Trip were falling, falling, right into each other's arms.

~

SHE AWOKE SOMETIME LATER to the sound of carols drifting through the closed door, along with talking, laughter and the tearing of paper.

Trip shifted, mumbling something about sweetness and light, then rolled over onto his back. She made a sound of protest in her throat – she wasn't ready to let go of him yet, to let go of the warmth, the feeling of completion – but then he pulled her to him, her head nestled on the firmness of his broad chest, hand over his heart.

A heart that beat in time with hers; a heart that pumped with her blood alongside his, as hers pumped his blood alongside hers; a heart that now held her deep inside.

She'd been so stupid to hold herself back from this; to let old fear rule her so completely. But now none of that mattered because she was home.

"That's nice," she muttered.

"What?" he murmured, moving his hand to brush her hair back from her face and tip up her chin.

She opened her eyes to see his, the light green glowing in the dark and filled with his love for her. His trust in her. His happiness in her. She smiled up at him. "This. Being here like this. It feels like home."

"It does. Being with you will always feel like that for me now. I love you."

"I love you too."

He bent down as she reached up, their lips meeting in a soft, longing kiss. She would have deepened it, but the sounds from outside the door got louder and he pulled away. "We better not," he said softly. "They might come through that door to check on us at any moment."

She nodded. She didn't want to get caught making love to him; the first time they truly made love, she wanted it to be just them, so she could lose herself in him completely.

She settled beside him, both turned on their sides, staring into each other's eyes.

She still couldn't believe this had happened; that after everything, she'd found her soulmate, had tied herself to him in every conceivable way and was filled with light and joy because of it.

For the first time in her life, she was peaceful. Next to realising she was in love with Trip and the magnificence of sharing blood with him, it was the most remarkable feeling she'd ever experienced.

"Should we go out and join them? Let them know we're awake? Sounds like it's Christmas morning with all the paper tearing."

"Can we just stay here a little longer?" she asked.

"Sounds perfect to me." He touched beside her eyes, the longing and love in his warming all the places inside her that had been so cold for so long. "Beautiful. So beautiful," he whispered as he ran his finger over her brow, down her nose and along her cheek.

"So are you." She mirrored his gesture. "Your eyes are glowing."

"Are they? So are yours. Like sunlight over a mountain peak at dawn, all purple and golden. In fact, all of you is glowing."

It was then she realised that the light she could see his face by was coming from her. She looked down at herself. Trip was right. She *was* glowing. But it wasn't the worrisome glow that had emanated from her chest because of her fury. This was like after Dawn had turned her spirit form into a corporeal one at Easter.

She growled deep in her chest. "Damn it. Not again!" It had taken a few months for that glow to dim enough so that she could go outside and not be subject to people's stares.

"You look like an angel. Like you'd be more at home perched at the top of a Christmas tree."

She growled louder. "Not funny." She sat up slowly, a little stiff but surprisingly okay for someone who'd been close to death not so long ago. "I am nothing close to an angel. I'm a thing of broken edges and angles. I'm a mess." She went to tuck her hair behind her ear, then stopped as her fingers tangled in the rat's nest of knots and mess that had taken up residence on the side she'd been lying on. "Agh! Look at my hair! Actually, don't look at it!" She quickly tried to smooth it down, but stopped when he chuckled and replaced her hands with his.

"You are beautiful as you are, mess and all. I'm not exactly perfect either."

"But you're a God – or something like one."

"Given you drank my blood like that, so must you be."

She grimaced. "I don't know how."

"Don't you?" He waved his hand at her chest. "You spent thousands of years in a piece of a Goddess' heart. Then you were remade with Goddess-gifted energy. You, like me, have had more than one Goddess' power responsible for remaking what you are now."

"You remember where you came from?"

He sat up beside her, grasping her hands in his, sliding his thumbs over the pulse point in her wrists. "Yes. Much is still foggy, but I can remember where I came from. I can remember Demeter and Persephone and Gaia. I can remember first hearing the prophecy and about Perses. I remember coming up with the idea to create the Eleusinian Mysteries to help others fight the coming darkness." He swallowed hard. "I remember what it felt like to leave my Innia, pregnant with Korinna, how it felt to know I might never know my daughter or see the woman I loved again."

"Oh. Trip."

He smiled softly at her. "It's an old pain, one that barely hurts now I know you. What I felt for Innia – it was the stuff of youth. What I feel for you is deeper and so much more encompassing. I will always love Innia, but that love is nothing to what I feel for you."

"I know," she said softly, brushing his hair from his forehead. "I know. And I am glad you remember her." She blinked tears from her eyes.

"As am I."

"It is not too much? Remembering all of it?"

He tipped his head. "I remember only a small portion as yet. I think that's as it must be. I don't think it would be comfortable to have everything come rushing back all at once."

"Do you think we might need to drink each other's blood again? To gain back your memories completely?"

He tipped his head to the side, looking warily at her. "Will you mind if we do?"

She glance down at their linked hands, chewing on her lip – careful not to break the skin with her newly pointy eye-teeth – as if she was considering it.

"It's okay if you don't. I'm sure they will come back eventually with what we've shared. I can already feel them at the back of my mind, like a cloud of fog just waiting to clear."

She looked up at him through her eyelashes, unable to hold back the mischievous smile. "I think I might be able to handle it. As long as we get to do it in a private place with nobody watching on, because next time we do, I'm not going to be able to stop from jumping your bones."

His mouth wobbled as he tried to hold back his smile. "I could get on board with that."

"Good." A noise from the lounge room made her glance at the door. "I wish we were alone now."

"So do I. But we're not. Although," he frowned a little. "I think I remember how to whisk us away to somewhere private if that's what you wish."

"You would do that for me? Miss out on your precious Christmas morning with your daughter and her family – the first Christmas you've ever shared with her?"

"I would. In a heartbeat. There will be other Christmases. But there won't be another first morning that I wake with you in my arms. And making love to you now would be the best Christmas gift I've ever given or received."

Her lips quirked. "Oh really? You think it would be the best Christmas gift you could give to me? Got tickets on yourself, I see."

"With what I'm remembering I can do, you bet."

He lunged and she laughed as his arms wrapped around her, taking her down to the bed, their lips meeting in a kiss that was all tongue and tasting and passion. She felt him deep inside her, but she wanted even more. She'd always want more. But could she ask him to give up his precious Christmas after everything they'd been through? No, she couldn't. Couldn't do that to him, or to herself.

She wanted to share this Christmas with him and everyone out there too.

The shock of that realisation had her gasping.

He pulled back. "What is it?"

CHAPTER 18

$\mathcal{B}$efore she could answer, the door banged open and they looked up as a body shot across the room to bounce on the end of the bed. "Trip! You're awake."

"Gideon! Come back here." Daphne appeared in the doorway.

More bouncing as Gideon shouted, "He's awake! I said I could hear him awake."

"Stop that. They don't need you bouncing on the bed!" Daphne entered the room, obviously with the intent to grab her youngest son.

Before she could, Trip pulled Gideon to him, giving him a hug and ruffling his hair. "It's fine. I'm used to this rascal bouncing on my bed first thing Christmas morning. It's a tradition."

"Dad?" The question had him looking up as Korinna entered the room. The others appeared in the doorway behind her, delight and relief in their eyes and smiles. Korinna edged closer, hands wringing in front of her, Tamuel at her back. "Do you ... do you remember?"

"Oh, my dear. My darling girl. I'm sorry. I'm so sorry I left you and your mother like I did. But I had no choice. I hope you understand I had no choice?"

"I do. I do!" She rushed to him, hands stretched to take his. Gideon moved so Trip could pull her close, enfolding her in his arms. "Dad. Dad. You remember? You remember."

A lump rose in Ilia's throat, her chin wobbling as she blinked back threatening tears.

"Not everything. But it's coming back." Trip kissed his daughter's head, holding her close for a moment before pulling away to look down at her. "It's all coming back." He reached out to grab Ilia's hand while holding Korinna to his side in a hug. "Ilia and I will share more blood to make certain I get all of my memories back."

"You will?" Korinna asked, gaze flying to Ilia's.

Ilia nodded. "Of course. It's the least I can do after all you've done for me. Besides ..." She shared a secret smile with Trip. "It wasn't as bad as I thought."

"That's such a relief," Jules said, as she came to the other side of the bed, Dawn in her arms.

"Oh!" Ilia said, gaze raking over the baby. "She looks so well. As if nothing ever happened."

Dawn held her arms out, leaning towards Ilia. Jules handed her over. Ilia hugged the baby to her, kissing her downy head, breathing in the smell that was baby powder and fresh soap with a hint of lavender and something else that was all Dawn. "I'm so glad you're okay, Dawny. So very glad."

Dawn placed her hand on the side of Ilia's face. In her mind she heard, *"I'm happy you well now too."*

"What?" She blinked, uncertain if she'd imagined what she thought she'd just heard.

"It'th me!" Dawn smiled brightly.

"That's ... that's impossible!" Their communication had always been in images and feelings, never words. Dawn was too young for anything else.

"She spoke to you?"

Her gaze snapped to Jules. "What?" She glanced around as the others all nodded. They'd heard her too. "How? Mind speech at such a young age is unheard of."

Jules shrugged. "It seems that in separating from you, her powers have grown. She can now speak to us all if she touches us. Bas thinks she'll be able to do it soon without even having to do that. Some form of Goddessly mind-speak she inherited from Ostara."

"That's ... amazing?"

Jules' mouth twisted into something that wasn't quite a smile. "We'll see." She shared a worried look with Bas. Ilia couldn't blame her. This was just one more thing to make the Gods look Dawn's way – and that wasn't something anyone wanted. They'd all suffered from too much attention from the Gods and Goddesses in the past. It seemed that the Eternal Well wasn't done with them.

Even if she hadn't already made up her mind to stay and help, she wouldn't be going anywhere now. She couldn't leave Jules and Bas and the others to deal with any of this alone.

Nothing could make her leave the family she'd found.

Trip gripped her hand tightly, as if he could feel what she was thinking, and when she met his gaze, he said, "I'm glad you feel that way. So do I."

She nodded. Neither of them were ever leaving their family again.

"I guess that means I'm bequeathing the farm early to Daphne and her boys."

"What? No. You can't!" Daphne said, putting her arms around Gideon as he bounced to the foot of the bed, Charlie and Harry coming to stand behind her.

"Of course I can. It was going to be yours anyway when I left. It's just going to be a few years early."

"What do you mean you're leaving and it was going to be mine anyway? Does this have something to do with you being a God?"

Trip gasped, his gaze flying to Korinna and Tamuel.

Tamuel shrugged. "We had to tell them. Our spells didn't work on them for long – on Daphne and Gideon not at all for some reason. They came in after you and Ilia started the blood magic and saw it all – bit hard to hide, given it whipped up a magical storm of light that flowed out of the house brighter than your Christmas lights.

He stared at Daphne and the boys. "You're ... you're okay with it?"

"It's fantastic! I always thought you were like Santa but this is even better," Gideon enthused from his place at the end of the bed.

Daphne's arms tightened around Gideon as she smiled at Trip and Ilia. "It explains a lot."

He looked to the other boys, his hand tightening around Ilia's as he waited.

Harry nodded slowly then smiled and said, "Gideon's right. It's super cool."

Charlie's smile was a bit slower. "Will I be able to grow the trees without you?"

Trip blew out a breath. "Of course you will."

"So, no Godly powers were used in the making of this farm," Charlie said, lips quirking a little.

Trip chuckled. "No. Well, maybe the trees won't grow quite as fast. That was a magic I couldn't seem to help using. But I've shared with you all my growing tips. You are more than capable of keeping this place going – if you want to?"

"I want to," Charlie said. "I love working the land." He glanced down and then back up again. "It's something I learned from you."

"You won't go and never come back though, will you?" Gideon asked, eyes shadowed.

Trip glanced at Ilia, his eyes asking her what she thought.

His sharing of this decision filled her with happiness. "We can come back as often as you want. As often as they need you. They're your family too. I wouldn't ask you to abandon them. And maybe, after we've finished all this, we can come back and live here."

"Really?"

"Of course. I mean, it's not like Korinna and the others can't just open a portal and visit at any time. So, we'd all still be together."

He smiled wildly, cupped her face and gave her a smacking kiss.

Tamuel wolf-whistled.

Korinna said, "I'd say get a bed, but you already have one."

Bas suggested, "Maybe we should leave them to it."

Ilia pulled back from the kiss and, smiling said, "No way. We've got Christmas presents to unwrap! And a feast to prepare and eat."

"You want to stay for Christmas?" Trip asked, eyes wide.

"My first proper Christmas? I can't think of a better place to spend it or better people to spend it with."

Trip leaned in to give her another kiss. Then, leaning back a little, hands still cupping her face, he said, "Loki was so wrong. I knew you'd get this Christmas spirit thing!"

She smiled crookedly at him. "Christmas with a family like ours ... what's not to love?" There would never be anymore bah-humbugs from her.

She dragged him up and out of the bed to lead everyone out of the bedroom and into the sunlit lounge where a huge Christmas tree sat in the corner, twinkling at them.

Everyone gasped as they entered the room. A truckload of presents had appeared under and around the tree, crushing the few that hadn't already been opened.

"What the Hells?"

"Where did they come from?"

Ilia raised her brows at Trip and he shook his head, as baffled as the rest of them.

Gideon whooped and dived in to the pile as Daphne said, "A Christmas miracle."

Ilia leaned in to Trip, loving how his arm went around her shoulders so naturally, tucking her into his side. "You're my Christmas miracle," she said, looking up at him.

"And you're mine." He kissed her lightly before he was pulled forward by Harry who, even though usually evincing teenage cool, couldn't keep his enthusiasm at bay.

The next few hours were spent opening presents – there were some for everyone in the miracle pile – clearing the torn wrapping paper and find places for all the gifts so they could bring in the trestle tables and start to load them up with the Christmas feast that Daphne, Jules, Bas and Tamuel were creating in the kitchen.

Ilia had never laughed so much as she worked. She sang carols with everyone as they tidied up – even though she didn't know most of the words – and rearranged the furniture and set the table. At least, she did when she wasn't being waylaid by Trip every few minutes – he seemed to feel the need to touch and kiss her as much as she did him.

When they sat down to the meal, Trip raised his glass to give a toast, but Ilia put her hand on top of his, stopping him, and stood. All eyes went to her.

"I just wanted to say, I thought Christmas was stupid and the idea of the Christmas spirit even worse. I thought it was all about taking and wanting – kind of a reflection of my life before I was freed from the HeartsBlood Gem." She swallowed, eyes pricking with tears as she looked around at all of their dear faces. "But you have all shown me over the last few months what friendship and family and love truly is. You gave me your trust and never asked for anything from me I wasn't willing to give. Even then, I was still wary of how I could ever be a part of something so good. I felt so broken and angry and cold."

Her gaze landed on Dawn, sitting in a high chair that Daphne had grabbed out of the storage shed. "But a little baby, full of dawn's light of renewal, started warming my heart and then all of you crept in with her, starting to heal my heart and soul in a way I never thought I wanted or deserved. Because of that, I was ready to open myself up to trust and believe when I finally met the man we'd all been looking for; the man who is the other part of my soul." She smiled at him, then at everyone at the table. "Thank you for sticking by me and sticking with me and never giving up on me, even when I had given up on myself. You helped to lead me here, to this moment, and I will be forever grateful. May the Eternal Well guide you and keep you safe and help us as we face what is coming. Together."

They all stood, raising their glasses. "Together."

They drank and as they did, there was a rolling knock in the distance – the Eternal Well accepting their vow to fight together to defeat the rising tide of evil that was Perses.

Ilia's gaze met Trip's – and instead of feeling worried at another vow having been made, she felt strengthened by it.

Like Demeter's vow to get Trip back, this one would work too.

How could it not when they were not only all working as one

towards a common goal, but had the bonds of love and family and friendship to strengthen them and carry them through?

"We'll win the day," Trip whispered to her.

"We will."

Then they proceeded to have the merriest of merry Christmases.

EPILOGUE

"That was nice of you to give them all those gifts. Especially given Christmas is hardly part of your pantheon's religion."

Loki turned to see Demeter come up behind him, then looked back at the glimmering mirror he watched Trip and Ilia through. "After years of watching Trip and nudging him along, I kind of see the appeal." He frowned as Trip started talking to an empty chair at the table next to him. "I'm a little worried though that I broke him. He seems to be talking to imaginary people." He pointed to Ilia who was also talking to the empty chair beside her. "I think I might have broken her too. Does drinking blood lead to some kind of madness for their kind?"

Demeter sighed. "I suppose it's time." She waved her hand over the image. At first, nothing happened, then there was a wavering in the spaces where he had seen nothing but empty chairs.

As the wavering clarified, he leaned forward. "Fuck me! No. It can't be." He stared at the woman who'd appeared in the chair next to Trip. It looked like her but … it couldn't be. She was long lost to him. "Have I gone mad too? Did I spend too long in the in-between?"

"No. You're not going mad. It's her."

He glanced at Demeter to see sad resignation in her eyes, but then couldn't stop his gaze from being drawn back to the woman in the image. "Callie?"

"Yes. Your Callianthe. Although, she's called Daphne now."

"But ... how? She died. My father killed her." Not Odin, his adoptive father, but his real father, that evil bastard who had been relegated to Tartarus for his crimes.

"No. He didn't. I found her and saved her. She was supposed to die alongside her sisters and their people, but I couldn't allow it. She was needed. So I warped her fate and brought her to this time."

"What? Why?"

"You would never have become what you needed to become if she stayed."

His mind reeling, he stumbled back from the vision. "I have to go to her." He raised his hand to call a portal, but Demeter stepped in front of him. His magic died with a little puff.

"You cannot go to her. Not yet. There are things to do. For you and for her."

"No. I have to go!"

She stopped him from moving past her, her grip firmer than it had any right to be – damn she was strong! "She is not ready to remember you yet. It will hurt her. It will hurt your child."

"My child?"

He looked back at the image, at the three boys who had appeared in the other previously empty seats at the table. Two of them he recognised as the children she had borne by the man her father had tied her to. A man long dead, killed in the raid that had brought Callianthe to Loki's attention. The boys were only ten or so years older than when he'd last seen them. How could that be? It had been thousands of years.

But the question didn't get asked of Demeter, because his eyes landed on the youngest one.

The boy's eyes were a startling, almost violet blue, like his powerful demi-God Warlock grandfather, but his hair was dark as night and there was the whisper of sharp cheekbones and pointed chin that would be identical to his father's one day.

"My son?"

Demeter's hand landed on his shoulder. "Yes."

He had a son! A roar of need burst to life inside him. "How could you have kept this from me?"

"I had to."

"I have to go to them."

"No. It isn't time."

"I don't care. I have to go."

He struggled against her grip, lifted his hands to use his magic, but it was a useless gesture in this place that was hers, filled with her magic, giving her dominion over all who stood here with her.

She whispered a word, and his magic fizzled out.

"Loki. I'm sorry. I know you want to go to them, but you can't. Not yet. It isn't time. They won't accept you. She won't even remember you."

"What do you mean?"

"I took her memory too when I placed her here to be a help to Trip. To be family for him. He needed that so he could be ready for Ilia."

"Why didn't you tell me!"

"I couldn't do that either. You had to live your life thinking she was gone. And for all intents and purposes, she has been, until now." She gripped both his shoulders and looked deeply into his eyes. "You are like my son, Loki, and I love you, but if you try to go to her now and ruin everything we've worked towards, I will smite you down without hesitation."

He shivered, seeing in her eyes her determination that would let nothing – not even her love for him or Trip or Persephone or even the long dead Innia – to get in the way of stopping Perses from coming back into the living Realms. She was right. He too had thought he would never let anything get in the way of that goal. But this … He closed his eyes, shutting out the sight of his love. "How long?" he finally managed to ask.

"Not long in the scheme of things. Ilia and Trip have a bit more work to do to solidify their bond and be able to use their magic side by side to strengthen everything Trip and Korinna must do. There is also the issue of Dawn's growth and training. Once we have taken care of those issues, you will be able to go to Callie and remind her of what you once were to each other."

"She will remember me then?"

Demeter nodded. "The spell on her is not the one I placed on Trip. She will remember when the Fates align and she is ready. Then you will go to her and your son. You will train him as I trained you and he will help in the fight ahead."

"But he is so young."

She pointed at the image, at the baby in her highchair. "If that baby can help, your son is not too young."

"You ask a lot."

"I know. But it is necessary." Her eyes blanked as she stared off into a future he couldn't see. "Once all the threads I have woven are in place, you will all see the bigger picture and you will know what I know. That only united by the hearts curse, can we beat back the evil that is coming."

"The hearts curse?"

She nodded. "Love."

He frowned at her. "Love is not a curse."

She smiled, the expression nothing comforting. "To Perses, it will be the greatest curse of them all."

~

I HOPE you enjoyed this first part of Trip and Ilia's story. There will be more to come later next year with *Fates Cursed: Gods Cursed Series Book 5* – to be featured in *A Perfectly Paranormal Prophecy*.

IF YOU'VE GOT A MOMENT, I would love it if you could leave a review for *Hearts Cursed*. Reviews can help readers find books, and also help tell me where I'm going right and where I'm going wrong. I am grateful for all honest reviews. Thank you in advance for taking the time to let others know what you've read, and what you thought—you can leave your review at Goodreads, BookBub or the ebook retailer where you bought your copy.

You can find links to the ebook retailers here: https://www.leislleighton.com/paranormal-romance-novels/#APPC

IF YOU HAVEN'T READ any of the other Gods Curses Series, or are interested in finding out about my other books (I write both paranormal and romantic suspense books) and where you can follow me on social media, then please keep reading.

LOVE A FREE BOOK?

YOUR FREE BOOK IS WAITING

One Fate, one mate, a bond too strong to deny ...

Paul Collins, duty-bound Pack Warlock and seer, must marry a strong witch for the good of Pack McVale. But his hidden feelings for his best-friend's sister, maternal wolf Ivy McVale, make this a more difficult pill to swallow every day. Especially when they begin to mate.

Then Paul has a vision: If they mate, Ivy will die. Desperate, Paul uses his powers to change destiny and make Ivy think she's always hated him. He can deal with any punishment the Fates make him pay for tampering with destiny, as long as Ivy lives.

After recovering from a bewildering month-long illness, Ivy notices her nemesis, Paul, is tormented by something. And strangely, she is the only one who can feel it. Unable to endure such unhappiness—even if he does call her Poison Ivy—she is determined to help him, no matter the cost. Because Pack McVale cannot survive without him, and curiously, neither can she ...

Simply sign up to my newsletter and I will email your free copy of Witch Bound to you. You will also receive the latest on upcoming books, sales, giveaways and relevant bookish news.

Get My Free Copy of Witch Bound Here:
https://www.subscribepage.com/w2g6b9

ALSO BY LEISL LEIGHTON

GODS CURSED SERIES

Love Cursed

Soul Cursed

Blood Cursed

Hearts Cursed

Fates Cursed

(Coming in A Perfectly Paranormal Prophecy - late 2023)

~

PACK BOUND SERIES

Pack Bound

Moon Bound

Shifter Bound

Wolf Bound

Witch Bound

(A Pack Bound Series Prequel Novella)

~

DAWN OF THE CURSE: A PACK BOUND PREQUEL SERIES

Soul Bound

Alpha Bound

(Coming in late 2023)

~

As well as writing sexy, dark paranormal novels, I write mysterious and emotional romantic suspense novels.

Storm Haven Series

Need You Tonight

(Coming April 2023)

~

CoalCliff Stud Series

Climbing Fear: Book 1

Blazing Fear: Book 2

~

Echo Springs Series

Dangerous Echoes: Book 1

Books 2-4 in this series, (written by Daniel deLorne, TJ Hamilton and Shannon Curtis) are also available now at all ebook retailers.

ABOUT LEISL

Leisl Leighton is a tall red head with an overly large imagination. As a child, she identified strongly with Anne of Green Gables, and like Anne, is a voracious reader and born performer. It came as no surprise when she went on to a career as a performer, script writer, script doctor, stage manager and musical director for cabaret and theatre restaurants.

After starting a family, Leisl stopped performing and began writing the stories plaguing her dreams. She now writes emotional stories mixed with mystery and a little bit of what goes bump in the night. Her novels have won and placed in writing contests here and overseas. She is a passionate advocate for the romance genre, was President of Romance Writers of Australia from 2014-2017 and when she's not writing romantic stories of redemption, she is helping other authors reach their dreams with her Author Services.

You can contact Leisl through her website www.leislleighton.com or sign up to her Newsletter and be the first to find out about new releases, appearances, special deals and exclusive giveaways.

You can sign up here:
https://www.subscribepage.com/w2g6b9

And if you want to get to know the Perfectly Paranormal Anthology authors a bit more, get sneak peeks of what's coming up for the APP

Anthologies, as well as giveaways, special offers and just some PNR fun, then join our Perfectly Paranormal Paramours Facebook Group.

Find us here:
https://www.facebook.com/groups/251663560162131

facebook.com/LeislLeightonAuthor
twitter.com/LeislLeighton
instagram.com/leislleightonauthor
bookbub.com/authors/leisl-leighton

ACKNOWLEDGMENTS

Getting this book ready for publication was more of an adventure than I'd bargained on. In the middle of the writing process, I had a bad car accident and fractured my sternum and a vertebrae in my back and spent four days in hospital with many months of recovery ahead of me. Then just after I was able to sit up for a few hours in front of my computer and get back to my editing, my son brought Covid home and promptly gave it to my husband and me. I felt truly sorry for myself. But so many people, both family and friends, helped out with food packages and running errands and keeping us all going and it filled me with a sense of such love and support that despite how sick I felt, and despite the Covid coughing and sneezing kept my fracture from healing for a month—extending my healing time by another 4-6 weeks—I was able to kick myself in the butt and get up and do the work I needed to get this one finished and out in time and still have multiple rests during the day.

So huge thanks have to go to my mum and dad, Kerrie and Jim, who did so much for me during this difficult time, and to all the friends who cooked for me and sent messages of love and support. This wouldn't have happened without you.

Of course, my hubby, Mark, and my two beautiful boys, Jacob and Nathaniel, all stepped up too and when they were all feeling better, did so much to help me get back to work and took on extra duties (especially Jacob) in cooking and cleaning and washing so the house was kept in order given I wasn't able to do it.

Aside from great family and friends, a writer needs a Coven of writing peeps all their own. Thanks to my friends in my writing groups for encouraging me in this endeavour and giving me the strength to push on through all the highs and lows of doing this crazy writing thing— Laura, Chris, Marnie, Frana, Anita, Samantha and Helen. I couldn't have gotten here without you. Especially Marnie and Anita who did all the hard yards so that we could still have our retreat together even though I was recuperating from my accident and was unable to help in the ways I usually do.

Thanks once again to the insanely talented Samantha Marshall for her brilliant covers. Every day I thank the universe for bringing us together and for being able to count you friend.

Thoughts and thanks also to my bestie, Helen, and to the first writing friend I ever had, Liz. You are both gone but never forgotten and a part of you will always live on in my stories.

And a big shout out to all my friends in Romance Writers of Australia —you are inspiration and mentor rolled into a big ball of supportive writerly love. Thank you.

The final person I have to thank is my agent, Alex Adsett, for believing in me and my work and always backing every decision I make. Your confidence in me helps me believe I can actually do this writing thing. Eternal thanks.

THE RED RIBBON

MARNIE ST CLAIR

THE RED RIBBON

An Uncanny Knack Series
Book 2

Marnie St Clair

ABOUT THE RED RIBBON

Home for Christmas …

Kitty-Rose Frost has a magical Knack for persuasion; she can talk anyone into anything. But after a disaster at school that alienated her only friend, and Woodleigh's favourite son, Sam Wells, she doesn't use her power anymore. That doesn't stop her being viewed with suspicion by everyone in her hometown. Which is why she needs to escape – go somewhere no one knows about the Frost legacy. But first, she has to rescue the family's failing dressmaking shop.

When a Christmas parade in a neighbouring town offers a massive first prize, Kitty sees a way to revitalise Woodleigh's struggling main strip. She starts to put together a show-stopping float – but she needs help. In particular, she needs Sam Wells, now the town mechanic and general handyman. But not only is Sam determined *not* to help Kitty, he's the only one immune to her Knack …

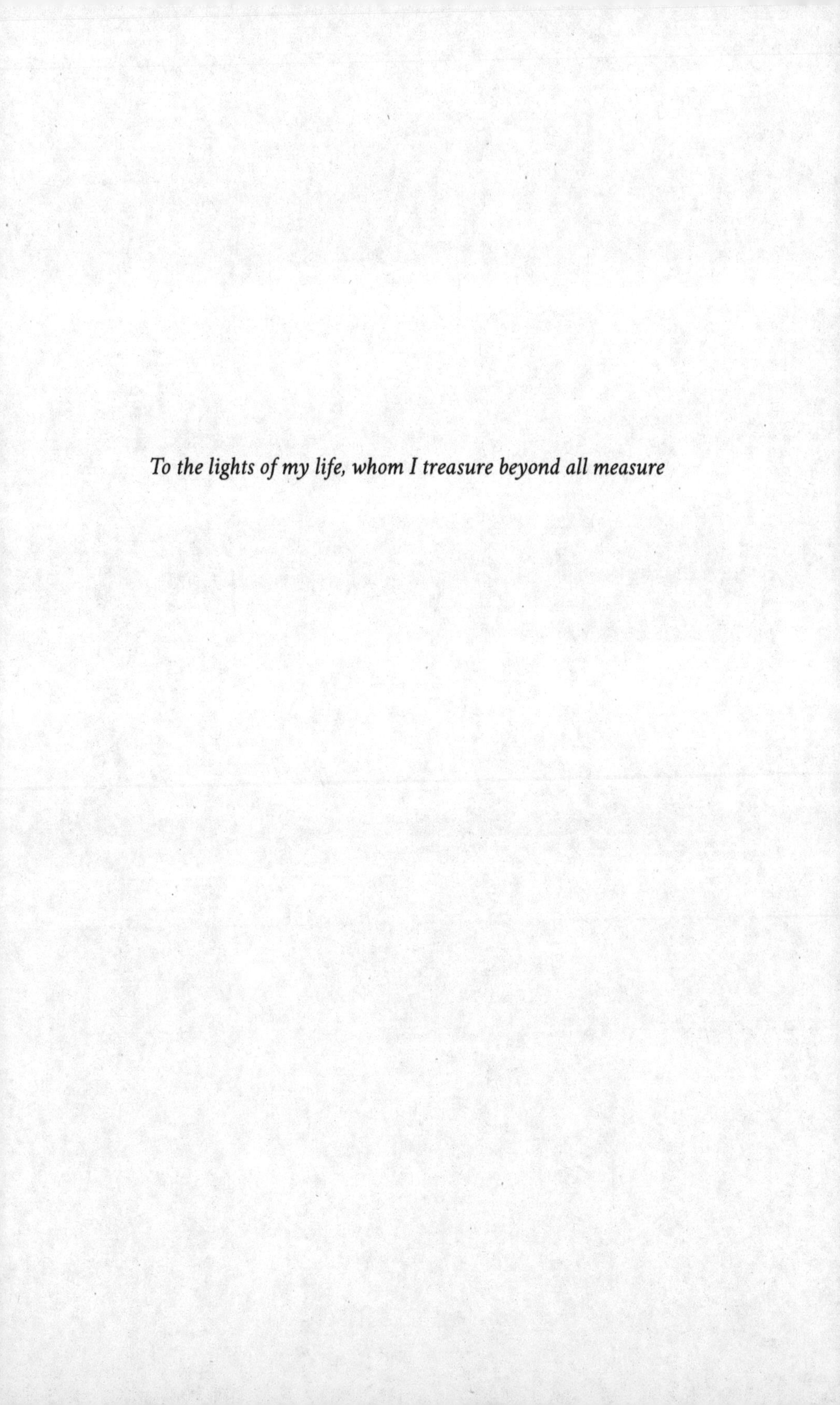

To the lights of my life, whom I treasure beyond all measure

PROLOGUE

Kitty-Rose Frost could count three defining moments in her twenty-five years of small-town life.

The first occurred at eight years of age, just before the war, when Susie Wells accused her of stealing Mrs Well's new Cartier watch – which Susie had brought to school to show off without her mother's consent. Despite Kitty's protests and a lack of any kind of proof, the whole class – bar one – had turned on her.

"Where is it, Kitty-Rose? Tell us where it is."

They'd surrounded her, hands in fists, faces strained and ugly. All except for 'Saint' Sam Wells, who'd stated with his typical calm confidence that Kitty-Rose didn't have the watch – which his sister shouldn't have brought to school in any case – taken Susie through her movements and organised parties to search for it. In that moment, watching him, Kitty knew she'd take a bullet for Sam Wells. He'd do the same for anyone – it was just the way he was – but he'd done it for her, and it counted.

The watch had quickly been found and the matter forgotten. But not by Kitty.

Until that day, she hadn't understood the true reality of her situation. Sure, there were birthday parties she wasn't invited to. At lunch, in their imaginary games, there sometimes wasn't even another servant required in the castle, and she had to play a wild horse, galloping through nearby hills. And when they paired up for Mary Mac, she sat cross-legged and alone, watching.

But when they'd surrounded her like that, seeing the naked fear and loathing in their eyes, shock and hurt rose through her like cold, murky floodwaters, and she realised that no matter what, she was, and always would be, an outcast in Woodleigh.

The girl with no father, a crazy mother, and rumours of witchery hanging over her head.

Everyone knew about the Frost women; how could they not, with that tell-tale Flare of otherworldly colour they all had in the corner of one eye? Kitty's was a violet fan in otherwise summer-blue eyes; Sophie's was emerald amid a deep sapphire blue.

Some even knew of their Knacks; the 'gift' each Frost woman grew into. Kitty's grandmother, Mary, had been able to change people's fortunes by reading them a story. Sophie could sew the most miraculous creations, which always fit to perfection. And Kitty ... Well, she loved her Knack. At first.

The second moment came eight years later.

Woodleigh didn't have a high school; everyone going on to Leaving caught the bus to nearby Belleville. Released from the confines of the town that knew too much, everything had changed. Without the stigma of her name and history, Kitty was merely pretty, clever and charming. She'd quickly become the most popular girl at Belleville High.

She saw Sam, a grade ahead, most days – at school, on the bus, around town – but they never spoke. She hadn't forgotten what he did for her, but she was busy putting space between herself and all things Woodleigh.

Her Knack was slow to come in, but once it started, there was no stopping it. The power of persuasion – so different from her mother's ability to work with fabric – and Kitty couldn't have been more thrilled.

By sixteen, she could talk anyone into anything. She got top grades, no matter if she was a little late submitting work, and plum roles in school plays. She had the best seat in the cafeteria; got invited to all the best parties by all the best guys.

Eventually, there was nothing she couldn't have.

She hadn't intended to steal Susie's boyfriend – she didn't even want him – but when Chad broke things off with Susie to pursue Kitty … given how Susie had treated her, could anyone blame Kitty for the thrill of victory that sparked through her?

When he'd gifted Kitty the brooch he'd been saving up to buy for Susie, Susie had been unable to control her jealous rage; she'd stolen it, like she'd accused Kitty-Rose of doing to her mother's watch all those years ago, and thrown it in a bin.

Full of sweet vindication, Kitty'd been ready to see justice served. She'd been in the process of compelling a hysterical Susie to accompany her to the principal's office to confess her sins when Saint Sam had shown up, brooch in hand.

Her gaze narrowed on him. "You know she stole it."

"And now you've got it back."

He tried to get her to take the brooch, but she kept her arms crossed, didn't bother even looking at it. "You should come too, tell the principal what she did."

His jaw hardened. "She's my sister."

"So? You're not doing her any favours by protecting her, you know. She should own up to her actions."

Coldness crept slowly across his earth-and-amber eyes. "When'd you get to be such a horrible person?"

She wanted to die. Her heart froze, then shattered to fall in shards around her, but she'd shot back a reply. "I don't know, Sam, maybe it was growing up in Woodleigh!"

His head jerked, and they'd regarded each other a long moment.

She wasn't ready to quit. She softened her tone, allowed her Knack to rise in her – golden and powerful – and sweep out. "Susie'll feel better once she's confessed. Look at her, she's crying. She feels terribly about what she's done. She needs to pay for it. You'd be doing the right thing by coming with us to the principal."

She put every ounce of compulsion she had into it.

His eyes closed and he exhaled, hard. Then he opened them again. "Doesn't work on me."

It worked on everyone! She stood, frozen, shocked into silence.

Sam put an arm around his sister's shoulders. "Come on, we're going home. Kitty-Rose's going to forget all about this, aren't you."

She'd let them walk away, but his words rang over and over in her head, each time stinging her more.

"When'd you get to be such a horrible person?"

She wasn't a horrible person, was she?

And if she was, it was only because everyone had always been so horrible to her. Susie *had* stolen from her, which was more than Kitty-Rose had done when Susie'd accused her.

And she'd realised, no matter what, she'd never win in Woodleigh.

A desire had formed, swift and strong – to leave; to leave that very day and never come back. Aunt Eleanor had persuaded her to bide her time, to stay at home until she finished high school.

Sam, being older, stopped catching the bus the following year. She saw him around town from time to time, but always pretended she hadn't.

Still, she never used her Knack like that again.

The third moment came some six years after that.

When she finished school, she'd made good on her promise, getting a job in women's clothing at Carmody's Department Store and moving to Belleville, with a plan to one day make it to Melbourne. Times were tighter then; the whole country, along with the rest of the world, was still reeling from the war. Everything was rationed, no one had much to spend.

But as the years ticked by, things picked up. She loved the work. She'd grown up with two dressmakers, spent long afternoons as a child at Manson's Dressmaking, so she knew how, but she didn't have the patience for cutting and sewing. However, she loved to help women dress themselves, pick out their best colours and cuts. Occasionally, she'd let her Knack shine, just a little, to get a customer to make a purchase – but only a little, only when they were wavering and she genuinely believed it was in their best interest.

Her talent had seen her progress through the ranks of shop girls and brought her to the attention of Frank Carmody – the owner's son. She knew who Frank was, of course – he wandered around the store, checking on it and checking on her. Good-looking and ambitious, he saw something in Kitty-Rose. But he had a girlfriend, so when he asked her out, she refused. He said he'd break up with Janice if he knew Kitty was a sure thing; Kitty said he had to break up with her before they could even have that conversation.

When she scored a job in a big, prestigious department store in Melbourne, she'd put in her notice. A day later, Frank ended things with Janice and made a counter-offer, sharing his plans for the store and Kitty's role in them. Kitty would take over as head buyer. Together, they'd take Carmody's to new heights. There'd be international travel and everything.

He was telling her everything she wanted to hear. She'd been nineteen; she'd believed him.

She'd given herself over to the business, delighting in each and every success she and Frank won. And if he sometimes made questionable decisions ... he was learning, and so was she. He asked her to marry him, and she said yes.

But despite how close the towns were, she never took him home to Woodleigh.

He'd heard about Redthorn – the grand mansion her family owned that now lay abandoned, eerie and alone, with her mother its only visitor. And when he'd pressed, and pressed, she'd taken him there – and from there, to visit Aunt Eleanor and Sophie in town.

She'd known, when they'd pulled up in his racing-green sportscar, that it was over.

She couldn't marry Frank – she loved the life he'd promised, full of plans and aspiration and excitement, not the man himself. She'd been happy, free of Woodleigh, and excited by life – and she'd confused that with being in love.

She'd known it, but still, she'd taken him in.

She hadn't liked the expression on his face when he was introduced to Sophie. That would have been enough perhaps, but then, the look Sophie gave her … She didn't say anything – it wasn't her way – but she didn't need to.

"You're a princess, Catherine," she always said, and it was pretty clear she didn't think Frank was any kind of prince.

Kitty broke it off with Frank, moved to Melbourne like she'd planned to three years prior, and started all over again.

But not long after, Eleanor had got sick, and Kitty'd moved back to care for her, taking over the running of the shop. The next eight months had passed in a blur of worry and appointments. When she'd emerged from grief enough to assess the situation at Manson's, she'd seen that it was failing. She couldn't allow the shop – Eleanor's life's work – to go bankrupt, to disappear; before she could leave again, she'd have to find a way to rescue it.

Apparently, Woodleigh wasn't done with her, and maybe, she wasn't done with it.

She was stuck in town for the foreseeable future.

With everything everyone thought of the Frosts.

And Sam Wells.

1

"That's what I'd like."

Kitty-Rose looked from the glamorous model draped in an exquisite form-fitting cocktail frock, up to Lynette Wells, and back down again. Even with the most exceptional dressmaker – which she had in her mother – the two images were difficult to reconcile.

But what was the life of a dressmaker but a constant balancing of tact and truth? "I know just the one." She crouched to retrieve a pattern from the wooden filing cabinet, then placed it to cover the magazine picture.

Lynette leaned forward. "You think?" she queried sceptically after a moment.

"We'd make alterations, of course. Add a little volume to the skirt. But in terms of the basic fit …" She tapped the pattern twice with a long, red nail. "This'd be lovely on you."

Lynette shifted it firmly to the side, revealing her choice once again. Her gaze travelled between the two images and her frown deepened.

"You know Sophie will make you look like a queen."

Her mother had a knack for sewing – she could make anything

533

look good on anyone, and her creations always fit perfectly. If only that were enough to run a successful dressmaking business! But as Kitty had learned over the past six months, since Aunt Eleanor had died and she'd taken over the running of the shop, there was more to it.

Like customers.

With everyone buying off the rack these days, her savings and the money Aunt Eleanor had left them were shrinking to nothing at an alarming rate. But Eleanor had kept Manson's Dressmaking open through the Depression and both wars – no way was it going to fail under Kitty's watch.

"And if I might suggest a fabric …" she continued, as if she had Lynette's approval for the pattern. She turned and pulled down a bolt from the high stacks behind the counter. "This satin would be gorgeous. Have a feel, it's divine." The warm peach tones would suit Lynette much better than the pastel pink the model wore. Kitty might not be the dressmaker her mother was, but she liked to think she had an eye for cuts and colours. "Leave it to us, Lynette, and you'll be the chicest mother of the bride on record."

A contented smile crossed Lynette's face. Her younger daughter had recently snagged herself the new bank manager, Roy. In a town that saw few newcomers, Roy was considered quite the catch, and Lynette couldn't be more pleased.

Neither could Kitty. A bridal gown and bridesmaid dresses, along with Lynette's mother of the bride, would go a long way to tiding them over for another couple of months.

Lynette glanced once more between the picture she'd brought in and the pattern Kitty had pulled out, and let out a sigh. "Alright." She looked Kitty up and down, a brow arched. "You certainly know how to dress yourself."

"Wouldn't be much of an advertisement for Manson's if I didn't," she said lightly, ignoring the not-so-subtle judgement in Lynette's tone.

She knew what Lynette thought, what the whole town thought – that her dress was too tight, her heels too high, and her nails and lips too red. Single women were viewed with suspicion. Especially ones like Kitty. Kitty-Rose Frost was fast – that was the assumption. She must be out to seduce – husbands and fathers, most likely. If only! It'd been over two years since she'd ended things with Frank, and there hadn't been a skerrick of romance in her life since.

But hell, no one in Woodleigh would ever approve of her anyway. If she was going to be the town outcast, she might as well look good doing it.

She reached into the shelf under the counter and pulled out the measuring tape.

Lynette pulled a face. "Don't you have my measurements already?"

"Better take them again." As much as anyone might wish it wasn't so, measurements could change. She walked around the counter. "Arms out, s'il vous plait."

Measuring was close business. Kitty kept her focus on the tape, but she could sense Lynette inspecting the light violet that fanned across the top section of one blue iris.

Her Flare.

All Frost women had one. Her mother's was emerald against an otherwise dark blue iris; her grandmother had apparently had the opposite – sapphire against merry green.

Lynette cast her eyes down at the tape wrapped around her waist and grimaced. "Wait till you're my age. You won't have that tiny waist anymore."

"Tell that to Sophie." Her mother was as slim as a reed.

"How is your mother, dear?"

There it was – that special Frost tone. Pity, scorn and just a touch of fear. No wonder she planned on getting Manson's back on its feet, training Sophie to run it, and leaving again.

"She's … Well, she's Sophie. Arms back down." Kitty-Rose turned to note down a set of measurements.

"Is she out the back?"

"Not today." There was no work for her to do; Lynette was their first customer all week. Kitty didn't much like leaving her mother to her own devices, but she couldn't ask her to sit around all day with nothing to do.

"How's she coping without Eleanor? I've been meaning to call around and check on her."

Pain stabbed at her. She swallowed around a sudden hard lump. "Pretty well, all things considered."

But the truth was, she was lost – and so was Kitty. Sophie'd had Kitty when she was seventeen; Aunt Eleanor had raised them both. She'd been mother, father and grandmother in one, and her passing had left a gaping raw hole.

"I still remember your mother as a child. Such a pretty thing. All that dark hair she got from Mary."

Kitty made a murmur of agreement though she'd never known her grandmother. She'd disappeared – literally disappeared – when Sophie was still a girl.

"And you so blonde."

Kitty could feel Lynette's eyes on her – on the golden hair that required neither peroxide nor permanent wave to fall like waves of sunlight down her back – but she just made another noncommittal sound. She knew better than to get drawn into any discussion about her colouring and where it might have come from. Finished with the tape, she walked back around to her side of the counter and changed the subject. "So, how are the plans for the big day coming along anyway?"

Lynette beamed. "Oh wonderful. Josie's so excited. And you know her, she's in her element with all the planning."

As Josie was four years younger, Kitty didn't really know her – not like she knew her siblings. "When's the wedding again?" She started to tally up a price for the dress.

"Not until spring. If you're busy with Christmas coming up, we can leave the frock until after."

If only! "We'll make a start right away."

"Good. As far as I'm concerned, it's never too soon to start planning a wedding."

"I couldn't agree more. When will we see Josie in here?"

She was estimating how long it would take Sophie to make Lynette's dress – she'd double it for the quote, Sophie was supernaturally fast – but Lynette's lengthy pause had her raising her head from the page. It was a rare event, but Lynette appeared uncomfortable.

"Well, the thing is, Kitty-Rose … she's got her heart set on a boutique in Melbourne."

Cutting disappointment almost had her fumbling with the pen in her hand. She and Josie didn't have any beef – not like she had with Sam and Susie; she'd really thought Josie'd be coming to Manson's for her dress. "They can't do better than we can."

Lynette made a tutting sound. "You know young people. Always wanting something new and different."

What Kitty knew was that she couldn't afford to lose that order. Bridal work was one of the few remaining reliable sources of income for dressmakers.

If she could get Josie alone, she was sure she could talk her around. She'd worked in womenswear in a department store in nearby Belleville and in a higher-end version in Melbourne before Eleanor got sick – she could say with full confidence that no one could sew like Sophie.

She could … *persuade* Lynette to prompt Josie to come into Manson's.

She could do it right now.

She felt her Knack rising in her – a strong golden glow that vibrated with intent and power. She could make Lynette get Josie to come in; she could make Josie pick Manson's to do her dress. She could do it with such ease.

I will not use my Knack.

I will not use my Knack.

She didn't use it anymore – she'd made that decision long ago – but by golly, sometimes she was tempted. She worked to shove the glow back down.

"You know, I always thought Sam would be the first to marry."

Something inside her clenched at the mention of his name. She examined the page in front of her, distracting herself by checking over her numbers. But she couldn't stop the image that formed in her head, of how he'd looked that day – eyes cold and hard, mouth curved in disapproval. The last time they'd ever spoken, when she'd lost his good opinion for ever.

When'd you turn into such a horrible person?

The memory should bore her by now, the number of times it had come back to haunt her over the years, but it was as vivid as ever and still cut as deep.

"He was serious about Delia," Lynette continued, oblivious to Kitty's turmoil. "Or at least I thought he was. Such a wonderful couple. Such a lovely girl; a total delight. I couldn't believe it when he told me they'd called it off. Just before you moved back, wasn't it?"

"Just after," she murmured, careful not to lift her gaze.

"And he hasn't found anyone since. I don't know why – there's a lot of willing takers, if you catch my drift. And doing so well with the garage since he took it over. He bought the lot next door, you know. To expand."

"Uh-huh."

"And not only that … Well, I probably shouldn't say anything, but … Rob's stepping down from mayor next year. Sam's name is already being put forward by those in the know. He's made for the role, everyone agrees."

Of course they did.

"And with Delia being Rob's daughter … Just imagine how perfect it'd be if she and Sam … Well, just between you and me, I think he knows he made a mistake. A little case of cold feet. I wouldn't be at all surprised if they were to take up together again – Delia'd have him back in a heartbeat. They might even beat Roy and Josie down the aisle if they got a wriggle on!"

Kitty couldn't listen to another word about Saint Sam and Lovely Delia. "And how is Roy finding town?" She'd yet to pay the new bank manager a visit.

Lynette tutted again. "Not too easy, is my impression. Tim left things in quite a state."

Kitty's chest tightened. "Oh?"

"Bless him, but he was a little too … understanding, shall we say. One of the difficulties in being a bank manager in a small town, I imagine."

"I suppose so." She'd have to speak to Roy – soon. She shelved her worry and smiled. "We're looking at around ten pounds for the dress."

"Fine." Lynette waved a hand. Hers was one of the better-off families in town and, to her credit, so long as the quality was commensurate, she didn't quibble on price.

Kitty could charge more. She *should* charge more.

There was a good chance Manson's was one of the businesses Tim'd been too understanding with. When she'd moved back, she'd convinced Eleanor to take out a loan to get new stock in. Not that they didn't have rolls and rolls of old fabric – Heaven knows how it'd all made it through the war – but it was hopelessly outdated. Wrong colours, wrong patterns, wrong textures. Fabric for fashion of a different era, and no one wanted the reminder of all those hard times. How could they hope to attract customers if they didn't have up-to-date offerings?

But things hadn't gone as well as she'd hoped, and right before he'd retired, Tim had agreed to pause the repayments, so all they were paying was the interest. A one-year grace period that was nearing its end. She needed to get it extended, but it sounded like Roy was tightening up.

We'll be fine. We'll be fine. She just needed a little more time to get things moving again. "Alright. I've got everything I need. We'll need you in for a fitting in a fortnight or so. And remind Josie we're here," she added brightly. "We can do anything she wants – better, cheaper and faster than anywhere else."

Lynette gave her a forced smile. "I'll do my best. You take care, Kitty-Rose." She turned to leave.

Kitty bit her lip. Lynette hadn't sounded too hopeful.

Dammit. They needed that business.

A buzz in her head that crackled like flame, and it rose in her again, a sweeping, sweet temptation. Bubbling up in her like finest champagne, threatening to flow out over the whole shop.

And what would it hurt? Manson's really could do anything better and cheaper. She'd be doing Josie a favour.

"Lynette."

The older woman turned.

Temptation was riding her. She made fists of her hands, squeezed them tight, while she shoved the impulse down, as hard as she could.

I will not use my Knack.

I will not use my Knack.

"I'll give you a bell when we're ready for your fitting."

Lynette tilted her head and left.

Kitty exhaled hard and slumped, dropping her elbows onto the counter. Her mouth quirked.

What had she been thinking? They needed that work!

She should have used her Knack.

When'd you turn into such a horrible person?

Damn Sam Wells!

2

Kitty-Rose closed the shop door and twisted the key in the lock, wishing she could lock her worries in there for the night too. She'd spent hours scouring the books, trying to make money appear where there was none. Why couldn't that be her Knack? Then they might stand a chance of keeping Manson's going.

She walked home through the warm, humid summer evening. This time of year in Woodleigh always smelled like jasmine and Christmas lilies. But despite the heat, her time indoors and general lack of sleep had her shivering, and she wrapped her arms around herself, tucking her bag into her side.

She knew she had the makings of successful business owner. She was great with figures – but there were no figures to play with.

They needed more customers. It was as simple as that.

And if Lynette was right about Roy being ordered to tighten the screws …

Was anyone else in town doing any better? Well, Sam was, according to Lynette. But being a mechanic, that was no surprise. Everyone was getting a car these days.

Getting a car, and then driving to Belleville to do their shopping. If

Woodleigh folk were driving to Belleville to shop, why couldn't Belleville folk drive to Woodleigh?

And people from farther afield.

But of course they wouldn't. Not with how drab and faded Main Street looked. She wouldn't exactly describe it as buzzing. Even now.

She cast a sweeping glance about her … and stopped. She'd been stuck in her head, and it had taken half a block to notice the huge golden stars that hung from the streetlights and the big tinsel-covered pine that'd sprung up in the roundabout at the top of the street. The nearby shopfronts had added decorations of their own. It was the first of December; the season to be jolly.

Her shoulders hunched, a queasy sensation roiled through her belly.

She hated Christmas.

Not surprising, given what her mother had put her through every year growing up. She hadn't thought she'd have to experience another depressing Woodleigh Christmas – she'd thought she'd be long gone by now – but somehow, she was still here.

She continued walking, investigating the different shop fronts as she passed. But all she could think was, even with the decorations, the street appeared drab. Dark, old and shabby, like they were still stuck in the Depression. It was the fifties! The modern era – and shoppers had different expectations.

Noise drifted from the open windows of the pub. Walking past, she cast a glance inside and caught Roy's eye. He was sitting by himself at a small table.

She smiled at him. He raised a hand and smiled in return.

Maybe he hadn't encountered all the rumours about the Frost women yet.

Surely he'd be reasonable about the whole repayments thing. They just needed a bit longer. A bit more grace. It wasn't like she didn't have the most talented dressmaker in the state on hand – she just had to find a way to let people know about Manson's.

If she used her Knack, she could convince him to extend the interest-only period.

She pulled up sharp, bit her lip.

She didn't use it anymore. She shouldn't use it now. And she wouldn't.

But she could have a word with him.

It was an ideal opportunity. He was alone – relaxed and out of the bank. Away from any sternly worded letters from head office. Surely that would help.

She swivelled, passing through the entrance and into the noise and the smoke- and hops-laden air of the front bar. Strictly speaking, she wasn't supposed to be in here, but it was such a stupid, patronising law, she couldn't bring herself to respect it. What exactly did they fear would happen if a women ordered a drink? In any case, she wasn't asking to be served; she just wanted a minute of Roy's time.

And besides, people expected a Frost to be doing all kinds of unconventional things. They believed the worst; she might as well prove them right.

She stalked through the bar, head held high. When she met their gazes – hell if she was looking away – the men gave her a brief nod but turned quickly. Were they uncomfortable at having a woman invade their territory, or was it because of her name, her Flare? Oh well, she wouldn't be staying long, and she didn't think anyone would actually throw her out. They weren't sure what the consequences might be.

Sometimes the Frost reputation came in handy.

Roy's back was to her; he almost jumped out of his skin when she appeared at his side and he realised she was there for him.

"Good evening, Mr Prescott."

"Good evening. And please, Roy." He was well-groomed, with a neat compact build, clear skin and white teeth. She could see why the Wells were crowing about adding him to the family.

"Roy." She smiled. "And I'm Kitty Frost, from Manson's Dressmaking. Might I have a quick word?"

"Oh. That is …" His gaze swivelled about him as if he was lost.

She took the seat beside him. "It won't take a minute. I haven't had a chance to congratulate you on the engagement yet. Josie's a lucky girl."

"Thank you, but I'm the lucky one," he replied gallantly.

"I bet you didn't anticipate this time last year you'd have a fiancée. I wanted you to know how much we appreciate you in this little town of ours."

He blushed. "I'm happy to be here."

She shifted her chair a little closer. "There's a special relationship between small business and banks, wouldn't you say?"

"I would," he replied, but he cast a glance around him.

"A mutually beneficial one. When we profit, you profit. And of course, when times are tough, a little latitude is also mutually beneficial."

"Well, we have our processes—"

"Of course! And you must follow them. But, as they say, context is everything. And if a particular business couldn't make a payment one time …" She arched a brow.

"Rules is rules, Miss Frost. And we really shouldn't—"

"Kitty, please. But in a town like this … I know you're relatively new to Woodleigh, but we take a more individual approach. I'm not sure if you've come across our file yet, but Manson's had an arrangement with Tim—"

"We really shouldn't be discussing this. Business should be conducted during business hours. At the bank." He attempted – with limited success – to inject a stern note into his voice.

"Absolutely." She brought out her best smile, did everything bar flutter her eyelashes at him. "But this isn't really business."

A streak of bright golden energy flowed through her. Oh, it had got away from her! She pulled it back, pushed it down. "I'm just wondering whether a short extension to our grace period might be applied."

"I really think we need to leave business to business hours," he squeaked, starting to look red and flustered.

"I agree. But I'm not even talking about a long time. Three months, shall we say? The thing is, it's actually in the bank's interest. If we stay in business, we eventually make our repayments." Another wave of golden energy. Gosh, it really was insistent. *I will not use my Knack. I will not use my Knack.* She fought to keep it under control, and continued with her point. "And not only that, we build a stronger town – everyone makes their repayments. But if we go bankrupt, the bank might not even get its money back in the end. You wouldn't want that."

"No. No, we wouldn't want that."

"And you know, when you think about it, the bank makes more money if we extend the interest-only period, because we're paying more overall."

"Well, yes. I suppose, strictly speaking, that is true."

"So what do you think? It'd just be a short extension, no big deal. You probably don't even have to consider it too hard."

"You might be right."

"So, we've come to an understanding?"

There was a certain desperate light in his eyes. "I really can't discuss business at the pub."

"But we're not really—"

"Sounds like business to me," a voice rumbled to her right. Deep and smoky-smooth as the world's best whiskey.

She stiffened; a thrill rose straight up her spine.

Turning, her gaze trailed up over a long, big-boned body, to a square, even-featured face with an unwavering gaze. Sam Wells, holding two foaming pints.

Saint Bloody Sam. Just what she needed.

Lord, he towered over her. Six-four, at least. It was enough to steal the breath from her lungs – just a little. A flush threatened to crawl up her throat.

"Evening, Kitty-Rose." This time, that rumble almost sent a shudder through her.

Her gaze dropped to his lips, which were just a little fuller than she ever expected. Her mouth went dry. "Sam," she replied, tilting her chin up. "I'm just having a word with Roy."

"Don't mind me."

She narrowed her eyes. That was an obvious hint to go away, and he'd ignored it. "We're just finishing up. We won't be a moment."

"Go right ahead."

He put Roy's drink in front of him, walked behind Kitty to the other side of the table, sending another thrill up her spine – she didn't like him at her back – and took a seat. She stared at him; he stared back, hard and expectant.

Well, she was hardly going to continue now that he'd joined them.

"What are you doing in here anyway?" he asked when she didn't say anything.

She cast a glance at Roy, smiled and shrugged. "Roy was sitting here by himself; I thought I'd come and say hello."

His gaze flickered. "What a kind heart you have." He turned to Roy. "You should go ahead and disregard anything and everything Kitty said before I got here."

Roy's mouth dropped open; his eyes were suddenly dinner plates.

She huffed out a breath; her arms came across her chest. "You don't even know what we were talking about."

"I can take a pretty good guess."

Roy's gaze travelled between herself and Sam in rapid succession, unsure of what was going on.

"We were just talking."

"Sure, but I know what that means, even if Roy doesn't."

She glanced at a confused Roy. "Nothing happened, did it, Roy?"

"Um …" Roy looked like he wanted to believe this whole conversation was a joke, but Sam's face didn't hold a hint of humour and she was pretty sure hers didn't either.

"It's not like Roy'd know if it had. But he had that dazed appearance to him that comes from spending any amount of time around you." He turned to Roy. "No offence, mate."

Roy raised his hands, palms out.

She narrowed her gaze. "I'm surprised you haven't warned him."

"Maybe I should have."

"Why don't I save you the trouble?" She turned. "Sam wants you to know that I'm a witch, Roy. Powerful and poisonous. Never to be trusted." Roy had given up trying to work out the joke. He now seemed as if he'd like the earth to swallow him whole. "That about sum it up, Sam?"

"Sounds about right."

They did nothing but stare at each other for a long moment, the air between them heavy with history. Saint Sam Wells. Her only friend when she'd need one the most. Her harshest critic when she'd crossed the line. The one person her Knack didn't work on – for some baffling reason.

And the only man who'd ever got her flustered like this.

She'd spent a long time building up a hard outer shell; she prided herself on her poise. How did he undo her with such ease?

And he did.

A flicker of his eyes and something flipped upside down inside her. It was so disorienting, she didn't know if she was falling or flying.

She stood suddenly. "I'll leave you to it. Enjoy your evening."

Her legs were none too steady, but she made sure she walked out the same way she'd walked in – back straight, unhurried, not a care in the world.

Eighteen months she'd been back in Woodleigh, and it was eighteen months too long.

She couldn't wait to leave.

3

When she was back inside the old weatherboard she shared with her mother, she eased off her heels and rested back against the front door.

Ugh. It was so humid she was dripping. She unbuttoned her frock and let it drop to the floor, leaving just her slip on, then picked up an envelope from the sideboard and fanned herself, trying to generate a breeze.

Sam Wells had a hide!

She might as well use her Knack if that was the attitude she faced.

And what was it to him if she got her arrangement extended? Anyone would think he wanted the shop to fail.

He probably did.

Lord, she'd kill for a frosted margarita right now. When she'd been engaged to Frank, she'd become accustomed to an aperitif, as Frank called it, in what even she knew was a terrible French accent, but she hadn't maintained the habit. She doubted there was anything to drink in the house. Eleanor hadn't ever taken anything more than the occasional sherry and Sophie never touched the stuff.

Fanning herself slowly, she surveyed their faded home. The carpet was worn threadbare, the paint peeling in places. She'd love to freshen it up a little – a lick of paint in a fresh pastel green or a sweet pink – but that, like everything, would have to wait. Funny to think that, once upon a time, her family had been by far the richest anywhere in the vicinity of Woodleigh.

She put the envelope back down, took another deep breath, and attempted to shake off the evening. Soon, she'd be out of here for good, and she'd never have to see Saint Sam again.

Once she got the shop up and running.

To be honest, the finances weren't her only problem. There was also the question of who was going to run it when she left.

Initially, her plan had been to improve the balance sheet, get a steady book of customers coming in, and hand it over to her mother. But Sophie had never run the shop by herself, and Kitty wasn't entirely sure she'd be able to. Or even want to – Sophie had her own priorities, ran to her own schedule.

Kitty'd had to continuously revise down her expectations. Perhaps her mother could commit to opening the shop for appointments just once a week? Perhaps Kitty herself would have to take an active role, even from Melbourne? Do the accounts, even take bookings in absentia.

And if that were so, maybe she wouldn't return to Melbourne – Bendigo or Albury-Wodonga were closer. She could start there and work two jobs while Sophie became accustomed to running Manson's.

Or maybe they could hire someone to run the shop. Goodness knows how they'd pay the salary, but the point wasn't really to make money.

She just didn't want Eleanor's shop to disappear from the face of the earth.

She listened for the sound of the old Singer treadle – Sophie kept it in her bedroom and used it to finish jobs – but the house was silent. She poked her head into the sitting room, the first room off to the right of the hall, and then knocked on the next door along. "Sophie?"

No response.

A frisson of apprehension ran through her. She shouldn't worry; Sophie'd be back soon.

In the meantime … looked like she was on dinner again.

She padded through to the back of the house, contemplating her options. She wasn't any kind of cook, so there weren't many. Out the window above the sink, ominous clouds rolled through the encroaching ink of night. A violent summer storm threatened.

She turned, resting back against the counter, a sinking feeling dropping through her.

But Sophie always turned up before nightfall.

It was a curfew of sorts, set by Eleanor before Kitty'd been born, to make sure Sophie remembered to come home. She spent whole days at Redthorn, their creepy old mansion ten miles from town. In the house, in the gardens with the ravens, venturing further into the fields and the hills behind, disappearing into the wilderness for hours on end. Eleanor hadn't liked it but knew she couldn't stop her going. The curfew was a compromise, which Sophie abided by out of love and respect for her adopted aunt.

And today was the first of December.

That's why she was late tonight. She was probably pulling out all the Christmas decorations. She'd turn up eventually; she always did.

Kitty busied herself in the kitchen – dicing onions and peeling potatoes. But when the rain started to pelt down, drumming like a battlefield on the tin roof, and the night had taken on a dense gloomy quality, and her mother was still not home, she gave in to her worry.

Lightning flashed across the sky, followed shortly after by the rumble of thunder.

That's it. She was getting in their ancient, unreliable car and driving out.

She'd just turned the rissoles off when she heard the front door.

Christ! About bloody time.

She hurried to meet her mother, watching with crossed arms as she removed her wet, muddy boots. "You're late."

Sophie rose, pushing back the hood of her dark blue cloak. Long dark hair hung in wet strands, her eyes glowed in a pale, heart-shaped face – deep sapphire blue, except, of course, for the emerald fan that covered the top outer corner of one iris.

Even half-drowned, she looked like something straight out of a Pre-Raphaelite painting – full of tragic and unearthly beauty. Fay-blood, according to Aunt Eleanor, that's what Frost women had running in their veins. Gazing at her mother, Kitty believed it.

Sophie ignored the water dripping down her face and neck. "Catherine! I have something for you."

Sophie was shivering. It was late in the year but she was soaked. "Christ, Mum, you're going to die of pneumonia."

She stepped forward to help remove her cloak, but her mother gripped her forearm, talon-like. There was a manic gleam in her eyes. "And I have a message for you."

A message for her. Crap.

The ravens had gone with her grandmother, Mary, to Redthorn and lived there ever since. Every day, they flew over the town, observing and learning all the secrets. They felt an ownership over Woodleigh and its people, and took their interests to heart – giving messages to Sophie to pass on to the relevant parties.

Which were received with varying degrees of interest and understanding.

Most people in town thought her mother was crazy. All her life, Kitty had watched people cross the street to avoid her; Kitty'd always sworn that wouldn't be her. But Sophie didn't let it stop her – she'd follow regardless, determined to tell them about some dire fate. Some, knowing her tragic background – and a little about her Knack – were kinder, but even those who were inclined to believe the messages were real had a hard time interpreting what they might mean. No one, including Sophie, understood what she was saying most of the time.

"It'll have to wait. You need to get out of those clothes."

"Catherine—"

"Or even better, straight into a warm bath."

But her mother wasn't budging. She started to ferret around in her big sack-like bag. "I found it today, when I was getting out the box of decorations. It'd got mixed up in there somehow. But now I can't find it."

"It can wait."

She attempted again to unbutton her mother's dripping cloak but it was impossible with her continuing to rummage around in her bag.

"Where's it gone?" she muttered.

"What are you looking for anyway?"

"Your red ribbon. From your father. It's time."

Just when Kitty thought her day couldn't get worse. Her father – that mythical creature no one except Sophie had met.

She'd encountered him at seventeen, wandering the fields behind Redthorn, and fallen in love with him instantly. He'd told her he was a prince; she'd believed him. When he'd asked if she'd return with him to his kingdom, she'd said no. When he'd asked her if she wanted a child, she'd said yes. Three days she'd had with him, and at the end of the third day, he'd told Sophie to give his daughter a name fit for a queen and left her with a ribbon; a parting gift for his unborn child.

And that was all Sophie would say of him.

Kitty'd asked Eleanor but she hadn't known any more. Sophie was never known to have had a young man, despite her beauty. Eleanor had thought at first some man from town had taken advantage, and racked her brain trying to work out who it had been. But all the Woodleigh men vehemently denied it, and when she was born, Kitty didn't bear any resemblance to any of them. Eleanor had eventually concluded it was a stranger passing through; it'd been the Depression, there'd been a lot of itinerant workers on the move.

"Mum! You're dripping puddles on the floor." Not to mention, the shivers were turning to shudders.

Sophie stopped rummaging, regarded her with wide luminescent eyes. "Catherine, you must take this seriously! The ravens told me you'll need it, when you least expect it. But soon. Before Christmas."

Kitty rolled her eyes.

"Catherine!"

"Okay! But it's not in there." It couldn't possibly be; her mother had thoroughly investigated every nook and cranny.

"There's no need to shout. It must still be out at Redthorn. I'll be back out there tomorrow – there's much to do." She met her gaze head on. "You will come out on Christmas Day, won't you?"

Kitty suppressed a grimace. She didn't like the thought of Sophie out there alone, but she hated going. They'd gone every Christmas when she was young, and she'd loathed everything about it. Sophie's pointless hoping and waiting for her missing family to finally arrive home; her quiet anguish when she realised they weren't coming, that yet another year had gone by without their return. Then the stupid candle in the stupid wreath – her way to make contact with them. They thought of her on Christmas Day, just as she thought of them.

And when Kitty'd been really little, she'd really thought she felt them there, in the room with her and Sophie and Eleanor.

Now she knew it was just the power of suggestion.

And it wasn't Sophie's fault, but it was a morbid, depressing Christmas to inflict on a kid, if Kitty did say so herself. The Christmas after she'd turned nine, she'd sworn she'd never go again. But this would be their first Christmas without Eleanor. "We'll discuss it over dinner."

Her mother sniffed at the air, grimaced delicately. "Rissoles."

"It's about all I know how to cook."

"Lord knows neither of us is blessed in the kitchen." She turned to Kitty. "We will find your ribbon, there will be an occasion on which you need it, and you will use it."

"Okay. I believe you." She smiled. "Go put dry clothes on. I'll finish up here, and tell you what you missed today. We got a new order."

4

The bad thing about living in a small town? Everyone knowing everyone else's business.

The good thing?

Kitty knew, as did everyone else, that Wednesday was Lynette's bridge afternoon, during which time Josie manned the general store.

So that was the time she'd chosen to pick up groceries. And spruik her wares …

Kitty understood where Josie was coming from. She herself had felt the lure of the big city, of believing everything must be bigger and better there. And maybe there was some truth to it … but not as far as Josie's wedding dress went.

There was only one Sophie, and she was here to convince Josie of that.

She could hear a group at the counter when she entered so she took her time collecting a basketful of staples – butter, ham and tomatoes – before heading back. But emerging from an aisle, she saw the group still huddled, talking in excited tones, bursts of laughter breaking through.

Josie didn't bear much resemblance to Sam or Susie. She was attractive in a thin, sharp-featured sort of way, with mousy hair and eyes the light grey of her mother's. Susie had more of Sam's height and build, along with his eyes and thick chestnut hair. And Delia ... Kitty might be the one with Fay-blood, but it was Delia who looked like a fairy – she was tiny, with long strawberry-blonde hair, pale skin and blue eyes. She'd been a ballerina until recently, and it showed in her graceful lines and precise, elegant movements.

Kitty hovered. She'd never be comfortable approaching a group in Woodleigh – particularly one that included Susie Wells. But more to the point, she couldn't talk to Josie with a crowd listening in. Perhaps she'd pretend some excuse to leave her groceries, come back later.

But Josie turned at that moment, eyes growing sharp when she saw her. "Kitty-Rose," she called, making a come-here motion with her hand.

Well. Looked like she was buying her groceries now. She walked over, stiff smile on her face.

"Have you seen today's *Tribune*?" Josie asked as soon as she was near.

"No." She dropped her gaze to see what was causing such a fuss.

A handsome face grinned back at her.

Frank Carmody. Her ex-fiancé. It was a punch in the guts.

He looked as slick as ever. Hair in a fashionable wave, teeth toothpaste white. Debonair and shiny. He'd always looked good. If she was honest, that, along with his ambition, was a good part of the attraction.

"Didn't you used to run around with him?" Josie asked.

"A long time ago." It'd been over two years – closer to three – since they'd broken up. It wasn't like she was nursing a broken heart but still ... it was a shock seeing him on the page. A reminder of how much her life had changed. Everything she'd given up to return here.

She could feel eyes on her, watching closely for a reaction, but she wasn't giving them the satisfaction. "What's he in the paper for anyway?" She was pleased at how cool and detached she sounded.

"Carmody's gives back with super-sized Christmas gift!" Delia read the headline out loud.

Intrigued, Kitty dragged her attention from Frank's face to the text below.

"Much-loved Carmody's Department Store is going from strength to strength. After opening a new store in Wangaratta in April, 1956 promises even more excitement, with the addition of a Melbourne store imminent! To celebrate and share in Carmody's good fortune, Frank Carmody is giving back to the region, announcing a fifty-thousand-pound prize for best float in Carmody's always eagerly anticipated Christmas parade."

Kitty drew in a breath. Fifty-thousand pounds! It was a small fortune. And typical of Frank. He was all about grand gestures, unwavering self-belief, and the dream of a bigger, better life.

"With that kind of prize, they're going to be flooded with entrants," she said.

"No. Wait – that's covered later." Delia's finger mover lower on the page and she resumed reading. "Entries for the competition have closed and no new entries will be accepted. But existing entrants now have the added motivation to really hone their floats. 'Get your thinking caps on,' says Frank. 'We'll be looking for truly outstanding entries.' Smaller prizes will be awarded for other categories, including most creative, funniest, and reddest."

Her mouth twisted.

Well, he'd done it. Like he – they – had always planned.

"What's he like?"

She met Josie's avid eyes. She was the one who dared to ask, but flicking quick glances at Delia and Susie, she could see they were no less interested.

She shrugged. "He makes an impression."

He'd certainly made an impression on her. When she was nineteen – young and naïve and desperate to believe everything he told her about how their lives were going to be.

"He must be doing well," Susie said.

Susie's eyes were guarded, her expression neutral, as she imagined her own must be. "He must be," she replied, and peered back down at Frank's smiling face.

Doing well; unlike Manson's.

They'd been going to take on the world together. She'd never been in love with Frank, she could acknowledge that now, but oh, she'd loved their plans. Meanwhile, here she was. Stuck in a small town she couldn't escape from, trying to keep her Aunt Eleanor's shop from going under completely. Bitterness welled in her.

"Well, I think it's exciting," Delia said.

"Imagine if Woodleigh won," Josie added.

Something pinged in Kitty. "Is that possible?"

"I don't see why not. We put in a float every year. Through the Chamber of Commerce. Mum's always Mrs Claus. Don't you remember?" Susie said.

When Kitty looked her way, she caught Susie scrutinising her make up; her trademark winged eyeliner and red lips.

"Yeah, I remember." An image of Lynette dressed as Mrs Claus, waving at the crowd in a tired costume from the back of a regular pick-up truck graced her mind. She must have gone to the parade at least once, when she was little. "They'll use the same float this year?"

"It gets trotted out every year."

Kids tended to remember things as bigger and better than they appeared to adults. If Kitty's memory of the Woodleigh float served her correctly, there was no way it would win.

Delia's mouth skewed; she seemed to be thinking the same thing. "I've got to run."

"Me too," Susie added immediately.

"See you girls later," Delia said with a sparkling smile that extended to Kitty as well.

"See you," she replied, swapping a glance with Susie as well. Not much but it was something. The first time she'd talked to Susie in almost ten years.

"Did you want to get those?" Josie asked, bringing her back to the present moment.

She hauled the basket she was still carrying up onto the counter. Josie rang up her groceries and she exited the store into bright sunshine.

Eleanor had been a member of the Chamber – a founding

member; she'd gone to every meeting ever held, until she was no longer able to. Kitty didn't know much about what the Chamber did exactly, but surely, taking care of the town's small businesses must rank highly.

If Woodleigh were to win, the money would be spent to improve the town's prospects. Which would surely benefit Manson's. She had a few ideas – more than a few – on where they could start.

But they wouldn't win if they didn't have a winning float.

Maybe she had a few ideas about that too.

If Woodleigh was going to win, for a start, they needed a much bigger tray. A bright red tractor wouldn't go astray either.

Kitty knew where to find both.

She sat in the old rust bucket Eleanor had bought second-hand just before the war, trying for the fourth time to get the engine to start. With all the petrol rationing over the years, it'd barely been driven. It gave a few promising coughs, and then died.

If only her Knack worked on inanimate objects!

She gave the dash a couple of firm pats. "Come on. Start for me."

Fifth time was the charm. She sighed in relief when the engine chugged to life.

She headed south-west out of town, in the direction of Redthorn. It wasn't long before she was climbing into more hilly territory. The bush off the sides of the increasingly rough road was dense in places, gums looming high to form a canopy over the road; ferns and wattle below. It was wilder landscape out here than the pretty flats along the river that Woodleigh occupied.

She turned off before she arrived at Redthorn, through a simple set of wooden gates, onto a drive that wound through cleared paddocks. She was heading to the Botham farm, which bordered Redthorn – a large grazing property Fred ran by himself.

In town, Fred was known as a cantankerous codger, with a chip on his shoulder deriving from having to complete home duty as a farmer as part of the war effort. But he'd always been kind to Kitty, and he always said he owed Sophie a debt – one she was cashing in now.

Knowing he came in for tea and two biscuits at precisely ten each morning, Kitty timed it perfectly. She was waiting at his door when he stepped up onto the verandah – a small man, made to appear smaller by the oversized pants held up by suspenders he wore. "Hi, Mr Botham."

He came to a sudden stop, took the hat off his head. It'd probably been years since anyone other than him had graced this verandah. "Catherine, is it?" He made a whistling sound with his teeth. "You've grown up real pretty."

She grinned. For once, it didn't sound like an insult. "You're looking pretty dapper yourself."

He let out a sound that might have been a chuckle. "Sophie okay?" There was a note of concern in his gaze. He'd always had a sweet spot for her mother.

"She's fine. Mind if I come in a moment?" She pulled a packet of Iced VoVos from her bag; Fred's favourite. "Brought these for you."

"Well, you better come in while I put the kettle on. Better call me Fred, too."

She followed him through his sparsely furnished worker's weatherboard to the kitchen. When he fussed about, making tea and putting the biscuits on a plate, she didn't see any reason not to launch straight in. "Well, Fred, it's like this. I'd like to borrow the tractor and your biggest tray for a day. Maybe two."

He froze, plate of Iced VoVos out in front of him, eyes almost bugging out of his head.

"Or even three?" She took the plate from him, placed it on the small table. "It's for the Christmas parade. You know the one Carmody's runs in Belleville every year? I don't know if you've heard, but there's a big prize on offer this year, and I want Woodleigh to win it. I'm thinking about putting a float together."

"You want to take my tractor to Belleville?"

"Could it make the journey?"

His chest puffed up. "'Course it could! No better tractor."

"Well, that's what I thought." She grinned at him and sat.

"But I don't know, Catherine," he said, placing a chipped cup of weak black tea in front of her. "It's an expensive piece of farm equipment. I couldn't do without it."

"I'll take good care of it, I promise. No damage will come to it."

He made a sucking sound with his teeth. "It's not that I don't trust you, love, but those Belleville characters ..."

She nibbled on an Iced VoVo. "It'd be of great benefit to the town."

He harrumphed, taking a seat near her. "What would I care about that?"

"I don't suppose you would."

"Surprised you do, to be honest."

Everyone dismissed Fred, but she wondered how much he saw, how much he knew. "The thing is Fred, that money'd do the shop – Sophie's shop – a world of good."

He went very still.

"You know we run Manson's together now? If the shop goes under, we're both out of a job. No way to bring money in. Sophie wouldn't want to leave but ..." She shrugged.

It was an exaggeration. Sophie would never leave Redthorn, no matter the circumstances. But the risk to the shop was real.

Fred considered it carefully. He picked up his tea and slurped at it. Kitty wasn't surprised. It must be scalding hot. He put his cup back down. "Won't ever forget what she did for Olly."

Kitty put a hand on Fred's shoulder and squeezed. She still remembered that day. She'd only been three or four; still at an age when Sophie dragged her out to Redthorn almost every day. They'd come across Fred's beloved Kelpie down by the creek. He'd escaped somehow, run off and got bitten by a snake. He was in a terrible state, whimpering and shuddering. Sophie had picked him up carried him the half-mile back to Fred's house, so he could say goodbye and shoot him himself.

Kitty could still picture Sophie as she'd appeared when Kitty'd looked up at her, trotting alongside her, knowing something was very wrong. Face pale and serious, tears flowing down her face, determinedly putting one foot in front of other. Funny, to Kitty then, she'd been an adult, but she wouldn't have been much past twenty. Sometimes she forgot how young her mother had been when she had her.

"Who'd be driving the tractor?" he asked finally.

"Santa Claus, of course."

He grinned. "Not sure I'd let anyone else drive it."

"Well, if you're volunteering …" Fred wasn't much over 5 foot, skinny as a rake, and had a sallow and craggy face that was a mile off Santa's round, rosy beaming countenance. "I think you'd do a great job. Is that a yes then?"

"So long as I'm in charge. Wouldn't trust anyone else with it."

"Thanks, Fred. I really appreciate it. Sophie'll make you a costume."

She left him with rest of the Iced VoVos, managed to get the car to start again.

Was she really doing this?

Until she had the tractor and tray lined up, she hadn't even allowed herself to think that she'd go through with it, but now … It appeared that the idea for a float she'd spent all weekend working on might actually become a reality.

If she could get the Chamber of Commerce to agree to let her take over their existing entry.

Looking out the window, she caught glimpses of the imposing red-brick neo-gothic Queen Anne through gaps in the trees that lined the fence. Each time it appeared, a fresh wave of goosebumps broke out over her skin and her belly flipped. When she got to the road, instead of heading left back to town, she turned right, then right again, in through the gates to Redthorn.

She pulling up when the house came into view, about half-way along the drive.

Stopping was a risk, given the car's tendency towards not starting, but while she was out here … She could at least make it this far.

It was a magnificent house, she could admit that, despite how else she felt about it. Built by her grandfather, Reginald, for himself and his son, Arnold, to live in when they'd moved from Melbourne. Reginald had fallen in love with Arnold's teacher, Mary, and Sophie had been born a few years later.

Kitty didn't know how her mother took such comfort from being out here – it gave Kitty the creeps. The whole place was a morbid mausoleum, everything exactly as it had been in 1919, when Reginald and Mary voyaged to ravaged northern France to find Arnold, who'd sign up to fight as soon as he was old enough and had gone missing in the last bloody stages of the war. They'd left Sophie with Eleanor, Mary's dearest friend, for safekeeping, promising to be home for Christmas. But they'd never come back – any of them. They'd disappeared into thin air, like Kitty sometimes thought Sophie would, out at Redthorn.

Sophie was convinced they were still alive. She said she felt close to them at Redthorn – especially at Christmas. She kept the house immaculate, and every Christmas, she cleaned and decorated and cooked, in case this was the year they made it back.

But it never was.

"They were so happy, the four of them," Eleanor had told her when she'd been a child and full of questions about her strange vanishing family. "Until the war."

5

The Woodleigh Chamber of Commerce had met the first Tuesday of every month since October 1933, when it was established to help the town exit the Depression. Given that Eleanor had been one of the founding members, Kitty supposed that, having taken over the running of the store, she should have continued the tradition. But she'd had her hands full caring for Eleanor, and then, there'd been those terribly long months, just before and after her passing, and now … Well, she hadn't been planning on still being here. She also wondered if she'd be welcome.

She left her entrance until the last moment before the door closed and the meeting officially started to avoid having to talk to anyone prior to. When she walked into the large meeting room, with its white walls, dark wood floors and geometric plaster ceiling rose, she attracted looks. But she smiled brightly and, poster rolled in a large bag under her arm, walked confidently to take a seat at the back, as if she had every right in the world to be present.

For the most part, people smiled back.

To be fair, many had probably known she was coming. She'd gone into the pub in the afternoon to ask Douglas, the publican and current President, if she could speak at tonight's meeting. Of course, she'd had to tell him why. She was sure the whispers had spread through town like wildfire.

Others appeared surprised but not unwelcoming.

Until she got to Sam.

When their gazes locked, her heart skipped a beat and her pulse raced. He continued to watch as she made her way to the centre aisle. He was upright in his seat but not stiff, holding himself with perfect confidence, naturalness. Still, a certain stillness to his big body let her know he wasn't one of the ones who knew she'd be here.

She, on the other hand, had definitely known she'd see him tonight. So why were her legs threatening to freeze on her?

To make up for it, she smiled extra-bright at him.

His mouth made a funny half-twist in return. Not a movement that could be described as a smile.

And then she was out of his line of sight, heading for the back where she could wait in peace until it was her turn. Douglas had said he'd squeeze her in at the end if there was time – her not being on the agenda and all.

And then the meeting started, and Kitty could no longer remember why she'd thought she wouldn't find this interesting or relevant. It was both.

Mrs Bushell, who ran the bookstore, attempted to rally interest in the production of a town brochure to entice people to visit – which Kitty gathered had been her particular bugbear for the past three years. Mr Farquharson, who ran the farm supplies store, reported on progress on lobbying the state government to build a town swimming pool. And Lorena Pickett, of Pickett's wool shop, talked about setting up a roster for volunteers on the drop-off desk for the Christmas food drive, which Kitty hadn't even realised was a thing.

All in all, it was fascinating.

She almost forgot why she was here. Until Douglas called on her. She lurched to her feet, and, poster tucked under her arm, made her way to the front of the room.

Shoulders back. Smile broad. Steps unhurried.

When she reached the front, she took a deep breath. She had every right to be here. She had an idea that would benefit all members, so why shouldn't she present it? Still, she was careful not to meet Sam's gaze. She didn't need him putting her off.

"I'm sure by now you've all heard the news. Carmody's has announced a prize for the winner of best float in this year's Christmas parade of fifty-thousand pounds." She allowed her gaze to travel around the room. They were interested, and why wouldn't they be? It was a hell of a lot of money. "I'd like to see Woodleigh win."

"We've never won," Lorena said.

Of course they hadn't. Not with Lynette's float.

"But we could, with this float." With a dramatic flourish, she held the rolled poster high, then let it unfurl. It came to its conclusion with a satisfying slap. Holding it to her chest, she looked down, then around the room. "I'm no artist, but I'm proposing that Woodleigh puts forward something like this. It's just the idea, of course; if anyone has other suggestions, we can accommodate that."

People craned forward in their seats, trying to see more clearly.

"As you can no doubt tell, it's bigger than previously. A lot bigger. And the shape is like a sleigh, see? We'll add a frame on top, and cover the whole thing with a fabric cover that Sophie and I will make." She raised her head. "Can everyone see?" Most were still forward in their seats; some were squinting, others were moving their heads up and around, trying to see over the person in front. This wasn't working. "Here, wait." She walked to the large wooden table pushed against the side of the room and, with another flourish, spread the poster on top. "Come and have a closer look."

A couple of people left their seats immediately, others followed close behind to examine what she'd come up with. A Christmas wonderland with curved sleigh ends, a huge throne, Christmas trees along the back, and fluffy clouds along the bottom, like the sleigh was racing through the night sky. Once enough of a crowd had gathered, she said, "So these elves ... I thought I'd ask Delia if her ballet class would like to make an appearance. Sophie and I will do the costumes." She stepped back, making room for more people to gather around and see. "And they'll be dancing a little routine, popping in and out of these big gift boxes, which Sophie and I will also make. And there'll be a Mrs Claus, here at the back, waving and throwing candy—"

"Lynette does the float." It was Sam, interrupting her flow.

She turned to find him in his chair – the sole person who hadn't left his seat – arms crossed, jaw set.

When she met his hard gaze, she felt her cheeks heat – and prayed it didn't show. She didn't rattle easily, but this man … he sent everything to chaos inside her.

She looked from Sam to Lynette, who was standing at the back of the crowd around the table. It was difficult to judge what she thought of Kitty's idea, and she didn't offer anything additional to Sam's comment.

Kitty narrowed her gaze at him. "There's a fifty-thousand-pound prize this year." And they weren't going to win with Lynette's usual float. They needed something bigger, and frankly, better. "If Lynette doesn't mind of course. Just this year …" She flicked another glance at Lynette. "This is just to give an idea. If anyone had anything they wanted to add or change …"

"I think it's marvellous," Mrs Bushell said, taking tiny steps over to Kitty and clutching her forearm.

Kitty smiled down at her. "Thanks, Mrs Bushell."

She wasn't the only one. Most people in the room appeared to agree. They were leaning over the table, investigating. She could hear murmurs about various features – the cuteness of the elves, the softness of the snow, the sparkliness of the lights on the trees behind Mrs Claus.

"The prize was such a late announcement, entries had already closed. So we pretty much know who the competition is. I'm sure everyone will attempt to up their game, given the money on offer, but if we can pull this off—"

"Correct me if I'm wrong, but the date of the parade hasn't changed. You really think it can be done in two weeks?" It was Sam again, voice gravelly, tone almost rude, and still attempting to rain on *her* parade.

She wrapped her arms around her chest. "If you actually came up and had a look, Sam, you'd see that most of the design is soft elements." Was she trying to rile him, make an enemy? She softened her tone a little. "You know what Sophie's like. She can make anything in next to no time."

"I don't need to come any closer to know it's not going to work. There's only one person who has a tractor like that and he won't let anyone touch it."

She shrugged, striving to keep victory off her face. "Fred's already agreed to lend it to me, along with the tray. He's going to drive it, as Santa."

A scowl crossed his face. His brows were low and furious, as furrowed as brows could be. "It's not possible; not in the time frame."

Really, he was impossible. He hadn't even bothered to come to the table; he was just arguing for the sake of it. "If it's not ready in time, we go back to Lynette's float. There's nothing to lose."

She turned away from him, back to the crowd, most of whom were drifting back to their seats or standing, waiting for what came next.

"I think we can do it, and we can win. If everyone's happy for me to take over, I'll take full responsibility for the whole thing."

"What do you get out of it exactly, Kitty-Rose?" Sam rumbled.

"It's a big prize. And I have a few ideas of what to spend it on."

"Here we go."

Douglas gave Sam a disapproving look, but then shifted the same disapproval to her. "You'd be entering on the Chamber of Commerce ticket. It'll be up to the Chamber what we do with the winnings."

"Of course! I just meant I have ideas that I think would be good for the town."

Sam let out a grunt.

"What did you have in mind?"

"That we spend the money sprucing up the main strip to attract more shoppers." She turned to canvass the whole group. "You know I worked at Carmody's for years before I came back here. And then Melbourne. So I know that the reason why Carmody's can afford to offer this prize is that they're riding the wave of consumer spending. There's no reason why Woodleigh couldn't do the same. Keep more dollars in town, attract customers from all around the region. But we have to be ready; make sure we look the part. We've got a good selection of shops, we just need to present them to best advantage. We could get rid of all those dark, decrepit Victorian shopfronts and add light and colour. Give them a modern edge; lots of glass. Plant some flowers, make sure there's generous parking. We could even do a 'Shop in Woodleigh' week – offer discounts and prizes. This money could give us a head start to getting some of the prosperity of the times flowing here. Just imagine how it could be—"

"Kitty-Rose." It was Sam, growling at her. "Stop."

Too late, she felt the force behind her words, invisible golden light twining around each person in the room, compelling them to see the logic of her words. She pulled it back as hard as she could, but she had a feeling she was too late.

She swung to face him.

He knew. She didn't know if anyone else did, but he knew.

The whole thing left her feeling a little sick. She should have kept better control, but the idea was good. She'd just got a little too enthused.

"Well, there's a lot to discuss there, Kitty, and first we'd have to win it …" Douglas cast his gaze around. "I for one think it's worth a shot."

"So do I," another person agreed.

"I'm in. Let us know what you need, dear."

"Lynette?" prompted Douglas, but it was just a courtesy. With so many people already having agreed, what could Lynette say? Insist on using her sure loser?

Sam stood. "You don't have to listen to her," he said to his mother. Then scanned the room. "No one has to listen to her," he ground out.

"Of course we don't. But if Kitty is willing to take this on, I think we should back her."

"Yes, alright," Lynette said. "The money would be good for the town."

Sam turned slowly to stare at her. The moment grew denser, heavy and electric as a storm cloud, and just as likely to rent the air, to crack it open and pour.

She didn't think Sam's frown could deepen, but it did. "For the record, I'm a no."

He strode out of the room, every line of his body signalling anger.

There was a lot Woodleigh could do with fifty-thousand pounds. Was he really voting no just to spite her? Well, he couldn't keep it up. He was a crucial part of the plans. She'd just have to wear him down.

Kitty coughed as she inhaled a wave of stale mustiness. The storeroom hadn't been opened in months, and it was evident in every breath. Lining the walls were rolls and rolls of old fabric in every conceivable fibre, weight, colour and pattern. Generations worth of unsold stock.

They had all they needed for the float and more right here. She turned. "Let's start by—"

But Sophie wasn't listening. She hurried across the room to grip a bolt of magenta shot silk with a small, white hand. "I remember this one. Not long after you were born, Catherine. We made a frock and two capes. Eleanor said afterwards we shouldn't have got so much of such a distinctive fabric. Woodleigh's too small."

Kitty's heart squeezed but she smiled. "That's why we've got all this just sitting here now."

"And this one." She ran a finger down a sturdy navy and red checked wool. "Eleanor had a suit in this."

"Yes." Kitty could still picture her in it. Her chest ached.

Her mother walked around the room, sighing and touching fabrics.

Perhaps it was a good thing they'd be getting rid of some of them, Kitty mused – give everyone a chance for a fresh start.

She left Sophie to her memories and started pulling and stacking anything red, white or green. "What do you think, Sophie? Is this going to be enough?" she asked when she'd amassed her first-pass finds.

But Sophie was across the room, hand on another bolt. She laughed, soft and low. "The fuss that Gloria – Lynette's mother, you didn't know her – but the fuss she made when she found out I was the one making her suit for Lynette's wedding. I don't blame her really. I was only fourteen."

Kitty put her hands out to encompass the stack in front of her. "Can you work with these?"

"My Knack had come in, and I just had to sew, sew, sew. And this one ... this one was a challenge to—"

"Mum!"

Her mother turned, brows arched.

Something about her expression of surprise got to Kitty. "Don't you want to save Eleanor's shop?"

"Is that what we're doing?"

Kitty breathed out. "I showed you the design. Is this going to be enough?" She tilted her head at all she'd gathered.

Sophie's gaze narrowed. "You're assuming I'll sew the whole thing?"

"Well, won't you?" Of course she'd assumed she would. She'd assumed Sophie cared as much as Kitty about Manson's. But looking at her mother, she was no longer sure. "Don't you care?" Her voice was high and loud.

"Eleanor's gone, Catherine."

For a moment, all she could do was stare at her mother, gaze shifting from one eye to the other, trying to make sense of her words. Then a strange sound ripped from her chest. "You think I don't know that? I know she's gone. But she left us Manson's. She loved this shop." Frustration added to grief. She stared at her mother – always so lost in a world of her own. "And I can't leave until the shop is up and running again."

"Why?"

Again, Kitty had no words.

"Don't stay on my account. I'll be fine."

"So you don't care if the shop fails."

She glimpsed the hurt in Sophie's eyes. "Don't take that tone with me. I loved Eleanor every bit as much as you did. But she's gone, and I've let her go."

"Six months, and you've over it. But Redthorn … It's been thirty-five years!" Thirty-five years, and her mother was still forever trapped between this realm and … wherever the hell her parents and brother were.

"That's different. They're not gone."

Frustration made Kitty's skin itch. She didn't want to get drawn into the whole Christmas Day thing. She attempted to keep the conversation on the immediate issue at hand. "The shop's how you use your Knack, Mum. What would you do if you couldn't use it?"

"You don't use yours."

"But yours is good."

And it brought her joy. She'd seen her mother at the old Singer treadle at home, humming as she let her imagination fly free. It was an escape for her; it always had been. It's why her Knack had formed like that in the first place – as an escape from her grief at losing her family. What would Sophie do if the shop shut and she didn't have her sewing in her life?

"There's no such thing as a bad Knack, Catherine."

She huffed out a soft indeterminate sound. How could the ability to manipulate others be a good thing? No one thought it was; no one.

Sophie came closer. "Show me that sketch again."

Kitty took a breath, then turned to retrieve the paper. She pointed to the different elements. "So everything on and around the float to make it look like a sleigh racing through clouds. A Santa costume. A Mrs Claus costume. Elf costumes and gift boxes. Twelve; I'll get you exact sizes later. The cover for the frame – it has to go over the throne and three trees. Clouds along the bottom. Anything else you think of; any changes you want to make. But we need something that will get everyone's attention and make sure we win. A real show-stopper."

She pointed to her rendition of herself as Mrs Claus. It was over the top, completely over the top, but ... they were going to give that judge no choice but to award the prize to them.

Sophie glanced between the stack Kitty had gathered and the sketch in her hand. Kitty watched her mother mentally allocating fabric to components of the design, amazed as she always was at her ability to 'see' the final product before she'd even started. She had no doubts about her mother's ability – Sophie'd make sure it was even better than her sketch.

Eventually, Sophie nodded. "I'll need more stuffing and a lot more red."

Kitty scanned the room, but she'd already grabbed the reds. She did a second round, adding anything pale. "If I dye these?"

Again with the back and forth of the head, and then Sophie nodded.

"And you could get it done in the next two weeks?"

"I could ... for the right price."

"You're blackmailing your own daughter?" She thought she'd have to bargain with others – Sam, for example – she didn't think she'd have to bargain with her mother.

"You leave me no choice. Promise me you'll come out to Redthorn for Christmas day, and I'll do it."

Kitty groaned. "Mum."

"It's important," she sniffed.

"Alright, alright. Deal." She'd go if she had to. She'd hate every second of it, but it wouldn't kill her. "I'll do all the dyeing over the next couple of days. Start with the costumes. We'll move onto the cover later. When I've got Saint Sam to play ball. He's making the frame."

"Sam Wells?"

"The one and only." A frown furrowed her brow just thinking about him.

"Oh hush now, Catherine. He always says hello to me."

Of course he did. He was a saint.

To everyone except her.

Her attitude must have shown on her face, because her mother continued. "Not everyone does, you know."

Yes. She knew.

KITTY-ROSE SLIPPED through the open door of the church hall, waiting just inside. Before her, her little elves raised their arms in wide circles and plié-d, as Delia, moving gracefully in front of them, counted the beats of the song. Their gazes were fixed on her and Kitty could tell they were trying their absolute best. Delia clearly had a wonderful way with them.

She turned, saw Kitty and smiled – a warm and sparkling smile that was impossible not to return.

Delia had been in primary school with Kitty – she, Kitty and Susie had been a tight group at one stage – until she'd moved to Melbourne to live with her aunt and attend the prestigious Blavatsky Ballet School. She'd been doing well, earning a place in the Australian Ballet, until an injury had her retiring well before her time. She'd returned to Woodleigh and started a ballet school of her own.

Somehow managing to find the time to also get engaged to, and then break up with, Sam.

When the class was finished, Delia issued final instructions to her pupils and made her way over. "Kitty-Rose! It's so wonderful to see you!"

Kitty was a little taken aback at the warmth of the greeting. "Hello."

"You look fantastic. I love this." She ran her hand down the sleeve of Kitty's frock. Today's was a fitted cap-sleeve number with a knee-length pencil skirt; white, covered with pairs of red cherries. "You don't believe in letting personal standards fall by the wayside, do you?"

"Well, it helps having Sophie. Listen, I have something to ask you …"

"Everyone's talking about it." She grinned. "The kids are going to be beside themselves."

Relief washed through Kitty "You'll do it then?"

"Are you kidding? Of course we'll do it!"

"I know they're little, and there's not much time to come up with something and practice it …"

"It'll be fine. It's a parade. We'll keep the routine short and just repeat it however many times we need to."

Of course. "Perfect. Sophie'll make each of them an elf costume."

"I didn't know she did costumes."

Kitty shrugged. "Sophie can make anything."

Delia's expression turned curious. "I mean I'd heard the rumours —" She broke off, gave Kitty an awkward smile. "Not rumours exactly. That makes it sound so … gossipy." She broke off again, flustered. People did gossip about Sophie – Kitty knew it and so did Delia. "You know what small towns are like."

Did she ever. "How are you finding it being back?"

Delia had lived in Melbourne for years. Surely she missed the action and excitement of the big city.

"I love it. I'm really happy to be home."

"But your dreams …" The words were out before Kitty could help it.

She laughed. "Well, they changed. It was hard at first. But this is my dream now; establishing a dance school." She surveyed the hall with a contented expression. "I'd forgotten how much I missed Woodleigh when I first went away. I don't regret leaving – I had to take my shot – but it would have been better if I could have stayed at home for longer. And hopefully, now any budding Woodleigh ballerinas will be able to."

Whereas Kitty had had a whiff of freedom and longed for more. It was starting to feel like she'd been back in Woodleigh forever; like she'd never left.

"I better go talk to the parents. But say, there's a dance on Friday night. In Belleville. Why don't you come along?"

Shock had her stammering. "O-oh. Th-thanks. For the invitation. But …" She blinked, trying to make sense of it. But of course, Delia had been away during those high school years. She didn't realise the situation between her and … well, Susie, for one. "It's just I'm so busy, trying to get the float together."

"That's a shame. It's the last one before Christmas. Maybe next year?"

Kitty wouldn't be here much longer. There was no point putting down roots when she planned on leaving again as soon as she could. "Maybe. Thanks again." She'd leave it at that.

She walked out into the evening and had to bite back a groan. Next stop, if he was still there: Sam.

7

She walked up the shrub-lined concrete path to the office at the right of Woodleigh Motors. It was after five; all his guys had knocked off for the day, but Sam's car was parked in the lot at the front. She expected to find him at his desk, poring over accounts or work logs, but when she knocked and opened the unlocked door, the room was empty.

A clang of metal reached her ears. He must be working on something.

She walked through to the open door on the other side of the room, into a large, high-ceilinged shed – a place of concrete and heavy steel, but no Sam. Then she heard metal on metal and followed it; to find two heavy work boots poking out from under a chassis.

"Sam?" Her voice rang through the echo-y space. "That you under there?"

There was a sound of a spanner being dropped onto concrete, followed by a muttered cuss. He pushed himself out from under the vehicle on a low, wheeled tray, large hands still on the chassis above him. Her gaze trailed over well-worn denim and a navy singlet that revealed the broad shoulders and heavily muscled arms of a man who used his body all day every day.

Mouth suddenly dry, she lifted her gaze to meet his. An indescribable look crossed his face; he pushed out further and came to his feet in a practised motion that brought him close. So close she could see the flecks of bronze and olive in his eyes.

Predictably, her insides turned to mush and her heart started thudding. She searched his honest, square face, trying to work out what it was about him that got to her like it did. It wasn't that he was unattractive, but there was nothing pretty about him. And his feelings about her were abundantly clear. So why, why, why? It made no sense.

"Kitty-Rose." His tone was steely.

She pushed a breath out. "You can probably guess why I'm here."

He grabbed a rag from the roof of the car and wiped at his hands. "I'm going to take a wild stab. You want something."

"Well … as it so happens."

His gaze slanted away and he shook his head, a bitter half-smile on his face. The fact he'd walked out last night hadn't been a good sign. She wished there was someone – anyone – else she could ask to make sleigh frame but Sam was it. The only one she'd trust to do it right in the limited time they had.

"Woodleigh needs your help to bring our vision to life."

His mouth skewed. "Our vision?"

"Sophie and I can handle the costumes and other soft elements, but …" Her gaze dropped to his big hands. "You were there, you saw my design for the sleigh. I'm going to need help."

His implacable gaze narrowed on hers. "I'm busy."

"It's only a month until Christmas; everyone's busy." Her throat tightened. If only that were true of Manson's! "But we've got to pull together and get this done. It'll be worth it if we—"

"Count me out."

Her jaw dropped. She'd been dreading having to ask him. She knew he'd give her a hard time, but she thought he'd do it – not for her, for Woodleigh. "You're saying no?"

"I'm saying no." He tossed the rag onto the bonnet of the car. "Find someone else to do your bidding."

"Do my bidding? This is for the benefit of the town, for Pete's sake."

His mouth skewed, he gave a slight shake of his head. "If there isn't anything else, I need to get back to it."

"Hang on a minute," she said, voice rising. "You can't say no."

"I just did."

"The Chamber of Commerce overwhelmingly supported my idea."

"Do you recall how I voted?"

"Everyone apart from you voted yes. I'm sure you don't want to be the one standing in the way."

"You're sure, are you?" he said, low and husky.

A pause, and the air seem to shift around them, even though neither of them had moved. That voice, the intent way he looked at her … It turned her stomach upside down.

He frowned. "I was a no then and I'm a no now."

"But …" She took a step closer. "Don't you want Woodleigh to win?"

He chuckled, low and bitter. "You've got some nerve."

"What do you mean?"

"You think after what you did to my mother, I'd help you?"

"She voted yes!"

"What choice did she have, with everyone wanting her to step down? But she loves putting the float together and being Mrs Claus. It's *her* thing; she does it every year."

Her hands came out. "And Woodleigh's never won!"

"For most people, Kitty-Rose, the point of Christmas isn't winning."

She let out another huff. Why did he insist on believing the absolute worst of her? "This town needs that money."

He shrugged. "You're the only one I hear talking about it."

"So why did everyone vote for my float then?"

His gaze narrowed. He appraised her for a beat. "Are you serious?" Another beat. "Because you …" He waved his hand over her. "Did your thing."

It took her a moment for her to realise what he was talking about. Then her hands came to her hips. "I don't use it anymore."

His face turned incredulous. "You used it last night."

Her Knack had risen in her, yes, but she'd tried to keep it back. She had been distracted though, trying to convince everyone. "I didn't mean to. It just … Sometimes it sneaks out. It was only a little bit; not enough to change anything. I doubt anyone even noticed."

"I noticed."

"Well, good for you. I can always rely on you to stand and cast judgement, can't I, Saint Sam?"

His gaze only hardened.

She flung her hands in the air. "They would have voted yes anyway!"

"I suppose we'll never know."

They'd been craning forward in their seats from the second the poster had unfurled. And why wouldn't they vote yes? She was going to win them fifty-thousand pounds. "*I know.*"

He gave her a look that said he was taking her measure. "What about Roy the other night?"

"I didn't—"

"You did," he insisted. "I could feel it. Like I could feel it last night."

She pressed her lips together.

"I asked him what you'd been talking about. I told him not to do anything he wouldn't usually do. But when I checked the next day, he said on further consideration, it was better to give you a bit longer."

"We got the extension?" Maybe it was wrong, but she couldn't help the wave of relief at hearing that.

He tilted forward. "You had no right to ask for it. Not like that. I'm sure you've heard his head office is tightening the screws, expecting Roy to get things back in order. What if he gets in trouble because of you? Fired even."

She swallowed and looked away. She hadn't thought of that. Of course she didn't want Roy to get fired. "He's really under that much pressure?"

"Yes."

"Like I said, I didn't mean to. I actually try really hard not to—" She broke off. She didn't have to explain anything to him; not that he'd believe her anyway. "You think everything I do is wrong."

"It's not so much what you do, Kitty-Rose, it's the way that you do it."

She crossed her arms, as if that might offer some kind of defence against his assumptions. "It's a Knack, by the way," she muttered. "We call it a Knack."

Sam made a noise at the back of his throat.

How had this conversation got so out of hand? She was farther from convincing him than when she'd first walked in. She took a deep breath. "I know you don't like me, but it's not like the prize money will be coming to me personally. It's for the town."

His head tilted to the side. "You know what I think?" He waited a beat. "I think this is about you settling your petty grievances against Frank Carmody."

She let out a half-laugh. "It's got nothing to do with him." Rare for Sam, but he was way wide of the mark this time. She didn't have any grievances against Frank; she didn't have any feelings about him at all these days. Unlike the man in front of her. "Besides, isn't that exactly why you're saying no right now? I'd say you're settling some petty grievances of your own."

He grinned. "Is that what I'm doing? I should do it more often."

He was enjoying this. Saying no, raking her over the coals. "Not such a saint really, are you?"

"Not when it comes to you, Kitty-Rose."

She wished she could tell him to go to hell, but she needed him. How could he be the one person her Knack didn't work on? *Why* was he the one person her Knack didn't work on?

"Seeing as you already think the worst of me, I don't see why I shouldn't try to ... *persuade* you." After all, maybe it did now. She'd been sixteen last time she'd truly tried; her ability, not that she used it, had evolved, grown since.

"Forewarned is forearmed?"

"Something like that."

Something shifted in his gaze, some challenge accepted. "Go right ahead."

Well, okay then. She let it rise in her, a golden and powerful force, thrumming with desire. Then let it out, so it wound and curled all over him. She could tell, by the answering flames in his eyes, that he felt it.

She stepped closer, face tilted up. "I know you don't like me. That's okay. You don't have to. But be reasonable, Sam; this is for Woodleigh. It'll be great for the town." Was it working? He looked a little flushed. "You don't really want to say no. Don't say no just because of me. Sure it's ambitious, the timeline's tight – and I get that you're busy – but I know we can do it. We can get it done and win – for Woodleigh."

She nudged closer still, let her voice turn more intimate. "And I'm sorry about your mum. I honestly didn't realise what a big deal it was to her. I should have asked her first, got her blessing. It's a little late now, but I'll go see her, apologise." Her gaze dropped to his big hands. His arms were crossed over his broad chest, hands on his biceps, thumbs tucked under his armpits. When she looked back up, his eyes were dark, hot – penetrating. "I need you, Sam. I know you can build it. In fact, I don't think there's anything you couldn't do with those hands."

His gaze was serious. "Kitty-Rose, there's something I have to tell you."

"What?" Her pulse was racing, she felt a little light-headed.

He leaned forward, bringing him ever so slowly closer. Her gaze dropped to his lips. Those very un-saintly lips. Was he going to— Her eyes closed. But he didn't kiss her. His mouth brushed over her cheek, nuzzled at her hair. When he reached her ear, everything inside her exploded. Her hand shot out to his chest and she sucked in air, breathing him in, as a shiver of awareness travelled through her body.

"Your *Knack* ..." he rumbled, sending warm air into her ear. Goosebumps covered her everywhere. "Doesn't work on me."

She jerked back, stared at him while her mind caught up with his words.

Now his eyes were laughing at her.

She let out a breath in a frustrated, outraged huff. Who was doing the mesmerising here?

Why didn't it work on him? And why, oh why did he have this effect on her? Her gaze travelled over his face, but apart from those lips ... "You're not even handsome!"

His face hardened. "Lucky you're pretty enough for the both of us, Kitty-Rose."

"I didn't mean ..." She *hadn't* meant it the way it sounded. Oh, he brought out the worst in her! She was just trying to understand her own reaction, why her pulse raced like it did ... But as she continued to examine him and her heart only thudded faster, she realised that it was the honesty of his raw, even features that made them compelling. He had a kind of blazing, uncompromising integrity that was hard to look away from. "Sam—"

"I might reconsider."

Her breath caught in her throat.

"Go see Roy. Reverse whatever you talked him into the other night."

"Then you'll do it?"

"Then I'll reconsider," he corrected.

It wasn't much of a win, but she'd take it. It was as good as she was going to get tonight.

And he'd say yes eventually, no matter how sweet his pleasure in denying her. She turned and stalked from the room to the sound of his low chuckle.

8

When Roy saw who it was, his face blanched. He jerked to his feet, but Mrs Geller closed the door before he could stop her.

Not to be stopped, he came around the desk, pink and flustered. "Miss Frost—"

"Kitty."

"Kitty." He walked past her to the door, opened it and stood there firmly. "Unfortunately, I don't have time to meet with you today."

"Mrs Geller said you were free."

He brushed a hand through his hair. "Well, urm, she was mistaken. I'm sorry, you really have to go."

She wished she could. She'd had to grit her teeth to get herself in here. She didn't want to reverse her extension – Manson's needed it – but if talking to Roy was the only way to get Sam on board, they'd just have to make their meagre financial resources stretch.

Maybe she could raid the silverware at Redthorn and sell that to tide them over.

"I just want to talk."

He held out a hand. "I can't do a thing more. I've sent off the paperwork to extend your interest-only period for an extra three months and that's all I can do."

"Roy, I'm not—"

He was nervous – red-faced and sweating. "I can see that you're going through a tough time at the moment, and the bank would love to be able to offer you further support, but it's not going to be possible."

She frowned. "I haven't come to ask for another extension."

His eyes went wide with hope. "Really?"

"No. In fact I—"

"Like I said, I don't have time to talk at all today. You'll have to schedule a meeting for some other time."

"I'd love to, Roy, but—"

"I have to make a call. Right at this second. You'll have to come back later. Or rather, don't. Just talk to Mrs Geller."

"This will only take a—"

"Someone's waiting on a call from me right now. Right at this second."

She frowned at him. "Has someone told you to interrupt anything I say?"

His already wide eyes went wider. Yes, they had. Of course they had. And she knew who.

She walked to take the seat opposite his.

"Please don't sit!" Still hovering by the door, he called up the corridor, "Mrs Geller, come and collect Miss Frost. She's just leaving."

She hated to admit it, but Sam was right – she'd really raised this guy's blood pressure. "Roy, I don't know what you've been told but I promise none of this is necessary."

He still appeared wary.

"I don't even want to be here. Sam sent me."

"Sam sent you?"

At her nod, he ran a hand through his hair again, then slowly walked back to take his seat.

"In fact, I came to ask if you could … reverse the outcome of our last conversation."

"What do you mean?"

"Pretend it never happened. We don't want an extension anymore."

"That'd be swell, but like I said, I've already put in the paperwork." She could almost see the beads of sweat breaking out on his forehead.

"Can you un-put it in?"

He gawked at her.

"The thing is, I really need for it not to have happened. Can't you send off some new paperwork?"

"It was bad enough requesting it in the first place. If I send a follow-up straight away reversing the initial request … they might examine it a little more closely. I'm already praying that the first letter doesn't raise any eyebrows."

Oh dear. What had she done? Sometimes she hated her Knack, and she could understand why everyone treated her with suspicion. "Of course you shouldn't stick your neck out further. Forget it."

He slumped with relief. "That's good of you, Kitty."

It wasn't good of her. She shouldn't have put him in this situation in the first place. She breathed in deeply, then let it go. "I didn't mean to, you know. I didn't realise I was …" She trailed off, and shrugged. Roy appeared highly uncomfortable. Sam had obviously told him something, but she wasn't sure what. "I apologise. I'll be more aware in future. It won't happen again."

But her mind had already turned to the implications. What was she supposed to tell Sam? Was he going to accept that she'd done her best to get Roy off the hook? But surely, if his key concern was for his future brother-in-law's job security, he wouldn't thank her for doing anything that made that job less secure.

She sighed. Sam would just have to suck it up. "Could I ask a favour though?"

His expression turned suspicious.

"A simple favour," she pressed. "Could you tell Sam that I came in today? That I asked you to reverse the extension?"

His brow furrowed. "What's it got to do with him?"

She shrugged. "He was just looking out for you."

"He's a good guy."

"The best," she agreed, and to her credit, noted only a small degree of sarcasm in her tone. "Saint Sam. That's what we used to call him." Roy chuckled lightly, much more relaxed now that the conversation had moved on. "I can only imagine what he calls me."

He stiffened; his lips pressed tight.

She couldn't help seeing the humour. "It's okay. I'm well aware of what Sam thinks of me. Witch is probably the least of it."

"Oh no, Kitty. I can't have you thinking that. I asked him … Well, after what happened in the pub the other night, of course I was curious. He said that witch wasn't the right word."

"No?" she asked coolly, as if the thought of Sam having a right word for her wasn't threatening to liquify her spine. "What is then?"

Roy flushed to the tips of his hair. "I think you'll have to ask the man himself."

A smile crept across her face. She stood. "Thanks for your time, Roy."

She left the bank and headed home. She needed to get to Belleville and buy the dye.

"Kitty-Rose!"

She turned, to see Mrs Bushell leaning out of the bookstore, hand in the air, hailing Kitty.

Well. She couldn't ignore Mrs Bushell. She walked back to the tiny old woman. "Morning, Mrs Bushell."

A firm hand gripped her forearm, Mrs Bushell grinned up at her. "How are you, dear?"

"Pretty well. How's the brochure coming along?"

"Oh, that's exactly what I wanted to talk to you about!"

How had she guessed? "I would love to, but could we discuss it later? I've got a few things I need to get done for the float."

"Of course, dear." A squeeze of her arm. "Anything I can do?"

A vision of Mrs Bushell standing on a stool stirring enormous vats of dark-red dye came to mind. "Don't think so. Thank you for the offer though."

She was still grinning up at her. "You're a lot like Mary; anyone ever tell you that?" Kitty shook her head. "Well, I knew her well and you are. She was always getting involved with this and that. This is just the sort of thing she'd come up with."

"Let's hope I can pull it off."

Another squeeze. "It's going to be splendid."

She couldn't help it; she smiled. "Thanks, Mrs Bushell. I do hope so."

Her arm was finally released. "But we must meet before the next Chamber meeting."

"The next Chamber meeting?"

"Well, of course. That was the last one for the year, but you will be at the next one, won't you?"

Kitty hadn't thought that far ahead, but she supposed, if they did win the prize, that was when they'd start deciding on how to use the money. She'd better be there. "I think so."

"Twenty-third of January, it'll be. A Monday. It's always a small meeting. Some people say we shouldn't have one then, people still away on holidays, but I always think it's important to get a good start on things. Don't you think?"

There was no way she wouldn't still be in town in January. "I'll be there."

"Oh good. We can talk about my brochure then. Oh and dear, could you thank your mother for me?" Kitty blinked at her. "Tell her the ravens were absolutely right. It was the neighbour's cat stealing my unmentionables from the line."

As opposed to …? Kitty smothered a smile. "Sure."

IT'D BEEN a good while since she'd been to Belleville, and even longer since she'd been in Carmody's.

She'd been to the haberdasher and bought every packet of red and green dye they had, then she'd come to Carmody's, to check on their supplies. She hadn't been into the store since she'd resigned, and decided to explore a little, to see what had changed, before she paid and left. Just to remind herself of the good times.

And there had been good times. She'd felt free here like she never had in Woodleigh. Free from assumptions and rumours and judgements. She'd run into a few old colleagues, and they'd seemed happy enough to see her, but she couldn't say she'd made any true friends when she was here.

She'd taken her job seriously, and when she'd ascended the ladder so fast, and then started dating the owner's son, people had talked. But at least it was all based on Kitty and Kitty alone. Not her Frost legacy, not her unstable mother, and not her lack of a father. And because she knew she deserved every promotion she'd gained – through talent and hard work – it had been easy to ignore any disgruntled mutterings.

She'd been happy in those years. At least, she thought she had.

To be honest, Carmody's didn't appear any busier than it had when she'd worked here, and if anything, seemed a little drabber. It certainly didn't look like a store that had fifty-thousand pounds to give away.

And she didn't understand how it could give away that sum. When she'd worked here, she'd gradually become more and more involved in the buying side of the business. She didn't know everything and she hadn't been privy to any information for a couple of years, but ... how could Frank afford to give that much money away?

He'd always been ambitious – it was one of the things that had drawn her to him. He wanted to be doing that well, he wanted everyone to believe it, so lo and behold, he'd go ahead and do it.

"Kitty!"

She whirled to see Frank's handsome face. Speak of the devil.

"Little bird told me you were here. Lovely to see you." Ever urbane, he leaned in to kiss her cheek, drew back, one hand at her elbow, and dragged his gaze all over her. "You're looking well."

She disentangled herself. It was a little familiar, but she supposed they'd been an item for three years – engaged to be married for one of those. "Hi, Frank."

His gaze dropped to the packets of dye in her hands. "Big job?"

She laughed lightly. He didn't even know about the other packets she'd already purchased. "I suppose so. It's for the Christmas parade actually."

Confusion crossed his face. "Sorry?"

"I'm helping with the Woodleigh float."

His gaze raced between her eyes, trying to catch up. "You moved back?"

"Just over a year ago." She hugged her chest, stared at a nearby rack of hats. "Aunt Eleanor passed away."

His gaze grew serious. "Sorry to hear that."

She inclined her head in acknowledgement. "Anyway, I ended up staying on for a while, to get things sorted at the shop."

He looked at her for a long while, clearly struggling with something he wanted to say. "I wish I'd known you were back," he said eventually, a strain to his voice. "I would have ..." he trailed off.

Kitty didn't prompt him. She'd ended things with him a long time ago, and, as much as she might miss the excitement of that life, she knew it'd been the right decision. Instead, she went back to the former thread. "So, the big prize!" She jiggled the packets a little. "Business is good, obviously?"

A shadow crossed his face, so quick she almost missed it, then he beamed. "Business is great."

She couldn't help her pointed look around.

"We've had to pull back here to focus on our other openings."

"I read about it in the paper the other day. How many now?"

"Two in the past two years, another coming in the new year. And of course, the flagship store in Melbourne."

"You finally got the old man to listen, hey?"

Frank had been trying to talk his father into retiring – handing over the reins to Frank – ever since she'd known him. They didn't get on all that well, though Kitty had always liked Arthur Carmody. Maybe it was because she'd never known her own father, and she was touched by how kind he'd always been to her. Frank and Arthur though ... she'd witnessed some blazing rows. Arthur would have been happy just keeping his shop a Belleville affair. He certainly didn't have his son's pretensions, but Frank was always pushing to build the business. He must have finally succeeded.

He let out a funny laugh. "Took a while but yeah. Eventually got him to see the light. It's the decade of the retailer. There's a new mood sweeping the country, a new wealth. After all the hard years, people are ready for some convenience and luxury in their lives. We have a once in a lifetime opportunity to grow a whole new generation of wealth. This is the fastest growing consumer society in history – and Carmody's is riding that wave."

It was the same lines she'd always heard from him. She must have been young and naïve to fall for them like she had. Now it just sounded like horseshit. "Fifty-thousand pounds though."

He shrugged. "It's an investment. We need to make a splash, for the Melbourne store."

If nothing else, he'd always been an optimist. "You always had ambitions, Frank. It seems like you're making all of them a reality. Congratulations."

Another flicker of something passed over his face. "Well, thank you, Kitty. That means a lot, coming from you."

She offered him a smile. "Well, I better get going on my way. Pass on my regards to your father."

"He'll like that. He always liked you."

"It was good to see you, Frank." She turned.

"Kitty."

She turned back.

He took his time, a million expressions passing over his face. "I really do wish I'd known you were back. I don't suppose we could catch up for a drink some time?"

The interest was clear in his eyes, but she had no intentions of going back in time, and they'd never been friends. They'd been colleagues, working towards a common goal, and they'd been lovers, but they'd never been friends.

"I don't think that's a good idea." She said it as gently as she could.

"No. Of course not." He let out a strange, strangled sort of laugh.

"Congratulations, though, on the success of the stores."

She was extricating herself, and he knew it. If it was one thing Frank wasn't, it was slow on the uptake. He inclined his head. "I'll see you parade day. I look forward to seeing what you come up with."

With a tight smile, she walked out of the store and headed for her car. She needed to get back – she had a tonne of dyeing to do – but she just sat for a moment.

She knew she hadn't made a mistake breaking up with him, but seeing him succeeding like that, while her own life was in the crapper … understandable that it'd breed a little discontent.

Still, she had a plan to get things back on track; it was just going to take time. She started the car, breathing a sigh of relief the engine sputtered to life. All the way back to Woodleigh, thoughts raced through her head. She knew she was dwelling on a past she couldn't change, feeling sorry for herself about her present, but she couldn't help herself.

Squeal. Hiss. Sputter, sputter.

Something was happening with the car.

She hit the brakes, and sat for a minute or two. When the initial rush of adrenaline had started to ebb, and her breathing had normalised, she tried the engine again.

Sputter. Sputter. Dead.

She tried again. For a moment, it sounded like it was thinking about starting, then … nope.

After what felt like a hundred attempts, she hit the dash hard. Ouch! And damn.

She got out of the car. Taking in the surrounds, she judged she was more than half-way back to Woodleigh. She'd just have to walk.

Which would take over an hour.

And she was in heels. Her feet were going to be a mess by the time she made it.

She was about five minutes down when a rumble behind her had her stepping off the road and turning.

She recognised that vehicle.

Great. Just great.

9

There was nowhere to run to, nowhere to hide. All she could do was keep walking – and pray he didn't notice the woman in the red suit on the side of the road ...

She was not in the mood to deal with Sam right now.

But, inevitably, he slowed to a snail's pace alongside her, wound his window down, and called across the front seat. "Car trouble?"

"Just taking in the sweet mountain air."

"Need a lift?"

She shrugged. "It's not that far."

"Come on, Kitty-Rose, get in the car."

She tightened her arms across her chest.

"You know I'll just trail along beside you the whole way."

Lord, he would too!

She faced him, hands on hips. He stopped the car. Her gaze caught on the line of his arm and shoulder as he leaned sideways. Such a ridiculously big man. How did he even fit in that front seat?

"Quicker if you just get in."

Saint Bloody Sam. She stalked over, opened the door and slid into the seat. "Thank you." She strove to keep any begrudging element out of her tone.

"No problem."

They rolled off, driving in silence for a moment or two.

How was this her life?

"I'll send a tow truck back to get your car."

She glanced at him. "Don't do that."

He glanced her way, then back at the road. "You got some other way of getting it to town?"

She gazed out her window, refusing to dignify that with a response. But she could sense his scrutiny, and it was making her feel warm.

"Can't just leave it on the side of the road."

Couldn't she? "It's temperamental. I'll walk back out tomorrow. It'll probably start."

He frowned. "You shouldn't be driving it around if it's that erratic. I'll take a look at it."

Was the car heating up? She was getting more flushed – and more tense – as the seconds passed. How far were they from Woodleigh? Three minutes? Four? At this rate, she'd combust before they arrived. "I don't want you to do that."

His mouth twisted. "Who do you usually go to?"

She just shrugged. She didn't go to anyone. She just prayed the car would start each time.

She could feel him frown. "I'll send one of the boys out to tow it to the garage."

"I said I don't want you to do that."

"It's not safe—"

"I can't pay you!" The words exploded out of her. He glanced over, then back at the road. "Happy now you got me to admit it?" Wasn't he always wanting to pull her down a notch or two? Well, he'd succeeded. "I can't afford to get the car serviced, let alone towed. I can't afford anything. Eleanor's shop is going under and I don't know if I can save it. I just ran into Frank Carmody, and he was parading all his success in front of me. 'Don't you wish you were still with me? No, I don't, Frank.' But meanwhile, until I can get Manson's back on its feet, I'm stuck in Woodleigh, with a mother who still thinks it's 1919, a failing business, and a town full of people who hate me!"

His hands tightened on the wheel. He held her gaze for an extended moment, but she couldn't read his expression. "That's why you asked Roy to extend the interest-free term of your loan?" he asked eventually.

"You thought I was doing it for the fun of it?" She let out a frustrated huff, heat sweeping over her. "Lord, you probably did."

"I'll let you know when your car's ready to pick up."

"I can't—"

"I know," he said, with the faintest shadow of a smile.

Embarrassment was starting to creep over her. She could feel her shoulders bunching. Why had she said all that to Sam of all people? "I don't want your help."

He gave her a quick sardonic glance. "Could've fooled me."

Was that a hint of dry humour in his tone? Wonders never ceased. "That's different. That's for the town." What she'd meant was, she didn't want his charity. But knowing Sam, he'd tow her car anyway, and he was right – she couldn't just leave it to rust on the side of the road. "I'll pay you back. When I can." She swallowed her bitterness as best she could.

He changed gears smoothly, slowing down as they hit the town speed limits. "How bad is it? With the shop."

She sighed and stared out the window. "We just need a few more customers to generate a little positive word of mouth. We've kind of fallen off the radar … But women care what they look like, and no one can make them look as good as Sophie. A few beautiful frocks, and they'd be flocking to us again. I know they would." She hadn't answered his question but he didn't push. They drove in silence for a few moments. "Pretty bad," she said finally. "If things don't turn the corner in the next couple of months …" Heaven knows why she was baring the secrets in her heart to her enemy.

"So that's why you're doing the float? To save your shop?"

She shrugged.

"Well, at least that's something I can believe."

"If it means people don't hate me quite so much, that'll be a bonus."

They entered the town, houses on either side of the road. It was probably being back around Woodleigh folk but she became more aware of him next to her, how he filled the car with his presence.

"No one hates you, Kitty-Rose."

She gave him a hard look. "Oh, come on, Sam. Your sister does. Your mother does. You do. And that's just the Wells family."

"I don't hate you."

"You said I was a horrible person."

He studied her, square face serious, before breaking eye contact. He took so long to answer, she was pretty sure that he wasn't going to. Then he said, "That was a long time ago."

It didn't feel that long ago to her. Those words still cut.

"And you shouldn't have done what you did."

"Why do you think I stopped using my Knack?" She glanced again at him. "Mostly."

"You really don't use it anymore?"

She shrugged. "I try. I suppose it sneaks out sometimes. More than I realised, maybe."

Another loaded pause. She didn't look at him, but it made no difference. She felt the tension rising between them even so.

"So that's the plan? You get the shop on its feet again and then you leave?"

"Of course it is." She sighed. "It's not easy being a Frost in this town."

He was silent a long time, gaze flicking to her, watching her carefully in that patient, thoughtful way of his. "Do you hate it so much?"

"Wouldn't you? Is it so hard to understand? Maybe it is. Everyone loves you, Saint Sam. Reliable. Honest. Noble. All around good guy."

"I'm not that good."

Something in his tone forced her eyes to him. There was heat in his gaze, bringing the amber flecks to the fore. It sent a wave of sweet flame over her skin and she turned to examine the shopfronts they were passing.

Another tense silence.

"Did it occur to you that maybe part of the reason you feel like that is because that's how you think things are?"

"You're blaming me now?"

"I'm not blaming you, I'm not blaming anyone. But since you came back, until the Chamber meeting two nights ago, you hadn't made the least bit of effort to integrate. You don't talk to anyone—"

"No one talks to me!"

He pulled up his truck and met her gaze straight on. "Maybe it cuts both ways."

A soft hiss escaped between her teeth.

They'd arrived at her home. She turned to contemplate her street, not sure what to make of his words. Her instinct was to deny it, to argue, but she couldn't find anything to say.

"I went to see Roy," she said, changing the subject, voice only a little hoarse. "He didn't want to do it, said changing the paperwork would only make things worse." His mouth tightened into a knot. "I didn't … you know. Help him reach that conclusion."

His gaze bored into her. "I believe you, Kitty-Rose."

He'd answered the question she hadn't even known she'd asked. "So what? You'll help me now?"

"No."

"But you said if I talked to Roy—" She couldn't stop herself sounding dismayed.

"I said I'd reconsider if you got Roy to withdraw the extension." He looked out the window. "It's too late for that – fine. But now we're back to square one, and I need you to do something else."

"What?"

"You said you'd go talk to my mother, apologise for what happened."

She had. When she'd been trying to 'Knack' him. But perhaps it was something she should do. She nodded.

"And then go talk to my sister, sort it out."

She'd rather scratch her eyes out.

Heat rose in her. She glared at him, got out and almost slammed the door. But she wasn't letting this town – him – make her rude. So instead, she stuck her head back in. "Thanks for the lift."

10

She'd never been inside Susie's Emporium before; it'd only been open for a little over a year. A bell over the door tinkled as she entered. Like all the shops in Woodleigh, it was dark inside, courtesy of that Victorian lack of light, and it took her eyes a moment to adjust.

Susie, behind the counter, looked up, breath held – Kitty assumed in excitement at a customer, given she was the only one. But when she saw who it was, her suddenly enormous eyes signalled her startlement.

Kitty stopped just inside the door, a little surprised herself. Susie had adopted winged eyeliner and red lips – Kitty's signature look. She schooled her features to keep any trace of reaction off her face. "Hi, Susie."

Susie tucked a strand of hair behind her ear. "Kitty-Rose."

Awkwardness descended. Kitty headed for the far wall and started examining the merchandise. A ceramic eggcup in the shape of a duck. Soldier and owl wooden stacking toys. Decks of novelty playing cars. Boxes of glass Christmas tree ornaments.

A whole array of cute and quirky items, and being so close to the season of giving, surely this should be one of Susie's busiest times of year. But she was the only person in here. She wondered how Susie kept it afloat. Well, she could relate to that.

"Can I help you?"

She turned. Susie was hovering, hands clasped in front of her. "Just browsing."

"For anything in particular?" Susie asked, as if Kitty were any old customer who'd wandered in off the street.

"I'm not sure." She hadn't planned that far ahead. "A Christmas present for Sophie, if I see something," she came up with. A gift seemed a safe bet, and pretending she'd come in to buy something was a good deal less awkward than her real reason.

Susie nodded, and moved a little distance away. She started to sort through and adjust items on a shelf. Kitty had to admire her gumption; she must know she wasn't really in here to find a Christmas present.

Or maybe she didn't.

Ugh. This was excruciating.

How was Sam making her do these things? She was the one with the Knack!

She turned her attention back to the shelf in front of her and spotted a snow globe with a tall, spindly house and a crow inside. She picked it up – noting out of the corner of her eye Susie extracting something of her own – and examined the globe from all angles. Redthorn wasn't spindly, and a crow wasn't a raven, but it might make a good present for Sophie.

In truth, there was only one thing Sophie ever wanted for Christmas, and that was the return of her family. "I think I'll take—"

"What about this?"

They'd spoken at the same time.

Kitty's gaze dropped to what Susie held. A small crystal sculpture featuring a cat and a rose. It was much nicer than what she'd found. Her mouth tilted up. "You know, I think Sophie might like that. I'll take it."

A small smile graced Susie's mouth. "I'll ring it up for you."

She put the snow globe back on the shelf and followed Susie to the counter.

"The store's nice. I haven't been in here before."

"Yes, well … Wrap it for you?" When Kitty nodded, she bent and pulled out a couple of sheets of plain brown paper and a sheet of wrapping paper covered in wreathes and red bows. "I wish everyone thought the same."

"Not going so well?" Kitty asked, watching Susie's deft movements with the paper. She was adding layers of plain brown paper to protect the sculpture.

She tossed her hair back. "I didn't know it'd be so hard to sell anything!"

Kitty's mouth screwed sideways in sympathy. "It's not easy in a town Woodleigh's size. To be honest, Manson's is the same."

Susie met her gaze. "Really?"

Kitty nodded. What was there to be gained by not being honest?

She added the final layer of brown paper. "I thought, being so well-established and everything …"

Kitty shrugged. "Everyone's going off the rack. For everyday wear anyway. The world's changing. At the moment, we're not on the right side of it."

There was a moment of silence, broken only by the stretch and snap of sticky tape. "It's great, what you're trying to do – winning the prize and all. I wish I'd been there at the meeting the other night, but Mum told me about it. Said you wanted to modernise the shopfronts and advertise Woodleigh and everything. I hope it works."

She offered a faint smile. "Me too."

Susie put the finished product in a bag and rang up the total.

Kitty handed over the right change. "Look, Susie …" she ventured. "I didn't just come in to buy a present." She glanced at the bag in front of her a moment. "Don't you think it's time we patched things up? I'm sorry about what happened." She pressed forward against the counter. Susie didn't say anything, but her eyes were wide. "I was horrible to you in high school."

"Well, I was horrible to you in primary school." The reply was immediate.

They both appeared stunned by the speed of their confessions.

"I shouldn't have accepted that brooch from Chad," Kitty said, recovering. "And I shouldn't have tried to force you to the principal's office."

Susie shrugged. "I shouldn't have stolen it. And I shouldn't have accused you of taking mum's watch in primary school."

"Why did you?" Her voice quaked a little. She felt oddly vulnerable.

Susie's arms came across her chest, her head went down. "I was jealous."

Kitty felt her eyes widen. "Of me?"

"You're a princess, for Christ's sake."

Kitty blew out a breath and shook her head. She'd been jealous of that? "It's just something Sophie made up because I don't have a dad. And I repeated it all the time because … I wished it was true, I suppose." It hadn't been easy growing up an out-of-wedlock child in a small town.

"Well, I believed it." Susie's mouth quirked. "How could I not? There's this thing about you, Kitty … You're special. You look like a movie star, and you've got this magical power, and this big mysterious mansion out of town … Of course I was jealous. I'm just plain, ordinary Susie Wells."

Kitty shook her head again. "I was jealous of you too, you know."

Susie's face screwed up.

"You have everything I don't. A dad, who just happened to be the mayor. A normal family – with a brother and a sister. The Wells are respected; you're part of this town."

"You're part of this town too."

Kitty's mouth quirked to the side. "Sure. The town freaks."

"That's not what people …" But her voice grew weaker and she trailed off.

"Believe me, it's not that great being 'special'."

Susie bit her lip. "I suppose." She grinned suddenly. "I can't help but think that you did me a favour with Chad."

Kitty-Rose let out a snort. "I definitely did." She stuck out her hand. "Bygones?"

Susie took it immediately. "Bygones."

They stood back, smiling at each other.

"I can't believe we've both got shops now," Susie said, then grimaced. "For the moment anyway."

Kitty's mouth skewed up. "You and me both."

"Do you need help? With the float?"

"I've still got a million yards of fabric to dye, if you're up for that. But actually ..." She considered Susie. She hadn't thought to ask before she came in but ... "Could you talk to Sam? I really need his help with the frame."

"He's not doing it?"

She shook her head. "So far, he's just saying no. He said he'd reconsider if I talked to you, but that's not a yes, and we're running out of time."

"This was his idea? I should have known."

"It was his idea but ... I'm glad I came in."

"Me too." Her brow creased. "It's strange he's not helping."

Kitty shrugged. "I don't think he likes me much. He thinks I used my ... you know, Knack, to get everyone to vote in my favour."

Her eyes went wide. "Did you?"

"Not intentionally. But it might have slipped out a little."

"And you don't understand why I'm jealous," Susie said wryly.

Her mouth twisted. "It's not all sunshine and roses. Look at Sophie, how people treat her. It causes as many problems as it solves." She bit her lip. "Don't worry about it. He'll probably just think I used my Knack to force you to accept my apology."

Her brows went up. "Did you?"

"No! Of course not. I don't use it anymore. After what happened between us ..."

Susie nodded, then a strange expression crossed her face. "Still, he's not the type to not help when it's for the town."

"He doesn't like that I took over from your mum either."

"You know Mum, she wants what's best for the town." But she couldn't quite make eye contact.

So Sam was right. Kitty's mouth quirked. Next stop: Lynette.

~

SHE FOUND Lynette in the general store, restocking the biscuit shelf. When she saw Kitty, she flicked a glance at her, but kept on with her task. "You need me in for that fitting already?" Her voice with thin with barely suppressed indignation. Not the best of receptions.

"Ah … With all the float preparation, we haven't actually made a start yet." Lynette continued with her stacking. "Speaking of which, I was wondering … would you consider reprising your role of Mrs Claus?"

Lynette's mouth pursed. "Want my help now, do you?"

"You'll do Mrs Claus better than me anyway."

Lynette gave an of-course-I-would sniff.

"Lynette, about the float … I should have come to you first. I realise that now. It just happened really fast. The announcement of the bigger prize, then thinking about putting something together for it … I didn't think about how you'd feel."

Lynette sniffed again, her mouth framed by lines. "I certainly won't be donning what Mrs Claus had on in the poster."

Kitty grinned. "Sophie hasn't made the costume yet. She can make it different. She can make it whatever you want."

"Wouldn't like to put anyone to any trouble. I do still have my old costume. Looks a little tatty now but it'll do."

Lynette was definitely waiting for her to argue. "Nonsense. Sophie won't mind. I'll get her to make the most glamorous Mrs Claus costume ever. You can keep it for future years."

"Maybe you'll be doing the float again next year as well." The words came out stiffly.

Kitty shook her head. "I probably will have left by then. And even if I am still here … I know it's your thing."

"Alright. Well, a new costume would be very nice."

"Thanks, Lynette." She'd talked to Roy, she'd talked to Susie, she'd talked to Lynette – Sam must be running out of reasons to say no by now.

"I saw you talking to Ros Bushell yesterday."

Kitty nodded. "She wanted to discuss the brochure."

"Of course she did. She's been rabbiting on about it for years. Can't get anyone to take it seriously even though it wouldn't cost much to produce."

"It's not a bad idea, in my opinion. Everyone's buying a car and petrol's getting so cheap. I reckon people will be driving all over on weekends. If we had a brochure in the bigger towns, they might make their way to Woodleigh."

Lynette took a few moments to consider that. "You think so? We could all do with a bit of that."

Kitty nodded. "It's a new era, Lynette. There's opportunity everywhere."

"You going to support her at the next Chamber meeting then?"

"Twenty-third of January?"

Lynette appeared surprised Kitty knew the date.

"I thought I'd attend. I've been told it's a small meeting, with people away on summer holidays, so maybe …"

"Maybe we can push something through? Yes, maybe." She finished her stacking and turned to face Kitty. "So, you're back to the city soon?"

"That's the plan."

"Shame. We could do with you here."

Kitty looked down to hide the sudden warmth that brought. She could only assume she'd been forgiven.

She arrived home to find a Mrs Claus costume draped across her bed.

Sophie had made it already! And it definitely wasn't suitable for Lynette. Never mind.

But it was glorious – all red and gold brocade and a sheer cape with strands of gold running through. She wouldn't be wearing it anymore, but she couldn't resist trying it on. She stripped to her underwear and stepped into it, then put on the enormous crown-like headpiece with its fluffy white trim and the matching white fluffy cuffs to her wrists, and stepped back into her red heels. She added a fresh lick of red lipstick, just to complete the effect.

Stepping back to take in the whole ensemble in her cheval mirror, she put a hand to her mouth to hold in a laugh.

Well. She'd asked for a show-stopper. Sophie had taken her already risqué concept and run with it. The bodice was fitted at the top, nipping in tight at the waist, with a deep sweetheart neckline that left little to the imagination. Sophie knew her measurements – it fit like second skin. The tulip-flared skirt, in the same thick red brocade, stopped so high on her thigh, it barely covered her. The cape covered her arms in a layer of sheer sparkly fabric that looked like it'd been woven from strands of scarlet spider's web. It gave the illusion of decency, without actually covering much.

She couldn't have worn this; the parade was a family affair. Really, what had Sophie been thinking? Maybe she was trying to prevent heatstroke – no way she could overheat with this little on … Still, swivelling back and forward in front of the mirror, she couldn't say the effect was displeasing. Not at all.

She twirled. Everything lifted. Her hand came to her mouth again.

She heard the front door and went to greet her mother, hands out as she spun slowly. "Well, what do you think?"

But she pulled up when she saw Sophie's pale, stricken face and red-rimmed eyes. She was lugging a huge velvet sack over her shoulder. "Mum?"

Sam stepped through the front door after her. He froze when he saw her, hand on the door, eyes raking up and down her body. When he met her gaze again, the heat there liquified her spine.

"Thank you, Sam." Her mother threw over her shoulder and pressed forward.

Sam managed to shut the door.

Kitty stuck a hand out to stop her mother on the way past. "Mum, what's the matter?"

Sophie tugged free. "Not now, Catherine. I'm busy."

She watched, open-mouthed, as Sophie continued up the hall and around the corner. Her bedroom door opened and then shut.

Sam was still standing just inside the door.

"Twice in as many days you've had to drive a Frost woman home. Getting to be quite the habit. What happened?"

"I don't know. I found her on the side of the road, heading back into town, hauling that heavy sack. She seemed pretty upset."

"She didn't say anything?"

His mouth quirked. "Something about a red ribbon."

Oh. That again. "Well, thanks for bringing her back."

He nodded, gaze fixed on hers, as if he was fiercely determined not to let it drop. The streaks of colour high on his cheeks and his strained breath indicated the effort that cost.

Well, her appearance had almost made Kitty herself blush. And it appeared she had the upper hand for once; she couldn't resist teasing. "My costume for the float. You like?" She did a slow twirl in front of him.

A strange half-grunt was her response.

She struck a pose, smiled at him. "What do you think, will it be a hit with the crowd?"

He ran out of will to fight, his eyes suddenly everywhere, lighting up a path of fire all over her body. "They won't know where to look, but they won't be able to look away." His voice had a raspy, choked sound to it.

She tilted her head. "Like you, Sam."

The words crystallised in the space between them. In the dark of the hall, his eyes gleamed deep earth and amber. She could feel them all over her face, her eyes, the Flare of violet that spanned one corner.

"Like me," he agreed.

She stepped closer, and he went incredibly still. She swore he wasn't even drawing breath. She bit her lower lip, trying to keep her smile in. Finally, he was the one who was flustered; she wasn't going to pretend it didn't feel good. "I thought it didn't work on you."

He pushed a hand through his hair. "Your Knack doesn't."

She chuckled and took pity. "I'm not actually wearing this."

He raised his brows at her.

"I spoke to your mum today; I asked her if she'd play Mrs Claus."

He looked her up and down again.

She laughed. "Sophie will make her something else." She crossed her arms. "I talked to Susie too."

"Yeah?"

"Yeah." She tipped her head. "We just might get there."

His face softened into a smile. "Good."

"So. The sleigh. Unless you've got some other task you're going to insist on."

"No, Kitty-Rose. We're good."

He was going to do it. He was going to build her the sleigh of her dreams. The relief was dizzying in its intensity. But ... "It's going to be tight. We've got less than a fortnight. And I know you're busy—"

"I might have already started."

What? Shock had her without a single response.

"Why do you think I was out on the road to Redthorn? I was checking dimensions with Fred."

Relief was swept away by disbelief, and then indignation. Her jaw dropped. A sound of shock left her mouth. After pretending he wouldn't do it, making her jump through all those hoops, leaving her to stew and worry about it …

"You bastard!" She pounced, flailing at him with her fists, only half joking. "You *bastard*."

His arms came around her, pulled her in close against his chest. She could hear him chuckling against her hair, and she let out a peal of laughter too, though she was still more scandalised than amused. She breathed him in – earth and wood and man – then rested her cheek against his chest, hearing his heart thumping loud and fast like her own. She closed her eyes, just for a moment.

Then pulled back, just enough to pretend-glare up at him. "I'm never going to forgive you for that."

He was smiling outright – at her – and it almost stopped her heart. "Alright, Kitty-Rose, never forgive me then."

The smile changed as they stared at one another. Her breath caught in her throat; her pulse thundered in her ears. Her hands travelled from his chest to his shoulders, and Lord, the strength in them. His hands had closed around her waist, his fingers sure and warm. He was holding her, and it felt like something she'd been missing, something she'd longed for, ached for, all these years. He was so warm, it seeped into her bones. Something white-hot flared in her heart.

She'd feel stupidly, ridiculously vulnerable if not for the darkness of his eyes, the colour high on his cheekbones and on his neck, the pulse she'd just seen throbbing further down. Her gaze dropped to his mouth; she pressed forward, lifted her face.

A sharp crashing sound.

She tensed and looked behind her. "Mum? Are you okay?"

"Fine," was her only answer.

She gazed back at Sam; he squeezed gently and let her go.

"I better get going." His voice was a gravelly rasp.

She didn't want him to, but she nodded. She'd better check on Sophie. That 'fine' had sounded anything but.

"Come and see me after work tomorrow. I'll show you what I've got."

"Okay."

He smiled, broad. Wolfish almost. "Okay."

She closed the door after him, took a deep shaky breath. What the hell had just happened? Had she almost kissed Sam Wells?

Held against him, she'd had the strangest thought, that she could stay like that forever.

Except that she couldn't. Who was she kidding? This was Sam Wells.

She didn't know what was going on but—

Another crash.

She raced to Sophie's room and opened the door to find her rummaging through her huge sack, carelessly tossing items over her shoulder, eyes flashing.

"Mum!" Kitty tried to grab her wrists. "Stop!"

"It's got to be in here somewhere," she muttered.

"What does?"

"You can't go to that parade unless we can find it."

"What?"

"Your red ribbon."

A toy car went flying against the wall. "Mum, stop!" She managed to wrench the sack away from her mother. "This is ridiculous. Can't you just empty it onto the floor?"

Sophie breathed out, a look of astonishment on her face. "Doesn't work like that, Catherine."

Kitty jiggled the bag. It did appear to be empty.

"You stick your hand in."

Kitty appraised the sack apprehensively, then shrugged and shoved a hand in. She couldn't feel anything – her mother must have emptied it with her manic tossing of things. Then her fingers brushed against something delightful and satiny. Gooseflesh whispered all over her; her breath came out in a rush. She pulled it out, and there it was, in her hand.

A length of lustrous, gleaming ribbon.

Her mother smiled. "Now you can go to the parade."

12

"I wish I'd known you could make costumes like this!" Delia surveyed her class, spinning cartwheels and tumbling around in their elf outfits, squeals of delight and excitement ringing out at each turn.

"It's all Sophie. I just did a little dyeing."

Sophie had made the costumes in record time, working on them late into the night. Kitty-Rose had piled them into a bag and walked them to the church hall, dispensing as well as she could based on size.

They all fit perfectly. Of course.

"Could you make the ones for our autumn festival next year?"

Kitty-Rose froze, unsure of how to answer.

"We'll pay you," Delia added quickly. "Not much – not what they're worth – but something."

Any payment would have to come from parents. Who were probably already stretched from the cost of ballet lessons. Which Delia was probably undercharging for in the first place. But with Sophie's skill and their stock of fabric, it wouldn't take much to put them together. "I'll talk to Sophie. If you don't mind us using old fabric, like we did for these elf ones … We wouldn't need to make much to cover costs."

"Great." Delia's smile was huge. "I really appreciate that. And then maybe ... the Eisteddfod too?"

"When's the Eisteddfod?"

"Not till September."

September. Would she even still be here? She smiled against a strange pang she couldn't place. "Yeah. Sure." Sophie'd be here, and they'd be able to use up more of the old fabric, if nothing else.

A gleeful shout had them turning their attention back to the kids.

"Careful, Cynthia. We don't want any tears!" Delia turned back to Kitty. "They really are stunning. You should sell them. Mail order, maybe. Or into a store in Melbourne."

"Maybe." Not something she'd considered before.

"Okay, children. Time to take them off. Careful now! No tears."

"How's the routine coming along, anyway?"

Delia beamed a proud smile. "They're doing so well. We'll definitely be ready for the day. And the rehearsal."

They'd decided on a dress rehearsal the day before the parade – mostly to make sure the kids were happy up on the tray. Fred'd be driving really slowly, but they didn't want anyone falling off. "Excellent."

Kitty-Rose gave Delia another smile. There was something she wanted to ask her, but she didn't know how to broach it. She looked again towards the elves, helping each other with their costumes. Sophie had catered for their little fingers, making them easy to put on and take off.

"Oh, I can't control myself any longer!"

Kitty swung to face Delia, whose eyes were glowing with curiosity.

"I've been dying to ask: What's going on with you and Sam?"

"Nothing." Her automatic response sounded defensive, but it was true. Not yet, anyway.

Delia made a not-buying-it face. "I saw you in his truck the other day."

Did she still harbour feelings of her own? Was she upset, angry? But examining her face, all Kitty saw was curiosity. "My car broke down; he gave me a lift back to town. He was just being nice. Like he always is."

Delia rolled her eyes. "Saint Sam."

"Saint Sam," Kitty agreed with a wry chuckle.

Delia leaned in close. There was a hint of mischief in her smile. "He doesn't kiss like a saint."

A low flutter started in her belly, but she offered primly, "I wouldn't know." Delia had paved the way for what Kitty had wanted to ask. She drummed her fingers on her folded arm, working up to it. "Do you think you'll get back together?"

Delia gave a quick startled glance then laughed. "Not a chance. He's great but we're better as friends."

"So how'd you end up together?"

"Friendship. Convenience. Lack of other options." She smiled, but there was a touch of sadness in it. "It was hard when I first came back. With the injury and all, I was pretty despondent. Susie was amazing. I know she can be a bit … you know. But she really took care of me. She invited me out all the time, refused to take no for an answer, and it was just what I needed. Sam was often there too, and … I mean, we've known each other all our lives. We just kind of fell into it, you know? And we might have even ended up together. But something changed. About a year-and-a-half ago," she said pointedly, eyes twinkling.

When she'd moved back to town. But that had to be a coincidence, didn't it?

"When he said we needed to talk, I knew what was coming. And when he explained that he thought the world of me, but our engagement couldn't continue, I felt … relieved."

"Really?"

She nodded. "We weren't right together but I could see us getting married anyway. Especially with all the expectations."

"Lynette."

Delia laughed. "Honestly, my parents were no better."

"Lynette still thinks you might end up together. I just want to make sure that …"

"That I wasn't still carrying a torch for him?" Delia laughed. "No.

Really no." She tilted her head, gave Kitty an arch look. "I knew there was something going on."

"There isn't." Her mouth quirked. "Yet."

SAM WAS WAITING when she arrived at his shop after work that evening. Leaning over his desk, he appeared to be examining paper-work, but something in the lines of his body – tense and alert – told her he wasn't really paying attention to the page.

When he raised his head and saw her approaching, he straightened. His hair had a dampness to it, his skin a sheen … Had he gone home and showered?

And the way he was looking at her – intense, expectant.

She almost melted into a puddle. How did he do this to her?

He smiled – small, barely there – and tilted his head in the direction of the workshop. "Come on through."

She followed, close behind, as he opened the door to the work-shop. She brushed past him, and made the mistake of glancing up as she passed, at those warm brown and amber eyes focused on her. She was immediately flooded with heat. It spread across her neck, her chest – fire of the most delicious kind.

Oh Lord.

"Follow me."

There was something intimate in his tone, in the way he looked over his shoulder at her, slight smile pulling at the corners of his mouth. Her stomach clenched.

And then she saw it. He'd cleared a space – a large space – to house the frame for the sleigh. Oh! It was going to be perfect. She rushed past him, walked up and down the length of one side. "It's exactly what I had in mind."

The frame comprised two long, low lengths for the sides, a front piece that curved, up to about her waist, and a higher curved back. The whole thing would sit on the tray, providing a frame over which all the custom coverings would be draped. She ran her hands over the smooth, heavy metal of the front curve. "What Sophie's making is going to work fantastic with this."

"She's started? I haven't even given her the specs sheet."

She grinned at him. "I think you'll find it won't be a problem."

Sophie's designs always fit; it was part of her Knack.

Sam started to explain how the pieces fit together, the various features he'd incorporated, welding technique he'd used, how he'd tested for safety aspects, and she tried to listen, but all she could concentrate on were his hands – big and sure, gliding along the metal, as he inserted and then unlinked various parts. At the end of the day, she had full confidence – if Sam said the sleigh was good to go, it was.

"It's perfect. I love it," she repeated when he'd finished. She still had her hands on the frame, like she couldn't bear to let it go.

"Great," he said after a beat. He shifted to lean against one of the long, wooden counters that stretched the length of the brick wall.

They stood in silence a few moments. She should drag her gaze away, but she couldn't. Every second that passed, it got just a little harder to breathe.

"Fred called in to see it today as well."

She raised a brow at him.

"He's changed his mind on being Santa."

She stilled. "But he won't let anyone else drive his tractor." If the whole thing were to fall over now …

Sam shrugged. "I said I'd do it. He agreed to that."

She took a long drag, exhaled slowly. "Thanks, Sam. You're a good guy."

Another beat, like a held breath. "Like I keep telling you, I'm not that good."

She grinned. "Well, you know I'm not good at all."

"Thank heavens for that."

A long, heavy moment dragged out. They were done. She'd seen the frame; that's why she'd come. She could go now. Say thank you and goodnight and flee back to safety. But she didn't.

She didn't want to go.

She walked ever so slowly towards him, hand trailing over the sleigh. The large space reverberated with the sound of her heels, the slow click as she walked. He watched her – not saying or doing anything beyond watching. Their gazes were locked until she walked past where he stood. Then her back was to him, hand still trailing over the sleigh as she went, and she swore she could *feel* his gaze on her, hot and heavy as the sun. Blood thumping in her ears, she rounded the corner, then the next one, turning her head back to find him still watching.

Anticipation and excitement built as she made her way back to him. But she didn't hurry, and he didn't move an inch.

The look in his eyes had heat climbing across her cheeks. Her heart went into overdrive, she felt like she might explode out of her skin. "What am I if I'm not a witch?"

"Enchantress, maybe. Beautiful and beguiling. Sent to earth to torment mere mortals." A hint of a smile played at the corners of his mouth.

Her footsteps slowed as she neared him again. Then stopped.

One beat. Two.

Then she took her hand from the metal, and before she could even begin to comprehend her actions, stepped foolishly, recklessly forward, into his space.

It was a leap of faith that made her feel almost untethered, but his arms came to her waist, held her steady. Hands on his chest, her gaze roamed over his face. His hair was still slightly damp and spiky, his jaw was cleanly shaved. Her fingers itched with need to touch, to feel for herself.

He beat her to it. Lifting a hand, he traced a gentle finger down her cheek, over her jaw, down her neck.

She tipped her head back and shuddered, eyelids fluttering briefly. "I thought we hated each other."

"Did you?" he murmured.

She tilted her head back, opened her eyes. "You know what your mum reminded me of the other day?" She was so light-headed, a part of her was surprised she could still form words.

He stared at her in that focused way of his.

"When you broke it off with Delia ... it was a couple of weeks after I moved back."

A smile flashed then disappeared. "Sounds about right."

It was terrifying, how she felt right now. The only thing that made it bearable was the thought that maybe he felt the same. "Yeah?"

"I'm crazy about you, Kitty-Rose. Maybe I shouldn't be, but I am."

She drew in a breath. "Shouldn't be? Because I'm a Frost?"

He made a clicking sound with his tongue. "Because you burn so bright, it's blinding. You're made for bigger and better things than I ... than Woodleigh can offer. I've got no business starting something with someone like you."

He was right; she was leaving. And while that thought was usually her sole source of hope, this time, the idea of it fell flat. "I'll be here a while. Even if we win, it'll take a while to fix up Main Street and turn the shop around."

"So?" Such a little word, yet so long and drawn out, and loaded with so many questions.

In answer, she pressed closer, tighter into his embrace, winding her arms around his neck and going to her tiptoes. She was flush against him, against his big, broad warmth. She could barely breathe she was overcome at his closeness.

He tightened his hold. She let her gaze trail ever so slowly over his face. Watched the light in his brown eyes turn gold.

"Sooo. Don't be a saint, Sam."

There was a pause that seemed to last a long, long time.

And then his head dropped.

The second their lips touched, a spark exploded in her; all the breath left her lungs. She was stunned at the sensation. It' wasn't like she'd never been kissed before. She'd been engaged to Frank for two years. But it hadn't been so ... transporting. A hot slide of tongue sent her world into room-spinning giddiness and she whimpered.

Delia was right. He didn't kiss like a saint.

It was deep and passionate, and everything she'd ever wanted. She was in a stupor of bliss, blood rushing like a river through her veins. Her hands speared into thick hair.

When he drew back, she groaned. She opened her eyes. "Kiss me again?"

"Whenever you want, Kitty-Rose." His voice was as low and gravelly as she'd ever heard it; his eyes were dark, dark brown, flamed within like a volcano.

"What if I want it all the time?"

The corners crinkled. "Works for me."

A sound had them snapping apart. The door to the workshop. Someone had come in.

She attempted to calm her breathing, cool her blood, while she waited for the person to appear.

Lynette. Her lips pursed, eyes narrowed. How much had she seen?

Kitty edged further away from Sam. Her hands came to her hips. "Sam was just showing me what he's got."

Lynette's brows went skyward. A quick glance at Sam revealed a wry half-grin.

"For the float." She laid a hand on the sleigh, took it off again. "I better get going."

Sam reached behind to the counter and handed her a sheet of paper. She took it, looked down. Specs. "Thanks. I'll let you know if Sophie has any problems with anything."

"Night, Kitty-Rose," he said, in that honeyed gravel voice.

Lord, even now, with Lynette standing six feet away, she wanted to turn back to him. "Night, Sam. Lynette."

13

She was pleased for the time alone.

Just for today, she was pleased there were no customers.

She'd finished all her dyeing – Sophie was in the workroom out the back, working on the cover – so there wasn't much more Kitty had to do for the float. She'd spent a few hours tending to the store – going over stock, tidying shelves, dusting anywhere that looked like it could use it. Now she was sorting through the buttons rack, making sure she had a handle on what they had.

And trying to absorb the upheaval of the past two weeks.

It had been an upheaval. So much of what she thought no longer seemed to apply.

Including … whatever it was she had with Sam.

After what had happened in high school, she'd never imagined something happening between them was a possibility. And maybe it shouldn't be happening, but she couldn't bring herself to regret it.

The way she felt when she was with him … When he kissed her, she lit up inside, became a being of pure, radiant energy. She forgot where she was, what day it was. Hell, she forgot her own name.

He'd always been her hero. Which sounded silly, and Lord knows, she was no damsel in distress needing saving but … as much he sent her pulse racing and blood rushing through her veins, she also felt safe with him.

From his big, strong body to his blazing integrity to the way he cared for Woodleigh and everyone in it … She thought maybe he even cared for her.

He'd helped change things for her in this town. Who would have thought she'd be talking to Susie again? That she'd be plotting the production of a brochure with Lynette? Maybe he was right when he said that she herself was part of the reason she felt like an outsider. And she still did, but … things had changed. And part of that was him.

And that's why, if she was truly sensible, she shouldn't have let anything start between them. It was just supposed to be temporary, a couple of months, while she was still here, but she was going to be in too deep before she knew it.

She suspected she already was.

Leaving was going to hurt. It did already, in a weird way. This recent pang that sprung up in her when she thought about it.

She really needed someone to talk to. It was times like these she missed Eleanor the most. She always—

Kitty jerked upright as she heard the door to the shop opening. Turning around, she saw Susie, just inside.

"Hi, Susie."

"Hi." She looked around her, and Kitty realised it was probably her first time in the store in at least twenty years. Perhaps she'd come in with her mother as a small child, but not since.

"After a new frock?"

"Ha," she laughed, wandering slowly closer. "I will come in, I promise, but today I just wanted to talk."

That sounded serious. What on earth about?

They were still on strange footing. Not yet friends, but no longer enemies. Things were a lot better but still uncomfortable, especially given their history.

"Thanks for asking Mum to be Mrs Claus, by the way."

Kitty smiled. "She was happy about it?"

"I think so. Still a bit snooty, but you know Mum. She's always a little snooty."

They swapped a smile.

Kitty picked out a new bottle of buttons, emptied it carefully onto a piece of felted cloth on the counter. "She's a better choice for Mrs Claus. I don't know what I was thinking when I suggested I should play the part. I just wanted to win."

"Well, we all want to win." Susie stepped closer, then dropped her elbows on the counter beside her, tilting her head sideways, earnest eyes on Kitty. "I don't want the Emporium to fail. The general store is always busy, I never hear the bloody end of Sam's success, and now Josie is marrying Roy ... I don't want to be the one who couldn't make it work."

Kitty offered a sympathetic smile and noted down a number in her book. "You've got some great merchandise. There's nothing else like the Emporium in town. You just need some customers."

"Yes. That's it. It's really important that we win. We need that money."

Kitty picked up the buttons with nimble fingers. "Everything's coming together. Sam showed me what he's done for the sleigh, and it's fantastic. Delia says the elves are doing great. And I know whatever Sophie comes up with will be amazing ..."

Susie sighed. "You've got this town believing that we can win, Kitty."

"Good. I'll just have to make sure we do."

They swapped another smile.

"Who's the judge again?"

"The Belleville mayor."

"Do you know him? From when you lived in Belleville?"

"Not really. I've met him once or twice. That's about it."

Susie picked up one of the waiting bottles of buttons, turned it upside down and righted it again. "I've been thinking—"

A noise reached them – Susie jumped, almost fumbling the bottle.

"Just Sophie," Kitty said. "She's out back working on the cover for the sleigh."

She sent Kitty a look, then went back to playing with the bottle. "Your mum …" She bit her lip. "She has it too, right?"

They could only be talking about her Knack.

Kitty-Rose nodded. She wondered what everyone in town thought. Some knew, some didn't. Susie more than anyone had reason to know hers existed and how powerful it was – she'd been subject to the full brute force of it all those years ago.

"And your grandmother?"

She nodded again. "Eleanor told me stories about her Knack. She had a book. Fairy tales. When she read from it, she could make things happen. All sorts of things. Like making sick people better and finding things that were lost. Good things."

"Mum told me about it too. She'd heard it from her mother. She said everyone knew that if you were ever in a pickle, you could go to Mary. She must have been pretty amazing."

"Yeah."

"And you've got your Knack." She met Kitty's gaze then lowered her head. "Does anyone at Carmody's know about it?"

"No." She'd never told Frank. She'd never told anyone. Why would she? Part of the reason for her moving out of Woodleigh was to free herself of the burden of her family name and everything it meant. She returned a bottle to the rack. "No point. I don't use it anymore."

Susie's gaze went straight to hers. "What if you did?"

"Sorry?"

She drew in a deep breath, as if gathering strength. "I mean, we want to win, right?"

Kitty's hands froze on the new bottle, an unsettling sensation roiled in her belly. "I really think we have a shot. You should see how cute the elves look, and they've been working so hard on their routine."

She opened the bottle onto the cloth, counting, if only to distract herself.

Susie nodded then traced a finger over a knot of wood in the workbench. "But, you know … If you know who the judge is, you could … I mean, you have a Knack and all. Why not use it?"

Kitty felt like she'd been hit in the head. A cold sensation speared through her. She stared ahead, at a patch of sunlight that had somehow made it through into this dark shop. Disturbed by her dusting, dust motes hung suspended in the air.

Perhaps she should have thought of doing just that but she hadn't. She looked back to Susie, who was still staring at her.

"I mean, there's a good chance we're going to win anyway. Everyone's been working so hard … What would be the harm in, you know, giving a little nudge? Just to make sure."

Her back went taut. She couldn't find a single response. All this time, she'd worried people would hate and fear her for her Knack, and here was someone asking her to use it.

Some of her horror must have been on her face, because Susie rushed to speak. "Not much of a nudge! Not completely changing his mind. But think about it, Kitty. If he's on the fence, if it's going to be a tie … who's the mayor of Belleville going to give to it? Belleville or Woodleigh? But if you gave a little nudge, he might choose us."

"Like I said, I don't use it anymore." A quake had stolen into her voice.

"But you said it slipped out sometimes."

"By accident. I don't mean to."

"No one would have to know. You didn't tell Frank; no one would suspect."

Something in Kitty-Rose broke apart. Was this what the town thought of her, that she'd do something like that? Is that what they expected; that she should do it? Her skin crawled at the idea; she felt icky and uncomfortable. She needed fresh air. "I better get out back and check on Sophie."

Whatever Susie saw in Kitty's expression made her heave a sigh. "Oh well. Just think about it." But she gave Kitty a tight little smile, like this was their little secret.

Kitty didn't want to have that kind of secret.

~

IT WAS A BEAUTIFUL SUMMER EVENING, with a brisk breeze that made her glad for the light apple-green cardigan she'd added around her shoulders.

She'd called Sam earlier at work and asked him to meet her at the bridge in the park after dinner. She waited now on the small, wooden arch over the gurgle of the creek, lost in the achingly clear water running over the smooth rocks of the bed. The snows had long since melted, but the creek was still high and rapid; it'd been a wet spring.

It was pretty here, there was no denying it. Graceful bright green willows mixed with silver-grey gums lined the banks. Over the hills in the distance, streaks of pink cloud made for a gorgeous summer sunset. A radiant and serene early summer evening.

Still, she couldn't shake the tension in her back.

A snap of a twig.

She turned her head and saw him approaching in dark jeans and a button-up short-sleeve shirt in a red-and-green plaid. Her heart flipped before starting up a steady thud. So tall, so broad, with those warm brown eyes – just the sight of him did strange things to her insides.

She waited on the bridge, uncertain. How was this going to work? She'd just needed to talk to him, she hadn't thought through meeting in a public place. Should she go to him? But before she knew it, he'd joined her. His hands were cupping her face and he was kissing her. Every cell in her body rose up and pirouetted.

"Evening, Kitty-Rose," he said in his low rumble.

Her heart thumped, hot and staccato. Truly, it was too much how it beat for him.

As the haze of reaction cleared a little, she had the presence of mind to glance around the park. It appeared to be empty. She exhaled in relief.

He glanced around quickly. "All of a sudden you care what people think?" A small smile played at the corners of his mouth.

The idea clearly struck him as funny. She looked around again. "I just …" She hadn't realised how she'd feel about their budding romance until this very moment, but she wanted to protect it; the new and precious bloom. "Can we keep it to ourselves for the moment?"

His head tilted, his gaze narrowed.

"It's new, is all. I don't know how people will react."

"It's none of their business. Besides, they'll be fine."

She bit in her sigh. She only wished that were the case. "You're probably right," she said with a smile. "Walk with me?" She stepped down from the bridge, onto the path that ran along the creek, heading away from town.

He took her hand. The feel of his hand around hers and the idea of someone seeing them emptied the air from her lungs.

Even off the bridge and with the trees lining the path, they weren't protected from view. Anyone walking in the vicinity would be able to see them. And houses backed along the river on the other side. While there was some coverage, it wouldn't take much for someone watering their backyard or gossiping over the fence to spy them.

She just didn't want to share this. As soon as the town knew, it wouldn't be the same. She'd have to fight to protect it. He might not know it, but she did.

But his hand around hers, its weight and warmth – she couldn't say no to that.

"I'm finished with your car," he said, breaking the silence. "It's running well now. Should stand up. So long as you bring it back for servicing every so often."

She glanced sideways at him, smiled. "Thank you."

"Was Sophie okay the other night?"

"Just Sophie stuff." She looked up at a pair of colourful parrots chittering among themselves around their gumtree home – a hole made by a fallen branch. "This time of year gets to her."

"So that's not what you wanted to talk about?" He cut a glance in her direction, all hot brown eyes. "Or are you going to make my day and tell me 'talking' is just a euphemism?"

She sent him a look of apology. She wouldn't mind making out all evening either. But there were things she needed his input on. "It's about the parade. Do you think we have a shot?"

"Sure." He shrugged, squeezed her hand gently. "Why wouldn't we?"

"Because we're from Woodleigh." She cast a glance to her side to find him watching her. "It's a lot of money and the mayor of Belleville is the judge. Maybe they'd prefer to keep it in their own town."

He shrugged. "We can't worry about that."

She nodded but couldn't quite meet his eyes. "I'm sure the other floats have upped their game too. It might be close; maybe even a tie between us and one of the Belleville floats."

He let loose a wry half-chuckle. "You're overthinking it."

She bit her lip. "But don't you agree that in that case they'd give it to the Belleville float?"

"Couldn't say, Kitty-Rose." He held her hand a little tighter but he sounded … bemused. When she'd asked him to walk with her, this probably wasn't what he had in mind.

"Well, you have to admit, that wouldn't be fair. After all our hard work!" She turned her head, towards the rush of the creek, breathed in clean, cool air, and considered how to phrase it. "The thing is, I could do something about it." She met his gaze briefly, then looked away again. "I know who the judge is. I could pay him a visit. Make sure he's inclined to treat us fairly."

He didn't say anything. When she dared turn to him again, he met her gaze with assessing brown eyes, but he still didn't respond.

"Just to make the playing field even."

He strode alongside her, holding her hand, radiating heat she could feel in the cool evening. "So why don't you?" he asked eventually, voice quiet and carefully neutral.

She almost stopped walking. She'd not been expecting that.

"Well, I-I don't know," she started. "I just … I mean, it'd just be making it fair, but …"

She bit her lip. When Susie had suggested it, Kitty'd been so shocked that someone was actually recommending she use her Knack that she hadn't got much further in her thinking. Susie had made it sound reasonable, but it hadn't felt right at the time and saying it out loud to Sam … she was even less convinced. "Do you think that's what everyone in Woodleigh would want?"

Expect even?

His gaze narrowed. "Has someone said something to you?"

"Not as such." She wouldn't land Susie in trouble. "Why do you ask?"

"Because every other time we've discussed it, you've been strident about *not* using your Knack."

She breathed out, some of the tension leaving her shoulders. He'd clearly listened to her when she said she didn't use it, and on some level, he'd believed her. It meant a lot.

He stopped, turned her to face her. "You know what I think, Kitty-Rose?"

She looked up at him, hardly daring to breathe.

"I think you asked me to walk with you tonight, that you told me about this, so that I could tell you not to do it."

Another big breath. "So are you going to?"

His head tilted. "No." He lifted his hand, stroked the back of his index finger down her cheek in a way that made her shiver. "You don't need me to."

She exhaled, long and slow. The bad feeling that had been sitting like a lump of coal in her belly since Susie's visit disappeared. As his words sunk in, deeper and deeper, she felt a smile break across her face. "No."

But was it that simple? What about everyone else in town? Sam's shop was doing well, but many others weren't. And not everyone was a saint, always wanting to take the high road. Susie, for instance.

She turned and started walking, flicking him a smile when he took her hand again. "But if we don't win … If we have the best float but we still don't win …" How could she explain how it felt to have a Knack like hers in a small town where people knew what she could do? "Everyone's going to think it's my fault. And they'd be right, in a way. They know I can make it happen."

It was a new thing, this feeling of responsibility. And quite the burden.

"No one's going to think it's your fault. We wouldn't even have this float if it wasn't for you. And if they do, so what?"

She grimaced. "Easy for you to say. Everyone in Woodleigh loves you."

"Why do you care so much what they think?"

She wanted to lie, to say she didn't care. She'd spent eighteen months trying to prove it. Eighteen months keeping her distance, keeping to herself. Eighteen months, always with a big smile, a tough attitude and a quick quip. Eighteen months unapologetically dressing in her own style, knowing they thought it was too much. But the funny thing was, she did care. She cared a lot. She hid it, or tried to, but she did. She always had, she probably always would.

"Woodleigh's home," she settled on, and felt him squeeze her hand. She had a difficult relationship with it, but it was undeniably her home. It's not like she had another one. Nowhere else in the world would ever know her – her history, who she truly was. And didn't everyone want to feel like they had a home; somewhere they were accepted for who they really are? She wasn't, but it didn't mean she didn't yearn for it. "I've lived elsewhere. I've lived in Belleville, I've lived in Melbourne, and it's easier – it's a lot easier – but it's not the same. I can't explain it properly, but you're right, I care." She looked down at her cherry-print canvas sneakers. "I'm not stupid. I know it'll never be what I want. That's why the sooner I go again, the better."

He stopped again, this time cupping her face with both hands. His eyes were serious. "You never have to use it if you don't want to. You don't owe anyone that. And if anyone attempts to give you any grief about it … You send them to me."

She blinked, hard, as his words sunk in. Then she smiled, still a little sad. "Always were my knight in shining armour."

"Don't you forget it."

They walked in silence for another few moments before reaching the end of the path.

Sam inclined his head towards the huge old gum by the creek. And that smile … that roguish smile he got sometimes – so un-saintly, full of heat and lazy charm. It completely undid her. "I think I'm done with talking now."

He led her by the hand, down to the gum, held it as she sank into a patch of soft grass, then joined her. The tree offered privacy, as did the deepening gloam, but really, she wasn't sure she cared at this point in time.

He rested back on one hand, body turned to her, other knee up. She sat at his hip, body facing his. They were close. His heavy-lidded gaze was intense on her; the heat rising from his skin was palpable.

"Sam?" Her voice sounded strange to her own ears. Thin and strained. "Why do you think it doesn't work on you?"

"Maybe you don't want it to."

His words stole her breath.

Of course that was it. Of course she didn't want it to.

Because how could this possibly work if it did?

And 'this' – she really wanted this to work.

It struck her with the force of a body blow; a wave of energy crashing through her body; a roaring in her ears.

She was in love with him.

She was completely and absolutely in love with Sam Wells.

He'd staked out territory in her heart when she was eight and she'd never turfed him out.

The evening, even the cool muted blue of the evening sky, felt new and shocking. She felt raw, like she'd been stripped naked. With anyone else, it would be too much. But with him …

His forefinger stroked along her brow bone, just above her violet Flare.

"You know I've had no sleep in weeks." There was a hoarseness to his tone. His chest was rising and falling rapidly.

She swallowed against the sudden dryness in her mouth. "Kiss me."

His free hand came to her neck, drawing her closer, so his breath brushed her skin and she shivered, heart kicking against her ribs in the quiet of the twilight.

She was in love with him. And maybe, just maybe, it was the same for him.

14

"It hasn't sounded this good … ever." They were driving out to Fred's to pick up the tractor, and the car was all but purring. She turned to him with a smile. "Thank you."

"You're welcome. I expect to see it again in six months."

Her eyes darted to his. He'd said it as a nice thing, so she wouldn't feel bad about getting him to take another look, but she couldn't find a response. Six months … something ached inside her.

He realised why she hadn't replied a moment later, and his face shifted, like shutters coming down.

"If you're still—"

"If I'm not—"

They'd spoken at the same time.

Sam glanced out his window. "This is about where I picked Sophie up," he said after a moment. "Is she out at Redthorn again today?"

She shook her head. "She's putting the final touches on the cover." An image of how she'd left her mother had a smile rising on her cheeks. "It's so big by now, I'm surprised she can even find her way to her machine."

He grinned. "It's in one piece?"

"Pretty much. There's some extras that'll be pinned or tacked on later."

"She should go up on stage with you. When we win."

Kitty exhaled. She hadn't even thought about who would collect the cheque. "Sophie won't be there." He shot a questioning glance at her. "She doesn't leave Woodleigh."

A frown furrowed his brow. "Ever?"

She shook her head. "That's just the way it is for Sophie. She doesn't want to. In case …" In case her family came home. That's what Kitty had always assumed. She looked out over the road. "Anyway, once the float is done, she'll want to get back out to Redthorn. Focus on her Christmas cleaning and decorating."

"Big job."

He had no idea. "She has a lot of energy."

"Must be quite the sight, when it's done up."

"It is." That she could admit, despite how she'd hated those days. "Have you ever been inside?"

He met her gaze, shook his head.

"Do you want to?" She'd have to go in eventually, given the deal she'd made with Sophie. She might as well get it over with; hopefully, it wouldn't be as bad if she visited prior. She'd break the ice with Sam.

"Sure."

Instead of turning in, she drove past Fred's gates, up to the next set – the heavy brick-and-iron gates of Redthorn – and onto the long drive. It was lined with shrubs that bore long thorns and the remnants of red berries spared by the birds. Behind the house, there were cleared paddocks. Or fields, more like – Redthorn hadn't run livestock while her family had owned it. Mountains loomed in the distance. To Kitty, the whole place had a gloomy, gothic feel to it, but she wasn't sure if that was innate to the house and landscape, or just reflected her own feelings.

Memories, feelings, of another age came in like floodwaters. Dark, murky, dangerous. Her mother's great grief. The waiting; the death of hope for another year when her family's absence came crashing down again.

When the house came into view, she braked abruptly and killed the engine.

She couldn't do it; she couldn't do it.

She sensed rather than saw his confusion. Instead of explaining, she got out of the car and walked around to the front, leaned back against the bonnet. Arms across her chest, she stared at the mansion half a mile up the drive.

Sam's door opened and closed. His boots crunched on the drive, and then he was next to her, leaning back against the bonnet at her side, arm nudging against hers.

"You okay?"

She nodded, but she wasn't. "I haven't been out here for years."

"We don't have to go today," he said quietly.

Lord, this place. The weight of memories. Of people she'd never met. She knew how it'd be inside. A pristine decorated museum. A shrine to her missing grandparents and uncle.

But she'd never known them. She couldn't mourn them like her mother did.

"I hate this place. It's depressing. Just thinking about it makes me sad for weeks."

A breeze blew, sending air rustling through gum leaves. The plaintiff caw of a raven rent through the air.

"Let's go straight to Fred's," he said.

Arms crossed, she shrugged roughly. "I made a deal with Sophie, promised her I'd spend Christmas Day out here with her if she did all the sewing for the float. Might as well go now, get that first hit over with."

"You sure?"

She nodded.

He bumped his shoulder against her gently. "You know the good thing about sad?"

She shook her head.

A second later she was gently pulled to him, into his chest. It took a few moments, but she gradually let go, relaxed into him, until she was snuggled like a kitten against his solid warmth. She could just stay like this forever.

"Your mum drives a hard bargain," he said quietly.

She let out a shaky breath.

"Does she understand how you feel?"

"She doesn't usually insist. But she thinks ..." She paused, embarrassment hot on her cheeks. But Sam had been nothing but kind to her mother. "She thinks she can connect with her family out here. On Christmas Day. And this might be the last one." She drew back a little. "I mean, if they were alive, they'd be in their seventies; eighties even ... Anyway, that's why she wants me there."

He squeezed her closer. "I'll come with you. If you want."

She was so shocked she couldn't speak. Her hands went to his waist. "Don't you want to spend Christmas with your own family?"

"Kitty-Rose." There was something like admonishment in his tone. "Do you really think I wouldn't—"

She felt his body go stiff. Tilting her head up, she could see his gaze was narrowed, scrutinising something in the distance. "Is that a car?" he said.

She jerked around to stare in the direction of Redthorn. It took a moment, but then she saw it. Peeking out from the cover of a bush was the bonnet of a green sportscar.

A Jaguar, if she wasn't mistaken.

It wasn't exactly unfamiliar. In fact, she knew exactly who it belonged to. Her own gaze narrowed. What was he doing here?

"Let's go see."

They got back in her car and made their way up the drive.

She cast a quick glance at the Jaguar once she'd parked. Definitely Frank's.

The front door was unlocked. Sophie always locked up, but the key was kept under the urn to the left of the door, and Frank knew that. He'd seen when she'd brought him here.

She stepped in, striving for quiet. She didn't want to alert Frank to her presence before she'd had a chance to work out what he was doing here.

Sam followed her in, closed the door quietly behind him.

The atmosphere of the house – its great sadness – was a sinking sensation in her belly. It would usually threaten to overwhelm her, but this time, she had other things to worry about.

The sound of a muffled giggle reached her ears. She followed it – creeping past the opulent curved staircase to the formal sitting room beyond. The door was slightly ajar. She pushed it open and walked in.

Two bodies were tangled up on the green velvet chaise.

"What the hell are you doing here?" She'd never felt so outraged, so possessive. What would Sophie make of two strangers necking on the couch?

"Kitty!" Frank rolled and leaped to his feet so suddenly his companion fell to the floor.

"Thanks, Frank!" she complained as she tried to right herself and stand.

"Janice?"

"Hi, Kitty," Janice returned in a surly tone.

Janice had been Frank's girlfriend for the first two years she'd worked at Carmody's.

Apparently they were back together.

Sam joined her, and she was grateful for his steady warmth at her side.

Frank's gaze flicked between the two of them. He had the grace to look embarrassed. His hand came to the back of his neck, and his handsome face flushed beetroot. "Sorry, Kitty. I didn't think you'd mind."

"You thought wrong."

"Why would she care? It's not like anyone lives here."

She turned to the petulant woman. "This is my mother's house."

"I think you better leave." It was Sam, firm and implacable.

"Well, it's not like we were hurting anything but if you're going to be like that." Janice took Frank's hand. Frank didn't seem too thrilled about it. He shook it off, took a step forward, expression earnest, like he'd been waiting for this chance for eons. "Could I have a word, Kitty?" A pointed look at Sam. "In private?"

What could he possibly have to say to her? But she shrugged an okay.

She felt Sam stiffen at her side, but all he said was, "I'll walk Janice to the car."

Janice obviously couldn't believe what was happening – her mouth wide enough to catch a whole swarm of bees – but realising there was nothing else she could do, she followed Sam.

"Sam?" Kitty waited until he turned. "We won't be a moment."

He nodded, but there was something in his eyes. He turned and disappeared.

"I really am sorry," Frank said, as soon as they were alone. "I was under the impression that no one used this place. But when we got here, I realised …" He waved at the Christmas tree in the corner. "That was wrong."

Fair enough. She hadn't told him that her mother practically lived out here. She hadn't told him much of anything. But still … "I can't believe you brought a girl here. How many others have there been?"

"None! I swear. It's just … there's a situation with Janice."

"Don't come again, Frank. Ever."

"I won't. That I can promise." His expression was earnest. He stepped forward again. "Don't tell anyone, will you? About Janice and me?"

Her face screwed up. "Why would I?" Frank really thought he was the centre of the universe. As if she, and everyone one else in the world, walked around thinking about nothing but him all day. But something in his face – some fear – piqued her curiosity. "What's going on?"

He blew out a breath and swept his gaze around the room. Was he searching for words? How unlike gift-of-the-gab Frank. "The thing is, Janice is not one-hundred percent free of entanglements, and if word were to get out …" He pushed a hand through the floppy wave of his fringe, looked sorrowful. "Her fiancé told her he'd come for her with an axe."

Her gaze widened, her jaw fell open. "You have to go to the police."

"No!" He stepped forward, palms up. "No," he repeated more

calmly, hands coming to his hips. "That will make things worse. We have a plan, just … please don't say anything to anyone."

Her mouth quirked. "Okay. But you're going to have to find somewhere else to meet. And be careful, for heaven's sake."

"Thanks, Kitty. I really appreciate it."

She was done with this conversation. She started for the door.

He jogged a few steps, caught up with her. "It was, er, great to run into you again."

Frowning, she gave him a you've-got-to-be-kidding-me look. He was back to his exuberant, oblivious self in record time.

"Will I see you Saturday? At the parade?"

"I suppose so."

All smiles, he joined Janice in the car, waving as they set off, as if it had been some kind of organised visit.

Kitty-Rose bit her lip as she watched them disappear in a cloud of dust. Something felt off; an unease that sat deep in her belly. But she couldn't put her finger on it.

Maybe she was just edgy. She was at Redthorn, after all. She turned to Sam.

Who was assessing her intently. "What was all that about?"

There was a stiffness in his tone. Something that might even be … jealousy? "Nothing." She wanted to laugh at the absurdity of Sam feeling in any way jealous of Frank. "He was just saying he and Janice have to keep their relationship to themselves for the moment."

His gaze narrowed on the direction they'd driven off in. "Like us."

What was that supposed to mean? She studied his face. Something was going on with him. "Sam?"

"You seemed pretty upset in there."

"Of course. He shouldn't be at Redthorn." She felt herself getting indignant all over again.

"That's all there is to it?"

It took her a moment to get his meaning. "Sam. Jesus. You think I'm jealous of Frank and Janice?"

He shrugged. "You were going to marry him at one stage. Not that long ago."

She let out a long breath, stared out over the fields. She hadn't told anyone what happened. They'd drawn their own conclusions, and she'd let them. She met his gaze. "I was the one who ended it with Frank. Everyone thinks it was him, but it wasn't. It was me."

Hands low on his hips; he was listening.

"Took me a long time to realise I liked everything about Frank except Frank. I liked the attention I got from being with him. People would stare at the two of us like we were film stars or something. I liked his father. I never knew mine, and Arthur was really nice to me. I liked the job, the department store, the feeling of having a place I fit. I liked all the plans we made for Carmody's. You know I was training to be a buyer? I thought I'd be flying to Paris, Milan—"

"Is that what Frank told you? Carmody's was going to be stocking only the best from France and Italy?"

She laughed. "That's what he told me. What can I say? I was young and naïve. I wanted to believe him. What I'm saying is, we had a whole life planned, and that's what I loved; not him. It just took me a while to realise the difference." She looked between his eyes, then let out a long sigh. "Funnily enough, it was the day I brought him out here. I didn't want to, but he'd been badgering for ages. Apparently there's stories about Redthorn even in Belleville. I'd never taken him home. He'd never met Sophie and Eleanor. I knew it'd be over the second he did."

Sam's gaze narrowed.

She shrugged. "I took him anyway." She gave a little wry laugh. "It's funny, for ages, I thought it was because of the way he looked at Sophie … Took me ages to realise it was the way she looked at him. She didn't say anything; she didn't have to. Once I'd seen him through her eyes, I couldn't unsee. All it took was that one look, and I wondered why I'd stayed engaged to him as long as I had."

Sam looked down the drive, to where the dust was gradually resettling. "Fancy car he's got."

Her mouth pulled up at a corner. "Yep." All style, no substance. That was Frank.

He looked back at her. There was still something raw and vulnerable in his expression, something that made her heart ache for him.

She was about to say something, something she couldn't take back, but he beat her to it.

"Let's go get the tractor."

15

"One, two, three ... Go."

She and Sam were standing in the centre of the tray, next to the folded-up cover. They slowly unfolded it, smoothing it out to the edges and over the sides as they went, Sam working towards the back of the float, Kitty towards the front.

The red velour fabric gleamed like a ruby in the sun. The gold cord running along the edge and up over the rim of the front curve added a regal touch. Sophie had also made the throne gold – not that Mrs Claus was likely to do much sitting.

After they left Redthorn, Sam had driven the tractor and tray to the garage, parking it in the lot out the back. Kitty left him and his guys to install the sleigh frame and went home to help Sophie get everything ready. There was so much to bring, Sam had had to drive a truck around to pick up them up.

As they covered the frame in fabric, Kitty's excitement built. Everything fit perfectly.

Sam had the trickier end – he had to drape fabric over a throne, three Christmas trees and the much higher back curve of the sleigh. No surprise, she finished first. "Can I help?" she called up the sleigh.

"No. Go help your mum," he called back.

She sat on the edge of the tray and jumped to the ground. Sophie was working quickly, tacking big, fluffy clouds along the bottom of the red fabric.

"Over there, Catherine. No, that other bag."

She peered in to see canes and red bows. Not part of her original sketch.

"You know how I feel," Sophie said. "Can't have too much Christmas."

Kitty grinned, picked up a needle and thread from another bag, and trailed in her mother's wake, following her instructions to tack on two crossing canes and a red bow at intervals along the sides of the tray.

She'd worked her way up one side when something had her leaning closer. This bow … it was slightly smaller than the others; a different red. A darker, more intense red. More lustrous than anything in this world. "Mum! What's this doing on here?"

Sophie didn't even lift her head from her stitching. "I told you; it's time."

Well, who was Kitty to argue with the ravens? She crossed her arms, bit her lip. But what did that mean for the parade? Her mouth twisted. She supposed she'd figure it out. The ribbon was supposed to be a boon, after all.

Finished, Sam jumped from the tray, landing easily on the ground, and walked towards them. When he reached Kitty, he slung an arm around her shoulders, then one around Sophie's as well. Uncertain, Kitty darted a glance across his chest to her mother, but she was smiling.

They all stared for a moment at the finished product.

It was stunning. Resplendent. As if lit from within, the sleigh glimmered red and gold, like something out of imperial Russia. The throne was incredible, gold with ornate patterns all over it sewn in by Sophie. The three trees rose high in a dark pine green to span the back edge, and white clouds lined the bottom of the sleigh – as if it were racing through the night to deliver presents.

All it needed now was Mrs Claus and the elves.

Bit by bit, the vision she'd forged a fortnight ago had come to life. And it was mostly thanks to the two people next to her.

Her eyes filled. She turned and hugged Sam, then her mother. "Thank you. Both of you. It's the best thing I've ever seen."

"It was your idea – and your drive – that got us here," Sam said. "We're a good team."

"Yep." She blinked, hard. "We're going to win."

He grinned at her and turned to her mother. "Can you make it to the dress rehearsal, Sophie? It'd be great to see you there."

"When is it again?"

"Tomorrow afternoon."

Kitty was sure she'd say no, but instead she nodded, and turned to lift one more oversized bag. "Ornaments. For the trees. They just need to be pinned on."

"I'll do them."

Sam took the bag and climbed back up onto the tray, taking off his shoes and standing on the back curve to reach the tops of the trees. The globes went on with care – well-spaced, even colour distribution.

Man with a method. Kitty grinned.

He gave a grunt of exertion, reaching high and revealing a large swathe of toned abdomen. Kitty's cheeks heated, her mouth went dry. Out of the corner of her eye, she saw her mother looking at her, one eyebrow raised.

She blushed harder. Maybe she was a little obvious. "He's … Um. We're …"

"There's not many men worthy of you, Catherine."

She stifled a groan. Here they went with the princess talk again. A fierce defensiveness rose in her. "Sam's more than worthy. I don't want to hear any nonsense about him not being a prince."

Her mother shot her a quick, sharp glance, then smiled again. "As I was saying."

Sam stepped off the frame and started to fix on the lower globes. The ornaments, in bright purples, blues and gold, only added to the overall splendour. She hugged her arms around herself. "It really is amazing, Mum. You've excelled yourself."

"So long as you remember our deal."

Kitty rolled her eyes. "You've certainly kept your end of the bargain; I'm not about to renege on mine." She turned her attention back to Sam. He noticed and grinned. "Sam might come too. On Christmas Day. Just for a while."

There was a slight pause, then, "Very well."

The breath she didn't realise she'd been holding came rushing out. "You don't mind?"

"Why would I mind? It'd be nice having people out there; a proper Redthorn Christmas. Speaking of which … I've got things I need to get to." She cast an appreciative glance at Sam, crouching as he attached the final globes. "I like your young man, Catherine."

Warmth ran through her like honey. "I like him too."

"Well. See you at home." She turned rapidly, as was her way, and headed towards the gate to the lot.

"Want a lift out, Mum?" Kitty called after her.

Sophie didn't turn, just lifted one hand and pushed it down again in a don't-worry-about-it motion.

Finished, Sam jumped down off the tray and came to where she was standing. "Sophie's off?"

Kitty nodded. "Back to Redthorn. She's behind with her own preparations." She met his gaze. "I said you might pop around on Christmas Day. If you still want to, that is."

"I want to." His eyes burned hot, turned amber by the sun.

She smiled.

"How's she going to do when you leave again?"

A sharp pang inside her chest. "She'll be fine." Sophie was smart and resourceful; she'd figure it out. But if she was honest, Kitty didn't want to leave her. "I've been training her on how to run the shop."

"How's that going?" His tone was sardonic.

Kitty chuckled. "About as well as you'd imagine." She shrugged. "I don't know. Maybe I'll hire someone to do it. Or come back once a month to do the books. Melbourne's only half a day's drive."

It sounded good; it sounded reasonable. But thinking about it, her heart sank.

She turned away, pretending to examine the float to cover a frown. A sinking heart – that wasn't right, was it? She wanted to leave. She'd thought of little else these past eighteen months. Counting down the days.

But that was before. Before things had changed here. Before Sam.

For just a second, her mind became a whirlpool of possibilities, visions she hadn't dared allow herself to dream rushing through her. A life in Woodleigh. It wouldn't be perfect. It'd be hard in some ways, if she were to stay. She'd always be a Frost – no getting around that one. Even married, she'd always be a Frost in this town.

But there'd be rewards too. Such rich, sweet rewards.

Him coming home from the garage, her from the shop. What could she do with Manson's if she stayed? And she'd have more time with Sophie.

Making dinners, talking through their days. Lord, she hoped Sam could cook.

Long nights together.

Waking next to each other.

A whole life.

"Big city still calls, hey?"

She stiffened. His arms came around her from behind. "It's okay, Kitty-Rose. I know you're going. I get it. I'm not Frank. I can't give you all those things he promised."

A horrified sound emerged from her mouth. That's what he thought this was? "I don't want you to be Frank."

"You said it, out at Redthorn. That you hadn't loved him, but you'd loved the life you had. I can't give you that."

She had said that, and she'd meant it. She'd loved that life – at the time. And she'd always thought that's what she wanted – a big, exciting future. But now, something else had started to take shape. A different life – smaller in some ways, but bigger in others. Richer, deeper. A life where people really knew her – and all the good things that came with that, and all the bad.

The bad. Living here, with her name and her history and her Knack …

Would it be possible? She didn't know.

She needed more time before she said anything. She wouldn't make promises she couldn't keep. She leaned her head back against his chest, put her hands over his forearms, still wrapped around her. "There's nothing I want that you can't give me, Sam."

That at least was true.

"I'm not even handsome, remember?"

She let out a huff of shocked laughter. "You know why I said that?" She took his hand, moved it from her waist, up her body, to lay across her heart. "I was trying to work out why, how, you made my heart beat so fast it almost burst out of my chest. No one is more handsome to me than you."

He leaned down, kissed the side of her head.

"If you weren't such a pillar of the community, you could come with me."

"To Melbourne?" He sounded surprised.

"Well, sure. To start with."

He breathed out. "I'd give anything to see the world with you."

A curl of delight spiralled through her. "Where would we go first?"

"Greece."

"Greece?" She laughed.

He made a sound, a low huff that curled up around her spine. "What's so funny about that?"

She shook her head, a smile on her lips. "Nothing."

"I've never told anyone that before." There was a rare hint of vulnerability in his tone.

"It's perfect. I'd be honoured." She turned, pressed her forehead into his chest, wrapped her arms around his waist. "Melbourne's only a few hours away. If I come up here once a month, and you come down …"

"Yeah."

But they were grasping at straws and she knew it.

~

When the knock came at the door early the next morning, Kitty was still in a bathrobe, hair wet from the shower.

"Sophie?" she called from her bedroom. "Can you get that?"

But there was no answer. On a fine summer morning like this, Sophie was probably long gone.

She padded barefoot to the door and opened it to find Lynette on the other side, dressed in a dark suit.

"Good morning," She said, trying to cover her surprise. She'd no idea who it might be at the door, but Sam's mother was not who she'd been expecting. "Hope there's no problem with the costume?" Sophie was the best sewer, but Kitty could mend or make adjustments if required.

"No." Her mouth pursed. "The costume is wonderful."

"Oh." Why was she here then? She looked around, as if she'd find the answer lying on the ground. "Can I help you with something else?"

"We need to have a little chat."

A chill went through Kitty. A certain note in her tone, a certain hard spark in Lynette's eyes. Something snapped inside her, like a crisp green bean. "What about?"

"Your plans, shall we say."

She crossed her arms. "What about them?"

"How long do you think it will be before you're off again?"

"Not sure. A while." Her bones felt hollow because she knew what was coming, but part of her was curious. Exactly how would Lynette approach this? How long would it take her to wind and wend her way to her point? "Not until Manson's is back on its feet."

"But you still plan to go when it is?"

There was an acrid metallic taste in her mouth, her tongue felt swollen. "Why would you think my plans had changed?"

"I don't know, Kitty. Why don't you tell me?"

She could see Sam in her, in her square jaw, her unwavering gaze. But she had things Sam didn't – steely grey eyes and a mouth that turned down in disapproval so often that it had permanently cast that line to her face. "And if they have?"

"I think we both know that wouldn't be the right decision."

Kitty-Rose swallowed her instinctive desire to lash out. "And why would that be, Lynette?"

Lynette's gaze narrowed, her grip on her handbag tightened. "I know he's been helping you with the sleigh. I know he fixed your car for you. I know you've been out to Redthorn together."

She dredged up a smile. "We went out that way to pick up the tractor and tray." The side-trip to Redthorn had been incidental. Though why she was even justifying herself she wasn't sure. "Sam's a good guy. He's been helping me like he'd help anyone."

"Of course *I* know that. And you're right … he'd help anyone. I just don't want you getting confused."

"About what, Lynette?" Her breath was coming swift and hot but she kept her expression open and curious.

Lynette finally cracked. "I saw you two the other night! In his workshop. And I've no doubt there have been other occasions, Kitty-Rose." She said her name like it was an affliction.

"And?"

"It has to stop. And it will."

Kitty shrugged. "Sounds like you don't have anything to worry about then." She checked a non-existent watch. "If that's it, I better get ready. Big day today."

Lynette's face turned a little meaner, a little more irate. She took a half step forward, her grip on her bag tightening in a way that said she wasn't going anywhere. "You need to be realistic about the way things are. Sam is heading in a certain direction. He's on a certain path." She said it as if that explained everything. She was so close Kitty could feel her breath. "You're not right for him."

There at last. Out in the open.

"That's for Sam to say, surely." Her hands quaked; she folded her arms, hiding them.

Lynette's gaze narrowed. "So there is something going on."

She tucked a wayward lock of hair behind her ear. She wished she wasn't in her bathrobe. She always felt more confident when she was dressed properly. Lynette had had time to prepare – pearls on, her hair sleeked into a coiffure. "I don't see how it's any of your business either way."

"Of course it's my business," she said hotly. There was no doubt in her. She was a woman who knew what she wanted – and got it most of the time. The queen of this small town. "This is my son we're talking about."

"Your fully grown son. Who can make decisions for himself."

"Can he now? With you around."

Everything inside her shifted and dropped. She drew in an outraged breath. "You think I've—" Her cheeks were hot and flushed. The gall of her! All efforts at pretended indifference abandoned her. "Sam is acting of his own free will, I assure you. I would never use my Knack like that. And it doesn't work on him anyway."

Lynette tutted, clearly pleased she'd gained some advantage now that Kitty had lost her cool. "No man is going to say no to you. Of course he can't help himself. No man could. It's lust, pure and simple. But he'll tire of it soon enough."

It wasn't lust! Or at least, not just lust. What a horrible thing to say. She took a moment to regain control of herself, to calm the thunder in her head, her heart, so that she could once again feign cool bemusement. "Well, if that's the case, what are you worried about?"

"You're a distraction. Your presence here is preventing him from—"

"Getting back together with Delia? I don't think so, Lynette. I've spoken to both of them."

The older woman drew a shuddering breath. "Well, it's preventing him from finding someone else he could get serious about, then. And the more time he spends with you, the longer it'll take. I don't want you drawing him into your orbit."

Her orbit. Really. It was a little too late for that.

She saw him again, as he'd been at nine years old. Face serious; calm and confident. Standing up for her, directing the search parties. Something had happened that day; some bond had formed, and they'd been part of each other's orbits ever since.

"Kitty, I came here today to have a mature conversation with you.

Have you thought about Sam at all in this, or are you really that self-ish? If you know him at all, you know he's the marrying kind—"

"And you don't want him marrying a Frost." Her voice was tinged with a hint of scorn, but the truth was a hard knot in her chest. She'd never be an acceptable choice in this town.

"Of course I don't want him marrying you! Have you thought about the children?"

Children. No, she hadn't thought about the children.

Her heart started to fracture, slow but sure. It wouldn't be long before the shards fell.

Lynette drew herself up. "No doubt you think me cruel and I can see you're determined to take offence, but this isn't personal. Despite what you might think, I have nothing against you, and I certainly appreciate everything you're doing for this town. But this is about my son and what will make him happy. For more than a couple of months."

Discomfit rose in her. Uncertainty cast shadows. There was something in Lynette's words that was getting to her. Something in her dogged determination to 'protect' her son.

"You know who – what – you are. Your children …" She broke off and shook her head firmly. "I won't have Frosts in the family!"

Sudden pain ripped through her. Pain so intense, it felt like it might kill her. But she pasted a smirk on her mouth. "You know what they say, Lynette – never say never!"

Lynette stared at her in open-mouthed dismay. Then her lips pressed in a firm line. "You think about it, Kitty. You're a smart girl. I'm sure if you do, you'll see that the sooner you leave, the better. And in the meantime, you'd do well to stay away from my son. For his sake, and yours."

Concluding with an air of triumph, Lynette turned and walked away.

Kitty slammed the door shut, full of white-hot rage.

This thing she had with Sam – so new, so fragile – was the best thing that had ever happened to her. She'd just wanted to enjoy it, whatever it was. Protect it for as long as she could.

She hadn't got very long.

Her eyes felt raw, her heart no less so. She leaned back against the door.

She hated to admit it, but the truth of Lynette's words sank into her bones. Of course Sam wanted marriage; of course he wanted children. He'd never leave this town – or he'd never be happy if he did. It was who he was.

Children.

With her own strange history, what kind of mother would she be? What kind of legacy would she pass on to her children? Daughters, most likely. Daughters who would one day develop Knacks of their own.

She wouldn't wish it on her worst enemy.

16

Dress rehearsal, and it was chaos in the vicinity of the float. Elves jumped and squealed in the heat, quivering uncontrollably with anticipation, while Delia tried to coax them into order. Their parents chipped in with reprimands, in between chatting among themselves and oohing and aahing over the float. Sam, already in costume, had been waylaid by a group on his way over.

Kitty stood beside her mother, wearing a smile she could feel; stretching her mouth, her cheeks. She knew it appeared real; upturned red lips to match her red, fitted shirt-dress as she gave polite but distant thanks for compliments on the float. But on the inside, she was reeling.

She shouldn't have let Lynette's visit get to her – she'd sworn she'd never let Woodleigh get to her – but she was only human. Lynette's words had penetrated her heart like a slow-acting poison, and it was still spreading.

It was insanely hot in the sun. She wanted to retreat to cooler climes, away from everyone. The dress rehearsal would take less than half-an-hour; she couldn't wait for it to be over.

Her mother kept casting quick uncertain glances in her direction, squeezing her arm. But Kitty just shook her head; she didn't want to talk about it.

Lynette swept past; an empress in her costume. She must be hot but she was also totally in her element. Sam finished up with the group he was talking to and went to man the short ladder resting against the tray. He held it steady, and a hand out to support Lynette as she climbed onto the float. Watching them – the two of them – made Kitty hurt everywhere all over again.

Lynette took her seat on her throne, baskets of Christmas canes and other bonbons at the ready. Once Mrs Claus had taken her place, the elves rushed to Sam. He helped them up, keeping them steady as they climbed, encouraging the ones who needed the boost, then passed their box up to them. When one elf decided it was too tempting to jump straight off again, Sam caught her mid-air and lifted her back onto the tray, with a gentle but firm warning not to try it again. She giggled, but ran to her place.

He was going to make a fantastic father.

She met Lynette's gaze, and some understanding passed between them.

She looked away. A lump rose in her chest and she made a sound to clear it.

Sophie glanced up at her, puzzled, concerned, but Kitty just shook her head again.

Sam was who he was. And she was who she was.

She needed a change of scene. She turned and walked up this side-street, peeked around the corner to Main Street. It heaved with people. There was a buzz in the air. The whole town had come out to see 'their' float. She spotted Fred, by himself but evidently happy to be there.

She turned and headed back to stand beside Sophie. They were waiting for the final elf to arrive. It shouldn't be too much longer.

"Oh. Mindy Clarkson," Sophie said.

Sophie headed over to Mindy, whose daughter was in the parade. Kitty watched with a sinking feeling as Sophie tapped on Mindy's shoulder, face earnest, intent on delivering whatever message of doom and gloom the ravens had given her.

The expression on Mindy's face. Discomfit, then contempt. Barb, right next to her, barely managed to stifle her smirk.

Kitty looked around miserably. Today of all days did this have to happen? With so much else going on, and everyone there to see, couldn't Sophie have waited? But her mother didn't care about appearances, or what people thought. She was doing her duty, to pass the message on.

She looked away, stupidly met Lynette's gaze again before turning away.

To have her eyes collide with Sam's as he leaned against the tray. A slow smile unfurled across his face. It was electrifying. She tried to smile in return, but couldn't quite pull it off. His expression shifted.

He pushed away from the tray but the last child arrived, stopping him from walking to Kitty. Sending her a questioning look, he reluctantly turned to help the last elf up.

She blew out a shaky breath. She really needed to get out of here before he came over and asked that question in person.

Before she could take more than a step, Susie stepped in front of her, beaming.

Kitty withheld a sound of frustration and said, "You're supposed to be waiting on Main Street with everyone else."

"I know, but I couldn't resist." She linked her arm through Kitty's. "It looks amazing! It really does deserve to win."

Kitty breathed out, admiring the float again. Yes, if nothing else, the float was wonderful.

"Given any more thought to …" Susie winked at her.

Kitty glanced around and lowered her voice, though given the general level of noise, it was probably unnecessary. "I can't do it. It's not right."

Susie waved an arm to showcase the float. "But look at it – it deserves to win! It'll just be typical Belleville prejudice if it doesn't!"

Kitty shrugged. "You're probably right, but even so."

Susie withdrew her arm. Her eyes were bright with anger, her mouth had turned petulant. "I told you how the Emporium's going."

"I can't just pull out my Knack and make people do what I want whenever I want," she snapped. The sun was baking her eyes. The heat was terrible. It was stifling her lungs, prickling all over her skin.

A scowl crossed Susie's face. "Be like that then." She stormed off, towards the float.

Kitty watched her in disbelief. A numb ache spread through her, a growing feeling of hopelessness. Her hand came to her middle.

When she turned back, Sam was heading her way, a look on his face letting her know he hadn't missed that interaction.

"What just happened?" he asked when he was near.

"Nothing." But she couldn't quite meet his eyes.

"It was something. You're upset."

Of course she was upset.

Goddamn this town! She could never win.

His hand came up to cup her nape. But she stiffened, shied away. Then glanced, horrified, at the confusion in his dark eyes. A sick feeling grew in the pit of her stomach. The thought of hurting him made her feel ill. But here and now, she could feel everyone's eyes on them.

"We can't— It's not ... I—" Was the heat making her irrational? But when she glanced around, she saw her mother still gripping Mindy's wrist, Susie glaring at her, hot and sulky, and Lynette giving her a glacial look.

Strength deserted her legs. "This isn't working." It came out like a whisper, but the need to say it had been welling up for hours. She tried again. "This can never work."

His gaze was piercing. "What are you talking about?"

She couldn't stay in Woodleigh; she couldn't give him what he needed. Lynette was right; she was a distraction. He was a family man; a pillar of the community. His future was here. She was only wasting his time. "Everything. You and me."

Shock passed over his face, then it darkened like a thunderstorm. "Just like that, hey."

"What?"

He tossed his head in the direction of the float. "You got what you wanted. Now we're over."

His words caused a sharp pinch in the chest. For a moment, she was speechless. "It's not like that."

His breath was steady, in and out, but the set of his jaw, the coldness of his eyes, betrayed his anger. "I don't know what it's like, Kitty-Rose. What I do know is that when you needed something, that's when you kissed me."

She gasped; her jaw dropped. "That's what you think of me." Her words were quiet but her blood was pounding.

God, she was stupid. Of course that's what he thought of her. That she was always looking out for number one, that she was willing to manipulate anyone and everyone to get her own way. She was forever going to be the Kitty-Rose of high school to him. He'd never trust her.

"Tell me I'm wrong." His gaze was unwavering, and she could see something in it, something that pleaded with her to explain.

She should protest – loud, strong – she had every right to. But with everyone's eyes on them, and this swirling confusion and chaos in her head, she couldn't find the words.

Why should she always have to defend herself from untrue accusations? Let him believe it, if that's what he wanted. "Everyone's waiting. You should go."

He jerked back. Looked around as if he'd forgotten where they were, what was happening. He gave her a this-isn't-finished look, then turned and walked to the tractor.

With one hand, she shielded her eyes from the sun. Sam started the tractor and the float moved off. She'd planned to head to Main Street to watch, as the rest of the crowd were doing – including Sophie, still trying to get through to Mindy. But she stood still as it slowly rounded the corner.

He'd been her single wild wish; she'd fallen for him in a dream. And now it was over.

Reality sliced through her heart – painful, searing, but cold and clean. Her heart might ache but her head was clear. The only way she'd survived as long as she had was by building a hard shell of indifference. Over the course of the past two weeks, that shell had cracked. It was time she rebuilt it.

She'd said Woodleigh was her home, and it was true, but it wasn't a loving one, and it never had been. She'd leave, as soon as she could. Maybe even forget about Manson's – no one cared except her. She'd make a fresh start where no one knew who she was or what she could do. And hope that one day, she'd have forgotten all about him, the man who'd claimed her heart all those years ago.

SHE WOKE the next morning after a fitful sleep, puffy-eyed and aching. The feeling in her chest had dulled to a throbbing ache.

Peering out her window, bright threads of cloud signalled a beautiful day ahead for the parade; the weather was supposed to be cooler today. She got out of bed and dressed quickly. She'd been restless all night; by turns hot and cold. Miserable.

And she looked it. Skin pale, dark smudges under her eyes, hair an absolute bird's nest.

She took a little extra time to make herself presentable. She had a big day ahead.

Starting with Sam.

She owed him an explanation. Yesterday had been … intense. The heat, the crowd, the scrutiny … and coming off the back of her 'chat' with Lynette, she just hadn't been able to explain. She'd go to his house now – before they all had to drive to Belleville. He deserved to know her reasons.

She was just about ready when there came a knock at the door.

Sophie wasn't home – she'd heard her leave – so she went to answer it, praying it wasn't Lynette again.

When she opened the door, it was Sam. He was dressed in light trousers and a checked shirt. He looked about as rested as she felt.

"I'll go with you."

She stared at him stunned.

"I'll go with you to Melbourne."

"No. Sam, no."

He stared at her, a heaviness in his brown eyes. "I shouldn't have said what I did."

"It's not that."

"I still shouldn't have said it. Forgive me."

She breathed out, head tilting to the side. The problem wasn't that he'd said it, it was that he believed it. Somewhere in his heart, he believed that she was the kind of person who pretended she had feelings for someone to get what she wanted.

"Be honest. You don't want to leave Woodleigh."

"You're leaving," he said, as if that was the end of the conversation. "There's plenty of jobs in Melbourne. We could go together."

Her gaze roamed over his face; the even features, the square jaw and the earth-and-amber eyes. A part of her wanted to say yes. But he hadn't denied not wanting to go, and she knew he didn't want to. That he offered meant something, but she couldn't take him from Woodleigh, the foundation of his whole life, when she couldn't give him what he really needed.

She hadn't thought about children. It wasn't necessarily that she didn't want them, but she wouldn't put them through what she'd suffered. If they weren't living in Woodleigh, it would be better. No one need know anything about the 'gift' she'd be passing on; even they wouldn't need to know until they were older and developing their Knacks. It wouldn't be the same for them as it'd been for her. But she was still unsure. Sam wasn't, and she couldn't promise him anything in return for everything he'd be giving up.

She crossed her arms. "I can't ask you to do that."

"You're not asking. It's my idea." He shoved a hand through his hair. "I didn't come around after the dress rehearsal yesterday because I needed some time to think." He paused. "After sitting with it for hours, I know, for sure: I don't want to lose you. I don't want this to end. I'll do anything."

She didn't want it to end either, but better now than kidding themselves – only to have to go through greater pain later. As Lynette had said, she was a distraction, wasting time he could put towards his future. "This isn't going to work longer term." They hadn't made any promises. The writing had been on the wall since day one. "It was always just for as long as I was here."

"That's not what I want. Are you telling me you don't feel the same?"

Oh Lord. She didn't know how she felt. About anything. "It's not about my feelings."

"What then?"

She shrugged. Where to start? "You think I manipulated you to get what I wanted."

"No, I don't. I didn't mean it, Kitty-Rose."

"Some part of you must believe it."

"I don't. I really don't." He stepped closer, smoothed a thumb over her cheekbone. "I know what you said, but ... it's hard for me to believe that what I have to offer is enough for you. When you wanted us to keep this secret, when you didn't want me to touch you in public, when you said it was over the way you did ... It was just a stupid knee-jerk reaction. But I know what we have is real."

She let out a long, shaky breath. "You've got it wrong, Sam. It's not about what you can't give me; it's what I can't give you."

He waited for her to go on.

"Your whole life is here. A life you love. You're a family man, a leader. You're going to be the next mayor, and they'd never accept me by your side. I can't be responsible for taking you from Woodleigh. This town would fall apart without you. Be honest, you don't want to leave."

"I would. For you."

She couldn't do it to him. She shook her head. "You wouldn't be happy." She endeavoured to steady her voice. She beseeched him with her gaze. "You'll find someone better suited to you. Who can give you what you need."

"I don't want anyone else. I won't ever feel about anyone the way I feel about you. Ever." He shoved a hand through his hair. "How many people do you think I've told I want to go to Greece? No one but you.

Everyone thinks they know who I am but they don't. Saint Sam – I'm no saint. You're the only person I feel I can be myself around."

She felt the same but still … "I can't be responsible for taking you from your home."

"Because you're not sure about your feelings?" His face was taut. She could see every splinter of orange and green in his eyes.

"I'm sure of my feelings about you." She stared like a fool into his eyes. "But I'm also sure your place is here in this town." It was who he was, everything that made him who he was.

"You know what I think? I think your place is in this town too. Why else do you care so much about it?"

She looked at him, heart in her throat. "Our daughters would be Frosts, Sam. They'd have this same Fay-blood that I have running through me."

"So? You think I wouldn't welcome that?"

She just stared at him. He couldn't understand everything that meant.

"Okay, you're right, Kitty-Rose. You asked me to be honest. Here's what I want. I want you to marry me. I want us to stay in Woodleigh. I know it's been rough, but give people a chance to get to know you. Give things a chance to settle. Everyone will adjust to you and me; they'll have to. And you won't be alone anymore; you'll have me. And then eventually, when the time's right, we can think about children, raise them here together."

She let out a strangled sound. "Do you know what you're asking?"

"It wouldn't be like it was before. Not for you, and not for them. You'd have me. They'd have me. We'd protect them."

"I can't. Do you see I can't?" They'd hit an impasse. They couldn't stand here and argue about it any longer. There was no point. "It's going to be slow-going, driving the tractor to Belleville. You better get going. I'll see you there."

"This isn't over."

But it was.

17

She didn't have time to brood. Not everyone had a car, and Kitty found herself driving Cindy and a couple of the kids to Belleville. At least the car was driving beautifully – she had Sam to thank for that.

Belleville was heaving. At least it was cooler than yesterday. Fresher. Everyone should be much more comfortable in their costumes. She parked where she could and they made their way to the oval, where all the floats were assembled prior to the parade. She saw the Woodleigh float immediately – one of the biggest and certainly the most splendid, it was impossible to miss. She couldn't help but check out the competition as they passed. Effort had been made, but they were nothing compared to theirs. Not everyone had Sophie and her Knack at hand. To say nothing of how Sam had come through. And when Mrs Claus and the elves were also added in … surely they would win.

It was eleven-thirty. The parade started in half-an-hour. She hoped everything had survived the trip from Woodleigh in one piece, but she could do repairs if required.

When she got there, there was no sight of Sam. Lynette, Susie,

Josie and Roy were standing guard instead – they'd come together in a car.

She approached, somewhat reluctantly. "Morning," she said brightly. Roy and Josie smiled back. "Where's Sam?" she directed the last at Josie.

"Getting his costume on."

"Kitty, can I talk to you?" Susie stepped forward. She looked pale and wan.

Oh Hell. She didn't have the energy for this today. But Susie put a hand around her waist, drew her away.

"You were right to say no. I shouldn't have tried to make you feel bad. I just … don't want my shop to fail." Her expression was contrite; her huge brown eyes were dark and shiny.

"Let's just forget about it." Something snagged her attention. Turning her head slightly, she saw Frank, about twenty feet away. He was staring at their float – and for some reason he appeared … aghast? Appalled?

"I shouldn't have even asked. But you have to know, I'll never, ever ask you again. No matter what." Her eyes filled with fresh tears. Her lips trembled as she spoke. "But you've forgiven me once, you probably won't forgive me again."

She couldn't take her eyes off Frank. "Susie, I'm sorry. I need a minute."

Turning, she headed straight for him. Her gaze narrowed on him as she approached. That expression on his face … Why did he look like that? It made no sense.

But the whole thing made no sense. It never had.

"Hi, Frank," she said.

He started. He looked strung out, eyes almost popping out of his head. Too much caffeine. Or something. "Kitty." He forced a smile. "Lovely to see you."

"I see you're admiring our float."

"That's *your* float?" Again, it was more like he was appalled by the idea than impressed.

"That's our float." She frowned, studying his face. "I told you we were doing something different this year."

His gaze swung to her. He forced another smile. "So you did. Well, best of luck. You never know how things will pan out on the day. Perhaps there are other surprises in store."

When she gave him a look, he let out a manic laugh. A huge patent-Frank grin covered his face. "Must keep moving."

Kitty-Rose watched him disappear.

Well. That was … strange.

Just the excitement of the day?

She didn't think so. Mouth skewed, she looked around. And spotted Janice, in some sort of pale pink tutu, heading in the direction Frank had just gone, strange intense energy radiating off her.

That had to be a costume.

Janice was part of a float? But she was Frank's new girlfriend. Secret new girlfriend. Surely that was some kind of conflict of interest. Is that why they were keeping the relationship a secret? That whole ex with an axe story hadn't rung true.

She approached a lady in her fifties with a round face, heavy makeup and orange hair from the next float along. She had the air of someone who knew everything about everyone.

"Say, I just saw Janice. Her costume looks great. I didn't realise she was on a float."

"Oh yes. She's with The Belleville Belles."

"The Belleville Belles? I don't remember them from previous years."

"No, they're new. A cappella, apparently. Fancy way of saying singing, if you ask me."

"Fun!" she said. "Well, good luck today. And Merry Christmas."

"And to you."

She wandered a little further from their float, in the direction Frank and Janice had gone, heading towards Clunies Street, where the parade would take place.

She should get back. She hadn't spoken to Sam, checked that everything was fine with the float. Time was of the essence.

But she didn't. She stood, worrying at her bottom lip, and thinking.

Something was off.

It had been from the beginning; everyone was just too blinded by the prize money on offer to look too hard. But she knew Frank. And she knew Carmody's. It had been less than three years since she'd worked there, formulated plans for its future with Frank.

At the time, she would have said they couldn't afford to give that kind of money away.

Could things really have changed that much in such a short period of time?

She headed away from the oval, their float, towards Clunies Street. There were people everywhere – the whole of the northeast of the state had come out in force to enjoy the parade. They crowded around stalls selling food and toys and various other items. A group of carollers were belting out 'Silent Night' in harmony. She passed a juggler who'd attracted a following. The air was heady with excitement and sweet as sugarplums.

She reached the end of the main strip. In among all the activity, she hadn't seen Janice or Frank. Perhaps she should just head back to the float; make sure all was well. She wasn't even really sure why she'd come this way.

Turning, she headed back, walking the other side of the street this time.

Past the wide, open doors to Carmody's. There were a plenitude of shoppers inside, getting some Christmas shopping done before the parade started.

She thought she saw a hint of pink netting slipping around a corner at the back.

The change rooms were at the back. She had good cause to know; she and Frank had met there often enough. He liked to use them for rendez-vous, as he called them. She walked into the store, keeping her head down and moving quickly, so as not to attract attention and be trapped into a conversation she didn't have time for.

When she reached the back, there was a 'closed for the day' sign in front of the change rooms. She glanced around, but no one was paying attention, so she slipped in and into an open stall.

Listening.

Eavesdropping technically, but not because she wanted to hear anything sordid. She just had a feeling …

Nothing for a moment or two but the sound of bodies brushing against one another and sighs.

"Did you go see him?"

A bitter chuckle. "Trust me, after last night, there's no way he won't do it."

"One more time. Just to be sure." Frank, at his persuasive best.

"I can't. I can't stand it! That great fat belly."

Kitty could sense her shudder.

"I know, baby, but after today, you'll never have to see him again. Just one more little incentive. A reminder of what's coming to him. Or what *he* thinks is coming to him."

"I don't want to."

"Just to be sure. Soon we'll be free, baby. Fifty-thousand pounds free. We'll start again, build a new empire. Just show him one last time where his vote needs to go."

"I've shown him." Another shudder.

"Please, baby. For me."

A groan of acquiescence. "You owe me, Frank. I want to go to Macy's, the very day we arrive."

New York! A hand came to Kitty's mouth.

"And we will. You wait and see. We're so close, we just need to bring it home. Yes?"

"Yes, baby."

A rustling and steps.

Kitty held the door closed, standing still as a stone angel, waiting for two sets of steps to pass by. Then she wrapped her arms around herself, forcing air into and out of her lungs.

She hadn't been wrong to suspect the stores weren't doing that well when she'd questioned the prize money. It was pretty clear what was happening – Frank had set the whole thing up. The Belleville

Belles were going to win and Frank and Janice were running off with the money!

She couldn't know for sure, but she could guess what had happened. Frank's Carmody expansions hadn't gone to plan. The whole 'empire' was probably about to crumble to dust. So he was extracting as much as he could and doing a runner. Frank hadn't changed – same breath-taking, misguided optimism and self-aggrandising motives. Fifty-thousand pounds and a new life – he probably thought he could start something to rival Macy's itself!

Poor Arthur! He probably had no idea of what his son had been up to; what he planned to do.

And what was Kitty supposed to do? The parade was starting any minute. She could tell the police – if she could find any on parade day – but would they believe her? Frank was ripping off his own company.

If she could stop the parade … But did she have time? And who would stop it? Not Frank.

There was one way she could definitely change the outcome.

Find Mayor Jenkins. Do a little persuading of her own.

He'd be in the Carmody marquee, where the raised platform and MC were, waiting for the parade to start.

She made her way there as quickly as possible. Poking her head in, she saw Janice leaning towards him, tittering into her hand. Then, she waggled her fingers in a bye-for-now wave and turned. As soon as she was facing the other direction, the smile fell from her face, replaced with a scowl.

Not that Kitty could blame her for that.

She headed out of the marquee, through the exit on the other side to where Kitty was.

Mayor Jenkins appeared very pleased with himself. A very fat cat anticipating a whole lot of cream. Odious man. Little did he know he was being fooled, just like everyone else.

Now was her chance. She strode towards him, broad smile on her face. He gave her a good looking over, despite his … arrangement with Janice.

Someone called to him to come and sit on the stage, but she got to his side, drew him aside, making sure they were alone enough for her to get to work.

She didn't have much time. "I know about Janice."

It was like she'd slapped him. Then a sneer worked its way over his face. "I don't know what you're talking about."

"She's using you to win."

"I don't know who you think you are, young lady, but I am the mayor of this town," he said through his teeth. "I won't have my honour impugned like that."

She heard over the loud speakers that the parade was about to start. The MC dropped into view again, tapping at his watch. "First float is heading this way! You gotta get up here."

Panic rose in her. She was out of time. She couldn't risk him not believing her. She couldn't risk him choosing to do the right thing even if he did.

There was one way to stop Frank, and that was to use her Knack. She let it rise in her, so strong and golden, and blasted him with the full force of it. "The Woodleigh float is clearly the best. When you see it go past, I'm sure you'll agree. There really is no other possible winner."

His eyes almost rolled back in his head.

Maybe she'd hit him with a bit too much Knack. She put her hand on his arm, made him looked at her again. "Mayor Jenkins, the Woodleigh float is the best. I'm sure you'll agree and make it the winner."

His gaze cleared a little. "What was that you said?"

"If you think the Woodleigh float is the best, I'm sure you'll make it the winner."

"Well, of course I will."

Atta boy. She released his arm and strode out of the marquee.

And then stopped. How would she explain this to Sam?

The parade had started.

The first floats were rolling out along the street as she hurried back to the oval. Looking at them, a burn of frustration mixed in with the already uncomfortable sensation roiling around in her belly. They'd all worked so hard getting their float together but for what? They were going to win, but not because they had the best float – even though they did – and Heaven knows if they'd be able to keep the money.

She'd hated having to use her Knack like that, but what choice had she had? She could hardly stand by and do nothing while Frank fleeced his own company. This way at least the money would be safe with them; they could sort out what to do with it in due course.

Still, she'd struggled long and hard with her Knack, and she'd never thought she'd use it like that again. Should she tell Sam? Would he accept what she'd done?

By the time she arrived back at the oval, she estimated over half the floats had joined the parade already. Woodleigh, due to its position in the alphabet, was the second last, but there wasn't much break between each entrant – they'd be up soon.

Back at the Woodleigh float, Lynette sat regally on her throne, gaze fixed ahead in anticipation. The elves were ready to go too – some in their boxes, some out – but all in high spirits. She breathed a sigh of relief to see that everything looked to be in order.

Except where was Sam?

Susie and Josie came straight over. "Where'd you go?"

"Just checking out the competition," she said breezily.

Josie grinned. "Are we going to win?"

"You bet." It was all but guaranteed.

"You sound pretty sure."

She whirled to find Sam behind her. He was in costume, though his beard was pulled down.

There was something to his tone that she didn't like.

"Like I said, I've been checking out the other floats." She searched his open face and brown eyes.

"Really? Because it looked to me like you just walked out of the marquee."

All blood, all sensation drained from her. "You were following me?"

"Susie said you were upset. I wanted to check you were okay."

"Sam! It's time," Lynette called.

Kitty turned to see the float in front of them had just rolled out. "Go on, Santa," she said. "We'll talk later."

But he didn't move. "Tell me it's not what it looks like."

She scanned his face. Would he understand?

For a terrible moment, she could barely breathe, then she let out a shaky stream of air. She wouldn't lie to him. She mustered her courage. "It's exactly what it looks like."

His head tilted, his silence thick.

The second call for the Woodleigh float came through.

"Sam!" Lynette was getting frantic.

This was where she could set him free by making him think the worst. But something in her made her say, "When we walked along the river, you told me I didn't need to ask you what's right and what's wrong, and you were right. I *can* explain, but we don't have time. You need to go. Now. You're just going to have to trust me."

He looked at her, and as the moments passed, his stance lost its tension, his face softened. He cupped her face, leaned forward and kissed her – on the forehead, and then on the lips. Then he turned, walked to the tractor and started the engine.

He looked at her, smiled, and something bloomed inside; a flower opening its petals, spreading radiant joy all through her, sweeping all else before it.

There must be a good thirty feet between them, but she'd never felt closer to him than at that moment. He pulled his beard up and drove off.

She only wanted to be with him. He was driving so slowly, she kept pace with ease. Arms folded across her chest, she couldn't take her eyes off him.

He had to watch the road in front of him most of the time. But every time he found a moment to glance her way, and their gazes collided, it sparked that joy all over again.

And it came to her with sudden, astonishing force; piercing her to the core.

He'd gone to the tractor and started it – on her word. He knew what she'd done – that she'd used her Knack – but he'd done it anyway. She'd asked him to trust her, and he hadn't shown a single doubt. A new fount of joy, of hope, bubbled up in her, clear and pure as spring water.

He trusted her. He trusted her Knack.

When they reached Clunies Street, crowds lined it. She chose the sparser side, stuck to the far edge, closer to the shops, where she could keep pace with the float without having to push and jostle her way through.

Sometimes she couldn't see him, there were too many people in the way, but the next break, there he was, and their gazes would collide all over again, giving her that hit of wild energy that coursed through her whole body, lighting up her soul.

She beamed at him, and he gave her that wolfish grin of his.

She loved him, and she wasn't leaving him. She'd trust him, as he'd trusted her. She'd stand by his side, as he'd stood by hers. She'd protect him, and he'd protected her. And one day, if it happened, they'd protect their children. And shower them in this love.

Towards the centre, the foot traffic was heavier. The floats were blocked from view where she was, at the back. She surveyed the faces around her; the joy, the appreciation, the excitement that came with this time of year. They were looking at the Woodleigh float – that was how it was making them feel. It didn't matter about the prize money; all their effort hadn't been wasted. She and everyone in Woodleigh had given this crowd a Christmas present. The idea sent a spiral of happiness through her.

Across the street, sitting on the low stage, she saw Mayor Jenkins. He was looking down at the Woodleigh float with something approaching awe. She grinned at her Knack in action.

Frank stood next to him; he clearly still had no idea what was about to happen. He had the face of a man who thought he was leaving town very soon. She almost pitied his delusion; his world was going to come crashing down around him very soon.

And then they were through the busiest part of the street. The crowd thinned – and she could see Sam again. She beamed at him, then waved to the elves, who were showing no sign of flagging.

And then they reached the end; volunteers stood, waving the floats to the left, so they could loop back and park in their original berths on the oval.

She shooed him on – he could speed up a little now – and the gap between them widened as the float returned to the oval. When she arrived at the Woodleigh berth five minutes later, Mrs Claus and the elves had descended from the tray. Everyone in the Woodleigh contingent was gathered around, chatting in excited voices.

Sam walked straight to her. He removed his hat and beard. She opened her arms. And they met, in the middle of the open space and kissed. And she didn't care that everyone could see. She didn't care because she had him.

"You asked me to marry you," she said when he drew back.

He grinned. "You just realised?"

"Ask me again?"

"Kitty-Rose Frost, will you please marry me?"

"Yes. Of course I—" But her response was swallowed by another kiss. She broke this kiss. "Don't you want to know about the parade?"

"I'd rather keep kissing you, to be honest."

She play-slapped his arm. "Frank had the competition rigged. That's the reason he was making sure we didn't tell anyone about his fling with Janice. She, err, seduced the mayor – her float was supposed to win and they were going to run off with the money. I only pieced it together just before the parade began. The only thing I could think to do was to make sure we won instead. But I'm not even sure we'll end up with the prize."

"Doesn't matter."

She shook her head. "We won anyway."

"Come on, you two. They're announcing the winner." It was Lynette. And she sounded … indulgent?

They made their way back to the marquee. The level of excitement was high. Everyone wanted to know who the winner was. When they arrived, the mayor was midway through a lengthy preamble about the role of Carmody's in Belleville – its history, its future. Next to him, Frank was beaming.

She stood, holding hands with Sam, in the Woodleigh huddle. Everyone was clutching her arm, congratulating her, smiles broad on their faces. They were so confident they were going to win.

And based on how the float looked and everyone's reaction, they should.

Across the way, she saw Janice, batting her eyelids at the stage, then turning and grimacing. She was sure in for a shock.

Mayor Jenkins turned his ramble to the parade – the standard of the floats, how tough a task he'd been set to choose a winner. "But after careful consideration, I must say, there can only be one winner …"

She cast a glance at Janice, standing right in front of the stage, hands caught at her chest.

She knew what was coming, but she still held her breath, squeezed Sam's hand.

"Woodleigh Chamber of Commerce!"

Relief rushed through her. Around her the huddle burst into cheers. Other groups were also clapping, acknowledging that the Woodleigh float was the best.

Up on stage, Frank looked stunned – too stunned to hide it. Then he pulled himself together; pasting a semblance of a smile on his face and bringing his hands together in a slow clap. His eyes sought hers; at the expression in them, a chill darted through her.

The mayor took an oversized bankers' cheque from someone on stage, and looked towards the Woodleigh contingent, waiting for someone to come up and collect it.

Everyone was staring at her.

It couldn't be her. She wasn't the right person.

Lynette turned to her, glanced down at her hand in Sam's, then back up to meet her eyes. "Go on, Kitty. You go up."

Sam dropped a kiss on the side of her head and released her hand. She looked up at him to find him grinning back. She shrugged and climbed the three steps to the low podium.

She reached to shake hands with Mayor Jenkins. Confusion crossed his face. "Have we met before?"

"Long time ago," she murmured, then turned to the cheering crowd, holding the cheque stretched between her hands, before descending once again.

They were all clapping for her – even Lynette. And it seemed everyone wanted to hug her. Delia hugged her, Susie hugged her. She was stiff at first – but then warmth bloomed in her, gentle as the sun.

"Well, thank you. I do appreciate it. But let's remember, we're also clapping Sophie and Sam, who did so much work. And Fred, who so graciously lent us his tractor and tray. And of course, our Mrs Claus and Delia and all our elves."

The elves wanted to see the cheque, and Kitty let them touch it, read the words aloud. Their parents also wanted to have a closer look, and Kitty couldn't blame them. How often did anyone get to hold fifty-thousand pounds?

Everyone was so happy – Kitty-Rose didn't have the heart to tell them they might not be able to keep it. They'd take it with them to Woodleigh, for safekeeping, while the mess at Carmody's was sorted out.

Would Frank stick around now that his plans had derailed? Or would he and Janice take those flights to New York, even without the money?

"I've got to get back to the float. I don't like leaving it unattended." He leaned forward and kissed her. "I don't want to leave you but I have to drive it back to Woodleigh. Walk me to the oval?"

The cheque was still being passed around. "You're responsible for the tractor; I'm responsible for that." She pointed at where the latest people were looking at it, eyes wide.

He dropped a kiss on her forehead. "We'll talk later then."

She nodded, released his hand reluctantly, and watched him walk away.

She didn't realise Lynette was close enough to hear their discussion, but she turned. She met Kitty's gaze and smiled. "You go with Sam. I'll keep an eye on the cheque and bring it across in a minute."

She stared at Lynette, stunned.

"You forget where I was on the float. I could see you two the whole way. The way you look at each other!"

She smiled. "Thanks, Lynette."

She caught up with Sam and took his hand. They glanced at each other and smiled as they walked. The crowd was starting to thin. Parents taking their sugar-crazed and overstimulated children home. Disappointed float designers and builders were slowly rolling out.

She didn't speak until they'd reached the float. "I want to try. The two of us. In Woodleigh."

His gaze was bright on her.

"You were right, what you said. This whole time since I came back, I've had one thought on my mind – leaving again. I never gave

Woodleigh a chance to work out. I assumed it wouldn't, and I held myself apart. But I don't want to leave – not you, and not Woodleigh."

"It's going to work out. In time, everyone will love you just as much – almost as much – as I do."

A thrill sang through her.

When he pulled back, she saw Lynette walking towards them. Lynette had seemed much more ... welcoming today, but she wasn't sure that'd be the case if she knew Kitty now planned to marry her son. "I don't know if your mum's going to be happy."

Sam shrugged, unbothered. "She'll get used to it. She'll have to."

Kitty smothered a smile. "Sam, I lov—"

She broke off, stiffened. The back of her neck prickled. A sound reached in her ears, growing louder, into a roar. It was angry, reckless.

Frank's Jaguar.

There was a screech as it careened to a halt. Right between Lynette and where Kitty and Sam stood.

It was so fast, so unexpected, it was impossible to process. Frank flung himself from the car, ran the short distance to Lynette and snatched the cheque from her, his rough action shouldering her to the ground.

Shock had Kitty frozen in place, watching open-mouthed while he bolted back to his car.

Sam was quicker to move. He jumped in front of Frank's car, blocking his escape. Then rounded the car to his door – no doubt planning on dragging him out.

Deliberately or not, the car jerked forward, ramming Sam on the thigh. He let out a shout of pain and went down. "Sam!" Kitty's heart stopped, her hand came to her mouth, then she ran, praying the car didn't jerk forward again. It'd kill him.

But Frank threw the car into an erratic, full-throttle reverse. She heard a shout, distant and confused. Someone else had noticed what was happening.

She crouched by Sam's side, trembling hands on his shoulders, all over him, trying to assess where he was hurt, and how badly. "I'm okay, Kitty-Rose," he said, though his voice was low and strained with pain. "It's just my leg."

A sickening crashing sound made her flinch into him. She glanced over her shoulder. Frank had reversed in a wide arc, clearly planning to turn and exit the same way he'd come in, but the speed with which he'd careened backwards and his overall lack of control had meant he'd instead rear-ended with great force into the float behind theirs.

He was slumped over the steering wheel.

She turned back to Sam. "Are you sure you're okay?"

He nodded and looked towards the crash. "You want to check on Frank?"

"No!"

The ragged cry sent a fresh rush of adrenaline through Kitty. She jerked to Lynette, then followed Lynette's gaze to see what had caused it.

Frank'd not only wrecked his own car, he'd destabilised the float he'd crashed into. He must have knocked one of the base supports loose, because the massive tree they had atop their float was tilting, falling – on a direct path towards Kitty and Sam.

She watched it with horror. Time seemed to slow, to freeze. But it would fall faster as it went. Instinct screamed at her to flee but Sam couldn't move – not with his leg – and she couldn't move him – he was twice her size. She wouldn't abandon him. Braced over him, thinking only to protect him, she met Lynette's gaze and saw the truth there.

It wasn't looking good.

Bracing for the impact, she flung an arm overhead, teeth clenched so hard, it hurt.

"No!" Sam yelled.

She caught the stark horror on his face before he pushed her away from him, out of danger. Right by the float, her only thought was to return to him. But then she saw it. The red ribbon.

She grabbed for it. Fear made her butterfingered, but on a second desperate attempt, she caught it and pulled.

From out of nowhere an incredibly powerful gust of wind rose. It held the tree up, motionless in place like an eagle soaring before it spun sideways, and started falling again.

To land safely on the ground beside Sam.

People still in the vicinity came running towards the commotion. She could hear them ordering others to run to a telephone and notify the police and an ambulance.

Sam looked from the tree to her. She met his gaze – a moment that lasted an eternity seemed to pass between them – and then she ran to him. He caught her in a hug, somehow managing to keep hold of her as he managed to stand again by leaning against the float.

On her feet again, Lynette rushed over. "You should have waited for the ambulance," she fussed.

"It's fine, Mum."

"What just happened? That tree was heading right for you." She stared at the length of ribbon still attached to the float, then at Kitty. "I don't understand."

"The ribbon … I don't rightly know myself. But the ravens …" She shook her head. "Sophie sewed it on, told me to use it."

"A Christmas miracle. That's what it was." She'd taken Kitty-Rose's forearm, she was gripping it fervently. Her eyes were wide with wonder.

Maybe one day she'd explain everything to them. "Thank God no one was hurt."

"They would have been," Lynette said sharply. "I don't know what you did, Kitty-Rose, but you saved Sam's life." Whatever she had previously thought about the Frost women and their Knacks had been obliterated by having her son saved by one. She grabbed her in a tight hug. "I'll never forget it."

Behind them, Frank raised his head, starting to stir. He pushed his door open.

Lynette let go of Kitty and marched over, grabbed the cheque back, and slammed the door closed, locking him in again. "You are staying right there, Mister, until the police arrive."

He seemed unharmed but stunned – catatonic almost. Lynette clearly planned on guarding him anyway.

Kitty looked up at the man by her side. "As I was saying, Saint Sam Wells, I love you with all my heart, and I have for the longest time. I'm so glad my Knack is smart enough not to work on you. If you only knew how you make me feel."

He smiled. "I think I have a fairly good idea." He took her hand, put it over his heart. Then leaned down and rumbled low in her ear. "Do you still have that Mrs Claus costume?"

EPILOGUE

It was the best Christmas Day Kitty had ever had.

She'd risen at dawn and she and Sophie had driven out together. She'd been helping Sophie in the week since the parade – Sophie was behind with her preparations because of it, so Kitty had come out to Redthorn every spare second.

Every second she could spare from Sam, that is.

She grinned every time she thought about him.

All the Wells, including Roy, were coming for Christmas lunch at Redthorn.

Kitty didn't know how Sam had talked Lynette into it. Lynette was still so damned grateful that Sam was alive, she'd do anything for him, and Kitty. Kitty was sure it would wear off – probably just in time for the first Chamber of Commerce meeting of the year.

Where they'd have to decide what to do with the money.

Frank had confessed all, and it caused quite the scandal. He and Janice were planning on driving to Melbourne straight after the parade. They had an appointment at a bank for first thing Monday morning, with the equivalent of fifty-thousand in U.S. dollar bills already requested and waiting. They had flights booked for later that day.

After discussion at an emergency meeting, the Woodleigh Chamber of Commerce had offered the money back to Arthur Carmody, seeing as the whole thing had been offered under false pretences and Carmody's wasn't doing too well, but he hadn't accepted their offer. It was a question of pride. Arthur had said everyone, including him, agreed the Woodleigh float was the best, so they should keep the money.

But things may have turned the corner for Manson's anyway. A few days ago, a woman had come into the shop. She worked in the costume department at the Melbourne Ballet Company; Delia had sent her samples of the costumes they'd done for the Christmas float. She wondered if Manson's would be interested in providing costumes for their productions?

Nothing was set yet, but it was an exciting new avenue to explore.

It wasn't the only new avenue to explore.

She sighed in pleasure as she glanced around her. The house looked magnificent, every corner spruced, polished and decorated, ready for their guests. With a little flourish, she put the finishing touches on the table. Everything was ready. Except … "Mum? Put out the plates for, um, Mary, Reginald and Arnold?"

Sophie popped her head around the corner. She smiled but sadly. "They won't be coming."

"I'm sorry, Mum. I'm done with the table then. I can help in the kitchen."

Sophie's mouth quirked. "Sit with me?"

As she did every year, she'd made a gum-leaf wreath on the coffee table next to the Christmas tree. In the centre was an enormous white candle. At precisely one minute to eight o'clock, she struck a match and lit the candle.

They watched it burn together. Kitty reached for Sophie's hand.

"Can you feel them?" Sophie asked.

A sense of darkness, of cold. Then a presence; bright and caring and determined. Another, wry and unexpected. A third, gentle and so wise.

They were out there, somewhere.

Love flowed like a river through her. For Sophie, and for her.

"Yeah, Mum. I do." She opened her eyes. "I wish I'd known them."

Sophie squeezed her hand and leaned forward and blew out the candle. "They know you."

She tugged her hand back and stood. "Come on. This dinner's not going to make itself."

~

I HOPE you enjoyed Kitty and Sam's story, the second in my *Uncanny Knack* series. The first in the series – *The Blue Raven*, which tells the story of Kitty's grandmother, Mary – will be available soon.

SIGN up to my newsletter to stay notified of release dates and special promotions, and you'll also receive a complimentary copy of the first story in my *Owlscroft Coven* series, *Bad Batch*.

Sign up here:
https://dl.bookfunnel.com/h2t9161g5d

ALSO BY MARNIE ST CLAIR

OWLSCROFT COVEN SERIES

Bad Batch

(In A Perfectly Paranormal Valentine)

Good Riddance

(In A Perfectly Paranormal Halloween)

Sweet Hereafter

(In A Perfectly Paranormal Easter)

∽

UNCANNY KNACK SERIES

The Red Ribbon

(In A Perfectly Paranormal Christmas)

∽

CONTEMPORARY ROMANCE

No Place Like You

∽

ROMANTIC SUSPENSE

Blue Steal

ABOUT MARNIE

After years of forecasting the price of tea in China, Marnie St Clair finally shut down the spreadsheets and got serious about her passion for romance, especially the kind that blends charm, humour and a dollop of magic and mystery.

A country girl at heart, Marnie now lives in Melbourne, Australia, with two surprisingly civil teens and a weatherman husband. She likes prosecco, cottage gardens, driving at night, sandalwood-scented anything and a really strong cup of coffee. Or preferably two.

You can contact Marnie through her website www.marniestclair.com, where you can also sign up to her newsletter to be the first to find out about new releases, special deals and exclusive giveaways.

And if you want to get to know the Perfectly Paranormal Anthology authors a bit more, get sneak peeks of what's coming up for the APP Anthologies, as well as giveaways, special offers and just some PNR fun, then join our Perfectly Paranormal Paramours Facebook Group.

Find us here:
https://www.facebook.com/groups/251663560162131

ACKNOWLEDGMENTS

A big heartfelt thanks to the *A Perfectly Paranormal Anthology* contributors – Hellucy Howe, Leisl Leighton and Samantha Marshall – and former contributor Georgia Tingley for inviting me to be part of the group. *A Perfectly Paranormal* has been a blast to be part of and I look forward to future instalments.

Thanks as always to lovely Mady (no sister like you) and my writing group pals Leisl and Frana for the continued support and friendship.

A million kisses to my biggest support and own personal weatherman.

LOVE PNR? JOIN OUR PERFECTLY PARANORMAL PARAMOURS FACEBOOK GROUP

If you want to get to know the Perfectly Paranormal Anthology authors a bit more, get sneak peeks of what's coming up as well as giveaways, special offers and just some PNR fun, then join our Perfectly Paranormal Paramours Facebook Group.

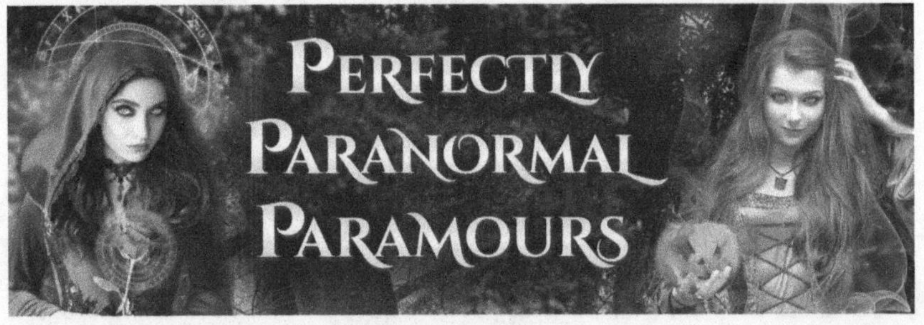

Find us here:
https://www.facebook.com/groups/251663560162131